Bittersweet
Christmas

Bittersweet
Christmas

*Christmas Spells Time for Change
in Three Romantic Novels*

JOYCE LIVINGSTON
GAIL SATTLER   JANET SPAETH

BARBOUR
PUBLISHING

One Last Christmas © 2004 by Joyce Livingston
Almost Twins © 2000 by Gail Sattler
The Candy Cane Caboose © 2001 by Janet Spaeth

ISBN 978-1-59789-494-4

All scripture quotations, unless otherwise noted, are taken from the King James Version of the Bible.

Cover art by Getty Images

Published by Barbour Publishing, Inc., P.O. Box 719, Uhrichsville, Ohio 44683, www.barbourbooks.com

Our mission is to publish and distribute inspirational products offering exceptional value and biblical encouragement to the masses.

ecpa Member of the
Evangelical Christian
Publishers Association

Printed in the United States of America.

One Last Christmas

I dedicate this book to all of you who are struggling to keep your marriage together.
I was eighteen when Don and I were married (a mere child!),
standing at that altar with my head in the clouds, smiling and repeating those vows
without fully realizing the lifetime commitment I was making.
Now, six children and oodles of grandchildren later, I am a widow.
The wonderful, godly man I married and happily shared all of my adult life
with is now gone, home with his Lord.
If you learn one lesson from this book, may it be this:
Love thrives in the face of all life's hazard, except one. Neglect.
Cherish your mate. You never know which day may be your last.

Chapter 1

Sylvia Benson hid behind the potted palm and tried to remain calm. Her intense gaze riveted on the man and woman seated at a table for two in the far corner of Dallas's trendy Fountain Place Avanti Restaurant. Hadn't her husband told her he would be having lunch with one of his key advertisers today? *That's no advertising client! That's Chatalaine Vicker, the woman who writes the society column for his newspaper. I'd recognize that gorgeous face and body anywhere. What is he doing here with her?*

"More coffee, ladies?"

Caught up in staring at the blond beauty seated across from her husband, Sylvia hadn't even noticed the waiter standing by their table, coffeepot in hand. She flinched, then covered her cup. "None for me, thanks."

The other women at the table, all friends from her church, bobbed their heads at the man without even a pause in their conversation.

Still trying to remain inconspicuous, Sylvia shifted her position slightly. Making sure the potted palm shielded her, she took another look at the pair in the corner. Surely, Randy hadn't lied to her. Not her Randy. Although he *had* been spending more time than usual at the *Dallas Times* office, occasionally even working weekends. *Come on, Sylvia, give that husband of yours the benefit of the doubt,* she told herself as she stared at them. *Maybe his client had to cancel their luncheon appointment at the last minute.* But even if that were true, what would Randy be doing with Chatalaine? And why hadn't he told her he would be free for lunch? After all, she was his wife. If he had wanted someone to go to lunch with him, she could have cancelled her luncheon appointment with her friends.

She leaned back in her chair and tried to shake off her suspicions. *It's probably all perfectly innocent, and I'm making something out of nothing. Business associates have lunch together all the time. Maybe they're discussing Chatalaine's column. After all, Randy is the* Times's *managing editor.*

"What *are* you looking at, Sylvia?"

Sylvia turned quickly toward the question and found her friend, Sally, staring at her. "Ah, nothing. Just thought I recognized someone."

Sally rose, placed her napkin on the table, and picked up her purse. "I'm going to the ladies' room. Anyone want to go with me?"

Without missing a beat in their conversation, Denise and Martha rose and headed for the ladies' room, still talking.

Sally gave a slight giggle. "You're not coming?"

"No, I'll wait here. You go on."

"Don't let that waiter get away if he comes with the dessert cart while we're gone," Sally said with a mischievous lilt. "I need chocolate."

Sylvia snickered. "You're terrible!"

She waited until her friends were out of sight, then turned and tipped her head slightly, parting the palm fronds again and peering through them. What she observed went a long way toward fueling her suspicions. The two were talking and giggling like two teenagers. *If this is supposed to be a business luncheon, those two are enjoying themselves entirely too much! Maybe I should just march right over there and confront them, ask them what they're doing together, and see what kind of an explanation I get.*

However, she didn't. Her pride would not allow it. Instead, she decided to wait until later, when she and Randy were alone. She sat there quietly, her nerves French-braiding themselves while all sorts of scenarios played themselves out in her mind. She flinched when the waiter filled her water glass, his close proximity pulling her out of her thoughts.

"Would you like to see the dessert cart, ma'am?"

"Ah—in a minute maybe." She motioned toward the hallway off to the left. "As soon as my friends come back from the ladies' room."

When he nodded and moved away, Sylvia twisted in the chair, unable to resist another peek. Randy was standing beside Chatalaine now, extending his hand to assist her as she rose. How long had it been since he had done that for her? Things were not looking good.

From behind her potted palm camouflage, she watched the attractive couple move across the restaurant toward the exit. After giving them enough time to reach the parking lot, she signaled the waiter and asked for her check.

I wonder how long this has been going on? She drummed her fingers on the table. *You're making too much of this, Sylvia. There's probably a perfectly reasonable explanation as to why your Randy and that woman had lunch together.* She dabbed at her misty eyes with a tissue. *If you confront Randy about this now, you may be sorry. Tomorrow is Thanksgiving, and the children will all be home. You don't want to ruin Thanksgiving for your family with your unconfirmed suspicions, do you? At least wait until DeeDee and Aaron go back to college. Then, if you still think there may be something going on between your husband and that woman, you can ask him.*

The plan sounded logical. But at this minute she felt anything *but* logical. Both she and Randy were Christians. Randy would never go against the commitments they had both made to God on their wedding day. Or would he? Had his faith slipped, and she had been so busy, she hadn't even realized it?

"He hasn't brought the dessert cart yet?" Sally slipped into the chair, eyeing Sylvia with a grin.

Sylvia scooted her chair back and placed her napkin on the table. "I—I really need to go home."

Sally's brow creased. "Go? You and I haven't even had time for a little girl talk. What's your rush? I thought you said you didn't have any plans for this afternoon."

Sylvia reached for her purse, pulled out a couple of dollar bills, and dropped them on the table beside her plate. "I'm sorry, Sally. We'll talk more next time we have lunch. I've developed a splitting headache."

Sally gave her a slight giggle. "Hey, that's the line we use with our husbands, not our girlfriends."

Sylvia frowned as her hand rose to finger her temple. "I'm really sorry, Sally. I hate to duck out on you like this, but I need to get home, take something for this headache, and lie down. Please tell Denise and Martha good-bye for me." She didn't have a headache before seeing Randy with that woman, but witnessing them together—after he had told her he was meeting with a client—had brought on a doozy.

Sally's face sobered. "Oh, sweetie, I'm sorry, I was only kidding. Do you feel like driving home by yourself?"

"Sure, I'll be fine. Don't worry about me." *Actually, I'm miserable!* Though Sally was one of her best friends, she simply could not reveal her unproven suspicions about her husband.

When he came home from his office, it was all Sylvia could do to keep from screaming out at Randy and asking him about his lunch with Chatalaine. But for the sake of the twins, DeeDee and Aaron, who had arrived home from college that afternoon, she kept quiet, pasting on a smile and brooding within herself. She had a difficult time even looking at Randy.

She waited expectantly at bedtime, hoping he would mention it. But he didn't. Even when she asked him how his day went, he simply replied, "Fine. Routine, just like any other day." Then he crawled into bed and turned away from her.

Okay, if that's the way you want it! Don't tell me. She yanked the quilt up over her head and gritted her teeth to keep from screaming at him, telling him she had seen the two of them having a cozy lunch together.

After a sleepless night, she crawled out of bed earlier than she'd intended and began to go mechanically through the tasks of baking the turkey and preparing the rest of their very traditional meal. Her mind still on the events of yesterday, she took out her anger and frustration on the celery stalks and onions as she mercilessly chopped them up on the cutting block.

Randy came into the kitchen about eight, his usual pleasant self. He rousted Aaron and DeeDee and even teased Sylvia about the bag of giblets she'd left in the turkey she'd prepared for their first Thanksgiving together as husband and wife. About eleven o'clock, their oldest son, Buck, and his wife, Shonna, arrived, bringing two beautiful pecan pies Shonna had baked. Randy greeted them warmly, then dragged both Buck and Aaron into the den to watch a football game while the three women finished setting the table.

"Is something wrong?" Shonna stared at her mother-in-law while removing the gravy boat from the china cabinet. "You're pretty quiet this morning."

DeeDee nodded her head in agreement. "Yeah, Mom, I noticed that, too."

Is it that obvious? "I'm fine. Just had a hard time getting to sleep last night." Sylvia forced a smile. It was nice having Shonna and DeeDee there to help her. "Maybe we'd better use that big serving bowl, DeeDee. Hand it to me, would you, please?"

By one o'clock, the Benson family gathered around the lovely table for their Thanksgiving feast. With everyone holding hands, Randy led in prayer. As he did at every Thanksgiving, he thanked God for their food, for the willing hands that prepared it, and for their family seated at the table. Sylvia found it difficult to keep her mind on his words. All she could think about was her husband having lunch with that gorgeous blond. Was this all for show? Inside, was Randy wishing he could be spending Thanksgiving Day with Chatalaine?

After he had consumed the last crumb of pie on his overloaded dessert plate, Randy pushed back from the table and linked his fingers over his abdomen. "Great Thanksgiving dinner, hon. The turkey was nice and moist, just the way I like it. As usual, you've outdone yourself." With a tilt of his head, he gave her a slightly twisted smile. "If my mother were alive, she would agree, and you know how picky she was."

"Thanks. That's quite a compliment." Sylvia nervously shifted the salt and pepper shakers, finally placing them on either side of the antique sugar bowl, a prize possession that had belonged to her mother-in-law. *Oh, Randy, how I hope I'm wrong! I know we haven't had much to do with each other these past few years, but surely that didn't drive you into another woman's arms.*

"Sorry, Mom. DeeDee and I have to go." Aaron tossed his napkin onto the table and nodded to his sister.

"You *have* to go this early?" Sylvia dabbed at her mouth with her napkin. "You just got here yesterday."

The good-looking young man, who looked so much like his father, gave her a quick, affectionate peck on the cheek. "I know. But you knew we'd planned to get back to school right after our meal. DeeDee and I promised we'd help our youth director with the lock-in tonight, and we've got a ton of stuff to do to get the fellowship hall ready before the kids get there."

"Great dinner, Mom." DeeDee pushed back from the table. "I hate to run and leave you and Shonna with the dishes, but if we don't leave now, we won't make it."

Sylvia rose and walked to the door with her children, with Randy following close behind. "I'm glad you're both active in the church you attend, but isn't there someone else who could—"

"Hey, DeeDee and I are the lucky ones. Most college students don't live within driving distance of their homes. Besides, we have to get back to our jobs." Aaron threw a playful punch at his father's stomach. "Maybe this old man'll help you with the dishes."

Randy let out an exaggerated "ugh" before wrapping his arm around his son's shoulders and pulling him close. "I'm counting on the two of you taking care of each other."

Buck shook hands with his brother, then kissed his little sister's cheek. "Yeah, Aaron, watch after this cute freshman. I know how those college boys can be. I was one of them once," he added with a chuckle. "Come to think of it, maybe I'd better have DeeDee keep an eye on you since you're a freshman, too."

Both Aaron and DeeDee kissed Shonna, then picked up their backpacks from the hall bench and headed for the door.

Sylvia followed them, then kissed each one on the cheek, giving them a hug as she struggled to hold back her tears. "I really hate to see you leave, but I'm so thankful the two of you get home as often as you do. It's just that—"

Grinning, Aaron tapped the tip of his mother's nose. "I know. You love us."

"We love you, too, Mom." DeeDee nudged her father with her hip. "You, too, Dad."

The two stood in the open doorway waving as their two precious children crawled into Aaron's beat-up old van. "Promise you'll drive carefully!" Sylvia called after them before its door slid closed.

"We gotta go, too, Mom." Buck motioned his wife toward the door. "Shonna's parents are expecting us. Can you believe we're gonna eat two Thanksgiving dinners today, and her mom's nearly as good a cook as you?"

Shonna rolled her eyes and pelted her husband with a pillow from the sofa. "Don't let my mom hear you say that, if you expect to win brownie points with her."

Randy and Sylvia watched until Buck's car was out of sight before shutting the door. For the first time since the restaurant incident, she was alone with her husband, and she felt as nervous as a tightrope walker wearing hiking boots.

Randy moved through the family room after grabbing the heavy Thanksgiving edition of the newspaper that lay on the hall table. "I wish the kids hadn't had to rush off. I really miss them and all the noise they make when they're here."

Sylvia followed, scooping up the pillow Shonna had tossed at Buck. With an audible sigh, she placed it back in its proper place on the sofa. "I like the kind of Thanksgivings we used to have, before they grew up. Thanksgivings where we spent the entire day together, just enjoying one another's company." She allowed the corners of her mouth to curl up slightly and managed a nervous chuckle. "I didn't even mind you and the boys spending most of the afternoon in front of the TV watching football."

He gave her another twisted smile; this one she did not understand. Was his demeanor sending up bells of alarm? Signals he hoped she would catch? He seemed nervous, too. Ill at ease. Was he going to tell her that he, also, had to rush off? Was he planning to spend the rest of the day with his girlfriend, now that their children had gone? *Girlfriend?* That word struck horror in her heart and made her light-headed.

"Those were good days, weren't they?" Randy pulled the newspaper from its bright orange plastic wrapper, tossed it into his recliner chair, then moved into the dining room. As he stared at the table, almost robotically he reached for the salt and pepper shakers and placed them on a tray. "But things change, Syl. People change. Life changes."

What does that mean? She began adding cups and saucers to the tray, eyeing him suspiciously. "My, but you're philosophical today."

Randy nodded but did not comment and continued to add things to the tray. His silence made her edgy. She wanted to reach out and shake him. *Say something. Tell me about your lunch with Chatalaine! Give me some excuse I can believe!* "Would you like another sliver of pumpkin pie?" she asked, biting her tongue to keep from saying something she might later regret. *What is it the scripture says? A tiny spark can ignite a forest fire?*

"No, thanks. It was great, but I'm full." He picked up the tray and headed for the kitchen.

"More coffee? I think there's still some left in the pot." She quickly gathered up the remaining silverware and followed.

"I've had plenty." He placed the tray on the counter, then sat down at the table. "Want me to help you with the dishes?"

Sylvia glanced up at the big, round clock on the kitchen wall. The one Randy had given her for Christmas two years ago. An artist friend of his had painted the words, *Sylvia's Kitchen*, across the face in bold letters and had even added a tiny picture of her where the twelve should've been. She had cried with joy at the thoughtful gift. Even now, with the tenseness she felt between them, just looking at the clock brought a warm feeling to her heart. "No football on TV?"

He shrugged. "I don't want to watch TV."

She pasted on a smile and counted his options on her fingers. "You don't want pie. You don't want coffee. You don't want to watch the game. But you want to help me with the dishes?"

Randy straightened in his chair and placed both palms flat on the table in front of him, his gaze locking with hers. "What I really want—" He paused and swallowed hard. "Is—is a divorce!"

Chapter 2

Sylvia's breath caught in her throat. All she could do was stare at him in disbelief. Her heart raced and thundered against her chest. *This can't be happening! Please, God, tell me I'm dreaming!*

"I—I didn't want to hurt you, Syl. But I couldn't think of another way to tell you other than just blurting it out like that. I've been trying to tell you for weeks."

He reached for her hand, but she quickly withdrew it and linked her fingers together, dipping her head and turning away from him. She could not bring herself to look at him. Not the way she was feeling. Her legs wobbled beneath her and, afraid they might not hold her up a second longer, she clutched onto the cabinet. *So what I witnessed in the restaurant and hoped was an innocent lunch was exactly what I suspected? You do have a girlfriend!*

She found herself anchored to the spot—speechless. She had been concerned there was something going on between Randy and Chatalaine. But had it gone this far? *No! Please, God. No!*

"Say something, Syl. Don't just stand there. I hate myself for telling you like this—"

"*You* hate yourself?" She sank onto the kitchen stool and looked up slowly, her shock turning to anger as her heart pounded wildly and her stomach began to lurch. "You can't begin to imagine the feelings of hurt and resentment welling up inside me! Why, Randy? Why? Has our married life been that bad?"

He stood awkwardly and began pacing about the room, his fingers combing through his distinguished-looking graying temples. "Like I said, Syl. Life changes. We change."

Sylvia spun around on the seat. Fear, anger, betrayal bit at her heart, and it felt like a wad in her chest. Her fingers clutched the stool's high back for both support and stability. "Of course, things change! The raising of our three children has taken most of my time, while you've been building your career at the newspaper! But our kids are gone now. Out on their own. We finally have the time for ourselves we've always talked about! It's our time now! Yours and mine! Why would you even think about a divorce?" *Say it, Randy. Be a big enough man to tell me you're leaving me for a younger woman!*

He stopped pacing and stood directly in front of her. The pale blue eyes she had always loved, now a cold, icy gray—eyes she barely recognized. He hesitated for what seemed an eternity, then turned away as if to avoid the sight of her. "Our marriage died a long time ago. Have you been so blind you haven't noticed?"

"Have *I* been so blind? Don't try to blame this on me, Randy Benson!" Sylvia felt like she had been sucker punched in the stomach as his words assaulted her and threshed away at her brain. "How stupid do you think I am? You're leaving me for that Chatalaine woman, aren't you?"

He flinched, and she could see he was startled by her mention of the woman's name. "Chatalaine? What made you say that?"

"I—I saw the two of you together." Why couldn't she cry? She wanted to cry, but the tears would not come. It almost seemed as if she were standing outside her body, watching this dreadful scene happen to someone else. "Yo–you've been having an—"

"Me? Having an affair?" He turned and grabbed onto the back of her chair. "I resent that accusation, Syl! How dare you even consider such a thing?"

She leaped to her feet and stood toe-to-toe with him. She wanted him to look at her when he told her his dirty little secrets. "Come on, Randy. Tell me. Admit to your little trysts!"

"Are you crazy? I have no idea what you're talking about."

She felt him cringe as her hands cupped his biceps and her fingers dug into his flesh. "You're a Christian, Randy! How could you?"

"Look, Syl, I'm sure you don't want to hear this, but the two of us—you and I alone—are responsible for the breakup of this marriage. I should have put my foot down—"

She felt the hair stand up on her arms. "Put your foot down? Exactly what do you mean by that?"

He stared at the floor. "Perhaps that was a poor choice of words. What I meant was—" He stopped, as if wanting to make sure his words came out right this time. "I—I should have complained more, instead of holding things back. Keeping things inside."

"Things? What kind of things?"

He gave a defeated shrug. "You were so busy with the kids, you never had time for me. I needed you, Syl, but you shut me out."

"I didn't shut you out, Randy. You were never here long enough to be shut out, or have you forgotten all the days, nights, and weekends you spent at the newspaper? What about the times *I* needed *you*?" she shot back defensively.

"I'd much rather have been at home like you, but as the breadwinner of this family, I didn't have that luxury."

"Oh, and I did have that luxury? Staying home with crying babies, doing a myriad of laundry each week, cooking countless meals, cleaning the house so things would look nice for you when you came home?" She could not remember the last time she had been so angry.

"I didn't want things to turn out like this. I—"

"Don't tell me the devil made you do it!" she shot out at him, suddenly wanting to hurt him as he was hurting her. He tried to back away, but she clung tightly to his arms and would not allow it.

"Syl, don't. You're only making this harder for both of us."

"Don't what? Cry? Scream? Get mad? You don't think you deserve to be screamed at? After what you've just said?" She continued to hold onto him, wanting him to feel her anger and frustration, to see it on her face. She wanted him to sense her fury. To feel her angst. What do you say to a man who just asked you for a divorce, when all this time you've had no idea he's been cheating on you?

He gave her a disgruntled snort. "If I didn't know better, I'd say you were jealous, but I don't think you care enough to be jealous."

She jammed her hand onto her hip. "Oh? Does that question mean I have a reason to be jealous?"

"Of course not. I was referring to your attitude."

She again held tightly to his arms, sure that if she ever let him go, it would be for good. She could not bear the idea of life without him. She inhaled a deep breath and let it out slowly, begging God to give her the right words to say and the right way to react, to make her beloved husband come to his senses. Why didn't he come right out and tell her about Chatalaine? That she was the real reason he wanted out?

After an interminable silence, she willed herself to calm down and said, trying to mask her disillusionment, "We can't do this, Randy. Divorce is not an option. We've both invested way too much in this marriage to give up on it now. Please, don't do anything you'll regret later. Have you prayed about this?"

He gently pried her fingers from his arm and walked away, turning when he reached the door to the hallway. "My mind is made up, Syl. For weeks, I have been trying to muster up the courage to do this. Now that I have finally said it, I am going to go through with it. You'll survive. I will continue to provide for you. I—I just want out."

"Would you pray with me about it?" she asked in desperation.

He shook his head. "No."

"Is Chatalaine married?"

"What's she got to do with this?"

His puzzled look infuriated her.

"You thought I didn't know your dirty little secret, didn't you?" she spat back, glowering at him.

"What secret?"

She felt her nostrils flare and her heart palpitate. "Come on, Randy, tell me about your lunch with your *client*! The one with the bleached blond hair and long, shapely legs that go up to her armpits. Did you make a sale? Is your social columnist going to purchase advertising with your precious newspaper because of your charms and your flawless sales pitch?"

He crossed the room quickly and grabbed onto her wrist, his nose close to hers. "Look, Syl. I have no idea what you're talking about. Yes, I had lunch with Chatalaine. A perfectly innocent lunch. The client called on my cell phone just before I reached the restaurant and said he couldn't make it. Since her column runs on the front page of that section and I was planning to pitch a succession of ads in the Dallas Life section, I thought it would be helpful to have Chatalaine there." He turned loose and stepped back with a shake of his head. "You're barking up the wrong tree if you're trying to accuse me of being unfaithful."

Like she always did when she was upset, Sylvia gnawed nervously on her lower lip, biting back words she knew she would be sorry for later if they escaped. *Is it possible I could have been wrong? Was it an innocent lunch like he said?*

"Face it, Syl. Another woman didn't break up our marriage. It's been dying for years, and we've both contributed to its death by ignoring it. I've realized it for some time. Maybe, if you were honest with yourself, you'd admit it, too. All we've been doing is marking time."

Divorce? That meant Randy would be leaving. She gasped at the paralyzing thought. "You're—you're not moving out, are you? Christmas is coming and the whole family will be—"

"There'll never be a good time. If there was, I'd have left months ago." He backed toward the hall again, as if wanting to put distance between the two of them, to pull away from her and all she represented.

This may be your only chance to try to save your marriage, she cautioned herself as she stared at the only man she'd ever loved. *Be careful what you say. Words, once said, can never be taken back.* "Please, Randy," she began, trying to add a softness to her voice when, inside, a storm was raging. "Give our marriage another chance. Just tell me what I'm doing wrong, and I'll change. I don't want you to leave. I—I love you!"

He did not look up. "I've worked long, hard hours for this family; now it's time for me. I'm going to get out and enjoy myself. Do some things I've put off for way too long."

His indifference broke her heart. "You could still do those things—"

"No." Keeping his gaze away from her face, he frowned and pursed his lips. "It's too late, Syl. I'm moving out. I packed up most of my personal things this morning while you were in the kitchen. I'll come back for the rest later."

Heaviness pressed against her heart and made it difficult to speak. "Yo–you're moving in with that woman?"

He gave her a look of annoyance. "No! Haven't you heard a word I've said?"

She rushed toward him and grabbed onto his arm, her fingernails nearly piercing the flesh. "You can't go! I won't let you!"

He pulled her hand away and rubbed at the red marks on his arm. "Hurting you is the last thing I wanted to do, Syl, but I can't keep living like this. The only fair way was to tell you this so we could both get on with our lives."

"Get *on* with our lives? How can I live without you, Randy? You expect me to believe you're not leaving me for another woman? Not for Chatalaine?"

His doubled up fist hit the palm of his other hand as his face filled with anger. "How many times do I have to tell you, Syl? There *is* no other woman! My lunch with Chatalaine was a legitimate, business-related luncheon, and I resent the idea that you would even think I'm cheating on you! Whatever happened to trust?"

"Trust? You ask *me* about trust?" Seeing the strange look in his eyes made her wonder at his words. Was that look guilt? Was he using anger and indignation to cover up his philandering? "Can you look me in the eye, Randy, and tell me this was the first time you and that woman have had lunch together?"

He did not have to answer. His face told it all.

"We've had lunch a few times but only to discuss her column—and those were on days you cancelled on me at the last minute because you were called to serve on some committee at the church or had to take a casserole to a sick person. You were always doing something for someone else when I needed you. Don't try to blame this on Chatalaine and a few business lunches."

Why hadn't she kept her mouth shut? "You're—you're really going through with this? Couldn't we maybe just have a separation for a while, so you can make sure you really want this before you take legal action?"

He gave her a flip of his hand. "A separation? Why? We've been living separate lives for years. I can't even remember the last time we—" He stopped midsentence.

His words hurt, and as badly as she hated to admit it, he was right. They'd both been so busy; they'd either been dead tired at the end of the day, she'd had one of her migraine headaches, or one of them had gone to bed early. But weren't there other ways of expressing your love other than physical? She had always thought taking good care of their children had been an act of love toward Randy. Keeping his house in perfect order and making sure his shirts were starched and ironed the way he liked them, to her, spoke of her love and adoration. Having good, nourishing meals on the table—sometimes having to reheat them because he got home late—all of those things and dozens of others were ways of saying *I love you*, weren't they?

"The children will have to be told," he said so matter-of-factly it only added to her already frazzled nerves.

She stepped back and crossed her arms over her chest, staring at him and seeing a stranger. "This is your party, Randy. Are you going to do the gentlemanly thing and tell them, or are you going to wait and let them find out for themselves? They'll hate you, you know."

"I'm hoping they won't hate me."

"They will. Our sons have always looked up to you as their role model. You've certainly fallen off that pedestal."

"I'll tell them," he murmured softly.

Sylvia pushed past him, rushed into the family room, afraid if she stood on her feet another minute she'd collapse.

Randy followed.

She shrugged and released a hefty sigh. "They say the wife is always the last to know. I guess that's because loving wives like me trust their husbands." She sat down quickly on the cushy green leather sofa, the one the two of them had selected together to commemorate their twentieth anniversary, and rubbed her hands over its smooth surface. "You certainly had me fooled. I thought we were getting along fine. I loved our life together."

He moved to the matching recliner, the roomier one they had specialty-ordered as his chair. But Sylvia reached out her hand and hollered, "Stop!"

He abruptly stepped to one side, giving her a puzzled look. "Stop what?"

She blinked her tear-filled eyes and pointed her finger at him defiantly. "Don't you dare sit in that chair! That chair is reserved for the head of this house. That wonderful, godly man I married. That description no longer fits you!"

Randy scooted over to a small, upholstered chair. "How about here?"

She nodded, feeling a bit chagrined, but he had to face reality. The breaking up of their marriage was something *he* wanted, not her.

Neither spoke for several minutes.

"I do love you, you know," she said finally, the tears now beginning to flow down her cheeks unashamedly. "I've always loved you. There's never been anyone else. Only you. Even if I haven't shown it much."

Randy hung his head and smoothed at the arm cover on the club chair. "I loved you, too, but—"

"But you no longer love me? Is that it?"

"I guess."

She glared at him, his answers not at all what she wanted to hear. "For a man who just asked his wife of twenty-five years for a divorce, you sure do a lot of guessing! Tell me outright, Randy. Do you or do you not love me?"

"I love you as the mother of my children," he said weakly, "and I care about you."

She bit at her lip until it hurt. "But you no longer love me as your wife? Your soul mate? Your lover? Is that the reason you never hug me anymore? Or touch me like you used to? Is that what you're saying?"

"I gu—yes."

"When did you make this amazing discovery? Before or after that woman came into your life?" She rose slowly, crossed the room, and knelt beside him. She had to find a way to make him change his mind. "Look into my eyes, Randy. See the pain I'm feeling. Think about the times we've shared together over the past twenty-five years—times both good and bad. Think about the struggles we've gone through together. And, yes, think about the times we've expressed our love for one another, though they may have been few lately. Then tell me. Tell me you don't love me anymore. Say the words. Convince me."

His gaze went to his lap, and for long moments he stared at his hands, methodically checking one fingernail at a time before he looked up at her. "I think whatever love I felt for you is gone, Syl, and has been for some time."

Those words cut so deeply, Sylvia was sure they had actually punctured her flesh and her blood was pouring from the cuts they had inflicted. Slowly, she stood and pulled herself up tall. She had to be strong even though her heart was breaking. Strong for herself and strong for her family, what there was left of it.

"If you're sure that's the way you feel and you're not willing to give our marriage another chance, then go, Randy. Go now. Give up the life the two of us made together. Give up your children, your home. Just remember, it was you who broke up this family. I have God to turn to, but I doubt very seriously He'll want to hear from you, unless it's to ask His forgiveness for what you're doing." She moved quickly to the double glass doors leading onto the patio, sliding one side open before she turned to face him again, her lips trembling. "It's your decision."

Without a word, Randy stood, started to say something but didn't, then hesitantly moved through the door and onto the porch.

Sylvia slid the door closed behind him and twisted the lock, shutting it on twenty-five years of marriage.

Chapter 3

Sylvia rushed to the narrow window beside the front door and pulled back the drapery just far enough to be able to watch Randy as he walked to his car, climbed in, started the engine, and drove away without even a backward glance. It was as though her very life ended with his departure. She wanted to pray, to ask God to bring her husband back to her, but the words would not come. It seemed even God had walked out on her. How could He have let this happen to their marriage?

Now what? Should she cry? No, she was too mad to cry. Throw things? Call the pastor? Go to bed and pull the covers over her head?

In robotic fashion, too numb to do anything, she moved to his recliner where the holiday edition of the *Dallas Times* still lay unrolled. How many times had she actually read the society column in the Dallas Life section? Probably not more than a dozen in all the years Randy had worked for the newspaper. Although her husband was constantly involved with community activities since he had been appointed managing editor, they rarely attended social functions together.

Maybe we should have, she told herself numbly as she lugged the heavy newspaper into the kitchen and poured herself that last cup of coffee before unplugging the pot. *Maybe that's one of the areas of Randy's life where I should have been more involved.* She tried to remember. *Did he ever ask me to go to one of those functions and I refused? Unfortunately, now that I think about it, he did. A number of times. But I had no interest in such things, and he never pressed the issue when I said no. If he felt they were important, he should have mentioned it instead of going on alone.* Her cup hit the table with a loud clunk, spattering coffee over the gingham placemat. *He went on without me!* That realization made her insides quiver. *I should have been with him! I should have bought that new dress he suggested and gone along, despite my lack of interest! For Randy's sake! Have I actually taken him for granted all these years, like he said? Is it my fault he's turned to someone else?*

She grabbed the dishrag from the sink and dabbed at the spilled coffee before settling down in the chair with the newspaper. Before she had seen her with Randy, she had never given much thought to Chatalaine. To her, the woman was just one of the many employees who worked for him. A columnist. Nothing more.

Until now.

Now she was reasonably sure Chatalaine Vicker was the reason their marriage was about to end.

Sylvia thumbed through the paper, discarding section after section, until she came to the one marked Dallas Life. There, glaring out at her with what she now perceived as a smirk instead of a smile, was the lovely, young face of Chatalaine Vicker, her nemesis.

Suddenly, feelings and emotions hitherto foreign to Sylvia came racing to the surface, and she wanted to go to that woman and scratch her eyes out. The woman who apparently wanted her husband and was more than likely willing to do whatever it took to get him. Did Randy really expect her to believe he wanted to leave her simply to find himself?

Blinking hard and trying to focus her eyes through the tears and terror she felt, she looked at the photograph again. She had to admit the woman was beautiful. The colorful picture, taking up a good portion of the first two columns, showed a full-length, enticingly posed view of Chatalaine's gorgeous, willowy figure as she stood leaning against a wall, her long arms crossed over her chest, a captivating smile adorning her perfectly made-up face. Even her name looked captivating, spread across the top of the page in an elegant, sprawling script. *What woman has a name like Chatalaine?*

Sylvia looked from the picture, to the half-empty cup of coffee, back to the picture, and back to the cup again. "Here's to you, you home wrecker!" she told the print version of her adversary as she slowly poured the remaining hot, black coffee over Chatalaine's face and body. "You wanted him. It looks like you got him! And I never even knew we were competing."

The ringing of the phone startled her, and the cup fell from her hands as she leaped to answer it, spilling the last few drops of coffee onto the floor. *Oh, dear God, let it be Randy calling to tell me it was all a joke!* "Hello!" she said eagerly into the phone, smiling and brushing away a tear.

"Hi. Just wanted to wish you a happy Thanksgiving."

She recognized the voice immediately. It was their pastor's wife, who was also her best friend. Sylvia's heart sank. "Hi, Jen."

"Hey, you don't sound so good. Are you coming down with a cold? Your voice sounds husky."

I can't tell her. Not yet. Not until I've had a chance to think this through. Do I want my church friends to know my husband has just asked me for a divorce? "May—maybe I am. I'm really not feeling up to par." She struggled to keep her words even, free of the raging emotions whirling inside her, when what she really wanted to do was cry out for sympathy. If she felt she could tell anyone, it would be Jen. But not now. Not yet.

"So? Is your family gathered around the TV set watching the game like my family is?"

Sylvia swallowed at the lump in her throat that nearly gagged her. Oh, how she wished they were in front of the TV. "No, DeeDee and Aaron both had to go back to college, to help out with the youth lock-in, and Buck and Shonna are spending the rest of the day with her parents."

"I'll bet Randy is glued to the set. I think the teams are tied. There's so much whooping and hollering going on in the other room, I can barely hear you."

"Ah—no. Randy isn't here. He—he had to—ah, to go down to the newspaper office." Although Sylvia had worked hard all her life at either telling the truth or just remaining silent, she felt she had to lie to protect Randy, still hoping he would change his mind and come home.

"On a holiday? Isn't that asking a bit much of the guy?"

"Ah—that's what happens—when you're the managing editor, I guess."

"Poor boy. His body may be at the paper, but I'll bet his mind is wishing he was there with you."

"I hope so." This time Sylvia's words were honest. She did hope he was wishing he was there with her, but after his dogged determination to get away from her, she doubted it.

"Well, that's all I called you for. To wish you a happy Thanksgiving and tell you that we love the two of you. So many folks in our congregation are experiencing marital troubles. It's refreshing to talk to someone who has accomplished twenty-five years of marital bliss. You two are a real inspiration to the rest of us."

Sylvia felt sick to her stomach as she clung to the phone with clammy hands, feeling like an imposter. "Ha–happy Thanksgiving to you, too, Jen. Thanks for calling."

After pressing the OFF button and placing the phone back on the table, she sat staring at it with unseeing eyes. *Marital bliss? That's what I'd thought it was, too, but apparently Randy thought otherwise.*

She glanced around the room, noting the stacks of dirty dishes still waiting to be loaded into the dishwasher, the roaster with the remnants of her famous pepper gravy clinging to its sides, and the pile of silverware she'd set aside to be washed by hand—the silverware she only used for special occasions. As she idly picked up a serving spoon, she had to laugh, despite her feelings of loneliness and despair. *Special occasions? Your husband asking you for a divorce is definitely a special occasion—one in which you never expect to be a participant.*

Placing her flattened palms onto the tabletop for support, she stood with agonizing stiffness, propelled herself one laborious step at a time across the spacious kitchen to the sink, and began to rinse the plates and place them in the dishwasher. Doing it the same way she had done hundreds of times before, but, this time, her mind was far from what she was doing.

Where is Randy this very moment? With that woman?

The question made bile rise in her throat. She picked up one of the delicate crystal goblets Randy had given her on their twentieth anniversary and flung it against the stone fireplace in the corner of the room. The glass shattered, sending shiny shards across the highly polished tile floor. Those glasses had been her prized possession, and she had always washed and dried them by hand to make sure none were ever broken. But today, somehow, the sound of breaking glass felt like a balm poured over her tormented soul.

Is he holding her hand?

A second glass hit the fireplace.

Is he holding Chatalaine in his arms?

The third glass missed its mark and broke against the wall, but she did not care. It was the sound she needed to hear.

Is he kissing that woman?

The fourth and fifth glasses broke simultaneously as she hurled one from each hand toward the fireplace. Sylvia jumped up and down, clapping her hands and laughing hysterically, relieving some of her pent-up tension in this unorthodox manner.

The last two glasses soon joined the others, and they all lay broken on the tile floor, their fragile beauty forever destroyed.

She stood for a long time, mesmerized as she stared at the broken pieces. Somehow, they symbolized the end of her marriage. Her dream. Her life. She wanted to turn and flee from the house she loved. The walls were permeated with memories. Memories she cherished. But today those memories seemed to haunt her, to ridicule her. To tell her she was a fool and a failure. If she had been the wife Randy had wanted, would he have been so easily lured away by that beautiful woman? It was a question she knew she would ask herself time and time again in the weeks to come. *I didn't have a chance,* she reasoned, looking for any excuse to absolve herself and her part in the failure of their marriage. *What woman wouldn't be attracted to Randy? He's not only handsome, he's also witty, charming, and highly successful.*

Her thoughts went to Chatalaine and how beautiful she had looked at the restaurant. Her gorgeous blond hair falling softly over her shoulders, her designer suit fitting her like wallpaper, displaying her perfect figure to the fullest advantage, her long slender legs, and fashionable high heels. The striking woman was a walking, talking, real-live Barbie doll.

Finally, willing herself to move, she pulled the dustpan and broom from the pantry, trudged across the kitchen floor, and began to sweep up the mess. Her body became as still as a mannequin when she heard the front door open and close. *Randy?*

"Mom, what happened?"

Disappointed it was not Randy, she turned to face her oldest son, sure that, after what she had been through, she must look like a mess. Even without checking the mirror, she knew her dampened mascara must have left dark streaks down her cheeks, her eyes had to be swollen from crying, and probably her nose was red from rubbing it across her sleeve.

Before she could stop them, two words escaped her lips. "Dad's gone!" She ran to Buck and buried her face in his chest, sudden sobs racking at her body, causing short gasps for air. Everything she had been holding back came gushing forth.

"Gone? What do you mean—*gone*? Is he hurt? Is he at the hospital? Did he have a wreck?" He grabbed onto her arms and pushed her away, staring into her face. "Mom! Tell me! What?"

Sucking in a deep breath, she blurted out, "He—he wants a divorce!"

"What?" Buck began to shake his head. "No, not my dad! He'd never do anything like that. Why are you saying this, Mom? Why?"

"He *is* doing it, Buck. I tried to talk him out of it, but—"

Buck doubled up a fist and plowed it into the palm of his other hand, looking eerily like his father. "It's another woman, isn't it?"

Sylvia nodded as she lowered her head and worked at keeping fresh tears at bay. "He says it isn't."

"That woman at the paper?"

Her eyes widened with surprise. "How did you know she was the one?"

Buck moved to the counter and checked the coffeepot. Finding it empty, he crossed to the cabinet, took out a glass, filled it with water, and took a long, slow drink before setting the empty glass in the sink. "I saw them together," he said, his back still to his mother.

She ran to him and circled her arms around his waist, pressing her face into his strong back. "Oh, Buck, no. You didn't."

He pulled her arms from about him and slowly turned to face her. "It seemed perfectly innocent at the time. I was having lunch with a friend at a little restaurant over in Arlington, and who walks in? Dad, with some woman."

"Did he know you were there?" she asked cautiously, wishing her son had not been forced to become a part of this fiasco.

"Yeah. I waited until they were seated and walked over to them. He introduced her as one of his employees—Catherine, Katrina—something like that. He said they had driven to Arlington to meet with some advertisers, and since it was lunchtime, they decided to have a bite to eat before driving back into Dallas. I believed him then, but now—with Dad talking about divorce, well, I just don't know."

Sylvia covered her face with her hands and tried to control her rekindled rage. "Oh, Buck. Why didn't you tell me? Give me a warning."

He patted her shoulder. "I tried not to give it a second thought. I wanted to believe him and his explanation seemed logical, the way women hold so many managerial positions nowadays."

She examined her heart. "I probably wouldn't have believed you even if you'd brought me back a Polaroid shot of him kissing her. I would've figured out a way to explain it. I trusted him."

"I—I asked Dad later if that was the real reason he was with her."

"You did? What did he say?" Did she really want to hear his answer?

"He really blew up at me. He told me I was a young punk with wild ideas, and he was insulted that I would even consider him being unfaithful to you. I felt like a jerk. He is my dad. The one I've looked up to all my life!"

"He says I should have seen it coming. That I'm to blame in all of this as much as he is." She slipped an arm around her son and hugged him tight. "I guess, if I'd had my eyes open, I should've seen it coming. He's been different for the past few months. Quiet and reserved sometimes, even spacey. Sometimes he was here—yet he wasn't. I should have read the signs. If only I'd—"

"Don't let him do that to you, Mom. Face it. Dad might be a Christian, but he's still a man. A mere mortal. We're all at risk for doing things we know we shouldn't." He gave her a smile that warmed her cold heart and began to melt some of the ice that had begun to form there. "You've been a terrific mom and, from my vantage point, the perfect wife. I can't imagine any woman being able to take your place."

Take my place? Oh, Lord—please—no! She mustered up a smile in return, not wanting him to know how much that phrase upset her. She was grateful for his words of consolation and encouragement, but his last words had pierced her soul. "Thanks, sweetie, but you've seen her. You know how beautiful she is. And young! I can't compete with Chatalaine Vicker."

"Hey, Mom, don't talk that way. You're a real knockout." He gave her chin a playful jab. "Get yourself a bottle of bleach and turn that brown hair of yours into a ditzy blond, take off a few pounds here and there, hit the makeup counters, add a couple of sexy, low-cut dresses and a pair of spike-heeled shoes, and she wouldn't have a chance at taking Dad away from you."

His humor cut through some of the insecurities she was feeling, and she laughed. But her laughter was soon overshadowed by the continual ache in her heart. "I wish I could convince myself it was merely her good looks that drew him to her, but I'm afraid it's much more than that."

Buck frowned, causing deep wrinkles in his forehead. "You—you don't think they're having—"

She reached up and quickly put her hand over his mouth. "Shh, don't even think it."

Buck gently pulled her hand away. "Would you take him back? After the way he's hurt you?"

"Of course, I would," she answered without hesitation. "On our wedding day, I promised before God that I was marrying your father for life, and I meant it. We both said, 'For better and for worse.' God never promised marriage would be easy, Buck."

Buck gave her that shy grin again. "But you had no idea how much worse, *worse* could be or that Dad would do something this bizarre. I'm going to ask Shonna to lock me in the closet if I ever start showing signs of a midlife crisis."

"Buck!" She giggled at his inane comment. "No, I never thought we'd have a problem like this, but I knew I'd have God by my side to help me work out the rough spots. I may have been young, but I wasn't stupid," she added through fresh tears. "I knew what I was vowing. I thought your father did, too."

He grinned a silly little grin. "You do know you look like a raccoon, don't you, Mom?"

She hurried to the little mirror on the back of the pantry door and gazed at her ridiculous reflection, summoning up a smile for his benefit. "I knew I looked bad, but not this bad! Why didn't you tell me?"

"I think you're kinda cute."

She grabbed a dishrag from the drawer, dampened it at the faucet, and began rubbing at the black circles and streaks around her eyes and down her cheeks. "What are you doing here anyway? I thought you and Shonna were spending the rest of the day at her parents' house."

"We are. I left my billfold in the bathroom after that fabulous Thanksgiving dinner you cooked. I came back to get it."

She patted his arm affectionately. "I'm glad you did. I needed someone to talk to. It seems God isn't listening to me."

"Come on, Mom, you know that's not true."

"If He is, why isn't He making your dad come back home where he belongs?"

"Who says He's not trying to convince him to do just that?"

She gestured around the room with a broad sweep of her hand. "Do you see your father here?"

He grabbed it and linked his fingers with hers. "You don't believe God is dealing with Dad? Think about it, Mom. Our father is giving up everything. You know he's got to realize, eventually, he's making a stupid mistake. You have to turn this over to God. Hasn't He promised He'd never leave you or forsake you?"

She pulled her hand free and cradled his chin. "My wonderful, well-grounded son. God does answer prayer. He already has."

He frowned. "What do you mean?"

"He made you leave your billfold in the bathroom, otherwise, why would you have come back here—just when I needed you?"

"See? I told you God answers prayer."

She had to smile at the silly expression on his face. What a joy Buck had been to her since the day he was born. "Yes, He does."

"What now, Mom? Are you going to tell DeeDee and Aaron?"

She crossed the kitchen, seated herself at the table, and began fumbling with the colorful basket of silk flowers she had put together in a craft class at the church. "Not yet. I don't want your brother and sister to know until it's absolutely necessary. And, please, don't tell anyone else about this—except Shonna, of course. I don't want there to be any secrets between the two of you, but ask her to keep this to herself until I'm ready to let everyone know. I want your father to have plenty of time to change his mind. If everyone knows, he'll be embarrassed, and I can't let that happen. Let's give him some time, okay?"

Buck planted a kiss on his mother's cheek. "My faithful, forgiving mother. What a treasure you are. I only hope Dad comes to his senses and realizes it before it's too late."

"Your father needs your prayers, Buck. So do I."

He kissed the tip of her nose. "You got them, both of you."

"Now," she said, trying to put up a brave front and pointing toward the door. "Go to your wife and enjoy what's left of your Thanksgiving Day."

"You gonna be all right? I can stay with you. Shonna will understand."

"I'm going to be fine. I'll call if I need you."

He pulled his cell phone from his belt and held it toward her. "You've got my number?"

She stood on tiptoe and kissed her son's chin. "Yes, I have your number. Go."

As he strode out the door, Sylvia kept the smile on her face, but the minute the door closed behind him, it disappeared, and the feelings of misery and betrayal she had endeavored to squash down deep inside rose to the surface. *Oh, dear God—what a mess we've made of our lives. Only You can straighten this out.*

After sweeping up the broken glass, she took a long, leisurely shower and let the hot water run over her face and body, washing away her tears, until she could stand it no longer. She toweled off and slipped into her pajamas, then dried her hair with the blow dryer and stared into the mirror. Though she fit nicely into a size twelve, her proportions were nothing like Chatalaine's. Giving birth and nursing her children had seen to that. Everything had gone south. She glanced at her reflection and the worn flannel pajamas—the comfortable ones she wore more often than any of her others—and thought about the three delicate, lacy nightgowns she had in her bureau drawer. The ones Randy had bought for her the past three Valentine's Days. Two of them still had the tags on them. The third had only been laundered twice. Why hadn't she worn them? Hadn't Randy told her he had bought them for her because he thought she would look beautiful in them?

Finding it difficult to pray and wondering how God could have let this happen to her, she muttered a few thank-yous, asked God to send Randy home where he belonged, and added a quick, "Amen." Many of the things Randy had mentioned, things that took her away from him, were things she had done at the church. For God. Is this the way He was rewarding her for her labors? By allowing her husband to walk out of her life?

As though God Himself were speaking to her, in her heart she heard, *It wasn't Me that let him go, my child. You turned your back on him and let other things take over your life and become more important than the relationship between the two of you.*

"But, God," she cried out. "Everything I've done has been for a good cause. The church activities. The children. Their school functions. Teaching my Sunday school class. Leading the women's prayer group. Heading up the Care and Share pantry. I did all of those things for You!"

None of it for your own glory? None of it when you should have been with your husband, being a helpmeet to him? When you made those vows before Me, you promised to do many things. Have you honored all of those promises, my daughter?

Sylvia stared at the Bible on her nightstand, remembering their wedding and the way the two of them had placed their hands on a Bible when they had made those vows. "But, Lord, Randy made those same vows. He's the one who is breaking them, not me! It's not fair that he's expecting me to take part of the blame."

Examine your own heart, daughter. Examine your own heart.

After turning out the light, she lay in the darkness, thinking. Pondering the words God had spoken to her. How many times in the past five years had her husband seemed aloof? Distant. Sometimes acting as if he had no interest in her *or* the children. Had an affair been going on right under her nose, and she had been so absorbed with her life she hadn't noticed? Looking back, the signs had been there. She just had not seen them—or cared enough to see them. The late nights at the office. Sudden trips to the newspaper on weekends to take care of some insignificant problem that cropped up. Calling at the last minute to say he couldn't attend one of the children's school functions. He claimed he was doing those things because of increased competition from both his competitors and the way more people were watching television news to keep them informed rather than the newspapers. Even on the few nights he was home, he would hole up in the den most of the evening and work at the computer. At least, she had *thought* he was working on the computer. Perhaps, instead, he had been talking to Chatalaine on that online instant message thing.

Had those excuses been simply that? Excuses to find a way to get out of the house? Away from her? Maybe to meet Chatalaine?

She flipped over onto her side with a groan, her tears flowing again. This would be Randy's first night of staying away from home. Was he having feelings of exhilaration? Or was he, too, feeling pangs of loneliness? She shuddered at how awful it felt being in bed alone. Surely, he was telling her the truth. That nothing was going on between him and that woman. *God, please keep him pure. Don't let him succumb to fleshly desires.*

Without Randy by her side, the bed seemed big. Overpowering. Like an angry giant. She closed her eyes and flattened her hand on his pillow, trying to convince herself that he would be there when she opened them.

He wasn't.

She tugged his pillow to her, drinking in the lingering fragrance of his after-shave and relishing its scent, draping her arm over it much as she did over Randy each night after they turned out the lights. *Oh, Randy. I love you so much. How will I ever live without you? You're my very life!*

Chapter 4

The last time Sylvia remembered looking at the clock on her nightstand, it was 5:00 a.m. She awakened at eight, feeling like she'd not slept at all, with the sheets askew, and the lovely old nine-patch quilt half off on the floor.

Randy!

She flipped over, her hand quickly moving to his pillow.

But Randy wasn't there.

It hadn't been a bad dream.

He had really left her.

Laboriously, she made the bed, dragging herself from side to side, though why, she didn't know. An unmade bed was the least of her worries. She brushed her teeth and ran a comb through her hair out of habit, not really caring how she looked. Visions of the long-legged blond on the front of the Dallas Life section of the newspaper blurred her brain and made her woozy. Her three children had left home. Buck to get married, and Aaron and DeeDee to attend college. Now Randy, her life's mate, was gone, too, and for the first time ever—she was alone. Really alone. Since she and Randy had married so young, she had gone directly from her parents' home to their little apartment, with no stops in-between.

She stood at the window for a long time, gazing into the backyard. With all her busyness, she had even neglected the flower beds she had at one time loved. When was the last time she had weeded and fertilized them? Even the perennials had quit blooming. If it weren't for the faithful geraniums, there would be no blooming flowers at all. Thanks to them and their endurance, every few feet a tiny blast of red spotted the otherwise colorless flower beds. She winced at the thought. Was her marriage like those flower beds? Had she let other things, like the weeds growing so prevalently, go unattended, get in the way, and crowd out the important things of her life until they had withered and died? At the thought, her stomach again turned nauseous, and for a moment, she reeled, clutching the windowsill for support. *Oh, Randy. How could I have taken our life for granted? How could I have taken you for granted? Did I really drive you into that woman's arms?*

Moving slowly into their walk-in closet to pull out her favorite pair of jeans, she froze. Except for a few garments he never wore, Randy's side of the closet was empty. Even the hangers were gone. Shoeboxes no longer filled the long shelves above the rods. No more beautiful designer ties hung from his tie racks. Even the prized rifle his father had given him when he was sixteen no longer stood in the corner behind the clothing where he had kept it so it would be out of sight of the children. Standing on tiptoes, she reached up and ran her hand along the top shelf, in search of the little .25 caliber pistol he always kept there in case an intruder entered their home.

It, too, was gone!

Randy was gone!

Everything was gone!

Her heart thudded to a sudden stop. Surely he wouldn't do anything foolish! Not her levelheaded Randy!

But the Randy who had told her he was leaving wasn't her levelheaded Randy. He was a stranger wearing Randy's body. She only thought she had known him. This new Randy was an unknown entity, and she had no idea what he might be capable of doing. *Oh, Randy, Randy! If only you would've told me a long time ago how unhappy you were with our marriage, maybe—* She banged her head against the window jamb, but it was too numb even to feel the pain. *If I'd been any kind of attentive wife to you, I should've known. Looking back now, I can see the signs. I'd attributed your silence to you having things on your mind about the paper. All those times when you seemed aloof, I'd thought you were tired. The many times you sat staring at the walls, I assumed you were too physically and mentally exhausted to talk. Were you deliberately ignoring me because you simply no longer wanted to be around me? How could I have been so blind? Why didn't I ask you if something was wrong? Were you seeing Chatalaine even then?*

The image of the elegant woman popped into her mind, uninvited, when she moved toward the bed, pausing at the full-length mirror on the way. Her breath caught and nearly gagged her as she stared at her reflection. *Can this be me? Where is that young woman my husband used to admire? The one whose hair was brown and shiny, instead of dull and graying? The one who was twenty pounds lighter and cared about her figure? Who always put her makeup on first thing in the morning and went out of her way to kiss her husband good-bye when he left for work? The one who hung on his every word, making sure she was there whenever he needed her?* She glanced down at her faded jeans and the well-worn T-shirt that had become the uniform she crawled into when she came home from one of her functions, eager to make herself comfortable. *When did I decide it was no longer necessary to look my best at the end of the day when Randy came home from work? When did I become so careless?*

Grabbing her robe from the chair where she had left it, she draped it over the mirror, shutting out the image that threatened to destroy what little self-esteem she had left. But it didn't help. The reflection remained etched on her memory, and she did not like the feeling.

She had to talk to Randy. To beg him to come back home where he belonged.

"Good morning. *Dallas Times*. If you know your party's extension, you may enter it now, otherwise listen to the complete list of options before making your selection," the canned recording said when she dialed the phone. She punched in the numbers by rote and waited for him to answer.

"Good morning. Randy Benson's office. This is Carol. May I ask who's calling?"

Instantly, Sylvia realized she had dialed the extension for Randy's office and not his direct line. "Ah—Carol—this is Sylvia. May I speak to Randy?"

"I'm sorry, Sylvia. He isn't in. He's in meetings over in Arlington most of the day. I don't expect him back until late this afternoon."

A meeting in Arlington or another one of his rendezvous?

"When he's out of the office, he usually checks in with me several times a day. Would you like me to have him phone home?"

"Yes, would you, please? I'll—I'll be here all day. I really need to talk to him."

"Would you like me to try and reach him?"

"No, just tell him when you hear from him." She thanked the woman, then hit the OFF button, and placed the phone back onto the charger, disappointed.

She had no more than lifted her hand from it, when it rang. She snatched it up, both hoping it was Randy yet not sure what she would say if he did call. "Hello."

"Hi, Mom. I've been concerned about you. Are you okay? Do you want me to come over?"

As much as she loved hearing her oldest son's voice, she was filled with disappointment. "No, honey, I'm—I'm okay. Just depressed."

"I love you, Mom. You know I'll come if you need me."

She smiled into the phone. At least her son still loved her. "No, I don't want you taking off work. Don't worry about me, sweetie. I'm still hoping, praying, somehow this will all work out."

"I still want to call Dad."

"I know, but please don't. Let's make it as easy as possible for your father to come back home, and I don't want there to be any rifts between the two of you."

"Okay, but if you—"

"I know, and thanks, Buck. Get back to your job. Your mother will survive."

"Survive?" she repeated aloud when she hung up the phone. "I'm not so sure I *will* survive or even want to if Randy doesn't come back home."

She busied herself doing several loads of laundry, weeping when she pulled a couple of Randy's favorite shirts from the hamper. Her tears fell softly onto the fabric when she cradled them close, the faint aroma of his aftershave tantalizing her nostrils. When the last piece had been pulled from the dryer and folded, she closed the laundry room door and made her way into the kitchen, checking the clock as she moved to the refrigerator and pulled out a bottle of cranberry juice. It was nearly noon, and she hadn't eaten a bite of breakfast or even had a glass of water.

Why hasn't he called? Surely Carol has heard from him by now.

She jumped for the phone when it rang about three, but it was not Randy calling; it was Buck, checking on her again.

An hour later, a telemarketer called, offering to give her an estimate on siding. Normally, she listened courteously to their spiel before saying, "No, thank you," and hanging up, but not this time. This time his call infuriated her, and she cut him off right after his "Are you the homeowner?" question.

For the next hour, she sat staring at the phone.

But it didn't ring.

Nor did it ring at six, or seven, eight, nine, ten, or eleven, other than two more calls from Buck.

When the doorbell rang at half past eight the next morning, she rushed to answer it, stubbing her toe on the ottoman on the way, but it was the UPS man bringing a package. Something Randy had ordered from a computer supply company.

Other than Buck's regular concerned calls, the phone did not ring a single time on Saturday, and Sylvia found herself in a deep pit of depression with the walls closing in on her. Why didn't Randy call? If only he had left the phone number where he would be staying. She was tempted to look up Chatalaine Vicker's number in the phone book but decided against it. Whether Randy was at her place or not, he would be furious with her for checking up on him. She tried watching TV to keep her mind off him, but that didn't work. Next, she pulled out the quilt she had started when their children were small and had never finished. Maybe the rhythm of working the needle would help sooth her jagged nerves, but she found she had misplaced her thimble, so she returned it to its box in the family room closet. The novel in her bedside chest held no more interest than it had a day or two before and ended up back in the drawer.

In desperation, she turned to her Bible for solace, but even it did not help. A bookmark fell out onto the bed as she closed its cover. Her gaze locked on the quotation printed there in a beautiful script. Its message ripped her heart to shreds. *Love thrives in the face of all life's hazards, except one. Neglect.* The words ricocheted through her being, replaying over and over, bathing her heart with guilt. She *had* neglected Randy! *Oh, dear Lord, what have I done? Help me, I pray! Help me put our marriage back together!*

At seven the next morning, after another sleepless night, she phoned Jen, her pastor's wife and best friend. "I won't be able to teach my class today," she told her, trying to make her voice sound raspy, as if she were coming down with something. She knew if she ran into any of her friends, her face would immediately tell them she had a problem without a word being spoken. Her swollen eyes and reddened cheeks, too, would be a dead giveaway, even if she could keep her tears in check, which she knew would be impossible.

"I'm sure Randy is taking good care of you, Sylvia, but if there's anything I can do—" Jen laughed. "Like open a can of chicken noodle soup, heat it in my microwave, and bring it over to you, I'd—"

"I know," Sylvia answered, interrupting, but the last thing she needed was to have to explain her appearance to someone. "There's really nothing you can do, but thanks, I appreciate the offer. I—I think I'll just rest and take it easy."

She stayed in her pajamas and robe all morning, mostly just sitting in Randy's recliner, rubbing her hands over the armrests, and staring out the pair of sliding glass doors, watching the birds feed at the bird feeder he'd built for her for Mother's Day four or five years ago. She had spent many happy hours watching the cardinals and blue jays sort through the seeds, picking out the kinds they liked best.

Buck stopped by about one o'clock, bringing her cartons of sweet and sour chicken, fried rice, and crab Rangoon from her favorite Chinese restaurant. Although she appreciated his efforts and concern and thanked him with an enthusiasm she did not feel, the food was tasteless and held no appeal. He took out the trash before leaving, telling her he'd be back the next day but to call if she needed anything in the meantime. He explained Shonna had wanted to come with him, but he'd told her it might be best if she waited until Sylvia was feeling up to seeing her. She thanked him, saying she would phone Shonna in a day or two. Maybe then she would feel more like talking about things.

After sleeping most of the afternoon, she ate a bit more of the rice about seven and crawled into bed at eight, facing another sleepless night without her husband by her side.

She phoned Randy's office again on Monday, this time punching in the numbers to his direct line. It rang four times before Carol picked up in the outer office.

"I'm sorry, Sylvia. He is in a staff meeting. I am afraid it is going to be a lengthy one. He has already asked me to call the deli and have box lunches delivered. But I'll tell him you called."

Sylvia let her head drop to her chest with an, "Oh. Of course. I forgot. He always has staff meetings on Monday."

Seeming to sense a problem, Carol offered, "If it's important, maybe I can interrupt."

"No! Don't do that. Just ask him to call, please."

She stayed by the phone the rest of the day, watching the hours tick by, waiting for his call.

But it never came.

When the phone rang Tuesday morning, she grabbed it up on the first ring.

"Mrs. Benson. This is Hank from Hawkins Flowers. Could you please tell Mr. Benson we were able to get the apricot roses after all? He seemed so disappointed when he ordered and had to settle for pink roses. I knew he'd want to know."

"Apricot roses?"

"Yes, and tell him we delivered them with his note attached, just as he'd asked. My driver said the lady was thrilled with them. Whoops, the other line is ringing. Thank you for conveying my message. Mr. Benson is a good customer, and we appreciate his business."

Sylvia stood with her mouth hanging open as the broken connection clicked in her ear. When the man had called, she had hoped the flowers were for her, and her heart had soared. Then he had said they had already been delivered. To whom had he sent flowers? Certainly not her! There seemed to be only one answer.

Chatalaine.

Why else would he go to all the trouble to make sure he was able to get roses of a certain color?

She staggered her way across the family room and plunked herself into Randy's recliner. When was the last time he had sent flowers to her? Her birthday? No, he had taken the whole family out to celebrate, but there had been no flowers for her. Usually, he sent her a gigantic poinsettia for Christmas, but this past year, he did not even do that. Mother's Day last year? No, Buck and his wife had given her a beautiful white orchid corsage, but Randy had barely told her, "Happy Mother's Day." She cupped her head in her hands, her fingers rubbing at her eyes wearily as the song "You Don't Bring Me Flowers Anymore" resonated through her head. No, her beloved husband did not bring her flowers anymore. Apparently, his flowers were going to someone else now. Someone who paid more attention to him and met his needs more adequately than she did.

As Sylvia lay in bed that night, she came to a decision. If Randy would not return her calls, she would go see him at his office. Yes, that is exactly what she would do.

By nine the next morning, her hair swept up in a twist, her makeup meticulously applied, and decked out in the dress she'd bought on impulse several weeks earlier, Sylvia was in the elevator on her way up to Randy's fourth-floor office. She had decided it was a bit too tight for her and a bit too short and had almost returned it to the store. Now she was glad she hadn't. She had purposely worn the necklace and matching earrings he had given her several Christmases ago, although she doubted he would remember. Normally, she wore shoes with less than two-inch heels, but this morning she was wearing the pair of strappy, spike-heeled sandals she'd purchased to wear to one of Randy's award banquets. She had ended up not going and staying home because DeeDee complained of a sore throat. She had never worn the shoes long enough to break them in, and her feet were killing her. However, if it meant catching her husband's attention, the pain would be worth it.

"My, you look nice," Carol said as Sylvia exited the elevator, "but I'm sorry. You just missed him. He hasn't been gone five minutes."

Sylvia wanted to cry. And nearly did. But knowing her tears would only upset Carol, she reined them in and forced a casual smile. "He didn't know I was coming. I thought I'd surprise him." Her heart broken and tears threatening to erupt despite her tight hold on them, she said a quick good-bye to Carol and stepped back into the waiting elevator. She had so hoped to see Randy and talk to him. Maybe then she could convince him to swallow his pride and admit he wanted to come home.

She exited the elevator and hurried out the front door toward the *Dallas Times*'s public parking garage to the left of the big building. But as she approached the entrance, a white minivan exited through the gate not thirty feet in front of her, her husband at the wheel and a gorgeous blond in the passenger seat.

Devastated by the sight, Sylvia leaned against the building for support, both hurt and angry. *He doesn't have time to return my calls, but he sure has time for his little cutie!* Lifting first one foot, then the other, she snatched off the offensive sandals from her aching feet and ran the rest of the way to her car in her stockings, not caring if anyone saw her or if she got runs in her new pantyhose. All she wanted to do was get home where she could hide out and unleash her overwhelming rage. *How dare he?*

Finally, she reached the house, not even sure which route she had taken. She flung herself across the bed and screamed out to God, asking what she had done in her life that was so bad she would deserve this kind of treatment.

When the doorbell sounded at four, she couldn't decide if she should answer it or not. It might be Randy, and at this point, she was not sure she even wanted to talk to him. If she told him she had seen him with Chatalaine, he would probably make up some ridiculous excuse. Or maybe he would just admit it, and she wasn't sure she was ready to hear those words from his lips.

The doorbell rang a second time. She stood pressed against the wall, weighing her options.

Whoever was there began pounding on the door. Since she had not changed the locks, she knew if it were Randy, he would just use his key. So rather than explain to whomever might be there, she opened the door.

"I knew you were here. Your car is in the driveway, and your keys are hanging in the front door. You'd better be more careful."

Chapter 5

J en!" Sylvia quickly wiped at her eyes with her sleeve. "I—I didn't know it was you!"

Jen moved inside and stood glaring at her, her face filled with concern. "Aw, sweetie, what's wrong? You look awful!"

Sylvia turned and led the way into the living room. "I–I'd rather not talk about it."

Jen took her hand and tugged her toward the flowery chintz sofa. "Look, Sylvia, you're my best friend. If you think I'm going to walk out that door before I find out what's bothering you, you're crazy. Now sit down here beside me and tell me about it, or I'm going to call Randy's office and ask him." Giving her a quick once-over, she continued. "You're all dressed up. Were you on your way out?" Spotting her stocking'd feet, she raised her brows and gave her a smile. "You forgot your shoes."

Sylvia leaned back against the sofa's soft cushions and closed her eyes. She needed to talk to someone. She hated to confide in Buck. After all, Randy was his dad, but she had to open up her injured heart to someone. The silence was driving her wild.

"Okay, out with it. What's wrong? You know you can trust me, don't you?" Jen placed her hand softly on Sylvia's arm. "You're doubly safe talking to me. As your best friend, I'd never betray your confidence, and as the wife of your pastor, I'm bound by God to keep my mouth shut."

Sylvia opened her eyes and stared at the ceiling. "I don't know who I can trust, Jen."

"Out with it, Sylvia. It'll make you feel better to talk about it. Are you sick? Has one of the kids gotten into trouble?"

"Worse than that."

Jen paused. "How much worse?"

Sylvia turned to her friend. She could be trusted, and she would never do or say anything that would harm either her or Randy. "Randy—he—"

Jen let out a gasp. "Oh, no! Is there something wrong with Randy? Harrison and I were just saying the other day, that man is the picture of health."

"No, he's fine. Healthwise."

Jen looked at her impatiently. "Then what about Randy?"

"He wants a di—divorce."

Her friend just stared at her in disbelief, as if words failed her. Finally, she slipped her arm about Sylvia and pulled her close. "I'm so sorry, Sylvia."

Sylvia gulped hard, then for the next half hour, she related the entire story about Randy's leaving and her suspicion he'd left her for another woman, even though he'd denied it. She was careful not to mention Chatalaine's name. "I'm at my wit's end. I've about decided to give up and let him have the divorce without contesting it."

When she finished, Jen asked, "You, Sylvia Benson, are going to give up? Without a fight? That is not like you. If you still love this man and want him back, you are going to have to slug it out for him. This pity party you're having isn't going to cut it. It only makes you look weak, and from my vantage point as a pastor's wife with experience in dealing with broken marriages, weak is never appealing or convincing to the spouse who walked out on the marriage. Especially if there is another woman involved. She's usually pulling out all the stops to get the man to leave his wife and marry her. It's her mission in life, her goal, and she won't quit until she gets him."

Sylvia looked at her with wide eyes, surprised by Jen's direct words. "If that's true, how do you expect me to compete?"

"That, friend of mine, is for you to figure out! But if it were me, and I loved my husband as much as I thought you loved Randy, I'd fight for him with every ounce of my being."

Sylvia pulled away from her and lowered herself into Randy's recliner. "I wouldn't begin to know how to fight. She—she's—" She selected her words carefully, even though she knew, as a pastor's wife, her friend would never go about telling tales and break a confidence. "She's beautiful, Jen."

Jen did a double take. "You've seen her?"

Sylvia nodded. "It's that society columnist from Randy's paper."

"Chatalaine Vicker?"

"Yes."

"Wow. You are right. She is beautiful!"

"Now you see why I said I couldn't compete with her."

Jen shook her head sadly. "I always thought, as happily married as the two of you seemed, Randy would be the last man to succumb to infidelity, but no man is safe. Or woman, for that matter. Many women leave their husbands and kids for so-called *greener pastures*, only to find they weren't as green as they'd expected." Jen seated herself on the sofa and leaned back into the cushions. "He sure wouldn't be the first Christian man his age to let his head be turned by a pretty woman. Is he wearing gold chains, leaving his top three buttons unbuttoned on his shirt so his chest hair will show, and talking about buying a motorcycle?"

Sylvia smiled through her tears. "Not that I've seen."

"Then there may be hope for him."

"You think he may be going through a midlife crisis?"

Jen shrugged. "Who knows? We women have menopause—men have a midlife crisis. We get grouchy. They get childish. All of a sudden, they need their space. We've seen it over and over again during our years in the ministry. I can't begin to tell you how many times my husband has had to counsel couples in this very situation. Usually, if both partners love the Lord, the husband comes to his senses before anything stupid happens, and if each person wants to revive the marriage and is willing to compromise and do their part, their relationship can be salvaged."

Sylvia sniffled as she reached for a tissue. "Salvaged? You make it sound like a battleship that went down at sea, was found, and pulled up later—battered and covered with barnacles."

"In some ways, that's what a broken marriage is like. But unlike the battleship, it sinks slowly—with the husband and wife barely noticing the leak that will eventually destroy it. Funny, you mentioned barnacles. I've heard my husband use those very words when he's been counseling a couple. He often likens them to wounds that married folks inflict on each other over time—like hastily said words, forgetting birthdays and anniversaries, neglecting to say I love you, taking each other for granted, not spending time together, and on and on and on."

Jen reached across and squeezed her hand. "The wounds are tiny at first, barely noticeable, but then infection sets in, and the wounds fester and grow until they actually threaten life if left unattended. Placing a Band-Aid over them merely covers them, but underneath the wounds remain infected, spreading wider and wider until they demand attention. At that point, drastic measures have to be taken. Though the wounds can probably be treated successfully with time and attention, many folks prefer immediate surgery. Cut it off and get rid of it."

"Divorce."

Jen nodded. "Yes, divorce. Sometimes those hurts go way deeper than we can possibly imagine."

The two women sat silently staring at one another. Finally, Sylvia spoke. "I–I've neglected Randy, Jen. I've put everything ahead of him and his needs. I realize that now."

"I'm afraid, as women and mothers, we all have a tendency to do that very thing. And for worthwhile causes. But that doesn't make it right," Jen confessed. "I have to admit, sometimes I feel neglected. Being married to a pastor doesn't mean everything is hunky-dory at all times. We get calls all hours of the day and night from people who need him. I've cooked many a supper only to have him call and say he won't make it home because someone is having trouble and needs him. As the pastor's family, the children and I always take the backseat in any situation. Harrison and I have our moments of conflict, too. We have the same pressures and problems our church members have; only we're expected to be perfect. The power of darkness would like nothing more than to see trouble in the pastor's home, and the enemy works twenty-four/seven to make it happen."

Sylvia stared at her friend. "You and Harrison? But—you two are perfect. I've never once heard you say a cross word to each other!"

"That's because we keep our best face forward and do our arguing within the four walls of our home." Jen leaned forward, bracing her hands on her knees, her face serious. "Look, Sylvia, no one is perfect. Not you. Not Randy. Not Harrison and certainly not me. Marriages are fragile things. We can't let them go unattended or take them for granted. I know Harrison and I have to work at it constantly. Several years ago, we realized, due to the demands of life, we were drifting apart and decided to do something about it. That's why Friday night is our night. Unless an emergency happens, which it does quite often, from five o'clock until midnight every Friday night, the two of us are together. Alone. No kids. No in-laws. No parishioners. Just my husband and me. One week I plan the evening. The next week, Harrison plans it. It's always a surprise. It may be as simple as hamburgers at McDonald's and a movie or a picnic in the park. Other times it's as complex as a dinner theater. But it's our time together. We've even sneaked out of town a few times and spent the night at a motel." Jen's eyes sparkled as she talked.

"I wish Randy and I had done something like that." Sylvia leaned back in Randy's recliner and stared at the ceiling, trying to remember the last time she and her husband had spent the entire evening together, just the two of them. "Maybe if we had, he'd still be here."

"Men try to act real tough, put on a façade. Rarely do they admit they're hurting. They pretend they have tough skin, but they're as vulnerable as we are, honey. If someone had asked me which man in our church would be least likely to do something like this, I would have said Harrison first, with Randy running a very close second."

Sylvia blinked back tears. "Me, too. I never dreamed—"

"That's the problem, Sylvia. Most of us don't even suspect a problem until it rears its ugly head. We're too caught up with life to see what's right under our nose."

"Do—do you think it's too late to fix it?"

"Let me ask *you* a question. Do you think God wants the two of you together?"

Without hesitation, Sylvia answered, "Yes! Of course, He does."

"Then fight, Sylvia! Fight with all you're worth. If you must go down, go down swinging."

"Fight?"

Jen doubled up her fist and punched at the air. "Yes, fight. Fight for your marriage."

Sylvia let out a sigh. "But I'm not a fighter. I wouldn't know how to begin."

"You? Not a fighter? I've always thought of you as a fighter. Aren't you the woman who went to bat with the city council over the zoning for the church's youth building annex and won? I was amazed the day you spoke at that council meeting. I never knew you had it in you. You were so passionate and articulate, they had no choice but to grant the zoning to you. I can't think of anyone who could have done a better job."

Sylvia smiled a small victorious smile. "I really wanted the youth of our church to have that annex."

"And you did all you could to make it happen, didn't you? You moved way out of your comfort zone. You have to do the same thing now if you want to win." Jen scooted to the edge of the sofa. "If you want to revive this marriage, you're going to have to face up to your part in its failure and do something about it."

"Like what? What can I do?"

"That question, my friend, is one you'll have to answer." Jen pulled her car keys from her pocket and rose to her feet. "I hate to leave you like this, but I have to pick up one of the children, and I'm already late. I will give you this bit of advice, though. Like you, I'm sure God wants the two of you together, so why don't you let Him help you with the answer? Pray about it, Sylvia. Listen to God. Read His Word. If your heart is open and you're willing to do whatever He asks, He'll tell you how."

Sylvia pushed herself out of the recliner and stood, her heart overflowing with love and appreciation for this godly woman. "I'm glad you came, Jen."

"Me, too, even though I had to pound on the door to get you to let me in." Jen gave her arm an affectionate pinch. "I'll be praying for you, you know that."

"I'm counting on it."

Sylvia stood in the doorway, waving at her friend and confidante as she drove off. God had sent her at just the right time. With renewed hope in her heart, she closed the door.

Reading her Bible that night, Jen's words kept coming back to her. *If you want to revive this marriage, you are going to have to face up to your part in its failure and do something about it.*

"But what, Lord? What can I do?" Sylvia cried out after she dropped to her knees beside her bed. "I've left messages nearly every day, and Randy hasn't returned any of my calls. I've gone to his office only to find he left with that woman. I don't know what to do. Jen says I have to fight for him, but how? How do I fight? Show me what to do. Surely You want Randy and me together. Help me, God! Give me wisdom. Give me guidance!"

No flash appeared.

No revelation from heaven.

As she lay there in the darkened room, Sylvia continued to pray, quoting every scripture verse she had memorized about God answering prayer. Eventually, she fell asleep, the pillow wet with her tears.

❄

It was after midnight when Randy crawled into bed in his new fifth-floor, high-rise apartment. Why hadn't he noticed the noise from the nearby set of elevators when he had leased it? And who could be going up and down in it this time of night, anyway? How did they expect a guy to sleep with all that racket?

He flipped onto his side and pulled the sheet over his head. Morning would arrive soon enough, and he needed to be at the office early to prepare for a meeting with one of his key advertisers. Unable to fall asleep, he ran the meeting's agenda over in his head, hoping to come up with a few more reasons why the client should up his advertising budget for the coming year. Circulation was down as more and more people turned to CNN for their daily news. And with the cost of production going up every day, it was becoming harder and harder to meet the anticipated yearly profit margin. Maybe he should have gone with CNN when they had given him the chance. They'd made him a good offer, but that would have meant moving to Atlanta.

Though he'd known she really didn't want to, Sylvia had even said she was willing to make the move.

Sylvia! Why did his thoughts on any subject seem to end up with Sylvia, when he had finally gotten up the courage to move out of the house and put an end to their stagnant marriage? Now that he was going to be free to do whatever he chose, maybe he should contact CNN again and see if they were still interested in his joining their staff. The kids were grown. He could always hop on a plane and come back to visit them whenever he wanted, and he could send them tickets to come and visit him. Atlanta was an exciting city, with lots of things to see and do. Sylvia would love the Antebellum Plantation and shopping at the trendy Lenox Square Mall.

Sylvia! There I go again!

He kicked off the covers and rolled onto his back, staring at the tiny slivers of light creeping in around the edges of the Venetian blind. *I wonder how she's doing? I guess it was pretty lousy of me to tell her I wanted a divorce on Thanksgiving Day, but I've tried several times to tell her, and there never seemed to be a right time. She'll get used to me being gone. No more picking up after me, doing my laundry, cooking my meals.*

His thoughts went to the pile of dirty shirts, underwear, and socks piled up on the chair. He would have to take care of them this weekend. The apartment manager had told him there was a coin-operated laundry room on the basement level. Maybe he would just wash them himself. How hard could it be? Toss them in, add the soap, and pop in a few quarters. In all the years they had been married, he had never once done a single load of laundry. Sylvia had always done it. His clean clothes were always either hung in his closet or folded neatly in his bureau. He had never even taken his suits to the cleaners. She had done that, too. Had he ever thanked her? Surely, he had. No, come to think of it, he hadn't. Doing laundry had been part of her job, just as getting to the newspaper office by seven had been his. Had *she* ever thanked him for bringing home *his* paycheck?

As he lay there, other things Sylvia had done over the years played out in his mind. The house had always been clean, with things put in their proper places even though, at times, she'd had a sick child to tend to or felt ill herself, but she'd done them without complaining or asking for credit. The meals appeared on the table as if by magic. He'd never given a second thought to when she'd had time to do the shopping. Not once had he stopped to calculate the time she'd spend in the kitchen peeling vegetables, browning meat, preparing casseroles, baking pies and cakes, or trying out new recipes she thought he'd enjoy.

She had become quite handy around the house at doing repairs, too. She'd even asked for a cordless drill and screwdriver for Christmas a few years ago so she could put a decorative molding up in their bedroom and a chair rail on the dining room wall. At the time, he had laughed, then humored her by buying them for her. Why hadn't he put those things up for her himself? Didn't she have enough to do? Well, he was busy, too. Working ten-hour days took its toll on a man. *Come on, Randy, be honest with yourself. You could have done those things for her, but you'd rather play racquetball with a client or watch a football game on TV. You weren't exactly a model husband.*

He rammed a fist into the empty pillow beside him, then flipped over onto his stomach. *Enough! I've got to get some Zs! I've made my decision, and there's no turning back. I waited way too long as it is. It's my time now, and Sylvia is just going to have to learn to live with it!*

❄

The ringing of the phone brought Sylvia out of a fitful sleep.

Chapter 6

She dove to answer it, hoping it was Randy.

"Good morning, Betty," the voice on the other end said cheerily. "This is your wake-up call."

Quickly sitting up on the side of the bed, Sylvia stared at the red numbers on the clock. Five a.m. "What? Who did you want? Betty? There's no Betty here."

"Whoops, sorry," a male voice said apologetically. "I must've dialed the wrong number. I promised my girlfriend I'd call at five. She has a plane to catch at seven. I hope I didn't wake you."

"It's okay," she mumbled before dropping the phone back into its cradle. After blinking several times, she stared at the clock, then lay back on the bed, snuggling under the covers and into the twisted nest of sheets and blankets she'd created by her night of tossing and turning.

"Okay, God. It's You and me here, and I need help. What can I do? I need a plan." As she lay there, praying and waiting on the Lord, she began to, once again, go over the scripture verses she had learned as a child and in her adult Sunday school classes. At one time, she had even enrolled in the Navigator's Scripture Memory Course.

"All things work together for good to them that love God. . . ."

"Trust in the LORD with all thine heart; and lean not unto thine own understanding. . . ."

"Now abideth faith, hope, charity, these three; but the greatest of these is charity. . . ."

"Who can find a virtuous woman? for her price is far above rubies. The heart of her husband doth safely trust in her, so that he shall have no need of spoil. . . ."

"Spoil," she said aloud. "Could that mean another woman? Umm, let me see. What else does the thirty-first chapter of Proverbs have to say about the perfect marriage?"

"She will do him good and not evil all the days of her life."

"Haven't I done that for Randy?"

Delving into the recesses of her memory, she continued into the chapter and quoted each scripture as she'd learned it from the King James Version of the Bible.

"Her children arise up, and call her blessed; her husband also, and he praiseth her.

Many daughters have done virtuously, but thou excellest them all."

Not me, Father God. I put everyone else's needs above those of my husband.

"Favour is deceitful, and beauty is vain: but a woman that feareth the LORD, she shall be praised. Give her of the fruit of her hands; and let her own works praise her in the gates."

She tried to go on to other scriptures she had learned, but the last verse of Proverbs thirty-one kept ringing in her heart, and she began to repeat it over and over. *"Give her of the fruit of her hands; and let her own works praise her in the gates. Give her of the fruit of her hands; and let her own works praise her in the gates."* "What are you trying to tell me, Lord? What am I missing here?"

"Give her of the fruit of her hands; and let her own works praise her in the gates." Why was He impressing this verse upon her?

Suddenly, it came to her. The plan she needed. Of course! It was perfect. She and Randy needed to go back to where they started. Learn to love each other all over again. Learn to appreciate one another and what they had each contributed to their marriage! Let their own works praise them in the gates!

✳

Randy sat behind his big desk and stared at the business plan he had spent hours preparing for his key client. Well, things happened. It wasn't the man's fault his wife had to be rushed to the hospital with a drop in her sodium levels. He glanced at the open book on his desk. His next appointment wasn't until one o'clock, which gave him time to work on several other pressing things he had put aside in order to work on the business plan.

"Mr. Benson." His name crackled over the intercom on his desk.

"Yes, Carol, what is it?"

"Your wife is here."

Randy frowned at the intercom. Sylvia was in the outer office? He had refrained from returning her calls, unable to face the crying scene he knew would come if he talked to her. "Ah—" he said slowly, trying to think quickly of an excuse to turn her away.

"I told her your nine o'clock appointment cancelled."

Carol! You shouldn't have done that. Now I don't have an excuse for not seeing her. "I'll—I'll be right out." *Maybe she won't cause a scene if I talk to her in the outer office,* he reasoned as he rose and headed toward the door.

He was not prepared for the sight that greeted him.

✳

Sylvia tugged at her skirt, then smoothed her jacket. *Why didn't I wear the taupe pantyhose instead of this black pair? I wonder if my hair looks okay? Should I have put on more lipstick? Is the neckline on this blouse too low cut? Why didn't I check myself out in the mirror in the ladies' room before coming up here? Oh my, I'm a nervous wreck!*

BITTERSWEET CHRISTMAS

Her heart was pounding way beyond the speed limit as the door to her husband's office opened and he stepped out, dressed in his black Armani suit, starched white shirt, and the black and white polka dot tie she had given him for Christmas. He badly needed a haircut, making the long silver streaks combed back from his temples even more attractive. "Hi, Randy," she said, conjuring up the sweetest voice and smile possible and holding up a white bag with the words *Moon Doggie's Bakery* emblazoned on it in big red letters. "I hope you've got time for a coffee break. I've brought your favorites. Chocolate Éclairs from Moon Doggie's!"

"Well, lucky you," Carol told her boss with a smile, "to have such a thoughtful wife."

Right away, Sylvia knew Randy hadn't told anyone at the office about their breakup, unless he had told Chatalaine. Without waiting for him to invite her in, she brushed past him and into his office, going to the little counter where Carol kept his coffeepot turned on all day. "Sit down," she said, grinning at him. "I'll put these on one of your paper plates and pour us each a cup of coffee." She could feel Randy's eyes boring into her.

"What are you doing, Syl?"

She turned slowly and gave him a coquettish grin and a tilt of her head. "Pouring my husband a cup of coffee."

"You know what I mean. Why are you here?"

Placing their cups on the desk, she scurried back to the counter for their plates and napkins. "Can't a wife surprise her husband once in a while?"

"Don't you think that it's a bit late for games? We are not teenagers."

His retort was cool, but she ignored it and continued to smile as she pulled a chair up close to the desk and settled herself into it. Her feet were killing her in the spike heels, but she kept smiling anyway, ignoring the pain. "Napkin?" she asked, reaching one out to him.

"I don't get it." He took a swig of coffee after blowing into his cup, and all the while, he stared at her. "I've never seen you like this. You're so—dressed up—for nine o'clock in the morning. Is that a new dress?"

Yes, it's a new dress. I bought it several weeks ago, because I knew it was your favorite color, to wear to the awards banquet you wanted me to attend with you. But instead, I ended up going to the hospital with old Mrs. Taylor when she had her heart attack, and you went on alone. "It's pretty new. I haven't had it very long." She stood and, smiling, did a pirouette. "You like it?"

His eyes widened, and he continued to stare at her. "Yeah, I like it. As a matter of fact, you look terrific."

Good, that's what I wanted you to think. Otherwise, I wouldn't have worn these ridiculous shoes. "It's a bit more youthful than I usually wear, but hey, I'm still young!" she said, adding a merry chuckle. "I have years ahead of me."

"We both do." His tone seemed a bit melancholy to her, or was she imagining it and hoping he was as miserable without her as she was without him?

"I'd like for us to spend those years together, Randy."

He cleared his throat loudly, then rose from his chair. "My mind is made up, Syl. If you've come here thinking you'll change it with a bag of éclairs, you're wrong."

"Sit down, Randy, please. I haven't come here to make a scene. I'm not planning on having a shouting session, unless that's what you want. Your news hit me hard, I'll admit that, but I now realize many of your reasons for wanting to end our marriage were valid. Neither of us has been doing our part to make this relationship succeed." *But at least I don't have a boyfriend waiting in the wings!*

He slumped back in his chair with a look of defeat. "So what do you want, Syl? I told you I still planned to take care of you and the kids."

"I'm not concerned about that, Randy." She reached across the desk and covered his hand with hers, relieved when he made no attempt to pull it away. "I—I love you. I always have. I always will, even if you go through with the divorce."

"I've already talked to my attorney, Syl. He's drawing up the papers."

"Randy, I've thought over the things you said, and looking back, although my heart was in the right place, my body wasn't. I should have been there for you. Instead, I've put the needs of others, the children, and the church ahead of you and your needs. But you were always so self-sufficient and didn't seem to need me. I just assumed you didn't mind when you had to go places and do things alone. You never complained. Not really. And *you* served on the church board. That took you away many evenings while I sat at home alone. Was that so different from what I was doing? We both accepted Jesus as our Savior, and we both love the Lord and want to serve Him—sometimes His work takes us away when we'd like to spend the evening at home."

"I'm going to resign from the church board, Syl," he admitted in an almost whisper. "When the word gets out we're getting a divorce, I doubt Harrison or any of the members of the church will want me serving as their deacon."

Especially not if you're leaving me for another woman! It hurt her that he avoided her gaze.

"I—I haven't told anyone here at the office or at the church yet—about us, but I suppose you've told Jen, since she is your best friend."

She wanted to lie, but she couldn't, not if she expected him to be truthful with her. "Yes, I told her, but I'm sure it will go no further than Harrison."

"You're probably right. They're good people."

"People who have the same problems as anyone else."

He nodded as he fidgeted with the handle on his cup. "I guess. They're human, too."

"I've come here today, Randy, prepared to make you a deal."

He raised his head and stared wide-eyed at her. "Short of saying *yes* to a divorce, I don't know what kind of a deal you can offer."

"Like I said, I still love you and don't want our marriage to end. So—here is the deal. I'll give you your divorce, uncontested, if you'll do one thing for me."

The look of relief in his eyes nearly made her cry. "What?"

"I want us to have one last Christmas together."

He shook his head slowly. "You mean you want me to move back in until after Christmas? No way! Leaving this time was hard enough. I'll not do it a second time!" He rose and moved around the desk toward the door.

"Your call, Randy. Do you want me to make a scene here in your office?"

He turned back to her. "Of course not!"

"Then sit down and listen to me."

❄

Randy did as he was told and settled back into his chair, staring at his wife of twenty-five years. He had never seen her like this, and her demeanor confused him. This wasn't the Sylvia he knew, the one who always walked away from him rather than have a confrontation, the woman who could never refuse anyone who asked for help.

And what was she doing dressed like this? She rarely wore short skirts that revealed her knees. And she was right. It was much more youthful than she usually wore, but in all the right places. She looked like she had just stepped out of the beauty shop. Every hair was perfect. Her makeup, which she rarely wore, made her skin look—oh, he couldn't think of a word to describe it, but she looked good. Really good.

"Before we shut the door on our marriage and we each go our separate ways, I want us to spend the week of Christmas together."

"Impossible. Christmas is a busy time here at the—"

"You haven't taken a day's vacation yet this year, Randy, and I know you have at least three weeks coming. Surely, if you want a divorce as badly as you say you do, you can manage a week off." She stood and stared at him, waiting for his answer.

"I—I suppose, if I wanted to—"

"Then want to. If you'll spend from December the nineteenth to midnight, December the twenty-fifth, with me, doing whatever I ask of you, and you still want the divorce, I'll give it to you, uncontested."

"Like—do what?"

"Like I said—whatever I ask. That should be simple enough, and remember, your children will be with you some of that time. If you go ahead with the divorce proceedings now, you know they won't have a thing at all to do with you over the holidays. This way, you'll be able to have a lovely Christmas with them, then file for divorce after Christmas is over." *That also means you won't be able to see your little cutie during that time, but I'm not going to mention that now and start another argument. I want you home for Christmas.*

"The children still don't know?"

She shook her head. "Only Buck. He came back about an hour after you left me on Thanksgiving Day. He'd left his wallet in the bathroom. I'm afraid I was in pretty bad shape. I had to tell him, but I made him promise not to say anything to anyone other than Shonna. I'm sure he's kept that promise. He's not happy about this, Randy, but for DeeDee and Aaron's sake, I'm sure he'll treat you civilly. At least until December the twenty-sixth."

"You're making this really tough, Syl." Randy leaned back in his chair, locking his hands behind his head and closing his eyes.

She knew her offer had come as a shock. "I don't plan to place all the blame on you when the kids are told. I'm sure I had a part in the failure of our marriage, too. I—I may not have been the wife you wanted me to be, but I did try."

"This is the craziest idea I've ever heard! I will *not* move back home, even for a single night!"

She worked hard at maintaining her cool. He had to say yes. She was counting on it. *Don't blow it now!* "It'd be a way to avoid a knockdown, drag-out in court."

"If you kept your end of the bargain."

"I guess you'll have to trust me," she answered, willing her voice to remain calm, at least on the surface. "Randy? What do you say? If you want this divorce, you'd better make up your mind real fast. Once I walk out that door, you can consider this offer withdrawn, and our lawyers can handle everything. Take it or leave it."

He inhaled a couple of quick breaths.

"Make up your mind, Randy. Think how nice it'd be to have at least one more peaceful Christmas with the kids."

"But what good would spending another week under the same roof accomplish?"

She glanced at her watch. "Time's a wasting."

Looking pressured, he leaned forward and folded his hands on the desktop. "You know this is only going to prolong things."

"Perhaps."

"And I'm supposed to move back into the house during that time?"

"Yes. I want your undivided attention every minute of those seven days. It's a small sacrifice if you want to avoid a nasty divorce court battle."

"You're leaving me no choice, you know."

"That was my intent."

Agitated, he rose and began to pace about the room, frantically running his fingers through his hair. Finally coming to a stop in front of her, he leaned toward her, his voice shaking with emotion. "Look, Sylvia, we've been living separate lives for years. The only thing we haven't done is the paperwork making it official. This whole thing seems a bit silly to me."

She wanted to shout at him, but she held her peace, pulling out the one last card left in her deck. Moving to the other side of the desk, she gave him a smile as she shrugged, slung the strap of her purse over her shoulder, and headed for the door. "Okay. If you'd rather do things your way, I'll see you in court."

She had only taken a few steps when Randy grabbed her arm and spun her around.

"All right, you win. I'll do it, but I'm not happy about it."

She pulled her arm from his grasp. "Sorry, that's one of the conditions of the deal. You at least have to act as if you're happy about it. I won't have you sulking around our house like a spoiled child who didn't get his way. Christmas is a happy time, Randy. The celebration of the birth of our Savior, Jesus Christ. I won't have you ruining it with a downtrodden face and a smart mouth."

He lifted both palms with a look of defeat. "Okay, okay. We'll do it your way."

Her heart did a flip-flop. Randy was going to agree! "You'll at least act like you're enjoying being home for Christmas?"

"Yeah, if you're a good sport about this, I guess I need to be one, too."

She had to get out of there before she shouted *Hallelujah!* "Good, I'll expect you in time for supper on December the nineteenth, and don't be late. No excuses, Randy, or the deal's off. Have everything taken care of at the office by the nineteenth. No running to the paper. No meeting with clients. None of that. Because if that happens, like I said, I'll see you in court, and I can assure you it won't be a pretty sight. I'll take you for everything I can get!"

He gave her a guarded smile. "You drive a hard bargain. I didn't know you had it in you."

She grabbed hold of the doorknob and smiled over her shoulder. "Only when my marriage is at stake, then I can be a wildcat!" She did an exaggerated *meee–ooow*, showed her claws, then moved out and closed the door behind her.

"I'm so glad you came, Mrs. Benson," Carol told her from her place at her desk. "Mr. Benson has seemed a little down the past few days. I'm sure your surprise visit cheered him up."

"I—I hope so." Sylvia had to smile. *If you only knew, Carol.*

❄

For the next couple of weeks, Sylvia rushed about like a madwoman on a mission, cleaning the house until it sparkled, readying their bedroom for Randy's return, shopping for Christmas presents, and a to-do list full of other things. She was busy from early morning until late at night, and for the first time in days—happy. She'd even printed out a small banner on her computer's printer saying, "Give her of the fruit of her hands; and let her own works praise her in the gates," and taped it on the mirror in her bathroom as a reminder, claiming that verse as her own, confident God had given it to her. She made out a carefully choreographed schedule for each day Randy would be with her and planned the important activities they would do together. Just knowing Randy was going to be back home with her, even for a few days, made her feel giddy and young again. How long had it been since she had planned something special for just the two of them? Too long!

Each night as she knelt beside her bed and prayed in Jesus' name, she asked God to give her wisdom and guidance and for the strength to keep her mouth shut when the need arose. It would be so easy to tear into her husband about Chatalaine, but now that she was convinced that her own negligence and not just Chatalaine's youth and good looks threatened to end her marriage, she found it easier to put the woman out of her mind. She needed to concentrate on herself and the devotion and dedication she had pledged to Randy on their wedding day.

Other than talking to Jen and Buck, she kept things to herself. At first, Buck was skeptical of her plan. He felt she was getting her hopes up and did not want to see her hurt anymore than she'd already been hurt. But at her request, he and Shonna agreed to go along with her plan and to treat his father as if nothing had happened.

Finally, December the nineteenth arrived. Sylvia spent part of the morning at the beauty shop having her long hair cut into a pixie style with wisps of hair feathering her face. "You look years younger," the beauty operator had told her as she gave her the hand mirror and swung her chair around. "I left a few wisps along your neckline, too. I think you'll like it that way."

Sylvia had gazed into the mirror and had to agree. The style did make her look several years younger. She was sure Randy would like it.

She was too excited to eat lunch and opted for a banana and a glass of cranberry juice. By two o'clock, she had baked a lemon meringue pie, piling the heavily beaten egg whites high and creating curly mounds just like Randy liked them. She hadn't baked a lemon meringue pie since she'd made one for the Fourth of July picnic at the church, although Randy had always claimed it was his favorite dessert. When she pulled the pie from the oven and placed it on the counter to cool, she looked at the deliciously browned meringue and experienced terrible pangs of guilt. Why hadn't she baked more of those pies for Randy? The children loved them, too. They took no time at all. She had baked several of them to take to the church bake sales, but had not made a single one for him in years.

By four, the table was set with the stoneware she usually reserved for company. The few freshly cut flowers she'd purchased at the market had been arranged in a colorful vase as a centerpiece, the crab casserole he liked was in the oven baking, and everything was in readiness. All she had to do was take her shower and get dressed.

When the phone rang a few minutes later, she cringed. *Randy, if that's you calling to say you're going to be late or that you can't make it, I'm going to be furious.*

"Hello."

"Hi," Jen said on the other end. "I just want you to know I've been praying for you all day, and I'm going to keep praying right on through Christmas Day."

Sylvia's heart soared. With a praying friend like Jen, how could things not go right? "Thanks, Jen. You don't know how much that means to me. I'm as nervous as I was on our first date."

"You'll do fine, honey. Just be your natural sweet self."

Sylvia huffed. "You wouldn't have thought I was sweet if you'd heard me threatening Randy in his office that day. I wasn't about to take no for an answer. Jen, I know God gave me that verse."

"I know it, too, and I think your plan is marvelous. If Randy doesn't see what he's giving up by the time Christmas Day arrives, I'll be mighty surprised."

"I'm counting on that. I don't even want to think about failing."

"You won't fail. Not with both of us praying about it. God knows your heart, Sylvia, and He knows the two of you belong together."

Sylvia thanked her for praying, said good-bye, and rushed up the stairs to take her shower.

❄

Randy stared into the mirror at the stubble on his cheeks and chin. Like his father, he had been blessed with a head of thick hair, but with it came the proverbial five o'clock shadow.

What a week he'd had. It seemed everything that could go wrong—did. Two of his key employees quit to go to work for the state government, where they would get better benefits. One of the main presses broke down as they were running the Dallas Life section for the Sunday paper, and Carol had tripped on the stairs and broken her arm. To top it all off, his rechargeable razor had quit on him when he had started to shave, and now he was going to have to use the emergency disposable razor he kept in his shaving kit. The way things were going, he would probably cut himself.

Well, trouble or not, he had taken off a bit early to get ready to move back into the house for the next week, and he was committed to going through with it. The paper would have to get along without him for a while. The only good thing going for him was his assistant manager, a young man who showed great promise. Randy had spent most of the day going over last-minute details with him, and, hopefully, the guy would be able to handle any crisis that might develop in his absence. Sylvia had made it perfectly clear she wasn't about to accept any excuses that would take him away from her for the next week, and he certainly did not want to end up in an expensive court battle if he could avoid it.

It was hard to believe she hadn't made any attempt to contact him since that day she'd appeared in his office, other than to send him a short handwritten note reminding him she'd be looking for him at six that evening. He had expected her to call him at the office continually, bemoaning the fact that he had asked for the divorce, but she had not, and he appreciated it. Maybe they *could* get through this divorce without all the hullabaloo he had expected, after all. He should be so lucky.

He jumped when his cell phone rang, almost afraid to answer it for fear there had been another fiasco at the newspaper.

"Hi, Randy," a male voice on the other end said pleasantly. "I have a favor to ask."

Randy recognized the man's voice immediately. It was Bill Regier, a fellow deacon.

"I know you've been so busy at the newspaper you haven't been able to attend church the past few Sundays, but my wife is insisting we go visit her folks over New Year's, and I wondered if I could talk you into teaching my junior high Sunday school class? They're a great bunch of kids, and I know they'll like you."

Teach Sunday school? Me? When I've just asked my wife for a divorce? Randy rubbed his free hand up the stubble on his jaw. "I—I don't think so, Bill. I've been kinda out of the loop lately—you know—with too many things going on in my life. It's a busy time of year, and—"

"Hey, this isn't rocket science. It won't take that much preparation. You can just tell the kids how you came to Christ. You know, when you accepted Jesus and what's happened in your life since. It'll be an inspiration for them. These kids need role models in their lives. Some of them are from the bus ministry and come from broken homes. They need to see what a real man is like. A man like you—with values and principles."

Randy was glad their conversation was on the phone so the man couldn't see his face—a face he was sure betrayed his guilt. "I—I'd like to help you out, Bill, but—but I'm afraid I can't do it this time. Year-end stuff, you know?"

There was a pause on the other end, then, "Well, okay, but it's these kids' loss. Maybe another time, when you're not so busy, huh?"

"Yeah—maybe another time." Randy tapped the OFF button, but continued to stare at the receiver. *Role model, Bill? You won't think so when you hear about the divorce.*

✳

Sylvia opened the Dillard's shopping bag and dumped the assortment of new cosmetics she had purchased several days ago onto the dresser. She'd never worn much makeup, never thought she'd need to, but after seeing the beautiful Chatalaine in the restaurant that day, she'd felt dowdy and washed out. Colorless. The woman at the department store's makeup counter had been extremely helpful and had given her all kinds of tips on applying moisturizer, foundation, blusher, eyeliner, mascara, and even lip liner. Now, if she could just remember all she had learned. *Beauty is only skin-deep,* the old saying her mother used to quote, popped into her mind as she gazed at herself in the mirror. She let out an audible giggle as a second quote came to mind. This one she had heard while playing one of Billy Graham's videotapes. *Every old barn can use a little paint now and then!*

"Well, this old barn certainly can!" she chided as she picked up the bottle of moisturizer. She began to apply it freely to her scrubbed-clean skin. After smoothing on the foundation and blusher, she picked up the eyeliner pencil and, using a finger to pull each eyelid tautly to one side, she carefully made a narrow line, one above and one below her lashes on each eye. *Umm, not bad for a beginner!* Next came the mascara, something she rarely used. "One light coat, let it dry a few seconds, then apply a second coat more freely," the woman had said. Once that was done, she reached for one of the new lip-liner pencils she'd purchased and chose one in a deep mauve shade. "Frame your mouth, staying right on the very edge of the lip line," she could almost hear the beauty consultant say as she applied it. She had never used lip liner before, but she had to admit, it did define her lips. Next, she reached for the mauve lipstick, in a shade a bit lighter than the liner. Sylvia applied it generously, then blotted it carefully on a tissue before looking back into the mirror. The woman who smiled back at her looked nothing like the woman who'd faced her in that same mirror the day before. What an improvement!

"Man looketh on the outward appearance, but the LORD looketh on the heart!" The words she had committed to memory so many years ago echoed in her heart. *I haven't forgotten that, God, but I want to look my very best for Randy. I want to knock his socks off!*

She spritzed her hair with the setting mist and used her fingers to lift and separate the wisps, pulling a few of them toward her face, just like the beautician had shown her when she'd cut her hair. A few puffs of hair spray, the addition of her new gold hoop earrings and a fine gold chain about her neck, and she was ready to slip into the gorgeous, rose-printed silk caftan she'd bought for their first evening together. She had already done her fingernails and toenails in the same rosy-mauve color. She gave herself a quick spray of the perfume Randy had given her for Christmas two years ago—the one she'd never even bothered to open. Then she slipped into her gold, heelless sandals, took one last glimpse at the mirror, and headed downstairs. She felt giddy, almost like a fairy princess on her way to the ball. Now if only Randy would behave as she imagined Prince Charming would behave. She laughed aloud as she whirled her way into the kitchen for a few last-minute preparations, visualizing Randy appearing at her door dressed in all white with gold braid at his shoulders and astride a fine white horse.

She turned on the coffeepot, checked the oven, gave the salad another toss, shifted the fresh flower vase a half inch to make sure it was centered just right, then moved into the living room to await his arrival.

At exactly six, the doorbell rang. She straightened, her heart pounding. If it was Randy, why didn't he simply use his key? After all, this *was* his home.

Chapter 7

Randy stared at the door, suitcase and garment bag in hand. Maybe he should have just used his key and gone in rather than ringing the doorbell like a visitor. But he *was* a visitor! He had moved out of this home he had known and loved. He glanced toward the west, to the three-bedroom addition they had added nearly twenty years ago, after DeeDee and Aaron became toddlers. He looked to the east at the big bay windows of the family room where the garage used to be. How they had needed that extra space when the kids started school and began bringing their friends over. Fortunately, their house had been on a corner lot, making it possible for them to expand the kitchen and build a nice attached three-car garage onto the back side of the house.

He remembered when they had nearly sold this home and simply bought a larger one in another neighborhood, but both Sylvia and the kids had wanted to stay where they were, near all the friends they had made and their church. As the managing editor of the newspaper, he could well afford to buy a bigger house now, but this home had always filled their needs. It was warm and comfortable, thanks to Sylvia and her decorating talents.

Realization smacked him between the eyes as the door opened and Sylvia appeared. He no longer lived here. He *was* a visitor!

❋

"Hi," Sylvia said, her voice cracking slightly with pent-up emotion. "Come on in." She watched Randy move through the door and place his things in the hall. It was obvious he was feeling every bit as awkward as she was.

He gazed at her, looking first at her hair, then her face, then the new caftan she was wearing. She liked the look she saw in his eyes. Though she felt herself trembling, she willed her voice to remain pleasant and calm. "Supper is nearly ready. Would you like a glass of iced tea or maybe a cup of coffee?"

"Ah—no. Nothing, thanks."

She laughed within herself as she gave him a purposely demure smile. He was wearing a burgundy knit polo shirt that nearly matched the dark burgundy lines surrounding the huge mauve roses in the print of her caftan.

"You've cut your hair," he said, his eyes still focused on her. "I like it."

A flash of warmth rushed to her cheeks at his compliment. "Thank you.

I like it, too. The hairdresser said it made me look years younger." *That was a stupid thing to say!*

"It does."

But not as young as your precious Chatalaine?

She gestured toward the living room and his recliner. "Would you like to sit down? I put a couple of your favorite CDs on to play." *Christian CDs. Or don't you like that kind anymore?*

"Sure. I guess."

He followed her into the living room and sat down in what used to be his chair. "Pretty dress. I guess you'd call it a dress. Looks good on you."

She lowered herself gracefully onto the chintz sofa and smoothed at the long caftan. "Thank you."

"It's new? I've never seen it before."

"Yes, new." *I bought it to impress you, hoping you'd like it.*

"How are the kids? I haven't heard from any of them."

"They're fine. DeeDee and Aaron are working hard on finals. Buck and Shonna are busy getting ready for Christmas. He's working lots of overtime." *Buck is furious with you! And DeeDee and Aaron will be, too, when they hear you're deserting your family for that woman!*

"I guess—you're doing okay. You look wonderful."

Doing okay? No, I'm not doing okay! I'm awful! I can't sleep, can't eat, cry all day and all night. I'm miserable without you! "I'm—managing. Thank you for the compliment. How are you doing?"

"Okay. Busy. At the office, you know. Busy time of the year."

"Yes, I remember," she said, fully aware of his rigid position. *He must be feeling as awkward in my presence as I feel in his. Two strangers, instead of a man and woman who've been married for twenty-five years and have three grown children.* "How is your apartment working out?"

"Other than hearing the elevator go up and down all night, it's working out fine. I need to get some furniture. The place is still pretty empty."

"Is it near your office?" She had wondered where he had moved, but he had never even given her a hint, let alone the address.

"About a mile. I could walk it, I guess. On nice days."

They sat in silence, listening to a gospel medley about God's love, each avoiding the other's eyes.

"I—I think the casserole should be done by now," Sylvia said, rising. "It's your favorite."

"Not the crab casserole you used to bake for me?"

The enthusiasm on his face made her smile. "Yes. The crab casserole."

He rose and rubbed his hands together briskly. "Sounds like I'm in for a treat!"

She crooked a finger at him, adding the demure smile once again, and headed for the kitchen, knowing he was following at her heels.

"Umm, does that smell good." He made an exaggerated sniff at the air. "I can't remember the last time you made that casserole."

"Far too long ago." *I'm ashamed to admit.*

He moved into his usual chair as she pulled the casserole from the oven and placed it on the iron trivet on the table. "Need any help?"

She shook her head. "No, I just need to get our salad bowls from the refrigerator, and we'll be ready to eat." Once the salad bowls were set in place, she lowered herself into her chair and bowed her head. Normally, Randy prayed at suppertime, but after a few moments of silence, she prayed aloud, a simple prayer thanking God for their food and asking Him to be with their family. She wanted to thank God audibly for bringing Randy back home, but felt it better left unsaid. At least aloud. The last thing she wanted to do was make him feel uncomfortable. She wanted to "let her works praise her in the gates"—her own home.

When she lifted her eyes, she found Randy staring at her. Was it a look of admiration, or resentment, or even tolerance? She couldn't tell. All she could do was her very best to make him see what he was giving up by moving out. One last look at the life they had shared. *Oh, God, make him want to come home for good! Please make him want to come home.*

She offered him the serving spoon. "Go ahead and help yourself while I get the rolls from the oven."

"This looks wonderful," he told her, scooping a huge serving from the casserole dish. "I wasn't sure you even remembered it was my favorite."

I remembered, Randy, I just didn't care, I guess. I always fixed the things the kids liked, putting your wants and needs aside. You never complained. I just figured it wasn't important. "I remembered."

He took the first bite and chewed it slowly, appearing to savor it by the looks of his contented smile. "I know the kids never liked crab. I sure couldn't have expected you to go to all the trouble to fix the crab casserole for me. You had enough to do."

"I like it, too. I wish now I *had* fixed it for you."

He looked up, his dark eyes fixed on her. "I do, too, Sylvia."

"Have a roll. They're nice and hot," she said quickly, needing to change the subject.

"Thanks."

"Are you ready for coffee?"

He sent a gentle smile her way and pointed to her still empty plate. "Eat, Sylvia, while everything is hot. I can wait on the coffee. The water is fine."

They finished their supper in near silence, their only conversation forced.

Sylvia tried to relax, but it was hard. She wanted to throw herself into Randy's arms and beg him to come back to her.

When they had finished and nearly all the casserole was gone, Randy leaned back in the chair with a satisfied sigh, linking his fingers across his chest. "That's the best meal I've had in a long time. Thanks, Sylvia."

"You're welcome." She gave him an impish grin. "If you had your choice of desserts, what would it be?"

"Lemon meringue pie, of course," he answered without hesitation. "Don't tell me—"

"Yes," she said smiling with pride as she rose and pulled her beautiful pie from the cabinet. "Lemon meringue pie." For a moment, she thought Randy was going to cry. The look he gave her was one she had not seen in a long time, and it tugged at her heartstrings.

"I know you're doing all these nice things in hope I'll change my mind—about the divorce—but, Sylvia, I am going to go through with it. I don't want you to get the idea that things are going to change just because you've fixed my favorite foods."

Now *she* wanted to cry, but instead, she pasted on a smile. "Let's not discuss the divorce. For this week, that word is off-limits. We made a deal, remember? And I plan to honor my end of the bargain. Give me this one week, Randy, as you've promised. This one last Christmas together, okay?"

He nodded, and she could tell his smile was as false as hers.

"Good, let's enjoy our pie." She cut generous wedges for each of them, then filled their coffee cups.

"Oh, babe, that's good," Randy said, taking his first bite. Then he seemed embarrassed that he had called her *babe*, the pet name he had used the first few years of their marriage.

She ignored his embarrassment as she forked up her own bite of the delicious pie. She had to admit it was one of the best lemon meringue pies she had ever baked. She hadn't lost her touch. "I'm glad you're enjoying it, Randy. I'd hoped you would."

"I guess I should offer to help load the dishwasher," he said, placing his fork on his plate and folding up his napkin.

"I'd like that." Normally, before she had gone off to college, DeeDee helped her mother with the clearing of the table and the dishwasher loading. To her recollection, Randy had never helped with the dishes. He had been too busy with his studies the first four years of their marriage. After he graduated, he had worked at two jobs to make ends meet so she could quit work and stay home to raise their family. Since that time, she had always been a stay-at-home mom, and he had never needed to take part in household chores.

Maybe he should have! Then he'd have a better idea of what I've been doing for this family all these years. Things, apparently, he's taken for granted.

He gave her an I-really-didn't-mean-it smile, stood, and began stacking up their plates and silverware. "You'll have to show me how to do it."

"It's quite simple." She took the plates and silverware from him and rinsed them off under the faucet before handing them back to him. "Plates stand on end in those little slots on the bottom shelf. Silverware goes in the basket. Glasses and cups upside down on the top shelf, saucers same place as the plates."

She watched him awkwardly place the dishes where she had told him. "One capful of dish soap goes in the dispenser, then swing the lid closed, shut the door, and latch it."

Once the dishwasher was in operation and the rest of the table cleared, with things put where they belonged in the cabinets and refrigerator, she shook the table-cloth, stuffed it into the laundry basket in the utility room, and placed the colorful basket of silk flowers back on the table. "That's that! Let's go into the family room. A letter came in today's mail from DeeDee addressed to both of us. I haven't opened it yet."

He followed her, heading for the cushy green leather recliner—his recliner. But he stopped midroom as if remembering the last time he had tried to sit in that chair and she had chastised him, saying he no longer belonged in it.

"Go ahead," she said, trying to sound unconcerned, but remembering that same incident as vividly as if it had happened that very evening. "We bought it especially for you. Remember?"

He moved into the chair cautiously, settling himself down and propping up the footrest.

Sylvia watched with great interest, wishing she had a camera to capture his picture. He belonged in that chair, in this house, not in some high-rise apartment. She pulled a footstool up close to his chair and opened the note from their daughter, reading it aloud.

Dear Mom and Dad,

I was sitting here in my room, listening to my roommate complain about her parents, and I suddenly realized how lucky I am to have been born to the two of you. Mom, you're the greatest. You always put your kids' needs ahead of your own and were always there for us, doing the little things that made our childhood so happy and carefree.

Sylvia's heart swelled with happiness at her daughter's words. She went on without so much as a sideways glance at Randy. She knew one look in his direction and she'd lose it.

Dad, you work too hard. I wish you hadn't had to spend so much time at the newspaper, and I know I used to gripe about it all the time, especially when you had to miss my volleyball and basketball games. But now that I am older, I realize you did it because you loved me, and you wanted to provide all the things for us kids that you never had and to be able to send Buck and Aaron and me to college.

Sylvia was sure she heard a distinct sigh coming from the cushy green leather chair, but she read on, sure their daughter's words were affecting him as much as they were her.

I've never thanked you two properly, but I want you to know I love you both and appreciate you and everything you've done for me. If my life ever amounts to anything, it'll be because of the two of you and the way you love the Lord and the witness you have been to me. Maybe now that Aaron and I are gone, you two can do some of the things you've put on hold while we were growing up. I pray for you every day, asking God to protect you and keep you both well. I'll see you December twenty-fourth.

With love, your daughter,
DeeDee.

When she finished, she folded the note and slipped it back into its envelope, not sure what to say or if she should just remain quiet. When Randy didn't speak, she rose, crossed the room, and placed the envelope on the coffee table.

"She's—she's a great kid, isn't she?" he finally asked, after clearing his throat.

"Yes, she is. All three of our kids are great kids."

"You've done a good job with them. I'm—I'm afraid I can't take much of the credit."

She moved back to the footstool and seated herself, smiling up at him, ignoring the ache in her heart. "I wouldn't have been able to be a stay-at-home mom if you hadn't worked so hard to provide for us."

"But it took me away from home. I missed the kids' games, their school activities, so many things."

She gave his arm a tender pat. "But you were at church with us most Sundays, and you've served faithfully on the church board all these years.

"You—you still haven't told them—about—"

"No, I haven't, and I'm sure Buck hasn't either, and I don't intend to, Randy. When and if the time comes, you'll have to be the one to do it."

He leaned his head against the headrest and stared off in space. "It is going to happen, Sylvia. I've been thinking about this for a long time. I nearly asked you for a divorce last summer, before you and the kids went to Colorado to attend that Christian camp, but I thought it might be easier on everyone if I waited until DeeDee and Aaron went off to college."

"Easier on them? Or easier on you?" she prodded gently, wishing right away she had kept her question to herself. "Don't answer that," she added quickly. "We're putting all that behind us now. I had no business even asking."

He gave her a faint smile, then closed his eyes. "This chair is comfortable. Feels like it was made for me."

She reached out and pulled his shoe off, and when he didn't protest, she pulled the other one off and placed them on the floor beside the chair. "I know."

"The music's nice."

"I thought you'd like it."

For the next few hours, they sat listening to the stack of CDs she had put on the player. Randy in his recliner, Sylvia stretched out on the chintz sofa. As the last song played and the room became silent, Sylvia heard a faint snore coming from the recliner. Randy was fast asleep.

She tiptoed into the hall, quietly picked up his suitcase and garment bag, and carried them up the stairs and into their room. She hung his garments in his nearly empty closet, then placed his suitcase on the bench at the end of the bed. She nearly unpacked it for him—and would have before their separation. But now it seemed like an invasion of his privacy, and she did not want to upset him by doing something that might offend him.

After washing her face and reapplying a faint trace of the rose-colored lipstick, she rubbed a sweet-smelling body lotion on her face and arms and slipped into the pink, lacy gown she had bought when she had been shopping for the other items she planned to wear during their week together. Before she left the room, she fell to her knees by the bed and asked God to be with the two of them and to give her the grace to be patient, loving, and kind. Lastly, she asked Him to keep her from saying things she shouldn't and to bring Randy back home for good—home where he belonged.

He was still sleeping in the chair when she came back into the family room, his head twisted to one side, his arms resting on the armrests. He looked like a little boy, and she wanted to kiss his sweet face. She could not remember the last time he had fallen asleep in that chair.

"Randy," she said softly, giving his shoulder an easy shake. "It's nearly eleven. Time to go to bed."

He sat up with a start, blinking as if he had to get his bearings. "How—how long have I been asleep?"

She reached out and gave his hand a tug. "Probably an hour."

He lowered the footrest and allowed her to pull him to his feet. "I–I'll get my things," he said, heading toward the front hall.

"They're already in our room."

He gave her a wild stare. "I—I was planning on sleeping in the guest room."

"This is still your home, Randy, at least until midnight Christmas Day. You'll be sleeping in our bed tonight, where you belong."

Chapter 8

He backed away from her, holding his palms up between them. "I—I don't think so."

She stepped toward him, determined to make her plans work out as she had envisioned them. "We *do* have a king-sized bed. There's plenty of room for both of us. I'll sleep on my side. You sleep on yours."

When he did not respond with more than a doubtful grunt, she added, trying to keep her voice sweet and on an even keel, "You do plan to keep your part of the bargain, don't you?"

He gave a defeated shrug and headed for the stairs without answering. As soon as he reached their room, he unzipped his suitcase and pulled out what looked to be a brand-new pair of pajamas, still bearing the creases from their packaging. Sylvia muffled a laugh. Although she'd bought him a number of pairs of nice men's pajamas during the years they'd been married, he'd always refused to wear them, opting for a T-shirt and boxers, saying only old men in hospitals or care homes wore pajamas.

She waited patiently, sitting on her side of the bed while he showered, using the time to read her Bible. Minutes later he emerged, his curly hair damp, and wearing the new pajamas. "Shower feel good?"

He nodded. "Yeah, I've always loved that big showerhead. Makes a guy feel really clean."

Is that a faint tinge of aftershave I smell? Did he put that on just for me? "I like that showerhead, too, especially when I rinse my hair," she added, closing her Bible. "I put a glass of water on your nightstand."

He glanced toward the glass. "Thanks."

"I'm not going to bite, Randy," she told him, giving him a raise of her brow.

"I—I know, I just feel—awkward, that's all, now that things are—different —between us."

"I still love you," she reminded him gently, not wanting to add to his discomfort.

He took a swig of the water, set the glass back in the coaster, and lowered himself onto his side of the bed, keeping his back toward her.

Sylvia quickly scooted across the bed on her knees and cupped her hands on his shoulders. Although he flinched and gave her a what-are-you-doing look, he did not move away. "You've been working too hard. Let me rub your shoulders."

"You don't have—"

"I know I don't have to—I want to. Now sit still." She began gently kneading his deltoid muscles, letting her fingers perform their magic.

"Umm, that feels so good."

"You're way too tense, Randy. Come on, relax."

"I don't want you to tire yourself."

"I'll quit when I get tired. Now let me work those neck muscles."

He bowed his head low and, oohing and aahing with each stroke, he let her fingertips press into his strong neck.

"I used to do this when we were first married, when you came home from your classes, remember?" she asked, leaning against him.

He nodded. "Yeah, I remember. Knowing you'd be waiting for me at the end of a hard day at college, ready to massage my weariness away, was what kept me going those last few hours."

Finally, he reached up and took hold of her hand. "Stop. That's enough. As much as I'm enjoying it, I don't want you to get hand cramps."

She leaned over his back and planted a kiss on his cheek before scooting back over onto her side of the bed and slipping under the quilt. As he turned to look at her, she flipped back his side of the covers, then turned her back to him. "Good night, Randy."

She felt the bed move slightly as he crawled in, pulled up the covers, and turned out the light on his nightstand. "Good night, Syl."

Sylvia arose early the next morning and carefully slipped out from under the covers, leaving Randy sprawled on his side of the bed, tangled up in the sheet and quilt. She had to smile. Parts of his thick hair stood in mounds where he had gone to sleep with it wet from his shower.

She wiggled into the new pair of jeans she had bought and topped them with a bright fuchsia T-shirt, a color she never wore. Most of her life, she had opted for beige, white, or soft pastel colors, never gaudy ones. But this week called for extreme measures, so many of the new things she'd bought were way out of her usual color realm, colors more like what she thought Chatalaine would wear.

Chatalaine.

She was glad Randy had not mentioned that woman's name. She did not plan to, either. The less he thought about Chatalaine, the better, as far as she was concerned. She had him on her turf now, and she planned to keep him there all week.

After spritzing her newly cut hair and finger combing it as the beautician had shown her, she painstakingly applied her new makeup and added another dash of Randy's perfume. By the time he arrived in the kitchen, also dressed in jeans and a T-shirt, the table had been set and she had breakfast well underway. "Good morning," she called out cheerily. "I hope you slept well."

He ran his fingers through the hair at his temples. "Extremely well. I like that mattress. The one I have at the—"

She put a finger to his lips on her way to the refrigerator, silencing him. "We're not going to talk about your apartment this week," she said as she pulled the bottle of cranberry juice from the fridge and filled their glasses. "The bacon is ready, and I'll put the eggs-in-a-basket on a platter as soon as we've prayed, so they'll be good and hot. Would you pour the coffee?"

He moved to the coffeemaker, lifted the pot, and filled their cups. "Umm, that smells good. New jeans?"

She froze. She had bought the faded ones purposely so he would not think they were brand-new. "I haven't had them very long."

"Nice T-shirt."

"I've decided I like bright colors."

"Looks good on you."

Sylvia smiled, then bowed her head and prayed. Though he usually prayed at breakfast, she knew he must feel awkward doing it under the circumstances, and she wanted him to be at ease.

"I thought we'd take a walk after breakfast," she said lightly as she placed her napkin in her lap.

He picked up his fork with a quizzical look. "Oh? Where to?"

She grinned. "You'll see."

"Ah, Syl?"

"Yes?"

"Could—could I have a piece of that pie for breakfast before we leave?"

They finished their breakfast, pulled on their jackets, and headed out the kitchen door and through the garage. Randy seemed surprised when Sylvia stopped and opened her car door.

"I thought you said we were going for a walk."

She motioned him inside, crawled in herself, and hit the button on the garage door opener. "Too boring to walk around here. I thought we'd walk around the Lakeside Park area. It's pretty over there."

He closed the door and buckled his seatbelt. "I haven't been to that area in years."

"I know."

It was a beautiful day. The sun was shining, and there were just enough breezes to make the leaves on the trees sway gently. Sylvia parked the car along the curb, and they set out walking.

"You don't have your cell phone on your belt," she said almost jubilantly.

"I didn't think you wanted me getting any calls."

She grinned. "I don't, but I don't want you to cut yourself off totally, in case there is an emergency at the newspaper."

"I think things will be all right. That young man I told you about should be able to—"

"You never told me about any young man."

His pace slowed and his brows rose. "I didn't?"

"No, you didn't, but I'm glad you have someone to help you at the paper. You've needed a dependable assistant for a long time."

"I hate turning things over to someone else."

"I know."

"Did I tell you Carol broke her arm?"

She stopped walking as her jaw dropped. "No! When did that happen?"

"Yesterday. About noon. I had to take her to the hospital. It happened right after they called and told me one of our big presses went down."

Guilt hit her like a Mack truck. "Oh, Randy, I'm so sorry to hear that. What a day you must've had. Is she okay? Did you get the presses rolling?"

"I guess she'll be all right when the swelling goes down. She'll be off at least until after New Year's, but she still won't be able to type when she comes back. I'll have to hire a temp to help her. And no, the presses were still down when I left the office, but two guys from the company that sold it to us are flying down from Cincinnati to help get it back in operation." He took a few more steps, then turned to her again. "I guess I didn't tell you two of my key men in the newsroom quit this week. They got jobs with the State Department. They gave them much better benefits than I could offer. I don't blame them, but it sure left me high and dry. They were good men."

Her eyes widened. "No, you didn't tell me about them. Oh, Randy, I had no idea how hard it was for you to take this entire week off. If you need to call the office—"

He placed his hand on her arm. "No, they aren't expecting a call from me. I've told everyone *not* to call me, short of a real emergency. I've put the newspaper first in my life for way too long. From now on, I'm looking out for Number One. Me. I'm going to do the things I've always wanted to and never had the time or the money."

Like buy a motorcycle and wear gold chains around your neck?

"I may even take up golf or fishing, maybe even hunting. I haven't decided yet. I might even do some traveling."

Alone? Please don't tell me you plan to take Chatalaine with you!

"I've even considering taking flying lessons; maybe buy myself a small plane."

"My, you do have plans. I hadn't realized you were interested in any of those things."

"Most of them were only pipe dreams—things I wanted to do when I retired, but too many men I know—guys my age—have been dropping like flies. Never even making it into their sixties. I don't want to be one of them."

Is that what this is all about? Your mortality?

"My dad died just a few months before his sixtieth birthday, his dad in his late fifties. I want to do things while I'm in good enough health to enjoy them, and I figure now's as good a time as any. From what my older acquaintances tell me, it ain't gonna get any better."

You are in a midlife crisis! "But your grandfather on your mother's side is still alive, and he's in his eighties!" she countered. "That's in your favor."

"But my body is much more like my father's side of the family."

Sylvia grabbed his hand and tugged him toward a nearby park bench. She sat and pulled him down beside her. "No one is invincible, Randy. Only God knows when He's going to call us home."

Randy ignored her comment as he looked around, taking in the park, the chip-lined walking path, and the park bench itself. "Hey, this is all beginning to look very familiar," he said, eyeing her with a laugh. "We didn't just happen to stumble onto this particular bench, did we?"

Her heart rose like a kite caught in an updraft. "You remembered!"

"I proposed to you in this very spot nearly twenty-six years ago."

"Yes, you did. And I gladly accepted your proposal, Randy. You're the only man I've ever loved. That little diamond you placed on my finger that day was the most beautiful ring I had ever seen. I'll never forget how excited I was. I was going to be Mrs. Randy Benson!"

"Boy, were we naive. A couple of kids who had no idea what we were doing or what the future held for us."

She cupped her hand on his shoulder and smiled into his deep blue eyes. "A couple of kids in love who were willing to face anything to be together."

"Your parents weren't too happy when they saw that ring on your finger as I recall."

"No, they much preferred that I attend college and get a degree in nursing, but marrying you was all I wanted out of life. Once they realized that, they accepted it." She scooted a tad closer to him. "Our life and our marriage may not have been perfect, but I never wanted it to end."

He stood quickly and glanced at his watch. "Hey, it's nearly noon. I'm hungry; how about you?"

"Sounds good to me, and I know just the place to have lunch."

She took his hand and led him across the street and down two blocks, to the little all-night diner where they used to eat hot dogs when they could afford to splurge and eat out.

Randy opened the door and stood back to allow her entrance. "Boy, I didn't even know this place was still in business."

"Then you do remember coming here?"

He nodded, stepping inside. "Yeah, I remember. You were pregnant with Buck, and you continually seemed to have a craving for foot-long hot dogs with pickle relish and loads of mustard. I wonder if they still have them on their menu."

They crowded into the only booth that was available, a small single-sided bench in the far corner.

"Yep, they're still on the menu! You up to it?" Randy asked when the waitress brought their water glasses.

Sylvia smiled back at him. "You bet!"

They giggled through lunch like two junior high kids, consuming their hot dogs and even ordering chocolate shakes to go with them.

"I'm stuffed," Randy said on their way back to where they had parked the car. "Why didn't you tell me to stop when I ordered that second hot dog?"

"Would you have listened?" she answered, slipping her hand into his as they walked along.

He gave it a slight squeeze but did not pull away. "Probably not!"

When they reached the car, Sylvia handed Randy her keys. "You drive."

He opened her door and waited until she was safely inside before jogging around to the driver's side. "Where to, lady?"

She could not hold back a smile. "How about our home?"

When they reached the house, the answering machine was blinking. Sylvia rushed to it and punched the button. A man from a florist shop was calling, and he sounded very much like the man who had called before, about the apricot roses. "Just wanted you to know, Mr. Benson, the lady loved the red roses. She said to tell you they were so beautiful they made her cry!"

Sylvia's blood ran cold. Randy may not have mentioned Chatalaine's name, but he was making sure she received flowers from him while he was away from her.

"Wow, am I ever glad to hear that," Randy said, moving up beside her. "I wanted those flowers to get to her as soon as possible. She needed to know someone cared about her."

Sylvia wanted to reach out and slap him. Hard. How dare he? When he had promised the week was to be hers?

"Poor Carol. I know she's hurting. No one ever sends her flowers. I hope those roses make her feel better."

Carol? He sent those flowers to Carol? Of course, he did! She's been his secretary for years. Sylvia nibbled on her lower lip, glad she had not blurted out something she would have regretted later. Feeling riddled with guilt, she picked up the phone and held it out to him. "You want to call the office? See how things are going?"

He took it from her and placed it back in its cradle. "I'm sure things are fine." He looked about the room, his gaze fixing on the venetian blind. "While I'm here, you want me to fix that window blind? I know it's been driving you crazy. I'm—I'm sorry I haven't gotten around to repairing it for you."

She nodded, grateful for his offer. The blind had been driving her nuts. Something in the mechanism was broken, and she had not been able to lower it to block out the late afternoon sun. "If you're sure you want to."

"Looks like I've got the time," he said with a grin, heading toward the garage, where he kept his tools.

She watched from her place on the sofa as he unfolded the stepladder and strapped on his tool belt, amazed at how handsome he was. *Women age. Men mature.* Where had she heard that silly saying? But it was true. Randy had matured, and on him, it looked good. No wonder that society columnist had gone after him.

"There you go. Good as new!" Randy crawled down and folded the ladder. "Go ahead. Give it a try."

Sylvia quickly moved to the window and gave a slight tug on the cords. As smooth as glass, the shade lowered into place. "Hey, thanks, that's great. Now the sofa won't fade."

"You're welcome. I'm just sorry I haven't done it before now. Got anything else that needs to be fixed?"

"The drain thingy in the lavatory in the half bath off the kitchen won't lock down."

He gave her a mock salute before heading toward the little bathroom. "Tool-time Randy and his trusty tool belt are on their way!"

In ten minutes, he was back. "Why don't I check that filter in the furnace while I'm at it?"

For the rest of the afternoon, Randy made the rounds of each room in the house, replacing lightbulbs, tightening screws, checking cabinet hinges and knobs, all sorts of manly me-fix-it projects. What impressed Sylvia most was the joy he seemed to get out of doing those things, the very things she had been at him for months to take care of.

By the time he finished, she had supper on the table.

"I knew it!" he said, coming into the kitchen after a quick shower. "Broccoli soup with garlic toast! I could smell it clear up in our bedroom!"

"I was hoping you'd be pleased." She checked the pot on the stove one more time and made sure the soup was not sticking to the bottom of the pan. "It's ready."

Randy rubbed his hands together. "Umm. Let me at it."

"You're not too full from those two hot dogs?"

He grinned. "What hot dogs?"

Again, Randy helped her clear the table and load the dishwasher when they had finished supper. Sylvia could not believe he had actually eaten two big bowls full of the broccoli soup and consumed four pieces of toast.

"What now?" he asked as they turned off the kitchen light and headed for the family room.

"I thought we'd watch a movie."

He wrinkled up his face. "Not a chick flick."

He headed for his recliner. She shook her head and pointed to the empty spot beside her on the green leather sofa. "Not there. Here."

He gave her a shy grin and settled himself down beside her while she punched the PLAY button on the remote control.

The tape began to roll, and Randy leaned forward, his eyes narrowed. "Naw, it can't be! An action movie? Surely not!"

Sylvia quirked a smile. "Don't tell me you've seen this one!"

He leaned back with a satisfied look. "Nope. I didn't even know it had been released to the video stores yet. I've been wanting to see it but—"

She rolled her eyes. "I know—you've been too busy."

"Exactly. But no more. From now on—I'm going to—"

"Take care of Number One," she inserted quickly, though it broke her heart to say it.

"Right! I didn't think you liked action movies," he said as the credits finished and the story started.

I hate them! "They're okay. Some of them have good story lines." *If you can weed them out from all the car chases and noise!*

Before long, Randy was so into the movie, he barely seemed to notice she was sitting beside him. *Will this thing ever end?*

When the movie ended, Randy took her hand in his and looked into her eyes. She held her breath, sure he was going to say something romantic.

"Is there any lemon meringue pie left?"

Men! She wanted to pick up one of the sofa pillows and pelt him like she had seen Shonna do to Buck, but instead she smiled sweetly. *Maybe the way to a man's heart is through his stomach after all. Hopefully, Chatalaine is a lousy cook!*

"Sure. I'll cut you a piece."

Randy finished his piece of pie with an appreciative sigh. "That's the best pie I've ever tasted."

"Think you can sleep on a full stomach?" she asked him as she pointed to the clock on the fireplace. "It's after eleven."

He let out a big yawn, stretching his arms first one way, then the other. "Oh, yeah. I'm so tired I could sleep standing up. I can't believe how far we walked this morning."

They turned out the lights and made their way up the stairs to their room. This time, Randy did not question their sleeping arrangements. By the time Sylvia had washed her face and slipped into her gown, he was already sitting on his side of the bed in his pajamas. "Is that a new gown?"

She nodded. "Yes. Do you like it?" *I had it on last night. Were you so worried about sharing the bed with me you didn't even notice?*

"Yeah, I like. What happened to those—"

"Granny gowns, as you used to call them? They're in the back of my closet. I'm thinking of giving them to Good Will. They're all cotton and would make wonderful rags," she added with a chuckle. "I'm making some changes in my life, too, Randy. Getting rid of my granny gowns and fuzzy slippers is one of them."

He gave her a quick once-over. "Well, you're a knockout in that gown. You should wear that color more often."

She moved across the bed on her knees and began her massage routine. Again, Randy did not protest. He just leaned over and let her willing fingers work on him again. "This has been a good day," he finally said when she moved back to her side of the bed. "Thank you for it."

"You're welcome." Giving him a playful grin, she slid under the covers and flipped onto her side, facing away from him, praising the Lord. Randy seemed mystified by her calmness, which is exactly what she wanted. "Good night, Randy."

"Good night, Syl."

Chapter 9

They awoke the next morning to another perfect Dallas day. After a hearty breakfast, they loaded into the car and headed for the zoo.

"Do you have any idea when I last visited a zoo?" Randy asked when they stopped at the gorilla section.

"I remember exactly. You were pushing DeeDee in her stroller, so I'd say that was about seventeen years ago. As I recall, you tilted that stroller up onto its rear wheels and jogged around the alligator pit, making motor sounds while she giggled and clapped her hands."

"Then, when she fell asleep, I carried Aaron on my shoulders while you pushed the stroller."

She threw her head back with a raucous laugh. "Poor little Buck! We made him wear that harness thing your mother bought so he wouldn't get lost. Remember how he hated that thing?"

"Do I! I finally had to take it off him. I couldn't stand his crying. Then he complained because we held onto both his hands."

"I guess—sometimes—we were overprotective."

"Hey, you!" Randy made a face at one of the gorillas, sticking his thumbs in his ears and wiggling his fingers at the animal.

Sylvia tugged on his arm. "Randy, people are staring at you!"

He shrugged complacently. "Who cares? Remember, I've turned over a new leaf! No more inhibitions!"

She eyed him with a shake of her head. *Turned over a new leaf? Sounds to me like the whole tree has fallen on your head!* "Oh, yeah. For a minute there, I forgot." She pointed to an area past the gorilla section. "Look, there's the duck pond."

Randy bought a bag of feed from the little vending machine, and they sat down on a nearby bench, tossing the feed to the many ducks that gathered. "We sure had three cute kids, didn't we? It seems like only yesterday little DeeDee was letting the ducks eat out of her hand. Those were good times, Syl."

"Yes, they were. We didn't have much in the way of worldly goods, and at that time, neither of us knew Jesus, but we had each other and nothing else mattered." She let out a deep sigh. "How I wish we could go back to those sweet times."

Randy threw the remaining feed onto the ground, watching a dozen ducks scramble to snatch it up before the others got it. "But we can't, Syl. What's done is done, and there's no undoing it."

It could be undone, if you were willing to give it a try!

Randy suggested they stop by the sandwich shop near their house for lunch since Buck and Shonna would be coming for dinner in a few hours. By three, they were back home, with Sylvia tying an apron about Randy's waist so he could help her prepare dinner.

The minute Buck came through the door, Sylvia rushed into the living room and pulled him to one side, warning him to behave and not mention one word about the divorce or seeing his father with Chatalaine.

"How's it going?" Buck asked in a whisper.

"I'm not sure, but we've been getting along extremely well. He may be humoring me, but at least I'm having a chance to spend time with him—just the two of us—which we haven't done in a long time."

He doubled his fist and gave a playful blow to her chin. "Hang tough, Mom. Shonna and I are praying for you and Dad."

She stood on tiptoe and kissed his cheek. "I know, Buck. God is able. I'm counting on Him answering our prayers."

Randy came into the room, pulling off his apron. He cautiously extended his hand toward his son. With a huge grin, Buck took his hand and shook it heartily as his mother breathed a sigh of relief. The last thing she wanted was for her husband and son to have harsh words.

After greetings all around, the four moved into the dining room, where the candles were already burning brightly, to share the dinner Randy and Sylvia had prepared. The dinner conversation was light and cheery, with both Randy and Sylvia relating their experiences of the past two days. Everyone laughed when Sylvia told them about Randy making faces at the gorilla.

"You're lucky they didn't stick you in the cage with him," Shonna said with a giggle. "After a trick like that."

By ten, the couple left after much hugging and kissing. Randy lingered at the door until Buck's taillights disappeared into the darkness. "What a good guy our son has turned out to be."

"We can be very proud of our kids," Sylvia said, gathering up the empty glasses that had accumulated in the room and carrying them to the kitchen.

"So, what's on the agenda tomorrow? A trip to the local museum?" Randy asked as they climbed the stairs. "Are we going to check out the mummies or look at abstract paintings?"

"Neither. Tomorrow morning, I thought we'd stay home, but I have something planned for the afternoon."

Randy stopped on the landing. "The whole morning at home? That sounds nice."

"But you have to make me a promise." She could see by his face that he expected a caveat. "I want you to call the office and make sure everything is going well."

He tilted his head quizzically. "You sure you want me to call? That wasn't part of the deal."

"It's my deal, which means I have the right to change the rules anytime I like," she said, pinching his arm playfully before turning and scurrying off to their room.

When she came out of the bathroom wearing another new nightgown, Randy noticed immediately and gave her a "Wow!" She did a quick turn around, twirling the long flowing skirt like DeeDee always did when she was a child playing dress-up in her mother's clothes.

Randy let out a long, low whistle. "I'd say getting rid of those granny gowns was a vast improvement!"

"You—you don't think it's too low cut? Too sheer?"

"No, ma'am. Not one bit!"

She crawled up onto the bed and pulled her Bible from the drawer. "If you don't mind, I thought I'd read a couple of chapters before going to bed."

He propped his pillow against the headboard and leaned against it. "Fine with me."

"That is, unless you're ready to go to sleep. I don't want the light to keep you awake." She gave him a coquettish smile again. "If you don't mind waiting a bit, I'll massage your neck muscles again. I noticed you rubbing at them when we were all sitting in the family room. Has your neck been bothering you, Randy?"

His hand rose and stroked at his neck. "Some. I asked a doctor about it. He said it was tension."

She put her Bible aside and crawled across the bed, moving up beside him, her hands kneading into the tight muscles. "You poor baby. Why didn't you tell me?"

"Nothing you could do about it. He said the only thing that would help was getting rid of some of the stress in my life, and that's not an easy thing to do."

Is that why you're trying to make such radical changes in your life? Because the doctor advised it? I'll bet he didn't tell you to get rid of your wife of twenty-five years. Did you tell him you had a girlfriend? "I'm sure it's not easy, with the job you hold at the paper."

"He said I'd better start getting more exercise, too. That long walk you and I took yesterday was just what the doctor ordered."

She worked his deltoids until her fingers began to cramp. After bending to kiss his cheek, she moved to her side of the bed and crawled under the quilt. "I'm really tired, and I know you are, too. Maybe we'd better put off reading the Bible until morning. Let's get some sleep. We have lots of work to do tomorrow."

Randy crawled into his side of the bed, propping himself up on his elbow. "Work? What kind of work?"

"You'll see." She gave him her sweetest smile before scooting to the edge of her side of the bed. "Good night, Randy."

"Good night, Syl." A second later, she heard the snap of the light switch, and the room fell into utter darkness.

"Syl?"

"Yes."

"Thanks for the neck rub."

"You're welcome."

"Syl?"

"Yes."

"Thanks for another great day."

"It was great, wasn't it?"

"Yeah. It was."

❄

Randy's eyes opened wide when the alarm sounded. Surely, it was not morning yet. He flinched! *Oh, oh! What am I doing?* His arm draped over Sylvia's shoulder, he was on her half of the bed. He froze when she moaned and reached toward her nightstand to turn off the alarm. He quickly withdrew his arm and scooted to his side, sitting up with a loud, exaggerated yawn. "What time is it?"

"Seven," she droned sleepily.

"Seven? I'm usually wide awake at five. You realize this week is going to throw my entire routine off whack, don't you?" He watched as she stood, reached her hands toward the ceiling with an all-out stretch, then headed toward the bathroom. *Boy, did I goof. I can't believe I was on her side of the bed after making such a big deal about sleeping in the guest room. But, wow! She looked so cute with that new haircut and wearing that fancy, low-cut red nightgown.* He shook his head to clear it. "Wanna tell me about today's project?" he called out to her.

She appeared in the bathroom doorway. "Not yet, but it'll be fun."

As he sat on his edge of the bed, waiting for her to return, his gaze fell to the Bible on her nightstand. How long had it been since he'd read his Bible? He shut his eyes tightly, trying to block out its vision. A shudder coursed through his body. *Are you sure you want to leave your wife?* a small voice seemed to ask from within his heart.

"I don't love her like I used to," he answered in a whisper.

You don't love her like you used to? Or are you turning your back on that love, trying to block it out to excuse your childish behavior?

Randy crossed his arms over his chest defiantly. "I've made up my mind. It is time for me now. For the past twenty-five years, I have sacrificed for my family, putting their needs first. I've worked round the clock to attain the position I have at the paper, spent every free hour I could find serving on the church board, and where has it all gotten me?"

You are in reasonably good health. You have a beautiful, loving wife, terrific kids, a great home, more than adequate income, and you are a born-again Christian. What more could you ask?

"Time for me! Time to do the things I'm interested in, before I either die or simply cannot do them because of poor health or because I'm too old. There's so much I haven't experienced. When I come to the end of my life, I don't want to have regrets for the things I never did. Why can't people understand that?"

"Randy?"

His wife's voice brought him back to reality as she came out of the bathroom. "Were you talking to someone? I heard voices."

"No, just talking out loud. Bad habit I seem to have picked up lately." He gave her a smile he hoped she did not perceive as guilt. "Among my other bad habits."

"See you downstairs," she said with a grin. "Gonna be a simple, quick breakfast this morning—juice, coffee, and cold cereal. We have things to do. Wear your jeans and a T-shirt."

Sylvia was already sitting at the kitchen table, sipping her juice when Randy arrived—showered, shaved, and ready for the day. Once the dishes had been loaded into the dishwasher, she reached for the two clean aprons hanging on a hook on the back of the pantry door. "One for me," she said, tying it about her waist, "and one for you."

"An apron? What's this for?"

"We're going to bake Christmas cookies!"

He gave her a skeptical stare, then allowed her to tie his apron about his waist. "This should be an experience!"

"It'll be fun, and remember, our kids will be home in a few days, and they'll be expecting homemade cookies. Think how proud you'll be when you tell them you helped me bake them!" She gave him a gentle swat on his seat. "Now go wash your hands. I'll get my cookbook."

He did as he was told, and by the time he was finished, Sylvia was already beginning to assemble the things they would need. "What kind are we going to make?"

She gave him a mischievous smile. "Actually, we're going to make three kinds. Chocolate chip, of course, since all the kids—and you—love them. My famous spritz cookies run through the cookie press and decorated, and lastly, it wouldn't seem like Christmas without sugar cookies cut into all those wonderful shapes and sprinkled with red and green sugar crystals. So we'll have to make those, too."

"Wow, we are going to be busy." He rubbed his hands together briskly. Just hearing the names of the cookies made his mouth water. "What do you want me to do?"

She handed him a tall canister from the counter. "Take that big bowl and measure me out six cups of flour."

He placed the canister on the island, pulled a clean coffee cup from the cabinet, and began to measure out the flour. "Like this?"

Her eyes widened. "No, you can't use a coffee cup! You have to use a measuring cup!"

He gave her a shrug. "Why? A cup is a cup!"

"Oh my, I can see I'm going to have to watch your every move."

Using the proper measuring cup, Randy began again to spoon out the flour. "Here you go," he said, trying to conceal a grin as he pushed the bowl toward her. "I lost count, but I think there are six cups in there."

Again her eyes widened.

"Just kidding, Syl, just kidding. There *are* six cups of flour in there. Honest."

She took the bowl from his hands and placed it on the counter next to the mixer. "I doubt it. It looks as though some of it went onto the floor, and you have to have at least a fourth of a cup on your apron!"

He looked quickly down at his apron, and she giggled aloud. "Just kidding, Randy. Gotcha!"

"What do you want me to do next?"

She motioned toward the kitchen wall phone. "Call your office."

He eyed her with a questioning smile. "Only if you want me to."

Fortunately, there were no major catastrophes going on at the office. A few minor ones, but the man he had left in charge was doing an admirable job of handling them. Randy was glad she had insisted he call. It set his mind at ease and made him realize it was only reasonable that he turn some of his responsibilities over to someone else. There was no way he could do it all.

They laughed their way through the three kinds of cookies, and by the time the last cookie sheet went into the oven, the kitchen was an absolute mess. Chocolate chips, red and green sugar sprinkles, and several colors of icing adorned the counters, the floor, and even the two cookie bakers, but the cookies looked beautiful spread out across the dining room table.

"I did it! I actually made cookies!" Randy said proudly as he stood beside Sylvia surveying their handiwork. He slipped an arm about her waist. "But I have to admit, babe, I never realized how much time and work you put into making all those Christmas cookies that seemed to appear by magic on Christmas Day. I don't think I ever thanked you."

❅

Sylvia blinked hard to hold back tears of gratitude as God's Word filled her heart, giving her renewed hope. *"Favour is deceitful, and beauty is vain; but a woman that feareth the LORD, she shall be praised. Give her of the fruit of her hands; and let her own works praise her in the gates."*

"Syl? Did you hear me?" Randy asked, giving her a slight squeeze.

"I—I heard you, Randy, but I want you to know—I never expected any thanks. They were my gift to my beloved family. Yes, they took time and work, but I loved every minute of it. I made those cookies because I knew you and the children would enjoy them."

They had a quick bite of lunch, then worked side by side cleaning up the kitchen until it once again sparkled.

"You still haven't told me what we're going to do with the rest of the afternoon."

She tapped the tip of his nose with her finger. "You and I are going shopping!"

He responded with an unenthusiastic groan. "I hate shopping, you know that."

"You'll like this shopping. We're going to buy a Christmas tree!"

By the time they reached the third Christmas tree lot, Randy was a basket case, ready to accept any old tree, but Sylvia insisted they had to find just the right one.

"I know exactly what you want," the elderly man at the YMCA Christmas tree lot told them as she described the tree she had in mind.

Randy's excitement revived when he saw the tree the man selected for them. "It's perfect, Syl. It'll look great in the family room!"

She had to agree, it was perfect. The right kind, the right height, the branches were densely filled with needles, and the color was an exquisite, healthy dark green.

"We'll take it," Randy said enthusiastically, almost snatching the tree from the man's hands.

"Don't you want to ask how much it is first?" the ever-frugal Sylvia asked.

Randy shook his head vigorously. "I don't care what it costs. It's exactly what we were looking for!"

It was nearly four o'clock by the time they got the tree mounted in the tree stand and placed in its majestic position in the corner of the family room. His hands on his hips, Randy stood back to admire it.

"Guess what you get to do!"

He turned to her with a frown. "Not the lights!"

She nodded. "Yes, the lights. Like you did on our first Christmas."

Together, they made several trips to the attic, bringing down all sorts of boxes and bags, until the entire family room floor was cluttered with decorations. As soon as they located the big box containing the lights, Randy began winding them around the tree, with Sylvia sorting out the various strings and handing them to him. Once the last string was connected and the extension cord in place, Randy proudly placed the plug in the wall and the beautiful tree came to life, with hundreds of tiny twinkling lights sparkling and blinking.

"Oh, Randy. It's beautiful! I've never seen a prettier tree. You did a great job with the lights."

His eyes surveyed the tree from top to bottom. "I kinda messed up there at the top. I should've put more lights up there."

She gazed at the tree, not caring if the lights were even. Randy had put those lights up—willingly. That is all that mattered. "I think it's perfect," she said dreamily.

He bent and kissed the top of her head. "You're biased."

For the next hour, they opened boxes, pulled out ornaments, and hung them on the tree. As they worked, they reminisced over each one, remembering where and when they had purchased them or who had given them to them as a gift. Some the children had made. Some Sylvia had made. Some others had made, but each one had its own special story.

"Remember when you bought me this one?" Sylvia asked, pulling a fragile, clear-glass angel from its fitted Styrofoam box.

He carefully took the ornament from her hand and stared at it. "Our tenth Christmas together?"

She nodded, surprised that he remembered. "Yes. You—you told me—"

"I—I told you that you were my angel. I bought it in the hotel gift shop when I was on a business trip to New York City. That face reminded me of you. You were supposed to come with me, but both DeeDee and Aaron came down with the chicken pox at the same time, and you had to stay home."

She felt her eyes grow misty. "I—I should've left them with my mother and gone with you. They would probably have been fine without me. Just like your office is getting along fine without you." She moved toward him, her hand cupping his arm. "Why didn't we find time for each other, Randy?"

He swallowed hard, then placed his free hand over hers. "I don't know. Life's demands, I guess."

Suddenly, he pulled away, and she was sure he did it to change the subject and break this melancholy mood they both seemed to be in. "Are—are you hungry?" she asked, wanting to put him back at ease. "I've got a pot of chili simmering on the stove."

His smile returned. "With grated fresh onion, cheese, and chips?"

"Just like you like it, and apple crisp for dessert."

After supper, when the kitchen had been restored to order, Sylvia led Randy back into the family room. "Tired?"

"A little. Stringing lights is hard work." He moved into his recliner and propped up the footrest, then sat staring at the tree. "Pretty, isn't it?"

"Absolutely beautiful! I've never seen a prettier tree." Sylvia punched the PLAY button on the CD player, and Christmas music filled the room.

"Me, either. It's nice just sitting here, watching the lights, listening to Christmas carols, and relaxing. Surely you don't have a project for tonight."

She smiled and shook her head. "Not really. I've already wrapped all the Christmas presents. I want to put them under the tree, that's all. You sit right there and watch me."

"You work too hard, Syl. I never realized how hard."

"Give her of the fruit of her hands; and let her own works praise her in the gates." "What I do isn't work, Randy. It's a labor of love." She bustled about the room and, after spreading around the base of the tree the Christmas skirt she had made several years ago, she pulled dozens of beautifully wrapped presents from the closet and arranged them on top of it. "There. All done."

He stared at the vast array of gifts. "When did you do all of that?"

"I started the week after Thanksgiving. Shopping for our family was like a—therapy—for me. It kept my mind off—things."

"I get the message," he said, leaning his head against the headrest. "I'm sorry, Syl, but there wasn't an easier way or a better time to tell you that I—"

She quickly pressed her fingers to his lips. "Shh. We're not going to talk about that this week. That was our agreement."

"I—I just don't want you to get your hopes up."

Though Sylvia remained silent, her mind was racing. *My hopes are up, Randy! I can't help it. However, I can see, if I am going to win you back, I'm going to have to give it everything I've got. Hopefully, what I have planned for tomorrow will bring you to your senses!*

Chapter 10

By the time Randy crawled out of bed the next morning, Sylvia had strung a long evergreen garland along the top of the mirror over the fireplace, arranged the fragile Nativity set on the dining room buffet, and placed dozens of Christmas decorations and Christmas candles all over the house. Many of them were things she herself had made over the years.

"Hey, why didn't you wake me up?" he asked, looking from one decoration to another. "I would've helped you."

She pointed to the empty boxes standing in the hall. "You can carry those boxes back up to the attic, if you want to help."

He grinned as he shoved up the short sleeve of his T-shirt and flexed his bicep. "Glad to. Easy task."

By ten, Sylvia was instructing Randy to pull the car into the parking lot of Dallas Memorial Hospital.

"Why here? I'm not sick, and you haven't mentioned feeling bad."

She smiled as she pushed her door open and climbed out. "Indulge me."

Once inside, they walked to the bank of elevators opposite the reception desk. As they entered the open one, Sylvia punched the button marked FIVE. She could feel Randy's eyes on her as the elevator ascended. She led him down a hall to a long set of plate glass windows with a sign above them that read NEWBORN NURSERY. "This look familiar?" The look on his face told her he well remembered the place.

❄

Randy pressed his cheek against the cool glass as memories flooded his mind. "Oh, yes," he answered in a voice that sounded raspy, even to him. "Especially that little bed over there in the far corner. I thought we were going to lose him, Syl, and we nearly did." He felt her move up close to him and lean her head against his shoulder. "I'd never been so scared in all my life."

"The birth of a child is truly a miracle. God took the love of two young people who thought they had the world by the tail and, through their love, created a tiny image of the two of them and breathed the breath of life into him. Our little boy. Our precious first child. Our Buck."

Randy closed his eyes, his head touching hers, and tried to shut out the memory of the tiny baby as he had gasped for life with each tiny, laborious breath. "He—he was so small. So helpless. I could've held him in my palm."

"But God intervened and strengthened his little lungs. Our baby lived, and look at him now. Buck is tall, straight, and healthy. A real answer to prayer." She slipped her hand into the crook of his arm. "I can remember us both begging God to spare our child, making Him all sorts of promises. That was an emotional time for us, Randy, one I'll never forget. But there were happier times right here in this nursery, too. Remember when the twins were born?"

He rubbed at his eyes with his sleeve. "Do I ever! I was so afraid of losing you, I must've driven the doctors and nurses crazy. After the trouble we'd had with Buck, I couldn't imagine you giving birth to two babies!"

She snickered. "I was so worried about you, I had trouble concentrating on my breathing. I was afraid you were going to faint on me."

He wrapped his arm about her waist. "And I did! I was never so embarrassed in my life."

"You were only out a few seconds. Good thing that male nurse caught you, or you might've ended up on the floor having to have stitches in your head."

"I'll never forget the experience of seeing our children born. How did you ever go through it, Syl? The pain must've been excruciating."

She leaned into him and gazed at the newborn in the little bed nearest the window. "Our babies were worth it." Watery eyes lifted to his. "They were *our* babies, Randy. Yours and mine. I loved them. I loved you."

For long moments, neither of them said a word, just continued to stare through the glass. Finally, Sylvia took his hand and silently led him back to the elevators. "There are several other things I want to show you," she said in a mere whisper as the elevator doors opened.

When they reached the corner of Fourth Avenue and Bogart, Sylvia instructed Randy to turn left.

"This looks very familiar. I think I know where we're headed. Are you sure this is a good idea, Syl?"

"Humor me, Randy, okay?"

He pulled through the cemetery gates, made a quick right turn, then a left, and parked at the side of the road. "Wanna reconsider?" he asked as she pushed open her door and made her way between the gravestones.

By the time she reached her destination, Randy was at her side. She knelt beside the tiny grave marked ANGELA RENAE BENSON and bowed her head. Seconds later, she felt Randy kneel beside her.

Sylvia tried to be brave, to keep her emotions under control, but she could not, and she began to weep.

"I'm sorry, Randy. Maybe you're right. Maybe coming here wasn't a good idea, but I wanted you to remember all the things we've gone through together.

All the love and the joys and the heartaches we've shared."

"I—I do remember, Syl. I tried to be strong—for you—when we lost our little Angela, but inside I didn't feel strong. I felt like a failure. I wasn't even there for you when she was born. I was—too busy—at the newspaper, tending to some unimportant problem when you called and said your mother was taking you to the hospital. I should've dropped everything and rushed to your side, but I didn't."

She leaned against him, needing his strength. "It—it wasn't your fault, Randy. We would've lost her whether you made it or not."

"I—I wonder if she would've looked like DeeDee? With lots of dark curly hair and that cute little button nose?" He leaned forward and traced their baby's name with the tip of his finger.

"Angela was a product of our love, Randy, just like Buck and DeeDee and Aaron. She—she would've been ten years old in February."

"Let's go, Syl," he said tenderly as he rose and offered her his hand.

She stood slowly, giving the tiny grave one last look. Then she leaned into Randy as his arm encircled her, and they walked back to her car.

"Now where? Home?"

She pulled a tissue from her purse, blotted her eyes, then blew her nose loudly. "Not yet. Head on down Fourth Avenue and turn onto Lane Boulevard."

They rode silently for several miles, when suddenly Sylvia grabbed onto his arm and said, "Pull over."

"Oh, Syl. Not here!"

When he braked, she crawled out of the car and motioned for him to follow, carefully moving down a slight embankment toward a grove of trees. When she reached her destination, she stopped and turned to him. "I nearly lost you here, Randy. I'll never forget that day."

He reached out and ran his fingers across a long diagonal scar on the nearest tree's trunk. "I thought for sure I was a goner when that drunk ran me off the road. It felt like I was doing ninety miles an hour when I left the boulevard, but I was only doing around forty according to the witnesses." He bent and rubbed at his knee. "I wasn't sure I was ever going to walk again."

"You could've been killed."

"I know."

"It was a miracle you lived. God spared you, Randy. He had a purpose for your life."

"I may never have walked again if it hadn't been for you and all those months of physical therapy you helped me with. How could you do it, Syl? With everything else you had to do, you put aside two hours a day to help me work my leg."

"Give her of the fruit of her hands; and let her own works praise her in the gates."
"I wanted to do it, Randy. I loved you."

He took a couple of steps back, stuffing his hands into his pockets. "If you're trying to make me feel bad, you're succeeding."

"Making you feel bad is not my purpose, Randy. I just want you to remember the things that make up a marriage. Both good and bad."

He extended his hand, and they climbed back up the embankment. This time, Sylvia moved into the driver's seat.

They crossed town to an area near the college where Randy had attended school and obtained his degree in journalism. Sylvia brought the car to a stop in front of a rundown old tenement building.

Randy shielded his eyes from the sun as he stared at the place they had once lived, pointing up to the third floor with his free hand. "That was our apartment right up there. I can remember you standing in that very window, smiling and waving at me when I came home from class every afternoon."

"Seeing you coming up that sidewalk was the highlight of my day. What fun we had," Sylvia said, waxing nostalgic. "Remember those old wooden crates you got out of the dumpster at some warehouse. We used those for end tables and a coffee table and thought they were grand. I don't remember who gave us that old brown frieze sofa bed, but it did the job. I loved that apartment. Our very first home. I was so proud of it."

He laughed, and his laughter made her smile. "You were easy to please." His smile disappeared. "I always hated it that you had to work nights to put me through school. As I sat in that apartment each night, studying, I kept thinking about you waiting tables in that all-night restaurant and the creeps that must've come in there. I should never have let you support me like that, and you sacrificed your own education to make sure I got mine."

"But you sacrificed, too! You cared for Buck while you were studying. Otherwise, I couldn't have worked. We sure couldn't afford a baby-sitter, and neither of us wanted to leave him with one anyway." She gave his arm a reassuring pat. "I didn't mind. Honest."

His fist pounded into the palm of his other hand. "That place was a dump! I can't believe we lived there."

"That *dump* was an answer to prayer, Randy. Remember how excited we were when we finally found something we could afford?"

"I remember promising you we'd be out of there and in a better place in a year. We ended up staying there nearly all four years!"

"Just knowing you wanted a better place for us and were working to get your education so we could eventually have one was enough for me." She grabbed onto his hand and tugged him to the little drugstore on the corner. Once inside, she went to the soda fountain and ordered two root beers, a delicacy they had only been able to afford when she had worked a little overtime at the restaurant or some customer had left an overly generous tip. They sat side by side on the tall soda fountain stools and sipped their drinks the way they had done it nearly twenty-five years ago. On the way out, Sylvia bought a bag of red licorice, the long, stringy kind, another delicacy they had indulged in from time to time. She opened the bag and handed several strings to Randy.

He bit off a long piece, then winced. "We actually liked this stuff?"

She gave him a wink. "Come on—you loved it and you know it!"

He grinned. "Yeah, I guess I did."

"Beat you to the car," she hollered over her shoulder as she took off down the block. He did not catch up with her until she had reached the car.

He threw his arms around her as they both stood leaning against the car, panting and breathless. "What are you trying to do, lady? Throw me into a heart attack? I haven't run like that since—since—"

She chucked him under the chin with a giggle. "Oh? It's been so long you can't even remember when?"

"Maybe!" He pulled open the passenger door. "Who's driving? Me or you?"

"I'll drive." She crawled in, started the car, and waited until he had his seat belt fastened. "One more stop, then we can go home."

She only had to drive a few blocks to reach their final destination for the day—a little redbrick church on a crowded lot, surrounded by a tall wrought-iron fence. She expected Randy to protest, but when he did not, she opened the door and climbed out. As she had hoped, the big wooden doors were standing open. Slowly, she walked inside, hoping Randy would follow.

An elderly woman who was waxing the pews smiled up at her as she entered. Without a look back to see if Randy was behind her, she moved slowly to the altar and knelt on the worn kneeling pads, folding her hands in prayer.

When she finished praying and looked up, she found Randy kneeling beside her. "This is the exact spot where we gave our hearts to the Lord, Randy. Do you remember?" she whispered.

He nodded.

"Though we used to attend church here occasionally, until that morning, neither of us had much interest in the things of the Lord, but when the pastor brought that message—"

"About engraving us on the palms of His hands and how God has a plan for each of us, a plan to prosper us and not harm us?"

Sylvia turned to him in amazement. "You do remember!"

"Isaiah 49:16 and Jeremiah 29:11. I'll never forget those verses. They've helped me through some hard times."

Tears pooled in her eyes, making it difficult to see his face. "Hard times, like now?"

Randy stared into her eyes for a moment, and though she could not be sure, she almost thought she saw traces of remorse. But he turned away and walked back up the aisle, leaving her alone at the altar. She quickly bowed her head once more and poured out her heart to God. "Lord Jesus, only You can put this family back together again. Please soften Randy's heart, and God, make me be the kind of wife You would have me be. I so want to serve You. I want to know that perfect plan You have for me and for Randy. Forgive me for the many times I've sinned against You. Only now, since Randy has been back home and I've examined my own life, have I seen how I, too, have been responsible for the problems we're facing. Help me to do Your will. Please, God, please!"

They stopped at Randy's favorite steak house for dinner and, although steak was not Sylvia's favorite, she ordered the same thing Randy ordered and willed herself to enjoy it. When Randy excused himself to go to the men's room, Sylvia held her breath, hoping he was not going to phone Chatalaine. Funny he had not mentioned her name, not once since he had arrived on the nineteenth. But why should he? No doubt he knew even the mention of her name would start an argument. No, Randy was too savvy for that. As long as she did not mention the woman's name, she was sure he would not, either. However, he was back in no time. No way would he have had time to phone the woman.

When they reached home, Randy plugged in the Christmas lights while Sylvia cued up another Christmas CD. They stayed up long enough to watch the nightly news and one of the late night talk shows before heading upstairs.

"Big day tomorrow," she told him as she climbed into bed. "The kids will be here for Christmas Eve, and we—you and I—have gobs of food to prepare. DeeDee and Aaron promised to be home by four, and Buck and Shonna are coming as soon as he gets off work."

Randy set the alarm on his side of the bed and flipped off the light before sliding under the covers. "Syl?"

"Yes."

"I can't say I exactly enjoyed today, but I have to admit it was an eye-opener."

"Oh?"

"I mean—I'd almost forgotten some of the things you and I have gone through together. I guess I—put them out of my mind."

"That's understandable. I wanted to forget some of them, too."

"Syl?"

"Yes."

"I don't want you to get the idea that I'm hard-hearted, but at the same time,

I don't want you to get your hopes up. I'm still planning on going through with the divorce."

"Good night, Randy. I love you."

Silence.

Suddenly, she felt Randy's weight shift in the bed, then his warm body snuggle up next to hers, his arm draping over her. "Good night, Syl."

Her heart pounded so furiously, she was sure he could feel the vibration. "Good night, Randy. Sleep tight."

Sylvia jerked out of Randy's arms and sat up with a jolt as his alarm sounded at seven. *Today is December the twenty-fourth! I have less than forty-eight hours to convince Randy to forget about the divorce and move back home where he belongs! Help, Lord!*

"Why don't I fix breakfast today?" Randy asked as he crawled out from under the covers and stretched his long arms.

Sylvia glanced at the Bible on her nightstand. "You sure you don't mind?"

"Not a bit! I'll come back up and take a shower later. Just don't expect anything too fancy."

She waited until she heard him go down the stairs, then picked up her Bible and began to read. *I'm sorry, Lord. Although it seems I keep shooting prayers up at You continually, I've neglected my Bible reading since Randy has come back home.* She turned to one of her favorite chapters, Psalm 139, and began to read. "O, Lord, thou hast searched me, and known me. Thou knowest my downsitting and mine uprising, thou understandest my thought afar off." She read through the few verses silently until she came to the twenty-third verse. "Search me, O God, and know my heart: try me, and know my thoughts: And see if there be any wicked way in me, and lead me in the way everlasting." *That's my prayer, Lord. Please, show me how to make these last few hours count. I can't lose my husband!*

As Sylvia reached for her jeans, she thought she heard the front door close. But deciding the noise must have been Randy working down in the kitchen, she went into the bathroom to put on her makeup and fix her hair. By the time she reached the kitchen twenty minutes later, he was sitting at the table waiting for her, a large white sack resting in the center.

"How does an Egg McMuffin sound?"

"Wonderful," she responded happily, meaning it, as she sat down beside him and reached for the sack.

❄

The strains of "Silent Night" filled the house as the six members of the Benson family gathered around the dining room table. Randy, Sylvia, Buck, Shonna, DeeDee, and Aaron. Sylvia's heart was so filled with gratefulness that they were all together like this—this one more time—she thought it would burst. Her wonderful son, knowing the secret their parents were carrying and apparently wanting to take the strain off his father and mother, offered to say the blessing on their food. Sylvia had hoped Randy would insist on doing it. However, when he kept his silence, she gave Buck an appreciative smile and a nod, and they all reached for one another's hands, forming a circle. Buck's prayer was brief but sincere, as he asked God to bless the food and the hands that prepared it and to bless each one assembled, especially his mom and dad.

"Your dad has been helping me all day," Sylvia told her family as she passed the carving knife to her husband.

Aaron gave a teasing snort. "Hey, Dad, why've you been hiding your culinary talents all these years? This stuff looks pretty good!"

DeeDee slapped playfully at her twin brother. "Be quiet, Aaron, or he may never do it again."

"Tell me what you fixed, Dad, so I can avoid it," Aaron added, backing away from DeeDee as she swung at him again.

"I'm not telling," Randy said with a chuckle as he began to slice off thick wedges of the roasted turkey. "You'll either have to take your chances or starve. Your choice."

Aaron cocked his head as he weighed his options. "You win. I'll take my chances. Pass the mashed potatoes."

"I think everything looks wonderful, Father Benson," Shonna said as she held out her plate. "You and Mother Benson make a great team."

Sylvia gave her an exaggerated bow. "Thanks, Shonna. It's nice to be appreciated."

"We all appreciate you, Mom," Buck interjected with a quick sideways glance toward his father. "Don't we, Dad?"

"We sure do. I'm just beginning to realize all your mother does for this family. Giving us great meals like this is just a small part of it."

Sylvia's heart pounded erratically. "Thank you, Randy. It was—was sweet of you to say that." *"Give her of the fruit of her hands; and let her own works praise her in the gates."*

"Hey, are you going to give me a piece of that turkey, Dad," Aaron asked with a playful frown, "or am I going to have to arm wrestle you for it?"

The meal continued pleasantly with good-humored bantering going on between Randy and his sons.

After the last bite had been consumed and everyone's napkin returned to the table, Shonna and DeeDee volunteered to clear the table and help Sylvia clean up the kitchen, suggesting the men go into the family room and relax. Once everything was back in shape and the dishwasher humming away, the women joined them. Buck was already at the piano playing a Christmas carol.

"Hey, all of you," he told the gang, gesturing for them to join him, "it's time for the Benson family sing-along."

The five gathered around him and joined in as he led off with "O Holy Night." Sylvia's breath caught in her throat as Randy moved next to her, harmonizing with her as they had done so many times before. They sang three more carols, then Aaron suggested it was time for their annual reading of the Christmas story from the second chapter of Luke before they turned to the opening of the presents.

"Why don't you read this year, Buck?" Randy said, reaching for the big family Bible on the bookshelf. "My throat is a bit husky."

As her son gave his father a frown, Sylvia felt her mouth go dry. *Don't say anything you'll be sorry for, Buck. Please!*

Buck reached out and took the Bible from his hands without comment and opened it to Luke 2 and, after allowing everyone time to be seated, began to read.

"I love that chapter," DeeDee said as her older brother closed the Bible and returned it to its place. "You helped me memorize it when I was a kid, Dad. Remember? The first year I was on the church quiz team."

All eyes went to Randy. "Yeah, I guess I did. You were a quick learner, as I recall."

"Just think," Aaron said, dropping down on the floor near the tree and drawing his knees up to his chest, circling them with his arms, "God sent His only Son to earth as a baby, knowing He would die on the cross to save us from our sins. Isn't that an awesome thought?"

Sylvia moved to the leather sofa and settled herself beside her daughter-in-law. "It's hard to fathom He could love us that much, when we're so unworthy."

"What do you think of the tree your mother and I picked out and decorated?" All eyes turned to Randy as he abruptly changed the subject. "Pretty, huh? I put the lights on."

"It's beautiful, Daddy," DeeDee said, leaning over her father to kiss his cheek. "You did a good job."

"I didn't know the old man had it in him," Aaron chimed in with a wink. "How come Mom's had to decorate the tree by herself all these years?"

"I—I like decorating the tree," Sylvia inserted quickly, not wanting Randy to have to explain himself. "But it was nice to have your dad do it for a change."

"Whose turn is it to distribute the presents this year?" Aaron picked up the gift nearest him and gave it a shake. "Looks like the man in the red suit has already been here and gone."

Sylvia leaned forward and swatted at him. "Don't talk that way, Aaron. I've always thought talking about Santa and pretending he's the one who brings the presents takes the glory away from Jesus and the real meaning of Christmas."

Aaron did an exaggerated double take. "You mean there really isn't a Santa Claus?"

"Just for that remark, young man, you can pass out the gifts," Sylvia said, hoping this wouldn't be the last Christmas her family would all be gathered like this. She could not imagine Christmas without Randy sitting in his chair.

"Okay, if you insist." Aaron began picking up the presents, reading the name on each tag out loudly, shaking the package, and predicting what he thought might be inside before handing it to the person for whom it was intended.

"Here you go, DeeDee. I'm guessing Buck and Shonna are giving you—a Barbie doll!"

He turned to his older brother. "Buck, inside this present DeeDee is giving to you, I predict you have a—a—a teddy bear!"

Randy's present came next. "Wow, Dad, what do you suppose is in this little box from Mom? Maybe that new set of golf clubs you told me you wanted?"

Sylvia watched with expectation as Randy opened her present.

"Oh, Syl," he said as he tore the last bit of paper off and opened the box. "You shouldn't have."

"What is it, Dad?" DeeDee asked, sliding closer to his chair.

"It's—it's the palm-sized video camera I've been wanting. How did you know—"

Sylvia grinned. "Buck told me you'd mentioned it to him. I hope I got the right one. You can exchange it if—"

"It's exactly the one I wanted. Thanks, Syl. Now I can take pictures of this motley crew as they open the rest of their presents."

Sylvia breathed a contented sigh. He liked her gift.

On and on and on it went, with each of Aaron's gift predictions sending the group into fits of laughter. Sylvia wanted to remember those sounds forever. As she glanced at the clock, she felt panic set in. Only twenty-eight hours to go, and although she and Randy had experienced some wonderful times since he'd arrived on the nineteenth, he seemed no closer to changing his mind about staying than when he'd arrived.

"And this last one is for Dad," Aaron said as he stood and hand delivered it to his father. "Another one from Mom. How many does that make? Looks like you came out better than the rest of us this year."

"That's not true. Each of you—"

Aaron held up a finger and waggled it at his mother. "Just kidding, Mom. Don't get bent out of shape. After all, that old man is your husband. He'll be around long after us kids move out for good."

Randy sent her a quick glance that chilled her bones.

"Well, that's it!" Aaron reached for the big trash bag Sylvia had brought in to hold all the torn wrapping paper and ribbons.

She looked down at the presents piled on the coffee table in front of her. Each of the children had given her wonderful gifts, and she was grateful for each one of them, but none of the gifts had been from Randy, and she wanted to break down in tears.

"Actually," Buck said, rising and taking Shonna's hand in his, "there's another present coming, but it won't be delivered for some time. Shonna and I are going to have a baby! In July!"

Sylvia's heart leaped for joy. How she had longed to have a grandchild to cuddle and care for. She was going to be a grandmother! Her gaze went to Randy, who was just sitting there, as if in a stupor.

"Hey, old man!" Aaron said, punching his father in the arm. "You're gonna be a grandpa!"

Randy donned a quick grin and stood as both Buck and Shonna hurried to his side. "Congratulations, son. You, too, Shonna. That's gonna be one lucky baby. You two will make great parents."

"Aw, they won't be half as good as you and Mom," Aaron said, hugging his mother's neck.

"Who wants dessert?" Randy asked as he surveyed the group. "Your mom and I made her famous Millionaire Pie."

Buck raised his hand. "I'll take a very small piece. I'm stuffed with those fabulous Christmas cookies you and Mom baked. Those things are good!"

"Thank you, thank you, thank you!" Randy bowed low, then asked, "Small pieces of pie for everyone?"

The entire group shouted yes in unison.

"I'll help Dad," Buck said, motioning Sylvia to remain seated.

A cry choked in her throat. *Buck, no! Please don't say anything to your dad about Chatalaine or the divorce. Or about him not giving me a gift. Please!* She watched in fear as the two men headed for the kitchen.

Seeming to sense her fear, Shonna slid over on the sofa and wrapped her arm about Sylvia's shoulder. "It'll be okay. Buck won't say anything," she whispered so only her mother-in-law could hear.

A few minutes later, Buck and Randy came back into the room carrying six plates with small wedges of pie on them. Buck passed out the plates while Randy handed each person a fork and napkin.

As Sylvia started to rise again, Buck shook his head. "I'll get the coffee and cups, Mom. You eat your pie."

She gave him a slight grin, thankful for his thoughtfulness.

"Buck and I had quite a talk in the kitchen," Randy told everyone as he forked up his first bite of pie.

Sylvia nearly choked.

"He tells me he's thinking about going back to college for his master's."

"I think he should," Aaron said, nodding. "He's a smart guy."

They continued with good conversation until, eventually, the pie was gone. "I have to get up early, Mother Benson, so we'd better be going. We're due at my parents' house at ten, and I still have to make two pies tonight."

"You are going to be here for breakfast, aren't you?" Sylvia asked quickly.

Buck bent and kissed his mother's cheek. "Sure, Mom. We'll be here by eight. We wouldn't miss your famous cinnamon rolls."

Aaron rose and tugged his sister to her feet. "We'd better get to work, too, little sister."

"Work? You two?" Buck asked with a teasing smile.

Aaron nodded. "Yep. Our friends are picking me and DeeDee up at ten for our ten-day skiing trip to Colorado, and we haven't even started packing our gear."

DeeDee took her mother's hand and patted it with concern. "You and Dad going to be okay? Being here by yourselves on Christmas Day?"

Sylvia nodded. "We'll be fine, honey. Just enjoy yourselves. I know you two have been looking forward to this ski trip since last year. Just promise me you'll be careful."

Everyone walked Buck and Shonna to the door. After hugs all around and more congratulations to the expectant parents, the couple left, and Randy closed the door.

Aaron and DeeDee each kissed their parents, thanked them for a wonderful Christmas, and headed up the stairs to their rooms.

"I—I think I'll go to bed, too," Sylvia said, as she gathered up her gifts. With a heavy heart, she climbed the stairs, leaving Randy to turn off the lights and check the doors, a job she had taken over in his absence.

I have to forget my husband didn't even give me a present. I can't let him see me sulking like this. Maybe, since he's spent the week with me, he simply didn't have a chance to do any shopping. I have to stop feeling sorry for myself. Deciding a quick shower might lift her spirits, she gathered up her gown and slippers and moved into the bathroom. When she came back out fifteen minutes later, Randy was sitting on the side of the bed in his pajamas, reading the instructions for his new video camera.

Sylvia pasted on her cheeriest smile as she sashayed across the room toward him. *If Randy does leave, I want him to remember me smiling and looking radiant and more like the woman he married twenty-five years ago.*

He looked up with a broad smile, as if nothing whatsoever was wrong. "Hey, another new gown? I really like this one! Even better than the red one."

She twirled around, holding her hands out daintily like a ballerina, and ended up sitting on the bed beside him.

"Oh, I like that perfume!"

She lifted her head, offering her neck to him. He bent and took in an exaggerated whiff. "Zowie! Now that's what I call a perfume!"

She gave him a coy smile. "You bought it for me for Christmas two years ago."

"Do I have good taste, or what?"

"Thanks for another wonderful day, Randy," she said as she crawled onto the bed beside him, her fingers cupping his neck. "I think the kids had a good time tonight. I know I did." She began to knead his muscles as he tilted his head to one side. "That was some present Buck and Shonna gave all of us. Can you believe we're going to be grandparents?"

"I always wondered what it would be like to hold my first grandchild in my arms. I guess we'll find out in July."

She loved touching his skin, wafting in his manly scent, feeling his hot breath on her hands. She longed to leap into his lap and smother him with kisses, but if she did, she knew he'd probably run for the door, and she wouldn't have that one last day with him, so she restrained herself.

"There, does that feel better?" She scooted off the bed and bent to kiss his cheek. Suddenly, Randy grabbed her and pulled her to him, kissing her more passionately than he had done in years. Although surprised by his sudden action, she melted into his arms, fully participating in their kiss.

"You are so beautiful," Randy whispered in her ear as he held her close and nuzzled his face in her hair. "I've missed the closeness we used to share." He kissed her again, holding her in his arms tighter than ever.

"I've missed it, too," she whimpered breathlessly against his lips.

"This has been one of the best weeks of my life, Syl. I'll never forget it."

She clung to him, wishing this moment could last forever, but just as quickly as he had pulled her to him, he pushed her away.

"Hold me, Randy! Please! I love you!"

"I—I can't! Don't you see? I'll be leaving tomorrow night! Holding you and kissing you like this—well, it isn't fair to either of us. Our marriage is over, Syl! It died a long time ago! What we're having this week is make-believe."

She could not believe what she was hearing! She had been so sure God was answering prayer. "But, Randy, you said this was one of the most wonderful weeks of your life! We've had a great time together! We're going to be grandparents!"

"You don't get it, do you, Syl? Just because we've both been bitten by the festivities and hoopla of Christmas doesn't mean things won't return to what they were before when we get back to normal. We've both been like Ken and Barbie this past week! On our best behavior. Working to please each other and avoiding having words. We've been blinded by the joys and frivolity of the Christmas season. Bright lights, candles, ornaments, music. What happens when Christmas is over and the lights and ornaments are put back in their cardboard boxes and returned to that drab attic? I can't take that chance. It took me nearly two years to get up the courage to tell you how I really felt—how unhappy I've been. I can't go through it again!"

She wanted to slap him, scream, hit a door, something, anything to wake him up. "Can't you see I love you, Randy? This hasn't all been your fault. I see that now! However, we can both change. We can work out our problems and differences if we really want to do it. We can't throw this marriage away like last week's copy of your newspaper. Our marriage is a living and growing thing!"

"A living thing that has been dying a slow death, Syl. It's time for the burial." He snatched up his pajamas and headed toward the bathroom, closing the door behind him.

Sylvia had never felt so hurt and rejected. Why hadn't she seen this coming? How blind and stupid could she have been? With tears flowing, she climbed into bed and pulled the sheet over her head. She heard Randy come out of the bathroom, felt him crawl into bed, and heard the click of the lamp.

Twenty-four hours. If I can't convince Randy to stay by then, it's all over. I promised I'd let him have the divorce, and I have to keep my word. Father God, are You listening, or are You forsaking me, too?

"Syl?"

She wanted to pretend she was asleep, but she could not. "Yes."

"Good night."

"Good night, Randy."

Sylvia lay awake until the red numbers on the clock showed 3:00 a.m. From the even rhythm of Randy's breathing, she was sure he was asleep, though she herself had barely closed her eyes. She crawled carefully out of bed and padded gently down the stairs, mumbling to herself. "Someone has to put the stockings up and fill them with little gifts and candy. Since Santa isn't real, I guess I'll have to do it."

"Give her of the fruit of her hands; and let her own works praise her in the gates."

Chapter 11

December 25 dawned even more beautiful than any other day in the week they had been together. Although Sylvia was dead tired from lack of sleep, she jumped out of bed with a smile. *This is your last chance, girl. Make the most of it!*

Randy turned over with a frown. "You're chipper this morning."

"Why shouldn't I be? It's Christmas morning, and my family will all be gathered around the table for breakfast." She snapped her fingers, then yanked the cover off him. "Rise and shine, Grandpa!"

He covered his face with his hands. "Grandpa? That term sounded nice last night, but this morning, just the mention of it makes me feel old."

She crossed the room and opened the blinds, letting the room fill with sunshine. "Not me! It makes me feel young. I can hardly wait for the patter of little feet in this house again."

He pulled himself to a sitting position and ran his fingers through his hair. "Are you forgetting dirty diapers?"

"I don't even mind those." She poked him in the ribs with the tips of her finger. "Hustle, hustle! Buck and Shonna will be here soon. You don't want them to see you in those hideous pajamas, do you?"

He looked down at his pajamas. "What's wrong with them?"

"The colors are nice, but have you looked closely at the pattern?"

He raised an arm and squinted at the sleeve. "No."

"Randy! Those yellow dots are little ducks!"

"Ducks? I thought they were polka dots. Why didn't you tell me? I was in such a hurry when I bought them, I guess I never really looked at them."

"No, I'm sorry to tell you, but those are not polka dots; those are ducks. Cute little yellow duckies." She hurried to the door. "The kids will be here in ten minutes. If you don't want them to tease you about your ducks, you'd better get dressed."

"Is that another new T-shirt?" he called after her. "Looks good on you. I like purple!"

She had to smile. "Yes," she called back over her shoulder. "I bought it because I thought you'd like it!"

By the time she had filled the coffeepot and put the rolls in the oven, the front door opened and Buck and Shonna came bustling in. Within seconds, DeeDee and Aaron came down the stairs, with Randy two steps behind them. "Well," she said with a joy that overwhelmed her sorrow, "looks like the gang's all here. Anyone want to check their stockings?"

Buck, Shonna, DeeDee, Aaron, and even Randy, all made a mad dash to the family room, pulling their stockings from the fireplace and rummaging through their contents, pulling out the little wrapped gifts, whistles, paper hats, balloons, bubblegum, trinkets, and candy canes. Randy put on his paper hat, looped two candy canes over his ears, and paraded through the room loudly blowing his whistle while the whole family laughed hysterically. Buck soon joined him, followed by Shonna, DeeDee, and Aaron. Sylvia could stand it no longer, pulled on her hat, draped her candy canes over her ears, and stuck a whistle in her mouth, too. Following Randy's lead, the little battalion made their way through the house, traipsing through nearly every room, until they were all too weak with laughter to keep it up any longer.

"Now that we've made complete fools of ourselves," Sylvia said, pulling the candy canes from her ears, "does anyone want breakfast?"

The Benson family laughed their way through breakfast, enjoying the huge platter of homemade cinnamon rolls Sylvia had baked, along with juice, coffee, and the large slices of the country ham she'd put in a slow oven when she'd gotten up to fill the stockings.

Buck and Shonna left at nine thirty to go to her parents' house. At ten, DeeDee and Aaron kissed their parents good-bye and joined the group of eager skiers honking in their driveway. Sylvia cast a cautious glance at the clock. *Fourteen hours to go.*

As soon as the door closed behind them, Randy tugged on her hand. "Come on, Grandma. I'll help you clean up the breakfast mess."

Putting on the best smile she could muster, she followed him into the kitchen and began gathering the dirty dishes and carrying them to the sink while he put things in the refrigerator. *I've got to stop counting the hours!*

"You outdid yourself again. These cinnamon rolls are the best you've ever made." He unwound a rounded section of the last roll on the plate, broke it off, and popped it into his mouth.

"Thanks. I'm glad you enjoyed them."

"So, what's the plan for today?" He slipped the empty plate into the dishwasher, then placed a hand on her wrist with a winning smile. "By the way, Merry Christmas."

She reached up and planted a quick kiss on his cheek. "Merry Christmas to you, too, Grandpa." *Why didn't you get me a present, Randy? Am I that unimportant to you? Do you hate me that much? I'll bet you got your little cutie a wonderful present!*

"And by the way, we're staying home. All day."

"I was hoping you'd say that."

Once the kitchen was cleaned up, Sylvia pulled a covered dish from the freezer and left it on the counter to thaw for lunch. Then the two of them headed for the family room. To her surprise, Randy plunked himself down on the sofa instead of moving to his recliner. She picked up the copy of the *Dallas Times* that Buck had brought in when he and Shonna had come for breakfast and sat down beside Randy. "I put on a fresh pot of coffee," she said trying to sound casual as she pulled the oversized Christmas Day paper from its wrapper. She shuffled through the various sections, finally coming to the sports section, which she handed to Randy. As soon as his attention was focused on it, she quickly pulled out the Dallas Life section, bearing that spectacular picture of Chatalaine and her willowy figure and Cheshire cat smile, folded it, and placed it on the lamp table on her side of the sofa, facedown. Compared to that woman, Sylvia felt dowdy, rumpled, and old. As soon as she had a chance, she planned on putting it in the trash container. No need for Randy to be reminded of his paramour on this, her final day with him.

Randy scanned through the sports section, then placed it on the coffee table. "Not much sports news today." He gazed at her for a moment, then cautiously slipped an arm about her shoulders and pulled her close. "I want you to know, Syl, how much I appreciate everything you've done to make this Christmas special for all of us. The kids, me." He hesitated as he raised a dark brow. "I—I hope we can always remain friends—for our children's sake."

Her heart dropped to the pit of her stomach, and she swallowed both her pride and a hasty reply. *Hold your anger! You have less than thirteen hours left. Don't blow it! Make every minute count. This may be your last chance to woo him back.* Instead of snapping his head off, which was what she would have liked to do, she smiled up at him, cradling his freshly shaven cheek with her hand. "Can we put this conversation off until later? I don't want to even think about it now."

He gave her a puzzled look, apparently caught off guard by her unexpected response. "Ah—yeah—I just wanted to make sure you—"

Deciding to make her move, since she really had nothing more to lose, she whirled about and climbed onto his lap and began to stroke his hair, her face mere inches from his. Though he eyed her suspiciously, he did not move. After giving him an adoring smile, she tenderly kissed first one eyelid, then the other. One cheek, then the other cheek. Slowly, she let her lips move to his mouth, his closeness playing havoc with her senses. "I love you, Randy. You may leave me, but you'll never be able to forget me," she murmured softly as her mouth sought his again. She nearly screamed out as his arms circled her, pulling her against him. *Please, Randy, say you love me, too!*

When their kiss ended, she rested her forehead against his, her fingers twined about his neck. "Don't do it, sweetheart, don't leave me. We have so much for which to be thankful. Some of our best years are yet to come. Don't let them get away from us."

As if her words suddenly brought him back to reality, back to his unshakable resolve, he pushed her away and turned his head. "Don't, Syl, don't do this!" Literally picking her up and setting her off his lap onto the sofa, he stood to his feet, clenching and unclenching his fists at his sides.

Tears of humiliation and hurt stung at her eyes as she struggled to meet his icy glare. "But, Randy—"

"Is there any coffee left? I need a cup."

She drew a quick breath through chalky lips. Brushing her tears aside, she stood, her heart thundering, and hurried toward the kitchen. "I think we both could use a good, strong cup of coffee. I'll get it."

Once in the kitchen, she worked frantically to pull herself together, dabbing at her eyes with a dish towel and mulling over what had just happened. *Come on, Sylvia, get hold of yourself. Maybe you moved too fast, too aggressively; after all, that's not your style. You probably frightened him.* She gave a snort. *And that Chatalaine woman wasn't aggressive? If not, how did she manage to snare my husband away from me so easily and so quickly? She was probably all over him. Telling him how handsome he was. How smart. How successful—batting her baby blues at him.* She filled their coffee mugs, lifted her chin, and moved back into the family room, determined to keep Randy from seeing how badly his words had hurt her. "Here ya go! Strong, just like you requested."

She watched as Randy took the cup and seated himself on the floor in front of the sofa, sticking his long legs out in front of him. "Mind if I sit down beside you?"

"Of course not."

She sat down, crossing her legs at the ankles and took a long, slow sip of her coffee, hoping the tension between them was surmountable. Suddenly, she noticed a Christmas CD was playing. Randy must have turned it on while she was in the kitchen. "I love that CD."

He leaned back against the sofa and tilted his head as if listening to the song with rapt attention. "Folks should play Christmas carols all year. Seems a shame to play them only in December."

"I think I could sit here forever, watching the lights blink on the tree and listening to that music." She made a nervous gesture to brush her hair away from her face.

They sat silently until the CD finished playing, then picking up their empty mugs, Sylvia rose. "I—I guess I'd better get us some lunch."

"Need any help?"

She shook her head. "Thanks, but no. I'll bring our trays in here." Fifteen minutes later, she returned, handing Randy his tray as he moved up onto the sofa.

"Umm, your barbecue ribs? I hoped that was what I smelled."

"And the mustard potato salad you always liked to go with the ribs."

She started the CD player again before sitting down with her tray in her lap, hoping the lovely Christmas music with its message of God's love would calm their spirits. They ate in silence as the music played. When they finished eating, Sylvia carried the trays back into the kitchen.

"Good lunch. Thanks. No special projects for this afternoon?"

She caused a smile to dance at her lips. "Of course, I have a project! A relaxing one I think you'll enjoy. On and off this past year, I've been working on our family scrapbooks, mounting many of those pictures we've been tossing into that big drawer all these years. I thought you might like to take a look at them." She was pleased when he gave her an enthusiastic smile. After taking three scrapbooks from the shelf and placing them on the coffee table, she sat down by Randy and opened the one on top. "This first one starts the year we began dating. Look at this funny picture of the two of us on that parade float. Can you believe we ever agreed to wear those silly costumes?"

He leaned in for a better look. "You were a real looker. No wonder I fell for you."

"Well, you were quite handsome yourself. All the girls thought so."

He flipped the page and pointed to a photo in the top corner. "I'd nearly forgotten about that old bicycle. I wonder what ever happened to it."

She leaned into him with a giggle. "Remember how you used to ride it backwards? I could never figure out how you did that."

"Oh, look, here's a picture of my mom in that old car my dad had."

"And here's another one of the two of us paddling that old canoe we rented at the boathouse."

Randy let out a raucous laugh. "As I recall, you lost hold of your paddle and turned us over when you tried to reach for it."

She punched his shoulder playfully. "Me? I wasn't the one who lost that paddle; it was you, Randy Benson! You turned us over!"

"Oh, there's a picture of Buddy Gilbert. Remember him? He spent more time in the principal's office than he did in the classroom. That kid was always in trouble."

She flipped over several pages and pointed to a full-page picture of the two of them, taken after their wedding by the photographer. "We made a handsome couple, didn't we? Look how happy we were. I was so excited about being Mrs.

Randy Benson, I couldn't get the smile off my face. I felt like a fairy princess in that dress. And look at that flashy tuxedo you were wearing. What a handsome groom you were."

"I'll never forget how beautiful you looked in that dress."

Her pulse quickened. "I—I don't want you to forget, Randy."

The lines bracketing his mouth tightened, and she wondered if, once again, she had gone too far. "Do you have any of Buck's baby pictures in here?"

She flipped a couple more pages, then pointed to the picture of a preemie wearing the funny little hat they put on tiny newborns. "He's only a few hours old in that picture. Can you believe that tiny baby is now over six feet tall and extremely healthy? God did a miracle in his life."

Randy gazed at the picture, touching it with his fingertips. "I was so scared, Syl. I was so afraid we'd lose him."

She carefully leaned her head onto his shoulder, hoping and praying he would not push her away. "Me, too. I knew how much you wanted a son."

"And now we have two sons."

"And DeeDee." She sat up and flipped another page. "Look, there's a picture of our twins. So many of the nurses remarked how cute they were. Nothing skinny about those two."

"I expected you to have a hard delivery when the doctor told us how big they were. Look at Aaron's fist! That boy came out ready to do battle."

"Aaron has always reminded me more of you than Buck. He and DeeDee both have your coloring and your dark, curly hair. Buck is more like me."

Randy took her hand and gave it a pat. "He not only looks more like you, he has your same patience and disposition. Lucky kid!"

"Here, I want you to see the pictures we took that time we all went on vacation to Branson, Missouri." She flipped a few more pages.

"What a trip that was. Why did we ever decide to camp out in that big tent rather than stay at a motel? It rained every day we were there."

She let out a giggle at the thought. "Everything we owned was drenched. As I remember, that tent molded before it dried out, and we had to throw it away. Your idea of camping out wasn't such a good idea after all, but the kids had fun."

He reared back. "My idea of camping? It was your idea."

"But you're the one who always talked about the fun you had camping out when you were a boy!"

"In the backyard! If it rained, all I had to do was grab my pillow and blanket and go in the house."

Sylvia planted her hands on her hips. "I never wanted to camp out. I only suggested it because you had talked about it so much. I never realized you'd only done it in your backyard!"

"I guess the joke was on both of us."

They went through all three albums, reminiscing with each page, laughing, sometimes crying, sometimes just remaining silent, and enjoying their memories. So many times, Sylvia thought Randy was on the brink of saying something, especially when she could see tears in his eyes. Sometimes she thought she saw a flicker of love, but he remained silent. Close to her at times. Withdrawn at other times.

"Our twenty-five years might not have been perfect, Randy, but they were ours. Yours and mine. We created a life together because we loved one another and wanted to spend our years together. I've never once been sorry I said 'I do,' and I've never stopped loving you, and I never will, no matter what happens."

"Syl—"

"Don't say it, sweetheart. I know you don't want to hear that right now, but I have to let you know how I feel." She motioned toward his recliner. "Why don't you take a little nap while I fix dinner? I'll wake you when we're ready to eat."

"I can help—"

Deciding her emotions had already been yanked around enough for one day and needing a few private minutes to herself, she held up a palm. "Not this time, Randy. Rest."

"But—"

"Please. Let's do this my way, okay?"

She hurried into the kitchen and checked the oven. The beef roast she had put in to bake that morning was just right. She scurried into the dining room, put her lace tablecloth on the table, and set it with her most delicate china and silverware. In the center of the table, she put a fresh pine candle ring, the one she and Randy had purchased at the YMCA lot when they had bought their Christmas tree, and added a big, fat red candle in the center. She lit the candle and stood back, admiring its beauty, then lit the candelabras on the highly polished buffet, giving the entire room a soft, romantic glow.

Once the gravy was made, the potatoes and carrots put into their serving bowls, squares of homemade cranberry salad placed on lettuce leaves, and the corn bread browned just right and everything placed on the table, she removed her apron, checked her appearance in the pantry mirror, and went into the family room to awaken her husband.

"I couldn't sleep," he told her as she came into the room. "I've been thinking about all those pictures you've put in those albums. It must've taken you weeks to arrange them like that and add all those notes under each photograph."

"Give her of the fruit of her hands; and let her own works praise her in the gates."
She grabbed his hand and tugged him to his feet with an inward smile as she

remembered the verse the Lord had given her. "Like most of the things I do, Randy, it was a labor of love. Come on. Dinner's ready."

He stopped at the archway leading into the dining room, his eyes wide. "Wow, you're going all out. Is that round thing what we bought when we got the Christmas tree? That thing around the candle?"

She moved to her place at the table, pleased that he noticed it. "Yes, do you like it? It smells wonderful. It's bayberry."

He hurried around the table and pushed her chair in as she sat down, then moved to his own seat. "Umm, brown gravy."

"I—I thought maybe—rather than having one of us pray—we might recite the Lord's Prayer together."

"If you want to."

She bowed her head and closed her eyes, folding her hands in her lap. "Our Father, which art in heaven." She paused, but not hearing Randy, went on. Eventually, he joined in with her, but she could tell there was no enthusiasm in his tone, and she almost wished she had not suggested it. "For thine is the kingdom and the power and the glory forever. Amen."

"This is nice, the two of us eating in the dining room like this." He heaped a huge helping of mashed potatoes on his plate, then reached for the gravy boat. "We should've done this more often."

"I tried a number of times, even had the table set and a special meal fixed, but then something would happen at the newspaper, a press would quit working, a paper delivery didn't show up on time, or some other catastrophe would happen, and you'd call and say you weren't going to make it home for dinner."

His face grew serious. "I'm sorry, Syl, I didn't know. You never complained about it."

"I didn't want to add to your problems. You had enough to take care of."

"Guess you haven't been too happy these past few years, either."

She shook her head vigorously. She had to make him understand. "That's not true! I *have* been happy. However, I would have been happier if you and I could've had more time together; but I understood, sweetheart. Honest I did! I knew you would've preferred being home with your family—" She drew in a deep breath as visions of Randy asking her for a divorce on Thanksgiving Day came back to haunt her. "Or—or at least I thought you would."

"I—I used to want that, but I never realized you did, too. You seemed to have more interest in the family cat than you did me. I've felt like an outsider in my own home for more times than I can remember, Syl. You shut me out. You *and* the kids. Sometimes I felt like none of you cared if I lived or died, as long as the paycheck continued."

She bristled. "That's a rotten thing to say, Randy Benson! I'm just glad the children aren't here to hear you make such a ridiculous statement! Do you have any idea how that makes me feel? Or do you even care about my feelings?" She swallowed hard and let out a long, low breath of air as she glanced at her watch. "We have to stop this. We only have three hours until midnight. I want those three hours to be pleasant, not a shouting match."

He nodded but did not look at her, just moved his carrots around on his plate.

"How's the roast?"

He raised his head slightly and gave her a weak smile. "Perfect. Best I've ever had. You're a terrific cook."

"Thank you." Sylvia tried to appear calm on the outside, but inside she was seething. *Why did I let him bait me like that? I wanted this evening to be perfect, one that would make Randy see what he was giving up if he left me, and what did I do? Nagged at him like some cartoon figure! Three hours! Lord, what shall I do? I'm all out of ideas. I felt sure that once Randy spent this week in our home, being reminded of the vows we took and the lives we've lived for the past twenty-five years, he'd want to come home. But now—I'm wondering if he, too, is counting the minutes until midnight—so he can get out of here, away from me!* She could not stop them. Tears flooded down her cheeks like a sudden rainstorm on a spring day.

Randy noticed and, hurrying around the table, put his arm about her. "Syl, are you okay? Aren't you feeling well?"

She turned away from him and got up from her chair. "I'm sorry, Randy. I never meant to spoil our evening. Give me a few minutes, okay? I'll be fine. Finish your dinner." With that, she rushed from the room and up the stairs, seeking the solitude of their bedroom.

❈

Randy stood by, helplessly watching her leave the room. *Randy, old boy, that was some smooth move. Are you so concerned about how you feel that you've forgotten other people have feelings, too?*

He sat back down and tried to eat, but the guilt he felt for mouthing off made the food wad up in his stomach. Sylvia had been nothing but kind to him all week, going out of her way to prepare the foods she knew he liked, taking him to places he hadn't been in years, and doing so many other things.

He placed his fork on his plate and leaned back in the chair, staring into the flame of the candle. She didn't deserve this kind of treatment, yet what else could he do? It was not fair to get her hopes up. Their marriage was over. Had been for years, as far as he was concerned. She did not care about him. Not really. Otherwise, she would have realized how he felt long ago. She would have changed and done something about it.

She would have changed? She would have done something about it? That still, small voice said from deep within his heart. *What about you? Did you make any attempt to change into the man she wanted you to be? Did you once even consider her happiness, as well as your own? Don't let these last three hours slip by. This is Christmas Day, Randy. You're not a selfish man. Surely, one day of the year you can put Sylvia first and forget about yourself.*

"I'm sorry, Randy. Please forgive me."

He turned to see Sylvia standing in the archway, and she was smiling. "Nothing to forgive, Syl. I was as much to blame as you, maybe more."

She reached out her hand as she moved toward him. "Can we start the evening over?"

He took her hand, lifted it to his lips, and kissed it. "I'd like that."

Once they were seated, Sylvia picked up the platter of corn bread and passed it to him. "It's kinda cold now. I could heat it for you."

He took it from her hands with a genuine smile. "It's fine, Syl, just like it is."

The rest of the meal was pleasant as each of the Bensons went out of their way to avoid confrontation or any mention of the divorce. "Would you like to wait a bit before having dessert?" she asked him when they had finished. "Later, in the family room with another cup of coffee?"

"Sounds good to me." He rose quickly. "Let me help you with the cleanup."

"I don't want to waste a minute of the few hours we have left," she told him as she picked up the roast platter. "I'm going to put things in the refrigerator and leave the dishes until later." They carried things to the kitchen, placing the dirty dishes in the sink, then headed back to the family room.

❅

"Sit by me, Randy." Sylvia patted the sofa cushion beside her.

He glanced at his watch, then stood gazing at her for a few moments before moving to her side and resting his head on the sofa's high back. "Sure hope the kids made it to Colorado okay."

Scooting a tad closer to him, she leaned her head on his shoulder, taking in his nearness, the smell of him, and the slight sound of his breathing. No matter what the future held, she wanted to capture this moment forever in her memory. She and her beloved, sitting close to one another, watching the lights twinkle merrily on the tree, listening to Christmas music extolling their Savior's birth. Would there be more nights like this, or would this be the last one?

Taking her hand in his, he caressed it with his thumb, causing her heart to do a flip-flop. Even after all these years, just his touch made her tremble.

"Are you cold?" Randy slipped an arm about her shoulders and pulled her to him. "That better?"

She nodded and snuggled up close. She wanted so much to tell him how she loved him, how much she wanted him to stay, but the words would not come.

Maybe you've said too much already, My child. She flinched as the still, small voice spoke from deep within her heart.

But, God, I have so little time left! I have to make Randy see how important it is that we stay together as husband and wife!

Perhaps, if you'd worked as hard at trying to please Randy these past few years as you have this week, he wouldn't have considered leaving you, the voice answered in a kind way. *Yes, raising your children was important; it was a job I called you to do. And all the things you did for other people, to please and serve Me, were important, too, but not at the cost of putting your husband last.*

I—I never meant to put him last, and part of it was his fault. He was always so busy—

And you weren't? the small voice asked.

Yes, I was busy. Too busy. However, I can't take the whole blame. What about that woman? That Chatalaine person?

"Syl, are you sure you're not coming down with a cold or something?" Randy asked.

His voice pulled her from her thoughts. "A cold? No, I—I don't think so, I'm just—just, well, you know. It's nearly midnight."

He checked his watch again. "I know."

Pressing back tears, she forced a smile and jumped to her feet. "Why don't I fix us some hot cocoa? Doesn't that sound good? With marshmallows on top like we used to fix for the kids."

He gave her the sideways grin she always loved. "Only if we can have some of those cookies we baked to go with it."

"You got it!" She gave him her sweetest smile and hurried into the kitchen, hoping to regain her composure. A few minutes later, she was back with the tray, setting it on the coffee table in front of them.

"Here ya go!"

They enjoyed their treat while talking about their children and Christmases past. Though Sylvia chattered on happily, panic was clutching its fingers tightly about her throat, and a jagged piece of her heart was breaking off with each stroke of the second hand on the clock. There was nothing in Randy's speech or demeanor that gave even the slightest indication he planned to stay beyond midnight. *Is he wondering about Chatalaine? Where she is and what she is doing? Oh, God, please, no! Don't let that woman break up our marriage! I love him so! I need him! My family needs him!*

Finally, Randy stood and walked to the hall closet, pulling something from his coat pocket. "I have something for you." He lowered himself back down beside her, holding a small, beautifully wrapped package in his hand. "It's actually my Christmas present to you, but I felt funny giving it to you Christmas Eve with everyone there. I—I decided I'd rather give it to you in private."

Feelings of joy and happiness flooded over Sylvia as he placed the package in her lap. Halting a compelling urge to weep, she carefully pulled off the paper, making sure not to tear it, revealing a square white box. She smiled up at Randy, both pleased and relieved he had actually bought a gift for her. It did not matter what it was. She would have been happy with the empty box, just knowing he had not forgotten her after all.

"Open it." He took the wrappings from her hand and placed them on the table.

Inside was a deep blue velvet box. Her hands shook as she lifted the lid and gasped. "Oh, Randy!"

"It's the diamond heart necklace I always said I'd buy you but couldn't afford. Like the one we saw in the jewelry store window, remember? The store where I bought your gold wedding band." He lowered his head sheepishly. "I—I should have bought it for you years ago."

Sylvia was so deeply touched, she could barely breathe as she stared at the spectacular necklace. They had joked about it for years, but she had never actually expected him to buy it for her. "Oh, Randy, I love it. It's so—so beautiful! Are you sure—"

He took the box from her hands, removed the necklace from its bed of white velvet, and opened the clasp. "Here, turn a bit and let me fasten it on you."

As she turned, she heard the clock on the fireplace chime a single chime. *Eleven thirty!*

"There!" Randy said, leaning forward to admire the necklace. "You look as beautiful in it as I knew you would."

"Does—does—" She lifted watery eyes to his, her voice raw and shaky with emotion as she fingered the necklace. "Does this mean you're staying?"

Randy looked into her eyes for some time before he answered. "No, Syl, that necklace is not only a Christmas present; it's my going-away gift." He glanced quickly at his watch, then said without preamble, "I—I'll be leaving at midnight."

Sylvia grabbed onto his arm, tears of humiliation and hurt blurring her vision. "No, Randy, no!"

His hand covered hers as her world tilted off its axis. "This week has been wonderful—I won't deny it, but there's no going back, Syl. I think we both know that. Our marriage has been on the skids for a long time. One week together, taking a walk down memory lane, could not resurrect it. Let's face it. It's dead and ready to be buried."

"But, Randy, there's more at stake here than you and me! What about our children?"

He blinked hard, then looked away, as if he didn't want her to see how this thing, this giant that was tearing them apart, was affecting him more than he'd admit. "They'll recover."

"They won't, Randy," she said, sounding stronger and more rational than she had dreamed possible. "Don't expect them to understand, because they won't."

"I'll—I'll have to deal with that. Try to make them understand. We're not the first couple to divorce. Over fifty percent—"

"Don't try to excuse this by quoting statistics! Do you think God will accept your statistics as an excuse when you stand before Him?" She grabbed onto his chin, forcing him to look at her. "You're a Christian, Randy! You know this is displeasing to God!"

He shrugged but did not pull away. "Lots of things are displeasing to God, Syl. Not just divorce."

She tried to find a snappy retort, some scripture she could quote to him to prove he was in the wrong, but her mind went blank.

Randy reached up and slowly pulled her hands from his face. "I'm sorry, Syl. Honest, I am. I've struggled with this thing for the past two years; now it's time for action. I have to try my wings. I know it'll take time, but I'm hoping, eventually, we can at least be civil to one another—for our children's sake. After all, we managed to spend this week together."

"Only because I thought there was hope for us." Sylvia shot a quick glance at the clock. One minute to midnight.

"You promised, Syl. One week with you, and if I still felt the same way, you would give me the divorce—uncontested. You are going to keep your word, aren't you?" he asked softly, as if he expected her to go into a rage and back out on her deal, maybe even take a swing at him.

She had no choice. She'd done her best to try to get Randy to change his mind, and despite the many times she thought he was being swayed during their week together, he was as determined as ever to go through with the divorce. To go back on her word now would only make her look foolish and like a liar. Stunned and shaken and assailed with emotion, she stood to her feet. "I won't back out. I did give you my word, but I want you to remember one thing. I never wanted our marriage to end this way. I love you, Randy. I'll always love you."

He took her hand and held onto it tightly for a moment, then backed away.

"Not so fast. I still have fifteen seconds. I have one more request."

His brows rose in question.

"Hold me, Randy. Kiss me good-bye like you used to when we were young and so much in love nothing else mattered."

"But—"

"Time is getting away—"

He stepped forward awkwardly and pulled her into his embrace, his lips seeking hers. To her surprise, his kiss was warm, passionate, and lingering as he pulled her so close it took her breath away and their kiss deepened.

As the clock chimed midnight, he pulled away and walked out of her life.

Sylvia watched him go through that door and close it on twenty-five years of marriage. She wanted to die.

Chapter 12

The next few days were the saddest days Sylvia had ever spent as she closed herself up in the house, keeping the shades drawn to shut out the sunlight.

DeeDee and Aaron were still gone. Buck and Shonna had visiting relatives at their house and were only able to spend a little time with her. They had invited her to come to their home, but she did not feel up to it and certainly not up to putting on a happy face and visiting with strangers.

And, worst of all, the God she loved and trusted had not answered her prayers. He, too, had forsaken her, just like Randy. She had never felt so all alone. In less than two days, she devoured the two-pound box of chocolates Buck and Shonna had given her for Christmas. Good, nourishing food remained in the refrigerator. She had no interest in it whatsoever. Chocolate was the only thing that seemed to satisfy. She did not want to talk to anyone, not even Jen, and especially not God!

Television held no interest, not even the Sky Angel Christian channel with its twenty-four hours of music, preaching, and talk shows.

She leaped to the window at the sound of every car going down the street, sure it was Randy coming back to tell her the whole thing had been a mistake or a bad joke that went too far.

She grabbed up the phone each time it rang, hoping to hear his voice. But it was never Randy. She even screamed into the phone at the next telemarketer who called, threatening to report him if he ever called her again, which was definitely not her true nature.

Each day, she rushed to the mailbox hoping to find a letter from Randy or a card, even a simple note, but none ever came.

She wanted desperately to call him, to beg him to come back to her, to give her another chance to show him how much she loved him and wanted their marriage to succeed. She wanted to tell him she was even willing to forgive his infidelity and would never mention it to him again. But then, just the thought of Randy and that woman together made her want to throw up, and she knew how hard it would be to keep that promise.

But what if Randy had been telling her the truth about Chatalaine? That there really hadn't been anything between them? As far as she knew, he had not made a single attempt to call the woman during the entire week. How would she have felt if Randy had falsely accused her of cheating on him, and she had been innocent? The thought struck horror to her heart. Could Randy have been telling the truth all along? Had he really simply been tired of being married to her as he had said? And wanted out? And there had never even been a relationship with Chatalaine?

No, she could not call him, not even to tell him she forgave him. A call from her, after he had finally made his move and walked out on her, would only anger him, especially if Chatalaine was there at the office with him. She glanced at the phone. It was so tempting to call, but she turned away.

Jen phoned several times, but Sylvia always ended their conversation as quickly as possible without being rude, leaving her friend to wonder how she really was. She had even refused Jen's offer to pray for her. Why should anyone pray for her? God did not care about her. If He had, He would have brought Randy to his senses and healed their marriage. *No, prayer doesn't change anything,* she told herself as she shoved her Bible into the drawer with plans to leave it there. *No more daily Bible reading—no more praying for me. If God were real, He would have shown Himself and kept Randy here where he belonged.*

Late the afternoon of the thirtieth of December, the doorbell rang, and Sylvia rushed to answer it.

"Are you Sylvia Benson?" the man standing at the door asked.

She nodded. "Yes, that's me."

"This is for you." He handed her a plain-looking envelope and, without another word, hurried to his car and drove off.

She carried it into the house, tearing it open on the way. As she pulled the paper aside, she let out a loud gasp and collapsed onto the sofa, one hand resting on her forehead, her heart beating fitfully. *These are the divorce papers Randy had said would be coming!* After taking several restorative breaths to calm herself, she lifted the pack of papers and read the first few lines. "Oh, Randy, how could you? I never thought you would actually go through with it, especially this soon. Not until you'd had a chance to tell the children!" She tossed the papers aside, too weak and too wounded to read another word. "God," she called out shaking her trembling fist. "Why—why have You forsaken me?"

She wandered about the house aimlessly, not knowing what to do or where to turn. Should she call Buck? Tell him about the divorce papers? What good would it do? There was nothing he could do to help her other than hold her hand to console her. He and Shonna had a house full of relatives. It would not be fair to her son and his wife to upset them at a time like this. Especially since Shonna was pregnant. She could just imagine the happiness and festivities going on at Buck's house as he and Shonna shared their good news with her parents and aunts and uncles. No, she could not do anything to take away from their joy.

She skipped supper, barely remembering she should eat, and went to bed early, pulling the covers over her head, touching the pillow where, only a few days ago, Randy had laid his head. Just the thought of his never being there again sent her into wild hysterics of crying until her eyes were so red and swollen, she could barely open them.

The next morning, Jen phoned again, this time trying to talk Sylvia into coming to the New Year's Eve service at the church. "You can't lock yourself away like this, Sylvia. It's not good for you."

"Not good for me, Jen? What *is* good for me?" she spat into the phone. "I don't think any of my church friends want me crying on their shoulders—the poor little woman whose husband left her for another woman because he didn't want to be married to her anymore."

"That's not true, sweetie. Your church family cares about you. You are not the first person whose marriage ended in this way. You didn't want your marriage to break up. You were the innocent partner."

Sylvia grasped onto the phone tightly, her knuckles turning white. "You're wrong about that, Jen. There was nothing innocent about me. Stupid, maybe, but not innocent. I see that now. Even if that woman hadn't come along, our marriage wouldn't have lasted. I—I put Randy last in my life. Behind our children, the church, my activities. I was never there when he needed me. It took our week together for me to realize that. If only I could go back and do things over."

"Well," Jen drawled out, as if not knowing what else to say, "I'm praying that you'll come tonight. I'm sure you need God and the church more than you're admitting. We all need Him, Sylvia. If you don't want to have to talk to anyone, sneak in after the service starts and sit in back. You can even leave a few minutes before midnight, if you want. Just come, though. Start the New Year out right."

"Don't waste your time watching for me, because I probably won't be there."

As Sylvia hung up the phone and gazed about the room, Jen's words drilled into her heart. *I'm sure you need God and the church more than you're admitting.* She shrugged as she pulled her robe tighter about her and settled down in Randy's chair to finish her cup of cold coffee, idly picking up the remote and hitting the On button.

"You may think no one loves you, no one cares what happens to you, but God cares," a gray-haired man with a kind face was saying as the Sky Angel channel lit up the screen. "Oh, He isn't some magical genie who snaps into being when you summon Him, eager to grant your every wish. However, He has a plan for you. A plan to prosper you and not harm you."

Her ears perked up, and she began to listen in earnest. *That's the very verse Randy quoted!*

"God has engraved you on the palms of His hands. His plan for you is perfect. Oh, at times it may seem like He's not listening when you call out to Him. Even as a born-again Christian, you may feel praying is a useless thing. Sometimes, you may have doubts about His existence and even wonder if there is a God. Satan puts those doubts in your mind. You must not let him have the victory."

Sylvia leaned forward with rapt attention.

"We who are Christians and claim His name must always remember," the preacher continued, "God has His own timing for everything. Only in His appointed time will He bring things to pass. All we can do is wait upon Him, pray, and seek His will. If you are listening to my voice right now and you feel God has forsaken you, it's time to give up your pity party and start living again. Seek God's face. Confess your sins. Turn to Him. Trust Him. His plan is always best for you."

Sylvia stared at the screen. It was as though the man was speaking directly to her. *I have been having a pity party! It's time I faced up to the fact that I have done everything I could to save our marriage and I failed. It's time I turned it all over to God. My life. Randy's life. If God cannot put things back together, no one can!*

She glanced about the darkened room. Dozens of the little fluted white papers that separated the chocolates she had consumed lay scattered about the floor. Empty coffee cups adorned the coffee table. Tissues she had used to wipe at her eyes and blot her nose were strewn everywhere. Two days! She had two days to get things back in order before DeeDee and Aaron came back from their skiing trip. She could not let them come home to the house in such disarray. It was going to be bad enough to learn their father had left their mother and had served her with divorce papers.

Putting her sorrow and heartache aside, she flung open the drapes, lifted the blinds, gathered up the trash, cups, and dishes, putting them in their proper places. The kitchen was still a mess from the dirty dishes, pots, and pans she had left on the cabinet and in the sink the night Randy had left. Rolling up the sleeves on her robe, she dove into the mess with zest and soon had the kitchen looking the way she usually kept it—spotless. She ran the sweeper in the family room, leaving the tree standing in the corner, waiting for either Buck or Aaron to help her get it out of its stand and to the curb where the trash man would pick it up. She dusted and waxed until the whole downstairs shone.

Next, she hurried upstairs, changed the sheets on the bed in their bedroom, even scooting the bed to a different wall to give the room a renewed look.

By eight o'clock, after eating a bowl of soup, she was in the shower with plans to attend the New Year's Eve service. The cool water falling onto her face from the showerhead was invigorating, and she knew, though life was going to be hard in the coming days, she would make it. She still had her health, a beautiful home, a terrific bunch of kids, her church friends, and, most importantly, God. Granted, she and God's relationship was a bit strained, but in time, she knew He would soften her heart and the two of them would be on good terms again. She knew now—she had left God—He had not left her.

She slipped into the service shortly after ten o'clock, just after the song service had begun, and took a seat way in the back in an empty area under the balcony. Thankfully, the lights in the sanctuary were turned low since candles burned in the candelabra on either side of the pulpit. Her gaze went to the third row from the front on the left side of the sanctuary, the row where she and Randy sat when he wasn't too busy at the paper to attend church. She would have to find another pew to sit in on Sunday mornings. That one held too many memories. Maybe she would just sit with Jen from now on. She always sat alone or with one of the widow women since her husband was always up on the platform preaching.

The song service was wonderful, as was the special music. It was as though all the worship team's songs had been chosen with her and her needs in mind. When the pastor asked for those who wanted to give a testimony of what God had done for them this past year, at least a dozen people responded. As Sylvia listened to their words, her own problems seemed to fade. With some, the Lord had brought them through a life-threatening disease. With others, an injury—one that had robbed them of a way to support their families, but God had been faithful and supplied their needs. With one family, it was the loss of a child through an accident. One couple's marriage had been ripped apart by infidelity. However, through confession of sin, apologies, forgiveness, and God's grace, the family had been reunited and was happier than ever. Each story was different, yet each ended with victory through the Lord Jesus Christ.

Sylvia didn't even try to keep the tears from flowing as she listened. Their stories were like a soothing salve on her troubled mind. If they could make it, surely she could.

The pastor's New Year's message was exactly what she needed to hear as he spoke about putting old things aside and beginning things anew. He talked about restoration with God and renewing your joy in Jesus. He even encouraged making New Year's resolutions, not in the way the world makes them, but as goals we should set to make us the people God would have us to be. Goals like daily Bible reading and prayer and serving Him.

A few minutes before midnight, the pastor invited anyone who wanted to pray the New Year in to come forward and kneel at the altar. Sylvia watched as a number of parishioners stood and moved forward. This was the time she had planned to duck out and leave. However, as she stood, to her surprise and dismay, her feet led her forward, and she found herself walking toward the altar. She no longer cared if anyone saw her tears or realized she would soon join the ranks of the divorced people who attended the church. All she had on her mind was getting to that altar, kneeling, asking God's forgiveness for ever doubting Him, and turning her life over to Him.

When she reached the front, she immediately dropped to her knees, folding her hands and resting them on the curtained railing. With a broken and contrite heart, she began to pray silently, talking to God, spilling out her heart to Him in Jesus' name.

As she prayed, she felt a hand on her shoulder. Without even needing to glance back, she knew it was Jen. She continued to pray, thankful for such a good friend. Remembering the pastor's challenge, she let her tears of surrender flow down her cheeks, her heart filled with gratitude to God for the many blessings He'd given her throughout her life and for the blessings He'd promised in His Word to continue to pour upon her. *I am not much, Father, and I have made so many mistakes, but take me, use me, mold me into whatever You want me to be.*

"I love you," a male voice whispered softly in her ear.

Startled, since she had assumed it was Jen who had kneeled beside her, she turned quickly toward the voice. "Ra—Randy? What are you doing here?"

His cheeks stained with tears, he warily slipped an arm about her, whispering, "Although you and I have grown apart over the past few years, Sylvia, I want you to know there has never been anyone in my life but you. I have so missed the closeness we used to have. You were always so wrapped up in our children's lives—I guess I was jealous of the time you spent with them."

She rubbed at her eyes with her sleeve. "Jealous of our children?"

He nodded, wiping at his own eyes. "I—I was so busy at the newspaper, we never had time for each other. I have acted like the typical midlife-crisis male and let my ego cloud my judgment. I responded like the old fool that I am, wanting to move out and find myself. I knew better, Sylvia. I knew I was going against God's will. Looking back, I cannot imagine how I ever let myself try to put the blame for our failed marriage on you. But thanks to you and our one last Christmas together, I now see what a fool I have been. I didn't fully realize what a mistake I was making until I got back to my apartment after leaving you that last night we had together. I have been miserable ever since. Spending the week with you and realizing what I was about to give up made me see things in a new light, but I was too proud to admit it."

"But—but the divorce papers! They were delivered to me just yesterday."

He scrunched up his face and drew in a deep breath. "I didn't know my attorney was going to have them delivered that soon. I was sick about it when he told me. What that must have done to you! I'm so sorry, Syl."

"But—but what about Chatalaine? What are you going to do about her?"

"I—I know you don't believe me about Chatalaine, but sweetheart, honest, there never has been anything going on between us. You can talk to her if you want and ask her yourself. We're both invited to her wedding next week."

Sylvia's jaw dropped. "Chatalaine is getting married?"

"Yes. She's been engaged for nearly a year and madly in love with the man she's going to marry, almost as madly in love as I was with you when we were young—and as I am now." He dipped his head shyly. "You're the only woman I've ever loved, Syl. I've asked God's forgiveness for my stupidity."

"But the apricot roses? I thought they were for her. When the florist called—"

"He called you?"

She nodded. "Yes, and he said you'd made a big deal about making sure they were apricot roses when you'd ordered them."

Randy let out a slight chuckle. "And you thought they were for Chatalaine?"

"Who—who else would they be for?"

"Syl, do you remember when we attended old Nick Bodine's funeral last summer?"

"Yes, but what has—"

"I spoke to his wife after the service, and she mentioned Nick had sent her apricot roses on her birthday every year since they'd been married and how much she was going to miss receiving them on her next birthday. I asked her when that was, then wrote it down in my appointment book."

"You sent the apricot roses to Mrs. Bodine?"

"Yes, I always liked Nick. He was a good worker and always had a kind word for everyone. I sent them to her on her birthday, with a note telling her to pretend Nick had sent them to her and to have a happy birthday."

Fingering the heart-shaped necklace, she leaned into him, overcome with his thoughtfulness. "Oh, Randy, that was so sweet of you. No wonder you insisted they be apricot roses. I'm sure she loved them."

He slipped his finger beneath her chin and lifted her face to his. "Syl, do—do you think you can ever forgive me for walking out on you like that?" He hugged her tightly to him.

She smiled through tears of happiness and caressed his face with her fingertips as she rested her forehead against his. "Oh yes, my beloved husband. I can forgive you, even as God has forgiven both of us. Despite everything that has happened between us, I have never stopped loving you. I, too, had my priorities all mixed up. While I loved our children and wanted them to have the best lives possible, they were a *product* of our love and not a *substitute* for it. God never meant for them and all the other things in our lives to become a wedge between us. I'm the one who let that happen, and I'm sorry. So sorry I ever doubted you."

After falling on each other in a loving embrace, they suddenly realized, except for Harrison and Jen, who were sitting on the front pew smiling with happiness, the church was empty. Everyone else had gone. They had been so caught up with each other and their love for one another, they hadn't even noticed.

"You have no idea how excited and happy we are to see the two of you together again," Jen said, her eyes clouded with tears as she hugged both Randy and Sylvia. "We've been praying for you, asking God to bring the two of you back together where you belong."

Randy kept one arm about Sylvia but extended his free hand toward his pastor. "I—I'd like to keep serving on the church board, if you think it'd be okay. That is, if my wife agrees. I'm going to make many changes in my life, but leaving my wife isn't going to be one of them."

He turned to Sylvia, squeezing her hand between the two of his, his eyes filled with tears, his voice cracking with emotion as he spoke. "Would you—could you even consider taking me back? Let me move back home—after what I've done to you?"

Sylvia, too, succumbed to the tears that pleaded to be released. Though he spoke the words she had longed to hear, prayed to hear, she found it difficult to speak. Each heartbeat told her she could trust him. He would never leave her again. "Oh, Randy, of—of course, I'll take you back," she said between sobs of joy. "Spending my life with you is all I've ever wanted." She grabbed onto his shirt collar with both hands and drew him to her, placing a tender, loving kiss on his lips. "Come home with me, darling, where you belong. Where I want you. Where God wants you."

"That's exactly where I want to be."

Sylvia leaned into her husband as Randy kissed her again.

"Hey, you two, break it up," Jen said, rubbing at her eyes and reaching to touch Sylvia's arm. "You're making Harrison and me cry, too."

"Yeah," Harrison added, circling his arm about his wife's waist. "We tough guys aren't supposed to cry."

Randy planted one more quick kiss on Sylvia's lips, then wiped his sleeve across his face. "From now on, I'm setting limits on the time I spend at the newspaper. It's time I get my ducks in a row."

Sylvia let out a giggle at the word *ducks*, as Randy sent her a smile at the little joke only the two of them understood—about his pajamas.

"Of course, we still want you on the board, Randy. You have always been an important part of this church. You're a great asset to us—and to God."

Randy nodded toward their friends. "Well, I'd better get my wife home before she changes her mind. Thanks for caring about us, you two, and for praying for us."

Harrison reached out and gave Randy's hand a hearty shake. "Our pleasure. It's always nice to see God answer prayer and bring a couple back together. Guess I'll see you two sitting in the third row next Sunday morning?"

Randy nodded. "You bet. Right where we belong."

As Randy turned his key in the lock when they reached home, he leaned over and kissed his wife. "Until I spent that week with you, babe, I never realized all the things you did to make our house a home."

"I loved every minute of it." The scripture God had given her the night she had prayed and asked God Himself to give her a plan flooded her memory and gave her cause to thank Him. *"Favour is deceitful, and beauty is vain: but a woman that feareth the LORD, she shall be praised. Give her of the fruit of her hands; and let her own works praise her in the gates."*

Once inside, they walked hand in hand up the stairway and into their bedroom. Randy paused in the doorway, his eyes scanning the area. "You've moved the furniture! I like it this way."

"Moving the furniture is only one of the many changes I plan to make, Randy. Remember what Aaron said Christmas Eve when he was passing out the gifts?"

Randy frowned, as if he was not sure what she meant.

"When he saw the various presents I had given you and acted as though he was upset because he didn't get as many, he said, 'It's okay, Mom. After all, that old man is your husband. He'll be around long after us kids move out for good.' He was right, Randy. It's time you and I began to think of the two of us as a couple and not only as a family. We need to concentrate on us and our needs, as well as those of our children. I want us to do things together, sweetheart. To grow old together."

He gave her a toothy grin. "Will you still love me when we're in a care home and I'm wearing my yellow ducky pajamas?"

"Even then!" She wrapped her arms about his neck and planted a kiss on his lips. "Will you love me when I'm wrinkled and my breasts droop to my waist?"

He laughed, then returned her kiss. "I'll probably be so senile by that time, I won't even notice!"

She tangled her fingers in his hair, much like she'd done when they'd first begun to date. "I hope God grants us many more years together, Randy. We've lost so much time. I want us to make up for it."

"We will, dearest. We've been given a second chance. I want to make the most of it, too."

She leaned into him, enjoying their intimacy. This was where she belonged. In the arms of the man she loved. How close she'd come to losing him—losing everything she held near and dear.

"Syl," he said, his voice taking on a low, throaty, tender quality as he lovingly gazed into her eyes. "Thanks to you and your love and patience with me, this didn't turn out to be our one last Christmas together. I love you, babe."

"I love you, too, Randy."

JOYCE LIVINGSTON

Joyce has done many things in her life (in addition to being a wife, mother of six, and grandmother to oodles of grandkids, all of whom she loves dearly), from being a television broadcaster for eighteen years, to lecturing and teaching on quilting and sewing, to writing magazine articles on a variety of subjects. She's danced with Lawrence Welk, ice-skated with a chimpanzee, had bottles broken over her head by stuntmen, interviewed hundreds of celebrities and controversial figures, and done many other interesting and unusual things. But now, when she isn't off traveling to wonderful and exotic places as a part-time tour escort, her days are spent sitting in front of her computer, creating stories. She feels her writing is a ministry and a calling from God, and she hopes Heartsong readers will be touched and uplifted by what she writes. Joyce loves to hear from her readers and invites you to visit her on the Internet at: www.joycelivingston.com

Almost Twins

Dedicated to Dave and Marthe.
Thank you for answering all my questions and not running
when you saw me coming with my map in my hand, once again.

Chapter 1

Another man might curse at the building snowstorm. Dennis knew little Raymond couldn't understand the nasty words. But God would.

Dennis turned off the radio in order to concentrate on his driving. He didn't need a weatherman to tell him how hard it was snowing. He enjoyed the white Christmas, since it snowed so seldom back home, but this was whiter than need be. Any other time, with Raymond asleep in his car seat, Dennis would have taken this opportunity to think. Today he had all he could handle just keeping the car on the road.

Another harsh gust of wind buffeted the car. Sections of the mountain highway had iced over with snow covering most of the pavement. Visibility lowered with each passing mile, and the snowdrifts grew larger.

The car slid on an icy patch beneath the blowing snow. Dennis gripped the wheel tighter and slowed his speed. He had no idea where the nearest motel might be, but he planned to stop at the next one he saw. Until then, he had no choice but to keep going. He knew he shouldn't drive under these conditions, especially since he wasn't used to mountain driving at the best of times, but he hadn't paid any attention to the worsening weather until it was too late. Now his only thoughts centered on getting home, although his life would never be the same again.

Up ahead and on a secondary road to his right, an old pickup approached the highway at a speed Dennis thought much too fast for the blustery conditions. Rather than slowing at the intersection, the pickup began to swerve, then slide.

Instinctively, Dennis stomped on the brake. Instead of stopping, the car fishtailed on the slippery road, turned clockwise, skidded sideways for a short distance, then continued to spin until he was careening backward toward the edge of the mountain road.

"Lord God, help me," he prayed through clenched teeth as he fought with the steering wheel, to no avail. He frantically pumped the brake, but nothing slowed the car's trajectory as it spun toward the edge of the cliff.

His heart pounded as the back end of the car reached the edge of the mountainside and crashed through the wooden guardrail, slowing him only slightly. As if in slow motion, the back end went down, sending the nose of the car into the air, akin to the sinking of the Titanic. He squeezed his eyes shut and prayed for either a miracle or that death would come quickly.

"I'm sorry, Raymond," he said aloud as the nose of the car tipped higher and the car began to slide down. Dennis held his breath, preparing himself for the worst. Suddenly, the rear of the vehicle slammed into something solid, bringing the car to a crunching halt. In that same instant, the engine died. A sickening silence hung in the air for a brief second before Raymond let out a terrified howl.

Dennis felt as if a fist had slammed into his gut. His heart thudded in his chest. The car shifted slightly, then settled midway with the undercarriage resting on the edge of the cliff, the front tires spinning above the ground. A mass of snow fell onto the car from above, landing with a muffled thump on the hood. The car shuddered once. Then all was silent—except for Raymond's crying.

In a rush of air, Dennis released his breath. With trembling fingers, he unbuckled the straps of the infant seat and held Raymond tightly with unsteady arms. Pressing Raymond's tiny head against his chest, Dennis closed his eyes in a prayer of thanksgiving for their spared lives and absence of injury.

He opened his eyes when Raymond's cries subsided to ragged hiccuping. The pickup truck was nowhere to be seen, the driver evidently oblivious to the destruction he had caused.

Very gently, he stroked the baby's back. "There, there," he mumbled. "The only thing that's hurt is the car." With more patting, the whimpering eventually stopped. Slowly, he lowered Raymond back into the car seat, buckled him up again, stuck a pacifier in his mouth, and cautiously climbed out of the car to survey the damage.

The entire back end was completely squashed and molded around a huge tree all the way up to the now-bent rear axle. Fortunately he didn't smell gas. The odd angle of the car left the front tires hanging off the ground by about a foot and a half, accenting his predicament.

His stomach churned when he looked down the mountainside, to where he had almost gone. The car rested on the only tree in the area large enough to hold the vehicle's weight. Besides that one large tree, nothing would have stopped their plunge to certain death. Dennis closed his eyes, again praising God that both he and Raymond survived unscathed.

Snow continued to fall around him, drifting in the wind and building a layer of white against the car as if something so beautiful could hide the accident's carnage.

Dennis looked back to the road, only five feet away. The tire tracks leading to the side of the mountain were already covered. As the shock subsided, reality sank in. He was stranded. With a one-month-old baby. In a snowstorm. In the middle of nowhere.

Dennis shivered as snow melted around his ankles and the cold seeped into his sneakers. He hugged himself and slapped his upper arms, then pulled the collar of his leather jacket higher. At home in Vancouver, the weather seldom dipped below freezing, so he was unprepared for the cold. When he got the call to rush to Hinton, buying a winter coat hadn't entered his mind. He had just gone.

He studied the car as he blew warm breath into his hands and rubbed them together. Even if the car was driveable, there was no way he could get it back onto the road. Nevertheless, standing outside until the snow covered him, too, wasn't going to get them out of this predicament either.

He scrambled back into the car, shutting the door quickly. If he couldn't drive it, he hoped to at least run the engine to provide some heat. The motor chugged and sputtered when he turned the key, but it wouldn't catch. After a few minutes, he gave up, rested his elbows on top of the steering wheel, and buried his face in his hands. He had a few blankets in the trunk, but he couldn't open it without a crowbar. And the crowbar was also in the trunk, along with his emergency roadside kit.

He spread the map over the steering wheel and calculated a distance of approximately twenty-five miles to the nearest town. He tried to recall if he had passed a house or any building recently, but couldn't remember. His total concentration had been on the road as he struggled to drive through the worsening storm. He hadn't bothered to pay attention to the scenery.

He stared absently out the car window. If the road was impassable, someone would have to get him by air. He wasn't sure it was possible, but there was one way to find out. He reached into his pocket for his cell phone and dialed but couldn't get a signal.

A long sigh escaped at the thought of going back into the freezing snow, but he had no choice. If he held the phone just right, he may be able to pick up a signal. Dennis clambered outside and, holding the phone in the air for a better chance at a signal, hit the SEND button again. The phone looked like it was connecting, but when he lowered it to his ear, it lost the signal.

Dennis shivered as he looked around. Maybe if he got more height. . . He surveyed the roof of the car and the tree he had hit.

He chose the tree. Clutching the leather phone case in his teeth, he struggled to find any place to hold on, then get a toehold to raise himself higher on the frozen trunk. He struggled to climb the tree as high as he could go and still have it support his weight without tipping, or him falling off.

The wind was worse with the added height. Dennis shivered from head to toe as he leaned his body into the tree to maintain his balance, hugging it with only one arm while he dialed with numb fingers. His teeth chattered as he held the phone above his head, praying for that elusive signal to human contact and rescue.

Without warning, a strong gust of wind whipped from the north. Already in a precarious position, his slight movement to counteract the force of the wind compromised his balance. His toes slid off the slick branch, and with the tree swaying, he couldn't hold himself up using only one hand to support his weight. Dennis felt himself starting to fall. He flailed his arms but couldn't regain his balance. Again, Dennis felt like everything was moving in slow motion. As he fell backward, he watched the phone arc gracefully in the air and hit a tree. As Dennis hit the ground, the phone tumbled down the mountainside and into the snow somewhere far below.

Dennis lay on his back in the soft, cold snow, unable to believe what had just happened.

The snow continued to fall on top of him, into his face and open mouth. What little heat was left in his body caused the snow on his neck to melt, as well as some that had gone up the back of his jacket.

Rather than freeze to death on the ground, Dennis scrambled back into the car, where he watched the blustering wind and drifting snow outside.

If he hadn't considered himself fully stranded before, he surely was now. Alone, he might have walked—however foolish. But he couldn't take Raymond into a blizzard, despite the infant's warm layers of blankets and clothes. At least the car would protect them from hypothermia until someone found them. *If* someone found them.

With the blizzard in progress and it being a mere three days before Christmas, except for the idiot in the pickup truck, most people were home preparing for the holiday or already with their loved ones.

If they didn't freeze first, Dennis wondered how long it would be before they starved to death. As an adult, he could go for weeks before he died, but babies couldn't. For now, cold formula was better than no formula, but he couldn't remember how much he had in the diaper bag. A case was in the trunk, along with everything else, save one suitcase that hadn't fit, which he now considered a blessing in disguise. The suitcase contained clothing he could use for extra warmth. He didn't want to think about how cold it would get overnight. Already the windows were fogging.

Dennis grasped the steering wheel with both hands and let his head drop as he slumped forward, wondering if by Christmas Day they'd both be dead. He thanked God for the miracle of not going over the cliff. Now he prayed for another miracle—to stay alive until someone found them.

Hours passed with no vehicle in sight. Inside the car, the temperature was cold enough for Dennis to see his breath. To his left, the blowing snow had drifted up as high as the lower portion of the window. To his right, ice had formed on the portion of the window not covered by snow. Dennis wrapped Raymond as best he could, using the clothing out of his suitcase. Nevertheless, within hours it would be dark and the temperature would plummet. The phrase from the old "Batman" shows drifted through his mind that the worst was yet to come.

He wondered how long it would be before the snow covered the car, which would insulate them somewhat from the storm. However, if on the remote chance a car came by, they wouldn't be seen. He didn't want to lose what little heat his body had produced inside the confines of the car, but he couldn't let the car become covered.

Dennis shivered just thinking about going outside. His feet were numb from being wet inside his sneakers, and he didn't want to think about standing in the snow again. After he cleared some snow, he wondered if he might be warmer by removing his sneakers and socks, and wrapping his freezing feet in dry clothing from the suitcase.

As he pushed the door open and leaned out, the movement caused a lump of snow to shift on the roof of the car and land on his head. Instead of brushing it off, Dennis froze, straining to listen. Unless his imagination was playing tricks on him, in the distance, he heard the drone of another car.

Not caring about the snow on his head, he jogged through the knee-deep snow, clambered up onto the road into the middle of the snow-covered highway, and waved his arms, leaving the driver no choice but to stop or run him over.

The car slowed, then came to a halt. He wrapped his arms around himself in a futile attempt to warm up, and waited.

A woman exited the car. Her knee-length wool coat and heavy black boots made him wonder if the seventh commandment included not coveting thy neighbor's winter outerwear.

The scarf wrapped around the large collar of her dark-blue coat was pulled up so to cover most of the lower half of her face. Between the fluffy scarf, the hat, the large collar, and the distance between them, all Dennis could see of her face was her eyes.

At that moment, they were the eyes of an angel. He paused to thank God for sending this stranger, and then prayed that she would help him.

❄

Adelle came within ten feet of the man in the middle of the road. She was about to ask how he got there, when out of the corner of her eye, she spotted a car with its front end sticking up in the air and the back end wrapped around a tree.

She turned to the man. "Are you okay? Are there any injuries?"

The man shivered. "I'm cold, but otherwise unharmed. Thanks for asking. Most of all, thanks for stopping."

She could only guess how cold he was. His short leather jacket provided little protection from the wind and snow and he had no hat or gloves. She couldn't see his feet because the snow was almost to his knees, but judging from the way he was underdressed for such conditions, she doubted he wore boots, either.

The wind blew his dark brown hair up in the air, flinging it helter-skelter onto his forehead and into his eyes. His nose was red and his teeth were chattering.

"Where were you going?"

He hunched his shoulders and blew into his reddened hands, then rubbed them together. "I was headed for Vancouver. But now I think my only choice is the nearest motel, which, I imagine, is in the next town."

Adelle shook her head. "I've just come from there, and they've closed the highway. I was the last one they let by, and that was only because I had chains. I'm on my way to my family's cabin; in fact, it's not far up that road." She pointed to the nearby road. "I'm sure they wouldn't mind a guest until the storm clears."

"If they wouldn't mind, I'd really appreciate that. Thank you."

Adelle smiled. "No problem. After all, it's Christmas."

This year, her parents were spending Christmas with her brother and his family in California, so it would just be her, Aunt Min and Uncle Bob, Rachel, and now, this sad, stranded stranger.

Many local businesses were already shutting down for the holiday, since it was only three days before Christmas. She doubted he would find anyone willing to tow his car anytime soon, especially in blizzard conditions.

"Is there anything you need out of your car?"

Without a word, he turned and ran to his car, slipping and sliding all the way. First he slung something over his shoulder, then pulled out an infant car seat with a baby in it.

Adelle gasped. Now she understood why God had allowed her to be delayed on her trip to the cabin.

She had left early that morning, but on her way out the door, the heel of her boot had snapped off. Since she planned to stay with her aunt and uncle for two weeks at the mountain cabin, she couldn't be without her boots for that long in the snowy wilderness. So she had made a stop at the mall to get it fixed. She underestimated the amount of people who would be shopping so close to Christmas and her task had taken much longer than expected, especially since she'd run into someone she knew who wanted to see her baby. Once she finally managed to leave the mall, she had been surprised to see the snow falling, and even more surprised as it worsened into blizzard conditions as she continued.

By the time the roads were so bad that she should have turned back, she was closer to the cabin than home, so she decided to forge ahead. Besides, if she returned home, she and Rachel would be spending her baby's first Christmas alone, and that was too depressing. She had convinced the police officer at the roadblock, who fortunately knew Aunt Min and Uncle Bob, to help her put the chains on and let her pass.

She slogged through the snow to where the land began to drop and accepted the baby-laden car seat. As she did, the stranger stuffed a suitcase full of various articles of clothing that were strewn about the front seat of his car. Soon the man followed behind her with a diaper bag and the bulging suitcase.

His hands were shaking so violently from the cold that Adelle buckled the infant car seat into place for him, after unwrapping several men's shirts from around the baby. She stood back while he tossed everything else on the floor of the backseat.

"Is that everything?" she asked.

He slapped his arms, blew into his hands, then wrapped his arms around himself. "Unfortunately, yes."

She returned to the driver's seat. He pushed aside the items that had been tossed in her backseat and climbed in next to his baby. Soon they were on their way.

Even above the sound of the motor, Adelle heard his teeth chattering. Although she was already too hot in her wool coat, she flipped the heater on full blast for him. Fortunately, the heat didn't bother little Rachel, who had already drifted back to sleep.

Adelle smiled. Not having to worry about her baby fussing would make driving in blizzard conditions less of a strain.

"I don't know how to thank you. You've probably saved our lives. My name is Dennis Bancroft, and this is Raymond."

"My name is Adelle Wilson, and this is Rachel. We're on our way to my aunt Min's and uncle Bob's cabin, but I guess I already told you that."

She looked in her rearview mirror to see him nod his head. His teeth had stopped chattering, but he was still shivering violently, so she didn't change the setting on the heater. She estimated that they would be at the cabin in less than an hour, where a roaring fire and Aunt Min's special holiday hot cocoa would be waiting for them.

❋

Dennis shivered silently in his seat, clenching his jaw so that his saving angel couldn't tell his teeth were still chattering. When the lump of snow had fallen on top of him, some had fallen down the back of his neck. From his earlier fiasco losing his cell phone, more snow had gone up the back of his jacket and down the back of his pants and melted. His back was wet, his underwear was wet, his eyes were still watering from being blasted by the frigid wind, and he couldn't feel his toes. Again he praised God for sending this woman his way. He knew that, for months, he would be having nightmares about what nearly happened.

They were traveling up the road from which the idiot who was driving the pickup truck that nearly had him killed had appeared. He hoped the driver wasn't her "Uncle Bob."

"We'll be there in less than an hour."

As they started up another incline, he stiffened. The curvy mountain side road they turned onto would have been treacherous at the best of times. In the snow, it was terrifying. Usually he didn't feel chauvinistic, but he wondered why Adelle was driving this treacherous road with a baby, and why her husband wasn't driving instead.

Rather than engage in meaningless conversation, Dennis kept silent so she could concentrate fully on her driving. He didn't know how or why, but Raymond had drifted back to sleep not long after they started moving. Dennis was almost jealous of the infant, wishing he could simply close his eyes and not worry about what was happening outside the car. He had no idea where they were, but his ears popped a few times from the changes in altitude as they continued their ascent up the mountain road.

"We're almost there."

She then turned onto a long, steep driveway that was not much more than a path sliced through the trees. His heart nearly stopped a couple of times as they slid, but the car recovered and continued along what Dennis hoped was the middle of the path. When they slipped one more time, he had to remind himself that she had chains on the tires. The thought buoyed his nerves enough that he released his iron grip on the door handle.

The car slid to a stop in front of a small, rough-hewn, wooden cabin, surrounded by snow-covered pine trees. The lights were out, no smoke came from the chimney, there were no other cars, and the pristine snow surrounding the building suggested no recent activity.

"We're here." Adelle said on an exhaled breath, indicating her relief at their safe arrival. "This is odd. They should have been here by now."

She quickly glanced at him, then lowered her head to unbuckle her baby's car seat while Dennis unbuckled Raymond.

With the movement, both babies began to cry. Simultaneously, they lifted both car seats out of the car; then Dennis followed her through the snow and into the small dwelling.

The interior consisted of a large room furnished with long-ago out-of-style furniture and an old black cast-iron woodstove in the center. A white fridge, circa 1950s, sat in a corner that served as a rustic kitchen area. On the other side of the room were two doors, leading to a bedroom and a bathroom. The odd combinations of age, wear, and practicality gave the place a uniquely homey feel. In addition to the relief at finally being safe, he instantly felt better when he saw a lime-green rotary dial telephone on the wall.

They lowered the babies in their car seats to the floor, unbuckled the infants, and both stood in unison, each cradling a crying baby.

Dennis nearly choked when she handed Rachel to him, leaving him with two fussing babies in his arms.

"It's so cold in here. I have to start a fire quickly," she said as she stripped off her gloves and stomped the snow off her boots. "This will only take a minute."

The door of the old woodstove creaked when she unlatched and opened it. She crumpled some newspaper, tossed in some kindling, a few logs, and lit it. Dennis felt warmer just watching the paper catch fire.

She removed her baby from his arm.

"How can I heat up a bottle?" he asked, over the squalling.

She shuffled her baby from her arm to her hip as she walked into the kitchen. She removed a pot out of the bottom cupboard, then set it under the tap.

"The facilities here are rather limited. We're on well water and septic tank, and since my aunt and uncle aren't here, the hot water tank isn't turned on yet. I'll pump some water for you, and you'll have to wait for it to heat up." She placed the pot of water on the stove, pulled a barbecue lighter out of the drawer, turned the knob for the propane burner, and lit it.

Dennis swayed back and forth, holding the now-screeching Raymond as comfortably as he could. "I don't know how to heat a bottle without a microwave. Can't we do both bottles together?"

Her cheeks reddened. Instead of making eye contact, she focused on her baby's head. "Rachel doesn't take a bottle."

"No bottle? But how. . ." Dennis felt his face heat with the realization of what she meant. "Oh," he mumbled.

Without further comment, she hurried into the bedroom and shut the door. Rachel stopped crying almost instantly, but Raymond continued to screech in his ear.

With one hand, Dennis fumbled with the zipper on the diaper bag to remove a bottle of formula. While Raymond screamed, he tried to figure out how to open a bottle with one hand. The words of the public health nurse echoed in his head, instructing him that there was nothing wrong with putting a baby on the floor, as well as her lame joke about a baby never falling off the floor. How he wished that dear woman was with him now.

Carefully, Dennis lowered the open bottle into the center of the pot of water while Raymond continued to holler in his ear; then he waited.

And waited. And waited.

He learned the hard way the true meaning of the cliché, a watched pot never boils.

Countless times, he dipped one finger into the open bottle to test it. When the formula was at a barely acceptable temperature, he screwed the nipple on and stuck it in Raymond's gaping mouth.

Instant quiet filled the room, except for the ringing in his ears. He walked slowly to the couch and sat down on the side closest to the woodstove while Raymond greedily sucked on the bottle.

The fire slowly heated the surrounding area, but with his clothing wet, even wearing his leather jacket, Dennis was still chilled to the bone. Another shudder wracked his body, and he clenched his teeth and stiffened in an attempt to control the chill. Unfortunately, he couldn't move until Raymond finished his bottle.

On Christmas Day, Raymond would be exactly one month old. Dennis wondered how old babies had to be to hold their own bottles.

A loud burp drifted from the bedroom. The door opened, and Adelle walked out with Rachel propped against her. She sat beside him with a happy Rachel cradled in her arms. "When you're finished you can use the phone over there and call your wife to let her know you're okay, so she won't be worried about you and your baby."

He smiled down at Raymond, who was still greedily sucking down his formula. "There's no rush. I'm not married, and Raymond isn't mine."

Chapter 2

Adelle stiffened, and she scooted back on the couch. She didn't know a lot about babies herself, being a relatively new mother, but from the awkward way Dennis held Raymond, it appeared he knew less than she did, which supported his remark about not being the baby's father. She tried to think of a reason why a single man would be alone on a country road with a baby who wasn't his and in no rush to contact the parents. She couldn't think of anything except for a kidnapping.

She tried to stifle her fear and convince herself that she was being unreasonable. She didn't know anything about him except that he was stranded and, unless she picked him up, both he and the baby would have frozen to death in the blizzard.

She wanted to do the Christian thing and give him the benefit of the doubt. He did see to the baby's needs before his own, and he seemed much too nice to be a kidnapper, but then again, she had never met a kidnapper before. She didn't know anything about him, including if he was telling the truth about his name. She had thought that Shawn was nice, too, and she had never been more wrong about anything in her life.

The wind howled outside, reminding her that she needed to go gather some firewood, but now she didn't want to leave Rachel unattended with him.

Adelle shook her head and stood. Dennis wasn't going anywhere. Nor was she. The force of the wind had increased, and the snow was coming down harder than ever. The drive to the cabin had been more difficult than she had anticipated and now it would be impossible to get out until the storm abated. Realistically, it would be days, maybe even a week, before they would be able to dig out.

The wood in the fire popped, again drawing Adelle's attention to the fact that there was only one log inside the cabin. With conditions continuing to worsen she would need to gather a large enough supply of wood to last the length of the storm, however long that might be. The longer she waited, the worse it would be, and she only wanted to go outside once. In addition to the wood, she also had to bring in the groceries, her suitcase, and the baby supplies from the car before nightfall. Already, the sky had darkened, and it would be pitch-black within an hour.

She laid Rachel down in the car seat and tucked a flannel blanket around her. "If you'll excuse me, I have to get everything inside while I still have the chance."

He looked down to Raymond and the bottle, which was still half full. "I can do that. It's okay."

Adelle shook her head. "I'm dressed for these conditions, you're not. Besides, Raymond hasn't finished his bottle, and I have to do it right away, before the groceries freeze."

She slipped her boots back on, fastened her coat, donned her hat, scarf, and gloves, and stepped outside, needing to get away from Dennis so she could think without being too near him.

The force of the wind made her stagger until she braced herself against it and forged through the knee-high snow. Instead of thinking about her problem, all she could think about was protecting herself from the cold and carrying as much as she could each time.

The first few trips back and forth from the car to the cabin were the most difficult, but once she created a path for herself as she plowed through the snow, the trek became easier. First she brought in the groceries, which were half of what she and her family would have needed without going back to the city for two weeks. Now Aunt Min and Uncle Bob weren't here, and she had a second mouth to feed. While she was in the kitchen, she flipped on the fridge and hot water tank, and went back outside to get everything else.

The suitcases were easy to carry, but Adelle struggled with the playpen, the only baby accessory she brought. She planned to set it up near the woodstove to provide a safe and warm place for Rachel to sleep.

After emptying her car, she plowed through the snow to the woodpile stacked against the tool shed. The mountain snow was powder fine, but it had been drifting against the building and had already covered the wood. She worked hard to dig through it and filled her arms with the limit of what she could carry. The snow was now past her knees, making it difficult for Adelle to trudge through as she made a new path back to the cabin carrying the extra weight.

She didn't care that she was panting when she reached the door. Her only thoughts focused on how many more trips she had to make. She nudged the door with her foot to open it, just as she had done when unloading the car. But this time, it didn't budge.

She squeezed her eyes shut. She had been careful not to fully close the door so that she could get back in easily. The wind must have clicked the latch shut.

A fresh gust of wind sent a frigid blast beneath her coat and whipped her scarf into her face. Despite the heavy wool coat, Adelle shivered. Rather than drop her armload, she kicked the door a few times and waited.

Inside, Dennis called out that he was coming. Through the closed door, she heard the old springs of the couch creaking, followed by muffled footsteps. Instead of the door opening, she heard the thunk of a bottle hitting the wood floor, followed by a barely audible "oops," and the start of baby whimpers.

The door squeaked open. Adelle shuffled in and pushed it closed with her foot. Dennis stood to the side, struggling to cradle Raymond with one arm. In his free hand, he held the bottle at a most awkward angle.

"You're making me feel so guilty. I should be doing that," he said, then returned to the couch, where he began to lower himself by just bending his knees, not using either hand to support himself, as he was still feeding Raymond. In the process, he lost his balance and flopped down, struggling not to jostle the baby as he landed.

Adelle stomped the snow off her boots, piled the wood against the wall, and then left the cabin for another load. Again, she left the door slightly ajar and prayed that, this time, it would remain unlatched.

Fortunately, when she returned, the door was as she left it. The bottle lay on the floor empty. Dennis sat with Raymond in his lap half perched on his knee, but mostly leaning crooked against his chest, and he was diligently patting the baby on the back.

She'd never seen anyone try to burp a baby like that but kept her thoughts to herself.

Along with the burp, Raymond spit up all down the front of Dennis's shirt. Dennis froze, staring at the smelly white trail oozing down his shirt. His face paled and his chest jerked as he inhaled sharply then held his breath.

"Let me get something to wipe that with," Adelle mumbled as she tried to quickly empty the logs from her arms. When he gulped for air, his color worsened. Adelle let the logs drop and ran to the kitchen to find the roll of paper towels. Quickly, she ripped open the plastic wrap, tore off a wad of paper towels, and ran across the room.

The closer she got, the more rancid the odor became. She arrived in front of him just as he started to gag. She reached for the baby and handed him the paper towels in one motion. In trying to wipe the mess, he only smeared it worse.

Even more color drained from his face. He looked up, his face white and his teeth chattering. "I think I need some fresh air," he mumbled.

In the blink of an eye, he ran out the door, without his jacket. Except for the odd crackle from inside the woodstove all was silent inside the cabin, but outside, over the howl of the wind, she could hear Dennis retching. Between the lingering stench of the baby spit-up and having to listen to what was happening outside, Adelle's own stomach churned.

She couldn't force her feet to move, so she simply stood in one spot, holding Raymond.

After a few minutes the door burst open. Dennis strode in without a shirt, visibly shaking. Without a word and barely slowing his pace, he grabbed his suitcase and strode into the washroom. The door closed behind him with a bang.

Rather than stare at the closed door, Adelle lowered Raymond to his car seat and tucked one of Rachel's flannel blankets around him, then removed her coat and headed to the kitchen.

Fortunately, he hadn't dumped the water he used to heat the bottle. Until the hot water tank finished the cycle, it was all the warm water they had. She began to wipe down the counter so she wouldn't have to set the groceries into the dust that had accumulated since the cabin was last used.

Dennis emerged from the washroom wearing a sweatshirt and jeans.

He shivered again, rested his suitcase beside the washroom door, and walked to the woodstove, where he set out his wet sneakers and a pair of socks. He then ran his fingers through his hair and approached Raymond in the car seat, bent as if to pick him up, then halted. Raymond gurgled, but didn't cry.

Dennis straightened with his arms empty, looked down at the baby, and rammed his hands into his pockets. He stared for a few seconds out the window, then turned back to her.

"He seems okay, so I think I'm going to leave him there. I'm not very good at this baby stuff," he mumbled, staring at a blank spot on the wall.

For the first time since she picked Dennis up, Adelle had a chance to really look at him.

He was quite a handsome man, now that his color had returned. She figured he was around thirty years old, and since she'd seen him without a shirt, however briefly, she knew he was trim and reasonably fit. His dark brown hair was slightly wavy, and the color almost perfectly matched the color of his eyes. Together with his long, straight nose and strong eyebrows, the combination gave him quite a regal appearance.

She couldn't think of a thing to say.

"Need some help? I don't want to stand here doing nothing."

Adelle nodded as she began to empty the contents of the grocery bags onto the counter. "I've put a bunch of stuff that has to go into the fridge over there." She pointed to the section of counter nearest the fridge. "Can you put it in for me?"

He picked up a package of frozen meat and smiled hesitantly at her. Adelle nearly dropped the spaghetti. When he smiled, she wanted to trust him, but logic told her that she knew nothing about him. She didn't know if she was being an accessory to some crime by having him at the cabin.

He tucked a few packages of frozen food into the freezer. "This seems so strange. The freezer motor is still running, but it's colder outside than it is in there."

Adelle forced herself to nod and concentrated intently on stacking the canned goods before she loaded them into the cupboard. "I just turned the fridge on a few minutes ago. I thought of putting the frozen stuff outside, but I worried that it wouldn't be too long and I'd never find anything again. It's snowing even heavier than it was an hour ago." She also thought of his soiled shirt, which he'd discarded outside, and wondered what her aunt and uncle would think when they found a man's shirt in the yard when the spring thaw came. Especially if, by that time, she was dead by mysterious causes.

"Do you have a radio? Maybe they'll have some kind of idea how long this will last."

She crossed the room to the corner designated for the living room and turned on the radio, which was the only form of entertainment available besides the portable CD player she had brought.

Before she returned to the kitchen, Adelle parted the curtain and looked out the window. The night was pitch-black, with no moon or stars visible through the heavy storm clouds or blowing snow. The force of the wind had increased again, and every once in a while a branch hit the cabin's outer walls. "It's getting worse," she muttered to herself more than to Dennis, who was still on the other side of the room, in the kitchen.

She was stranded, with a stranger.

At the end of the song, the announcer advised of the road and highway closures, repeated the weather warning, and instructed people in the area to stay indoors. Adelle stiffened when he announced that the Weather Advisory Branch said the storm was expected to last for at least another forty-eight hours, probably into nightfall of Christmas Eve.

"I really should phone my aunt and uncle and let them know I'm here."

He nodded and turned his attention to loading the last of the groceries from the counter to the cupboard.

Adelle wondered who she should call first, her aunt and uncle, or the police.

❄

Dennis watched Adelle as she dialed. He concentrated not on what she was doing, but on the woman herself.

Without the bulk of winter clothing, Adelle Wilson was tiny. She had to stand on her tiptoes to reach the higher cupboard, and her lack of height was equally matched by her small stature. While she wasn't thin, he acknowledged the woman recently had a baby, so he really didn't know what she was like before. He guessed her to be about twenty-eight years old, which was only a year younger than himself.

Her curly brown hair framed a face with kind, brown eyes and soft, full lips. She wasn't all that pretty, yet she wasn't ugly, either. But when she smiled, she had the face of an angel.

Dennis praised God for Adelle as his angel. The situation he found himself in could have been very different. Not only were he and Raymond safe and warm while the blizzard raged outside, but Adelle had enough food to last a week, even if he wasn't going to be here that long. The minute the snow stopped, he would call for a helicopter to come and get him. As soon as he found out exactly where they were, he and Raymond would be airlifted home. Of course he would offer the same to Adelle, but since this was her family's cabin, he had a feeling she would stay. When the roads were cleared, her family would be able to come. They'd just be a little later than planned.

He was curious about her phone call. She said she was phoning her aunt and uncle who owned the cabin, but didn't mention calling her husband. Dennis wondered why.

She turned her back to him as she dialed. He wished he could have given her some privacy to make her call, but the cabin was small, and not being able to go outside forced them into close company. He expected things to be awkward since they were strangers, but so far, she was being gracious. Dennis planned to do all he could for her while he was here.

Again he praised God that he was safe and wondered what he could do when he got home to thank Adelle and her family for what she had done for him and the shelter they provided.

Not wanting to overhear her conversation, he walked back to the ugly '70s style orange couch and sat down. He tried to focus his attention on the babies, but they had both fallen asleep and weren't very interesting to watch.

Within the confines of the small, quiet cabin, he could still hear every word Adelle spoke, despite her lowered tones.

"Hi, Aunt Min. I'm at the cabin. I didn't hear the weather advisory until I was already here." Adelle nodded her head a few times as she listened to her aunt. "Don't worry, I certainly have enough food, and everything is okay here. I'll be fine." She paused. "Yes, I heard. We'll just have to see what happens and hope it ends Christmas Eve like they predict." Another pause followed. "Uh. . .I'm, ah, not exactly alone." Adelle laughed nervously. "I sort of picked up a stranded motorist and his baby on the way, expecting you and Uncle Bob would be here. Except you weren't."

This time the pause was longer, and Dennis could see that she nodded a few times, which he thought kind of funny, since her aunt couldn't see her.

"I know, but what could I do? He'd had an accident and his car was wrecked. I was the last one your friend Officer Paul let pass. If I didn't pick him up, he would have frozen to death in the blizzard." Her voice dropped to a bare whisper, but with so little distance between them and the perfect quiet, he could still hear what she said. "He said that his name is Dennis Bancroft. He says he's from Vancouver, and he has a baby with him."

As she listened to her aunt again, she hunched her shoulders, and her voice dropped to a forced loud whisper. "I know. I'd appreciate it."

He had a feeling that Adelle's aunt was going to check him out to make sure he wasn't an escaped felon or something, except she wouldn't find anything, because his phone number was unlisted. He stood, ready to take the phone and give Adelle's aunt his phone number, as well as the numbers of some of his friends and his pastor, so both Adelle and her family could be assured that he wasn't a serial killer.

Before he'd taken a step, she said a quick, "I'll phone often. Bye," and hung up.

She turned to face him, and then froze when she saw him standing. She cringed almost imperceptibly.

Dennis shuffled back as far as he could, without having to sit down again. "I couldn't help but overhear your end of the conversation, and I really can't blame you for being nervous. After all, you don't know me or anything about me. I wish there was a way I could assure you that you're perfectly safe, and that I'm an honest and trustworthy man. I wouldn't do anything to jeopardize you or your baby's safety. Quite the opposite, in fact, since you saved our lives and took the chance on having us here. I'm deeply moved by your generosity and trust. I'll be forever in your debt. Please relax, I'm quite harmless."

"It's okay," she mumbled.

Dennis resisted the urge to run his hand down his face. Instead, he checked the time. It surprised him that it was already dark out, yet it wasn't really that late, although it was suppertime. "Actually, there is a phone call I have to make. No one is expecting me until tomorrow so no one will be worried, but I guess I've kind of been putting it off."

He paused and sucked in a deep breath. "If you don't mind, I have to call my fiancée."

Chapter 3

A million thoughts roared through Adelle's head, none of which explained the baby.

He walked to the telephone but didn't begin to dial. "I have no idea where we are. Does this place have an address or something?"

"Address? I have no idea what the address would be. I don't even know if the road has a name. It's just an old logging road. I've come here all my life, so I know how to find it without asking directions."

He silently studied the phone. "I wonder. Someone should be able to trace the address with the phone number." He turned back to her. "I know the roads are impassable, but is there anywhere nearby with enough clearing to land a helicopter once the snow subsides? I need to be airlifted as soon as I can get out."

Adelle could only stare. For someone who was in no rush to make a phone call, suddenly he was in an awful hurry to leave. She couldn't even guess the cost of chartering a helicopter, nor could she guess his reasons for wanting one, but she pictured a ransom figure far above her total income for the next decade.

Adelle cleared her throat and forced herself to speak normally. "I don't know if there's a clearing nearby. I've never thought about it."

"I guess that will be up to the company who owns the helicopter to find out, then. I'll reimburse you for the call."

He dialed and waited.

"Hi, Joanna. It's me."

He winced at the other person's response, which Adelle thought quite odd considering he said it was his fiancée he was calling.

"Yes, I've got him, and I know what you said, but this is the way it's going to be. However, I'm not going to discuss that right now. I'm having a bit of a problem, and I need you to do something for me."

This time, he held the phone away from his ear while the other person shouted.

His voice became low and stern, and although Adelle didn't know him, she could tell he was angry. "Knock it off, Joanna. I've run into some trouble here and I need your help. I got caught in a blizzard and had an accident in the mountains. A very kind lady rescued me, and I'm at her cabin right now. I have no idea where we are and there apparently isn't an address, but I'll give you the phone number.

Someone should be able to have the location traced so you can send a chopper to pick Raymond and me up."

Again he listened in obvious frustration. Briefly, he raised his eyes and made eye contact with her.

Adelle felt her cheeks flush, embarrassed at having been caught eavesdropping on his conversation. She turned and crossed the room to sit on the couch, but she could still hear every word he said.

"I told you before, I'm not abandoning Harv's baby. He's the only family I've got left."

At his words, Adelle didn't care whether she was caught watching him. She noticed he held the phone so tight his knuckles turned white.

"I can't believe you're being so self-centered. Can't you put that aside and do this for me as a favor? We can deal with everything else later. The most important thing now is. . . Hello? Hello?"

He flicked the button on the phone a couple of times. "There's no dial tone. The phone's dead."

"I guess it's the storm. That's really odd. The power goes out frequently here, but usually the phone line is okay." In unison, they both looked up at the light fixture on the ceiling, which was shining brightly.

Dennis sighed. "Praise God for small miracles. Still, I need the phone more than I need the light. It's really important that I get home because—"

The lights flickered once, and everything went black.

"Uh oh," Adelle muttered. "I think I spoke too soon."

The only light now came from the glow inside the woodstove. As her eyes adjusted to the darkness, she could make out Dennis's shape. He hadn't moved.

"What now?" he asked.

"First I have to switch the fridge over to propane."

"Is that difficult?"

Adelle shook her head. "No, it's much the same as a camper, the kind that you can set to run on either electricity or propane. The only problem is, I have to go outside to do it."

They both looked out the window at the same time.

"Is there anything I can do?"

Adelle shook her head. "Usually my Uncle Bob does it, but it's not difficult. I can do it myself."

If a blizzard weren't raging outside, she would have asked him to hold the flashlight, but she didn't want him going back out, as now it would be even colder than it had been during the daytime. "It's just like lighting the fridge in a camper."

"I wouldn't know. I've never lit a fridge in a camper."

Adelle grinned. "I haven't either. When my uncle showed me how to do it, that's what he said."

Again Adelle donned her coat and boots. She found the flashlight and lighter and braved the weather to light the pilot light from outside. The wind was blowing so hard it took her a number of tries, but once it was lit and the cover was back in place, it would stay lit until the electricity was restored and she turned off the propane supply.

Since she was already outside braving the elements she brought in a few more armloads of wood.

The small cabin warmed quickly, but due to the nature of the only source of heat being in the living room, Adelle bundled herself in a sweater and her big fuzzy slippers. Then, with Dennis holding the flashlight over her shoulder, she searched the cupboards and drawers for candles.

Considering the storm and their remote location, Adelle feared the power could possibly be out for days. Therefore, she lit only one candle and set it on the coffee table to ration the supply. Since she didn't know how much propane they had, she didn't change the hot water tank over to propane, meaning they didn't have an endless supply of warm water.

Adelle turned her attention to the kitchen. "I haven't eaten since breakfast, and I'm really hungry. I'm going to start making supper."

"Want some help?"

She shook her head and was about to begin when Raymond awoke. His crying also woke Rachel.

Ignoring the grumbling of her empty stomach, she laid a thick quilt on the floor near the fire and picked up her diaper bag.

Dennis stood next to the woodstove. "You're going to change her diaper, aren't you?"

She nodded as she laid Rachel down.

"I guess I'd better change Raymond, too."

"Yes. You haven't changed him since we arrived, have you?"

"No. And I didn't change him in the car, either, because it was too cold."

She didn't want to think about how wet the baby was. Adelle almost suggested that Dennis bathe him in case his skin was irritated, but then remembered that they didn't have hot water. It would take too long to heat enough water for a bath on the stove, and he needed to change Raymond now.

Dennis laid Raymond down on the quilt beside Rachel. "I'm not very good at this."

Adelle wasn't as frightened as before, now that she knew he had a fiancée and that somehow, the baby was family. Still, she distanced herself as much as she could without arousing suspicion.

While she changed Rachel, out of the corner of her eye she watched Dennis fumble with the tiny snaps on the sleeper. The diaper was so soaked it had leaked, so he removed the sleeper entirely, as well as the diaper-shirt. She'd never seen anyone so carefully pick the tape off the disposable diaper. Once the tape was loosened, he opened it very, very slowly, as if he was afraid of what he would find.

His relief that the diaper was only wet seemed almost tangible.

By this time, Adelle had Rachel completely changed. She picked her up and continued to watch Dennis.

He tucked the diaper with the wrong end up under Raymond's bottom and then poffed out triple the amount of baby powder Adelle would have used. When he discovered the tape was at the bottom instead of the top, he delicately grasped both of Raymond's ankles and lifted him so his little bottom cleared the diaper enough to switch it around.

Because he'd used too much powder and got it everywhere, the tape wouldn't stick. Rather than throwing the diaper away, he pulled a roll of duct tape out of the diaper bag, and taped the diaper shut by going all around Raymond, once again lifting the baby by the ankles so he could get some tape underneath.

Adelle struggled to keep quiet, first wondering how he was going to get the diaper off with all that tape sealing it together, and then wanting to tell him that if he was equipped with tape because of difficulty closing the diaper, he should simply use less powder. Instead, she continued to watch.

It took him four tries to align the snaps on the clean diaper-shirt. After the third try to align the snaps on the new sleeper, Adelle couldn't stand it any more.

"It works better if you start from the feet and work your way up, instead of trying to go down."

"Oh. Thanks," he mumbled, unsnapped it again, and followed her instructions.

When Raymond was finally redressed, Dennis cradled his tiny head with one hand, wiggled his other hand under the baby's back, and awkwardly picked up Raymond.

He smiled at Adelle once he had the infant resting against his chest. "That's a new record for me, the fastest I've ever done it. I don't know who invented those things, but there has to be a better way to dress a baby."

"Not really." If Dennis was this bad at changing Raymond, she was now glad she hadn't suggested that he should have bathed Raymond before putting him in clean sleepers. They would have been there till midnight.

Adelle's stomach growled, reminding her that they still hadn't had supper.

She couldn't decide if she should give Rachel to Dennis to hold while she started cooking, or if she should offer to take Raymond and let Dennis cook.

Since they were stranded together for at least twenty-four hours, she hoped he was better in the kitchen than he was at caring for a baby.

Rather than make the choice, she propped Rachel up in the car seat. Since Rachel didn't cry immediately Adelle quickly set to work to prepare supper. She was so hungry, she began to prepare the first thing she saw, which was a package of macaroni and cheese. She hoped Dennis wouldn't be too picky, either.

He stood to the side and watched. "I wish I could help, but I don't think I should put him down."

"It's okay," she mumbled as she flicked the ignition over the propane element, then turned it to full when it flamed. "I understand."

"I haven't had macaroni and cheese in years. Probably not since I was a kid."

"It's become a staple for me in the last month. It's amazing how having a baby changes your life, even down to eating habits."

He looked down to the top of Raymond's head then back to Adelle. "Yeah. I guess."

They stood in silence. When the water boiled, she dumped in the raw macaroni, waited for it to boil again, then checked her wristwatch so she could time it.

"I think I have a lot to learn about babies. I've only had him for a couple of days. It's nothing like I thought it would be."

Adelle wanted to ask a million questions but didn't know where to start. Before she could formulate her first question, he continued.

"Raymond is my brother's baby." He squeezed his eyes shut, swallowed hard, then opened them again. "Was my brother's baby. A week ago I got a call that Harv and Katie were badly injured in an automobile accident. They both lived for twenty-four hours, never regained consciousness, and died." He paused to swallow hard again before he continued. "And now I'm Raymond's legal guardian. I started the wheels in motion to care for their estate, and I was taking him home when the storm hit."

Adelle didn't know what to say, so she said nothing.

"And if you're wondering why I was doing something so stupid like driving in conditions like that, well, I wasn't thinking. I just wanted to get home for Christmas, to something familiar."

"Maybe you can still be home in time for Christmas. And even if you're not, I'm sure your fiancée will at least be happy that you and the baby are safe." She knew it wasn't likely anyone would be able to move his car for a while, nor was it likely a helicopter would come unless it was for an emergency, which didn't include getting someone home for Christmas.

Despite the argument she'd overheard, Adelle envied Dennis's fiancée. She wished she had someone who loved her enough to go through such extremes to be with her. Not that she would allow someone she loved to do something foolish to risk their safety, but the knowledge that someone would have wanted to would have been a great comfort.

He stared down at the floor. "Actually, I don't know what she thinks. I'm not sure I even care. We just split up."

Adelle almost dropped the spoon into the pot. "I'm so sorry!"

He shrugged his shoulders and stroked Raymond's tiny back as he spoke. "Don't be. I'm seeing her in an entirely new light since this happened, and it's been a rude awakening. I guess I've been ignoring the truth until now. When I left to be with my brother and his wife, Joanna plainly told me she wanted me to stay home, to be with her for Christmas. But how could I not go? He's my brother, and he was going to die. I couldn't abandon him. So I went. I basically threw what I could into one suitcase and drove away because I couldn't get a flight sooner than it would have taken me to drive there."

Raymond had fallen asleep in Dennis's arms, soothed by having his back stroked, but Dennis didn't put him down, which impressed Adelle.

"She was really mad that I didn't stay to be with her for Christmas, but that's not all. When Harv died that left me as Raymond's legal guardian. Joanna told me she refused to raise someone else's kid. The only children she wants will be her own, and she doesn't want to start a family for five more years. She said she doesn't want to be tied down by kids underfoot. Now that I think about it, I really don't think she wants kids at all. When five years comes around she still wouldn't want kids, and then it will be too late. She told me I had to make the choice between her and Raymond. So that means the wedding is off."

He cradled Raymond's head in his large hand, lowered his own head, and softly brushed his cheek to Raymond's soft crown of baby hair. "I may not know exactly what to do with babies, but I do like kids." He raised his head and smiled at her. Adelle thought it was the saddest smile she'd ever seen. "Even kids that aren't mine. But Raymond is my nephew, so he's kinda mine."

"Really, you are good with him. You just need more practice."

He gently kissed the top of Raymond's head. "I guess. However, I must say I like him best when he's sleeping like this. He's quiet."

Adelle smiled.

"So what about your husband? I guess he's having fits that he probably won't be spending Christmas with you and Rachel. But at least your aunt and uncle can pass on the message that both of you are safe."

Adelle lost her smile. "I'm not married. And her father really doesn't care where either Rachel or I am at any given moment. You see, he's in jail."

Chapter 4

Dennis tensed. While she hadn't mentioned anything about a husband or significant other, it hadn't occurred to him that Adelle might be a single mother. What threw him even more was the status of the baby's father.

The man she, at one time, must have loved was in jail.

His mind raced with possible reasons for the father's incarceration, ranging from petty theft to assault with a deadly weapon.

"I'm sorry," Dennis muttered, unable to think of anything to say. He wasn't sorry that someone who had committed a crime was being punished, but he did feel badly that a woman who would put herself at potential risk to help a stranger would be emotionally attached to someone like that.

She lowered her head and concentrated far more than necessary to stir the macaroni as it cooked. "I'm not sorry. I'm the one who put him there."

He didn't trust himself to speak, so he waited in silence for her to continue. But she didn't say anything. Instead, she slowly stirred the macaroni, then covered it again.

Minutes went by with the only sounds the crackling of the fire in the woodstove, the slight hiss of the propane burner, and the sound of the lid moving up and down as the contents of the pot bubbled.

Finally, he couldn't stand it any more. "Don't you think he'll want to see his daughter?"

"No." She stirred the macaroni, checked her watch again, then turned the burner off, lifted the pot, and dumped the boiling water down the drain. "Can you get the milk and butter out of the fridge, please?"

Dennis knew when to take a hint, so he didn't press it further. One thing he did know was that tonight, when he was alone and all was quiet, he would pray for this woman. He'd met many women who had been either widowed or abandoned while caring for young children. While loneliness was often difficult to deal with, what added to the trials of single parenthood was lack of support, both emotional and financial.

He balanced Raymond with one arm, necessitating two trips to deliver the milk and butter.

Adelle sighed loudly. Even in the near darkness he could see defeat written across her face. "I know you're curious. I might as well explain because I don't want you to be asking me questions about Rachel's father, or think that I'm in any way emotionally attached to him. He's in jail because he raped me. But I am a Christian and I don't believe in abortion, even in a case like this. Murdering a child for the sin of another person isn't what God would have us do. I know many people would argue with me, but that's what I believe."

She stirred the macaroni mixture vigorously. "I know what you're thinking. But I know that God loves me, and although her conception wasn't under ideal circumstances, Rachel is God's child, as am I. God will take care of us both. I really believe that. And don't be like everyone else and tell me I should have given her up for adoption. I may not like her father, but she's my child, and I love her very much."

Dennis swallowed hard. "I'm not going to insult your intelligence and tell you that I know exactly how you feel, because I obviously don't. I can't even imagine what you must have been through. But I think I can understand at least a little bit about not terminating the pregnancy, because I'm a Christian, too."

Her eyes widened, and she stared at him with her mouth hanging open.

He shook his head. "I'm not just saying that to get you to trust me. I love God with all my heart, and I go to church every Sunday, but I don't blame you if you don't believe me. The only way to see that is by my actions and to get to know me better."

She narrowed her eyes. "Okay. Then what's your favorite verse? And don't quote me something obvious like John 3:16.

Dennis smiled. "How about Matthew 6:9 through 13? And I can recite that in three versions."

She remained silent for a few seconds. "I'm impressed. I'm listening."

"This is from the NIV." He cleared his throat. " 'Our Father in heaven, hallowed be your name, your kingdom come, your will be done, on earth as it is in heaven. Give us today our daily bread. Forgive us our debts, as we also have forgiven our debtors. And lead us not into temptation, but deliver us from the evil one.' Now which one do you want next, King James or NASB?"

She stared blankly at him. "Nice try but not funny."

He couldn't stop smiling. "Hey, I knew the reference; you didn't. I thought you'd catch me before I even started."

She didn't comment.

"Seriously, I could quote you some of my favorite verses, but I'd probably get the references wrong. I'm not very good at memorizing, but my Bible study group just finished a session on the Lord's Prayer and we all memorized the Lord's Prayer from three translations. I picked the NIV, the King James, and the NASB. I guess this is God's way of telling me I should be better prepared to defend my faith, although it's a different reason than I could ever imagined."

"Well, I guess you earn some brownie points by being able to name three versions of the Bible and catching me off guard with the reference for the Lord's Prayer."

"If you want me to quote a lesser-known verse, my dad drummed into my head a verse somewhere from I or II Thessalonians, I forget the exact reference. He said it a lot when I was a teen and I complained about my chores. It says, 'if a man will not work, he shall not eat.' And did you know that the famous 'Golden Rule' doesn't appear anywhere in the Bible?"

She covered her face with her hands. "The idea was for you to quote me something that *was* in the Bible, something you knew yourself, not something repeated to you over the years."

"I can sing a song and name all the books of the Bible in order. Not just the New Testament, but the Old Testament, too. Does that count?"

Finally she smiled, which Dennis thought a welcome relief. It was also a reminder to get more serious with his Bible reading, including real memorization.

"The macaroni is ready. Are you going to eat with one hand, or are you going to put him down?"

"I guess I probably should put him down."

Dennis walked to the playpen. Very slowly, he leaned over, and lowered Raymond to the padded bottom. He rolled up a flannel blanket and wedged it in behind Raymond's back to prop him up on his side like the nurse had shown him, tucking a second blanket over top of him. Then he joined Adelle at the small table.

She folded her hands on the table in front of her. "Would you like to pray?"

He didn't know if the test was over or not, but he couldn't blame a woman who had been a victim of such a violent and personal crime for not trusting him.

Dennis took a moment of silence to prepare himself to pray. He didn't do eloquent prayers, but what he did pray was heartfelt. He cleared his throat, and reminded himself that he was supposed to be praying only for the food, no matter how much he had to be thankful for at that moment. He would do that when he was alone, in his own private time.

"Dear heavenly Father, thank you for this humble meal. Thank you also for the shelter You've provided and, most of all, for the kindness of a stranger, who turned out to be another one of Your children. Thank you that we can share Your blessings together to Your glory. Amen."

"Amen."

Dennis didn't look up. He couldn't remember ever being so hungry in his life. He immediately dug into the macaroni in front of him, thinking that he'd never tasted anything better, including a week before when he'd taken Joanna out to one of the best steak and lobster restaurants in town.

"This is really good," he mumbled around the food in his mouth. "Thank you."

He speared more food onto his fork, but just as he raised it to his mouth he looked up at Adelle, who hadn't yet taken her first bite. She was openly staring at him.

He didn't lower the fork. "I don't do long prayers before meals. Don't you just hate it when you go out for lunch after church and whoever is praying goes on and on, while you're hungry and your lunch is getting cold?"

"I guess. . ."

He continued eating. Thankfully, Adelle followed his lead.

Except for the slight glow coming from the woodstove, the only light in the room came from the candle between them. With everything beyond the candle on the small table increasingly shrouded by darkness, their world became very small. With no distractions except for the howling wind, all his attention focused on Adelle's face. The uneven light played on her features, giving an unexpected intimacy to the sharing of a simple meal.

Adelle wasn't particularly pretty, but the kindness radiating in her eyes far outweighed any flaws in her appearance. Her concern for him as a stranger carried beyond simple kindness, it stepped into genuine risk. Knowing nothing about him except that he needed help, she stopped to pick him up, even though she could have driven on and phoned for the police or someone else to go get him. For all she knew, he could have been an escaped felon.

He knew he shouldn't compare. Still, he wondered what Joanna would have done, had she been in this situation. He doubted Joanna would have even stopped.

The flame flickered.

He thought back to a week ago, eating out at the restaurant with Joanna by candlelight. She'd tried to make the most of the close setting, batting her eyelashes at him, and smiling sweetly when the light from the candle cast its moving shadows. Instead of acting coy, Adelle's brows furrowed as she laid down her cutlery and cupped her hands near to the flame. "Did you see that? I never thought the cabin was this drafty. That wind must be really intense out there."

He wanted to get to know Adelle Wilson better.

He couldn't hold back a smile. "When I get home, I don't think I'll ever feel the same about those candles in the middle of the table when I eat out."

"I suppose not."

"Except for the lack of electricity, this cabin seems pretty cozy. Do you come here often?"

"Yes, I do. More in the summer time."

"I'll bet it's beautiful here. There are probably lots of animals."

"Yes, but it's not like a big city park. The animals here are real wild animals, and have to be treated with respect and caution. Bears and cougars, especially, can be dangerous."

He hadn't considered the dangerous animals; he'd mostly pictured squirrels and deer. His idealistic picture of the quaint mountain surroundings began to change. "I wonder how long the power will be out. You mentioned earlier that it's fairly common out here."

She nodded. "Yes, this area is very remote. Usually, when the power goes out, we can at least phone. But this time, since the phone went out first, and since not many people are in this area in the winter, they may not even be aware that it's out until they do some kind of routine check."

Dennis didn't care as much about the power as he did the phone. He tried to hold back his anger at Joanna for starting an argument before he could give her the phone number so that someone might trace it and locate him. For now, he was grateful for their safety, but he had to get home with Raymond very soon. Since Adelle wasn't speaking, he prayed silently for a miracle.

❄

Adelle wasn't as frightened as she had been earlier, but she still wasn't comfortable with the situation in which she found herself. Even if the radio's weather advisory predictions, that the blizzard would be over in forty-eight hours, proved true, that wouldn't mean an end to their predicament. For when the snow stopped falling, they would still be without electricity or telephone service. And the roads would not magically clear.

Even if the snow ended on schedule, not much would be done on Christmas Day. Once the plowing began, the cities and the main highways would be plowed first, then the small towns. She didn't remember ever seeing a snowplow on the old logging road to her aunt and uncle's cabin, especially the quarter mile path her uncle laughingly called a driveway.

Since Dennis wasn't talking anymore, Adelle silently praised God that she had convinced Aunt Min to let her bring half the food. Otherwise, they'd been in a worse predicament.

"So what do you do for fun when you're here? I imagine you use this place both in the summer and winter."

She smiled. "Usually we have electricity, so it's different. Of course we have the radio or the CD player going. As you've no doubt already noticed, we don't have a television here. We just relax and talk. In the summer, when the sun doesn't set until late, we go for walks."

"Since this is in the mountains, I guess there isn't a lake nearby."

"No. But there is a running stream at the edge of the property. It's really beautiful in the spring, and in the summer the deer drink from it."

He smiled, and his eyes glazed as he stared into nothing. "I'll bet it is. It sounds so perfect. I don't get away enough. I spend too much time working. But it sounds like it makes a nice getaway."

Adelle didn't want to think of her job. That was one of the things she needed to discuss with her aunt and uncle. For now, she was on maternity leave, but when that ran out, she had some very important choices to make, decisions she couldn't leave until the last minute. Besides wanting to be with her favorite relatives for her first Christmas with Rachel, she needed this time to hide from well-meaning friends, so she could sort out what she was going to do.

"Yes, it's nice and quiet here."

"I guess it's quieter than ever with no electricity."

Adelle sighed and absently stared across the room to where both babies slept. Her aunt had offered to watch Rachel in order to give her more time to think and provide a break from the exhausting responsibilities of single parenthood. It was difficult not knowing what the future would bring. Now, instead of a break, she had the added responsibility of entertaining a stranger, and instead of getting help with her own baby, she had a feeling she would have to help him with his baby.

She stood. "There aren't many dishes to wash, but we should still hurry to get them done before Rachel and Raymond waken. They've both been sleeping most of the day, and I have a feeling that means they're going to be up a good portion of the night."

Her guest's smile fell. "Why do you think that? I've been told that babies sleep a lot."

"Just exactly how long have you been caring for your brother's baby, Dennis?"

"You mean all by myself? This will be the second night."

"You mean he slept all night last night? At under one month of age?"

"Well, no. I couldn't sleep last night, so I was packing some things and moving stuff around, getting ready for my trip home. I figured I was too noisy for him, because he didn't sleep much at all, poor little guy. I know babies are supposed to sleep a lot, and I felt really bad. That's another reason I wanted to get him home today, so we could get used to each other before I have to go back to work after the holidays."

"So you don't know if he sleeps through the night or not?"

"I hadn't really thought about it. Why wouldn't he?"

Chapter 5

Dennis stuck the pacifier back into Raymond's mouth and stared into the glow of the woodstove. "Do you have any idea what time it is?"

He could tell Adelle was yawning without looking at her.

"Nearly midnight."

The pacifier fell out again. Fortunately it only fell onto the couch instead of the floor. Dennis gave up and let it lie beside Raymond. "I think he yawned, but I'm not sure." Just the thought that Raymond could have yawned made it impossible for Dennis to hold back a yawn of his own. He didn't know how Raymond could be so wide-awake, because he couldn't remember ever being so tired.

The tragic events of this past week had left him numb. The fact that he would never see his brother again didn't hit him until after the funeral, when he was alone that night at Harv's and Katie's house with only Raymond to keep him company.

Rather than sleeplessly tossing and turning all night, he started packing everything to get their house ready to sell. That was when the realization finally sank in that Harv and Katie were never coming back. Going through their belongings with the house in the disarray of normal life stressed the abrupt finality of their deaths. It felt as if they should be walking in the door at any time, except he knew they wouldn't.

The only thing that eased the pain was knowing that both Harv and Katie were Christians and that, one day, he would see them again in heaven. Still, his heart was heavy at the loss. All their lives, until Harv moved away, they'd been best friends as well as brothers. Their parents had died five years ago, and now Harv was gone, too. Raymond was all the family Dennis had left.

He yawned again and brushed his cheek on the top of Raymond's fuzzy head. Dennis was exhausted, but Raymond was wide-awake.

In addition to waving his arms around and kicking his tiny legs, something about the flickering glow from the woodstove held Raymond's attention. Since Dennis no longer had the energy to keep Raymond occupied, he just held Raymond in his lap, letting him watch the flame.

"He'll go to sleep soon, right?" he mumbled through another yawn.

"Maybe, maybe not. They've both been awake for a while. I know Rachel usually falls asleep after I feed her in the evenings.

Dennis could barely keep his eyes open, so he was ready to try anything. "Let's try that then, if you don't mind. I'm really beat."

"It helps if you change them before you feed them, because then babies stay sleepy after they eat, and it's easier to get them to settle down."

He nodded, and they carried both babies to the quilt, still on the floor near the fire. Dennis carefully snipped the duct tape off the diaper and tucked a clean one under Raymond's bottom. He was just about to apply the baby powder when Adelle spoke.

"You've got the diaper wrong side up again."

He mumbled his thanks, turned it around, then lifted Raymond's bottom, ready for a second attempt to apply the powder, but she spoke again.

"You really don't have to use much powder. And if you sprinkle it from closer, it won't pouf all over the place, and then you'll have no trouble getting the tape to stick. See? Like this."

"Oh. Thanks."

Dennis gritted his teeth while he applied what he hoped was the correct amount of powder. He was counting on help from his married friends when he got Raymond home, including the art of changing diapers, until he could figure out suitable day-care arrangements. He had also unrealistically hoped that Joanna would assume a portion of the responsibility, but her response before the phone went dead only confirmed what he should have accepted before he left.

She had been more than willing to accept the perks and benefits of his lifestyle and financial status. However, now that partnership with him involved some sacrifice to the easy future she expected, he could see her true colors. And he didn't like them. Whatever relationship they had was over.

He was still working on the goofy little baby undershirt when Adelle picked Rachel up, completely dressed and ready to be fed. He felt more inept than ever.

"Don't feel bad, Dennis. Remember. I've had a month at this. Give it a week, and you'll be an expert at changing babies. With or without the duct tape."

Her little grin did funny things to his stomach, but he attributed it to being overtired.

Fortunately, this time Raymond wasn't screaming in his face while Dennis waited for the bottle to heat up. As before, Adelle came out of the bedroom with a very tired Rachel when Raymond was only halfway through the bottle.

"Watch me," Adelle said quietly. She sat beside him and sat Rachel on her knee, supporting her head between the 'V' of her thumb and index finger. Rachel was all scrunched up and didn't look at all comfortable, but she wasn't complaining. "This is how you burp a baby. See how I'm supporting her head? And see how she's leaning forward on my hand?"

Dennis nodded. It wasn't the way he'd been shown, but what he'd been doing hadn't exactly worked very well, and he didn't want to repeat his earlier experience. Not only had he already embarrassed himself enough for one day, but he only had two more shirts in his suitcase.

"If she spits up anything with the burp, it will be on the floor instead of me. If this was a carpet instead of linoleum, I would have a receiving blanket or a towel tucked under her, so if she spit up, she'd spit up on that."

When she was finished speaking, Adelle gently patted Rachel on the back until Rachel let out a contented little baby burp.

"There. See?"

Adelle gathered her baby up, tucked her into a tight bundle inside a receiving blanket, and gave her a cuddle. Rachel was sleeping before Raymond was finished with his bottle. Adelle carried Rachel to the playpen and settled her in.

"I think Raymond will be asleep soon, too, so we should figure out sleeping arrangements for ourselves. There are only two beds here, one in the bedroom, and the couch, which is a hide-a-bed."

He'd never slept on a hide-a-bed, but he knew people complained about them being uncomfortable. However, after being given shelter from the raging blizzard, everything else was a bonus, including a soft surface to sleep on. "I'll take the hide-a-bed. I'm sure the bed in the bedroom will be more comfortable, and you deserve it. And please, don't argue with me, I insist."

"I'm too tired to argue anyway."

To his dismay, she hung around to watch as he burped Raymond the way she had shown him. He couldn't quite get the hang of it, so she had to pick Raymond up by his armpits to help position him properly.

"The trick is to support him with one hand, so you can pat him with the other."

Between the two of them, they maneuvered Raymond into what she termed the right position. Then, to his horror, she let him go. Surprisingly, Dennis really did have Raymond balanced properly.

"This doesn't look or feel right."

"Don't worry. The point is that it works. One of the elderly ladies in my church showed me this. Now burp him."

Very gently, he patted Raymond's tiny back until a burp resounded. Thankfully, it was a dry one.

"There! See?"

"I guess I can't argue with success."

Before Raymond became fully alert, Dennis laid him on the couch and tried to tuck him into a blanket. He tried three times to wrap him properly, but the cover wouldn't stay snug.

"Would you like me to do that for you?"

"If you don't mind."

In seconds flat, she had the blanket snugly around Raymond. In the time it took to walk the few steps to the playpen, Raymond was asleep.

Without speaking, Dennis unfolded the mattress out of the hide-a-bed as quietly as possible. He accepted the sheets, blankets, and a pillow, and whispered insistently that he would make his own bed. After a murmured, "good night," Adelle disappeared into the bedroom with a similar pile, and the door closed.

❅

Adelle dreamed of a baby crying way off in the distance. She didn't have to worry. It was far away, and her fuzzy brain told her it was the television.

Suddenly, Adelle jerked her head up and blinked. Complete blackness surrounded her, but the muffled baby cries didn't end. It took her a couple of seconds to realize that she wasn't at home. She was in the cabin bedroom, and the door was closed. Rachel's crib was not beside her bed. Rachel was in the living room in the playpen next to the woodstove.

And that meant Dennis Bancroft was also beside the woodstove on the hide-a-bed. Where she should have been.

Quickly, she slipped her feet into her fuzzy slippers, which were as cold as the room since the closed door shut off her heat source. She ran her hands over her sweat suit in a fruitless effort to rub out the slept-in wrinkles. Then she stumbled to the playpen.

Not only was Rachel awake, but Raymond was crying, too. Dennis was sitting on the edge of his bed. First he shook his head, then rubbed both fists over his eyes.

"What time is it?" he asked through a yawn.

Adelle tilted her watch toward the muted light of the woodstove. "It looks like it's about five. Right on time."

The crying increased in volume as they both leaned into the playpen to lift their respective babies.

"I guess they're hungry," he murmured.

She didn't think he really expected an answer, so she didn't comment.

Adelle carried Rachel back to the bedroom with her, while Dennis headed to the kitchen with Raymond.

While Rachel nursed contentedly, she could hear Dennis fumbling about in the kitchen and Raymond fretting in his own little baby way.

She'd been told that formula-fed babies often slept through the night sooner, but Adelle wasn't going to change her mind about breast-feeding Rachel, even if it did mean less sleep for a while longer. She had no idea if Raymond slept through the night, as some babies did. It was her fear that Rachel's cries woke

Raymond, rather than a full case of hunger.

Finally, at about the time she switched sides with Rachel, Raymond suddenly quieted.

Adelle smiled. This was the third time Dennis had prepared a bottle the old-fashioned way, rather than in the microwave like he had been doing previously, and she was sure he had already improved.

When Rachel was finished feeding, she fell asleep and Adelle tucked her back into the playpen. Whispering a good night to Dennis, who looked like he was struggling to keep his eyes open while Raymond drank his bottle, she tiptoed back to bed.

❄

The morning didn't bring the sunshine she wanted for her Christmas vacation. The wind had stopped, but the snow continued to fall heavily, just as the Weather Advisory had predicted.

Adelle stood at the window with Rachel in her arms, surveying the property. The gusts from yesterday had piled the snow high against the tool shed door. She'd been so distracted with Dennis being there that she hadn't thought to get the shovel out while she could open the shed without much digging. Now the only way to get the snow shovel was to dig through the massive snowdrift by hand. The woodpile against the shed wall was also covered with snow, but fortunately they had enough wood inside to last for days.

An ever-increasing pristine blanket of white evenly covered everything on the property, including her car.

Layers of snow decorated the tall pine trees, all but shouting the majestic beauty of God's creation. This quiet grandeur of God's handiwork was the authentic version of what the department stores attempted to artistically recreate in their Christmas displays. The real thing was far more impressive and didn't cost a dime.

Inside, all was safe and warm, but she would have felt more peaceful if her aunt and uncle were with her, rather than a stranger. Granted, she did feel less uncomfortable with him today than when they first arrived. By his actions, he appeared to be exactly as he claimed, and she couldn't help but feel sorry for him.

As if he knew she was thinking about him, Dennis appeared beside her, his attention also fixed outside.

The dark circles under his eyes told her what she wanted to know, but decorum dictated she should be polite and ask anyway. "Good morning, Dennis. Did you sleep well?"

He smiled politely. "I slept well, but not long enough. I guess it's something I'll get used to, like every other new parent. Can we turn on the radio? I'd like to hear an update on the forecast."

They continued looking out the window while the music played in the background.

"It never snows like this in Vancouver. Sometimes a whole winter goes by and it doesn't snow at all. When it does, it melts quickly. In fact, most of the time it doesn't even stay on the ground. It's kind of a wet slush. You can't even call it real snow. This is really pretty."

"It can be very beautiful, but the snow can also be dangerous. You have to treat it with respect."

"I think I found that out the hard way."

They stood in silence watching the snow fall. After a few songs, the announcer made a bad joke about a very white Christmas, but nothing was mentioned about the forecast.

"What do you think? Will the snow continue for another day and a half?"

Adelle nodded. "It's possible. It's happened before, but it's bad timing to have it happen at Christmas. Usually we don't get a blizzard like this until later in the season."

"Will the phone and electricity be fixed soon?"

She sighed. "I hate to be the bearer of bad news, but since this area is so remote, it's all but deserted this time of year. It's likely that no one knows it's out. And even if they did know, they're not going to risk the lives of their crew to fix it during the blizzard.

"You mean we could be without power or phone until Christmas Day, and no one would know?"

She kept her gaze fixed out the window. "That's exactly what I mean."

❄

A wave of dread hit Dennis so strongly, he felt his stomach lunge.

He wished he could pinch himself and awaken from this nightmare, but he knew the situation was very real. So he prayed for a miracle. Actually, he prayed for many miracles: first that the phone service would be restored; secondly, that the snow would stop; and thirdly, that somehow, he could find a way to get home quickly.

"I put a pot of water on top of the woodstove earlier. I figured that instead of having to use so much propane every time we need warm water, we can use the woodstove, since it's a never-ending source of heat. I'm going to need lots of warm water soon, because I bathe Rachel every morning. Do you have a routine in place yet?"

He tried to keep the cynicism out of his voice. "Are you kidding? I've never bathed him, never mind set a routine in place. I had planned to be home yesterday, where I would have help with all this stuff and someone who knew what they were doing."

What he had planned was for Joanna to help him. He knew she didn't have much more experience with babies than he did, but between the two of them, and perhaps a part-time nanny, he thought they could manage. After all, they were formally engaged. Or at least they had been, until yesterday.

Their families had lived next door to each other since before he could remember. They had played together as children, dated as teens, and continued their relationship as adults. When Dennis found himself approaching thirty years old and still single, Joanna had suggested that it was time to get married, and at the time, he thought it was a good idea. All their friends thought it was natural when they announced their engagement.

Since they had been a part of each other's lives since childhood, Dennis thought that although he didn't feel the sparks and fireworks of love and romance shown in the movies, that didn't mean they weren't right for each other. It only meant such things were highly overrated.

Now he looked at it from a different perspective. He'd dated a few women besides Joanna but none of them ever lasted. Joanna had always managed to show him some fault he hadn't been aware of, or she convinced him that he didn't need anyone else because he had her. He'd been so busy with his business he hadn't realized until now that he was being manipulated.

She was more than eager to share in the benefits of his business and his successes, but accepting responsibility for his nephew was work and raising a child would cut into her social life.

Dennis stared out into the snow without really seeing it. Joanna didn't really love him. She was just using him in order to have a privileged future. If he had to think about it, he didn't love her either. He was more accustomed to her constant presence than feeling any deep emotional need to share his life with her.

When he thought of the traits a partner perfect for him would have, in hindsight, Joanna didn't posses many. Her selfishness in refusing to help with Raymond stung. Joanna had been the first person he'd called when Harv died. She'd expressed her regrets, and then when he told her he now had legal guardianship of Raymond, instead of sympathy for an orphaned infant, she became adamant that she wasn't going to raise someone else's baby. He had been in such shock that he didn't want to argue with her, but she'd pressed on to make him choose between her and the baby.

In the past he'd always caved in to her because nothing she'd ever asked had been that important, or at least he hadn't thought so. It stunned him to think that she thought she had the power to influence him to abandon a baby—the only family he had left.

He praised God he had been able to see what was happening before it was too late. Even if it meant that he would be a single dad by default, it was better than marriage to someone who only wanted him for the material gain and comfortable lifestyle he could provide.

"Dennis?"

He blinked and turned to Adelle, who was looking at him as if she expected him to say something.

"I'm sorry. I was thinking about something else. Did you ask me something?"

Her cheeks flushed. "I asked if you wanted to watch me bathe Rachel. The same lady who showed me how to burp Rachel also gave me the handiest thing for bathing a baby. I just know you'll want one."

He sighed. He had so much to learn, and if he was going to do it alone he supposed this was a good place to start.

She pulled a large roasting pan out of the closet. Her cheeks flushed again, which he thought was kind of cute. "I'm not going to roast her," she mumbled as she set the roaster on the counter beside the sink. "Aunt Min told me to use this instead of lugging my baby washtub all the way here."

He smiled back. "I'm glad."

His heart nearly stopped when it looked like she was going to give him Rachel to hold. She hesitated, then fortunately for him, placed Rachel in the infant car seat on the floor, and filled the tub with the water she had in the pot on the woodstove. She then put what looked like a terry-towel ramp into the tub, undressed Rachel, and laid her on it.

"That looks kinda comfy."

She nodded as she soaped the baby. "Yes. And it also lets me use both hands while she's supported."

Before he knew it, she was done, and Rachel was dressed in a clean sleeper. Adelle smiled at him. "Your turn."

He laid Raymond in his infant car seat. Then together they dumped the used water and refilled the roasting pan. When everything was ready, he began to undress Raymond. But, as he opened the diaper, his stomach churned. Dennis held his breath. Still, the war in his stomach continued.

"It looks like you picked just the right time to bathe him."

"Uh. . .yeah. . ."

He did his best to wipe Raymond up as quickly as he could, hoping he wouldn't pass out. This was what he had dreaded, and also what he would have appreciated help with, but Adelle didn't offer to help, nor did she offer to dispose of the soiled diaper.

When the mess was taken care of, he lowered Raymond into the warm water and laid him on the ramp. At first he thought Raymond was going to cry, but he didn't, which buoyed Dennis's confidence. With far more self-assurance than when he'd begun, he dressed Raymond in his last clean sleeper.

He cradled Raymond against his chest and stood at the window to watch the nonstop snowfall. Clothes for Raymond weren't the only things he was running out of.

The next time he fed Raymond, it would be the last bottle of formula, and he didn't know what to do.

He again turned his attention to what was happening outside. The heavy snowfall hadn't changed since the last time he looked at it. On the outside chance that something had changed, he picked up the phone.

"Anything?"

"No." He hung up and stared at the phone. He really didn't know what to do. In his business he always had a Plan B. Out here in the middle of nowhere, there was no Plan B. "We're really going to be stranded out here for days, aren't we?"

"It looks that way."

"Is there any way to contact anyone, any way at all?"

"I'm afraid not."

He lowered Raymond into the car seat on the floor, calculating the time since he'd been fed. He'd be hungry again in approximately two hours, and that would last until suppertime. Then he would have to trust God that a miracle would happen, because a miracle was all he had left.

Chapter 6

After Rachel's afternoon feeding, Adelle sank to the couch. If she were at home, she would have crawled into bed for a nap while Rachel slept during the daytime. Now that she had to entertain a guest, she didn't have that option.

Dennis requested she turn on the radio again, just in case there was an update to the weather forecast. While the music played, he stood at the window with Raymond, talking to him and explaining the difference between the snow and the rain in the wintertime, which Adelle thought rather sweet. It was also quite an education.

Having been raised in Blue River and never having gone far from home, she found his stories fascinating. She had never been to Vancouver and couldn't imagine living in a place that didn't get snow in the winter. She imagined it would be boring with green all year round and no winter snow to enjoy.

He was silent when the announcer's voice came on between the songs with the news that no change was expected in the forecast. They turned the radio off to conserve the batteries.

Since she had nothing to do, Adelle heated a bottle for Dennis and then sat beside him as he fed Raymond and put him into the playpen to sleep.

With both babies asleep, they were forced to talk to each other. They stood in the kitchen, away from the sleeping babies, so as not to disturb them.

Dennis checked again for dial tone and then toyed absently with the phone cord, not looking at her as he spoke. "I have a problem. That was my last bottle of formula. I don't know what I'm going to do."

Adelle looked toward the fridge. "I know plain cow's milk isn't great for babies, but it will do in an emergency. I have a couple of gallons of milk. That should last for a while if we don't drink it and leave it all for Raymond. As soon as the phone is back, there must be some kind of emergency service we can contact that can either have someone come out here by snowmobile, or maybe when it stops snowing they could drop a case of formula out of a plane. I don't know what they call that. Kind of like an airlift, except they don't lift anything, they drop it out. By parachute or something."

He shook his head and continued to stare at the dead phone. Now, more than ever, he felt the loss of his cell phone. "I can't give Raymond milk. I remember Harv telling me that Raymond is lactose intolerant. I asked the health nurse what that meant, and she told me that he'd get really sick if he drank cow's milk. Not just sick. He'd have severe cramps. He'd vomit and have bad diarrhea. That also means dehydration, which for a baby is really bad, not including the pain he'd be in. I need your help, Adelle. I'm sorry."

Adelle didn't know what to say. She'd been told about that kind of thing in prenatal class, but since she'd already decided to breast-feed her baby she hadn't really paid much attention when the teacher had spoken on the different kinds of formula and the possibilities and ramifications of lactose intolerance. Now she wished she would have.

At least now she knew why Dennis had been so concerned about getting home. It was not to get away from her, but because of Raymond's dietary requirements. She didn't know what she could scrounge up to feed him if he couldn't drink milk. Even if a baby so small could eat applesauce or pureed apples, they didn't have a blender. And if they did, there was no electricity to run it.

A sick feeling of dread came over her as she imagined what it would be like trying to help little Raymond, not just to try to soothe him, because he wouldn't understand why he was hungry or why his tummy hurt from eating the wrong thing. Knowing how much he would be suffering broke her heart for him already. The poor darling didn't know what was in store for him. For now, he was sleeping soundly, expecting in his own little baby way that all his needs would be met.

Adelle wondered if his mother, before she died, gave him formula, or. . .

Her heart sank as she fully realized what Dennis was asking when he said he was sorry.

The only way to help Raymond was for her to feed him. He wanted her to nurse someone else's baby.

She turned to watch Rachel as she slept. Adelle had her own baby to feed. He was asking her to nurse both of them until help arrived or he found some way to get Raymond home.

She turned toward him and noticed he made very direct eye contact, as if he dared not look elsewhere. She couldn't help crossing her arms over herself.

He didn't say a word, but he didn't have to. The regret in his eyes said everything he couldn't put into words.

She didn't know if she could do it. She was. . .small.

Her gaze drifted to Raymond, asleep in the playpen, right beside Rachel. They were born only days apart. They could have been almost twins.

Many women breast-fed twins. And it wasn't like they were big. They were only one month old. A baby that size couldn't possibly eat much, although she had never measured.

Adelle realized she didn't have a choice. She couldn't let Raymond suffer, and she certainly couldn't let him starve, which was what could potentially happen if he couldn't digest cow's milk.

Dennis's voice came out in a low, gravelly sound. "I'll never be able to thank you, Adelle. I don't even know what to say. But if you ever need anything from me, anything, just name it."

She knew she would never ask him for anything. Given the circumstances, she couldn't refuse to help.

She tried to speak clearly through the tightness in her throat. "Don't worry about it."

His whole body sagged, his relief almost tangible. "I know it will be hard on you. Please, tell me what I can do to give you a hand."

Adelle shuffled her feet. "There isn't much to do."

She felt silly just standing in the kitchen. The polite thing to do should have been to sit together on the couch and talk, but that was too close to the sleeping babies and she didn't want their voices to disturb them. She also didn't want to get too close to Dennis. Not that he had said or done anything threatening, he'd been nothing but a gentleman. She just couldn't sit beside him.

They stared at each other, glanced around the small cabin, then back to each other.

Adelle cleared her throat. "You know what we need? I was thinking about it when I was on the way here. Before I picked you up, I mean. Every Christmas, when my family comes to the cabin Aunt Min makes her secret recipe holiday cocoa. It's only two days before Christmas, and I think that's what we should do. We need a holiday treat to get ourselves in the holiday mood."

"I've never made cocoa before, all I do is dump the package in a cup, add some water, and put it in the microwave for a couple of minutes. I wouldn't know what to do."

"The microwave? You can't make real cocoa in the microwave. You've got to use real ingredients and heat it in a pot. It tastes different. I don't know why, it just does. What you're talking about isn't real cocoa, that's processed hot chocolate." She started searching through the cupboards for what she needed. "I have milk, and I know there is sugar here. If the other ingredients were left the last time they used the cabin, I can show you the best cocoa in the world."

When the two steaming cups were ready, she set them on the table. They both cradled the warm mugs in their hands across the table from each other. Adelle felt like she could have been looking in a mirror, except it wasn't herself looking back.

He held the cup under his nose, sniffed the warm beverage, and sighed. "This smells so good. Is that a hint of mint in there, besides the cocoa?"

Adelle nodded. "Yes. I hope I've done it right. I've not made this for a whole year. I sometimes wonder if Aunt Min has withheld the last secret ingredient. It always tastes better when she makes it."

"She makes this every Christmas? Only at Christmas?"

She took a slow, cautious sip, so she wouldn't burn her tongue. "Yes. I look forward to this every year. I come to the cabin every year for Christmas, and my parents come here every second year. They alternate between this and my brother's house in California. This year is the year for California."

"That's too bad. It would probably have been nice for them to be with Rachel on her first Christmas."

"I have to admit that I was a little disappointed with their decision. My brother Andrew has two kids, a boy and a girl, and there's been a couple times where they've gone to California two years in a row. I wonder if part of what draws them, besides their obvious love for their grandchildren, is the weather. They're getting close to retirement, and I think they might be considering moving south for the winters."

"I hear lots of people do that. Snowbirds."

She stared down into her mug. "They do," she mumbled. "But I thought they would want to spend some time with Rachel, especially while she's young."

Adelle bit her bottom lip, then quickly took anther sip of her cocoa. She couldn't believe she had told him that. She had never mentioned what she just told Dennis to anyone, not at church, not even to her closest friend. He just seemed easy to talk to, and she couldn't put her finger on why. Perhaps, because he was a Christian.

"You know, drinking my aunt's cocoa makes me want to decorate. There should be something around here to remind us of Christmas. Aunt Min was going to bring all the decorations, but there's probably something around here we could do to get us in the mood for Christmas."

"I thought they spent Christmas here every year. Wouldn't she store the decorations here?"

Adelle laughed for the first time in too long, and it felt good. "This place is really small. There's barely enough room for the necessities, never mind a box of decorations. You also have to know my aunt. Since the cabin is in a really remote area, she keeps some necessities here, but nothing she really values, as you can see by looking around the place. She does that in case a vagrant breaks in and either steals everything or trashes the place. There is a special story behind every single one of my aunt's ornaments, and she would never take the chance anything could happen to them. Before we go home, everything is carefully packed and taken back to their attic at their house."

"That sounds really special. I bet there are homemade things in there, right? Things made by her own children?"

"They never had kids, unfortunately. Maybe that's one reason I've always been really close to them." Adelle couldn't hold back her grin. "I must admit, they spoil me."

Dennis grinned back, and it took her by surprise. It occurred to her that this was the first time since they'd been together that she'd seen him smile like he meant it, not just for the sake of good manners. He really was a good-looking man. Adorable little crinkles formed at the sides of his eyes when he smiled, and when he smiled so broadly, a pair of very attractive dimples appeared in his cheeks.

She wondered if he smiled more often when he was in familiar surroundings. He didn't seem to be the shy and silent type, but at the same time, he wasn't exactly sharing the intimate details of his life either. Of course, they'd met less than twenty-four hours ago, so she didn't expect to suddenly get a life history from him. She wondered what he did for a living and how long he'd been a Christian.

His voice broke her out of her daydreams. "Everyone needs to be spoiled, sometimes."

She forced herself to remember what they were talking about. "Yes. I had the best dressed Barbie on the block. My parents couldn't afford extravagant doll clothes and my mom didn't sew, but Aunt Min did. She made so many beautiful clothes for my Barbie that my Barbie was better dressed than I was."

He never lost his grin. "I find that hard to believe."

"It's true. I was a bit of a tomboy, and my mother gave up trying to make me wear dresses. The only place I ever wore a dress was to church, and that was entirely under protest. But enough of that. Let's start decorating before the babies wake up."

She tried to remember some childhood Christmas craft idea. All she could think of that might be available in the cabin was aluminum foil—which wasn't colorful, but at least it was shiny.

She found scissors, although she couldn't find any cardboard to cut for shaping. Dennis watched without offering to help as she cut and scrunched enough foil to fashion a crude but recognizable star.

"Tah-dah!" she sang out, holding her masterpiece up for him to see.

One of the babies gurgled at the sound of her voice. Dennis froze, and Adelle slapped her hands over her mouth, with the star dangling from her fingers.

"See?" she said in a stage whisper. "Now to put it by the window, because that way is north."

"I really don't think it matters."

"But it does! Every year we set out a special nativity set and, instead of just putting them out for decoration, we reenact the Christmas story. We put the innkeeper in the stable, and Mary and Joseph and the donkey start by the couch over there." She pointed to the couch, and he actually turned his head to look where she was pointing.

"Every day we move them a bit closer toward the stable. When we were kids, Andrew and I had lots of fun moving them. The shepherds and sheep went beside the coffee table, over there, and the wise men and their camels were in the kitchen, which is the easternmost part of the cabin."

"This sounds like quite a process."

"It is. And then on Christmas morning we brought out the star and put it on top of the tree. Mary and Joseph got moved all the way to the stable, and we brought out Jesus like he'd just been born. Then we prayed before opening our gifts. I'd like to do the same thing as Rachel grows up."

Dennis nodded. "That sounds like a good way to start Christmas Day."

She nodded back. "Yes. And after we tore into the gifts and cleaned up the mess, then we moved the sheep and shepherds into the stable. The day after Christmas, we started moving the wise men and their camels across the room until New Year's Day, when they would finally make it to the stable. And then we'd pack everything up until the next year."

"It sounds like a special way to remind the family, especially the children, of the real meaning of Christmas, which is the celebration of the birth of Jesus Christ."

Adelle sighed. "Yes. I really am going to miss not putting everything out this year. That set is getting a little more tattered as time goes on, but it seems to make it more special. Of course, that set is my Aunt's favorite Christmas decoration, and that's why she couldn't bear it if anything ever went missing."

"My family never had any real tradition like that."

Adelle walked to the window and tied the star onto the cord from the mini-blinds as best she could, and then patted it for effect when it was in place. "I really miss Aunt Min's decorations. The cabin doesn't feel like Christmas. But I guess this is a start."

She stood back to admire her handiwork. There wasn't any sunshine to reflect on it, since the heavy clouds obliterated the sun. The constant snowfall made the world appear pasty white.

Dennis stood by her side at the window but kept a respectable distance.

"I wonder how deep it is out there. It's been snowing nonstop for twenty-four hours now, with still no end in sight."

"That lump over there is my car. It looks like it's almost halfway up the door, but it's hard to tell."

The sound of stirring behind them signified the end of their efforts to make the cabin more festive.

Adelle checked the time. She didn't know how mothers of twins did it, but she imagined that feedings must be staggered. Rachel usually wanted to be fed approximately every four hours, so she would have to try to feed them two hours apart. She also didn't know how long it would take for her own body to increase the supply with the new demands.

Since Rachel was awake and Raymond had been fed most recently, Adelle retired with Rachel into the bedroom and shut the door. Whatever happened, she would do her best with whatever God put before her.

✳

Dennis tried to relax, but he couldn't. As little as he knew about babies in general, he knew less about this.

One thing he did know was that Raymond wanted a bottle every four to six hours and Rachel would likely be just as demanding. That meant Adelle would have to alternate feedings, and using simple math, he figured that every two to three hours, she'd be at it again, as the babies took turns.

His stomach clenched at the thought of what he was asking her to do, but there was no other way. He couldn't see it lasting more than a few days, but at that rate, by the time they were either rescued or they could contact someone to deliver a case of formula out here in the middle of nowhere, Adelle would be exhausted. However, while he knew it was going to be hard on Adelle, it was life or death for Raymond.

The knowledge gave him little comfort.

Raymond woke while Adelle was still behind the closed door with Rachel, which gave Dennis the chance to change Raymond without her watching his every wrong move.

He cradled Raymond and stroked his tiny back, but all of his attentions were fixed on the closed bedroom door. He wasn't going to be of much use with the baby care beyond changing diapers, and he still wasn't much good at that. But he had his roll of duct tape when all else failed.

However, even if he couldn't help much with the babies, there were other ways he could give Adelle a break. For starters, he could make today's supper.

Chapter 7

Dennis turned the burner down just as Adelle walked out of the bedroom.

"What are you doing?" she asked as she lowered Rachel to the quilt and began changing her. "I thought you already used the last bottle."

"I'm making supper for us. I don't see a turkey here, so I guess we should save that nice little ham you brought for our Christmas dinner. Out of the choices I have left, I'm making my specialty, spaghetti, for supper."

"Thank you. I don't know what to say."

He nodded in response. Usually his housekeeper left him dinner every day, hot and ready for when he got home from the office. Most weekends he went out with Joanna for supper. For the rare times he had to fend for himself, spaghetti was the only thing he could cook with any proficiency. He wondered what Adelle would say when he cooked spaghetti for supper again tomorrow.

"I put Raymond in the car seat and left him in the middle of the counter so he could see me. As long as I kept talking, he didn't cry. I just might make a spaghetti fan out of him. I wonder how long it will be before I can feed him spaghetti."

"A long time, I think. Don't get your heart set on it anytime soon."

He shrugged his shoulders. "This fatherhood thing is making me look at my life in a whole new way. I've always thought that one day I'd have kids of my own, but I've never really considered what I'd do once I got one."

She smiled, and Dennis nearly dropped the spoon into the pot. When she first picked him up after his accident he had thought her appearance rather ordinary, but he could see now that he'd been wrong. She wasn't a classic beauty, but she had an honest charm that made her flaws unimportant. For starters, she had beautiful brown eyes that sparkled when she smiled.

She lowered her head and continued the process of changing Rachel. "I didn't expect to be a parent, either. But at least I had nine months to get ready for it."

He had thought about Adelle for a good portion of the night when he should have been sleeping. He didn't think that most women would keep a baby to love and cherish when the baby had been the result of a rape, yet that was exactly what Adelle had done. It made him want to know more, but at the same time, he mentally kicked himself for being so morbid.

He swallowed hard, then pretended to concentrate on stirring the spaghetti as it cooked. Finally, he could no longer hold back. "Did you know the father?"

"Yes. Not well, but I did know him. I worked with him. Worst of all, I trusted him. He was giving me a ride home from work. Then, at the last minute, we decided to go out for dinner. The next thing I knew I was in bed with my mother beside me, worried to death because I had passed out. Shawn had taken me to my mother's house and told her that I had an allergic reaction to something I ate and passed out. She managed to give me my allergy medication, and she was about to take me to the hospital because I wasn't responding, when I woke up."

Dennis knew the answer, but he had to ask the question. "He gave you a date rape drug?" He'd heard of date rape drugs, but he'd never actually spoken to anyone who had experience with them, either to use them, or to use them on someone else. The very idea made him sick.

She held Rachel close as she spoke and wouldn't look at him while she was speaking. "Yes. Looking back, he would have slipped it into my drink when I went to the washroom. I remember thinking it odd that he adamantly insisted on not leaving the drinks behind when we were ready to go. It happened so quickly I don't even remember passing out, but I obviously did. I didn't know I was pregnant for the longest time. It took even longer to figure out how it happened, but as soon as I did, I laid charges against him."

Dennis was speechless. His thoughts and emotions bounced around inside him, from rage to sympathy to a flood of other feelings he couldn't identify. He knew there was nothing he could do, but he wanted to help her in some way. Instead, she was the one helping him.

"Is he going to be giving you some kind of child support?"

"I don't know. I have to think about what I'm going to do. He wants no part of me or the baby, but his parents desperately want to be included in their grandchild's life. They've offered me support, but I don't know yet if I'm going to take it. If I did, that would tie me to obligations I'm not sure I want. That's the main reason I needed to come here, and why I said a little snow wasn't going to stop me. I wanted to have some time away from everything to think about it."

"And now you're stuck with me and my problems. I'm so sorry, Adelle."

Her sad smile nearly broke his heart. "It's not your fault. I'm sure God can use this for our good somehow. We might not understand why it happened, but there is a reason for this."

Dennis already knew the reason. In fact, it was two reasons. First, it was a lesson to use his common sense, which had completely deserted him when he left Hinton. He'd wanted so much to go home, as if getting out of his brother's house and back into familiar surroundings would somehow ease the pain of losing Harv and Katie. Instead, he'd ignored the forecast and the falling snow and chosen to discount his inexperience in driving in it. By doing so, he had made a bad situation worse.

The second lesson was a difficult one to learn. Although Joanna had given him the ultimatum to chose between herself and Raymond, he had hoped that when Joanna actually saw Raymond and held him, she would change her mind. He hoped if he hurried home, before she had too much time to think about it, if she spent Christmas Day with Raymond as an infant, she would fall in love with him and change her mind about being an instant stepmom as soon as they got married. Her selfish response to his phone call was a real eye-opener. She wasn't concerned about his welfare, or even where he was. She only wanted his assurance that he was going to commence with adoption procedures. The only adoption procedure he would start was his own adoption of Raymond.

His only regret was that because of him, Adelle's first Christmas with her lovely daughter would be tainted by his presence and what he was forcing her to do for Raymond's sake.

"I think the spaghetti is ready. Time to eat."

After he dished out the food, she bowed her head, waiting for him to pray the blessing on the food. He had previously joked about food cooling while waiting for a prayer to be finished, but he truthfully had so much to pray for that their food would be stone-cold by the time he was done. So once again, he prayed only for the meal before them.

He cleared his throat. "Dear heavenly Father, thank you the shelter and safety you've provided, this meal before us, and for new friends to share it with. Amen."

"Amen." Her smile told him that she agreed with him.

Despite the questions he wanted to ask, Dennis limited their conversation to pleasant small talk. When they had finished eating and cleared the table, they sat together on the couch and continued their conversation where they left off. He discovered they enjoyed the same books and found the same things funny. Both of them were actively involved in their churches, and they had a shared love for youth ministry.

About an hour after they had finished with supper, Raymond started to get fussy, which could only mean one thing.

Raymond was hungry.

❄

As Raymond became increasingly fussy, Adelle's stomach became increasingly queasy. She had lost count of the number of times she repeated in her head the fact that, throughout history, many women nursed babies who were not their own. Many women also nursed twins.

When they were all acutely aware that nothing short of food in his tummy would quiet Raymond, Adelle sucked in a deep breath, laid Rachel in her car seat, and took Raymond from Dennis.

Dennis's face paled, and when she actually lifted Raymond from his arms, the paleness turned to a deep shade of red in his cheeks, extending to his ears.

She knew from the heat in her own cheeks that she was blushing, too. Rather than making the situation any more awkward, Adelle turned and walked silently into the bedroom.

Before opening her blouse, Adelle snuggled Raymond close, rocking him gently while she talked, keeping her voice low. She told him her name, and that she was from Blue River, and that Rachel was the same age as he was, and that his uncle Dennis loved him very much.

For a while her voice calmed him, but when talking alone no longer soothed him, she opened her blouse and prayed that it would work, for both of them.

He didn't take long to catch on to the idea. He ate well, but she feared that he would be hungry again soon because she wasn't yet producing the volume required for two babies.

While he ate she ran her fingers over his soft cheeks. He was a darling baby, and her heart went out to him, losing his parents before he really could know or appreciate them. She burped him, but rather than leaving the sanctuary of the bedroom, she held him close and stroked his tiny back.

Since Dennis had just broken up with his fiancée, that would mean Raymond would not have the love of a mother figure in his life beyond paid child care while Dennis was at work. Knowing this made Adelle want to do what she could for him in the short time she was a part of his young life.

When she returned to the living room, Dennis was holding Rachel beside the window, staring out into the last of the daylight, watching the steady snowfall. He kept his gaze focused out the window as he spoke.

"She started to get fussy, so I thought I'd pick her up. I think she missed you."

She wanted to tell him that Raymond had missed him, but she really didn't know. Truthfully, she doubted that Raymond had proper time to bond to Dennis. She knew Dennis already loved Raymond, but it was more the connection to his brother than a personal one-on-one relationship with the child.

When earlier she had said she didn't know the reason for being stranded together at her family's cabin, she now knew. Dennis and Raymond needed this time together with no distractions and nothing to concentrate on except each other.

With both babies being so young that she couldn't risk not supporting their heads as she and Dennis traded babies, she walked to Rachel's car seat, still on the floor between the couch and the woodstove. "If you put Rachel down, I'll give Raymond back to you. I think he needs you."

Dennis turned. "Why? Is he wet?"

Her breath caught at the sight of the way Dennis was holding Rachel. He had her leaning into his chest, using one hand to hold her up by her padded bottom, his other large hand splayed across her back, with two fingers supporting her head. Rachel was limp against him, on the verge of falling asleep. Despite his inexperience with babies, his touch was gentle but firm. They were completely relaxed with each other, like it should have been if Dennis was Rachel's father rather than a stranger.

Watching Dennis with Rachel only magnified the absence of a man in her life. She had fully accepted that she would probably never marry, as there were plenty of single women in her small community without the added encumbrance of a baby. As much as she wished Rachel had a father who loved and appreciated her, Adelle missed the presence of a man to cherish her as a woman. She longed for a man she could love and who would love her back as a partner.

What little social life she had drastically declined when she was pregnant, and in the past month, since Rachel's birth, it had dropped to zero. With the added stigma of charging Shawn with rape and putting him in jail, she didn't expect many men would risk going out with her, especially since she did not intend to explain what had happened.

Counseling sessions had helped her to deal with the situation, but she still lacked the ability to trust except in rare instances. So far, Dennis was one of those rare men whom she felt she could trust. She believed that he was a Christian, as he claimed, and his honesty of his shortcomings made her want to trust him.

"I think I'll put her down in the playpen. She seems to have fallen asleep. I hope you don't mind."

"Of course I don't mind. I just can't let her sleep too long, or she will be up all night."

Dennis hesitated in the middle of lowering Rachel. "So far I've only heard what it's like to be up all night with a crying baby. I don't think it's something I'm looking forward to. Maybe I shouldn't let her sleep."

"It's okay. Really."

He continued to lower Rachel until she was settled. She transferred Raymond to him, lit the candle on the coffee table, and sat beside him on the couch.

"I couldn't help noticing the way you were holding Rachel. You're going to make a good father to Raymond. Really."

"I don't know. I hope so, and of course I'll do my best. I still really don't know what I'm in for. I don't even know what I should call myself. I know he won't remember his father, so he wouldn't know the difference if I had him call me, 'Daddy.' But I'm not his daddy. I'm his uncle Dennis. I want to figure out some way for him to think of his father in love and never forget Harv. I'm so confused. For a while I thought of having him call me, 'Uncle Daddy.' Isn't that ridiculous?"

He smiled a very humorless smile, and her heart went out to him. She didn't know how she would feel if anything ever happened to her brother, Andrew. Although they lived thousands of miles apart, she still loved him very much.

"I don't know. You still have lots of time to decide."

"I suppose. As time goes on, I expect that he'll look a lot like me, because Harv and I looked a lot alike. Right now, though, I can't say he looks like anybody, either Harv or Katie. At the funeral, lots of people, especially the older ladies would look at him and say how much he looked like his father, then burst out crying. At least we're going to look related."

"I don't think it really matters. Lots of adopted kids obviously don't look like either parent, but no one cares. The important thing is that you love him. I think you're going to do just fine with him."

"Yes, I guess so."

Rachel started to wiggle, so Adelle picked her up, and they both sat on the couch with their babies, serving almost as chaperones, in their laps.

"It's still snowing so hard that your car is covered. It's just a white lump. I've never seen snow like this in my entire life. It makes me wish I could take some home and spread it on my lawn for my neighbors to enjoy."

Dennis gritted his teeth. He was starting to babble, but he had to change the subject. He knew Adelle was sincere in her support. Again, he was comparing her to Joanna. Every time he'd spoken to Joanna, including when he phoned her for help, all she did was remind him that he didn't know what he was doing, and it was a big mistake if he thought he would be able to handle a baby.

Adelle, on the other hand, did everything she could to encourage him and help him to learn.

He couldn't figure out now why he'd thought he and Joanna would have been suitable marriage partners. Like him, Joanna had been raised in a Christian home, she attended church regularly with him every Sunday, but other than that, he couldn't see much that reflected the fruits of the Spirit. She was pleasant on the surface and did all the right things, but below the surface, she was self-centered and shallow.

He shook his head and stared at the glow of the woodstove. His relationship with Joanna was over. When the day came for him to get married, he would choose someone with a warm heart, someone who could put her own needs aside for others, a woman who laughed not to stroke his ego, but when she really thought something was genuinely funny. A woman with whom he shared common interests and goals for ministry. Someone who would do what was right in the eyes of God, no matter what.

He turned to watch Adelle play with Rachel, wiggling her tiny hands and feet and humming a Christmas carol.

One day, he would fall in love with a woman like Adelle.

Chapter 8

Adelle hummed "Joy To The World" as she gently swayed Rachel in her arms, but the carol soothed her own spirit more than it calmed the baby.

The only Christmas decoration, the lone foil star hanging from the blinds, reminded her just how sparse the cabin was this year and that not only were the Christmas decorations absent, so was her family.

But at least she was spending Christmas with another Christian.

Without warning, Rachel made a strained little grunt and stiffened. Instantly Adelle knew what just happened.

She stood and laid Rachel on the quilt, which now seemed to be a permanent changing area. She didn't look up as she spoke. "Since she needs changing, after I'm done I'm going to feed her and see if I can put her to sleep. Then I'm going to go to bed, too. I think it will be a busy night for me, so I'm going to get some sleep while I have the chance."

Dennis checked his wristwatch, twisting his arm until he could see the time in the limited lighting. "You're probably right. I think Raymond is ready to fall asleep, so I'll hit the sack, too. Good night." His last word trailed off, like he was going to ask a question. Adelle turned her head to look at him.

He looked straight into her eyes and whispered, "Thank you."

❄

Adelle opened her bleary eyes to the sound of a baby's cries. She struggled to get her bearings in the dark as she rose to her feet and followed the glow. She'd lost track of whose feeding it was, since this was the fourth or fifth time she'd been awakened to nurse. Although it was nearly daylight and nearly eight hours of nighttime had elapsed, she was as exhausted as if she hadn't slept. Every time she finally managed to doze off, she was awakened again. She'd never been so exhausted in her life.

Adelle dragged her feet all the way to the living room.

As before, Dennis was in front of the playpen, leaning to pick up whoever was crying. At first, she had told him not to get up, but they soon learned that if the crying baby was picked up quickly, the other baby might stay asleep. So far, the plan had worked. However, soon it would be daylight. She didn't know what time Raymond woke up in the morning, but Rachel seldom slept past 7:00 a.m.

When daylight arrived, both babies and Dennis were awake and alert, but Adelle felt like she'd been dragged through the mill. She nearly fell asleep feeding Rachel until the growing aroma of food nudged her awake. As soon as Rachel was done, Adelle nearly ran into the kitchen, where she found a plate filled with two fried eggs and a piece of bread alongside a glass of juice. Dennis had also set out a napkin for her.

"I took a guess on making coffee in this percolator. It's not ready yet, and I've never done it this way before. And sorry about the bread. I couldn't think of a way to make toast without destroying it. I really am not a very good cook. I couldn't find any bacon, either."

"You look like you're doing fine."

He grinned, and Adelle's heart did a little flip-flop. She was sure it was because she was overtired.

"Thank you for the juice, but I'm supposed to drink milk while I'm nursing." She began to open the fridge, but Dennis appeared beside her.

"I don't think that's a good idea. I remember Harv telling me that Katie couldn't drink milk because of the thing with Raymond. She could get away with some milk in her coffee, but not much more."

Adelle knew that while she was nursing she wasn't supposed to eat things like onions or cabbage, so she supposed it only made sense to include milk in the list when Raymond was lactose intolerant.

"I'm sorry, Adelle. I seem to be saying that a lot lately."

"Don't worry about it. I guess I wasn't thinking."

"Let's eat while it's still warm. Better yet, let's eat before anyone starts crying."

Adelle thoroughly enjoyed the eggs for breakfast. She almost asked Dennis if he ate like this every morning but stopped herself. If he said he wasn't a good cook she suspected the only reason he did this was so she could avoid her usual breakfast of milk and cereal.

Dennis sighed at the pile of dirty dishes. "I don't know which is more scary. Doing the dishes or watching the babies."

"They both seem happy for the moment. Let's do the dishes together to get it over with quickly."

Adelle had never shared the chore of cleaning the kitchen with a man. She found it strange.

By the time they finished, the coffee was ready. So they moved the babies and retired to the couch.

Dennis checked his wristwatch. "About this time, I would normally be on my way to church. I can't remember the last time I missed a Sunday service."

"Same."

"How long have you been a Christian, Adelle?"

"I guess about six years. A friend took me to a Christian outreach program for young adults on Sunday nights. I initially went because of the music. Then I started paying attention to the words we were singing. I couldn't help but notice the joy of the people there, and I wanted what they had. I accepted Jesus into my heart not long after that. How about you?"

"I was born and raised in a Christian home. I made my decision at a youth group meeting when I was in my early teens."

"I guess that's why I try to help in those programs, because of the ministry there."

He smiled. "Same."

They both turned to look at the foil star at the same time. Dennis let out a wistful sigh, and she wondered if he was thinking about everything he missed in his home congregation. "You know what we should do? We should have a small prayer and worship time here, just the two of us." Adelle glanced down at the babies in their car seats on the floor, then back up to Dennis. "Well, I guess technically it's four of us."

"I'd like that."

"Great. What should we sing?"

He laughed to himself and looked out the window. "My first thought was 'White Christmas' but that's not exactly suitable for worship. How about 'Joy to The World'?"

Adelle hummed the first note. He joined in, and they found their pitch. She always enjoyed Christmas carols, but when Dennis harmonized in his rich, deep baritone, she was enthralled. They picked a few more carols, ending with "Silent Night," then sang a couple of contemporary choruses they both knew.

They sensed together when it was time to stop singing and pray. Dennis gently brushed her hand as though asking permission to touch her. In response, she grasped his fingers to let him know it was okay. He smiled, gave her hand a gentle squeeze, and bowed his head. Adelle did the same.

His prayer touched Adelle's heart. First he praised Jesus for coming to earth knowing what was going to happen to Him. He thanked Him for paying the ultimate price and sacrificing His own life to bring salvation to sinful humanity. He thanked God for the safety and shelter of Adelle's family's cabin. Then he thanked God that he'd been stranded, because he'd been forced to make personal decisions which he might not have made had he been at home.

Adelle's throat clogged, and she fought back tears at his heartfelt thanks to God for the way she picked him up as a stranger and for being able to care for all Raymond's needs.

When he was done, she had nothing to add because she didn't think she could speak without breaking down, so she simply mumbled an "Amen."

Right on cue, Raymond began to fuss, providing an excuse to break contact.

Adelle wasn't doing anything special, she was only doing what needed to be done. When she was going through the heartache and tribulation of the court trial and the events leading up to it, and then the birth of her fatherless baby, she knew many of the people in her church were praying for her. She needed their prayers and appreciated them greatly.

This was different. No one had ever prayed about her like Dennis had, and she didn't know how to handle it.

Dennis picked up Rachel while she disappeared into the bedroom with Raymond.

In the light of day, and since her brain was more alert now than in the middle of the night, she studied him as he nursed. He was a darling baby. Raymond wasn't fussy, and he had settled right in to her without squirming in the arms of this "stranger." She found herself getting rather attached to him, despite the unique circumstances that forced them together. Already she knew she'd have a hard time saying good-bye.

Dennis was waiting for her when she returned to the living room. "I think we forgot to bathe them this morning."

"You're right."

Adelle bathed Rachel first, then supervised as Dennis bathed Raymond. He did well, and she was proud of him.

She waited while he searched through all the pockets of his diaper bag.

He sighed and tossed it aside. "I'm out of diapers."

Adelle gave him one out of her diaper bag, and he cringed as he dressed his boy in a pink diaper. When he fastened the diaper, without the aid of any duct tape, he looked up and gave her a very sad smile. "Thank you, Adelle."

"Please, quit thanking me for everything. It's not a big deal. It's just a diaper. You're making me feel funny, you've thanked me so often for every little thing."

"Sorry."

She buried her face in her hands. "And quit saying you're sorry, too."

"Oops."

"Forget it. Now let's make lunch. I'm hungry."

Dennis insisted on making sandwiches, claiming it was something he actually could do in the kitchen with some degree of proficiency. Frankly, Adelle hadn't seen anything wrong with what he'd done with last night's supper, or today's breakfast.

Rachel had her lunch after they ate theirs and promptly fell asleep. Adelle couldn't stop yawning as she laid Rachel into the playpen.

"Why don't you have a nap, Adelle? You look like you could use it. I'm sure I can find something to occupy my time without getting into much trouble."

From what little she knew of Dennis, she imagined the likelihood of him getting into trouble anywhere, either here or at home, was negligible.

She smiled through another yawn. "I think I'll do that. Catch you later."

❄

Dennis had almost finished tying the last knot when he heard the bedroom door creak open.

"What in the world are you doing?"

He jumped to his feet and stood in front of his creation. "Nothing."

She craned her neck to the side, so he shuffled over a few inches, trying to block her view.

"That doesn't look like a nothing, but I can't tell what it does look like."

Dennis shuffled again so she couldn't see it.

While Adelle and Rachel were sleeping, Raymond had also fallen asleep, leaving him with nothing to do in the little cabin. Thinking about it being Christmas Eve Day reminded him that he had missed his own company's Christmas party, as well as many of the festivities at his church, when he took off to Hinton to be with his brother.

He thought of his nine-foot cedar tree at home, decorated with hundreds of ornaments, colored blinking lights, and shiny tinsel. That made him think about driving around at night to see the outdoor Christmas lights in his community.

The cabin held no signs of Christmas, save the lone foil star that Adelle had made. It distracted him. It taunted him. It called out to him. It dared him to do more.

And so he had. At least, he'd tried.

He had wandered through the cabin, first trying to overcome his uneasiness and guilt over snooping into what didn't belong to him.

Just as he feared, he didn't find anything that inspired him. Feeling like a failure, he stood in the silence of the small cabin staring out the window, watching the never-ending snow pile up on the pine trees. In the end, he couldn't stand it. He couldn't find anything inside. But he knew what he could do outside.

The door to the tool shed was nearly buried in snow. He didn't have clothes suitable for digging through the deep cold to uncover the door, so he couldn't gain access to an ax. Therefore, he had slogged through the drifts to the outer edge of the forest and started breaking branches off the trees. He had no idea what the temperature was, he only knew he'd never been outside in such dire cold in his entire life, but determination and vision kept him going.

While he fought with the branches, just like in his experience at the car, the snow kept falling on top of him—only this time, in far greater volume. Snow made its way under the collar of his leather jacket and melted down his back, which was not a pleasant sensation. Likewise, with his arms raised and yanking

181

on the branches until they snapped, so much snow had gone up into his sleeves that his arms were numb.

Since he didn't have boots, the snow had caked into his sneakers and soaked his socks, and, once again, he couldn't feel his toes. His fingers were numb just from pulling on the frozen branches.

Nothing stopped him until he had enough branches for the project he envisioned.

When he had piled up as many pine branches as he could carry, he trudged back inside. By then he was half frozen. He pulled off his icy wet sneakers and socks, and changed out of his wet clothes into new jeans and the last clean shirt in his suitcase. After he laid everything on the floor close to the woodstove to dry, he pulled the best log out of the pile of firewood, sorted his broken branches, picked the dental floss out of his travel bag, and began his project. He had almost finished when Adelle awoke.

He stood back, no longer able to hide his pathetic attempt. He had tried his best, but his imagination and his vision had far exceeded his talent.

Dennis sighed. "It's supposed to be a Christmas tree."

Chapter 9

"Well, now that you mention it, it kind of looks like a Christmas tree. . . if I use my imagination."

He could tell she was being kind. He said nothing.

"I think all it needs are a few decorations. Honest."

She was being *really* kind.

"Seriously, Dennis. You had a good idea. And it's better than nothing."

Now she was being more accurate. Although his substitute tree wasn't *much* better than nothing. He sighed and turned to appraise his creation. "I don't know why I thought I could do this. I think I'll pull it apart and throw the branches in the fire. I couldn't cut down a real tree because I couldn't get into the tool shed for an ax. I thought if I poked holes in a piece of firewood it would be like putting an artificial tree together, but I couldn't get deep enough holes without my drill."

She stepped closer, squinting as she studied it. "How did you get the branches to stay on like that?"

"I tied them on."

She stepped closer still. "With what?"

"I couldn't find any string, so I used my dental floss."

She covered her mouth with both hands. He could tell she was trying not to laugh, but she wasn't very successful.

"Necessity is the mother of invention," he mumbled.

He noticed that she stopped laughing when she saw his wet clothes laid out near the woodstove. "Oh, Dennis! You must have frozen yourself in order to do this!"

"I'm warm now. Everything will dry."

She stepped up to his makeshift Christmas tree and leaned down to touch it. "It's kind of short, but considering what you had to work with I think it's a wonderful tree. It just needs a little help. You know, like the poor little tree in the 'Charlie Brown's Christmas' special."

He found himself starting to believe her.

"Oh, I know what our first decoration will be!"

Dennis watched as she untied her foil star from the cord for the blinds and tucked it into the top branch. It didn't fit right on top, and since it was all

183

scrunched up, it wouldn't sit straight.

"That makes it look worse."

"Nonsense. This is just the beginning. Let me see what Aunt Min has around here. I'll bet there are lots of things we can use to make decorations. I did VBS for a week this past summer. And if there's anything that teaches you, it's to make crafts out of things that are cheap and easily available."

Dennis followed her around as she peeked into every cupboard.

"We don't really need the foil for cooking, so we can use it for decorating."

"I guess."

"When I was a kid, we used to string popcorn. I know Aunt Min has popcorn somewhere. I have a sewing kit in my purse, so that's something else we can do. You just have to promise not to eat the popcorn."

"Aw. Too bad. I like popcorn."

She smiled at him over her shoulder. Something funny happened in Dennis's stomach, and he wondered if he was hungry or what.

"It's not very good to eat because there won't be any butter or salt on it."

Suddenly his throat became tight. He had to force the words out. "I was just kidding."

"Here it is. I'll get a pot and the oil. Do you want to pop it, or shall I?"

"I think I'll pass."

"Let me guess. You can't pop popcorn unless it comes in a little bag that you put in the microwave for five minutes."

He grinned. "How did you know?"

She mumbled something unintelligible under her breath. He thought it best not to ask her to repeat it.

Adelle poured a little oil into the pot, turned on the burner, and was just about to dump in the popcorn when Raymond woke up. Raymond's crying naturally woke Rachel, indicating the temporary end to their decorating spree.

Dennis parked himself on the couch and cradled Rachel in his lap while Adelle disappeared into the bedroom to feed Raymond. While she was gone he studied the pathetic tree and tried to think of something else they could do to decorate it. Not a single thing came to mind. He leaned back and sprawled little Rachel over his chest and resigned himself to the idea that a few strings of popcorn would be sufficient embellishment.

When Adelle returned, they swapped babies so that they each had their own again. He hugged Raymond and patted his fuzzy little head.

He expected Adelle to sit with him on the couch, but instead she stood in front of him. "You have a choice. You can either hold both babies, or pop the popcorn."

His mouth opened but no sound came out.

"Come on, Dennis. If we don't do it now, it will never get done. Take your pick."

He glanced around the stark and functional cabin. He was used to gaiety and decorations galore at Christmas, including never-ending Christmas carols playing in the background. From the way time disappeared so quickly when tending to the babies, he had a feeling she was right. If they didn't squeeze in the time it took to do the popcorn now, there would never be time between sleeping and feeding schedules and other baby duties. At this rate, they wouldn't finish decorating until next Christmas.

He turned to the stove. Judging from his past cooking experiences, if he was the one to pop the popcorn it would only be a color suitable for a snowman's eyes and buttons, not for decorating a Christmas tree.

Supported in Adelle's arms, Rachel gurgled and made some other baby noises he couldn't describe, but at least she wasn't crying.

Dennis gritted his teeth and forced himself to smile. "I'll take the babies."

He didn't want to analyze her expression as he shuffled Raymond to make room for Rachel in his lap. Before he was completely sure he had them both securely nestled, Adelle turned and ran into the kitchen. He heard the pouf of the flame, and a minute later, the sizzle when she dropped a handful of popcorn into the pot. It fizzled and crackled, and the unpopped kernels rasped in the bottom as she shook the pot back and forth over the flame.

Dennis wanted to turn and watch Adelle, but he was too scared to move. His heart pounded in his chest when one of the babies made some kind of goo-goo sound, and they both wiggled. Not one, but two tiny lives were literally in his hands, both depending on him, trusting him not to drop them or hurt them in any way, trusting that their needs would be met.

He wondered if this was what married life was like before the availability of electricity, with the wife in the kitchen and the husband sitting in the living room next to the woodstove with the children.

Not daring to move, he kept all his attention focused intently on the babies in his lap. He could feel the glow of the heat on his face. After his adventure outside in the bitter cold, he was grateful to be near the source of heat. Behind him a few kernels exploded. The popping tempo increased to a constant nattering against the pot lid. He didn't dare to turn his head to look, as much as he wanted to.

It felt homey and comfortable, and he liked it. After the rat race and the bustle at the office, he liked to come home to a quiet house. Although, with a baby in the house, he doubted his home would ever be quiet again. Often the only reason he'd gone out with Joanna was because his home was too quiet and too empty, especially on the weekends, when his housekeeper wasn't there. He couldn't picture Joanna settled into the kitchen, happily cooking something so mundane as popcorn, especially the old-fashioned way.

Dennis squeezed his eyes shut. He had promised himself that he would no longer think of Joanna. However, he wasn't really thinking of her in a way of missing her or in any way regretting that it was over. Every time he thought of her, it was another realization of how they really weren't suited after all and thankfulness that he'd seen it in time.

"Popcorn's ready. Now all we have to do is wait for it to cool and we can make a chain and hang it on our new Christmas tree."

Her words made his heart skip a beat. She had said *our* tree, not *his* tree, or *the* tree, but *our* tree.

Adelle appeared in front of him and removed Rachel from his lap, smiling as she gave Rachel a tender little hug. Inwardly, Dennis wished she would smile at him like that.

He lifted Raymond to his chest, cradling his padded bottom with one hand and bracing the back of his head with the other. Together, he and Adelle walked to the pathetic assembled mass of branches and firewood. She was right. It was *their* tree, and this was going to be *their* Christmas.

A Christmas he would never forget.

He cleared his throat, but he couldn't get rid of the tight sensation. "I'm thirsty. Do you mind if I have something to drink before we continue?"

"Help yourself. I think I'll make myself some tea. Do you want some?"

"No thanks, I'm not really a tea drinker. If it isn't coffee, I'd prefer something cold."

Adelle cradled Rachel with one arm while she filled a pot with water and turned on the burner. Dennis walked to the fridge and, using his newly acquired balancing skills, held Raymond with one arm while he opened the fridge with the other. He searched for the milk, finally finding it at the back. He awkwardly piled the containers that stood in front of the milk onto the counter.

"Dennis! What a great idea!"

He blinked and stared at the milk carton in his hand, which he had finally reached. He thought he would drink the milk since Adelle couldn't have it, and leave the apple juice for her. He didn't think his idea worthy of comment or praise.

"We can have red popcorn!"

He closed one eye and stared at the milk container. At least he thought it was a milk container.

Before he could figure it out, Adelle appeared beside him and picked up one of the containers he had stacked on the counter.

"We can color the popcorn red with the juice from the beets!"

"You've got to be kidding."

"Red is a Christmas color. Think of how pretty it will look."

"I think white will look just fine. Like snow. It's popcorn."

She made a sound almost like a snort, which he found rather amusing. "Come on. There's enough white snow outside. We need some color. Besides, where is your sense of adventure?"

"I used up all my adventure getting the branches from outside."

"Then you can hold Rachel, and I'll do it myself."

This time, he gathered his wits before it was too late. "Never mind. I'll help you. Just tell me what to do."

"We need something to spray the beet juice on the popcorn without getting it too wet, but using enough to color it."

"Really, Adelle, I think white will be just fine. Think of how nicely the white will show up against the dark green branches."

Her enthusiastic smile dropped, and her suddenly-sad eyes tore at his heartstrings. "Okay, I give up. You're right, red popcorn will look much better."

She smiled again, and he thought he'd been set up. For some reason, he didn't mind.

He moved aside while she rummaged through the cupboards. Her voice echoed while she poked her head into a lower cupboard, sitting on the floor with Rachel in her lap. "I can't find anything. I think I'll have to sprinkle it on by hand."

"What do you mean?"

"I'll end up with red hands for a while, but it will be worth it. I'll use my fingers. But you'll have to hold Rachel again."

He still wasn't used to holding one baby, never mind two, but he couldn't refuse her, not after all she'd done for him. Besides, he didn't want to end up with red hands.

"Do I get to watch?" This time he remained standing while he balanced Raymond, then waited for her to position Rachel. He wondered if, once he arrived at home with only one baby after spending the Christmas season juggling two, he would find handling one not so bad.

Adelle cupped a hand and carefully poured a few spoonfuls of beet juice into her palm. She dipped the fingers of her other hand into the juice and began to splatter it onto the popcorn. She repeated the process until she had used all the red liquid in the beet jar.

"This didn't work as well as I hoped. The popcorn isn't really red, it's more spotted with pink, but it's still kind of pretty."

Dennis glanced at the beets in the jar, which didn't look the same without the liquid. "I'm never going to be able to think of beets in the same way again."

He turned back to the tray of popcorn. "It's not really pink, either. The sleeper Rachel is dressed in, that's pink. But the popcorn isn't really red, either. I don't know what color it is. Now your hands. They're red."

She wiggled the reddened fingers of her right hand in front of his nose. "It was worth it. As soon as the popcorn is dry we can string it together. While we're waiting, we can decorate something else. By the time Christmas Day comes, you won't recognize the place."

Dennis doubted that, but he didn't have the heart to contradict her.

To his surprise, she pulled a bucket out of the closet. "I thought we were going to decorate, we've already cleaned the place up."

She pulled a sponge out of the bottom of the bucket. "Look!"

"Uh-huh. . .it's a sponge."

"Isn't this a pretty color?"

It looked like an ordinary blue sponge.

She tossed it back into the bottom of the bucket, then pulled out a bag containing three brand new sponges from the back of the cupboard, one blue, one green, and one yellow. "This is our next decoration project."

Dennis couldn't hold back a smile. "That's a great idea. I'll get the scissors."

He rested Raymond in his car seat, Adelle laid Rachel into her car seat, and they got to work, Dennis cutting sponges into varying shapes, and Adelle making popcorn strings.

Dennis did his best to use every piece, wasting nothing. By the time he was finished, he had a pile of twenty-four colorful decorations, leaving him quite proud of himself.

They walked in circles around the tree, carefully positioning the popcorn garland until it was set exactly right. Although it was only thread holding the popcorn strings together, Dennis thought it added some stability to his questionable construction.

Rachel started to fret, so Adelle picked her up, leaving Dennis to position the sponges as he saw fit. Adelle offered several suggestions, but it took two hands to poke the sponges onto the pine needles, sometimes taking many tries before the sponges would finally adhere to the branches.

"She's getting too fussy. I'll be back in fifteen minutes."

Dennis wasn't ready to give up, especially since Raymond was being cooperative. The only other item Adelle had left out for future decorating was the roll of foil. He picked it up and unwound the roll to discover that only a few feet of foil remained, meaning whatever he made, it would have to be single thickness to make it go farther.

Very carefully, he cut the length into twelve squares, folded them, and began to cut snowflakes, just like he had done with construction paper in grade school.

Cautiously, he poked holes and created intricate snowy shapes. Then, slowly and delicately, he picked the layers apart and opened his first foil design.

By the time he heard the bedroom door creak open, he had completed three snowflakes.

She lowered the sleeping Rachel into the playpen. "Those are nice. You've done a lovely job."

Dennis grinned, feeling rather silly about how her compliment of his questionable artwork on this children's project affected him.

Adelle ran her fingers on one of the branches. "I think they're too big to put on the tree. Why don't we use thread and hang them to decorate the rest of the cabin?"

"Don't you think there's enough snow outside, without making it snow inside?"

"It's going to stop snowing sometime. It's not going to last forever."

Dennis stopped cutting and turned his head toward the window. For now, the snow was still falling fast and thick, but she was right, it wouldn't last forever. And when it stopped, this small part of the world would start to dig itself out. The power would go on and the phone service would be restored, and he would be that much closer to being able to go home. Strangely, not only was he no longer in a rush to leave, he didn't want to leave at all.

"How would you like to keep doing that, and I'll make supper? I'm really hungry."

"That sounds great. But don't go to a lot of trouble. Just do something simple and quick, so we can finish doing this while it's still light. The light is already starting to fade."

He lowered the snowflake-in-progress to his knee. "Oh, and Adelle, thank you."

"Dennis. . ."

He couldn't hold back his laugh. "Oops. I forgot, I wasn't supposed to thank you for anything anymore."

"That's right."

He put down the scissors and the folded piece of foil and followed Adelle, who was already in the kitchen and starting to prepare supper.

"In that case, instead of thanking you, let me do this."

She backed out of the fridge, her arms full, balancing a package of lunch meat, a loaf of bread, jars of mustard and mayonnaise, a couple of wrapped slices of cheese, and a head of lettuce.

Dennis stepped closer. He had never met anyone like Adelle. At first he had thought her appearance rather ordinary, but after spending so much intense time with her, he'd changed his mind. She was quite pretty, but not in a movie star or fashion-model sense of beauty. Between her messy hair, the casual and rumpled clothing, including her pink fuzzy slippers, an armful of groceries, and the total lack of makeup, she was the antithesis of what anyone could call sophisticated.

"What?" she asked.

What she lacked in elegance, she more than overcame with her honest charm and caring heart.

He cupped her cheeks with his hands and rubbed his thumbs into her hair behind her ears. She had the kindest eyes he'd ever seen, and when she smiled, he felt its warmth all the way down to his toes. He'd never experienced such beauty from the inside out.

"This," he whispered, his voice thick. Before he thought fully about what he was doing, he leaned down and covered her soft mouth with his.

Chapter 10

Adelle didn't know how she managed not to drop anything, nor did she know how her knees kept her upright.

She also didn't know why he was kissing her. The only thing she did know was that she shouldn't have kissed him back. But knowing that didn't stop her from feeling the loss when he stopped.

Very slowly, his hands drifted away from her face and he backed up a step. His smile told her he had enjoyed the brief encounter as much as she had.

Adelle tightened her grip on her groceries. Part of her wanted to know why he did it, but a greater part was too afraid to think about it.

Although she didn't know much about him, whatever she felt for him went beyond sympathy for the loss of his brother and the shock of instant adoptive fatherhood. They shared many common interests, and they were never lacking for stimulating conversation. Other than the functions of child care, there was nothing else to do but talk. Their discussions ranged from light and funny topics to downright serious ones. At the same time, they both knew when to stop—before they crossed an unspoken line that was too personal, too intense, or simply uncomfortable.

It had been a wonderful surprise when she woke up from her nap to discover his makeshift Christmas tree. Knowing how he braved the snow and subzero temperature to gather the pine branches made her appreciate the little tree even more. His ingenuity at using the dental floss to hold it together had impressed her. She certainly would have never thought of it.

She also couldn't think of many men who would actually sit down and make decorations, especially considering the limited choice of materials available. It pleased her to think he might have gone along with her because she wanted it so badly. The decorations were always a big part of the Christmas season and, this being her first Christmas as a parent, it was important to her that this year be special.

On the other hand, no matter how nice he seemed, no matter how well they got along, and even though he appeared to be a good Christian, she still didn't completely trust him. Her counselor had helped her deal with her mistrust of men in general, but she still had difficulties. That hurt, because she had always had a trusting nature before Shawn violated her. Now she always used extreme caution in dealing with men, especially strangers, but Dennis seemed to be stripping away her need to protect herself. . .

He smiled but made no attempt to touch her again. "I think I'll get back to my indoor snowfall before it gets too dark to see what I'm doing."

Making the simple sandwiches gave Adelle the opportunity to watch Dennis without him being aware that he was being studied.

He sat cross-legged on the floor, carefully and diligently snipping the foil snowflakes and then gently smoothing them flat when he was finished with each one.

Raymond watched him, almost as fascinated as she was. He watched every movement Dennis made, especially when he smoothed out a new snowflake and slowly waved it in front of Raymond's face.

"Hey, look!" he called out without turning to her. "I think Raymond likes them. I must be doing a good job."

She couldn't help but smile. "I agree with Raymond. They look really good."

He stood, brushing a myriad of foil snippets off his pants. "These snowflakes would rival those made by the most talented six-year-old."

He measured out pieces of thread for each and proceeded to distribute them around the cabin wherever anything could dangle, starting with the lampshade, the doorknobs, and a curtain rod. When he had only one snowflake left, he stepped into the kitchen area.

Adelle backed up, but he didn't seem to notice her reaction to his proximity. He tied the last snowflake to the fridge door handle, then rubbed his palm over his stomach. "That was a hard job. I sure worked up an appetite."

She looked at her sandwiches. Never had it taken her so long to make two little sandwiches. "Here you go. They're just waiting to be eaten."

He helped carry the plates and glasses to the table, talking over his shoulder as he walked. "It's still snowing."

"In these parts, it isn't unheard of for snow to fall for days. We're not that far from Jasper, as the crow flies. The skiing will be great for the Christmas holiday crowd. Do you ski?"

He shook his head as he laid the plates on the table, then pulled out a chair for her to sit down. "No. I've always meant to, but I never seem to have the time. If it's not one thing, it's another, and then the winter is over."

She glanced toward the living room before she sat. "It looks like Raymond fell asleep. We can eat in peace and with both hands."

He grinned. "And who said miracles don't happen?"

Adelle's heart caught in her throat. She did believe in miracles, despite the fact that none had ever happened to her. Either that or she'd been looking in the wrong things.

She'd wanted so badly to come to the cabin that she'd ignored the snow. If she hadn't picked up Dennis and Raymond at the fork in the road, she would have been here with just Rachel for company, and that would have been a very lonely Christmas. After the initial awkwardness she was enjoying her time with Dennis, and by his kind and gentle nature, she was learning that it was possible to trust a man again. When he had kissed her, he'd only touched her face, giving her the option to easily back away or resist. But she had done neither.

This time Adelle said grace. Remembering his comments concerning praying before a meal, she kept her prayer short, although the sandwiches weren't likely to grow cold if she took too long.

Dennis carried both plates to the sink when they finished eating. "I think I'll volunteer to do the dishes tonight. Then it's your turn tomorrow."

"Nice try. There are only two plates, two glasses, and one knife."

"Yeah. That means Christmas Day is your turn, so I get off easy."

He winked, then picked the glasses up off the table.

Adelle smiled. Despite his words, she knew he would help with both dinner and the cleanup tomorrow. She was beginning to know a lot about him, despite the short space of time they'd been together.

While he ran water over the plates, Adelle leaned against the wall and studied the cabin. It wasn't exactly the way the cabin was usually decorated at Christmas, but they hadn't done a bad job, considering. The daylight had nearly faded, and the foil snowflakes reflected the glow of the woodstove in the low light. The makeshift tree was near enough to the woodstove to catch enough light to be seen, but not near enough to create a fire hazard.

She had been correct in comparing it to Charlie Brown's Christmas tree. The colored sponge ornaments and the reddish splatters on the white popcorn strings added just the right amount of color to the dark green of the pine branches, and the crooked foil star provided the right touch for the top. All things combined, it possessed its own unique charm.

Dennis appeared beside her. Under other circumstances, it would have been the most natural thing in the world for him to slip his arm around her waist, but he didn't touch her. Nor was she sure she wanted him to. She could have escaped from his kiss, but she couldn't escape from his arms. Not because she thought he was anything like Shawn, not that she thought he would be forceful and hold her captive, but because she didn't think she would want to escape.

She turned to look up at him. Their time together had been short, but already she knew she would miss him when he was gone. She turned back to the tree but continued to think of Dennis.

Already, she knew many of his likes and dislikes, as he did hers. His home was in Vancouver, and he appeared to hold some kind of executive position which paid well enough that he had entertained the thought of being airlifted home. Adelle, on the other hand, worked as an office clerk for a local logging company, a job that was far from glamorous and farther still from well paid.

On the positive side, Dennis lived his life with Christ in his heart and was honest enough to admit he didn't read his Bible or memorize as much as he should. She was no different in that respect. In general, life made it difficult— and even more necessary—to put aside time for scripture reading.

Perhaps one of the reasons she entertained the thought of getting to know Dennis better was because she knew it was impossible. The mere geography of the faraway metropolis of Vancouver versus little Blue River was enough that if they did keep in touch, at best it would be a long distance friendship consisting of e-mail and an occasional phone call. She could handle that.

She continued to stare at the tree without really focusing on it. Adelle had learned the hard way that harsh reality often shattered idealistic dreams. She had always dreamed of a loving husband and a peaceful bungalow she could call home, complete with happy children and a frisky dog. She did have a happy child, but the father of her child had abused her and now hated her. She wasn't exactly fond of him either. And now she would soon have to move to low-rent housing as a single mother with a low income. In order to go back to work, she had to find satisfactory day-care arrangements. After all that, she wouldn't have money or time to care for a goldfish, never mind a dog.

Adelle suspected Dennis would make up with his fiancée upon his return, even though he was adamant that it was over. His feelings had been hurt, but he had a kind heart and he would forgive Joanna. After all, that was what God called His children to do.

Most important, Dennis needed someone to care for Raymond and the woman he had loved enough to ask to marry him was the best choice. He was a sweet and righteous man, and Raymond was a darling baby. Joanna would be a fool not to want to be a part of their lives on a permanent basis.

Soon Dennis would be happily married, with a loving wife and an adopted son and, no doubt, more children on the way, while Adelle would struggle through life as a single mother. Her only option was to take what Shawn's parents were offering her, but instead of being a relief from some of the responsibility, it would tie her into a lifetime of obligation, both financial and personal, in order to see that Rachel's needs were met. She wasn't ready to sell her soul to them, but she didn't know what options she had left.

Dennis's voice broke into her thoughts. "It sure looks good, doesn't it? I mean considering what we had to work with."

Adelle snapped her thoughts back to the little Christmas tree. She would worry about her problems later. While she was with Dennis, she would enjoy the celebration of Jesus' birth with him as a Christian brother. "Yes, it does look good. I think it's time for the presents."

"Oh. Presents." He rammed his hands into his pockets. "I only have one present with me. It's for Raymond. I wish I had something to give to you. You've done so much for both of us."

"Don't be silly. I certainly understand. I actually don't have much, either. I only have two gifts to put under the tree. One for my aunt and uncle, and one for Rachel."

He pulled his suitcase out from behind the couch, removed a small, brightly wrapped gift, and laid it under the tree. "I don't even know what it is. It's from Harv and Katie, for Raymond."

As he spoke, his voice skipped, so Adelle didn't comment. She busied herself with pulling the two presents out from the cupboard where she had stored them, then she returned to Dennis's side. They stood in silence looking at the small tree with the presents nestled underneath. Three presents seemed right.

Dennis sighed. "I had a really hard time packing up their Christmas stuff. They had gifts for each other under the tree, and I didn't even want to touch them." His voice skipped again, and he drew a ragged breath. "They had a number of gifts for Raymond, too, but they were too big, and I didn't want them reminding me what happened, so I didn't want them in my car. I put them all in boxes and had everything shipped to my house. I missed that small one and picked it up at the last minute and put it in my suitcase as I was leaving."

The guilt at her own selfish thoughts poked at her. She had been thinking so much about her own problems that she had forgotten about Dennis's. She couldn't imagine how difficult it had been for him to have lost his brother, especially this time of year.

When her parents had announced they were going to California to be with her brother's family again, Adelle had struggled with the hurt and the jealousy and the disappointment. Now it paled in comparison to the thought of the death of Dennis's brother.

Adelle walked back to the playpen and lifted Rachel out. "You should really wake Raymond. I'm waking Rachel right now. If they sleep too much now, they're not going to sleep tonight."

"They both wake up every four hours to be fed. You must define sleeping at night differently than I do."

"The point is that they go back to sleep after they're fed."

"I guess."

Dennis picked Raymond up and sat on the couch, but Adelle went into the kitchen and flicked on the radio. The announcer confirmed what she already knew, that it was still snowing, and then traded jokes with a caller about the over-white Christmas in store for the area. She flicked it off, lit the candle on the coffee table, and joined Dennis on the couch.

"It sounds like there's been no change in the forecast, huh?"

Adelle shook her head. "Nope."

"There hasn't been a mention of power or phone outages, either. This must have been the only area affected."

"It's possible. I told you before, this area is very remote. Most of the access roads leading to the cabins out here are old logging roads—some of them are in use during the logging season, but some of them aren't. I don't think the last road we used to get up here is even on the map. People come out here for privacy, and they get it."

"That's amazing. I don't know what it's like in Blue River, but where I live, I imagine you'd feel awfully claustrophobic. The houses aren't all that close together, in my opinion. But coming from Blue River, you'd probably think they were nearly touching."

She grinned. "Probably. I've never been to Vancouver."

"And I've never been to Blue River."

He looked down at her hands, giving her the impression that he would have touched her if she hadn't been holding Rachel.

"One day, I'd like you to come and visit me in Vancouver. I don't want to lose touch, Adelle. I'm not saying that just because I owe you my life—"

She opened her mouth to protest, but he quickly shook his head, stopping her from protesting.

"Please. Let me finish. I really do owe you my life. If you hadn't come by and picked me up, Raymond and I would have frozen to death. As I was saying, I want to see you again after all this is over. Not just out of gratitude, although I am eternally grateful, but more so, because I like you. I want to stay friends, special friends, even over the miles."

Adelle opened her mouth, but again, no sound came out. This time it wasn't because he stopped her, it was because her brain short-circuited.

"I know this is awkward for you, so I'm going to change the subject. It's Christmas Eve, and it's time to take it easy, time to relax, and time to reflect. Tell me about your best-ever Christmas."

She stared at him. She'd always enjoyed Christmas, and most of the time she came to the cabin for Christmas with her family. She really couldn't think of any year that really stood out above the rest.

Except this Christmas. There were almost no decorations, her family was missing, her future was uncertain, but so far, it was turning into a special Christmas, because of a very special new friend.

Chapter 11

Dennis couldn't hold back a yawn. It wasn't that late, but the atmosphere of the cabin was cozy. Sitting side by side with Adelle and cuddling a baby was comforting in a way he never would have foreseen. Not only that, but the heat from the woodstove was making him drowsy. From what little experience he had gained in the past few days, he thought Raymond was sleepy, too. It appeared Rachel was already asleep.

He turned to Adelle. "Do you think it's bedtime?"

She nodded. "Rachel probably needs changing, but I'm not going to wake her up to do it. How about if you change Raymond, and then I'll take care of him."

He liked the delicate way she said that. Dennis smiled. "Great."

As he touched the diaper bag, the lack of bulk reminded him that it only contained the wipes and powder. Everything else was used up, including his supply of sleepers.

He laid Raymond down on the changing quilt and waited while Adelle tucked Rachel into the playpen for the night. He opened his mouth to apologize for needing more from her but snapped it shut. It was becoming increasingly difficult not to extend his apologies or thanks as she continued to help him, both with Raymond and his own need of food and shelter. He'd never felt more helpless in his life, nor had he been so dependent on anyone since childhood. He wondered if there was a reason he needed to be taught to accept help gracefully, as well as to receive instructions. Usually he was the one who gave the orders and people depended on him for their needs, not the other way around. He wasn't sure he liked it this way.

Dennis gritted his teeth and forced himself to smile nicely. "I hate to ask you this, but can I borrow a sleeper?" It nearly killed him, but he bit his lip and didn't apologize.

Her answering smile told him his efforts at self-control had been worth it. "Sure." She reached into her diaper bag and pulled out a clean sleeper.

It was pink.

Dennis dressed his little boy, who was already wearing a pink diaper, in a pink sleeper. At least he still had a neutral yellow receiving blanket to tuck around Raymond, although he was sure it was also ready for the laundry. When it did go into the hamper, he had a feeling his little boy would also be wrapped in a pink blanket.

While Adelle was busy in the bedroom with Raymond, he carefully carried the candle to the kitchen, washed the few dishes, and placed another pot of water on the woodstove to warm. When she returned with Raymond, Dennis suspected that Adelle would want to go to sleep for the night, knowing what kind of schedule lay ahead of her. After a full day of baby care he knew she was tired and regretted that she wouldn't get much of a break. Her night would consist of a series of naps rather than a good, sound sleep.

Somehow, he wanted to show her that he appreciated her and tell her how much what she was doing meant to him. Already whatever was between them had grown into a friendship beyond that of a host and caregiver.

For one of the rare times in his life, he had no words to express himself. He wanted simply to be with her with no responsibilities or distractions for a couple of hours, but to keep her from what little sleep she would get would be selfish.

Raymond was asleep in her arms when she emerged from the bedroom, and Adelle was trying to stifle a yawn. She looked so sweet he wanted to kiss her again, but he didn't have that right. It had been a mistake to kiss her the first time because now he wanted to do it again. Given their circumstances, it was neither right nor proper to do so.

Instead, he merely smiled politely at the memory of how good it had been as he took Raymond from her. "If you want to go to bed, that's fine with me. I'm tired, too."

She smiled, and the puffy circles underneath her drowsy eyes twisted his heart. "Thanks. I think I'll do that. Good night, Dennis." With those few words, she returned to the bedroom, and the door clicked shut.

Dennis pulled the couch mattress out to make up the bed; changed into the same clothes he had worn at night previously, and crawled into bed, but by the time he lay down all the tiredness left him.

The fire in the woodstove cast its amber glow in the otherwise complete black of the night, reflecting on the little tree nearby, making it the only thing he could see with any clarity.

It was, indeed, a very special little tree, not by its components, but because of the experience of its creation—the process of assembling it with someone special. The broken branches, ragged sponges, and badly colored popcorn wouldn't be beautiful to anyone else but him. And tomorrow, they would celebrate the reason for assembling the tree.

In the morning, it would be Christmas, the celebration of the birth of the One who would become the Savior for a world fallen into sin.

A piece of wood popped in the fire, illuminating the shiny wrapping paper of the one small present for Raymond with its brief flare of light.

Dennis rolled over onto his back on the lumpy bed. His eyes burned and he squeezed them shut, but a few tears managed to push their way out. He gave up and let them flow. Now he was alone, and it didn't matter. No one could see him, and he could allow himself to grieve the loss of his brother. Tonight, he didn't have to be the strong one in the crowd as others wept around him. He also didn't have to worry about looking like a loser in front of Adelle, although he knew she would never feel that way.

As much as the loss of his brother and sister-in-law left a gaping hole in his heart, he knew they were now with Jesus in heaven. The knowledge gave him comfort and the strength to carry on and be a parent to Raymond for them.

Dennis rolled over and buried his face in the pillow. Nothing was going to stop him from adopting his nephew and making him a son. He prayed for help until he knew what he was doing, for guidance as Raymond grew up, and that they could be a happy family.

Sleep continued to elude him. When baby noises emanated from the playpen, he picked up the fussing infant and blinked a few times before discerning that this baby dressed in pink was Rachel.

He sat on the edge of the mattress to wait for Adelle to appear, but she didn't. It took a few minutes to figure out that since he had picked Rachel up so quickly, there hadn't been enough noise to awaken Adelle.

Dennis glanced toward the closed bedroom door. He had two choices. He could wait until Rachel got so hungry that she started screaming in his arms, or he could tap on the door loud enough to awaken Adelle and, hopefully, not wake Raymond.

He didn't want to invade Adelle's privacy while she was sleeping. But neither did he want Rachel's poor little tummy to hurt from hunger.

Rachel began to whimper again, indicating it wouldn't be long before she started wailing.

Dennis stood, and Rachel quieted as soon as he took his first step. Even with his limited experience, he knew the quiet was temporary. He tapped gently on the bedroom door. "Adelle?" he whispered as loud as he dared.

He put his ear to the door and thought he heard a slight creak of the bed moving, but not enough to indicate that she had actually gotten up.

He tapped again, louder this time. "Adelle? I've got Rachel. . . ."

This time, he didn't hear a thing, but he couldn't be absolutely certain because Rachel was starting to whimper.

Rather than let Rachel scream, Dennis sucked in a deep breath, opened the door, and poked his head in. "Adelle? Rachel wants you."

The room was in total blackness, and it caught him off guard since he was accustomed to the muted glow coming from the woodstove. A gasp sounded from what he assumed was the direction of the bed.

"It's only me. I've got Rachel. She started to fuss. She wants you."

The bed creaked, and Adelle's voice came from a bit closer. "Here. I'll take her. Thank you."

He couldn't see her, but suddenly the weight of Rachel was lifted out of his arms.

Quickly, he backed up a step, closed the door behind him, and hustled back to his own bed. He lay down, but his heart pounded in his chest. He'd only had the best of intentions, but he knew he had crossed some kind of personal line, and the guilt roared through him. For a married couple to hand a baby back and forth in the bedroom was a different set of rules. He wondered what it would be like to be so familiar and so comfortable with someone that such things were commonplace.

By the time Adelle returned with Rachel, he still wasn't sleeping, but he didn't move so she would think he was. She changed the baby with such tender care that Rachel didn't wake up. Then delicately, Adelle lowered the infant into the playpen. Before she returned to the bedroom, she ran her fingers along the top of Raymond's fuzzy little head, straightened the blanket he'd used to prop Raymond up on his side, and covered him up again.

"Goodnight, little darlings," she whispered.

Dennis imagined she'd spoken the same gentle endearment to him, and he felt himself drifting into sleep as her bedroom door closed.

❄

This time, Dennis didn't try to roll over and go back to sleep when Adelle disappeared with Rachel. Raymond was wide-awake, and not because of hunger. It was daylight. He tried to ignore the squawking while he folded the bed back into the sofa. When he was finally done, he picked Raymond up and waited on the couch.

He stood when she returned. "Merry Christmas."

She smiled back. "And a Merry Christmas to you."

Heaven help him, he wanted to kiss her. He didn't need a gift under the tree. A kiss from Adelle would have been present enough.

Dennis tried to push the thought aside as he squatted beside the tree and rested Raymond into the car seat. "It's a man's job to hand out Christmas presents."

Adelle nodded and sat cross-legged beside Raymond with Rachel nestled in her lap. "That must be true. My dad hands out the presents when he's here, and when he isn't, Uncle Bob does it."

He picked up the soft, squishy, cylindrical gift with a name tag for Rachel. It had a hard lump near the top, and the contents divided from a single mass into two long portions about two thirds of the way down. When he squeezed it, the contents giggled and said, "I love you." Dennis grinned and shook his head in mock disbelief. "She'll never be able to tell what this is, Adelle."

She laughed, and it was a wonderful sound. "Never mind. It didn't come in a box, and I didn't have one that size."

She held out her hands, but Dennis suspended the gift in the air over his head. "This isn't for you to open. It's for Rachel." He held it in the air in front of Rachel. Rachel gurgled and kicked her little legs.

Adelle harumphed and held out one hand, palm up. "Get real."

"Listen. Can't you hear her? She's asking for *my* help to open it."

Adelle rolled her eyes and sighed.

Very gently, Dennis pressed the present against Rachel's tummy to tickle her. She squealed and waved her arms, smacking the gift a few times.

Dennis very slowly ripped a piece of paper from it.

Adelle reached for the package, but Dennis yanked it away, again holding it over his head. "Patience is a virtue."

"I give up. Do it your way. Take your time. It's not like there are dozens of gifts. I only bought her one this year because I knew she wouldn't know the difference to open anything. Besides, when I did my shopping, I wasn't sure how much room I'd have in the car."

He took his time pulling off the paper, then gently laid the teddy bear on Rachel's tummy. She swatted it with her jerky movements, the same as before he'd unwrapped it.

"I think she likes it. After all, every girl needs a pink teddy bear."

Adelle's eyes narrowed. "Are you making fun of my selection? There were tons of Christmas bears with hats and scarves, and lots that said 'Baby's First Christmas' on them, but I liked the pink one best."

"It's cute. Really. I've just never seen a pink bear before."

Before he realized what she was doing, she grabbed Raymond's present out from under the tree.

She grinned. "Turnabout is fair play."

Just as he had done, she held out the present in front of Raymond until he managed to touch it with his jerky movements. He didn't know it was possible, but Adelle picked the paper off even more slowly than he had.

Dennis groaned. "Why do women do that? They always pick off the tape. It's not like you're ever going to reuse the paper."

"It's a law of nature—the way life was meant to be."

She laid a tiny pacifier with a candy cane pictured on it in Raymond's lap. "This is really cute. I've never seen one like this before. But then we don't have as big a selection as the bigger cities."

They both looked at the last present under the tree, the one for her aunt and uncle.

"I guess I'll take it home when I can get out of here and just give it to them later. I suppose your presents are all at home, too."

"Yes. I thought I'd be home on Christmas morning. What about presents for you and Rachel from your parents and your brother? Don't you exchange gifts?"

"Yes, we do. But since I knew I'd be lugging so much baby stuff up here this year, all those presents were at Aunt Min and Uncle Bob's house, and they were going to bring them. I think half my little car was filled with just diapers."

Dennis gritted his teeth. Pink diapers. Diapers which he was now going to be using up. "I wish I had a gift for you under the tree." All he had to give was the money in his wallet, which was useless at the moment. Worse than being useless for any of his current needs, he knew that if he attempted to give her money, she'd be terribly insulted.

"Don't be silly, Dennis. I'm just glad you're here with me. I didn't know it at the time I picked you up, but if you hadn't been there, I would have had a very lonely and probably a very scary Christmas here all by myself. Your presence and friendship for this Christmas has been a lovely gift. And after having said that, I wish I had a gift for you, too."

She smiled so sweetly that if he hadn't been a man, he might have choked up.

Dennis swallowed hard. "What you've done for me and Raymond is a gift beyond any material thing that could have been wrapped and put under a tree. I know you told me not to thank you, but there's no way I'll ever be able to repay you for this."

"Well then, isn't that the best gift of all? A gift isn't meant to be repaid. It's simply a gift. Just like the gift of God's Son, which is what we're celebrating today."

Now he really felt all choked up, and he couldn't stop it this time. He forced himself to smile politely. "Yeah. You're right," he said in a monotone. He stood and walked to the window, not that he needed to see what was going on outside, but because he didn't want her to see his face until he got himself under control.

She joined him at the window, which wasn't exactly what he wanted. She held Rachel cradled against her, along with the new teddy bear. "It looks like the snow is starting to lighten up, like the forecast said."

"Yeah," he mumbled.

"I wonder how much snow has fallen in town, if it's as much as here."

"I dunno."

"I doubt they'll call the snowplows out today except for the major roads and highways, but tomorrow they should be able to start digging everything out."

"Probably."

"You might even be able to go home by the day after tomorrow, if all goes well. That's assuming the phone comes back sometime soon. Then you can make arrangements to have someone come and get you."

"I guess." Strangely, he didn't want to go. He knew it was unrealistic to want to stay. They only had a limited supply of food and diapers. Even when the power came back, which eventually it would, they still wouldn't really have anything to do without television and only one radio station up here in the middle of nowhere. Yet even with the lack of things to amuse them, he hadn't been bored for a single moment.

He turned to watch Adelle as she stared at the snow out the window, and he realized that the main reason he wasn't ready to go home was because he might never see her again.

She spoke but continued to gaze out the window. "One thing I always love about being here is when it snows. A pure layer of white covers all the tracks and dirt and bad things. It's so clean and beautiful. Especially at Christmas." She turned her head and smiled. "Merry Christmas, Dennis."

He was going to wish her a Merry Christmas as well, but the words caught in his throat. Her smile warmed his heart and made it pound at the same time. Her eyes radiated the same inner beauty that had hit him the day before, when he kissed her. He longed to kiss her again. Only this time, he knew what would happen and how good it would be.

And this time it would be harder to stop.

Rachel made a little squeal, reminding him that the woman he wanted to kiss had a baby in her arms. The baby was as effective as any shield—he wasn't going to kiss a woman over the top of a baby's head. In the circumstances in which they found themselves, he shouldn't be kissing her at all.

He'd crossed the line twice already. Once by kissing her the first time and the other by walking in on her when she was sleeping. Both times his reaction had caught him off guard. This time he knew what would happen, and it scared him. His heart was getting too involved with a wonderful woman with whom there could be no future.

He wanted to kiss her, but he knew he shouldn't start something he couldn't finish.

She was still looking up at him with the same dreamy expression.

"Merry Christmas, Adelle. I'm starving. What's for breakfast?"

In a split second, he turned on his heel and strode into the kitchen.

Chapter 12

In the time it took Adelle to blink, he was gone. She tried to think of what she could have said that caused him to react so strangely, but all she'd done was wish him a Merry Christmas.

She pushed aside her bruised feelings and joined Dennis in the kitchen. "I'm hungry, too. Christmas morning, after we open the presents we always have omelets for breakfast. Then we're so stuffed we skip lunch, and have an early Christmas dinner midafternoon."

"It must be good to have so many traditions."

"Traditions?" She tried to think of all the things she had told him that usually happened in her family on Christmas morning. "I don't know if I'd go so far to call them traditions. More than anything, they are just habits we've fallen into over the years. I think the reason the omelets happen every Christmas morning is not for tradition, but because a set menu makes the grocery shopping easier."

"Whatever the reason, it's nice to be able to look forward to the same good times every year. I guess I'm going to have to start thinking of some traditions to do with Raymond as he grows up. Your moving nativity set is a great idea, but I think I'm going to like the omelets for breakfast the best."

He gave her a little grin, and something funny happened inside her stomach, which told her that she must have been hungrier than she thought.

"What do you want to do, hold Rachel or make the omelets?"

"I've never made an omelet in my life. I think I'll take Rachel."

"You've never made an omelet?" The more she thought about it, aside from making spaghetti and frying eggs, he didn't seem to be able to do anything else in the kitchen unless it somehow involved the microwave. "Just what do you feed yourself every day?"

He didn't look at her as he spoke but became overly interested in the nose on the pink teddy bear. "I get by. I'm obviously not starving."

The image of Dennis running through the cabin without a shirt flashed through her mind. Whatever he did eat sat well on him. Unlike herself. She'd gained some weight during her pregnancy, and it wasn't coming off as easily as it went on. She obviously wasn't starving either, but she wasn't going to comment.

About halfway through the preparation, Raymond started to squawk. So

Dennis deserted her for the couch and sat with both babies in his lap until she had the food on the table. After a short prayer, they began to eat—both holding babies in their laps.

"I have a bad feeling that I'm going to get really good at eating with one hand."

"Either that, or you'll learn to run your life by a baby's feeding schedule, which is always changing. As soon as you get used to the bottle schedule, babies start on rice cereal, and then not long after that you start them on baby food, and then more and more real food."

"Culminating with when they get to be teenagers and start eating us out of house and home."

"Maybe for you. I have a girl. That's not going to happen to me."

"No. You'll have to get an extra room built onto your house to store all the shoes."

"And you'll have to hide the car keys or get your own private gas pump."

They both laughed, and the banter continued throughout the entire meal-time. She couldn't remember the last time she'd enjoyed herself so much at the table.

Immediately after they were done, she took Raymond to be fed while Dennis did the dishes. Part of her wanted to tease him concerning his comment yesterday about being free of kitchen duties on Christmas Day, but the wiser part of her told her to leave well enough alone.

She could have sat on the couch while he bathed Raymond, but she didn't. Likewise, when she bathed Rachel, he held Raymond and remained in the kitchen.

When the time came for them to leave, Adelle knew, without a doubt, that she would miss Raymond. But she fought the idea that she probably would miss Dennis, too. She didn't know if that was good or bad and refused to think about it any more.

By the time both babies fell asleep in the afternoon, Adelle was tired. In a backhanded sort of way, she was thankful that most of the ingredients for their planned Christmas dinner weren't there. If they were, then she would have had to work to cook it. Now she no longer had to worry about preparing a fancy meal. If it wasn't for Dennis, at this point, she would have been satisfied with a hot dog for Christmas dinner.

She put the ham and a yam in the oven, lit the pilot light, and joined Dennis on the couch.

Resting her elbows on her knees and leaning forward, she gazed into the playpen at the sleeping babies. "They sure are sweet, aren't they?"

Dennis arched his back, pushing into the back of the couch with his shoulders as he stretched. He extended both arms along the top of the couch, then sagged with his legs extended in front of him. "Yes, they're sweet, but they're even sweeter when they're sleeping."

A yawn escaped, and she made no effort to hide it. She no longer had the energy. "I don't know how mothers of twins do this. It's only been two days, and I'm exhausted."

"Most mothers of twins have electricity and supplemental formula. Have I told you recently how much I appreciate what you're doing?"

Adelle turned her head. "Dennis. . ."

He grinned then let the corners of his mouth drop. "Sorry."

She refused to comment, unsure if he was goading her, or if it just happened that he was again apologizing for something without thinking of his promise.

It became too much effort to hold herself up in that position, so she leaned back on the couch, despite Dennis being sprawled all over the place. She even ignored the light touch of his fingertips on her shoulder. She was too tired to care. She was even too tired to turn her head as she spoke. "It's too bad they won't remember this. If they were a little older, this would be quite an adventure for a little kid."

"Never mind little kids. It's been quite an adventure for me, and I'm an adult. If only I had more suitable clothes and my camera, I could get some good mileage out of this."

The warmth of the woodstove relaxed Adelle from head to toe. She nestled into the soft couch, ignoring the fact that her head was now resting on Dennis's arm. "I still think it's fun to play in the snow, and I was born and raised here."

His fingers drifted down to her shoulder. "Back home, I have to admit that we don't get dressed up to go outside and play in the rain. We tend to ignore it unless it's pouring, but still, I spend most of the winter indoors."

"My uncle Bob said he was going to build Rachel a special toboggan when she gets a little bigger."

"And I'll probably buy an umbrella with cartoon characters on it for Raymond."

She smiled up at him, and when she did, he closed his hand on her shoulder and pulled her closer so that she was nestled into him. He was warm, and being with him on the couch next to the stove with the snow falling outside felt comfortable in a way she had never experienced. She'd never had a man hold her close like this. He made no effort to kiss her or do anything other than just sit together. It felt good, and it felt right.

His fingers brushed her hair, and with the gentle touch, she allowed her eyes to drift shut.

"You look tired," he murmured in her ear.

"I am," she sighed, then snuggled into his warmth. She probably should have opened her eyes, but she couldn't.

In just a minute, she would open them and then get up and make a pot of tea.

In a minute.

❄

Dennis smiled as he watched Adelle's eyelids flutter shut. It didn't take long for her breathing to become deep and even. Soon her weight pressed against him as her whole body relaxed.

He knew he was still smiling as he snuggled her in a little closer. She was exhausted and deserved the chance to rest comfortably, but he didn't want to move her. He couldn't remember the last time he exercised or participated in a strenuous activity, so he didn't dare try to lift her limp body as a deadweight to carry to the bed.

He leaned his cheek into the top of her head and inhaled the scent of spring flowers from her soft hair. He closed his eyes and tried, unsuccessfully, to remember what shampoo commercial claimed to smell like this.

If he couldn't carry her to the bed, then the best he could do to make her more comfortable would be to slide out from under her and let her lie down on the small couch.

He started to move, but she murmured in her sleep and nestled her head into his chest, immobilizing him.

Dennis couldn't wipe the smile off his face. He liked having Adelle lean on him like this. It was probably a chauvinistic thought, but he liked to think that, as the bigger and stronger of the two of them, he could protect her and see to her needs, even though she wasn't aware of it.

As he tried to think of a way to slide out without disturbing her, he yawned and thought he could use a nap, too. Again, he rested his cheek on the top of her head and inhaled her shampoo.

Dennis let his eyes drift shut. As soon as he figured out the commercial for the shampoo, he would wiggle away and give her the couch to herself. It wouldn't take long for him to remember it.

Only a minute.

❄

The sound of a baby fussing forced Adelle to open one eye. Through the fog in her head, she remembered she was in the living room. She tried to figure out why she was sitting up, and why the couch was so lumpy.

The other eye shot open as she realized she was leaning against Dennis. Quickly she righted herself and stared at him. He was sprawled out in a seated position, his legs fully extended and crossed at the ankles, his head all the way back at what appeared to be a very awkward angle, his mouth was open, and he was snoring.

He stirred with her movements, groggily righting himself as he rubbed the back of his neck with one hand. "Did I fall asleep? Sorry. What time is it?"

The whimpers of one baby fussing changed to the sound of two babies fussing.

Adelle tried to get her brain to function as she checked her wristwatch. "It's four thirty. I can't believe it's so late. I'll feed the baby whose turn it is, and you peel the potatoes and get them started, okay?"

Before he could protest, she picked up the hungry baby and hustled off to the bedroom. She could alternately hear the sounds of Dennis clanking about in the kitchen, interspersed with Raymond squawking, and then a bit of quiet with Dennis trying to convince him to keep his new Christmas pacifier in his mouth and quit spitting it out.

Upon her arrival in the kitchen, the potatoes were boiling nicely. Dennis had one finger in his mouth and was holding Raymond with the other hand.

"What happened? Are you okay?"

"It's not a big deal," he mumbled around his finger. He pulled it out, wiped it on his shirt, and inspected it. A few drops of blood seeped through a small cut on his index finger. He yanked off a section of paper towel and wrapped it around his finger. "I cut myself peeling the potatoes. But don't worry, I didn't get any blood on them."

"You cut yourself peeling potatoes?"

He unwrapped his finger, examined it, and satisfied it had stopped bleeding, repositioned Raymond to support him with both hands. "What part of my explanation did you miss? I was using that peeling thingie and it slipped and I cut myself. It's not a big deal, but it is annoying. It stings, too."

She wondered if she should have been surprised that he knew what a potato peeler looked like. She tried to figure out how in the world someone could cut themselves with one, but couldn't.

Adelle chose not to comment further and busied herself with the rest of the meal preparation and with setting the table while Dennis amused the babies.

"Hopefully we can eat our Christmas dinner with both hands," she called over to him.

"I wouldn't count on it," he grumbled barely loud enough for her to hear.

She amazed herself with the speed at which she had dinner ready. Knowing he was probably right and that they would both only have one hand available, she spooned a bit of mashed potatoes, a slice of ham, and a piece of baked yam onto both plates. She also took the liberty of slicing the meat into bite sized pieces, but left the yam whole, since that was soft enough to cut with a fork. "Supper's ready!"

His prayer was short, but still it was so touching with his thanks of Jesus' love and sacrifice that Adelle nearly had to fight back tears.

Dennis had barely taken a few bites when he paused. "This is really good, Adelle. And thanks for cutting up the ham. At first I felt silly having my food cut up for me like a little kid, but it turned out to be a great idea."

During dinner, their conversation stayed on Christmas related topics. She learned about what the big malls did for decorations, and she told him what the co-op did. They talked about their church Christmas functions which, this year, he'd unfortunately had to miss. She learned that her own church, which she thought was fairly big, was small in comparison to his, which seated five hundred people and ran two services every Sunday morning.

She didn't know if she would like worshipping God amongst such a large crowd, but at the same time she thought the sound of so many voices joined together in praise of their Lord would be wonderful. Her heart clenched when he said he would like to take her to one of his regular services, but she knew it could never happen. The drive from Blue River to Vancouver took approximately five hours, so it was not a day trip. With her expected raise in expenses and drop in income she couldn't justify spending the money on travel or two night's hotels. Neither would she accept his charity to cover her expenses.

This time, when they were finished eating, Dennis busied himself washing the dishes while Adelle played with both babies. Up until now, she had fed Raymond, bathed him, cuddled him, and put him to bed. She'd even changed him once, but she had not yet found any free time to relax and do nothing in particular with him.

Just as every other time she'd spent time with Raymond, he was an agreeable baby. He smiled freely, and she knew it wasn't just gas. He watched the colored objects with obvious interest, and when she picked him up, he responded happily to her touch.

By the time Raymond and Rachel were settled for the night, Adelle was ready for some relief from the responsibility of parenthood. However, since she had slept for so long in the afternoon, she wasn't yet ready for bed herself.

She made a pot of herbal tea, and Dennis begrudgingly agreed to share it, since he wasn't sleepy yet, either.

They both cradled the mugs of hot tea in their hands and watched the woodstove.

The words to "White Christmas" drifted through her head as Adelle looked outside. It was dark and she couldn't see anything, but she knew it had finally happened. "It finally stopped snowing."

"Yes. I guess we'll be able to see how buried we are in the morning."

She secretly wished that morning was more than twelve hours away. "Yes," she mumbled into her mug.

Dennis cleared his throat. "I hope you don't mind me asking, but I've been wondering why it is you wanted to come here so badly that you ignored the snowstorm. Why was it so important for you to come up here in the middle of nowhere? And what were you thinking so that you didn't consider the possibility of your family staying home and then wondering where you were?"

Adelle probably should have felt strange discussing it with him, but she didn't. So far, she hadn't talked about her problems with anyone, not even her best friend. Yet in talking about it with Dennis, she knew he would understand. The knowledge gave her solace. "I have some things to think about concerning Rachel's support. I've only got an office job, and it doesn't pay very well. To make matters worse, I'm going to be making less money when I get back from my maternity leave."

She could see him stiffen, but he otherwise didn't move. "They can't do that. Legally, your employer has to give you back the same job you left, provided you stay within the guidelines of the time frame for your maternity leave. Which I assume you are."

She nodded. "I know that. Technically, I was only working four days a week, but they gave me extra time, sometimes on Saturdays. As a single parent, I won't be able to do the extra time any more. It will be bad enough having to leave Rachel with someone during regular hours. I couldn't leave her for extra time. It's going to be tight, but I figured that I can do it if I count my pennies."

"What about the father? I know it's not a usual situation. Will he be giving you any form of support?"

Adelle sighed and tightened her grip on her mug. She fixed her gaze on the woodstove, not really seeing it as she spoke. "That's what I came here to talk about with my Aunt Min and Uncle Bob. Shawn won't be paying any support because his lawyer says I could have had an abortion, considering the circumstances. He said that if I try to get any support out of him, he'll drag me through court, and after the nightmare of what I've already been through in the rape trial, I just can't face that again."

"I can only imagine how hard it must have been."

"It's his parents who have offered support. Shawn is their only child, and they want a grandchild so bad that, although they are upset at how it happened, they want to be a part of Rachel's life as grandparents. It doesn't matter to them that Shawn doesn't want to ever see Rachel. They do. And they know what my job situation is like. I've known them all my life. They've offered some child support, but only if I grant them visitation and custody rights."

Dennis winced. "And you don't want to do that?"

"I don't know if I do or don't. I suppose eventually Rachel is going to discover that she's a product of a rape, and that's going to be hard on her. I only pray that, by then, she will know how much I love her, and that will make up for it. The hardest part will be spending time with her grandparents and knowing Shawn is her father. He hates her enough already. I can't imagine what kind of atmosphere that would be as she grows up. Her second set of grandparents will love her, and their son, who she will know is her father, hates her. Shawn doesn't live with his parents, but it's not realistic to think that, on an ongoing basis, she wouldn't be in contact with him when she's with them."

"That doesn't sound like it would be pleasant."

"No, I don't think it would be. The decision I have to make is to weigh the love her grandparents will have for her versus the hate of her father. Believe it or not, just to have a grandchild, they asked if I would consider marrying Shawn sometime in the future, for the sake of the baby. I don't know what they're thinking, but it's never going to happen. For starters, when Shawn gets out of jail, there's already a restraining order issued."

"Do you think he might be a danger to you?"

"He has threatened me, yes. But even knowing that, I know they will try to use her as a tool in the middle. I can't expose her to that. The other side is that they will love her very much, and is it fair of me to deny the chance of some good coming out of this when I can't really be positive of the future? And then again, there's the money. I know I'm going to struggle, and I know there are times when we'll have to do without. If we had that support, I'd be able to give her things that I otherwise wouldn't. Not just extras like nice clothes and dance lessons and stuff like that, but books, a college fund, and a decent place to live."

"I'd say you've thought about it a lot, and it sounds like there are good and bad to both choices."

"That's what makes this so difficult. They're pressing me for a decision, and that's why I wanted to come here, to get away from everything and be able to think about it from a distance."

"Would you like to pray about it? Right now?"

Adelle turned to see Dennis had repositioned himself on the couch to be ready. If she angled herself the same way, their knees would be touching, and they could face each other at an angle and hold hands as they prayed together.

"Yes. I'd like that very much."

They set the mugs on the floor, joined hands, bowed their heads, and prayed. Dennis prayed beautifully, his words showing he really understood the situation, her dilemma, and the weight of the future of her decision. He never once interjected his opinion, but always asked God for guidance and wisdom, and for a safe and happy future for both her and Rachel.

By the time he was done, Adelle was so choked up she didn't trust herself to speak. She made her prayer very short and very heartfelt and said, "Amen."

Dennis didn't release her hands, nor did he speak. Very softly, he ran his thumb up and down hers, soothing her with the relaxing motion.

"Thank you," she ground out, hating the huskiness of her voice.

He smiled more with his eyes than with his mouth. "Now let's talk about something else. Tell me about your favorite Christmas movie and why it's your favorite."

Adelle smiled, grateful for the change in subject matter.

For the rest of the evening, time passed quickly. They wouldn't have been aware how much time had gone by if it weren't for Rachel wanting to be fed, alerting them to the fact that it was past their own bedtime.

By the time she had finished feeding Rachel, Dennis had pulled the couch into the bed, changed, and had tucked himself in for the night. She tiptoed to settle Rachel into the playpen, blew out the candle, and began her trip back to the bedroom.

She was about to close the bedroom door behind her when she stopped. With her hand on the doorknob, she stood in the doorway, taking in the scene before her.

Rachel and Raymond lay asleep in the playpen, Dennis was fast asleep on the hide-a-bed, and the fire in the woodstove cast its glow over all of them.

It had been the strangest Christmas she'd ever had in her life. Instead of her family, she'd entertained a stranger. For the first time, there had been no turkey. She had to make do with what was available. The lack of electricity alone lent itself to a unique process for the day's activities. Most of all, she and Dennis had simply enjoyed the day for what it was, a time set aside to remember Christ's birth.

The absence of gifts hadn't made a difference. Perhaps she'd received the most special gift of all, a gift that had no monetary value, the gift of a special friendship. He understood her situation, yet was not judgmental, nor did he offer his opinion. He did what she needed, and that was to listen and then to pray.

She hadn't made a decision, but the sensation of it always hanging over her head, ready to overwhelm her was gone. She now knew that God would guide her when the time was right. The situation was fully in His hands, where it should have been in the first place.

Dennis made a grunting sound and rolled over, bringing her attention to him. Fully dressed, he lay sprawled across the small mattress tangled in the blankets, snoring softly. Between the presence of the children, a special man, and the cozy surroundings, in a convoluted way, it felt like what should have been home and a typical family.

Christmas was officially over.

Adelle sighed. It may have been the strangest Christmas in her life, but it had also been the best.

Chapter 13

Daylight came too quickly for Dennis. He didn't want to see that it had stopped snowing. That would mean this part of the world would be starting to dig itself out, and it would be digging closer to them.

First, he flicked the light switch.

Nothing happened.

He picked up the phone and listened.

Silence echoed in his ear.

Adelle appeared with Raymond in her arms. She handed the baby to him and watched him hang up the phone.

"I guess it's still dead, huh? Don't worry. Since it stopped snowing, someone will be working on clearing the roads soon. And when that happens, that will give access to fix the phone lines."

He smiled, hoping she thought he found comfort in her words. He didn't. He wasn't ready to go home.

Dennis held Raymond back out to Adelle, encouraging her to take him. "Since you made supper yesterday, how about if I make breakfast?"

As Adelle accepted Raymond her eyebrows scrunched in the middle. "What do you have in mind?"

"I'm not sure, but I'll be able to figure something out."

"That's what I'm afraid of. Since there's no microwave, how about if you watch them, and I'll make breakfast?" She handed Raymond back. Raymond squealed with glee at all the movement.

Dennis narrowed one eye. "I have the feeling that I should be insulted."

She had the nerve to laugh. "Don't be insulted. Think of it as realizing your limitations."

Although it stung, he couldn't feel insulted because the sad fact was, she was right. He didn't have a clue what he could prepare for breakfast, but he had the best of intentions. At home, he either had cold cereal, or he went through the drive-thru window at the local fast-food restaurant and picked up something he could eat in the car on the way to the office.

He retired to the quilt in front of the woodstove and did his best to amuse the babies, all the while inhaling the fragrance of something very delicious sizzling in the pan. By the time she called him to the table, he worried that his stomach had been growling so loud she would be able to hear it across the room.

"Wow. French toast."

He said a very quick prayer and dug in, savoring every bite.

"You're acting like this is such a big deal. French toast is easy to make."

"Never tried it," he mumbled around his mouthful. "But sometimes on the weekend I have waffles."

Her eyes widened. "Waffles? Waffles are harder to make than French toast. If you can make waffles, you can make this."

He tried not to choke and swallowed hard. "I hate to burst your bubble, but the waffles I'm referring to are the frozen toaster kind."

Her mouth opened, but no sound came out.

"Yeah. I don't even put them in the microwave."

"If the power ever went out, you'd starve in your own home. Do you know that?"

"Naw. I'd just go out for a burger."

"I think you missed my point."

He shook his head. "No. I got your point. I think you missed mine. Men don't need kitchens. We only need the closest fast-food restaurant, and we'll never go hungry."

She swished a piece of the French toast in a puddle of syrup on her plate and mumbled something he couldn't hear. He didn't dare ask her to repeat it.

"To show you how much I appreciate this fine breakfast, how 'bout if I do the dishes?"

"Nice try. Today was your turn to do them anyway."

Dennis smiled. He loved her quick wit and the resulting verbal banter. She did nothing to try to impress him, and she certainly didn't try to stroke his ego.

He hadn't thought about Joanna for a long time, but he couldn't help but compare. If this had happened at home, Joanna would have convinced him to go out. If they couldn't go out, she wouldn't have attempted to cook anything, although he would have. She would play helpless and let him do it, and even if he wasn't good at it, she still would have told him he was perfect just to stroke his ego so she could get her own way.

Dennis wondered when he'd become tired of it, and worse, when he'd become so complacent about it.

"We're starting to run low on wood. I'm going to have to dig some wood out of the pile this afternoon."

Instead of looking at Adelle, Dennis looked outside. He couldn't see a cloud in the sky. The sun shining off the stark white snow was so bright it nearly hurt his eyes. He'd never seen so much snow in his entire life.

"I don't think that's a good idea. It's pretty deep out there. It might be over your head."

Her silence made him bite his lip and wonder if he should duck to avoid flying objects.

"I'm not that short," she finally said.

"Then I think you'd better define 'short.'"

Her chin tilted up, and now it was even harder not to laugh, but somehow he managed.

"Short is under five feet tall. I'm taller than that, so I'm not short."

Dennis knew exactly how tall she was. If he wanted to hug her, she would nestle nicely right under his chin. In order to kiss her properly, she would have to stand on her tiptoes and lean into him, and he would envelop her in his arms and hold her tight. They would be perfect together.

"Dennis?"

He tried to stop the heat from rising in his cheeks and couldn't. "Sorry, I was thinking about something else. You were saying?"

"I said this would be a good time to bathe them, and then, while they're sleeping, you could do the dishes and I'll go outside and get more wood."

"But that doesn't seem right."

She harrumphed, crossed her arms over her chest, and rolled her eyes. "Oh, you mean because you're the big strong man, you should do the manual labor while the little woman stays inside doing the domestic chores?"

"That's not what I meant. Well, not really."

Her scowl told him she didn't believe him.

"It's not that. I just hate to see you doing such hard work."

He realized he'd just said exactly what she had accused him of, that he should be doing the man's work of the heavy lifting, and she should be doing the household chores.

"Okay, it is that, but I don't mean it that way."

She tapped her foot, which looked ridiculous when she was wearing those big fuzzy pink slippers, and since they were soft soled, he really didn't hear any tapping.

He dragged his palm over his face. "I meant that it would be easier for me, and I could carry more at a time simply because I'm bigger."

"But I'm the one with winter clothes."

Dennis turned his head and stared out the window. He hadn't exactly frozen to death when he'd braved the cold and snow to get the pine branches for their Christmas tree, although it had taken him three hours to stop shivering once he'd finally made it back inside.

"I really don't mind, Dennis. Remember, I was born and raised in this area.

I'm used to the cold. You're not."

He sighed. "Okay, but I'm giving in under protest."

She patted him on the arm, and he wanted to give her a hug.

"Let's get busy."

Just as they were finished with the second bath, the lights came on.

Adelle cheered. Dennis didn't.

Since Adelle was the first to be finished, she was the first to try the phone. "No dial tone yet, but I don't imagine it will be long."

He didn't care about the phone, he only cared that their time together was now almost at an end. Once the phone came back, he would have no excuse for not finding a way to go home. As unrealistic as it was, he wasn't ready to go home.

"When I'm outside, I'll turn the fridge back to electricity. In fact, I should do it now. I don't know how much propane is left, and I don't want to waste it now that we have electricity again. Even with the electricity, we still need the propane for cooking."

He accepted Rachel and sat on the quilt, a spot he was becoming very accustomed to, while Adelle kicked off her slippers and headed to the closet for her coat and boots.

In the background, a strange motorized hum sounded. Normally he wouldn't have noticed something so slight, but in the total silence of the cabin, it was out of place. "What's that noise? Is something wrong since we've got both the propane and electricity on at the same time?"

She tilted her head as she also listened. "No, it doesn't work like that. I have to physically switch the fridge over." She listened as the noise grew louder.

As suddenly as the lights had gone on, a wide smile lit Adelle's face. She clapped her hands in front of her, dropped her coat on the floor, and ran to the window.

"What is it?" Dennis asked.

"I don't believe this! It's Uncle Bob and Aunt Min!"

Dennis blinked, put Rachel down into her car seat, and walked toward the window to join Adelle. He didn't see anything, but the noise was getting louder. "I thought the roads would be impassable for at least a day or two."

She laughed. The hum continued to grow louder, turning into a sound much like a lawnmower, which Dennis thought quite bizarre, considering the amount of snow outside.

"The roads will still be impassable for at least a couple of days. But they're not coming by car. They'll be past the trees and into the clearing in a few seconds. They're on the snowmobile."

"Snowmobile. . ." His voice trailed off as his heart sank. The French toast that he'd enjoyed not long ago turned into a lump in the pit of his stomach.

If the snowmobile could get there with no trouble, he would have no trouble going back to Blue River, and from there, he would have no trouble finding transportation home. All he had to do was pack the few clothes he had into his one suitcase and bundle Raymond. They could be gone within half an hour.

Adelle ran back to the closet, yanked on her boots, pulled on her coat without doing up the buttons, then ran back to the door.

The noise grew to an annoying roar, then stopped.

Adelle threw open the door and ran outside. "Aunt Min! Uncle Bob! I'm so glad to see you!"

The door closed, cutting off whatever words were being exchanged.

Dennis didn't rush to the door. He didn't want to see her aunt and uncle, not because they wouldn't be nice people, but because they brought with them the means for him to leave.

Guilt for his selfish motivations roared through him. He should have been happy for Adelle, but he was too busy feeling sorry for himself. And it was wrong.

He settled both babies into their car seats, plugged the pacifiers into their mouths, and stood. He smoothed the wrinkles in his pants, straightened his sleeves, and walked slowly to the window.

An older man was unloading bags from something that looked like a combination between a sled and a miniature snowmobile. A tow bar attached the unit to a large and very sturdy snowmobile. An older woman and Adelle were wrapped together in a firm hug.

As he watched, the uncle handed both women a number of bags, he grabbed a box out of the trailer and the three of them turned toward the door and started slogging through the snow. He hurried to the door to open it as they filed in caravan style and closed it behind them when they were inside.

Dennis forced himself to smile. "Hi," he said as cheerfully as he could muster. "You must be Uncle Bob and Aunt Min. Thanks for the use of your cabin."

They dumped everything on the counter and approached him.

"You must be Dennis, of course. Welcome. As you can see, we brought everything. We're a few days late, but we finally made it."

The three of them scurried back outside to bring in the last of the contents of the trailer. Dennis was amazed at the volume being unloaded onto the counter. He didn't want to snoop, but in the piles of things they'd brought, he could see two packages of diapers—both pink.

Adelle's uncle disappeared outside one more time for a couple of minutes, and Dennis assumed he was turning off the propane to the fridge.

Instead of unpacking the bags on the counter, Adelle's aunt scurried to the babies. "Oh, they're so adorable together! How's my little pumpkin?" She sank to her hands and knees and patted Rachel, then Raymond, on their little tummies. "You have a beautiful baby, Dennis. She's almost as adorable as our little Rachel."

"Uh, he's a boy. His name is Raymond. I ran out of blue sleepers."

The woman giggled and tickled their tummies again. "Oops. Sorry."

Adelle's uncle wasn't in such a rush to see the babies. The man never broke eye contact, making Dennis feel very much like a bug under a microscope.

"You two been okay out here?"

Dennis stiffened from head to toe. He shouldn't have felt intimidated because he was at least two inches taller than Adelle's uncle, but in this case he had a feeling that his size made him more suspect. If they hadn't been worried, they wouldn't have come all this way under the present conditions, snowmobile or not. He thought he knew the real question, but didn't know how to answer. "Yes, sir, considering."

"Haven't seen a snowfall like this for nigh on twenty years. And on Christmas, yet. So you're from Vancouver. Don't get much snow there, do you?"

Dennis shook his head. He didn't think her uncle really wanted to talk about the rain in Vancouver at this particular moment, although he couldn't quite figure out what he was supposed to be saying. Dennis wondered if this was some kind of test and if he was passing. "No, and when we do, it's nothing like this."

He could hear Adelle in the kitchen unpacking and putting away the fresh supplies. In the background, her aunt was chattering to the babies that she couldn't decide which one of them to pick up and explaining that she would stay on the quilt and tell them a story, as if they could understand what she was saying.

"Dellie says you had an accident. We didn't see a car anywhere."

Dennis nearly choked. Dellie? Her nickname was Dellie? He didn't dare speak.

"So where is it?"

He tried to remember the original question. "The car's probably covered in snow, that's why you didn't see it." He also thought about the shirt covered with baby puke that he'd thrown into the snow shortly after his arrival. Like the car, it was well covered. The car was easy to explain, but he knew the shirt would be more difficult.

"Guess it will turn up in the spring thaw, huh?"

Dennis opened his mouth to warn him about finding the shirt, but Adelle distracted him when she clanked something on the counter. "Oh!" she exclaimed. "You brought formula! This is wonderful!"

Dennis's words caught in his throat. The thought of formula for Raymond pushed all else from his brain.

Adelle's aunt picked up Raymond, gave him a cuddle, and rubbed her cheek on his fuzzy head. "We know you won't need it, Dellie, but when you said Dennis had a baby, we didn't know how old the baby was, so we took a chance. You must be almost out of formula for this little darling now."

They had no idea, and he wasn't going to tell them what they'd had to resort to, and how hard it had been on Adelle. The last few days had been a lesson in trust and relying on God unlike anything he'd ever experienced. "Yes, I could really use it. Thank you. I don't know what to say."

The woman sighed when Raymond gurgled. "Think nothing of it. I just love babies. I'll do anything for them. I wish I could have had one of my own."

Dennis again opened his mouth to speak, but her uncle spoke first.

"It's been a long morning. Auntie and I are hungry. You finished putting everything away yet?"

"Yes. How about ham sandwiches? We had ham for dinner yesterday, and there's enough leftover for lunch."

"Good, because for supper, we brought the rest of the turkey. We cooked it at home for Christmas dinner yesterday, and so we'll still be eating leftovers until it's gone. You won't have to cook much for a few days. But I sure missed those delicious baked yams we have every Christmas. Right Min?"

"Whatever. I don't care about cooking right now. Oh, Dennis, your little Raymond is so sweet. He's talking to me. Can you hear him?"

Adelle's uncle responded with a grunt. "Babies don't talk. That's gas."

"You stop that. He's a wonderful baby. How would you like to put on some music so we have something nice to listen to?"

"Only if I can put on some Waylon."

"Just put on some Christmas carols, okay?"

Dennis gave up trying to follow any part of the conversations going on around him. "I think I'll help with lunch. Excuse me."

❄

Adelle tried not to let Dennis see her hands shaking. Part of her was happy to have her family arrive. Part of her was even happier that they had brought formula, just for the relief it would bring. But part of her suddenly realized their arrival meant Dennis and Raymond would soon be leaving.

She didn't know if she was ready for that. She'd finally gotten used to them; now she didn't know if she was ready to let them go.

"Want me to cut that tomato?"

Her hands froze midway through a swipe of adding mayo to the bread. "You cut yourself peeling potatoes. What makes you think you'd be better at this?"

"That was different. This time I'll be using a knife."

That didn't make it better. That made it worse. "I don't think so."

She noticed he ignored her protests and did it anyway, and he didn't do too badly. She completed the assembly of the sandwiches, Dennis set the table, and everyone sat for lunch.

This time Uncle Bob prayed before they ate. His prayer was more formal than Dennis's, and since it had been brought to her attention so many times, she noticed Uncle Bob's prayer was much longer.

During lunch, they talked about the snow and what the city was like as people started to dig their way out. With the Christmas season in mind, so far only the main roads had been cleared, and they had not finished clearing the main highway.

However, the condition of the highway didn't matter. Dennis didn't need the highway. He would be leaving in the snowmobile. The only thing that would stop him from leaving would be if the snow suddenly melted and the snowmobile didn't have enough snow base to drive safely. And if that happened, they would simply drive out in Adelle's car.

There was only one conclusion. He really was leaving.

They agreed that it made the most sense for Adelle to stay at the cabin with Aunt Min. Uncle Bob would drive Dennis and Raymond into town, get them settled either onto the bus or into a motel, and then return.

After lunch, Adelle stacked the dishes beside the sink and took Rachel into the bedroom to be fed. Dennis packed what few belongings he had while Aunt Min insisted on giving Raymond a bottle, not missing any chance to complain that she never got to feed her darling niece, since Rachel didn't take a bottle.

When Adelle came out of the bedroom, Uncle Bob was standing in the same place he had been before she went in, which was at the woodstove warming his hands. "Looks like we're going to need to bring in more wood, Dellie. I think I'd better do that now, before we go."

Dennis set his suitcase by the door, ready to go. Its presence was a sad reminder that it was over.

She didn't know how it had happened, but in the few days since she picked him up, they'd developed a friendship unlike any other. She couldn't see that letters or e-mail or even the occasional phone call would be satisfying after the lengthy and personal discussions they'd shared. More than likely, the time would grow longer between communications, until finally they never saw or heard from each other again. She didn't want to think about it, but she could think of nothing else.

Dennis joined her uncle in front of the woodstove.

"I don't know how I'll ever be able to repay you for the use of your cabin these past few days. For now, since Raymond fell asleep, how about if I go get the wood? I really would like to let him sleep for a little while, because if he doesn't, I think he'll probably be cranky during the trip on the snowmobile."

Adelle clasped her hands tightly and stepped forward. "Don't be silly, Dennis. You've only got that small leather jacket, and you don't have boots. Uncle Bob can do it. He does it all the time." For selfish reasons, she didn't offer to be the person to get the wood, as she had been ready to do earlier. If Uncle Bob brought it in, that would give her more time to say a proper good-bye to Dennis while her uncle was busy.

Just the thought of saying good-bye made her stomach churn.

Uncle Bob raised his eyebrows and turned his head toward Dennis, but Dennis spoke first.

"I don't think we're too much different in size. Would you mind if I borrowed your coat? You've had a long trip on that snowmobile, and you look like you haven't completely warmed up. You stay by the fire, and I'll get the wood."

She wondered if Dennis realized that he would still get fairly cold outside, even with Uncle Bob's heavy parka. And then Dennis would have to sit on the back of the snowmobile for over an hour in the wind, just wearing his thin leather jacket. She didn't want to think of how cold he would be.

Uncle Bob didn't move. "Don't be ridiculous, you'll freeze your feet. What size shoes you wear?"

"Size eleven."

"Hmmm. . .I wear a size nine, but I buy a size ten boot so I can fit extra socks in there. You might get away with it with regular socks."

Dennis looked down at his sock-clad feet and wiggled his toes. "Regular socks are all I have."

"I always wear good wool socks in my boots when I'm out. Not those funny acrylic ones, but real good wool. And then I have my regular socks underneath so my feet don't get itchy."

"I've never worn wool socks. Never needed to."

They both studied Dennis's feet.

"Those should be okay. Nice socks, by the way."

He wiggled his toes again. "Yeah. They're new."

Adelle nearly wanted scream. She was fretting about him leaving and never seeing each other again, and Dennis and her uncle were discussing socks.

She cleared her throat. "So are you going to borrow Uncle Bob's parka and boots, or not?"

They both looked up at her in unison. Adelle felt her cheeks heat up at their perusal.

At the same second, they both turned away from her and back to each other.

"By the way, do you have gloves I can borrow?"

"In the pockets."

As Dennis slid on Uncle Bob's parka, he turned to her. "So, Adelle, do you want to help me?"

She couldn't stop her smile. "Yes!"

Chapter 14

Adelle bit her bottom lip. It stopped her from laughing, but it didn't stop her from smiling. Dennis was trying so hard to be brave, but she could tell that even with Uncle Bob's boots and parka, his teeth were still chattering. The parka was a little snug and the sleeves were a little short, but he was covered much better than if he had been wearing the leather jacket. She also suspected the boots pinched his toes, although he said nothing. But the gloves fit okay.

The snow was powder-fine since it was so cold, but the sheer volume was daunting, especially since they had to dig through four feet of it to get to the woodpile. Since the door to the shed was completely covered all the way to the top, they decided the lesser of two evils would be to dig for the firewood by hand. The only reason they needed to get into the shed was if they ran out of wood and had to cut more, but Uncle Bob claimed he had enough wood piled up to last through the winter. All they had to do was get to it.

Dennis stopped digging and pressed his fists into the small of his back. He arched and blew out a long breath, which came out in a cloud of steam. "I feel like I'm digging for buried treasure. If I ever think of moving away from Vancouver, I'll remind myself of this."

"You have a bad attitude, you know that? Snow is fun."

"Snow is cold."

"Snow is pretty."

"Snow was prettier when I was inside and it was outside."

"You have to make up your mind to make the best of it. Think of all the wonderful things you can do outside in the winter. You can go skating, make snowmen when the temperature is right, and there's always snowball fights. Best of all, you can make snow angels and tractor treads."

He grunted, slapped his hands to his upper arms, and mumbled something she didn't think she wanted to hear.

"You're being such a cynic." Adelle grabbed his hand and tugged to lead him away from shed and to a flat area they hadn't messed up. "Watch me." She walked as carefully as she could for a few steps, trying to disturb as little of the pristine surface as she could. When she was a few steps way from Dennis, she spread her arms and fell backward, landing flat on her back in the snow. She swished her arms and legs to make the wings and the angel's skirt, and then climbed out of the indent as carefully as she could. Next, she would show him how to make tractor treads out of bootprints.

As she rejoined Dennis she brushed the snow from her coat and swiped what she could from her hair. "See?"

Instead of laughing at her childish artwork, he grasped her hands and gave them a gentle squeeze through the layers of mittens and gloves. "It suits you. You really are a little snow angel."

Adelle tilted her chin up to reply, but the words left her. His dopey little smile and the tenderness in his eyes caused her heartbeat to quicken and her brain to go blank. She didn't have a lot of experience with men, but behind the grin, she doubted he was thinking about anything that had to do with making snow angels.

He gave her hands a little tug, which made her step a little closer, close enough to kiss her.

Adelle yanked her hands out of his and placed them in the center of his chest. "Your turn," she called out and pushed with enough force to catch him off guard.

He flailed his arms, but it was too late. Dennis landed flat on his back, followed by a pouf of snow that flew up in the air on impact, then settled around him.

She looked down at him. "Did you know that, even though angels depicted throughout the years are always shown as women, in all the Bible references where angels appear, they're always men?"

He blinked and looked up. "So?"

"So it's much more fitting for you to make a snow angel than me. Consider it a guy thing."

He didn't move, but he didn't get up, either. "I feel silly."

"Think of it this way, if you don't do it now, you may never get the chance again."

"Pardon me?"

She rested her fists on her hips. "Do you ever get enough snow in Vancouver to make a snow angel? This right kind of fine-powder snow? Even if you did, do you have a place where you could do it with no one watching?"

"Okay, you win. Tell me if I'm doing this right."

Dennis swished his arms and legs in the snow and made the biggest snow angel she'd ever seen.

"How does it look?"

"First you have to get out of it so I can see it."

"If I move, I'll wreck it."

"Just the bottom. Come on, I'll help you." She extended both hands, and he reached up, first with one hand then the other. She held tight and pulled.

She didn't want to ask him how much he weighed, but since he was ten inches taller than she was she had to assume it was a lot more. She couldn't budge him.

Suddenly, he grinned. A dreadful feeling washed over her. Without warning, his grip on her hands tightened and he pulled. Hard.

Adelle flew forward, and just as she thought she would land face first in the snow, he extended his arms and she landed with a thud on top of him. To lessen the impact, his arms closed around her and he rolled them both through the snow a few times, ending up with her beneath him laying on her back.

Dennis grinned down at her, supporting himself on his elbows beside her head. "How does it feel, smarty?"

Adelle grinned back. "Not bad. How does this feel?" Before he could figure out what she was doing, she grabbed two mittfuls of snow and swooshed them up and rubbed them into his hair. The powder snow flew everywhere, including into her own face, but she didn't care because she was laughing too hard.

"Hey!" he called out.

His weight thumped down on her as he came off his elbows and grabbed her wrists, but before he squashed the breath out of her, he rolled the two of them over until he was on his back and she was lying on top of him.

He continued to hold her wrists, immobilizing her above him. "Apologize, or you'll be sorry."

She didn't like his sly little grin. He was up to something, and she would probably get the worst of it, but she was having too much fun to stop.

"Never!" Adelle shook her head so the snow fluttered out of her hair and into his face.

Panting from the exertion, his mouth was open. Some of the snow from her hair landed in his mouth, making him sputter. His mouth snapped shut. "That does it," he grumbled, fighting the grin, speaking with his lips barely moving. "I'm through being Mr. Nice Guy."

Before he could roll again Adelle spread her legs, bracing herself with her knees, preventing his movement. She'd played enough games in the snow as a child that she knew all the tricks.

Since he hadn't expected her to prevent whatever he was planning, his grip loosened for a split second. Adelle took advantage of it. Before he could think, she pulled her hands free, grabbed more snow, and mussed it into his hair, laughing the entire time.

When he caught her hands she couldn't stop laughing. Snow dotted his face, and the white in his hair almost made him look old and gray. For a second, she thought about how distinguished he would look when his hair started to turn gray with age. Dennis really was a handsome man, even lying on the ground and covered with snow. "Give up? I know all the tricks. You don't stand a chance."

She wiggled her arms and waggled her eyebrows, just to make him think she had something else planned, even though she didn't.

"I give up!" he said. "You win!" He released her wrists, raised his hands over his head, and lay perfectly still in the snow, like a submissive dog.

Slowly, she clambered off him. This time when she offered to pull him up, he rose with only a slight tug.

At the same time they shook whatever snow in their hair hadn't melted and brushed what they could off of their clothing.

"That was a blast. I guess you're right. Snow is lots of fun, when you're dressed for it."

"Except we wrecked our snow angels."

They stood side by side and studied the mess. She couldn't tell there had ever been snow angels.

Suddenly, he moved to face her, blocking her view of the carnage. "I wouldn't have believed it from someone so short, but you did it. You beat me."

Adelle grinned. "Well, if I won, then what's my prize?"

He stepped so close that he brushed against the buttons on her coat. She could feel his hands barely touching her hips through the layers of her coat, and she realized he was using her to steady himself as he bent his knees to lessen the height difference until his face was level with hers.

"The prize is that you get to kiss me."

❋

Dennis closed his eyes and hoped for the best. He prayed that he was doing the right thing. He wanted to scoop her into his arms and kiss her thoroughly, but he couldn't do that. With her history he didn't want her to think he was forcing himself on her or taking advantage of her in any way. The only reason he touched her at all was to keep his balance in the uncomfortable squat required to stay at eye level with her.

He hoped her family wasn't watching through the window, but he really didn't care. Soon he would be gone, and if he didn't act now, it would be too late. Just like his chance to make the snow angel, this fleeting moment would be gone forever if he didn't grab it now.

The next move was hers.

Something cold and rough touched his face, but he didn't open his eyes. He had to trust that she would take him seriously and not do something rotten to him in the snow.

It took him a few seconds to figure out that the rough texture was her suede mittens, and the cold pressing into his cheeks were little frozen lumps of snow stuck to them.

And then, in contrast to the cold hard lumps on his cheeks, her soft warm lips touched his.

Dennis could no longer maintain that ridiculous position, not with his heart pounding in double-time and fireworks going off in his brain. Adelle was kissing him and he was going to kiss her back. Properly this time.

He raised his gloved hands to her cheeks, not breaking the kiss as he slowly straightened his knees until he was comfortable again. He didn't want to have to think about maintaining his balance, not when her kiss was short-circuiting his brain. He slid his hands until they were behind her back so he could embrace her fully. A low groan escaped him when her mittens left his cheeks and slid behind his neck. He just might have died and gone to heaven; he was being kissed by the woman he loved.

Too soon, he felt her starting to pull away, so he reluctantly allowed the separation. It wasn't what he wanted, but it had to be. They were outside in the middle of the yard, in full view of her family.

Adelle's cheeks flushed red, and he knew it wasn't from the cold. "We'd better get that firewood into the cabin."

He wanted to tell her he loved her, but he couldn't. It was too soon. Everything had happened so fast he doubted she'd believe him, especially since there hadn't been sufficient time for him to earn her trust. He had done his best to prove himself responsible, honorable, and most important, to live his life by the standards God set before him. He wished he knew that she would take him seriously. "Yeah, let's get back to the woodpile."

They dug out enough wood and trudged back and forth until, again, there was a good healthy pile beside the woodstove.

"Parka keep you warm enough?"

"Yes, sir, thank you." Dennis smiled at Adelle's uncle but inwardly he cringed, half-expecting a comment about taking so long or about indulging in other activities.

"I've been thinking. Since the phone still isn't working, and I don't want to just drop you off without having made arrangements. I couldn't leave you in good conscience until I knew everything was taken care of, and you had a way to get home. Looking at the time, we don't have a lot of leeway. I can't be driving the snowmobile in this area in the dark. I don't want to take the chance that I won't make it back and leave the ladies alone out here all night. Would you mind staying another night?"

Dennis grinned. "Not at all."

"Oh, and one more thing."

Dennis cringed. By now her uncle had no doubt noticed that his parka was wet in spots from rolling around in the snow, and it didn't take a rocket scientist to know that they were outside much longer than necessary to bring in a small pile of firewood. Not that he had anything to hide. Everything they had done had happened in plain view for her aunt and uncle to see from the window, if they desired to watch. The only thing that bothered him was the lack of privacy, not for himself, but he didn't want Adelle to be put on the spot for what had happened between them.

"Yes, sir?" he asked.

"Quit calling me sir. And don't worry about this aunt and uncle stuff. The name's Bob. And my wife's name isn't ma'am, it's Min. We ain't old enough for that nonsense."

He grinned. "You got it."

Min's voice drifted from the couch. "I heard you talking about making arrangements. When was the last time you checked the phone, Bob?"

"Me? I thought you were checking the phone."

"No, you were supposed to be checking the phone."

Adelle picked up the phone. "It's working. There's a dial tone."

Dennis wondered how long it had been working and no one had known. Actually, he wished the phone lines were still down. Although, with transportation into town now available, he no longer had an excuse. "I guess I should make a few calls."

Bob shook his head. "Oh, forget it. It's too late anyway. It's nearly supper-time on the day after Christmas. Most everything will be closed. Phone in the morning. The cabin's awful small, but we can make do for the night. The girls can take the bedroom, and we can sleep, uh. . ."

Dennis glanced quickly at the small hide-a-bed, the only other place to sleep in the cabin. "You can take the hide-a-bed. I'll make do on the floor by the woodstove. To be close to the babies."

Bob nodded and smiled. "You play chess?"

❄

Adelle put away the last dish while Dennis drained the sink. She had thoroughly enjoyed her aunt's special Christmas omelets for breakfast, even though it was two days after Christmas. The best part was that she didn't have to cook. So she had offered to do the dishes while her aunt played with Rachel. What had surprised her even more than Dennis jumping in to wash the dishes was that her uncle didn't protest to being left with a baby in his lap.

Now that she thought about it, except for the times when she needed to be alone, Dennis had almost glued himself to her side. The strange thing was, she didn't mind. She had wanted to come to the cabin to be alone, but at the thought of his imminent departure, panic set in.

It was unrealistic, but she didn't want him to go. He had fit in well with her family, and when they discovered he was a Christian, they'd opened up to him in a way she'd never seen. Conversation hadn't stopped until it was time to go to bed, and even then, they'd gone to bed much too late.

She didn't envy him the long drive on the snowmobile. As a child she'd always enjoyed the joyrides her uncle took her on, but she'd never ridden it for as long or over such rough terrain as the trip to Blue River required. She knew from experience that any trip was more uncomfortable for the passenger than the driver, especially with the awkwardness of having to hold Raymond in the infant car seat the entire trip.

Dennis made all his trip arrangements by phone with his credit card. Blue River didn't have a real airport; it only had a 5600-foot asphalt airstrip, which was completely buried in snow. Therefore, he'd booked a ticket on the bus from Blue River to Kamloops, where they would connect with a flight home to Vancouver.

There was no delaying him, or he would miss his departure time. Too soon, his suitcase and the diaper bag were by the door, and Raymond was dressed in his baby bunting suit and strapped into his car seat, which sat on the floor at Dennis's feet. Fortunately Rachel was asleep, so she didn't have to deal with a fussing infant.

It was time to say good-bye, possibly forever.

Adelle stiffened her back to make herself as tall as possible. Since he wore his sneakers and she was in her fuzzy slippers, he stood an entire foot taller than her. She looked up at him and tried to keep her voice even as she spoke. "Phone me as soon as you get home, okay?"

"Sure."

She had so much to say, but all they did was stand near the door and stare at each other.

Uncle Bob joined them and picked up Dennis's suitcase. "Min and I will figure a way to load this. We'll also pack up some formula and diapers for you. You never know, right?" Uncle Bob and Aunt Min went outside, leaving Adelle and Dennis alone in the cabin to say their good-byes in private. One day she would thank them for it.

She reached up to play with the collar of his leather jacket, which didn't need fixing; she just needed something to do with her hands. "It's going to be a cold ride home. Make sure you drink lots of coffee when you get to the bus depot, okay?"

"Sure." His hands covered hers, and he massaged her wrists with his thumbs, with her hands still resting on his shoulders. "Give Rachel a big hug and kiss for me."

Her eyes burned, but she managed to blink it away. "Of course."

The roar of the snowmobile's motor began, the engine revved a couple of times, then ran smoothly.

Adelle forced herself to take her hands away, to start the withdrawal process. When she did, Dennis rammed his hands into his pockets.

She tried to clear the thickness out of her throat. "I think it's time for you to go."

"I know."

This time she couldn't stop her burning tears. She felt as though her heart was ripping in two. One tear overflowed and trickled down her cheek. "I'll miss you," she choked out.

His hand trembled as he reached up and wiped the tear away with his knuckles, then let his hand drop to his side. "This is so stupid. I can't just leave you here and go home. There has to be a way to keep seeing each other. We have something special here I can't explain, a rightness, even though we haven't known each other long. I can't let it end like this." He rammed both hands into his pockets. "I'm not saying this lightly; I want you to come home with me. I need you, Adelle. I need you to be my. . ." His voice trailed off.

Adelle's heart pounded. She'd never felt such a connection with any human being, ever. They'd only met days ago, but she'd shared things with him it had taken months to share with her best friend. Her words flowed naturally with Dennis. His responses weren't condescending, he didn't pretend to understand when he didn't. He knew when she needed a suggestion and when she just needed an ear.

Likewise, she could only guess at how he felt to lose the brother with whom he had been close all their lives. The combination of grief and the sudden shock of becoming an instant father was more than she could imagine, to say nothing of the sudden opening of his spiritual eyes concerning the heart of his fiancée, or rather, his now ex-fiancée. Yet, she could relate to him, and in the same way, she could give him suggestions when she thought he needed them, and she could tell the right time to keep quiet and listen when he needed to talk.

Adelle had never believed in love at first sight, yet she had no explanation for their instant bond. Was this love?

He'd kissed her twice, and it had been just like what she frequently read about in the Heartsong romance novels she subscribed to. Beyond the obvious attraction, they connected both on a spiritual level and with a deep personal kinship. She didn't want to be separated from him—she wondered what it would be like to stay with him forever, to be his friend, his lover, his soul mate. His wife.

Her breath caught in her throat. "You need me to be your. . . ?"

He cleared his throat. "I need you to be my nanny."

Chapter 15

Dennis sat in the boarding area of the Kamloops District airport. He didn't know how many hours had passed before he finally stopped shivering. He didn't think he ever wanted to see that stupid leather jacket again. Rather than the bus depot, their first stop in Blue River was the co-op, a place Dennis could only compare to a modern version of an old country store. They had everything from hardware and tackle to foodstuffs and clothing all under one roof. There he'd purchased a real winter jacket, boots, and padded gloves. Then they climbed back onto the snowmobile. At the door of the bus depot, they had exchanged addresses, said their good-byes, and Bob roared away on the snowmobile, back to the little mountain cabin. And Adelle.

The intercom buzzed and a garbled voice announced an arrival. The noise made Raymond murmur in his sleep, and Dennis sighed and stroked Raymond's back. After an hour and a half on the snowmobile, then the grueling two and a half hour bus ride from Blue River to Kamloops, he now had an hour to wait for his short flight home, which gave him lots of time to think.

He thought he was an idiot.

At the last minute, in that one fleeting chance he had to tell Adelle that he loved her, that he wanted her to come home with him forever, he had panicked. He didn't want her to be his nanny, his paid help. He wanted her to be his wife and all that went with it. When his mouth opened, in that one split second of hesitation, the wrong word had come out, and he would regret it for the rest of his life.

The shock on Adelle's face when he said "nanny" instead of "wife" cut him to the core, but by then, it was too late. Bob had walked in the door and said they had to leave right away, and the moment was gone forever. Just like the snow angels.

She had said she'd think about it. A classic brush-off—exactly what he deserved.

By the time he landed at Vancouver, his nerves were shot. The takeoff had been hard on his ears, which was normal, but Raymond had screeched in agony. His cries broke his heart. Every woman on the plane had poured out their sympathy to the two of them once they were at cruising altitude. A few of them even offered to hold Raymond while he collected himself. His inexperience with babies had never been more obvious.

The landing was as bad as the takeoff, maybe worse. When the time came to disembark, everyone remained seated, waiting for him and his crying baby to deplane first. Hopefully Rick, his best friend, had gotten his message and would be there to drive him home. Otherwise, after he changed Raymond's soggy diaper, he would simply call a cab. He'd never wanted to go home so desperately in his life.

With the diaper bag slung over his shoulder and a whimpering Raymond in his arms, Dennis headed straight for the luggage carrousel, wondering if the men's washrooms had baby changing facilities.

His heart nearly stopped as he entered the arrival area.

Rick wasn't waiting for him. Joanna was.

"Dennis! Over here!" She waved and ran toward him, her heels clicking on the floor.

Adelle would have worn more practical shoes.

"Joanna," he muttered.

She leaned up to kiss him. He didn't want her kiss. Whatever relationship they had was over. She no longer had the right to touch him, as far as he was concerned. However, he didn't want to cause a scene in the middle of the busy Vancouver International Airport, so he turned his head so that the kiss landed on his cheek. He would deal with her in a more private setting.

"So this is little Raymond. Can I hold him?"

"You sure you want to hold him? He needs to be changed."

He could tell her smile was forced. "Of course I do."

He was very close to telling her that if she wanted to hold him, then she could take him and change him while he waited for his one suitcase and the car seat to come down the luggage chute. He thought it would be poetic justice to let her change a wet baby, but he didn't want to mislead her. In his present mood, he was close to telling her to go home and that he would take a cab.

"Where's Rick? I thought Rick was going to come and get me."

"Oh, I was with Rick when he listened to your message. I told him I would come and get you."

He wondered what she was doing with his best friend, but then told himself he didn't care. As far as he was concerned, the relationship between himself and Joanna had ended the day before Christmas Eve.

The only reason he let Joanna carry Raymond was because he had his hands full. When they left the arrival area, he turned to the washrooms, and Joanna turned to the exit.

"Joanna!" he called out. "Where are you going? Remember, I just said he had to be changed."

"Oh."

Adelle wouldn't have forgotten. She would have seen to the baby's needs first.

Joanna returned but didn't offer to take the diaper bag. She just stood there, waiting.

Dennis laid the suitcase and car seat down but left the diaper bag on his shoulder. "I'll take him."

As they shuffled Raymond back into his arms, the engagement ring scratched his hand. He gritted his teeth. She was still wearing it.

Without a word, he took care of Raymond and they left. He barely said two words in the car, but Joanna chattered nonstop. She talked about what her parents gave her for Christmas, she thanked him for the gifts he had given her, then continued on about items he considered gossip and really didn't want to hear. He noticed she didn't ask how he'd fared in the accident, what it had been like being stranded, or how he'd managed with a baby. She did pass on her regrets that his nice car was wrecked. He made a mental note to call the towing place he'd contracted in Blue River for a final bill once they dug the car out and hauled it to the holding yard until the insurance was finished with it. They were also going to pry open the trunk and ship home anything that was worth salvaging.

Dennis stared out the window as Joanna continued to yak. He wondered how in the world he'd ever thought he could be happily married to this woman. She was more like a sister to him than a friend because they'd grown up together, a poor reason to commit the rest of one's life to someone.

As he walked in his front door, he looked at his ornate tree and all the gifts still beneath it. He was too tired to open them. With Raymond asleep in the car seat on the way home, he had allowed himself to relax, and the events of the past week had caught up to him, overloading his senses. He was exhausted and wanted nothing more than to fall into bed, but he couldn't. He had a baby to look after, and his housekeeper wouldn't be back until tomorrow. Fortunately Raymond was still asleep after the car ride, and Dennis wondered how long it would last.

He checked his watch. He'd given Raymond a bottle on the plane, which was two hours ago. After the day they'd had, Raymond would probably sleep for a while.

"See what I bought for Raymond?" In the middle of the living room sat a blue tricycle with a large red bow on it.

He hadn't expected Joanna to buy anything for Raymond considering she had told him to put Raymond up for adoption.

"Joanna, he's only one-month-old and can't properly hold his head up by himself yet. He can't sit by himself, and he certainly can't use a tricycle! What he does need is a place to sleep. If you went to all the trouble to buy him something, knowing I wouldn't have a chance to go shopping before I got home, don't you think something more practical would have been a better choice for his first night in his new home? Like diapers? Or clothing? Or a crib?"

"I don't know anything about cribs, but I found some really cute wallpaper."

"Joanna, I think we have to talk."

"And I asked around and got some recommendations for a nanny. You can start interviewing tomorrow."

"Joanna, listen to me. You made yourself perfectly clear when you said you wouldn't look after someone else's child. You told me to make a choice between marrying you or keeping Raymond. I chose Raymond."

"But. . .but. . .I might have been a little premature. I've decided to help you get a nanny for him."

"In other words, I called you on it, and you lost. I've done a lot of thinking and you were right all along. There is no place in my life for both you and Raymond. The woman I marry should want to care for Raymond as part of our family, not as a burden. I'm sorry, Joanna, but it's over between us. The wedding is off. Keep the ring. I don't care what you do with it. I think you should go home."

"Go home. . ." Joanna's beautiful face transformed into an ugly scowl. "Well, that's just fine!" She stomped to the Christmas tree, withdrew the gift that she'd set under it for him, and stomped to the door. "And you can find a nanny on your own."

The door slammed behind her, the sound echoing in the large room.

Dennis sank to the couch, all the strength drained from him. He'd already found his perfect nanny, a woman who would also be his perfect wife. If she would have him.

Beside him on the floor, Raymond whimpered, then began to cry in earnest.

Dennis ran his hand over his face. Since Raymond was awake, he knew what he had to do. Sleep would come later. For now, he had a family to take care of, and unless Raymond was going to spend the night in the laundry basket, a trick that Adelle had told him about, he needed to go shopping.

❄

The phone rang.

Adelle stood at the window, staring at the mess in the snow in the middle of the clearing. The sun was starting to set, and it was the last time she would be able to see it as a real reminder that the past few days had really happened.

"Aren't you going to get that, Dellie? You know it's for you. And you know who it is."

Part of her wanted to talk to him, part of her didn't, but she answered it anyway.

"Hi, Adelle. We're home."

"Did you have a nice flight?"

He let out a very strange, humorless laugh. "It was okay."

"Are you and Raymond all settled now?"

"Yes, he's now got a crib and a dresser and a changing table. You wouldn't believe the assembly instructions on those things."

She smiled. "Oh, yes I would."

His smile came through in his voice. "Yeah. I guess you would."

Silence hung over the line.

"Adelle, what I was trying to say before I left didn't come out right. I really want you to come. I need you. For a lot of reasons."

She gulped. "I told you I have to think about it." She'd been thinking of nothing else since he left.

"And?"

"I don't know."

A cry echoed in the background. "I think I have to go. May I call you tomorrow?"

Adelle's heart pounded in her chest. In other words, he wanted her to make a decision by tomorrow. Normally she didn't like being pressured, but in this case, she knew getting it over with was the best thing. Then it wouldn't be hanging over her head.

The crying became louder.

"Yes, call tomorrow. Good-bye, Dennis."

"Good-bye, Adelle."

She hung up quickly, and when she turned around both her aunt and uncle were watching her.

"What?"

"Did he ask you to go to Vancouver?"

"Yes."

"Well?"

"I don't know. I haven't decided."

"You know how you feel about him, Dellie. He seems like a good Christian man. Think he's got money, too."

"What's inside a man's heart is more important than his money."

Uncle Bob grunted. "Easy for you to say."

Adelle bit her bottom lip and turned to watch the last glow of the red sunset over the rumpled snow. Contrary to her uncle's words, it hadn't been easy for her to say. Unless she accepted Shawn's parents' terms for Rachel's support, she would probably be in a desperate financial position even if she counted every penny and nothing unexpected happened, which she knew was completely unrealistic. She did need money.

"We saw you two kissing out in the snow."

Adelle felt her cheeks grow as red as the sunset she was watching.

"Even after what happened, you trust him to touch you, 'cause unless we were mistaken, you weren't exactly fighting him off. That says something to us, Dellie. What does it say to you?"

They were right. He had treated her gently and with the utmost respect. What they had done, he had allowed to happen as she was ready.

Was she ready to take her chances and go to him as he had asked? And if she went, what would happen?

She continued to stare out into the darkness. She had fallen in love with a man who had asked her to be his nanny. If she did go, it would be a way to know for sure that this love was real, not an emotional overreaction to the unnatural situation they had found themselves in. She knew he felt some kind of affection for her, it was obvious in the way he treated her, and in the way he kissed her. But now that he was home, would he feel the same?

She was too scared to find out. But if she didn't go, she would never know. Adelle didn't know which was worse.

She turned back to her aunt and uncle, who were still watching her. "I don't know, I haven't decided. I'm really tired; I think I'll feed Rachel and go to bed."

Chapter 16

Dennis's hand shook as he dialed the phone. The time was later than he wanted to call, but this time he didn't want a crying baby in the background. He'd waited until Raymond was fed and sleeping soundly so he could convince Adelle to come without any distractions. If she said no, he didn't know what he'd do.

He counted seven rings, and when Adelle finally answered, he exhaled a long breath.

"Hi, Adelle. How are you?" Dennis squeezed his eyes shut. He'd said, "How are you?" *How lame could he be?*

"Fine. And you?"

He didn't want to plod through meaningless platitudes. He was so nervous he felt queasy. "We're fine. Have you decided to come?"

"Well. . ."

He wanted to tell her that, even during the confusion of settling in with Raymond, his life was empty without her. On the other hand, while this was true, he didn't want to chance her not believing him.

"I really need you, Adelle. A few of the older ladies from church have been helping me with Raymond. Still, I've had to take this week off work. Monday is New Year's Day, but by Tuesday I have to be back at work."

"This is a difficult decision."

His queasiness continued. He wasn't going to beg, yet he didn't know how to convince her. "If you're worried about being here by yourself, my housekeeper is here for four hours every day Monday through Friday. You won't be alone. I bet you two would get along great."

He heard her gasp. "You have a housekeeper?"

He grimaced at her response and hoped his reply sounded natural. "Didn't I tell you?"

"Never answer a question with a question. No, you didn't tell me."

"Well, she's a great cook, and she's here four hours a day, so that would take a lot of pressure off you."

"Now I know why you can't cook anything that doesn't go into a microwave."

Dennis slapped his palm to his forehead. "I thought it would make you feel better to know that you won't be alone all day when I'm at work."

More silence hung over the line.

"Rachel would have her own bedroom."

"She would?" He could hear her counting on her fingers. "You've got a four bedroom house?"

It was a five-bedroom house, plus den, family room, and sauna, but he didn't want to intimidate her. From what she'd said, her little house in Blue River was quite. . .modest. "Don't worry. It's a big house."

"Well. . ."

He sucked in a deep breath. "Raymond misses you."

Silence again hung over the line, but this time he forced himself to keep quiet.

"Oh, come on. Don't you think you're laying it on a little thick?"

He grinned. It was a little thick, but it was working. He could tell she was weakening. "Seriously, he really does miss you. He doesn't settle down for me the same way he does for you."

When she didn't respond, he stiffened his back and squeezed his eyes shut. He had one thing left to say, and then he would start begging. "And I miss you, too."

"Oh."

He waited, but he found it harder than ever to stay silent.

"To tell the truth, Uncle Bob is encouraging me to do it as a temporary thing, until I can decide what to do about Rachel's support and all."

Dennis didn't want this to be a temporary measure. He wanted her around permanently. Still, she seemed to be softening to the idea. He would deal with convincing her to stay once she arrived. "That's great. When are you coming?"

"The radio said the main highway is all clear, and Uncle Bob has a friend who can have the road to the cabin cleared by Friday so I can get my car out."

"Your car? But I can arrange all your travel arrangements from here. You don't have to drive."

"I want my car, Dennis."

Dennis sucked in a deep breath. He wanted to buy her another car, one in better condition and with less miles on it than the one she was presently driving. Although, her little old car had done well in getting them safely out of the blizzard and to the cabin. "All right. But I'll be nervous with you driving all that way by yourself. When can you be here?"

"I have to take care of some things at my place, and I should be able to leave after church Sunday. I could be there Sunday night."

"Sunday night? But that's so long."

"You said you didn't have to go back to work until Tuesday."

"I know. Sunday will be fine, I guess."

He gave her detailed instructions on how to get to his house, and they hung up.

"Yes!" Dennis yelled, raised both hands in the air, did a little two-step dance, and then froze, slapping his hands over his mouth. He listened, but no sound came from behind Raymond's closed bedroom door.

Sunday wouldn't come soon enough.

❋

Adelle double-checked the instructions and looked at the house again. According to what she'd written, this should be the place. The numbers matched, as did the color of the house, the description of the unusual tree in the front yard, even the decorative mailbox on the carved wooden front door.

Everything was right except the house. This wasn't, as Dennis implied, a "big" house. This was a mansion. The grounds were professionally landscaped. The driveway wasn't plain old asphalt. It was cobblestone.

The little house she rented in Blue River could fit into the attached three-car garage.

She almost turned around to try to find a telephone when Dennis ran out the front door.

"Adelle! Finally! I was getting worried about you."

She turned off the ignition and stood beside the driver's door but continued to stare at the house.

"Adelle? Your face is pale. Are you okay? You're not sick, are you? Do you want to lie down?"

She wanted to go home. The closer she got to his house, the more expensive the neighborhood had become. Not even in magazines had she seen such beautiful houses. One mortgage payment on any of these homes would probably pay her rent for an entire year.

She felt like the country mouse just arriving in the big city. "I'm fine," she mumbled. "A little tired is all."

"Let's put your car in the garage, and I'll get your suitcases out of the trunk. How did Rachel handle the drive?"

"Fine. She slept most of the way, so she's probably going to be up most of the night."

He ran into the house while she settled back behind the wheel. Within moments, one of the garage doors opened.

She studied the gorgeous new car parked next to hers. She didn't know what it was, which was an ominous indication of what it cost. The third space was empty.

"Why do you have a three-car garage when you only have one car? You do only have one car, don't you?"

He shrugged his shoulders. "The garage came with the house."

Dennis grabbed two of the suitcases out of the trunk, and she lifted Rachel in her car seat, then followed Dennis into the house. She'd never been inside such a house in her life. She couldn't believe this was his home. As they walked down a richly carpeted hall, they passed a high archway that served as the entrance to a massive living room. The room was expertly decorated in graduated shades of greens against a cream-colored carpet so thick she could see footprints on it.

Featured prominently in one corner stood the most beautiful Christmas tree she'd ever seen. At least ten feet tall, the top of it nearly touched the vaulted wood beamed ceiling. She glanced around the room. "How did you get that huge tree in here?"

Dennis made a strange sound that wasn't quite a laugh. "You don't want to know. Come on this way. I'll show you to your room."

Her feet wouldn't move. The tree held her transfixed. Multicolored lights flashed in time to an electronic Christmas carol playing from one of the ornaments. There had to be hundreds of brightly colored ornaments, yet no two were alike.

Dennis appeared at her side. "You know what? I think I like our little tree at the cabin better."

"This is beautiful." She put the car seat with Rachel still in it down on the carpet and reached out to touch one of the cheerful ornaments, as if touching it would confirm its authenticity. She thought the tree at her church was spectacular, but it was nothing like this. From her spot on the carpet beside her, Rachel gurgled and waved her chubby little arms.

Dennis made a low, comfortable laugh. "Look at her. Raymond likes the lights, too. Maybe I'll keep the tree up all year."

In a daze, she picked Rachel up and followed Dennis down the hall to a huge bedroom containing a big double bed and maple furniture. The gray carpet here was as plush as the living room, the spread and drapes were a blue, green, and pink combination, and the walls were the exact same shade as the blue in the fabric. The effect was gorgeous.

"This is the guest bedroom. It's yours."

The guest bedroom was bigger than her living room at home.

He stepped across and opened a door beside the walk-in closet. "And here's your bathroom. I hope you like it."

"This bedroom has its own bathroom?"

"It's just a powder room and shower. The bathroom in the hall has a soaker tub if you want to use it."

Adelle's stomach churned. She was out of her element. She wanted to go home to what was familiar.

"I'll show you Rachel's bedroom."

The bedroom next to the guest bedroom contained a pine crib with a matching dresser and changing table. The walls were a neutral off-white, and the curtains were the same shade as the teal carpet.

She looked at the new furniture. "Dennis, I can't let you give up Raymond's room. She can sleep in the playpen, just like she did at the cabin."

He shook his head. "This isn't Raymond's room, this room is for Rachel."

"But the baby furniture. . ."

". . .is for Rachel. Raymond has his own room, and his own furniture."

Now Adelle really felt sick. He had bought a room full of baby furniture and she wasn't even sure how long they would be staying.

"Why don't you start unpacking, and I'll finish unloading your car? I can put Rachel by the tree to keep her occupied with that annoying electronic music and the flashing lights. I'm learning a lot about babies, you know."

His little grin made her foolish heart flutter. She didn't know what to say or think so she nodded and ran into her new bedroom to be alone. It didn't take long to put away everything she brought, both for herself and Rachel.

By the time she was finished, Raymond was awake. Since she was now the official nanny, she didn't wait for Dennis to tend to him first but simply followed the cries into Raymond's bedroom. This room had the same colored walls and carpet as the one for Rachel and similar furniture in a darker wood.

"Hi, little darling," she cooed as she picked Raymond out of his crib. "I missed you. Your Uncle Dennis says you missed me, too. Are you hungry?"

She gave him a big hug. She really had missed him. She would feel strange giving him a bottle after all they'd been through together. But that's how it would be.

"I haven't had time to decorate the room yet. I guess it will be awhile before I know if he prefers sports or trucks or clowns."

"Quite awhile, yes."

She turned around to see Dennis in the doorway, holding Rachel. "I missed her. But I missed you more. You all settled?"

"Yes, thank you,"

"Then let's go relax in the family room."

She followed him back to the same room they were in before, the one with the Christmas tree. Since he called it the family room instead of the living room, she had to assume there was someplace else in the house he called a living room. The unbidden idea flashed through her mind that she should ask for a map.

He sat beside her on the overstuffed couch, not trading babies back to their rightful owners.

"I know you feel kind of strange here. I didn't want to tell you about the house because I didn't want to scare you. It's really just a big house. I'm not even sure why I bought it, except that I fell in love with the yard."

Now she was afraid to see the yard. If this mansion was what he called a house she had no doubt that what he called a yard, she would call a park. Fortunately it was already dark, and that gave her an excuse not to look until she was better prepared mentally.

"If you can afford a house like this, you must have a pretty good job. You never did really tell me what you do, other than that it's a supervisory position."

"Well, it's a little more than supervisory. I own my own company. I started it when I was twenty, and God has really blessed it; we've done very well. You're not mad at me, are you? I'm still the same old Dennis as I always was."

Back home, folks always considered the elderly couple who owned the co-op wealthy. The difference between their lifestyle and this was beyond her comprehension. She probably should have been angry with him for not telling her everything, but she wasn't. While he may have been evasive, he hadn't lied. She may not like his reason, but he was right. His affluence would have intimidated her, and she wouldn't have opened her heart to him. Likewise, she wouldn't have taken his problems and situation seriously, as wrong as that would have been.

Long after both babies had been put to bed, they continued to talk. Before they turned in for the night they prayed together, asking God for assurance that they were doing the right thing and for His blessing on their time together.

In light of the surprises the day had brought, Adelle thought she would lie awake for hours, but she fell asleep as soon as her head hit the pillow.

Monday passed in a blur, as the days had at the cabin. But, while much of their energy still focused on parenting duties, they now found more time to spent on each other, thanks to adequate facilities, hot water, and most of all, pizza delivery.

Before Adelle knew it, Tuesday arrived, and Dennis appeared dressed in dress slacks and a silk shirt, complete with a hand-painted tie and a briefcase in his hand.

"I wish I didn't have to go." He paused with his hand on the door to the garage. "But I'm so far behind from taking two weeks off, I don't know which end is up."

"It's okay, Dennis. I understand that you have to work. You're the boss, I know it's important that you get back to the office. If you have to stay late, that's okay, we'll be fine."

He stepped closer and cupped her chin with his free hand. "Knowing you're here, the only way I'd stay late was if the place caught fire. I'll be home just after six. See you later."

Before she realized what he was doing, he bent to brush a short kiss to her lips, then backed up. "The housekeeper will be here in an hour. Her name is Donna, and I think you're going to like her. I'll give you a little tip. If she cooks her special, secret recipe chili, don't eat it unless you've got a gallon of water beside you. Gotta run. Bye."

She watched him drive away as the garage door closed all by itself.

"Come on Rachel. Let's check on Raymond. I think we're going to have a great day today."

❈

Dennis signed the last approval sheet in the pile, pushed it aside, and pressed the intercom button for his secretary.

"Jennie, can you hold my calls for twenty minutes? There's something I have to do."

"Are you calling home again?"

He grinned at the speaker, unable to stop himself. "Am I that transparent?"

She muttered something he couldn't hear, and the speaker went dead.

Dennis reached out to dial, but his finger hovered over the numbered buttons. He wondered if this was what it was like to be married. Having two babies in the house presented challenges and responsibilities he could never have foreseen, but the past week had been the best of his life. For the first few days, Adelle had complained that, as much as she and Donna liked each other, she felt strange not doing the cooking, but that complaint didn't last long. He grinned broadly at the thought that Adelle never complained about not doing housecleaning.

Every day, he loved her more. He hadn't yet told her how much he cared for her, but every morning he kissed her good-bye before he left for the office, and every night they prayed together before bedtime. The only thing that would have made it perfect would be if they were married and didn't go into separate bedrooms.

He punched in his home phone number and waited for a response. Today was Friday. Tomorrow he would take Adelle and the kids out somewhere, just for fun, and Sunday, they would go to church together, just like a family.

And one day very soon, he would ask Adelle for her hand in marriage. When that happened, he would be the happiest man on earth.

Chapter 17

Adelle smiled as she hung up the phone. Dennis was such a sweet man. He phoned her at least twice a day just to talk about nothing in particular, and she liked it. She couldn't help but fall in love with him. Hook, line, and sinker. Uncle Bob had been right to suggest that she take the job and be his nanny, because that gave her the opportunity to get to know him in normal conditions. Normal for him, anyway. In the past, she had only dreamed of such luxury, but despite his obvious wealth, he worked hard. Nothing fell into his lap.

Donna did all his housekeeping and cooking, but she didn't cater to him. Dennis had been right—first that she and Donna would like each other, and second that Donna's secret-recipe chili really was awful.

Throughout the past week, Dennis had treated her well, not taking advantage of her in any way, either as a nanny, or as a friend.

Adelle sighed.

She had fallen in love with the man and wanted more than his friendship, but she didn't know what he wanted. For now, she would continue with the routine they had established, but eventually she wanted to know what the future held for them, if anything.

The doorbell rang. Usually Donna answered the door, but she had gone grocery shopping so Adelle picked Rachel out of her crib and hurried to the door.

A tall, beautiful blond woman dressed in clothes worthy of a fashion magazine stood on the porch.

"May I help you?" Adelle asked.

"You must be the nanny." The woman reached up to flick a blond curl out of her face, and in the process, Adelle caught sight of huge diamond ring. "We haven't met yet. I'm Joanna, Dennis's fiancée."

"Fiancée?" Adelle sputtered. "But. . ."

Her mind raced. They hadn't talked about Joanna since the cabin, when he had told her that the engagement was over. Yet the woman still wore his ring.

"May I come in? Where's Donna?"

Adelle stepped back to allow her entry. It hadn't occurred to her that the woman would be a friend of Dennis's housekeeper. "Donna's not home, she's gone grocery shopping."

Joanna checked her watch. "Oh, really? Should I wait?"

"Actually, you just missed her. She left about one minute before you got here."

"How about that." She reached out to touch Rachel's shoulder. "What a cute baby. So this is your fatherless child. Dennis has such a kind heart to help those in need. He always helps those less fortunate people at church when they go through a tough time. This must be a good job for you, much better than any work you could find in that quaint little town you came from. And it will be good for Raymond to play with someone his own age, too."

Adelle recoiled. She wasn't a charity case. At least she hadn't gotten that impression from Dennis. But then, she hadn't gotten any impression from Dennis. Except for a friendly peck on his way out the door, he hadn't touched her in any way except when they held hands to pray.

Joanna reached into her purse. "I guess I can catch Donna another time. I was just in the neighborhood. But when Dennis gets home, can you give him this? He left it at my house." Joanna handed her a man's watch. "Oh, and can you tell him that the jeweler phoned? They've finished sizing his wedding ring, and they want to know when he's going to pick it up. Thanks, sweetie. Tah-tah."

Without waiting for Adelle to show her out, Joanna pranced out the door.

Adelle's feet wouldn't move. Apparently, the wedding was back on. The rings had been ordered and were ready. She looked at the expensive watch in her hand and turned it over. Engraved on the back was a date about four months ago, and the words IT's TIME TO GET MARRIED. LOVE, JOANNA.

Adelle felt sick. If he had left his watch there, that meant he had been there recently. Not that he had to tell her everywhere he went, or who he was with, but that was something she would have wanted to know.

He should have told her that he was getting married after all.

Being in love with a man who was also her employer was one thing, but being in love with a married employer was wrong. Dennis and Joanna weren't married yet, but if the rings were ready, then the wedding date must be close. And she hadn't known.

Of course, he had been back home nearly a week before her arrival. She hadn't taken long to fall in love with him. In that same amount of time, there was no reason he couldn't have made up with the woman whom he had already said he would marry. He had known Joanna all his life. He had only known Adelle a few weeks. It didn't make sense for him to choose her over Joanna. Now she knew whom he had chosen.

She tried to fight back tears, but they spilled out anyway.

He hadn't said anything to her. So, by reconciling with Joanna, he had lied by omission.

She gently laid the expensive timepiece on the coffee table and hustled into the family room to lay Rachel beside Raymond in the playpen, where they could both watch the still-standing Christmas tree.

The tears flowed harder. This would be the last time Rachel would be with Raymond.

After making sure they were sufficiently amused with the blinking lights, Adelle ran to her room. Without folding anything properly, she rammed all her clothes into her suitcases and threw the rest of her belongings haphazardly into boxes.

As soon as Donna returned, she was going home.

Just as she closed the last lid, a car pulled into the driveway. She wanted to avoid any long explanations for her flight, so she grabbed Rachel's bunting suit from the closet and ran into the family room to get Rachel into her car seat while Donna put the groceries away.

The front door slammed. "Adelle! Where are you?"

Adelle froze. It wasn't Donna. It was Dennis.

She had no idea what he was doing home in the middle of the day, but whatever the reason, she couldn't face him. She probably should have known about the wedding plans. To run now was cowardly, but she couldn't let him know how stupid she'd been to fall in love with an almost-married man.

He stormed into the family room. "What are you doing?"

The front door slammed again. "Adelle? Dennis? Where are you?" Donna's voice called out.

If only Donna had arrived before Dennis, that one minute would have been enough to make a clean getaway.

Dennis came up alongside her. Out of the corner of her eye she saw his hand about to touch her, but then he yanked it back and held both his hands behind his back.

Adelle dropped the bunting suit on the floor and spun around.

Dennis stepped backed, leaving a couple of feet between them. His eyes widened, when he saw her tear-streaked face. "I heard that Joanna was just here."

Donna ran through the doorway. "Praise God, you're here. I can only imagine what she said." She squeezed in behind Adelle and scooped up both babies. "I'll go entertain them somewhere else."

"What happened, Adelle? What did Joanna say to you? And don't try to deny she said something. It's obvious you're upset."

"How did you know she was here?"

"Donna forgot the shopping list and had turned around to come back to get it when she saw Joanna's car in the driveway. Joanna knows that Donna wouldn't have been here because she goes shopping every Friday. She meets a friend and they shop together. Since Joanna's arrival coincided with the time she is usually gone, Donna knew she was up to no good. When Joanna pranced out the door with a smile on her face, Donna called me on her cell and told me to come home right away." He inched closer but still didn't touch her. "Tell me, what did Joanna say that's upset you so much to make you run out on me?"

Adelle swiped her face with her sleeve and stiffened to make herself as tall as possible. "She said your wedding rings were ready to try on and pick up. And you forgot your watch at her house."

His brows knotted. "Wedding rings? Watch? What are you talking about?"

"This is my own fault. I didn't know you two had made up. I can't stay here anymore."

"We didn't make up. And I know nothing about any wedding ring. Of course she has her wedding ring. It came with the engagement ring as a set. I told her she could keep it, but I never picked out a ring for myself."

"She said it was ready."

"If she ordered a wedding ring for me, I didn't know anything about it." His brows knotted, and he brought his left hand out from behind his back. "See? I'm wearing my watch. I certainly didn't leave it at Joanna's house. And I haven't been there since before Christmas. She drove me home from the airport, which was a complete surprise to me to see her there, but that was when I told her our engagement was over."

"She said I was a charity case. She knew I was a single mother and she knew all about me."

Dennis brought his right hand out from behind his back and ran his palm down his face. "It's not hard to figure out that you're a single mother. I told my friends that you and your daughter had moved in with me, that you were going to look after Raymond. I don't think a happily married woman would leave her husband to be a live-in nanny. Of course they all know you're a single mother, but that's all they know. They don't know the details. Only I know that. But I did tell my friends how we met and how you rescued me in the snow. Remember, Joanna and I grew up together. Most of our friends are mutual friends. It wouldn't be hard for her to find out all this information."

Adelle sniffled and backed up. She saw the watch on his wrist, but with his financial freedom, it wasn't unreasonable to think he owned more than one watch. He could well afford a different watch for every day of the week.

He caught her line of vision to the watch on the coffee table and picked up the watch. "I don't recognize this." He examined it closer, then flipped it over. As he read it, his lips tightened. "This is probably the date she told me it was time we got married. It was her idea, you know. I'll bet this is what she was going to give me for Christmas, because when she stormed out of here, she grabbed back the gift I still hadn't opened."

Dennis shook his head and sighed. "I'm really disappointed in her. I would never have thought she would stoop so low, to stage this as an act of vengeance because I told her I couldn't marry her. I'm sorry she hurt you like this, Adelle."

Her lower lip quivered, and more tears welled to the surface. She knew she should say something, but if she spoke she would burst into tears again.

Dennis stepped closer and extended his hands at waist level, waiting for her to touch him first. His consideration for her emotional baggage touched her very soul. She couldn't speak, but she could show him how she felt by touching him, as he was asking without words.

She sniffled, stepped forward, and shakily wrapped her fingers around his.

For a second he closed his eyes, and she could see the tension leave him as his stiff posture loosened.

"I don't love Joanna, Adelle. I don't know if I ever really loved her. I always thought we were close friends, although now I wonder if we really ever were. The woman I love is you."

She sniffled again. "Really?"

He gave her hands a gentle squeeze. "Really. I think I fell in love with you on Christmas Day because of your gentle spirit, your strength of character, and your solid faith, despite what's happened to you. I can't count the hours I've prayed about you and what's happening between us, especially since we haven't known each other long. I was going to wait, but I can't any more. I really feel this is God's will for us, both by the way we met and how much it felt like a part of me was missing when I came home alone."

Adelle raised her chin to stare into his eyes. The love she saw in them confirmed his words. "I know it's happened so fast, but I love you, too."

"You didn't know it at the time, but on Christmas Day I gave you the gift of my heart, and now I offer you the rest of me and my ready-made family. I love you, Adelle. Will you marry me?"

Adelle released his hands and, wrapping her arms around him, she sank into his chest with her ear right over his pounding heart. "You got the same gift—my heart—on Christmas Day. And if you'll take my ready-made family, yes, I'll marry you."

He wrapped his arms around her, buried his face in her hair, and kissed her cheek. "When?"

"Whenever you want."

"Soon. Before we take down the Christmas tree."

Adelle smiled. It had been a long Christmas season, but with it she had received the best gift ever, the gift of God's grace, a loving husband, and a family of almost twins.

GAIL SATTLER

Gail was born and raised in Winnipeg, Manitoba, and now lives in Vancouver, BC (where you don't have to shovel rain), with her husband, three sons, two dogs, two lizards, and countless fish, many of whom have names. Between looking after her active family, her day job, and playing bass guitar for her church's Worship Team, Gail says her days wouldn't be complete without finding time to write.

Gail writes Inspirational Romance because she loves happily-ever-afters and believes God has a place in that happy ending. She says—"I love to read something that will make me smile, remind me of the blessings God has for us, and forget about the troubles of life for a while, so why would I write any differently?"

The Candy Cane Calaboose

To M.E. Froelich
Friends 4Ever

This is the day which the LORD hath made;
we will rejoice and be glad in it.

PSALM 118:24

Chapter 1

N o, no, stop!" Abbey Jensen yelled futilely at the package that slithered off the towering pile of decorated Christmas socks. But the package continued on its wayward course, sliding through the slots of the grating that blocked the front entrance of Trends and landing on the highly polished floor of the empty mall just outside the store.

She looked around her as if a solution beyond the only obvious one would suddenly appear. But nothing materialized.

She was going to have to open the security gate and retrieve the package from the mall floor.

She just wanted to go home. She'd been at the store since shortly after seven that morning, and it was now—she glanced at her watch and nearly gasped—almost eleven at night. At this rate, she might as well just go ahead and set up a cot in the store—if she could find a spot that wasn't covered with racks or shelves. Her store was getting crowded with the holiday displays that arrived daily.

Abbey turned her key in the grid work's lock and winced as it groaned open. The sound echoed through the empty mall. The gate raised itself no more than a yard above the floor and stuck.

It wasn't the first time. She ducked under the gate and snatched up the socks from the gleaming tile of the outer mall. Glaring at the recalcitrant grid work, she kicked the bars angrily. "Piece of junk—"

As if in reply, the gate slammed shut.

Her keys were still dangling in the lock on the other side of the gate, tantalizingly just out of reach. Abbey tried to reach the keys, but her hand wouldn't fit through the grating. She was stuck inside the cavernous Cedar Mall.

What should she do? The mall doors were set up so that she could leave through any of them without setting off an alarm, but then what? The keys to her car and her house were on the same ring as the store's keys—on the other side of the grating.

Frustration rose in her like an angry fountain. She could see the keys, but they might as well be in Timbuktu.

She set off through the mall in search of a security guard.

That meant she had to run the gauntlet that the mall management had placed in her way. Cedar Mall looked more like it was situated at the North

Pole than in Northern Mills, Minnesota. The numerous Christmas decorations, normally so festive, now looked merely stupid. At Santa's workshop, an elf held a little silver hammer that was minus its tip. Santa himself, lit only from the faint glow of security lights, appeared old and tired. Only the plastic reindeer seemed to have any personality. One of them faced her as if ready to take a bite out of her.

The expression on the reindeer's face reminded her that she was hungry. If she didn't get something to eat pretty soon, she'd take a bite out of the reindeer. She hurried past the display.

It was just one of many ahead of her. The mall owners had decided that this year they would go all out. Games and kiosks, exhibitions and artwork, all jostled each other for room. She ignored them and headed toward the mall office. Security was usually there at night.

It wasn't that she had anything against Christmas. Christmas was, in fact, one of her favorite holidays. At least it had been when she was a little girl. Now that her family was scattered across the continent, she had to spend Christmas alone. As a store manager, she no longer had the luxury of leaving Minnesota to spend the holidays with her parents in their home in Connecticut.

And the specter of spending Christmas alone was enough to put a damper on even the most fervid Yule fan. The solution was easy: She didn't think about it.

What she needed to think about now was getting in touch with mall security.

A light in another store a bit further down gave her an idea. *Tuck's Toys, Mike's store.* . .she breathed a sigh of relief.

She and Mike Tucker had been friends since they were children. Not good friends, and certainly not as close as their parents would have liked, but friends nevertheless. He'd let her in to use his phone.

As she peered through the grating of Tuck's Toys, she saw a head moving behind a display, and she called out, "Excuse me? Is someone there? Mike?"

A familiar face popped up. "Abbey!"

Abbey breathed a sigh of relief. Never before had Mike's round brown eyes and dark blond hair seemed so welcoming.

"I'm locked out of the store, Mike," she said. "Can I use your phone to call security?"

"No problem." He turned the key in the grid work of his store.

His gate, she noticed, didn't groan and screech the way hers did. And it didn't catch partway up. She was going to have to talk to the mall management about hers.

She ducked in under the opening grid and followed him to the phone as he asked, "Are you working late tonight, too?"

Abbey nodded. "I wanted to rearrange the entrance displays. What about you?"

"Oh, I took a break earlier. I ran out to Golden Meadows to see Grandma, and I had dinner with her out there."

Her stomach growled in response to the word "dinner." "How's she doing?" Abbey had never met his grandmother, but she knew that Mike was devoted to her.

"Pretty good. She's a cool lady. You should come with me someday and meet her. I think you'd like her."

Not a chance, Abbey thought. Maybe Mike liked going to Golden Meadows—after all, his grandmother lived there—but for her it would just be a visit to a place where old people went to die. No, thank you.

"And then," Mike continued, as if he hadn't noticed her chill, "it was back to work." He motioned toward an open box. "More Wag-A-Muffins."

"Wag-A-Muffins?" She stopped and stared at him.

"Have you been living on another planet, or what?" He grinned and reached into the box. "This is a Wag-A-Muffin, the hottest toy in the universe. By noon tomorrow, we'll be sold out."

He held up a small brown stuffed dog. "Watch this." He stroked the toy animal's back, and the tail curled. "Neat, huh? There are about thirty-five different animals, although I doubt that I have all of them here."

She touched it, and the tail lifted into a curlicue. "It's really cute."

Silence met her statement, and she raised her eyes to see him leaning against a display of computer games, a contemplative soft smile on his face.

"What's the matter?" she said and immediately regretted the belligerent tone.

He shook his head and smiled brightly at her. "Nothing. It's just that for a moment I thought I saw a streak of humanity in you."

She glared at him. The old familiar taunt he'd leveled at her since they were children still hurt, although she'd never let him know it.

"The only warmth that flows through my bloodstream comes in at a steady 98.6, thank you very much," she shot back.

"What about when you get a fever? Oh, I know," he interrupted himself as she tried to speak. "You don't get sick. That's for wimps."

"I don't have time for it." Abbey shrugged off the argument. "Actually, I don't have time for anything right now except to head back to my store and get my keys. I want to go home. I'm hungry, and I'm tired. It's been a long day."

"And they're not going to get any shorter now that the Christmas season is gaining on us," he agreed amiably.

He handed her the phone, and within minutes the two of them were walking back toward Trends.

"What do you think of this Christmas Village idea?" Mike asked as they walked by Center Court, where an entire town was set up. Each tiny building was in fact a kiosk with a seasonal specialty. Stuff Your Stockings sold leg wear of all kinds, Lollipop Time sold candy, and Piñata Pete's sold piñatas in imaginative shapes.

"It's, well, a bit much." Abbey wrinkled her nose at the display. "I can understand why they're doing it, and it's already bringing in lots of foot traffic just to see it, but it's too busy for me."

"You know, it's not all that the mall management has planned," he said, but Abbey had lost interest.

She spied the security guard ahead and sprinted toward the gate.

She was dimly aware of the fact that Mike had dropped back, but all she could think of was what awaited her: a hot dinner, a warm bath, and a cozy bed.

❊

Mike watched her head for the guard as if the man held the keys to heaven itself.

Mike knew he was frowning, but he couldn't help himself. He'd always cared for Abbey, but her aloofness had kept him at a distance.

Still, she had a talent for fashion. With her sleek black hair, clear gray eyes, and willowy figure, she could be a fashion model. She also had an instinctive feel for business that he envied. When he'd heard that she was taking over Trends, he was delighted. The fashionable store had suffered under poor management and was near closing, but she had brought it back to life.

But she'd accomplished it at great expense. He'd seen the lines of exhaustion etched around her eyes. He wanted to take her in his arms and hold her, let her rest her head against his shoulder, while he breathed in the fresh scent of her perfume.

But that would never happen. She'd made that clear. No relationships, no ties. She was building her résumé, she'd told him, and she had no time for anything that would swerve her off that course.

He watched as she stumbled slightly. She was fatigued beyond even her capability. She was definitely too tired to drive, but he knew she'd never admit it, and she'd certainly never accept a ride from him. Abbey would insist on driving herself home.

Mike shut his eyes and offered a quick prayer. *Father, take care of her. See her home safely. She is so worn-out.*

His gaze stayed on her as the guard opened the gate and she reentered the store. It took him less than a second to know what to do. As quickly as he could, he hurried back to his store, switched off the lights, and closed the gate. Then he retraced his steps, looping around Christmas Village, and left through the door of the mall that was closest to Trends.

His breath froze in his nostrils as he stood outside, scanning the expanse before him. The parking lot was empty. Or almost empty.

His instincts had been right. He could see her car pulling out of one of the far-off slots where mall employees were supposed to park, and from the pause before she switched gears, he could tell how deep her exhaustion was.

He followed her home, staying a discreet distance behind, and left only as he saw her put the key in the door of her house. She would be safe. He smiled and let out a sigh of relief.

❆

Abbey leaned against the storm door, letting the cool metal refresh her tired forehead. Tomorrow she'd have to find some time to shovel the steps. The snow was so drifted, even this early in the season, that the door wouldn't fully open.

But the snow was more compacted than she'd figured. She dug into the drift with her toe to clear it.

It wasn't all snow. There was something there.

She reached down and burrowed through the snow until her fingers closed around a squarish form. It was a package, she realized, as she dusted the snow off. And, from the emerald green writing on the address, she knew immediately whom it was from.

Aunt Luellen. Loopy Aunt Luellen.

She opened the door and dropped the package inside the entryway as she shrugged out of her coat. She was so tired. But first she'd have to take care of this soggy package on her floor. It was already dripping into a rapidly spreading puddle.

Microwavable meatloaf was just moments away. Flannel pajamas were waiting for her. A nice comfortable bed was around the corner. A quick face wash—she was just too exhausted for a bath—a few moments to brush her teeth, and she'd be asleep.

It was a lovely thought.

But Aunt Luellen was, well, Aunt Luellen.

And the package was wet. Whatever was in it needed to be rescued. She sighed and opened the sodden package.

She blinked once. Twice. Three times. But the image remained.

Yellow fuzzy slippers with a grinning frog on the toe of each—that's what Aunt Luellen had given her. And the eyes on the frogs were bright blue plastic gems. Aunt Luellen was even loopier than ever.

A note fell from the toe of one of the slippers, and Abbey unfolded it. Maybe this would give her a clue as to why on earth her aunt thought that this was an appropriate gift for a woman who owned only one pair of jeans, for whom comfortable shoes were two-inch heels.

"Claire: Every time you wear these slippers, look at the toes and tell yourself that this day is a jewel, perfect, and ideal. If life at Golden Meadows is getting you down, look at where the jewels are—and smile! Wishing you great hoppyness always, today, and many tomorrows, Luellen."

Claire? Her name wasn't Claire. Aunt Luellen had gone from loopy to lunatic. Suddenly, through the fog of exhaustion, she realized what was going on. The slippers weren't meant for her. She had no idea who Claire was, although she was obviously one of Aunt Luellen's cronies if she lived at Golden Meadows.

Abbey sighed. She'd have to get the slippers to whoever this Claire woman was. But she didn't have the time to do that—she hadn't even had time to eat dinner. How could she fit in a trip to a retirement home? Besides, she told herself grumpily, she did not want to go to Golden Meadows. If her head weren't so clogged with a desperate need for sleep, she'd be able to figure it out.

She laid the slippers aside, planning to deal with them in the morning, and another bit of paper fell out of the other toe. "This is the day which the Lord hath made; we will rejoice and be glad in it."

The Bible. That sounded like Aunt Luellen. The woman had the whole book memorized, or so it had always seemed to Abbey. Aunt Luellen could quote scripture with an astonishing ease. Of course, she was a missionary, so she lived and breathed religion, but nevertheless, her ability was uncanny.

Religion. That was where Abbey and Aunt Luellen parted ways. Sometime, when Abbey was established in her career and had gotten her MBA, she'd look into it again. Clearly, religion took a lot of time, and that was one thing she didn't have.

Time—and sleep. "And food," she said to the frogs, whose bright blue eyes sparkled back at her. Meatloaf would take too long. She reached into a box of sugar cookies and held one out toward the slippers. "Froggy want a cookie?"

Abbey shook her head. Any longer with the slippers and she'd be as loopy as Aunt Luellen.

But a moment of clarity came right before sleep claimed her.

Mike.

His grandmother lived at Golden Meadows. He went there all the time. She'd give the slippers to him tomorrow, and he could take them out there to their rightful owner—whoever Claire was—and she'd be finished with the whole messy thing.

Abbey smiled happily. Mike would take care of everything. She just knew it.

Chapter 2

"No."

"What do you mean, 'No'?" Abbey asked as they stood outside Tuck's Toys where she'd come to visit Mike.

"Simply that. No. I won't take the present for you."

"But why not?" She could not believe what she was hearing. Why wouldn't he do this one little favor for her? "You're going out there anyway, right?"

He nodded.

"Then why not take it with you?"

"Nope."

His refusal had her flabbergasted. It didn't make any sense at all.

"You should take it out to her. For one thing," he said, "this Claire probably has your present. And besides, it just would be the Christian thing to do for your aunt Luellen."

Abbey barely restrained herself from snorting. Christian, indeed. Just because Aunt Luellen had turned her life over to the church didn't mean that she, Abbey Jensen, should act all holy. Religion wasn't one of those things that ran in the family, like red hair or big ear lobes.

"I'm going out there tonight, and I can give you a ride if you like," he offered.

"You're going out there? Just take the stupid slippers with you and be done with it, then. I can't understand why you won't." She knew she sounded like a petulant child, but she couldn't help herself. "It's no big deal."

"And I can't understand why you won't go," he parried. " 'It's no big deal.' "

His words, slung back at her like that, sounded terrible.

But the fact was, she did not want to go to Golden Meadows. The thought of being surrounded, even for a minute or two, by old people was awful. That's why she liked the mall; it was young and very much alive.

"I'm going at five thirty," Mike continued, as if he hadn't noticed anything wrong.

Abbey breathed a sigh of relief. She absolutely couldn't go. "I'm the only one in the store then."

Mike shrugged. "You deal with this on your own schedule. I go at five thirty so I can have dinner with my grandmother. It means a lot to her."

He turned to leave, but he paused and faced her again. "It really wouldn't take you long. For about fifteen minutes of your time—which I know is precious—you could make two women very happy."

Abbey could feel herself frowning. "Two women? Oh, you mean Aunt Luellen and this Claire woman."

He smiled at her. "That's right. I know that most of the people at Golden Meadows love visitors, but even if Claire is a total recluse who hates everybody and doesn't want to see anyone for the rest of her natural days, you do have her Christmas present from your aunt. Give it to her. Not only is it hers and not yours, but Abbey, it's Christmas!"

He was making this difficult, she thought as he walked away. What he didn't know about her, what he couldn't know about her, was that her heart was made of marshmallow fluff. She just had it cased inside steel.

She'd work on it. She'd figure out some way to get the slippers to Claire.

Abbey walked back to Trends, scowling at the mechanized group of carolers that sang outside the music store. Noise. Just what this world needed. More noise.

Once, just once, she was going to say it, and she did so at the Dickens village: "Bah, humbug."

Christmas didn't have to be all this complicated. And it certainly didn't have to be this loud!

❄

The evening shift crew arrived on time, and Abbey found herself with an hour and a half free. She had wandered back to the evening dresses and began unnecessarily straightening the already-neat rack, when she heard two teenaged girls giggling together.

"Look at these! Aren't these a hoot?"

One of the girls, Abbey saw, was showing the other one something in a bag.

Then, to Abbey's astonishment, the girl pulled out a pair of yellow fuzzy slippers, complete with frog faces on the toes.

"Those are like the coolest slippers ever!" the other girl gushed. "Where did you get them? I don't care if I am supposed to be shopping for my mutant brother, I've got to get some for myself!"

The two girls briefly examined a display of jewelry before ambling out of the store.

Abbey didn't believe in signs, not really, but she had to admit it: This was clearly a sign.

"Okay, that does it!" she said to the heavily-beaded green gown she was holding.

"Excuse me?" A woman browsing through the evening jackets on the other side of the aisle looked at her curiously and pulled her purse a bit closer to her side.

Abbey tried to disguise her embarrassment with a laugh. "Sorry! Talking to myself!"

The woman smiled. "I understand. I've got five kids and sometimes I talk to myself just to have an adult conversation. Honey, whatever it is that you've just decided to do, you go for it!"

Abbey laughed, but she watched thoughtfully as the woman moved on. Go for it. That's exactly what she was going to do.

❄

Mike smiled as the elderly woman next to him tugged on his sleeve. "Mike, dear, could you please play 'Red Sails in the Sunset'?"

"Sure, Grandma."

He was sharing a piano bench with her. His grandmother had lost her ability to walk, and her sight wasn't very good any longer, but her hearing was as sharp as ever.

She loved music, and soon after she had moved into Golden Meadows, she had enlisted him to play some old favorites on the shiny piano in the fireside lobby of the retirement home.

Usually he loved playing for her, but tonight his fingers were clumsy and found the wrong keys.

"Something bothering you, Sweet?" she asked him.

He grinned at her nickname for him. "Nothing really."

"There is something," she insisted. "I can tell. You know, I can almost smell it. You've got a guilty conscience."

"You can smell a guilty conscience?" He laughed.

"Yes, a bit. It's a kind of fear, you know, and you might not be able to notice it, but when you're like me and the only things you've really got left are your hearing and sense of smell, they get stronger." She touched his shoulder. "Want to talk about it?"

"Oh," he said, his fingers running lightly across the keyboard, "I committed a sin of omission."

"You didn't tell someone something?"

"That's right, and I should have. It wasn't fair to her either. But my intentions were good."

"Well, you know what my Arthur used to say. The road to you-know-where is paved with good intentions."

"I have no intentions of going to you-know-where," he said, unable to keep the amusement from his voice. "Guess that means I'd better take care of it, right?"

"Well, Sweet," his grandmother said, her thin papery cheeks dimpling with impish delight, "if this involves a woman, I'd say you'd better race to it and get this straightened out."

"If it were a man, I could take my time fixing my mistake, huh?" He couldn't resist teasing her.

"Sweet, there's no doubt in my mind that I have the world's best grandson. I couldn't ask for better than you. But I also want great-grandbabies one of these days. I'm not getting any younger, and neither are you." Her eyes, their brightness only partially dimmed behind thick glasses, followed him as he stood up and got his coat from the rack.

"I'll walk you to your room if you'd like," he offered.

"I'll be okay here. But you've got work to do. Go get her!" She shook a bony fist in the air. "Go now!"

"Yes, ma'am!"

He was still chuckling as he drove away from Golden Meadows and toward the mall.

❅

Abbey had driven by the sign for Golden Meadows countless times, but she'd never turned down the lane that led to it.

It was, like many retirement communities, near the hospital, but this was tucked back in a grove of trees. What seemed like several buildings were, she realized as she drove up, in fact one large building with connecting halls made primarily of tall, polished windows. On the front door hung a large wreath, its green boughs interwoven with twinkling lights. All in all, it was a bright and cheerful place, not at all like she had imagined it.

The true test would be what the interior was like, she told herself as she parked her car. Inside, it might be the dreadful place she'd imagined it to be.

But as she entered the door, she had to admit that she had been wrong. The front door opened into a great room, the high arched ceiling allowing the biggest Christmas tree she'd ever seen. And it was real. The clean aroma of the large pine tree permeated the air.

"May I help you?" A young woman behind the desk to her right beamed at her.

"It's somewhat hard to explain," Abbey began, suddenly nervous as she put the present on the counter beside her. "You see, I received this gift from my aunt Luellen, who is a dear but a bit on the, well, loopy side. And no big surprise to anyone who knows her, but the present wasn't for me. I don't know who it is for, but maybe you can help me."

"Your aunt Luellen lives here? Are you sure?" the woman asked her, turning toward her computer.

"No, no. Aunt Luellen lives in Brazil right now. She's a missionary."

"How very interesting." The glaze over the young woman's eyes told Abbey that she was perilously close to turning away.

"Let me start again. I have a gift for a woman named Claire. It came from my aunt Luellen. I don't know anyone named Claire, but apparently she lives here, and I'd like to give it to her." Inspiration struck. "Or I could leave it here, and you could give it to her."

The woman behind the desk pulled back a bit, and her eyes narrowed with faint suspicion. "You want to leave a wrapped parcel for someone you don't know? Oh, I don't think so. It's not our policy to do that."

"Okay, then can you let me know who Claire is, or where she is? I'd like to make sure she gets it, and I do have to get back to work." Abbey glanced at her watch as if to confirm that.

Never taking her eyes off Abbey, the woman dialed a number. "Claire? This is Nadine at the front desk. I have someone here. Her name is—excuse me, what is your name?"

"Abbey Jensen. Tell her I'm Luellen Gregg's niece."

The woman repeated the information into the phone. Her eyebrows rose as she listened to the response. "Are you sure?" she asked.

She paused then shrugged. "Fine. I'll send her down to your room."

She turned to Abbey. "Room 108. Take the hall on your right, and it's the fourth door down."

Abbey fled the desk and the woman's wary eyes and walked as quickly as she could to the door of room 108. She took a deep breath and knocked.

The door opened to reveal an elderly woman in a wheelchair. Her china blue eyes sparkled behind thick lenses, and she leaned forward a bit, as if to bring Abbey into focus.

"Abbey Jensen? Luellen has talked so much about you, I feel as if I know you! Come in, come in!" She wheeled herself back into her room, motioning Abbey to follow her. "What's Luellen been up to lately?"

"She's still a missionary in Brazil," Abbey said as her eyes took in her surroundings. The room was lovely, done in clean white and bluebonnet blue, and as neat as the proverbial pin. A white porcelain cross hung over a small table on which a Bible was neatly centered. It was bigger than any Bible Abbey had seen, and she realized that it was undoubtedly a large-print edition.

"Brazil? Last I heard it was Chile."

"It probably was Chile, then. I'm pretty bad with keeping up with her."

"Isn't it exciting, though? Traveling through the world, spreading the Word." The old woman's face appeared almost transfixed. "She and I are total opposites of each other. She's the world traveler, and the most I do is go down the hall for dinner."

But rather than sounding sorry for herself, she seemed quite happy.

"By the way, I'm Claire Thorson. Luellen and I have known each other since we were girls. I have a scrapbook I'd love to show you if you have time."

"Actually, I'd love to look at it," Abbey said, amazed that she really would, "but I have to get back to work. I brought your Christmas present from Aunt Luellen. She sent it to me by mistake."

Claire laughed. "Somehow that doesn't surprise me. Luellen was always the one with her head in the clouds, just to be closer to heaven, we used to tease her. I suppose that means I have your gift, then."

She wheeled over to the small tree that was set up by the window and picked up one of the many packages under it. She held it close to her face, trying to read the name.

"Don't worry about it," Abbey reassured her. "It's not that important."

"A Christmas present 'not that important'? My goodness, Abbey Jensen! Yes, it is!"

Abbey grinned at the elderly woman's honesty. Her eagerness about Christmas reminded her of Mike's comment. Christmas mattered quite a bit to Claire. "You're right. It is important, and here is yours." She held out the slippers, now completely rewrapped in bright red foil with a shiny gold bow on the top. "But now I've got to get back to work."

"Where do you work?"

"At the Cedar Mall. I manage Trends."

"Cedar Mall? My grandson works there. Maybe you know him."

"Maybe." Abbey impulsively dropped a kiss on the top of Claire's head. "But I've got to go now."

She opened the door to leave and there, in the hallway, still out of breath from running, stood Mike Tucker.

They all managed to speak at once, and for a moment, chaos reigned supreme. It ended with a sudden blanket of silence as their words settled on them.

"You've met Grandma, I see," Mike said at last.

Before Abbey could say a word, Mike took her by the arm. "Let's go have some coffee," he suggested as he steered her out of Claire's room. "We need to talk."

As they left, Abbey saw Claire lift her hand ever so slightly in a fisted salute. And perhaps her ears were playing tricks on her, but she was sure she heard the older woman whisper, "Wahoo!"

Chapter 3

Mike led Abbey into a small room that opened off the lobby. Several small round tables were clustered near a cozy fireplace, where a hearty fire burned. He poured them each a cup of coffee from the pot on the counter and dropped some change in the pottery piggy bank beside the coffeepot, moving with the easy grace of someone who knew the ropes of Golden Meadows.

A few surprised residents lifted surreptitiously interested glances at them. When he nodded at some of them, smiling and greeting them, Abbey said through closed teeth and a tight smile, "Why don't you introduce me to your friends?"

He nodded at a table of three gentlemen, then sat beside her, sliding a cup toward her. "Because this way you'll be the hit of the rumor mill. They'll all be speculating who Sweet's new girlfriend is."

"Who's Sweet?" she asked, momentarily diverted.

A stain flushed his cheeks with dark color.

"Mike, are you blushing? Well, will you look at that? You are!" She grinned. "Are you Sweet?"

"Yup," he said, ducking his head. "Grandma always said I was the sweetest grandbaby boy in the world, and that soon became Sweet."

"I like it," Abbey said truthfully. "It fits you, in a way. Plus, it's, well, sweet."

Their laughter broke the uneasiness only for a moment. They had serious matters to work out, and Abbey went right to the point. "Mike, why didn't you tell me that your grandmother was Claire?"

His dark eyes were serious when he studied her face. "Would it have mattered?"

"Yes," she replied. "Yes, I think it would have."

"How?"

She thought about her answer before speaking. "Well, I think I would have come out here right away."

"Really?"

Annoyance tinged her response. "Really. I would have at least given it stronger consideration."

He shook his head. "I'm not so sure about that."

"Michael Tucker, I would too have come out here!" she protested, her back straightening. "How can you say such a mean thing about me?"

Mike shifted in his chair. "Let's face it, Abbey. You and I have known each other since we were kids. We never were buddies even when we were children, and the years didn't draw us together; they emphasized our separateness. Your life has been focused on your career."

She tried to interrupt him, but he held up his hand. "Wait. Let me finish. I might as well be hung for a sheep as a lamb, and after all I've said, I'm well on my way to the sheep gallows."

Abbey settled back in her chair, but every nerve in her body tingled with anxious worry. She felt exactly the same way she did during performance evaluations at Trends, knowing that she was about to hear something she didn't want to and that it was unavoidable. The riot in her stomach turned and churned, and she had a fleeting thought that she shouldn't have had the evening special at Pizza Fair.

"We're friends, Mike." She congratulated herself on how even and calm her voice sounded.

"Are we?"

Abbey had heard people say that it felt like their world had been pulled out from under them, but it was a phrase she'd never really understood. But now she did.

"Yes, Mike, we are."

"And who else are your friends?" His words were deadly quiet.

"Well, let's see. There's Brianna and Selma at the store, of course, and, um, then there's Terri. Terri and I have been pals since we were in diapers."

"When did you last see Terri? Talk to her? Write to her?"

"Write to her?" She looked at him blankly.

"Terri moved to Rochester in August," he said gently.

She put her face in her hands. She hadn't known that. She'd been too busy to call Terri, too busy to drop by, just too busy.

This was terrible, absolutely terrible. The pain was almost too intense to feel. It was as if she were having major surgery—without anesthesia.

A touch on her shoulder startled her. "Is this young man acting like a cad?"

Beside her a thin elderly man balanced on a cane. His hands shook with palsy, and his eyes were murky with cataracts. But his voice was strong, and his meaning was clear as he glared at Mike.

"No, he's fine." She shot a furtive glance at Mike, then looked back at her defender. "He's just offering me some suggestions on how I might improve myself."

Abbey thought the elderly fellow was going to raise his cane and shake it at

Mike. But instead, older eyes glared at younger eyes, and the gentleman said, "If there's one thing you should learn, young man, it's that you can't tell a woman anything."

She tried to protest, but he continued, apparently unaware of her interruption. "You can't tell them anything because they know everything. My Eleanor, may she rest in peace, may not have gone past the twelfth grade, but she had a doctorate in Life. Good Christian woman, too." The man nodded. "Actually, you can't tell men anything either," he said to Abbey. "It's not because they know everything—they don't—but they've got this problem with their ears."

Abbey was fascinated by this man. "Their ears?"

"Yup. And the fanciest hearing aids in the world can't help with their problem. You can't tell a person anything they don't want to hear, whether they're male or female." He leaned on his cane thoughtfully. "So here I am telling you this, and you probably don't want to hear me either. Go figure. Just because you're old, don't mean you're smart."

"I think that you are extremely smart," Mike declared, "and I'm glad you stopped to talk to us. Right, Abbey?"

"It seems to me that Eleanor got a pretty good deal when she married you," Abbey said softly, suppressing the urge to give the man a hug.

She noticed Mike's quick glance at her as the gentleman walked away. "What?" she snapped.

"You sounded almost like a romantic for a minute there," he said, nearly laughing.

"Yeah, right. Your hearing is pitiful."

"Well, he did say that you only hear what you want to hear," he reminded her.

"And you wanted to hear that I'm a romantic?" She meant it lightly, as a quick and witty response, but as she said it, the meaning struck her.

Mike didn't know it, but his offhand comment—and it was an offhand comment, she was sure—had struck pay dirt. The problem was that this gushy romantic, which she had efficiently buried under the lacquered coat of her career, tended to surface at the most inopportune time, like whenever she watched *Miracle on 34th Street* or when she attended weddings or even when a certain greeting card commercial appeared on television. It was really quite inconvenient.

Hastily, she tried to cover the glimpse of her inner self that had escaped. She changed the subject to something she was more comfortable with: "I've got to get back to work," she announced. "It's late."

Mike glanced at his watch and nodded. "You're right. I'm supposed to meet a friend at Tuck's Toys in fifteen minutes, so I'd better hustle."

She couldn't resist it. "A friend?"

"Yes, Miss Snooper," he answered. "A friend."

"Big friend? Little friend?"

He laughed. "Are you trying to find out if I'm seeing someone? Well, not in that sense, no."

She stood up and busied herself with clearing away her coffee cup. "It's just that you work almost as many hours as I do. I don't even see my mailman, let alone get out to meet people. What do you do? Do you go to the bars after work?"

His expression was half shocked, half amused. "The bars? No, I don't go to the bars. They're not my scene at all. No, my dear, I find my friends at the best place in the world. I find them at church."

"Oh, that," she said dismissively. "They don't count."

He stopped midaction. "Why not?"

"Well, for one thing, they've got to love you. Kind of like parents."

He chuckled. "Not exactly. But in a way you're right. They do have to love you, because Christ told them to."

Abbey responded with a very unladylike snort.

"It's true. Oh, admittedly there are moments when we disagree, but that's just part of it all. That's how we grow."

He was so serious. Mike must take this religion stuff pretty seriously. Of course, his grandmother did, too, judging from her room décor.

He took her by the hand. "Abbey, want to come with me to church on Sunday, give it a try?"

"Nah. I need to be at the store early. We're starting our big Christmas promotion that day." For once, she was grateful for the signs and displays that had arrived earlier in the day. She had a ready-made excuse for not going with him.

"There's an early service. You could be out by ten o'clock."

She shook her head. "No, Mike. Thanks for inviting me, but I just don't go for this organized religion stuff."

He grinned. "Well, sometimes we're not so organized at the early service."

"You know what I mean. I believe in God and all that, but this church business is, well, not for me. If I want to say hello to God, I can go to the lake and do it."

"And do you?" His question was quiet and unnerving.

"I've got to get going, Mike." Abbey turned on her heel and left the room before he could say another word.

She fumed all the way back to the mall. Religion was one of those things that people were supposed to keep to themselves.

It was true that Mike had never proselytized. As a matter of fact, this was the first time he'd even mentioned anything having to do with church. But his invitation made her uneasy. And she had to admit that part of the feeling was born of the fact that this opened up another area of Mike that she didn't know existed.

For some reason, she wanted to know more about Mike.

A lot more.

❄

The evening mall traffic had picked up, and Abbey grimaced at the new booths that had gone up since she'd left. The latest one was a peppermint-striped building. Instead of a wall facing the mall corridors, the space was lined with black metal bars.

She edged closer. A large heart-shaped black lock hung on the door.

Abbey couldn't believe her eyes. It looked almost like a jail, but what on earth did a jail have to do with Christmas?

As if in answer to her unspoken question, a workman wearing a Cedar Mall uniform hauled a ladder up to the front of the building. Curiously, she watched as he set up the ladder and climbed it, balancing a large wooden sign. After a few quick taps of his hammer, she had her answer. The sign was lettered in Old West style: THE CANDY CANE CALABOOSE.

"Well," Abbey said to no one in particular, "that explains it." She shook her head. "Or not."

As she started to walk toward Trends, another worker joined the first. The second man carried a sign that was also immediately nailed to the building. She retraced her footsteps and read the new sign: THE MALL MERCHANTS INVITE YOU TO WATCH THIS SPOT FOR HOLIDAY FUN!

"Oh, right," she muttered to herself. "Well, not this mall merchant. I wonder what on earth they've decided we're going to have to do now."

She walked back to Trends, mumbling and grumbling about past mall endeavors, such as the potluck when everybody brought desserts and potato salad, and nobody brought a main dish. The mall office had been forced to buy meat and cheese trays from a neighboring grocery store. Then there was the picnic, scheduled for mid-July, prime mosquito season. Even the toughest repellent hadn't been able to repel the hordes of hungry buzzing insects. Next time, Abbey thought, they probably wouldn't have the picnic next to the river. Another one of their grand plans had been a talent show to raise money for a local charity. It soon became apparent that few, if any, of the mall merchants had any talent at all. The talent show had never been repeated, and she thought it was possibly at the charity's request.

No, whatever this Candy Cane Caloose was, it was going to prove to be an awful idea.

But Abbey hadn't gone to the potluck or the picnic or the talent show anyway.

And she had no intention of having anything to do with this latest brainstorm of the mall's management.

She shrugged. This Candy Cane Calaboose nonsense wouldn't bother her one way or the other.

Chapter 4

The alarm went off, and Abbey realized it was aptly named. The little torture device was truly alarming. Every morning its persistent buzz startled her into wakefulness.

She slammed her hand on the snooze button, hoping for a few more precious moments of sleep, but that was a luxury she'd never been able to manage. Once she woke up, she was awake, and there was no going back to sleep for her. Her parents had teased her about her hidden "on" switch.

She missed her parents, especially during the holiday season. But she was a realist. Connecticut might as well be on the other side of the moon this time of year. And they had their own lives, their own friends, and although she knew they'd have been delighted to see her, she also accepted that they were comfortable with their annual summer visits.

It was one of the sacrifices she made for her career, and they understood. The other sacrifice she made for her career was never having a leisurely morning. . .at least not at Christmas.

As she hurried through her morning routine at a pace that surprised her, she tried not to think about families, the night before, or her visit with Claire. But her thoughts kept returning to Mike and his grandmother.

Somehow it all fit together perfectly, with Aunt Luellen at the center. When things got crazy, her aunt was often the precipitator, with her well-meant actions and her impulsive engineering of situations. She was a kook, that one. Abbey smiled as she thought of what her aunt must be like as a missionary. What on earth did the people of Brazil—or wherever she was—think of her version of the gospel? She could only imagine how it would come out through the filter of Aunt Luellen's nutty brain.

Abbey gasped with surprise as her feet touched the linoleum of her kitchen. It was icy cold. Slippers. She needed to get some slippers. She was on the verge of making a mental note to buy some at the mall when the irony of it all struck her.

She could have had slippers—goofy frog slippers. At least Claire's toes should be toasty warm after Christmas.

That reminded her. She had to get out to see Claire and retrieve the package that Aunt Luellen had sent. That is, she corrected herself, if it were for her. Knowing Aunt Luellen, she might have her entire Christmas gift list scrambled beyond repair. The gift that Claire had could easily be a fishing rod meant for Uncle Kirby in Oregon.

But the sooner she got out there and straightened this whole mishmash out, the sooner she could get back to her own life again and shrug off this crazy business. Her conversation with Mike was still making her uncomfortable, and she didn't like to be uncomfortable.

She snatched her purse from the hook by the door and headed out into the cold. Yes, if she was ever going to have peace of mind, she was going to have to get this thing taken care of once and for all.

Her car groaned into life, and Abbey shivered as she sat in her driveway, waiting for the engine to warm up. There wasn't any new snow, and the sky was a bright, clear blue, but that didn't mean anything when it came to the temperature. It had to be below zero.

She glanced at the spot where an indoor/outdoor thermometer had been attached to her house, but it had fallen off during a late autumn windstorm, and she just hadn't had the chance to put it back up. Then she remembered: The thermometer had fallen off during the autumn of last year. She was really letting things slide.

Well, she countered as she continued her discussion with herself, it wasn't as if she had time. She was busy at the store. . .and looking into maybe going back to school. . .and life was just generally hectic. It was something she'd come to live with.

She rubbed her hands together. Even through her thick mittens—on sale at Trends, two pairs for eight dollars—the icy air pierced right to her bones. The defroster had cleared only a small section of her frosty windshield, and she impatiently turned on the wipers, hoping to hurry the process along. She did not want to get out and scrape the window off. It was just too cold.

But the windshield began to film up on the inside from the warmth of her body, so she knew she was in for a wait, and she was too edgy to sit in her car and wait patiently. She fidgeted with the wipers, monkeyed with the defroster, and tried to rub the frost off with her mittened hand, succeeding only in smearing the fog. At last the windshield was clear enough, and she headed off.

This was going to be quick, she promised herself. She'd run in, pick up the present from Claire, say a few bland and polite words, and be on her way. Five minutes, tops. And she'd be through with this whole bizarre slippers thing and able to get on with her life.

Whatever that might be, a nagging little voice whispered in her heart.

Mike? Surely, Mike didn't have anything to do with her life. He was just a friend—or not a friend, she thought as she remembered their conversation. It made her stomach hurt.

She pulled into a spot near the door of Golden Meadows. The tall windows sparkled in the morning light. From the parking lot, she could see the mammoth Christmas tree through the largest windows in the entryway. The lights were on, catching the sunlit crystals of ice on the edges of the windows. With the early morning frost lit by the tree lights' multicolored array, the building looked incredibly picturesque.

She briefly considered leaving the car running but decided against it. She was already low on fuel and about the last thing she needed now was to run out of gas in the parking lot of a retirement community. So she switched off the ignition, telling herself she'd be inside such a short time that the car would still be warm—or warmish—when she came out again.

Resolutely, she marched into the high arched lobby of Golden Meadows and approached the desk. Just her luck. The same woman who'd been there earlier was there again. Nadine, that was her name.

"Yes?" It was remarkable, truly remarkable, how much iciness the woman could pack into the single word.

"I'd like to see Claire. Claire Thorson."

"Is she expecting you?"

"Yes. No. She is, but probably not right this minute. I mean, she knows I'm coming, but not necessarily today. Well, really, she's not expecting me at all right now, since it's opening time at the mall and it's Christmas."

The woman behind the desk stared at her, her expression never wavering. What was it about her that made Abbey splutter and blither like this?

"You're the lady with the package," Nadine said at last.

Abbey nodded, unsure of what the woman was going to do.

She certainly didn't expect this: Nadine burst into a huge smile and leaned across the desk to capture Abbey's hands. "Thank you so much for bringing the gift to her. You know, Mike's pretty much the only family she's got here anymore, and while he is here daily, bless his heart, having a new young face in her life has meant so much. She's really perked up."

Abbey could feel the smile freezing on her face as the woman continued to gush. "I hope you'll be back more often. This is just doing her a world of good." Then the woman delivered the *coup de grace*. "Plus you're almost family."

"Almost family?" Abbey gulped.

"You and her grandson, Mike. You're, well, you know." Nadine stopped just short of a conspiratorial wink.

"We're what?" Abbey asked through nearly numb lips. "No, never mind. I have the feeling this is something I don't want to hear." She shot a wild smile at the receptionist. "So is Claire in her room?"

"No, honey. She's with the others, down in the Fireside Lounge. You can go ahead. It's just down this hall, take a left, then a quick right. You can't miss it. There's a fireplace the size of a Buick in there. And they're all in there singing their dear hearts out, so follow the music."

Abbey felt her face relax. Maybe she could make it through this after all. She started down the hall, and she could just make out the sound of voices raised in song. They finished the last triumphant notes of a hymn Abbey somewhat recognized and, after some murmured discussion, a series of chords led them into another song.

What the group lacked in talent, they made up for in enthusiasm. Some voices were quavering with age; others were strong and true, undiminished by the years. One clear tenor led them all. She knew even before she peeked around the corner who the voice belonged to. He motioned her in as he kept on leading the group in singing.

If only the song hadn't been a rather rousing rendition of "When the Saints Come Marchin' In." Abbey's face flooded with red when the audience's singing lagged as they turned around to stare at her with open curiosity. The voices faded out as the residents studied the newcomer.

She tried to cover her embarrassment by whispering loudly to an elderly gentleman in the back row: "I'm not a saint, and I'm not marching."

To her chagrin, he leaned back and said, just as loudly, "Could have been worse. The song before last was 'How Great Thou Art.'"

She knew she shouldn't, that she would be doomed if she did. But she couldn't help it. She looked at Mike.

His face was as red as hers but with suppressed amusement. As their eyes met, Abbey and Mike dissolved into laughter. It wasn't the genteel, tee-hee, hymn-sing kind of laughter either. Oh, no. It was the can't-catch-your-breath, clutch-your-sides, gulp-and-snort brand of laughter that takes over and won't let go.

Tears ran down her face, and she collapsed onto the nearest folding chair and wiped her eyes as she tried to control herself. The harder she tried, the worse she laughed.

Just when she thought she had mastered her laugh attack, she looked at Mike. His attempt to look as sober failed as their glances locked again, and once more they both gave way to the laughter.

"Hmmph!" A man in a plaid shirt settled himself into a posture of righteous indignation. "Such behavior! Have you ever witnessed such a scene in your life? This is a hymn sing, not a vaudeville show. They ought to—"

"Get married," a tiny lady with a lace scarf finished for him. She sighed happily. "Get married and have lots of little Sweets."

Abbey stopped midgulp. The woman's voice carried clearly through the room, and from the way that Mike froze in place, bent at a nearly impossible angle, she knew he had heard her. His hand was motionless on the strings of his guitar, and if she didn't know better, she'd think he was a wax figure from Madame Tussaud's.

Lots of little Sweets?

Mike was staring at her, looking at her with a strangled pain she knew mirrored her own shock. She knew she should get up and leave, but her muscles were apparently cemented into place. Dimly she heard sounds behind her, and a familiar tinkling giggle broke the silence. "Speaking of Sweet, how about 'Sweet Hour of Prayer'? Come on, everybody! I love that hymn. I'll start." Claire's wavering but true soprano started the hymn, and the others soon joined in.

Abbey could have kissed her as the crowd faced forward again. Mike, after a split-second pause to collect himself, joined in with his guitar.

As soon as the attention had turned from her, Abbey decided, she'd leave. She'd creep out, hoping no one would notice. She'd deal with the wayward Christmas gift later. She had to get back to the mall. Her fingers pushed back her sleeve, and she grimaced. She'd forgotten to put on her watch.

Surreptitiously she glanced around the room, trying to find a clock. Surely there'd be one on the fireplace. But nothing. There were no clocks in the room at all. Maybe, she thought, when you got to this point in life, time didn't matter. You just moved from Activity A to Activity B to lunch, then rested, then Activity C, Activity D, dinner, television, and to bed. She resisted the urge to shudder. This was definitely not the life for her.

The woman with the lace collar leaned over to her. "Need the time?" she asked as she held her thin wrist over toward Abbey.

Abbey realized she was the only person in the room without a watch on. That might explain the dearth of clocks. Golden Meadows supplied the activities, but each resident was responsible for his or her own time.

Maybe that was what Aunt Luellen was talking about. Maybe this was what rejoicing in the day meant.

She smiled at the woman with the watch. The group had begun another song, a Christmas carol. She should leave, but this was "Joy to the World." It had been her favorite when she was a child, and she couldn't resist joining in as the words came back easily to her mind.

She'd stay for this one song, and that was it. How long could a song take? A minute, two tops, right? She'd allow herself the luxury of one song, then she had to get to work.

But the lure of the familiar carols soon wrapped their magic around her, and she stayed for "He Is Born" and "Hark, the Herald Angels Sing." As the last note drifted into silence, she glanced at her neighbor's watch.

It was a few minutes after ten!

Trends was already open! She scooped up her purse and made a hasty, muted farewell to the members of the hymn sing and raced out the door, down the hall, past a surprised Nadine, and into the cold clear air of a Minnesota morning.

It wasn't as if no one was at Trends to open it. Selma was scheduled to be there at eight thirty, and she was so reliable that Abbey knew she was there by eight fifteen. But Abbey needed to be at the mall, at Trends.

Actually, what she needed was to be away from here, away from Golden Meadows and this whole bizarre scene with Mike. And away from all those hymns. Her mind swam with the memories of long-neglected melodies, and the words came back to haunt her. It was amazing how easily they sprang back into her mind, although it had been years since she'd set foot inside a church.

The carols, of course, she'd heard every minute of every hour of every day since November fifth, the official start of the holiday season at the mall. She could sing them in her sleep. Abbey snorted. She probably did sing them in her sleep.

She snapped her attention back to the road as a patch of ice nearly sent her car spinning off the paved parking lot. Now there was a metaphor she could understand: Be in control. Hold the steering wheel tightly and never take your eyes off the road ahead, and you will stay directed. For her, that meant staying on track, straight toward her MBA and a real career with megabucks in her bank account. If she kept her target in sight, as she had been, she'd stay on the path to her heart's treasure.

Somewhere in the back of her mind, she could hear Aunt Luellen saying something about heart's treasure. Abbey shrugged. If it was Aunt Luellen, it was undoubtedly something from the Bible.

She'd had her dose of religion for the day. A couple of rousing Christmas carols, and look at her. She was wrapped in that soft-focus, greeting-card kind of glow that retailers relied on to pull them through the Christmas season.

There were Christian retailers, she was sure, who looked upon the season as a time to celebrate Jesus' birth. But there were just as many, if not more, who saw this as a season of profits, and a tiny baby born in a stable played only a minor part in it. The thought saddened her, even though she wasn't a dyed-in-the-wool Christian like Aunt Luellen.

Christmas was the base of the retailer's year. It was what carried them though the lean times in other months and kept them going. Without Christmas to boost their sales, many stores would not be able to stay in business. And now that she was a store manager, she was part of the feeding frenzy when it came to Christmas. She had to be. She had a responsibility to the storeowners and the other employees. Abbey sighed and pushed away the thoughts that jostled around in her mind, arguing with each other. Why did Christmas have to be so complicated?

She pulled out of the Golden Meadows parking area and into the stream of traffic, trying to squish the not-so-tiny voice that insisted she didn't believe a word she was thinking—that Christmas was a time of holiness and joy, and that stores like Trends played only the most minor of roles in its celebration.

The wise men may have bought the newborn Jesus gifts of incomparable value, but somehow she didn't think they would have shopped at the Cedar Mall, with "forty-two individual stores offering the region's widest assortment of shopping pleasure," as the television commercial boasted.

As if on cue, she could hear Aunt Luellen's voice from many childhood Christmases: "The greatest gift of all was not what they brought Him but what He brought us."

Abbey sighed. That was true. What was a television set compared to everlasting life?

Or a pair of goofily grinning frog slippers?

Chapter 5

The mall was already filling with customers, even though it had been open less than an hour. Selma was busily refreshing the stock from one of the cartons that seemed to arrive every hour, although Abbey knew deliveries were only twice a day.

"Hey, stranger, good to see you! Don't tell me you overslept!" Her clerk grinned at her.

"Ha. I don't even sleep, so oversleeping is too much to ask for." Abbey said it lightly, but the weariness that seeped into her bones told her that her words weren't that far from the truth.

"No kidding. One of these days you'll have to try sleeping. It's vastly underrated, at least in your world," Selma commented wryly.

"After Christmas. Then I'll have time."

Selma snorted inelegantly. "After Christmas come the returns, then it's Valentine's Day, then. . ."

"Okay, I'll take a Wednesday off sometime and try sleeping."

"Wednesdays are Senior Citizens days here, remember?"

Abbey made a face at her salesclerk. "Whatever. I'm too tired to argue." Their eyes met, and both women laughed.

"Okay, lecture ended. Now, where do you want these?" Selma handed Abbey a box of brightly colored slipper socks, and Abbey gasped.

She'd gone all the way out to Golden Meadows to pick up the gift, but she'd left without it. She slammed her fist down on the counter.

"Okay," Selma said, drawing the two syllables out. "What just took you from mellow to mad?"

"These slippers."

In one smooth movement, Selma reached out, took the box, and tossed it under the counter, then smiled innocently at her boss. "What slippers?"

"No, no," Abbey responded with a frustrated sigh. "They just reminded me that I was supposed to pick something up, and I forgot. Now I have to go back, and I don't really want to."

Selma knelt to get the box again. "Anything I can do to help?" Her voice was muffled from under the counter.

Now there was an idea! Selma could go to Golden Meadows. . . . But before the thought took full root, Abbey dismissed it. She had to see this through to the end.

"No, I'm just busily berating myself. For some reason I can't seem to remember to pick up the gift my aunt Luellen sent to Golden Meadows."

"She sent your Christmas present to Golden Meadows? Isn't that a retirement home?" Selma threw back her head and roared with laughter. "Honey, I think your auntie is trying to tell you something!"

"You are not even a little bit funny," Abbey responded, although she had to smile. "All I need is a simple brain transplant, and I'll be fine."

"Would that be outpatient surgery?" Selma ducked the teasing swipe Abbey gave her.

The two spent the rest of the day companionably unpacking new arrivals and setting up the merchandise. As soon as they emptied one box, another arrived to take its place, or so it seemed. Between the two of them, they barely made a dent in the towering stacks of cardboard boxes, all marked URGENT: OPEN FIRST.

"I'm here!" The voice of the college student who worked part-time called to them from the front of the store.

"Hi, Brianna." Abbey groaned as she rose from the crouched position where she'd been retrieving an entire boxed shipment of rings that had broken open a few moments ago. Rings had rolled all over the store, coming to rest in the most difficult-to-reach positions. "What are you doing here so early?"

"Early?" Brianna looked confused. "I'm here to work. I'm supposed to be here at five, aren't I?"

Abbey and Selma exchanged glances. Selma said affectionately, "Yes, dear, but it's only—" She consulted her watch and gasped. "It's nearly five!"

"No wonder I'm so hungry. Selma, you can go on home, and Brianna, if you'll straighten that holiday sweatshirt display, I'll—"

"Get something to eat." Selma pushed Abbey toward the front of the store. "You haven't even had lunch, and I suspect you skipped breakfast, too. I'm on for another hour anyway, and Brianna and I can certainly cover long enough for you to get a decent meal."

Abbey opened her mouth to object when a familiar voice spoke from behind her.

"I'll take care of it, Selma. Come on, Abbey, let's go get some grub." Mike grinned at her.

"Some grub?" Brianna laughed out loud. "Man, you've got to do something about your romantic style."

It seemed to Abbey that everyone began to speak at once, and the mayhem ended only when she was unceremoniously shoved outside the open gate of

Trends, her coat in her hands, with Mike laughing at her side.

"I think we're going out to dinner," he said at last.

"I don't need my coat for that. Actually, I don't need dinner at all but—" As if on cue, her stomach rumbled loudly.

"The case of the tattletale tummy," Mike said. "Let's go."

"Just let me put my coat back. We can run down to the pretzel place and grab a stuffed pretzel and a soda."

He put his hand on her arm. "No pretzels. We're going to go out for a real dinner."

"A real meal?" A terrible thought struck her. He had said that he often ate with his grandmother. "Oh no, Mike. We're not going to eat at Golden Meadows."

He shook his head. "No, but I do go out there sometimes to eat with Grandma. I like to do that."

She shuddered. "I don't mean to be horrid, but I can't imagine that being anything you'd want to do."

"Well, I like it. But that's not where we're going tonight. We're going to a real restaurant, the kind where you sit down, they hand you a menu, you get a salad and a meal with vegetables. And maybe a dessert that doesn't come wrapped in plastic."

It did sound good. So Abbey allowed herself to be ushered through the icy-cold parking lot, then driven to a nearby family restaurant, Ginger's. The restaurant's brick and glass exterior was softened by chintz curtains and tablecloths, and Abbey detected the warm inviting scent of meatloaf. She had to admit it; this was a great idea. She was starving.

"This must be new. I've never been in here before," she said as she sipped the water the waitress handed her.

Mike shot her a curious look. "It's been here about a year and a half. I'd ask where you've been, but I know—working."

"That's not really fair," Abbey protested. "It's not like I don't have any life at all outside Trends."

Mike smiled ruefully. "I'm sorry. It came out sounding harsher by far than I intended. It's just that it's been true of me. I realized that my whole life was revolving around work. I'm trying to cut back a bit."

Abbey couldn't help it. She laughed. "You're cutting back? That's ludicrous."

He seemed surprised. "Why do you say that? I don't work nearly as many hours as you do."

"Who was the only person besides me at the mall at eleven o'clock at night when I got locked out of the store? You. Mike Tucker. Workaholic."

He had the grace to look abashed. "That's true. But I am trying to do better.

Like not grabbing a hot dog or a pretzel in the evening and calling it dinner."

"We're busy, Mike," she said in her own defense—their own defense. "It's not like we have the time to do full-course meals."

"We don't? I don't know about you, but I've been neglecting myself lately."

"Neglecting yourself?"

"I know. Sounds kind of selfish, doesn't it? But I'm starting to realize that I've got to take care of my body. And that includes eating right as well as getting some exercise."

Abbey glanced at him suspiciously. "Are you one of those exercise fanatics?"

He struck an exaggerated muscleman pose. "I'm in the running for Mr. America, hadn't you noticed?" He laughed, and for the first time she noticed that he had dimples. Actually very cute dimples. The kind that made his eyes light up like. . . She broke off that train of thought before it could go further.

He was still talking, and she pulled her attention back to his words. "So I promised myself that one day I'll join a gym, and I will, but right now if I can make a turn around the mall with the other mall walkers, I consider it my exercise for the day. No, right now I'm aiming for some sleep and some veggies. Baby steps first."

The waitress appeared with their coffee. "You ready to order?"

Her words took Abbey by surprise. She hadn't even looked at the menu. "What do you recommend?" she asked Mike.

"They have really good soup," he said.

Soup sounded wonderful. Nice and warm and filling, the perfect food for a cold December evening.

"I'll be right out with the bread," the server said as she collected their menus and left.

"We get a loaf of homemade bread with flavored butter. It comes with our meal," Mike said. "It's just this side of heaven."

"I haven't had homemade bread in years," Abbey commented. "Not since Mom made it, and that has to be, wow, four years ago? They've been gone that long?"

Mike's forehead wrinkled with concern, and it took Abbey a moment to realize why. "Oh, I didn't mean that kind of gone, I meant gone as in gone from Minnesota. They live in Connecticut now. Dad was transferred just shortly after I graduated from high school. I guess that's something you wouldn't have known."

He nodded. "Probably. Are you going to go out there for Christmas?"

"No." For the first time since she and her parents had been separated, she felt a twinge at being apart from them at the holidays, but she quickly suppressed it. "That's okay. We've only got Christmas Day off anyway. It's not worth it. What about you?"

"Well, Dad passed on last year."

Abbey felt herself flush. "Oh, I'm sorry. I didn't know. What a horrible thing to bring up at this time of year."

"It's certainly true I miss him, but I miss him every day of the year. It's still raw, and it hurts, but I know he's celebrating Christmas in heaven." He smiled contemplatively. "To be honest, that's what gets me through. I know you might not believe it, but it's enough."

His words took her by surprise, and her expression must have mirrored her feelings, because he continued, "I'm not saying that those first days didn't hurt with a pain as if someone had cut my heart right out of my chest, but my faith is strong, and his faith was stronger. He taught me that this life is great. . .and the next life is going to be even greater."

"How about your mother?" Abbey wanted to change the subject. She was in no mood for the turn the conversation was taking. She didn't want to think about things like religion, at least not now. She wanted to relax.

It wasn't that she didn't believe, not really. She did. She just didn't have the time to reason it all out. One of these days she would, when she had time.

Mike didn't seem to be bothered by her lack of interest in his family's faith. "Mom moved to Arizona, and she lives with her sister in a mobile home where she can reach out her bedroom window and pick an orange for breakfast. She says she doesn't care if she never sees another snowflake."

"So she's not coming up here for Christmas?"

He shook his head. "No. I won't get to see her at all this Christmas, sad to say. I have to stay here because of the store. This is the worst time of year for a toy store owner to take a vacation."

Abbey smiled. "I suppose you're right. It's the price you pay for owning your own store."

"Keep that in mind, Abbey, in case you decide to trade in managing for ownership. But I'll pop down there in February and visit. Right about then I figure I'll really need a blast of warmth. It'll be interesting to see what she thinks about celebrating Christmas in the desert."

"Arizona is a real change from Minnesota," Abbey commented. "I don't know if I could do it. I need snow and sweaters and mittens for it to be Christmas."

"I know what you mean," he agreed. "But there are times when I think I'd really like to try a Christmas without snow." He shivered. "Like last night. Did you hear how cold it got? Can you imagine what it must have been like to live here before electricity?"

"I remember reading about how people used to live in sod houses," Abbey said. "First off, I can't for a minute imagine what that was like." She shuddered. "Living in a house made of dirt? And what was it like to heat it by a stove? I'm glad to have my house, that's for sure."

"And my coffeemaker," Mike added, with a wry grin. "These cold mornings, I think I take all that for granted."

Their food arrived, but they barely noticed it, chatting companionably about the blessings of modern appliances, especially furnaces. All too soon, the soup was gone, the coffee cups drained, and Mike leaned back and rubbed his stomach. "I don't know about you, but I'm stuffed. We'd better get back."

They'd talked about nothing, but at the same time they'd talked about everything. Abbey thought that over as they rode in the comfortable dark cocoon of Mike's car. Somehow she felt she knew Mike better, but how on earth had that happened? The most personal their conversation had gotten was about their parents and where they lived now. Hardly the kind of thing that would qualify as an innermost secret. But now she felt closer to him.

And, she realized with surprise, she liked him. She really liked him.

He pulled into the snowy stretches of the mall's parking lot. As she opened the door on her side of the car, he pulled on the handle from the outside. Suddenly their faces were only inches from each other, and the strangest thing happened. Her mouth poised for his kiss, and she felt herself leaning in toward him, as if it were the most natural thing in the world.

Abbey hadn't had much experience with romance. Her knowledge was pretty much limited to some clandestine smooching behind the school with Edwin Carlson when she was fourteen. But she'd heard that a really good fellow and a really good kiss would sweep her off her feet.

Apparently it was true. She felt her feet leave the ground, as though she were floating, while Mike's arms grasped her shoulders, then her waist with a fervent intensity. The world spun around in a dizzying whirl, and the stars arched overhead.

"Aaaaaaabbey!" His voice echoed in her ears as they ascended quickly and just as rapidly descended.

Whomp!

With a very definite thump, she landed on the ground in an inelegant sprawl, with Mike nearby. Her long skirt was tangled in the heel of her boots, and her hat had slipped over one eye. Her bright yellow mittens were now smudged with black where she'd tried to stop her fall. The contents of her purse had escaped, and a lipstick was still skittering across the pavement.

"Are you okay, Abbey?" Mike said. "Wow, this parking lot is icy."

Her hip ached, and her arm, she knew, was going to sport a livid bruise in the morning. But it was nothing compared to her crushed ego.

This was why she had never been a ballerina, why she had never been chosen as a cheerleader. She had all the grace of a lumbering orangutan. She looked as if she should be a dancer, with her slender build, but somewhere between her brain and her feet, the message got scrambled. She was such a klutz. Mike undoubtedly thought she was clumsy, to the point of being dangerous to those standing near her, but what worried her most was something else.

Had she really wanted Mike to kiss her? What on earth had she been thinking of? And worse, what if she hadn't slipped? What if she had actually leaned in too far and kissed him?

He probably would have pulled away, and that would have been the end of their rapidly developing friendship.

Did he know she had been leaning in for his kiss? And if he did, did he think that she was forward, that she did this with anybody who took her to dinner? Being a recluse floating on an iceberg in the middle of the Atlantic Ocean was looking better by the minute.

❄

Mike cradled his head in his hands. He'd never been the most graceful gazelle in the herd, that was a given, but tonight he'd really blown it. He'd been about to kiss her and had lost his bearings completely

He had wanted to kiss her so badly that he'd lost whatever moral compass he had. He wasn't the kind of fellow to just kiss a woman because she was pretty, or because he'd had a good time being with her, or anything like that. No, for him a kiss was serious business.

That is, it was until his fancy footwork took them both down in a mall parking lot. The memory made him cringe. She must think he was a total idiot, or at least a complete clumsy Charlie. The next time he was going to get carried away by the moonlight, he'd make sure he wasn't standing on a patch of ice.

Chapter 6

Abbey woke up the next morning feeling a mixture of contentment and annoyance. She had enjoyed dinner far beyond what she'd expected. It was the kind of thing she could get used to. . .as long as she had someone to eat with.

Someone like Mike? a little voice nagged.

She'd known Mike since they were children. All through their teen years, when everybody of the opposite gender was a potential love interest, she had never thought of him in that sense, and she was sure the thought of going out with her had never crossed his mind either.

Not that it mattered. Even if she were attracted to him—which she wasn't—last night certainly made it clear that he saw her as a friend. A klutzy friend.

She mulled it over as she waited for her curling iron to heat. Although Mike had been ever-the-gentleman and helped her up, even retrieved her wayward lipstick from under a car where it had rolled and at last come to rest, he had to be wondering about her. What kind of woman would try to kiss somebody in a parking lot, then lose her balance in the process?

Could she be any more out of practice?

She hastily dismissed the thought. For one thing, she was perfectly capable of doing anything she wanted to do. If she'd wanted to make their dinner date an evening to remember, she certainly could have done so. She stood straighter and glared at her mirrored reflection. Yes, she could have knocked his proverbial socks right off.

The truth was, she had come really close. She'd knocked his hat off.

The image in the mirror glared back at her and reminded her of one important element that she was overlooking in this conversation with herself: this developing romance that she sometimes felt and sometimes didn't was completely one-sided. Mike was only trying to be her friend.

That brought her back to the second part of her morning thoughts. It hadn't been a date. Not even close. It had simply been two friends having dinner together.

Friends. The conversation at Golden Meadows sprang back into her mind, and for a moment Abbey felt uneasy. Maybe she—

She shook her head. No. She was fine. Just fine. All she had to do was quit mooning at the mirror like a lunatic and get going, or she was going to be an unemployed lunatic.

A light snow had fallen during the night, and while it made the main road to the mall a pleasant seasonal white, it also made it a crazy ride. The slicked roads forced her to drive slowly, because the fairly simple act of braking to a stop took at least half a block.

A blue four-wheel drive vehicle passed her, able to go faster because it had greater traction than her small car had. She glanced at it, then did a double take.

It was Mike's car, and by the way he was tapping his fingers on the steering wheel and moving his lips, she figured he must be singing along with the radio.

She didn't have time to react emotionally. She'd taken her eyes off the road just long enough to lose control. With a sick sensation in the base of her stomach, she tried futilely to bring her car out of its slide and back into the line of traffic.

"Don't let me hit someone," she said, and she didn't worry about who she was talking to. The message was more important.

The sensation of having her car skid, the steering wheel useless in her hands, was horrible. Then she saw a child walking on the sidewalk, completely absorbed in sliding on the slick pavement, gliding along as if he were ice-skating. The scream that rose in her throat died as her car slid sideways and launched itself, neatly and totally, into a snowbank, a few yards from the little boy.

She popped open the door of her car. As completely wedged in as she was, she could get it ajar just a few inches. "Are you okay?" she called to the boy, but he continued to skate on, the muffler and hat that covered his ears apparently preventing him from hearing her.

"Thank God," she breathed. That had been entirely too close.

The boy was all right. Now she had to get to the business of getting her car out of the snow. She drove into the snowdrift, she told herself, so logically she should be able to drive out again.

After futilely switching gears between reverse and drive, she gave up. She had two options. One, she could call the neighboring gas station to come and get her out. But who knew when they'd get there, and she could guess at how much that call would cost her. Or she could go directly to the second option. It was free. It was the shovel in her trunk.

The first challenge was getting the door open. It would only open about six inches before the snowdrift stopped it. She was thin, but not that thin.

How could she dig herself out when she was trapped inside the car?

Finally she settled on a successful combination of digging with her hand for a while, then slamming the door open and repeating the motion. Dig, slam. Dig, slam. Dig, slam. At last it worked, and she was able to escape from her car.

Her success was limited, however. She was still in the snowbank.

Abbey clambered across the snowdrift, wincing as a soft patch of it gave way, and her foot slid up to her knee in the icy crystals. The sharp pain from her hip as her leg turned reminded her of her elegant fall in the parking lot the night before. She opened the trunk, taking care not to drop her keys in the snow, and got the shovel.

She began digging the compressed snow from under her car. Her long scarf, which she'd purchased for its color rather than its utility, was much too short and slid down from the bottom of her face and hung loosely. After the fourth time that it got caught in the shovel and nearly decapitated her, she yanked it off and threw it aside in disgust.

Her nose was running, and she was sure that her hair looked like elves lived in it. Somehow, she knew, Mike Tucker was to blame for this.

❄

Mike whistled as he raised the grating that covered the entrance to Tuck's. He ducked under it, and as he turned the key to lower it again, he smiled to himself.

You've given me a good year, Lord, he prayed silently as he always did while he went about the opening process. He was in the store by himself, and it was a good time to visit with God. It wasn't his only time of prayer, but even though it was informal, he found it to be valuable preparation for the day—and he was able to focus more clearly for evening prayers.

He continued to talk to God as he restocked the displays, started up the tills, and dusted off the countertop. *The store is doing well, Grandma is settling in just fine at Golden Meadows, and my mother is adjusting to living without Dad in Arizona. Thank You for the blessings You've given me.*

Two thoughts popped into his prayers simultaneously. The first was simple: *How can I repay You?* The second was complex: *Watch over Abbey Jensen and touch her heart to open it for You. She needs You so much.*

Even as he prayed the words, he knew what was being asked of him. The second thought was the answer to the first.

Aw, God. I meant for You to watch over her. Not me. I'm not good at that. He paused and straightened an already straight display. *Here's a suggestion: How about if I serve on another committee at church instead?*

Silence. Not that he had expected God to answer him aloud. He could always feel the response in his soul. God wasn't a bargainer, he knew that, but maybe he just hadn't offered the right bait.

No, huh? Okay, I'll increase my giving at church. Surely You can't argue with that.

God didn't argue, but that resounding emptiness stayed hollow, and Mike had to accept the truth: God wanted him to do what he could to point Abbey toward God.

He thought about it as he went through his workday. He didn't want to get involved romantically with Abbey. It wasn't that he didn't like her—he did. Oh, as a friend, he hastily told himself. And he'd enjoyed their time together. But he certainly didn't want to get involved with her as deeply as he thought God was asking him to.

Besides, he could imagine what Abbey would say if he started hanging around her, watching over her both physically and spiritually. He laughed. *Are you sure about this, God?*

Well, he'd give it a try. The warm, loving glow that came over him told him that this was the right thing to do.

Caring for Abbey. . . He had to admit, the thought had its appeal.

❅

Thanks to having stuck her car in the snow pile, Abbey had pulled into the parking lot with only moments to spare before Trends opened.

Usually, her lateness would have made her tense—even more so after her unfortunate experience with her car—but today she welcomed the diversion. The morning scurry to have the tills ready by the time the front gate came up was intensified, and she was glad to see an early morning crowd already window-shopping in preparation for the stores to open.

"Honey, you look like you've been at hard labor," Selma said as Abbey rushed to have the store in perfect condition by opening time.

"That's not far from the truth," Abbey said. "A snowbank and I had a disagreement."

Selma clucked sympathetically. " 'Tis the season, that's for sure. The roads were in pitiful shape this morning, weren't they? I almost got to meet the fella down the street. You know I've been wanting to run into him sometime to introduce myself. Well, this morning I almost got my chance. In fact, I nearly ran him down when my car went out of control on an ice patch."

They chuckled. Selma's romantic life was a constant trial to her. She had more boyfriends than Abbey had been able to keep track of, but none of them seemed to materialize into husband material.

Selma got a sly look in her eye and asked with clearly faked casualness, "So how did it go last night?"

Abbey diverted her eyes and attentively arranged the Christmas jewelry display. "Last night? Oh, that's right. It was fine."

"Fine? That's all you have to say? Fine?"

"Okay, 'fine' may not be the best word to describe it. It was great."

Selma smiled happily and settled back onto the chair behind the cash register.

"Now we're talking! Did anything exciting happen?"

"As a matter of fact, it did. Something totally unexpected, and I was soooo glad." Abbey couldn't resist baiting Selma.

Selma's eyes got huge. "What? What?"

Abbey took a deep breath, then said melodramatically, "We went to Ginger's. I'd never been there before. They have good soup."

For a moment, she thought Selma might explode. "Never mind the soup. I want details. Give me details."

"You want details? What kind of details?"

"Boy details. Girl details."

"There are no details," Abbey said, bringing the conversation to an end. "The best part of the evening was the soup."

As she walked to the front of the store, she was sure she heard Selma mutter something under her breath that sounded not very nice.

Abbey raised the gate to the store, and a handful of customers wandered in. Those early customers got her total attention, and soon the conversation with Selma was ancient history in her mind. After all, the last thing she wanted to think about today was dinner last night with Mike.

❄

"Want me to get the mail?" Selma asked awhile later. "It's almost noon. It should be here by now."

"Why don't I do it, then you can take the first lunch shift," Abbey suggested. "I could use a break, and so could you."

"I'd argue," Selma said, "but I wonder if part of the reason for your decision is the chance that you might meet a certain toy store owner at the mailboxes."

Abbey didn't answer, partially because she knew Selma was teasing, but also because her assistant was right on the mark.

The mall mailboxes were clustered at the end of a service entrance on the opposite side of the mall, and all shop owners and managers watched for the mail arrival carefully, especially this time of year, when the pace of sales picked up in the afternoon. If she didn't get the mail now, it would be early evening before she'd have a chance to do so.

It was something all the managers knew, so between eleven thirty and noon, they tended to cluster down there and spend a few minutes sharing quick updates—and extensive gossip.

She could hear them laughing even before turning the corner to the service entrance. From the words that floated free of the general chaotic noise, she realized that the topic of conversation had something to do with a recent decision of mall management.

She slipped through the cluster of kiosks that broke the traffic pattern—when had that fireplace mini-store gone in?—and made her way to the mailboxes. The trip usually took her under five minutes, but now, thanks to the displays the mall management had put up, she had to run an obstacle course.

The managers motioned her into their group, and one of the women handed her a flyer. "Get this," she said to Abbey. "Honestly, what this new executive outfit won't do!"

"I've heard of stupid ideas, but this takes the cake!" added another.

"What's going on?" Abbey asked the woman who had handed her the flyer. "What have they done now?"

The woman just shook her head and threw her copy of the flyer into the nearby recycling bin. "You don't want to know. Oh, you've got one of their notices. Read it for yourself. I, for one, don't have time for this kind of nonsense. If they want to help the retailers, they could hire some extra help. But not this. The last thing I need is to be taken off the floor at Christmas!"

"Those people who come up with these ideas must have fruitcake for brains," another woman chimed in.

"Or reindeer tap-dancing on their heads," someone else agreed. "This idea is downright idiotic."

"Careful what you say," a man in a three-piece suit added. "Or you might end up in the slammer, er, calaboose."

The entire group burst into raucous laughter.

Abbey looked at the flyer to see what was causing this wild reaction on the part of the other store managers.

The flyer was the traditional mall office notice, with a candy-cane striped border around the edge, and on it red letters proclaimed: "The Candy Cane Calaboose is on its way!"

Candy Cane Calaboose? What on earth was that? She remembered seeing the construction going on down the mall corridor from her store, but she hadn't bothered to investigate further. She certainly didn't have the time to keep up with all the little "enhancements" the mall management had added this season.

Abbey shrugged, and her flyer joined the others in the recycling bin by the mailboxes. The Candy Cane Calaboose sounded like another one of the half thought-out ideas of the mall management, and certainly nothing she had the time or energy to deal with.

It was just silly, and it certainly had nothing to do with her.

Chapter 7

The pace of Christmas sales had picked up tremendously, and Abbey felt her spirits rising to meet the challenge of the increased traffic. The weather had been cooperative—except for the snowfall that had resulted in the brief skirmish she'd had with that snowbank—and the crowds in the mall had increased as Christmas approached.

The nice part about it was that she had a reason to stay at the mall from early in the morning until late at night, and when she went home she dropped into bed, exhausted, and slept. For others, that might be a nightmare, but for her, it was great. She was in her element at the store. She knew the rules, she knew the way things went, and she felt good about her abilities.

It's not the kind of life that most people dream of, she acknowledged to herself the next day as she waited for her car to warm up before leaving her house, *but it's perfect for me. Everything now is building toward a good future in business, and all the stress, all the struggle, is going to pay off, and pay off well.*

Still, a part of her argued back, *wouldn't you like to have someone to be there for you, someone to say, "Poor baby," when you complain about the shipment that didn't arrive or the salesclerk who forgets her shift? Wouldn't it be nice to have someone to talk to in the morning while your car warms up. . .instead of having to talk to yourself?*

She was clearly losing her mind. Sitting in her car, having a full-fledged conversation with herself about talking to herself—this was definitely not a sign of strong mental health.

She sent the wipers across the windshield in one last angry sweep. The glass wasn't entirely clear of frost, but there was a small window of visibility that she decided to take advantage of, and she backed out of the driveway.

As she crept along the road to the mall, the radio played Christmas carol after Christmas carol. She wanted to change the station, but she didn't dare take her hands off the steering wheel; she didn't want a repeat of yesterday's encounter with the snowbank.

"Joy to the World" began to play, and she recalled the hymn sing at Golden Meadows.

Golden Meadows!

She started to slap her head but remembered just in time not to let go of the steering wheel. In the bustle of the Christmas trade and the emotional chaos Mike had thrown her into, she'd forgotten to get the gift from Claire and get the mess straightened out once and for all.

For a moment, she considered writing the whole thing off as a loss, and if loopy Aunt Luellen inquired about her present, she could lie and say it had gotten lost in the mail. It was only a teeny white lie, Abbey reasoned, since Aunt Luellen had sent the gifts to the wrong address, and it was only through a momentary lapse on her part that the slippers had gotten to Claire.

Why, oh why, hadn't she simply tossed those dreadful slippers in the trash that evening?

Abbey tried to imagine how her life would have been different had she done just that. She wouldn't have met Mike's grandmother, and she probably wouldn't have gotten to know Mike better. Life would be calmer. More orderly. Peaceful.

And boring.

❆

Mike smiled as he listened to the voice on the phone. The store was packed with people bearing lists of Christmas wishes, some carefully detailed by organized parents, others crayoned haphazardly by anxious children. Nick, his assistant, was making frantic signs at him that his help was needed with customers.

Mike waved him away, but Nick was persistent.

"Not now," Mike wrote on a piece of paper and shoved it to Nick. "In a minute."

"Who are you talking to?" his assistant asked him.

"No one," Mike mouthed at him.

"Whaaaat?"

Mike put his hand over the mouthpiece and whispered, "It's my grandmother."

"Your grandmother is not 'no one.' Honestly, Mike, I thought more of you than that!" Nick told him indignantly.

Mike grinned. "I meant I wasn't talking. She talks. I just listen."

He returned his attention to the voice on the telephone. "Yes, Grandma," he said at last. "I'll be there. And yes, I'll do my best to do that. Yes, Grandma. I understand. Okay."

At last he hung the phone up. "I do love my grandmother," he told Nick, "but when she's got something on her mind, heaven and earth must stop until it's done."

"What's up?" Nick asked.

"The story I just heard was a long, convoluted saga about a plugged drain and a handyman shortage at Golden Meadows. I didn't follow it all, but I'll run over tonight during the supper lull and see what's up."

Any further discussion was stopped by a harried-looking woman bearing five wrinkled lists. "How does Santa do it?" she asked, juggling the packages she already carried while trying not to drop the stack of games and action toys she had picked up. "I've only got five kids, and I can't keep their lists straight."

"Volume," Mike answered. "He buys in volume."

She grinned at him. "I think that's what I'm doing today. At least, that's what my checkbook is telling me."

"Want some help? I could put those smaller packages into some larger ones with handles," he offered. "That would make them easier to carry."

"Oh, bless you. I love Christmas, even though it is a financial crunch." She heaved the packages and the toys onto the counter. "It reminds me to take another look at my children and see what miracles they are, what a fount of possibilities they are, what a gift they are. God trusted me with them—me! It humbles me every time I think about it."

"I like that," Mike commented. It was a refreshing change from the complaints he heard so often from parents who had overspent their budget to buy toys that their children wanted at the moment but might very well forget about in a week or two.

She blushed. "I know I should do this every moment of my life, but sometimes life gets in its own way, if you know what I mean. Christmas is a nudge in the side to look at those children. Okay, look at them when they're asleep, which is about the only time they're not fighting, but that's kids for you. Anyway, even with the wildest of the bunch—that'd be my Richie—I know I see the face of an angel in training."

She frowned as she looked at the pile of toys. "Could you do me a favor and add these things up? I have the dreadful feeling my Christmas Club account has run dry."

Mike totaled the items up. She sighed with relief as he told her the sum. "Just under the wire." She handed him the money. "Thank you so much for the bags—and for listening to me. Have a Merry Christmas!"

It was interesting, Mike thought as she left, how someone so unexpected could give you a gift. . .one you couldn't buy at any mall.

The thought of a gift reminded him that his grandmother had mentioned that Abbey hadn't picked up her gift from her aunt Luellen yet. This might be the perfect chance for her to do so. He'd stop by Trends on the way to Golden Meadows. That way Abbey wouldn't have time to think of reasons why she shouldn't go.

For some reason, there was a special lilt in his step that carried him through the rest of the day.

❊

Abbey put away the last of the new shipment of holiday earrings and stretched. The day had gone on endlessly. Maybe she should take a walk down the mall and get a cranberry Italian ice. It was one of the seasonal offerings the mall had that she actually liked.

"Abbey!" Mike's voiced hailed her from the front of the store. "You about ready to take a break?"

"I don't know when you started mind reading," she said, her voice only somewhat grumpy, "but I was just getting ready to go down to Italian N'Ice. Want to walk with me?"

"Sounds good, but I'm headed out to see Grandma. Would you like to join me? We can go through some hamburger joint drive-in on the way back if that's okay with you. I usually don't go for fast food, but tonight that's all I can manage—Nick is leaving early since he has a final exam at seven."

She paused, and Mike added, "Grandma isn't going to leave you alone until you go get your gift, you know. You might as well accept that. When she gets a project—and right now straightening out the confusion with the gifts is her project—she doesn't stop until it's resolved. She did mention that she has your present out there, and she suggested, as only my grandmother can suggest, that you could come out there and pick it up."

Abbey opened her mouth to object but then thought better of it. This might be the perfect chance for her. If they weren't going to stay long out there, she could get the package, wish Claire a Merry Christmas, and be on her way, back on track, within an hour.

It was the ideal situation.

"I'll go," she announced. The expression on his face made her add hastily, "But only to put an end to this maniac mix-up."

The evening was warmer than it had been during the day, and Mike commented on the mild temperature.

"It'll snow soon, then," Abbey said. "Didn't you pay attention to Mr. Lloyd's science class in high school, when he talked about weather?"

"He talked about weather?" Mike laughed. "Oh, that was the class that Eileen Jamison was in. No wonder I don't know anything about weather. There was no way I could concentrate on anything when she was in the room. I had such a major crush on her. Then she married some football player, like the day after graduation. My teenaged heart was broken."

"I didn't know you and Eileen were a couple," Abbey said with some surprise. Eileen had been the class president, a cheerleader, and a soloist in the chorus. Mike had always been in the background of activities.

"We were a pair in my adolescent dreams only." Mike sighed dramatically.

"I don't think she even knew I was alive. Well, maybe she did. Remember that showcase that had all those dusty old trophies dating back to the turn of the century—the nineteenth century, that is?"

Abbey nodded. "I don't remember seeing it after my junior year. Didn't they finally get rid of it?"

"They had some help. I was watching Eileen in the hall one day, being the googly-eyed lovesick teenaged boy that I was, and I wasn't watching where I was going. A staircase just appeared out of nowhere, and suddenly I was going head over heels down it. As if that weren't bad enough, as I started down the stairs, I grabbed her arm—why, I don't know—and she went with me. That showcase broke our fall. Or maybe I should just say that the showcase broke."

"What did she do?" Abbey asked, laughing over the image of them tumbling down the stairs together.

"She was very polite about it. She got up, helped me up since my long gangly legs were tied into a knot, or so it seemed, and asked me if I was okay. Then she grinned and said that she had never taken that particular set of stairs so quickly or so noticeably—and that once was quite enough. So if was all right with me, she'd be taking another set of stairs for a while—and she was doing so without my help. And that was it."

"Didn't you just about die?"

"I asked my parents to move so I could go to another school. They said no. I thought maybe I could go live on a mountaintop like those hermits but realized I would have trouble finding a mountain in this part of Minnesota. One of the troubles with being a teenager is that your range of movement is limited. So I stayed on and lived with the utter humiliation."

They discussed the trials and tribulations of being a teenager until Mike pulled into the parking lot of Golden Meadows. True to Abbey's earlier prediction, thick white flakes had begun their lazy drift from the sky. Residents were lined up at the large glass windows watching the snowfall.

It was pretty, Abbey had to admit that. The air was quiet, free from sound, and the evergreen garlands and wreath were frosted with the new snow. For this one moment, away from the bustle of the holiday mall, she could almost like Christmas.

✳

Mike took a deep breath. He needed to talk to Abbey about the other night and apologize for his clumsiness. Hopefully he could do it without taking a header on the parking lot of Golden Meadows.

Maybe he should wait until he was inside, he told himself ruefully. He seemed to have better luck staying upright when he was inside. But he knew that once he was inside, the residents wouldn't let him have a minute alone with

Abbey. Toss in the fact that the retirement home was one of Abbey's least favorite places on earth, and he realized that this wasn't the place.

He'd try the parking lot, but he just wouldn't touch her arm when he talked to her. Maybe that would help him keep his equilibrium.

It would also help if he didn't try to kiss her, he reminded himself. There was nothing wrong with being head over heels in love, but not in an icy parking lot.

Chapter 8

Mike paused a moment before entering the oversized entrance of Golden Meadows. "I want you to know that—"

He wasn't able to finish the sentence. The door was flung open, and a crowd of elderly laughing women yelled, "Surprise!" One of them held a bough of something over his head, then stood on her tiptoes and kissed him soundly on the cheek.

"Marlys, do you have mistletoe?" he teased.

She blushed and nodded. "Yes, I do."

"Can I borrow it?" he asked with a wink.

Abbey's stomach was twisted with anticipation and anxiety. Surely he wouldn't. . .surely he would.

Which did she want?

"Sweet's going to smooch his sugarplum," someone in the group crowed.

"That's right," he said, his eyes twinkling as he turned to look at Abbey.

Her heart and her mind waged war. She wanted him to take advantage of the mistletoe, and yet she didn't. For a moment, time held its breath.

Then he announced, his warm brown eyes twinkling, "The first kiss goes to my favorite girl."

All heads swiveled with one accord to look at Abbey. She knew she was blushing, but there wasn't a thing she could do but stand stock-still and wait for her fate.

Mike raised the mistletoe and turned to the woman who was watching from the corner. "Grandma, pucker up!"

Disappointment caught Abbey off guard. Of all the emotions she might have expected, this was not one of them. What had she been thinking? That they'd share their first kiss in front of a group of senior citizens—when they hadn't even really dated yet?

And besides, it wasn't as if she cared about him one way or the other. He was simply a friend, a fellow retailer, and no more.

Nevertheless, the image in front of her blurred, and the carols that were piped into the great room faded into the background. She blinked her eyes rapidly and willed her emotions back into line. This was just silly. He didn't matter to her, not at all.

Mike was bent over, talking to his grandmother, an attentive expression on his face, and she was reminded that he was a good, caring man. Then he stood up and walked away.

She realized that Claire was watching her, and she forced a smile. "Claire, it's good to see you again."

Claire reached out a gnarled hand. "How nice of you to come see me! At least, I'm assuming you've come to see me."

"Of course I'm here to visit you. Shall we go to your room to visit, or is there another place you'd rather go?"

"Let's go to the Fireside Lounge and sit beside the fire. There's a big picture window there, and we can watch the snow falling. Mike will be tied up for a while finding that reprobate handyman to unplug my drain. Can you stay?"

"Not for long. This is my dinner break."

"Have you eaten?"

"Mike and I will stop on the way back."

Claire made a face. "Not that dreadful fast-food stuff, I hope."

"I'm afraid so, but just for tonight. I think we'll live through it."

The Fireside Lounge looked different than it had before. The folding chairs that had been set up for the hymn sing had been taken down, and now small tables and comfortable chairs were scattered in conversational groups throughout the room.

Abbey helped Claire settle near the fire. It was a cozy setting, with upholstered wingback chairs positioned on either side of the native stone fireplace. A large picture window looked out on the rolling back lawn of the home, and the pines that ringed the clearing enclosed the peaceful world.

"How are you doing, Claire?" Abbey asked, and she was amazed at how much she really did care.

"Pretty good. Oh, there are days when I'd like to complain, and maybe I do, but for the most part I'm doing well. How are things with you?" Claire's china blue eyes fixed on Abbey from behind the thick lenses of her eyeglasses.

"The store is doing well, but of course much of that right now is the Christmas trade. It'll drop off in January, after the returns are done, of course."

"Sweet says the same thing about his store." Claire leaned back contentedly. "I'd have never thought that a grown man could make a decent living selling toys, of all things, but that boy sure did prove me wrong."

"Especially this time of year," Abbey agreed. "I think everybody buys toys at Christmas."

"He's going to make a fine husband for some lucky woman," Claire said with studied casualness. "He'll be a good provider, he's not bad to look at, and he's a Christian, which counts for everything in this world."

Abbey could feel a flush rising up her neck. Had Claire seen her get flustered when Mike was fooling with the mistletoe? "He's a nice person," she said, noncommittally.

Those bright blue eyes sharpened behind the thick lenses. "He's the best, and I'm not just saying that because we're related so I have to. He really is. And it appears to me that he thinks highly of you."

Claire was clearly matchmaking. In her mind, she already had Abbey and Mike paired off, probably with 2.5 children in a house surrounded by a white picket fence and morning glories that bloomed in the morning sun. Abbey knew she had to put that idea to rest. And the best approach was the direct one.

"I'm going back to school to get my business degree," she said gently. "First my undergraduate degree in business, then my MBA. I can't do that here. I'll have to move."

Claire's lips curved a bit in a secret smile. "There are plans, and there are plans," she said enigmatically.

"My plans are real," Abbey said. "I have a ten-year strategy all worked out. I know exactly where I'll be and what I'll be doing."

Claire's smiled deepened. "The certainty of youth. Oh, I'm not going to argue with you," she said as Abbey started to interrupt. "It's always good to have a plan, but it's like the Good Book says: God has His own set of plans for us. Just when you think you've got it under control, God comes along and shouts, 'Surprise!' right into your heart."

"You speak like someone who's experienced that firsthand." Abbey knew that the best way to derail Claire was to change the focus of the conversation.

"God's given me many a surprise in these years He's had me on this planet. Some are good, and some. . .well, some weren't."

Claire paused, and Abbey watched the wave of memories wash over the elderly woman's face—twinges of pain mixed with uplifting joy.

"I've had a good life, you know—not that I'm writing the last chapter to it yet, don't get me wrong on that! But I'm happy with what the Lord has given me."

"Did you always feel that way?" Abbey asked. "I don't know how to ask this, but did you have a career outside the house?"

Claire patted Abbey's hand. "You're a dear. Yes, honey, I was a teacher until I got married and had my children; then I took some time off. I went back for a while after they grew up and started their own lives."

"Did you have a plan?"

Mike's grandmother laughed. "A plan? I don't think they'd been invented yet! But I did have an idea of what I wanted to do and why. It's not quite the same as the life plans people do now, but it worked at the time."

Abbey stirred uncomfortably. She lived so tightly by her ten-year plan that she couldn't imagine life without it. But apparently Claire had done fine without one as detailed as hers. On the other hand, Abbey told herself, life had been simpler for Claire. Her life couldn't have been as complicated as the one Abbey led.

"We didn't have money for much of anything," Claire reminisced, "but we had lots of love. You hear that all the time, and sometimes it seems like they're just so many words. But with us it was true."

"What was your husband like?" Abbey asked.

"My Arthur was a God-fearing man—although he used to insist that he was also a Claire-fearing man. We had good times together. Lean times, sorrowful times, stressful times—they were all made better by the fact that we had each other. Abbey, don't get so caught up in your career that you overlook the importance of having someone to love—and to love you," Claire implored her with earnestness.

"I'm not overlooking that," Abbey answered stiffly. "I'll get to it when I have time. I just don't have time right now."

"Make time. Don't build walls around your heart. Your career is important, but don't let it become a prison. You have your whole life ahead of you, and I'm serious when I tell you that it's a whole lot easier when you have someone to share the burdens and the joys with."

"Claire—"

"Don't interrupt your elders, dear. I'm not through yet. Let yourself be open to love. Promise me you will."

"I will," Abbey said, but mentally she added, *In my dreams.* What Claire said had the flavor of truth, but it left a sour taste in her mouth.

"What are you ladies discussing so seriously?" Mike asked behind her.

"We're just talking about what to do with young men who sneak up and listen in on women's conversations," Claire said half-jokingly.

"I didn't hear a word," Mike said seriously, but the sparkle in his eyes made Abbey wonder if he was being completely honest. "Abbey, I don't want to hurry you, but we'd better get going."

"I'll go with you to the front," Claire said. "Mike, why don't you go ahead and start the car so it'll be at least a little bit warm for Abbey?"

Mike grinned at Abbey. "She's still trying to make me a gentleman. Okay, Grandma, I'll go." He dropped a kiss on her head. "I'll try to get over here tomorrow. Abbey, I'll pull up in front."

He left quickly, and Abbey and Claire proceeded at a more leisurely pace with Claire wheeling herself out of the room and down the corridor.

As they started down the hall back to the great room, a gentleman leaning on a cane turned toward them. "Is that Sweet's lady friend?"

Abbey recognized him from her first visit to Golden Meadows. He had been her champion when Mike had lectured her about friendship. She looked at Claire and grinned. "Yup, she's right here, sir. Claire's his grandmother."

He waved a hand twisted with arthritis. "That's not what I mean, and you know it, young woman. I mean you. Is that fellow treating you better, or do I need to give him a piece of my mind?" He shook his cane. "I'd be glad to do it, too. These young chaps have no sense of chivalry at all."

Claire grasped Abbey's arm. "Did Sweet treat you badly? What did he do?"

Laughter bubbled out of Abbey. These two darling senior citizens were ready to defend her honor, even at Mike's expense. It was utterly charming.

She leaned over and kissed Claire's furrowed forehead. "Don't worry. Mike has been a perfect gentleman."

Claire said something that sounded suspiciously like, "Rats!"

❄

The busy evening left Mike few minutes of quiet to reflect upon the evening's events. His grandmother had called him out there on some obviously trumped-up excuse. She'd given him some line about the sink in her room being plugged up, but by the time he'd gotten ahold of the Golden Meadows handyman and they'd gone to her room, the clog had miraculously taken care of itself.

It was almost, he thought, as if she'd been maneuvering to get some time alone with Abbey. And considering how things had been going lately, that was probably exactly the reason she'd engineered the whole thing.

And there was only one reason for her to want to have time alone with Abbey.

He probably should tell her that her efforts were futile, that Abbey was the ultimate businesswoman, focused on her career only. Although, he mused, lately she had seemed to be friendlier. Perhaps his talk—no, his lecture—about friendship had gotten through to her. He still felt a bit guilty about how heavy-handed he'd been that day.

Nevertheless, she'd needed to hear every word of what he'd said. He knew what it was like to feel so tired that exhaustion swirled through your body like a living thing. He'd been there himself, and he had to admit, there were times when he still overworked himself.

But friendship was the glue that held humanity together. Abbey needed a friend, and he was willing to be that friend. Just a friend, he told himself for the thousandth time that night. That was all. A friend.

He had the same uneasy feeling he used to get when, as a child, he tried to lie to his parents.

His mind leaped back to the moment with the mistletoe. He'd truly wanted to hold it over her head, but he knew he didn't dare. Friends didn't kiss under the mistletoe, the contrary voice in his head pointed out to him. And even if he had tried, she probably would have decked him on the spot.

But hadn't he, maybe, seen hope spring into her eyes like a flash of light?

Chapter 9

I don't have time to do it," Abbey said, staring at Mike as if he'd lost his mind. "You know perfectly well that I'm working eighty hours a week. And now you want me to do something like this? And in three days?"

He was out of his mind. That was the only reasonable explanation. He'd taken total leave of his senses. Asking her to give a presentation on career guidance, and during the busiest time of the year at Trends!

"It'd be fun," he countered. "A nice change of pace."

"Sleep would be a nice change of pace. Mike, really, I'm sure—"

"You'd reach so many lives," he interrupted. "The Jeremiah Group is a great program. We got the name from the Bible verse, Jeremiah 29:11–14."

When she didn't respond, he prompted, "The one where God says that He has plans for us."

"I'm familiar with the verse," Abbey answered, with a mental addendum: *Sort of.*

"The Jeremiah Group is made up of young women who need to hear what you have to say."

"Oh yeah, right." She snorted. "I don't know anything special. What do I have to talk to them about?"

"A lot. They don't have guidance from the outside, so I know they'd be interested in how you decided to go into retail, and how this job you have now is a steppingstone to your career goals."

"Mike, it's Christmas. You know what that means. We never have a minute to ourselves." She motioned around the interior of Trends and realized, too late, that they were the only ones in there. "Okay, so at this particular moment no one else is here. Come back in an hour or so. Then this place will be jumping with shoppers."

He didn't say anything, and she added defensively, "It's not like I could simply show up and give a talk. I'd need time to prepare. Three days isn't enough lead time. What happened to whoever was supposed to talk to them originally?"

"She went into labor."

"Some people will do anything to get out of a commitment, won't they?" Abbey said wryly. "I'm sorry. I just can't. Not now. Maybe next spring." She turned to refolding a table display of brightly striped sweaters.

"If you don't do it, the meeting will have to be cancelled."

"So? They probably have better things to do. . .like Christmas shopping." She smiled at him, but he didn't return her smile.

"Abbey," he said seriously, "these girls don't have money to shop with. That's the point of the whole thing. It's a career guidance group."

She couldn't do it, she reasoned. She kept coming back to the one irrefutable fact: She didn't have time. When would she squeeze something like this into her already overpacked day?

And besides that, she had no expertise when it came to guiding young women, especially those who were considered at risk. What would she say to them? She'd never addressed a group at all, let alone a selection of teenagers who were bound to be a reluctant and captive audience.

She knew how it would go. She'd bumble her way through, and they'd laugh at her. Maybe openly, but most certainly behind her back.

Actually, that was a best-case scenario. What if she said something terribly wrong. . .and messed up someone's life?

No, it was too much to ask of her. She couldn't do it.

"Plus I don't go to your church." She clutched at that straw. "I couldn't talk about religion. All I know about religion is what I got from Aunt Luellen, and loopy as she is, I wouldn't be surprised if she didn't mix up Jeremiah with Niemeier."

"Nehemiah. That doesn't matter. We'll do that part. All you have to do is come in, tell the girls a bit about how you decided what you wanted to do for a living, and talk to them about goal setting and career planning."

"That's all, huh?"

"Yup." He smiled at her winningly.

"How long would I have to be there?"

"An hour, hour and a half tops."

An hour? It loomed like a lifetime. She couldn't do it. She wouldn't do it. But her traitorous mouth opened, and she heard herself saying, "All right. I'll do it. Let's hope they're not expecting too much."

"You'll be great!" Mike said with enthusiasm. "I'll talk to you more about it tomorrow and see how you're doing, okay?"

"Okay." Abbey was sure she was making a monstrous mistake, but it couldn't be that bad, could it?

Mike turned at the entrance to Trends. "Oh, one more thing, Abbey."

"What's that?"

"Don't quote from the book of Niemeier."

❄

Abbey laid out her presentation as she worked. While she was arranging a shimmering display of vests, she organized her biography. As she positioned another rack of evening gowns in an impossibly tight corner, she prepared the steps of effective goal setting. She shifted sale purses to a table near the front of the store while she created questions sure to provoke vital and intelligent discussion.

As she drove home, she thought of the young women. She would have benefited from such a group, she knew that. Whether she would have listened when she was that age was another matter entirely. Well, all she could do was go and share what she had, and if something took root in even one girl's mind, it was a good thing.

For the first time in months, Abbey felt really good. She was energized. She was excited. She tried to ignore the fact that she was undoubtedly nuts.

❅

Mike picked her up at Trends an hour before the Jeremiah Group was to meet. "You look nice," he commented. "I meant to tell you not to wear a suit, so what you have on is perfect."

This was the seventh outfit she'd put on. Her bed was piled with discarded dresses, slacks, and skirts. She'd finally chosen a long denim skirt and fleece vest with a turtleneck. She hoped she exuded a sense of confidence she didn't truly feel.

"Thank you," she said.

There. She was in trouble. If her voice was going to waver and wobble like that, and she hadn't even left her store, she could only imagine what a nightmare her presentation was going to be.

Mike put his hand on her arm. "Abbey, these are girls who are starting from ground zero. Some of them may even be below that. Don't be afraid of them."

"I'm not afraid of them," she said defensively, lifting her chin just a bit. "What I'm scared of is myself. What if I blow it?"

"You'll be fine."

"I hope you're right." Abbey's hands were sweating as she pulled on her yellow mittens. Their bright wool reflected a cheerfulness she didn't feel.

Mike talked about everything except the presentation as they drove to his church, Word of Faith Community Church. She'd seen it before, but she'd never gone in. It was a simple pale brown brick building with a white-painted steeple and cross.

Every muscle in her body urged her to turn back as she and Mike entered the building. But the window of opportunity closed quickly, and she was soon enveloped with warm greetings of others who were waiting inside.

"It's so nice of you to do this," one woman said. "I have everything ready for you, even a laptop and a projector."

The woman took Abbey's coat and introduced herself as Mrs. Robbins. "I'm one of the counselors for the Jeremiah Group," she explained. "There are many people involved with the program. Mike, for example, coordinates the speakers. My specialty is helping the young women with filling out job applications and going to interviews."

"It sounds interesting," Abbey commented, realizing it was a bland statement that didn't really focus in on what Mrs. Robbins was saying.

"The girls in this group—and they are rather young this time—need this kind of assistance. Whatever we can offer them is beneficial. In some cases, their parents don't work, or they rely on seasonal or part-time employment. Two of them have been shuttled around in foster homes so much that they don't have a clear picture of what a career even is. That's why what you're saying to them today is so important."

Mrs. Robbins motioned to a nearby room. A green and gold plaid curtain hid the interior from view, but from the way the drape moved a bit, Abbey knew she was being observed. She was only faintly aware of the curious gazes studying her covertly. She was using all her energies to keep from passing out from stage fright.

Mrs. Robbins saw Abbey's glance and smiled. "They'll be very distant, almost detached, but don't let that bother you. That's their defense against a world that often makes them into outsiders. Being aloof is their way of turning the tables."

Abbey could understand that. She had been through a rebellious stage herself, although what she'd been rebelling against was still a mystery to her. It was probably just teenaged angst.

"Shall we go in?" Mrs. Robbins asked, leading her toward the curtained room. Abbey was sure that mortal embarrassment waited for her.

They had done all that they could to fill the requests she made and to make her feel welcome, and with fearful feet she went in to meet the Jeremiah Group.

A flurry of activity greeted their entrance as the young women scurried away from the window that looked out on the narthex. They made a great show of not being at all interested in the guest as they gathered in the far corner and talked lazily to each other.

"Don't let them deter you," Mrs. Robbins whispered. "They're dying to meet you."

I'm the one who's dying, Abbey thought. This was the modern day equivalent of being thrown to the lions. Didn't that happen in the Bible? She remembered seeing a vivid picture in her children's Bible of a man sitting amidst a group of ferocious lions.

Scrap that. Insert a picture of a completely terrified store manager surrounded by a small group of bored young women. Truly a horrific scenario.

She looked at her tormentors. There were fourteen of them in attendance that day, most of them in their mid to late teens. Some viewed her with hostility, some with smiles, some with suspicion.

Her mouth was suddenly very dry, and the first words she had formulated to speak wouldn't come out at all. The teens watched her with increasing interest, inquisitiveness edging into their expressions as she continued to stand in front of them, mute.

It was just as she had feared. It was like one of those dreams she used to have in which she was addressing Congress in her pajamas, the fuzzy white ones with the chickens printed in bright yellow. The women's faces faded in and out again, and for a moment she thought she was going to be sick. That might not be such a bad thing, she reflected, because then she could leave.

She turned pleadingly at last to Mike. He'd have to take over and save her.

Sure enough, Mike stepped into the breach. He introduced her, then said, "Let's open in prayer. Blessed Father, guide Abbey's words as she speaks to the members of this group. Guide our ears that we might learn from her. And guide our feet as we go forth with today's message. Amen."

Abbey shot him a look of surprise. "That was short," she whispered.

"Cool, huh?" Mike grinned at her and turned his attention back to the assemblage. One woman chewed on the edge of her fingernail while another curled a lock of her hair around her finger. They could not have looked less interested.

Yet Mike persisted. "You all know that this group got its name from Jeremiah 29:11–14, right? God has plans for you, but there's absolutely nothing wrong with helping Him along and making the most of the talents He gave you. That's what Abbey is here to talk to you about—maximizing your time and your talents. Let's welcome her."

Some lackluster applause accompanied Abbey as she faced the group again. She knew her first instincts had been right. She shouldn't be here. What on earth had she been thinking of? What kind of insanity had overtaken her when she agreed to do it?

I need some help here. If there was ever a good time for prayer, this was it.

The sea of faces swam into focus. One by one, she looked directly at each young woman and saw them as individuals, not a homogenous group of blasé girls. Their eyes met hers, and in that moment of contact, each teenager let Abbey see past the artifice. She saw the fear of rejection behind the bravado, the hurt behind the mask of boredom.

The words she had so carefully prepared vanished from her mind, and suddenly they were replaced by words from her heart. The group quit shifting in their seats and focused their attention on her. The young women watched her, transfixed, and her speech gained power. She talked about finding her talent and making the most of it, and the satisfaction of knowing that she was doing what she was meant to do, and doing it well.

The teenagers rarely looked away as she talked. And finally, she realized she was through. Her energy reservoirs were totally depleted, and she felt as limp as cooked spaghetti.

Mike stood and shook her hand. "That was wonderful. Thank you so much for coming today and sharing your expertise with us. Abbey will stay for a few minutes if you want to talk to her some more. I'm sure she won't mind answering any extra questions you might have."

There was a moment of silence before the worldly cloaks fell back over their eyes and they retreated to their façade of coolness. Yet as soon as Mike left the podium and the session was clearly over, in one wave of movement, the young women stood and came forward to surround Abbey.

❄

Mike sighed with relief. Abbey had done extremely well to get this kind of reaction from them. He offered up a quick prayer of thanksgiving for the success of her talk. Not only did the girls need it, he sensed, but Abbey did, too.

Finally the last teenager drifted away, and Mike moved over to where she was standing. "You must have been quite the success," he said. "These girls may be anywhere from fourteen to eighteen in chronological age, but in street years, they're much older. They're usually so blasé that we're lucky they're not doing their nails during the presentation. And you were worried!"

To his amazement, she sat down and put her head in her hands.

"What's the matter?" he asked.

"Are you ready for this? They all had the same question." Abbey shook her head in amazement, but she didn't look up.

"Really? What was it? Did they want details on how to find career counseling or something like that?"

"No." Her shoulders began to shake.

Mike ran his fingers through his hair. Why was she crying? He never knew what to do when adults cried.

"Did they have educational concerns, like where to find a school?"

"Not exactly."

"They were intrigued by a career in retail?"

"Um, sort of," she hedged. She raised her eyes, and he realized that she had not been crying. She was laughing. "They wanted to know where I got my vest."

They looked at each other, and together they howled with laughter. It was getting to be a habit with them, this roaring into uncontrollable laughter over the most inane things. But it was a nice habit.

"It's so absurd," Abbey said at last. "All of that emotion, that worry, that preparation, and all they wanted to know is where I got my stupid vest."

"It's good advertising for Trends," Mike said.

"No, it isn't." Abbey couldn't avoid the absurdity of the situation. "I got it at the discount store at the other mall about four years ago. I had no idea what to tell them, so I just said I'd had it for ages."

"Do you feel bad that you put so much work into the presentation only to have it turn out this way?" Mike asked gently.

It was a legitimate question, and Abbey's response was a bit surprising to her. "I've got to admit it would have been a lot simpler if I could have had them come over to my house and go through my closet, if that's what you mean. But yes, it's a bit distressing. All that planning, only to find out I'd been preparing for the wrong thing. Go figure."

"You know," Mike said, standing and reaching for their coats, "the verse in Jeremiah applies to you, too. We don't know what God's plans are for us. We can only trust that He won't do anything too rash to set things in motion. Maybe one of these teenagers has had her life changed today by that woman in the dynamite vest. It could be that's why you wore it today."

She remembered the many changes of clothes before she'd decided on this particular outfit, how often she'd tossed aside an outfit simply because it didn't "feel right." Could he be onto something? She'd heard that there were no true accidents.

Mike continued as they left the little church, "And who knows, you may very well have touched someone's heart here today in a way you can't know."

She'd touched a heart, all right, he acknowledged, *but God, did it have to be mine?*

Chapter 10

Abbey was still chuckling over the incident the next day. She was telling Selma about it when suddenly a man dressed in a Keystone Kops outfit, complete with a rounded helmet and a billy club, invaded her store.

"Officer Oliver P. Torkelson here. I have a warrant for Abbey Jensen," he said loudly. "I've come to arrest you!" His handlebar moustache tilted forward dangerously, and he shoved it back into place.

"What on earth?" Abbey asked. She'd never seen anything like this. "You must have the wrong place, or at least the wrong person."

"You're under arrest, young lady. The charge is—wait a second, let me check." He pulled a folded sheet of paper from his shirt pocket with great ceremony and proceeded to read: "Abbey Jensen is hereby placed under arrest for being a Holiday Hooligan."

"A Holiday Hooligan? What is that? This is crazy!"

"Got the warrant right here. All written out proper-like. You'd better come with me."

"I'm not coming with you," Abbey protested. "I have no idea what this is all about."

"Sorry, ma'am." Torkelson produced gigantic red plastic handcuffs. "Resisting arrest means I'll have to use these."

A strangled sound from behind her made Abbey turn her head. Selma was overcome with giggles. "Do you know anything about this?" Abbey asked her employee warily. "You do, don't you?"

Selma shook her head wordlessly.

"Mike. Mike had something to do with it," Abbey accused. "And from that grin on your face, you do too know what's going on."

Officer Torkelson cleared his throat loudly. "Enough chitchat. You'd better come with me to the Candy Cane Calaboose."

"The Candy Cane Calaboose?" Abbey repeated. "What is that?"

The policeman tsked and wrote something on the warrant. "I'm going to have to add Failure to Read Merry Mall Mail to the complaint."

"Merry Mall Mail?" Abbey couldn't believe her ears. "I've never heard of such a thing."

"That's because you never read your Merry Mall Mail," Officer Torkelson said logically. "If you'd have read it, you'd know what it was."

Abbey covered her face with her hands. "This is unreal. I never heard of Merry Mall Mail. I don't know what the Candy Cane Calabash is."

"Calaboose," Selma corrected. "A calaboose is a jail. A calabash is a gourd."

"Calabash, calaboose. This is insane."

Officer Torkelson stroked his moustache reflectively. "Trying to cop an insanity plea, eh? Are you insane? Do I need to get a straightjacket?"

"No, I'm not insane. They're insane, whoever 'they' are. And I certainly don't need a straightjacket." She paused as she realized what was transpiring. "Oh, for crying out loud. This is what the other managers were talking about down at the mailboxes, isn't it? Please tell me this isn't the brainchild of the mall management."

The policeman's moustache twitched dangerously.

She knew she had no choice except to go. Selma would watch the store, and besides, it would probably be just a few minutes. Even the mall administration wouldn't be as silly as to take people off the selling floor during the busiest season of the year for any extended period of time.

"This won't take long," she told Selma grimly as she left in the custody of Officer Torkelson. "And if it gets busy, call the mall office. This is their idea, so they might as well reap the results of it."

She'd walked by the Candy Cane Calaboose, but she hadn't paid much attention to it other than to note that it was another way of making use of every inch of the mall's space. The wooden structure was clearly modeled after an old-fashioned jail but with one crucial exception: the bars on the cells were painted in red and white spirals.

"Here, put this on." A woman dressed in a skirt and blouse printed with tiny candy canes handed her a bundle. "These are your jail coveralls."

Abbey shook them out. They were striped, like the prisoner outfits of the old movies, but instead of black and white, these were red and white, like candy canes.

"I can't put these on," Abbey objected. "I'm wearing a skirt, in case you hadn't noticed."

"Just pull them on top," the woman instructed her. "By the way, I'm the warden here, so don't get snippy with me." She shook the large key that hung around her neck, which was apparently used with the oversized heart-shaped lock on the cell door. The twinkle in her eyes softened her words, and she added in a whisper, "It could have been a lot worse. They started out with this being a dunking tank, so count your blessings."

Abbey shuddered at the thought of what havoc that idea would have wrought. "The mall management has had some nutso ideas," she muttered as she pulled the coveralls over her clothes, "but this takes the cake."

Her skirt bunched up around her hips under the coverall, and she was sure she looked as if she had the world's biggest caboose. The Candy Cane Caboose, she told herself.

"Did you see that you have company?" the woman added, pointing to a second chair in the cell.

Abbey had almost missed him, but how, she couldn't have said. Mike was also garbed in the candy-striped coverall.

"You look ridiculous," she said, plopping into the vacant chair. "Kind of like an oversized after-dinner mint."

"They don't call me Sweet for nothing," he quipped.

"Fill me in on this, please," she said. "Apparently I didn't read my Merry Mall Mail—whatever that is—but I have no idea who ratted on me. And I was certainly never aware that it was an offense that was going to get me arrested."

He chuckled. "Here's the scoop. Anybody at the mall—employees, customers, competitors, whatever—can pay to have you put in the slammer, er, calaboose. And there you stay until someone bails you out. All the money goes to charity."

"A noble goal," she grumbled. "So what you're saying is that somebody, some rat fink, paid to have me put here?" She glowered at him suspiciously.

"First of all, I don't believe I've heard someone actually say 'rat fink' in the past decade, and secondly, don't glare at me. I thought you were responsible for me being here, but since you are clueless about this whole Candy Cane Calaboose thing, I guess I have to blame one of my employees."

She recalled Selma's bout with hysterics when Abbey was "arrested." "I think I know who the culprit is. . .at least for me being stuck in here. Selma."

A sudden thought struck her. Selma was a one-person fan club for romance; it wouldn't be too hard to imagine her putting both Abbey and Mike in the Candy Cane Calaboose at the same time.

Mike leaned back and hummed along with the public address system, which boomed nonstop Christmas carols at top volume. Abbey craned her neck and noticed that they were positioned directly under a circular speaker embedded in the wall.

"I used to love those songs," she mused. "But somewhere around November tenth, they lost their appeal."

"You're kidding!" Mike seemed genuinely surprised. "I love the whole Christmas scene. Carols, trees, presents, the whole nine yards."

Abbey motioned at the mall outside their cell. "But look at this. 'Gaudy' doesn't even begin to describe it. They've added another scene. A purple plaster seal wearing a wreath around its neck. Isn't that charming?"

"The seal is inexplicable. I don't know what that's doing here." Mike cocked his head and studied the statue. "No, I can't say as I see any reason for it to be here. It's ludicrous at best."

"Well, that's my point. What does it have to do with Christmas?"

He leaned forward earnestly. "That isn't Christmas. That's profit margins, pure and simple—if there is anything pure or simple about profit margins. The seal has more to do with the mall manager and his exquisite artistic taste than the future of a major world religion. Christmas is about the birth of hope. It's the first day of our salvation."

"You sound like my aunt Luellen." The conversation made Abbey uneasy, but at the same time she craved talking about her confused feelings. And oddly, having this discussion about Jesus in the midst of this crazy Candy Cane Calaboose made it easier.

"Your aunt Luellen is pretty smart."

"My aunt Luellen is a kook. She's the reason we're even having this talk. If it weren't for her getting those packages mixed up, we'd still be going on with our lives. . . separately. And I wouldn't even be thinking about Jesus or God or anything except my own profit margins."

"Like I said," Mike said, so softly she had to crane to hear his words, "your aunt Luellen is a very smart person."

Abbey snorted in derision. "How can you say that? That would mean that Aunt Luellen would have done this. . .on purpose," she ended slowly as the realization of what he was saying dawned on her.

There comes a moment in love when time stands still—or wishes it could. And just as frequently, that instant is pushed away in the flurry of life.

She liked him, she told herself. That was all. He was a nice guy. Okay, he was a nice guy with very nice eyes and a very nice smile and a very nice way of approaching life. But she didn't love him. Love meant—well, she couldn't define it, not here in a makeshift jail in the midst of a busy mall filled with curious shoppers. She'd have to think about it. But the fact was that she was pretty sure she'd know if she was in love. At least there would be—or should be—fireworks and volcanoes and shooting stars. She didn't feel any of that when she saw Mike. What she felt was a pleasant warmth, like the good basic meal they had at Ginger's the other night. Nothing fancy. Plain home cooking didn't equal love.

The food analogy made her hungry.

She looked at him covertly. He was a bit pinker than usual. Was it possible? Was Mike Tucker blushing? Or was it only the reflection of his candy-striped jail coveralls?

She had to change the subject, and fast. "I wonder if they feed us in this Candy Cane Calaboose," she said. "I'm starving."

Mike seemed as equally grateful for the switch in the direction their conversation was taking. "Even a candy cane would be welcome. I think that woman who's supposed to be our warden probably has some. Want me to get one for you?"

Abbey shook her head. "I don't know if I'll ever be able to look a candy cane in the eye again."

Mike hooted with laughter. "I didn't know candy canes had eyes, but I get your point."

"How can you be so cheerful about this shenanigan?" she asked crossly, but before he could answer, a voice hailed them from the mall corridor.

"Yoo-hoo, Candy Cane captives!" Selma was approaching them and obviously enjoying their predicament entirely too much. "Ready to get out?" She waved a ten-dollar bill at them.

"Am I ever!" Abbey stood up. "Pay my bail, and let's go. Say, if you're here, who's watching the store?"

"I closed it."

"You what?" Abbey thundered.

"Oh, I'm just kidding. Brianna came in." Selma walked around and studied the jail from the outside. "This isn't too bad. I've lived in worse places."

Mike grinned. "It's about the size of my apartment, now that you mention it. Are you springing both of us, or just Abbey?"

"Both of you. You two ready to go?"

As Abbey sprang to her feet, Mike touched her arm. "It hasn't been that bad, has it?"

The sharp retort that sprang to her lips died, and the truth—in a single word—replaced it. "No."

❅

That evening, as Mike said his nightly prayers, he asked for reassurance. It wasn't something he often did, usually choosing instead to trust in his Father's leadership.

I'm trying, Lord. Every time I think I've taken a step closer, though, she steps back. This would be a lot easier if she'd just stay still. Am I doing this right? And, by the way, God, am I supposed to be falling in love with her?

❅

And across town, a young woman found herself in an unusual position, her head bent and her heart open. "Tell me what to do about the way I feel," she said quietly, although who she was speaking to, she couldn't have said.

Chapter 11

Abbey leaped out of bed, horrified at the bright light that shone in through her window. Clearly she had overslept. A quick glance at the clock beside her bed verified it. It was nearly eight. She pulled back the curtain and peeked outside. Already the first round of rush hour was underway, with the late-to-work drivers stretching the speed limit.

Usually she was up early, quick to get ready for her busy day and always the first one at the mall. What was happening to her? She hadn't overslept in a couple of years. Crazy dreams had haunted her sleep, dreams filled with dancing candy canes and prisons made of sweets.

And Mike. He'd been in all of her dreams, all night long.

Once when she was in high school, studying French, her teacher had told her that when she dreamed in French, she could be assured that she had total command of the language, that she totally understood it. What did that mean when she dreamed about Mike?

She'd never dreamed in French anyway, she told herself as she slurped down a gulp of too-hot coffee, so she'd never had the chance to test the hypothesis. She needed to wake up and quit worrying about such inane stuff.

Customers were already browsing through the sales racks as she slipped into her spot behind the cash register at Trends.

Selma glanced at her curiously. "Oversleep?"

Abbey nodded. "I couldn't believe it myself." She busied herself with rearranging the display of glittery necklaces and earrings. "I guess there's something about winter that makes me want to hibernate."

Her associate snorted inelegantly. "There's something about working sixteen-hour days that makes you want to hibernate." Selma put her hand over Abbey's and stilled her active fingers. "Quit dinking around with that stuff and look at me. You need to take a break. You're working too hard and too long—"

"It's Christmas," Abbey replied, as if that explained it all.

"So go have a Christmas. Even a couple of hours. Go shopping. Drive around and look at the lights. Sit at home and watch that Christmas special with Charlie Brown and Snoopy."

As Selma spoke, Abbey felt a hunger rise in her, almost palpably. She wanted to shop, to look at lights, to watch Charlie Brown with his pitiful little tree.

317

She nodded. "I will. I promise. Tonight I'll take a break."

Selma looked at her with unsure eyes. "You'd better. A promise is a promise, and I'm holding you to it. You're missing the best part of Christmas, hanging out inside this mall day in and day out."

"Okay, okay, you've made your point!" Abbey cried with exasperation. "I'll do it, I promise!"

❄

"It's four o'clock," Selma said pointedly when the afternoon rush had tapered off.

"I know. Did you want a break?" Abbey began sizing the sale blouses.

"Yes, I do, but not for me. For you. You promised."

"And I will." Abbey stooped to pick up a blouse whose hanger had broken. "Selma, can you get another hanger for this?"

"I'm going to keep after you until you go," Selma warned. "Brianna will be here in less than an hour, and then you have no excuses, m'lady."

"But who—"

"I don't know because I'm not going to listen to your question so I can't answer it. But you are going to go. How do I know? Because I can be the world's biggest pain in the neck when I need to."

Abbey grumbled under her breath.

"I heard that," Selma snapped. "I'm not sure what you said, but I can't think it was nice. Now go."

"All right." Abbey gave in grudgingly. "But first I'm off to grab a bite to eat. I'm just running down to that pretzel place, then I'll be back to do those markdowns."

Selma barred her way. "You will not. You promised me you were going to take the evening off, and I'm holding you to it. Brianna will be in to cover tonight, and there's that high school student backing her up. The store will be fine tonight. Go get some R & R."

Abbey couldn't summon the strength to argue. "You win. I'll be back tomorrow morning."

"Good. Now, at the very least, I want you to promise me you'll get in your jammies with some popcorn and veg out in front of the tube. Either the Peanuts special or *It's a Wonderful Life*." Selma almost pushed her into her coat.

"They might not be on tonight," Abbey protested lightly.

"Ha. It's December. They'll be on." Selma's laughter followed Abbey as she left the store.

❄

Mike smiled as he stopped at the door to Trends. He'd come to see if Abbey wanted to go back to Golden Meadows, but Selma's voice had stopped him. He was glad he hadn't barged on in.

Abbey didn't even see him as she swept out with her coat on. That was good. She needed to get away for a while, and it didn't matter where she was going: home, grocery store, Laundromat. Just as long as she wasn't living her life here in the mall.

He'd seen the little lines that were beginning to etch themselves around her eyes. She was far too young for that hard-worn look. Exhaustion radiated from her like an aura. Abbey clearly needed someone to make her leave the mall once in a while, someone to insist that she take some time to herself.

That's why he wanted her to go with him to Golden Meadows. That's why he was going to ask her to go to dinner with him tomorrow night. She was a child of the heavenly Father, and she deserved time to relax. That's why he was taking her away.

And it had nothing, nothing at all to do with the way her gray eyes made him feel suddenly warm and protective.

❄

Her car sputtered and bucked. Abbey's eyes darted to the dial on the dashboard. Gas. She'd forgotten gas.

Luckily the station by the mall was open, and she basically coasted into the bay.

"Fill 'er up?" the attendant asked.

"Oh no, I can—" she stammered in confusion. Then she realized she had driven into the full-service bay. A slow smile crossed her face. "No, go ahead. Fill it up."

It felt nice to let someone do this simple task for her. She leaned against the headrest and felt the tension try to leave her body. And she felt the resistance of habit. Go. Do. Get busy.

They were hard habits to let go of.

"Don't forget to plug in tonight."

The voice of the station attendant startled her. "What?"

"Plug in tonight. Supposed to be eighteen below." He clasped his hands together and rubbed them briskly. "Already twelve below."

She thanked him for the reminder. Minnesota winter evenings were sometimes so cold that cars needed block heaters so they'd start in the morning. Born and bred Minnesotan, Abbey thought briefly that any car without the plug hanging out of the front grillwork looked odd.

She paid for her gas and headed home. Popcorn and a television movie did sound heavenly. If she tried really hard, she might be able to get into this relaxing stuff.

But success isn't measured by how much you're relaxed, a nasty little voice whined inside her head. *It's measured by how much you've achieved, and you're not going to achieve anything by lolling around the house.*

One night, she told herself, *just this one night.* It was an experiment to see what it was like.

The wind whistled around her ears as she dug the plug-in out of the snow-bank. The fellow at the gas station was right: It was already cold enough tonight to plug in her car. She hurried through the task and was glad to get inside to the warmth of her small house.

One of these days she'd actually do something to decorate the inside. The house was still painted the same bland off-white it had been when she'd bought it. The furniture was, to put it bluntly, practical, and that was all. It was the same couch, chair, bed, and table that she'd had when she was in college.

But before she committed herself to anything, she would think about what kind of furniture she wanted. And that took time. She didn't have time.

She shed her suit and wrapped a thick terrycloth robe around her. Popcorn, then the television.

Abbey pulled open first one cabinet, then another. They seemed to gape at her. Where was the popcorn? Didn't she just buy some? She shook her head as she realized that she had last bought popcorn nearly a year ago.

"Okay, no popcorn." She shut the last cabinet door, perhaps a little harder than necessary, and opened the freezer. It was well-stocked with frozen dinners. "And this, my friends," she intoned to an imaginary group of visitors, "is what the larder of the busy career woman is like. Cabinets are empty while the freezer is stocked."

She'd make a list, she decided, and put everything she needed on it. She returned to the bare cupboard shelves. It was amazing how empty, how totally empty her shelves were.

"Okay," she continued aloud, "first item: everything."

She microwaved a macaroni and cheese dinner, figuring that was as close to popcorn as she was going to get, and sat down in front of the television with the remote control.

Click.

The screen lit up with fuzzy static. She tried another channel. It was no better. And on through all the channels, still no picture.

"Stupid cable company," she muttered, getting up to shuffle to the phone and call them.

Abbey punched in the numbers with a vengeance. "Hello, this is Abbey Jensen. My cable isn't working."

She gave them the pertinent information, then paused, aghast, at what she heard. "I haven't had cable since when? No, I guess I haven't turned on my television since then. Oh no, no need to come out. No, I don't want the service started again. Thanks, though."

She hung up the phone and stood motionless, staring at the mute television screen.

She hadn't had cable in five months. She'd been disconnected when she hadn't responded to a switch in service. And she'd never realized it.

Abbey sank to the kitchen chair beside her. She didn't know she was out of popcorn, and she didn't even know she didn't have cable TV. Could it be worse?

How had her life gotten so far away from her? No wonder she spent so much time at Trends. She didn't have a life at all.

That wasn't true, she argued with herself. She had a VCR, and she could rent a movie and watch it. The more she thought about it, the better the idea sounded. There was a video store just around the corner. Actually, she could even walk there.

She quickly changed from her robe to a pair of woolen pants and her thickest sweater and piled on a coat, boots, mittens, and hat. She stuck her VideoVideo card in her pocket and headed out.

The crisp air froze the inside of her nostrils. That, she told herself as she strode enthusiastically through the December night, was one of the best things about living in the north. Where else could you experience that?

The cloudless sky sparkled with a few random stars that were powerful enough to overcome the lights of the city. Abbey stood still and tried to pick out Orion's belt and the Big Dipper.

A sudden memory shot into her mind, like a long-forgotten message. She had been tiny, two or three perhaps, and on such a winter night as this, her parents had bundled her up and driven her out of town, far away from the streetlamps and house lights, to the absolute darkness of the countryside where her father pulled the car over.

Abbey could still remember the rush of cold air invading the heated car as they took her out. And there, as her mother held her, still wrapped in too many layers of quilts, her father pointed out the constellations in a sky that seemed to have too many stars.

"This is Cassiopeia. See her throne? Orion the Hunter: that's his belt, those three stars in a row. The Pleiades, the Seven Sisters. The North Star is at the end of the Big Dipper's handle. Sailors used it to navigate by, and it's still the first star our eyes see in the heavens."

On and on he talked, naming the magical constellations, most of which her young eyes could not take in, but even now she remembered her mother's warm breath on her cold cheek and her father's calming voice. She was cocooned in their love.

She missed them.

A tear threatened to slide down her face but began to freeze. Abbey swiped at it with her gloved hand. There was no time for this foolishness. And it would never do to step into VideoVideo teary.

The video rental store was so bright her eyes hurt after being in the dark night. A teenager, so tall and thin that his long-sleeved VideoVideo shirt could cover only part of his arms, approached her. "Can I help you find something?"

Abbey sniffled. The problem with that marvelous feeling of breathing in icy air is that when she got into a warm room, her nose began to run. "Yes. I'm looking for *It's a Wonderful Life.*"

"Right here." The boy stretched one long arm and snagged a video from the Christmas display at the register. "Can I see your card?"

She pulled the card from her pocket and handed it to him. The clerk frowned. "This expired three years ago."

"You're kidding me!" Abbey snatched it from his hand with more gusto than she intended. "How can that be? Why, I just—" She sighed. It had been that long. "Fine. I'll get a new one."

"Okay. I need a picture ID." The teenager handed her a clipboard with a pencil dangling from a grimy string.

"ID?" she asked blankly. "I don't have my ID with me. Can't you just reactivate my old card?"

"Not after three years. Sorry, but it's—"

"Company policy," she finished for him. "I know, I know."

"You know, you could buy it for only $4 more. There's a special right now, it being Christmas and all."

"Oh, I don't need to—" she began, then stopped. *Four dollars,* she told herself. *Four dollars. Bend, Abbey. Bend and breathe.*

"That sounds like a deal," she said brightly.

What's wrong with me? she asked herself as she hurried home, the video tucked under arm. She'd forgotten the present at Golden Meadows, she'd neglected to put gas in her car, she was out of popcorn and just about everything else to eat, her cable TV bill wasn't paid, and now her video card had expired.

What else could happen?

❄

She stared at the VCR. A tangle of cords emerged from the back of it, and somehow they were supposed to be hooked up to her television and who knew what else. Abbey sank to the floor and put her head in her hands as she remembered. She'd bought it, and as she was trying to put it together, she had been called back to Trends.

And she'd never gotten back to finishing it.

Well, she told herself, *it can't be brain surgery.* She bravely took a cord and studied the back of the television. There was no place that it fit. She checked the other end of the cord. Nope.

If she had the directions, she could figure this out. But she had no idea where they might be.

Call Mike. She knew she could do that. He undoubtedly knew how to put one of these monstrosities together, just like he probably put gas in his car, paid his bills, stocked his cupboards, and never let his memberships lapse.

Or, she told herself, she could do it herself. Not that she had any idea how to do it, but she could certainly sit down and give it a shot.

Surrounded by mysterious wires and cords, the VCR on her lap and her television turned out so that the back faced the living room, she put it together. It would have been easier with the directions, but it was possible.

Soon, *It's a Wonderful Life*—her own copy—was playing as she curled on the couch, snuggly wrapped in pajamas and robe, a bowl of freshly popped popcorn—purchased at the video store—in her lap. But Abbey was completely unaware of George Bailey's plight.

She was sound asleep, snoring lightly, with the remnants of a satisfied smile on her face.

Chapter 12

Abbey awoke from her exhausted sleep with the instinctive feeling something was wrong. Had she overslept again? She'd been doing that a lot lately, it seemed, even if only for fifteen minutes. She had her morning regime down perfectly, and the slightest variation threw her off. She glanced at the alarm clock.

It was still early. The alarm wasn't set to go off for another half hour.

She knew she couldn't go back to sleep, but she didn't want to get up. It was too cold. The only reason it would be this cold was because the power was out, and the way the window shook told her why.

Blizzard.

She sighed and resisted the urge to tunnel deeper into the covers. Instead, she threw back the blankets and shivered as her feet touched the frigid floor. She pulled her thick robe on and tied it tightly, a faint defense against the chilly bedroom.

The hall, usually brightly sunlit, was shrouded in grayish white, the color reserved for an intense snowstorm. Abbey padded into the living room and peered at the thermostat. Sixty-four degrees. Not bad. There had been days in August when sixty-four degrees would have seemed like a blessing, she reminded herself.

A gust of wind made the windows chatter in their frames. This was a major blizzard indeed. It must have just started, because the wind was picking up speed even as she listened.

She was a good Minnesotan. She knew what to do. The first thing was to determine if it was just her house that was suffering from the power outage, or if it was everyone. She crossed to the window and drew back the curtain.

The houses on her street could have been lit up like Las Vegas, and she wouldn't have been able to tell, the storm was that intense. She couldn't see anything except a wall of white.

Whiteout. She hated this part of winter storms, when she couldn't see more than an inch or two in front of her face.

As if angry, the wind rattled the panes of glass even more. White snow, once so fluffy and Christmassy, had become suddenly granular and menacing. She couldn't see past the curtain of white that blew sideways, obscuring even her car.

Almost idly she thought that she should have put it in the garage last night. Now she'd have to dig it out.

Then Abbey laughed out loud. At the rate this storm was raging, she'd be shoveling one way or the other.

One thing was clear: She couldn't tell if it was just her house or if the entire block was powerless. She checked the phone. It was dead, too.

What she needed now was light and some way to make coffee. She rummaged through her closet until she found what she was looking for. It was a centerpiece she'd gotten as a housewarming gift—from Aunt Luellen, now that she thought about it—and had never used. In the midst of a fuchsia raffia circle studded with oversized fake roses was a huge glaringly pink monstrosity of a candle, with three wicks and a definite strawberry scent. Right now it seemed lovely.

Abbey had a plan. All she had to do was find something to light the thing with, and she'd be in business.

She dug in the utensil drawer fruitlessly until she had an idea. Bracing herself against the cold, she zipped into the garage, grabbed the barbecue lighter off the hook on the wall, and tore back inside.

Abbey clicked it, and a flame sprang into life. She felt ridiculously happy to see it.

"And now, my strawberry-pink eyesore, you are about to make yourself useful."

She spent the next few minutes rigging up a metal measuring cup and a coat hanger. She did some quick pouring, measuring, and stirring, and after waiting somewhat patiently, was rewarded with a warmish cup of coffee. It was not Starbucks by any means, but she said to herself as she cradled the precious cup in her hands, it was coffee.

The next matter of business was getting warm.

She had a fireplace, but she hadn't gotten around to getting firewood. Her only option was to put on more clothes. Abbey pulled on another sweatshirt and wrapped the throw from the couch around her shoulders.

The batteries in her transistor radio were dead, so she shook one out of her alarm clock and commandeered another from the miniature calculator the bank had given her and finally tuned in a local radio station. The reception was uneven at best. Static cut through the announcer's words, but she hung on every syllable.

"Lines are down. . .neighborhoods south of. . .plows are waiting out the storm. . ."

The sporadic news was her link with the outside world. There was nothing quite like being in a blizzard to make a person feel isolated. The swirling snow shut out everyone and everything.

". . .Senior citizens. . .residents are urged to use caution . . .hypothermia. . . and small children. . ."

Claire. She hoped Claire was all right. Certainly Golden Meadows had a back-up plan—at least a better plan than she had. She grimaced at the gaudy pink candle and the rig she'd designed to make coffee. She was pitiful.

Anyone would have a better severe weather plan than she had. Mike, for example, was the kind who'd have flashlights with batteries. She didn't even know where hers was, and if she did find it, she was sure the batteries would be too old. No, she had to rely on a grotesquely pink candle for her light and heat.

Actually, knowing Mike, he probably had all the residents of his apartment building gathered in one room, singing "Kumbaya."

That was mean-spirited, she knew. It was just that she had let everything slide. Everything, except her career. That she had firmly in her grip. She needed to take comfort from that.

"Closed. . . Also the schools, the mall, the post. . ."

That was what she was listening for. The mall was closed.

❉

Mike pulled the drapes shut on the window of his apartment. He'd seen enough. This wasn't going to be one of those blizzards that blew through quickly. No, this blizzard was settling in for a while.

It was hard to concentrate when the walls of the apartment shook with every windy blast. That was one of the problems of living on the fourth floor. It seemed as if his floor took the brunt of the storms.

If the electricity were on, he could watch television, or maybe a videotaped movie. He told himself he could read a book, but the fact was he didn't want to. He couldn't concentrate on it.

He was glad he'd chosen this apartment. It had a fireplace, so he was warm. But despite the comfort of the fireplace, he couldn't shake a feeling of worry. He knew that his grandmother would be safe at Golden Meadows. The generator would keep the heating system going, and there were round-the-clock aides to reassure the residents. But he wished the phones were working so he could call Abbey. Something told him that this storm had caught her unaware. She didn't watch television and rarely listened to the radio. He knew that. The blizzard warning had come late, too. Had she prepared for it? Was she all right?

This was the first blizzard of the season. That wasn't too bad for Minnesota. He remembered years when the snows started coming in October. Maybe it signaled an easy winter.

He couldn't shake this worry about Abbey. He opened the curtain once again and looked out. The storm wasn't breaking, and it didn't seem to have reached its full fury yet.

He checked the clock. 6:00 a.m. Abbey was probably asleep.

God, could You please watch over her?

He felt better after asking for God's protection, but he remembered something from his childhood. A burden shared in prayer was halved. That's what his mother used to tell him. Any load was lightened by prayer, she'd explained, but that didn't let you off the hook. You still had to do what you could. It was a partnership.

Now he had to figure out what he should do. Blizzards limited his alternatives to, well, zero. But he'd figure something out. He had to.

❄

The announcer's voice continued with his broadcast, which arrived in intermittent sputters.

Abbey peered outside. The storm whirled on, pausing occasionally, then increasing its intensity. She couldn't tell if it was growing worse or not.

She shivered—and only partially from the cold. There was something elementally terrifying about a blizzard, although she'd lived through enough of them to know that the safest place for her to be was inside. The problems happened when someone went outside and got stuck in the snow, or perhaps got turned around and lost.

It had happened to her once. She had been in college, walking home from the part-time job she had at a restaurant. She'd lived only a few blocks away, but the wind-borne snow was so intense that she'd had to walk with her head down and somehow had turned mistakenly. She'd ended up in an unfamiliar alley and had wandered for over half an hour before stumbling upon her apartment. She'd managed to escape frostbite, although her face had been swollen for a day from the icy blast of the snow.

This forced seclusion was going to drive her crazy. She cooked herself another cup of coffee, but it tasted terrible. She walked through her house, picking up the newspapers from the past week that had piled up. Then she straightened the towels in the bathroom.

What she really wanted to do was go to the store. The weekly sales figures were due, and there was the box of sweaters that had arrived late the day before. If they weren't unpacked soon, they'd be irretrievably wrinkled.

Of course, the power was probably off at the mall, so the computers were down, and the steamer would be useless, but she could do some of the work by hand, and if she took the sweaters out of the box and laid them out on the workroom table. . .

There was a break in the wind, and she could see her driveway. The area behind her car was blown clear, and an idea began to form in her mind. She could back out.

"No travel is advised. . .snow gates on the interstate are closed. . .extremely slippery. . .finger drifts. . ." The radio crackled back into life.

The snow gates were huge metal gates that blocked the ramps to the interstate during a snowstorm, but they wouldn't affect her. She didn't use the interstate to get to the mall. And slippery? She'd go slowly. As for finger drifts, the long, narrow heaps of snow that stretched across a lane or two of traffic, they were no problem. She'd accelerate through them.

And besides, she reasoned, she'd stay just long enough to do the weekly report and take the sweaters out of the box.

She got dressed as quickly as she could, pulling on several layers. The temperature in her house was dropping, and according to the thermostat, it was already four degrees colder inside than it had been when she got up.

A blast of icy wind threw snow in her face as she opened the front door, and instinctively she tucked her head down as she scurried to her car. The man on the radio had been right. It was very slick, and she had trouble keeping her balance with the force of the wind.

She hurried around the back of her car and stopped. What she hadn't been able to see from the kitchen window was a huge drift that wrapped around the driver's side of the car, just out of her view. It was almost as high as the side mirror. It would take her forever to shovel it out, especially with this wind. She gave up and crept back inside, abandoning her plan.

The house, although there was a definite chilly edge to the air, was much warmer than outside. She kicked off her snowy boots and dropped her coat unceremoniously on the entryway floor. She was stuck here, and she might as well make the best of it.

Abbey wrapped herself in the throw from the couch and curled up. Maybe she could just sleep through it.

At first sleep seemed impossible, but the pound of the blizzard eventually lured her eyes to close and her breathing to even out.

Then the blizzard began pounding harder.

She sat up, groggily, and realized that the sound was coming from outside. Someone was knocking at her front door.

Chapter 13

Who could be at her door during a full-fledged blizzard?

Abbey paused for only a moment. On one hand, her visitor could be an ax-murderer, but on the other hand, this was a blizzard and no one should be out in it, not even an ax-murderer.

She peeked through the window in her kitchen. Another vehicle was parked beside hers. The snow was swirling so thickly that she couldn't tell what color the car was, just that it looked to be something with four-wheel-drive. Ax-murderers didn't drive four-wheel-drive vehicles, she was pretty sure of that.

She opened the front door a crack and saw a rather tall, huddled shape. It certainly didn't look like an ax-murderer.

He looked like Mike. A very cold Mike.

She threw open her door. "Come in!"

He stepped inside her entryway, and an eddy of snowflakes accompanied him. "Do you need firewood?" he asked without preamble.

"It's good to see you, too, and yes, I do," she answered. Her heart was ridiculously elated to see him.

"Wait a second, then."

He vanished back into the storm and went to his car. Within moments he was back, carrying an armload of firewood.

She took it from him. As he kicked off his boots and shed his coat and muffler, she arranged the logs in the fireplace and started the kindling.

"I'm impressed." He spoke behind her.

"Why?"

"It's not easy to lay a fire and have it start that quickly. At least I've never been able to do it. I have a fireplace in my apartment, but I go through a lot of matches getting it started, and even then it doesn't always work out right."

Abbey rocked back on her heels. "It'll take a couple of minutes to catch. The trick is where to put the kindling and to remember to put the logs in bark side down. My dad taught me how to do it. We used to camp out a lot."

"Really? You don't strike me as a camping kind of gal."

"I'm not. I never was. My parents were, though, so I got dragged along. I never did figure out the charm of cooking over a campfire. I always ended up with everything charred on the outside and raw on the inside. Plus sleeping in the woods is an open invitation to any biting, creeping thing to come along and bite and creep on you. What's the point?"

Mike stood behind her, rubbing his hands together, and she realized he must be frozen.

"Where are my manners?" she asked. "I have a visitor, and I haven't even offered him something to wrap up in."

He chuckled. "I wonder if Emily Post dealt with blizzard etiquette."

She gave him the throw from the couch. "Here, use this. I'm plenty warm here by the fire. . .er, the single little flame that will soon catch."

As if on cue, one of the smaller logs sparked into life. Abbey smiled. "Good. Now it's only a matter of time before the other logs catch, too, and we'll have a real rip-roaring fire."

Mike draped the woven throw around his shoulders. "Great. That wind is fierce."

Abbey looked out the window. "Is it really bad?" An idea was formulating in her mind. If he could get to her house, then he could take her to the mall. It wasn't that much further.

"The roads are awful. It took me forever to get here. I had to go five to ten miles an hour the whole time."

"But you got here," she pointed out, smiling brightly.

"I hope you're not thinking what I think you're thinking," he said, "because the answer is no."

"How do you know what I'm thinking?" she asked somewhat peevishly.

"Let me guess. You'd like a lift to the mall."

"Okay, you do know what I'm thinking. Please, Mike. I have so much to do." She felt like a child wheedling for a toy instead of an adult asking to be taken to work.

"No. The streets are dreadful." His voice was adamant, and he sat down squarely on the couch.

"But you got here," she repeated.

"And it was stupid, but I was worried about you."

"Which was stupid, driving here, or worrying about me?" The words were out before she thought about them.

His lips curved in a slow smile. "In this world, worrying about other people is not stupid, at least in my experience—well, I need to clarify. Maybe we're mixing up worrying and caring. Worrying is out of control, whereas caring is in control. When I start to worry, I know I need to take it to God. It's an alert to me that I'm not handling something well, but I know that God can."

She sat on the sofa beside him. "Only you would see worry as a call to prayer. The rest of the world worries about worry. Just check the cover of any magazine.

'Fifteen Ways to Worry Less.' 'Worried about What's Worrying You?' And I'm sure it's just a matter of time before someone comes up with 'Worry Your Way to a Slimmer, Trimmer You!' "

"Worry is a signal," Mike said, wrapping the blanket around him tightly. "Whenever you worry about someone, it's because you have a concern for them, usually for their welfare. Worry by itself is futile, but if you turn it into action and prayer, then it becomes helpful."

"I don't know about that," she said slowly. "I worry about a lot of things, like the store, for example. I was even worried about Claire when I saw the blizzard."

"You're sweet to think of her. They do have an emergency generator out there, by the way, so they're nice and warm at Golden Meadows."

Abbey felt her muscles relax. She'd been more apprehensive about the elderly woman's situation than she'd allowed herself to recognize.

"No, worry isn't good at all. It consumes you and does nothing for the person you're worrying about," Mike continued, as if knowing where her thoughts had led her. "What we do when we feel worried is up to us. If there's something we can do to ease our concern, then of course we should do it."

"That's the hardest part," she confessed. "What if we can't do anything—like today, when the storm prevented me from getting out?"

"That's when prayer comes in. We give it back to God, tell Him that we recognize our anxiety, and we trust Him. That's the sticky part—letting God do His work, having faith that He is at work, even when it isn't readily apparent to us. The problem is when we don't handle our concern well and let it take over our minds. That's worry."

The radio, which had been silent for some time, suddenly sputtered with static. "Situation improving. . .northern Minnesota. . .back to regularly. . ."

Abbey and Mike looked at each other and laughed. "Well," said Mike, "thanks for the update, huh? Sort of sums it all up."

She rose from the couch and looked out the window. "I think they may have been a bit optimistic about the storm. It looks as bad as ever."

She hugged her arms as she sat back down. "I don't know if I ever thanked you for bringing the firewood—I was so glad to see it. . .and you."

His warm brown eyes twinkled with a soft reflection of the fireplace's cheerful blaze. "My pleasure. See, this blizzard's not all that bad. You've got a fire burning; you've got a friend with you. What more could you ask for?"

"A cup of coffee."

He stood up and went back to the front door. She could hear him pulling on his boots and coat. Was he leaving? She stood up and joined him in the entryway.

"Was it something I said? Look, I can live without the coffee if that's what the problem is, although I personally don't see. . ." Her voice trailed off as she realized that under the muffler and pulled-up coat collar, he was smiling.

"I'll be right back."

"It's not that important—" she began, but he brushed away her concerns.

He vanished from the warmth of her house and was soon lost in the swirl of white. But within seconds he was back, and he held out a large blue vacuum bottle. "I made this before I left the house. The power did flicker back on for a while early this morning, and I made a pot just in case. I can't believe I forgot to bring it inside with me."

Within minutes, they were both seated again in the living room, cups of coffee in their hands. As the fire warmed their faces, she felt her tension ease.

"This is the life," she said, a bit surprised at how relaxed she felt. Her usual reaction to being housebound would have been restless energy, and she had to admit, if she had been here alone, by now she would have been a nervous wreck. "I suppose I could get used to it, but I'd really have to try."

"You should. God didn't mean for us to spend our lives at work."

She studied him covertly. He talked so easily about God. His life must center around his faith. It was something she couldn't quite understand.

"Everything with you is God, isn't it?" she asked.

He had his head back and his eyes closed, and for a minute he didn't answer. She couldn't tell if he was sleeping or praying or just resting his eyes.

At last he opened his eyes and looked at her with his clear amber gaze. "Yes, it pretty much is. He is my life. Make that a capital L: Life."

"How did you come to that?" she pressed, finding that she really did want to know. "I mean, was it always like that, or did you have some kind of experience, or what? And please tell me if I'm being too snoopy."

"I'm always glad to share my story. I was raised Christian. I went to Sunday school and to church. I'd accepted Jesus as in I accepted Him without thinking, the same way you accept a bit of snow in the winter or a pleasant day in June. But when I really accepted Him in my heart and my mind and my soul was in church one Sunday. Are you sure you want to hear this?"

Abbey nodded. "Please."

"I must have been growing aware of the lack of something in my life, but I couldn't put my finger on it. And then, one day in church, the gospel reading was the story of Jesus and the lame man. You know, where Jesus says, essentially, throw away your cane, your crutch, your mat, and get up and walk."

"That did it?"

"I realized at that moment that it was very simple. I had to put aside the 'canes' I used in my everyday life—for me, that meant the whole slew of excuses

I'd use to get out of anything that would require me to lay my heart on the line, like I didn't have the time, or it was someone else's turn to do the work—and get up and walk on my own, with Him."

"And that's what you did."

"That's what I'm doing," he corrected. "It's all a process, which is why so many people refer to it as a path. I'm still walking and stumbling."

"I can't believe that little Bible story did all that," Abbey said. "I'd always thought it would a big knock-you-off-your-feet experience."

"I was sitting down when it happened, so I can't speak to that," he answered, his eyes gleaming. "But even the little things are what make the big things happen. Like the fire. You started by lighting the kindling, little bits of wood that burn out quickly. But the kindling sparked the twigs, which lit the small sticks, which lit the logs."

"The Parable of the Fireplace."

He laughed. "Well, you get the idea. We now have a wonderful fire keeping us warm, and that's my point. From that one thin match came this great blaze."

"I don't know," Abbey said doubtfully. "I need to think about it."

"I'll pray for you," he said. "I can do it right now if you'd like."

The radio chose that moment to burst forth with renewed life and issue an updated weather bulletin: ". . .Storm has diminished. . .plows are out now. . . tomorrow. . ."

The lights flickered on, and the furnace clicked into operation.

"You don't need to," she said. "I think my prayers have just been answered."

❄

Mike concentrated as he drove along. He knew he shouldn't be out yet, but with his vehicle in four-wheel drive, he'd be all right. And Golden Meadows wasn't that far away.

He'd had to leave. He knew now that more than anything he wanted Abbey to know the Lord the way he did. *That's asking a lot, isn't it?* he questioned God. He knew what the answer was.

She'd have to do it on her own terms, in her own way. For everybody it was different. He could feel her hunger for faith, her thirst for salvation. All he could do was give her the kindling and hope the fire caught.

His vehicle still hadn't warmed up, and at the first stoplight he rubbed his hands together. Now that the storm was over, the sun was out, making the late morning seem warmer than it was. Once the snowplows got out and did their job, the only evidence of the morning's blizzard would be the deep piles of snow scooped aside by the plow blades.

God had asked him to watch over Abbey, and it was a burden he had accepted. Was what he had shared this morning too much—or not enough?

His advice to Abbey about worry came back to him. He could continue to worry, turning his thoughts over and over in his mind in the futile hope that he'd see something new there, or he could do what he should do. He could examine the reason for his concern and give it back to the Lord in prayer.

But the questions in her eyes did something strange to his heart, and for once it was very hard to take his own advice.

Chapter 14

A small snowplow was already clearing the lot at Golden Meadows. Mike pulled into a parking space and gave the snowplow driver a jaunty wave before dashing into the retirement home.

The snow had drifted against the west side of the doorway, and over the top of the pile he could just make out the curious faces of some residents who were checking the aftermath of the storm.

When he came through the door, they surrounded him, chattering about the excitement of the blizzard. One woman pushed her walker closer. "Wasn't that something, Sweet? We couldn't see past the edge of the parking lot!"

The fellow standing beside her frowned. "Snow is snow, Marlys. Don't tell me you haven't seen snow before."

The woman beamed at him happily. "Actually, I've never seen a blizzard before at all! I came here from Florida."

The grumpy man seemed somewhat abashed. "Well, a blizzard is just snow with some oomph, that's all."

Another woman, who stood behind him, rolled her eyes expressively. "It was exciting. They had to use the generator since the power went off. Did it go off where you were?"

Mike nodded. "But it's back on now."

He'd been scanning the group, but he hadn't seen his grandmother, which was unusual since something this exciting should have sent her down to watch the storm and its aftermath. Maybe she had gone to visit someone or to pick up an item at the small store here at Golden Meadows.

He asked about her, and the group discussed her absence with enthusiasm and concern. "I didn't see her at breakfast," the first woman said, "but a lot of people chose to stay in their rooms this morning. Storms do that to some folks. They just hole up."

"We had oatmeal with raisins for breakfast," the grouchy man offered. "There's some as what don't like that. Maybe that's it. I didn't come down because I can't abide raisins. Nasty little things. Stick in your teeth. Not a fan of oatmeal either. Horrid glop that tastes like somebody forgot to finish cooking it."

"Oh, John, you are such an old crank. Can't you lighten up?" Marlys said.

The man who had talked to Abbey and Mike about relationships joined the group. His long-sleeved shirt was neatly pressed, and he leaned on his cane. "Is Mrs. Thorson under the weather?"

"I hope not," Mike said, but he didn't like the sinking feeling in his stomach. Claire adored breakfast, especially oatmeal with raisins. If anything happened to her. . . It was too painful to even think about.

"I'm sure she's okay," Mike told them reassuringly, "but I'd better go up and see her."

"You do that," the man said, turning to leave. "She's a good woman, almost as good as my Eleanor, may she rest in peace. Tell her Albert Caldwell asked about her."

The group resumed their watch of the man on the snowplow as he continued to scrape the snow out of the parking lot.

❅

Abbey attacked the snowdrift that locked her car in. She really needed to get a better shovel than the one she'd inherited with the house. This one was ungainly, and as much snow slid back onto its original spot as was left on the blade of the shovel.

She probably should have insisted that Mike take her along to Golden Meadows. Then she could have easily asked him to give her a ride to Cedar Mall.

Her back protested as a sudden realization brought her upright. She had never picked up the present from Aunt Luellen.

This was getting ridiculous. How hard would it be to go out there and pick it up? She made a mental note to go out there and get the gift later in the day, once the snowplows had cleared the roads. . .and she'd gotten out of her driveway.

She jammed the shovel into the snow and looked at her handiwork. All she'd succeeded in doing was demolishing the drift from a smooth pile of snow into a ragged heap. But it was not a bit smaller.

Maybe if she backed out as quickly as she could, she'd clear it. It was worth a try.

She headed back inside to get dressed for work. There might even be enough hot water by now for her to take a shower.

The red light on her answering machine was blinking. She pushed the button and heard the voice of the manager of Cedar Mall, clearly reading a prepared message: "The lots are being cleared by snowplows, but to ensure the safety of the drivers as well as our employees, we are requesting that you do not come into work until the parking areas are done. The mall will reopen at 5:00 p.m. today."

She was tempted to ignore the dictum. Those reports were waiting, and she could get so much done before the mall opened. But she knew that mall management was serious when they made these policies, and she did not want to tangle with them. So she resigned herself to spending the rest of the day inside. There was a book on the end table that she had started reading in the summer that she could start in on again.

Abbey got the book and sat down with it. She opened it to the spot that was bookmarked and read for a few lines. It made no sense. She'd have to start it again.

Well, that was okay, she told herself. She could do that. She turned to the front of the book and began to read.

Coffee. Another cup of coffee would be nice. She made a pot and sat down once more with the book. Two pages later she was up again, looking for something to eat.

"Oh, give it up, Abbey," she scolded herself out loud. "You're more antsy than an August picnic." She paced through the house until she finally sank down onto the couch.

It wasn't just the forced house arrest that bothered her. It was Mike. . .and what he'd said.

What exactly was it about him? She'd known him, somewhat, for many years, but lately their lives had become conjoined, primarily because of those goofy frog slippers that Aunt Luellen had sent to her instead of Claire.

Abbey had long ago taken the idea of loving someone and shelved it in the back of her mind, right next to religion. She had always intended that one day, when she was settled in her career, her MBA in hand, she would look into love and faith. But with Mike, they came perilously close to arriving hand in hand.

This wasn't the way she had planned it, not at all. She had plans for her life, a career plan. It was what she had talked to the young women at his church about.

What made her life work for her, what gave her days shape and meaning, was her career. She was good at what she did. She'd brought Trends back from being on the brink of closing to one of the most financially stable businesses in the mall. She had done it because she was focused. She'd started young, identified her strengths, and built on them.

What was wrong with that?

Aunt Luellen used to talk about the parable of the talents. It was everyone's responsibility, Aunt Luellen had told her, to make the most of the gifts God had given them. Wasn't that exactly what Abbey was doing? And rather than running ahead, helter-skelter into the future, she'd laid out a path to follow.

The problem was that people kept stepping onto her path. People like Mike. And what had become painfully clear to her since her growing friendship with Mike was what she hadn't included in her plan: fun.

That Bible verse that was tucked into the toe of one of the slippers sprang to her mind: *This is the day which the LORD hath made; we will rejoice and be glad in it."* That was Mike. He certainly was having a good time with God. Was that his secret?

The phone rang, and she leaped to answer it. It was probably mall management, telling her that the parking lots were cleared, so she could go to work. . . assuming she'd be able back out.

But it wasn't the monotone voice of the mall manager. It was Mike, and he began without preamble: "Claire is ill. Very ill."

Chapter 15

Abbey paused in midmotion, the scarf she was knotting around her neck hanging from her numb fingers. She must have heard him wrong. "Ill? What do you mean? How ill?"

"She's feeling dizzy, and she says she has pains." Mike's voice was calm, but Abbey could hear the worry behind the words.

"What kind of pains? Chest pains?"

"No, stomach pains. Probably something she ate."

Abbey realized that the scarf was now trailing in her coffee cup, and she pulled it out and swabbed at it as she spoke. "Is she in the hospital?"

Mike hesitated a moment before answering. "She refuses to go."

"Refuses to go?" Abbey realized she was nearly shouting and forced herself to moderate her speech. "Why on earth won't she go?"

Mike's pause was even longer, and when he spoke, Abbey could hear his stark fear. "She says she wants to die at home in her own bed."

Abbey's world collapsed. "Die?"

He spoke so softly she had to struggle to hear him. "She always said that when she died, she wanted to do it in her own bed, and preferably around Christmas. She wants to spend Christmas in heaven. . .where there's bound to be a birthday party the likes of which earth has never seen."

"No, no. She's not going to die, is she? She's not going to die! Please tell me she isn't." This was not the way things were supposed to happen. Abbey had just gotten attached to Claire. She couldn't let her go.

He became reassuring. "It's probably not that major—at least that's the sense I got from the nursing staff. A doctor did come in and check on her. Praise God that he had been on ER duty at the hospital and had walked over to visit his own father at Golden Meadows. It's just a short trip, but I guess it took him quite awhile since he waded through snow. The plows hadn't been out yet."

"Well, if a doctor has seen her. . ."

"But I have to be realistic."

"I don't like realistic." She was aware that she sounded like a little child, but that was exactly how she felt—small and powerless. Realistic was sickness and pain and parting. It wasn't good, especially now.

"She's not young. Every illness is a stress for her. All we can do is pray for her." The words hung in the air. "Please pray for her, Abbey." Then he hung up the phone.

Pray for her!

Didn't you have to be a Christian to do that? She didn't know how to pray, not really. She'd learned as a child that it wasn't right to pray for a bicycle—her aunt had straightened her out on that one—but that was about the extent of her knowledge on the subject.

She didn't want Claire to be sick, and she particularly didn't want her to die. *Please, please, make her all right.*

Well, she'd just have to leave the praying to Mike.

Abbey poured herself another cup of coffee and carried it into the living room. She sank onto the couch and didn't even bother with the pretense of trying to read one of the magazines piled on the end table.

Make her better.

She couldn't abide sitting here a minute longer. She had to do something. Abbey put her cooling coffee on the kitchen counter and pulled on her boots. She was going to go to Golden Meadows.

The sky was a bright, clear blue now that the storm had passed, and the sun hurt her eyes. The world looked sculpted in snow. *A single storm can change everything,* she mused. *One storm blows through and another takes its place,* she thought. *First snow, and now this. Her emotions were battered.*

The demolished snowdrift was still behind her car, and she studied it briefly. At just the right angle, she could make it through.

But then she saw the impediment that she could not cross.

The snowplows had been by, and the end of her driveway was blocked with the snow the plows had pushed in. Heavy chunks of compacted snow and ice lay in a thick, impenetrable ridge. There was absolutely no way to get through that with her car. It had to be shoveled out, or preferably taken out with a plow or a strong snowblower. All she had was this insufficient shovel.

Once again, she was ill-prepared for the storm. Abbey sighed. Was everything a metaphor?

She mounded her hands over the end of the shovel and rested her chin on her knuckles as she surveyed her predicament. She was really locked in now. It would take her all afternoon to break through. . .if she were lucky. Experience had told her that she was not getting out any time soon.

Thwarted by a snowstorm.

Hot tears pressed against her eyelids. Why did she even care about this old woman? And what did she hope to accomplish by going to Golden Meadows, anyway? It wasn't as if she could help Claire. She was a store manager, not a miracle worker.

Why did Claire have to get sick? And why couldn't she just go to the hospital? That's what most people did. They got sick, and they went to the hospital to get better. Why wouldn't she do it? This wasn't fair!

Abbey slammed her fist onto the side of her car. It was all wrong. Claire needed to be well.

She abandoned the effort to dig herself out and put the inadequate little shovel back into its spot in her garage and went back inside. She poured herself a fresh cup of coffee, but it was bitter on her tongue.

The coffee at Golden Meadows was good. She remembered the conversation with the man who had spoken to them on her first visit. His Eleanor was lucky indeed. Would Abbey ever find a love as real as theirs?

God, save Claire.

She paced through her small house. All she could think of was a single phrase: *God, save Claire. God, save Claire. God, save Claire.*

Suddenly her feet stopped their mindless steps. She was praying. She, Abbey Jensen, was praying! For the first time in years, she was praying for someone else. And it felt terrific.

She continued: *God, save Claire.* The words were simple, but they said it all. In her mind, she could picture the elderly woman, her nearly sightless eyes still alert behind the substantial lenses. The Bible, such a sign of her faith, centered in her room—as it must have centered in her life.

And those slippers. Those goofy frog slippers with the fake gemstone eyes. Claire hadn't even opened them yet.

What had Aunt Luellen written on the note? "Wishing you great hoppyness always." That's what Abbey wanted for her, too. Great hoppyness.

"Don't spend Christmas with God," she whispered to Claire. "Spend it with me."

❋

Mike held the gnarled hand and gazed into his grandmother's eyes, which opened and closed irregularly. "Grandma, go to the hospital."

Claire shook her head. "I'm staying here. I'm around the people I know. Sweet, for us here at Golden Meadows, death isn't quite the scary ogre it is for you young folks. It's not wearing a big black cape and reeking of the grave. It's simply how we get from this life to the next. Kind of like a bus."

He laughed. "Only you, Grandma, would come up with that. Death is like a bus. But this bus isn't yours. Yours is waaaaaay across town."

She patted his arm. "When my bus comes, honey, I'm hopping on. Destination: Promised Land!"

"Plus it's almost Christmas," he reminded her. "You know how much you love Christmas. You wouldn't want to miss that, now would you?"

"Christmas! That reminds me. Help me sit up, Sweet."

"Oh, Grandma, do you think you should—"

"Hush your mouth and help me. I'd hope by now you'd know enough to listen to your elders. I'm not going to run a marathon. I just want to sit up." Her china-blue eyes twinkled weakly.

He gently lifted her thin shoulders and helped her edge up to a sitting position. "Good?"

"Super. Now, you have to get Abbey out here. I've got her present, you see. She never did pick it up." Claire leaned forward and whispered conspiratorially, "She's a bit absentminded, I'm afraid."

Mike smiled at that. "I suspect she likes coming out here to see you more than she lets on, and that present is just an excuse."

"Do you think so?" Claire seemed very pleased.

"By the way, a gentleman named Albert Caldwell asked me to relay his concern."

His grandmother sat up straighter and patted her puff of white hair. "He did? Did he say anything else?"

"We—"

A knock at the door interrupted them. It was the doctor who had checked on Claire earlier.

"Sweet, do you mind for just one minute?" Claire asked. "I'd like to talk to Dr. James for a moment alone."

Mike hesitated, but the doctor nodded and said, "Go ahead and wait in the lobby. I'll stop by before I leave and give you an update."

"Then you can come back up and see me. But if you can find me a piece of chocolate, that'd be nice," Claire said. Then, as if suddenly tired, she sighed. It was the sigh that worried Mike. His grandmother wasn't a sigher.

He did the only thing he knew to do: He prayed. *God, make her all right. If she needs to go, I'll try to understand. But I love her, and I want her with me a little while longer. I need her.*

This prayer came with a postscript that totally surprised him: *And Abbey needs her, too.*

❅

Dr. James joined him in the lobby and, after updating the other residents on Claire's condition, invited Mike into the Fireside Lounge. Most of the chairs were filled, and their arrival created a curious stir, but the two men managed to find a fairly secluded spot.

"I'll tell you what I know," the doctor began, "which is that I don't know. She seems to be as healthy as a horse, although, of course, the horse is eighty-two years old. She seems to have good moments and bad moments, but her mind is sharp."

"That's true," Mike agreed. "What concerns me is that she seems to be willing to let go so easily. She's not fighting any of it."

"In most patients, that would be a worry," the doctor said, "but with Claire, I see it more as a natural acceptance. She's certainly not hurrying toward death."

"Not racing to catch her bus," Mike murmured.

"Excuse me?" Dr. James was clearly confused.

"Just vintage Claire," Mike said.

❄

Abbey's pacing had slowed down, simply because her legs were getting tired. She hadn't heard anything more from either the mall or from Mike. How could all her worries come together like this on one single day. . .and just before Christmas too?

She stared at the phone, her arms clutched across her chest. If only she could will the phone to ring!

As if by telepathy, it did just that.

She lifted the receiver, dreading the mall manager's drone. But instead it was Mike.

"The doctor checked on her again, and they're going to keep her here at Golden Meadows tonight. If her condition worsens, they'll move her to the hospital pretty much whether she wants them to or not. The hospital is less than a block away, and for now she's comfortable in her own room. They can monitor her there for the time being."

Abbey breathed a grateful sigh. "It sounds like she's going to be fine."

"I'm still being cautious. She can still use our prayers."

She paused. "I prayed for her."

There was a long silence. Abbey wished she could see his face to know how he was reacting. Then he said, simply, "Thank you. By the way, she wants to see you. She still has your present."

"Oh, I forgot! I'm getting as loopy as Aunt Luellen. But I'm not going to be able to get out until I get ahold of someone to plow me out. The snow fairies didn't come in and dig out my car or my driveway."

Mike promised to come by the next day and either get her car out or give her a ride to Golden Meadows, then to work.

"Tomorrow's Christmas Eve," he reminded her.

Chapter 16

Abbey awoke to the sound of a snowplow outside her window. She leaped off the couch where she'd fallen asleep and stumbled to the front door. She opened it a crack. Mike was out there, a blade attached to the front of his four-wheel drive vehicle. He waved at her, and she wiggled her fingers back at him before retreating into the bathroom to pull herself together.

One look in the mirror confirmed her worst suspicions. She looked horrible. One side of her face was wrinkled where she'd slept on it, and her eyes were puffy and swollen. She hoped that Mike wouldn't hurry with his plowing outside. Maybe he'd go slowly and give her the necessary time to make herself presentable. Nobody, she reasoned as she splashed water on her face, deserved to see her looking the way she did when she first woke up. It was enough to scare a bear back into hibernation.

One side of her hair bent straight up, and no amount of combing would make it settle down. In desperation, she clipped a barrette in it. It didn't look very good, but this was no time for vanity. She wanted to get to Golden Meadows and see how Claire was doing.

She'd caught only a glimpse of Mike's face, but it had been enough to know that the news from the retirement home must have been good. Plus, he wouldn't have stopped to plow out her driveway if his grandmother was still gravely ill.

She had just pulled on a red sweater when he knocked on the door.

"Thank you so much," she said as she let him in. "How's Claire?"

He smiled. "Much better but still weak. She's holding her own, and I think we'll have her around to tell us how to live our lives for quite awhile."

Our lives. The words had a glorious ring to them.

"Are you ready to go?" Mike was wrapping his muffler around his neck.

She gulped down a final splash of coffee. "Ready."

It was odd, she thought as she rode to Golden Meadows with him, how much everything about her had changed. Just a month ago she would have done anything to avoid going to the retirement home. Now she couldn't wait to get out there.

And Mike. He had changed her in ways she wasn't yet ready to explore. What was especially strange, she mused, was that she was still changing, and it was a wonderful sensation, like a butterfly must feel when it finally emerges from its long cocooned sleep.

Perhaps she was just caught up in a generally good mood. It was the day after a storm, the sun was shining, it was Christmas Eve morning, and Claire was doing better.

Mike's car was already warm, and Abbey's lack of sleep began to catch up with her on the drive to Golden Meadows.

He glanced over and grinned as she yawned. "Big night?"

"I couldn't sleep, worrying about Claire, so I decided to watch *It's a Wonderful Life*. I just bought it the other day, and I still hadn't seen it all the way through."

"So what did you think?"

"A bit predictable."

"Really?" His eyebrows arched in surprise.

"But sometimes predictable is good, very good." Her smile threatened to wobble out of control as she added, "Last night I would have taken predictable."

"No kidding. I was so scared about Grandma. I must have talked God's ear off. I couldn't stop praying." He pulled into the parking lot of the retirement home. "Well, here we are."

He turned off the car engine and sat, his hands still on the steering wheel. "Can you give me a minute here? I need to get a little strength before I go in."

Abbey reached over and touched his arm. "Please, pray aloud."

"Dearest Father, thank You for another morning, for a blessed morning, as we approach Your Son's birth. Abbey and I ask that You keep Grandma in Your healing hands. We love this woman." He paused. "Amen."

"I'm not very good at praying out loud," he confessed as he helped Abbey out of the vehicle. "I know what I'm saying in my heart, but when I say the words out loud, it sometimes seems too little."

"I'm sure God listens to both your heart and your lips," Abbey said.

Mike's quick smile told her how much he appreciated her comment.

They were mobbed as soon as they opened the front door of Golden Meadows.

"How's she doing, Sweet?"

"Tell her I've been praying!"

"She'll pull through. She's a strong one."

"A good Christian woman."

"That Norwegian blood, it's going to keep her going, that's for sure."

Mike laughed as their voices assailed him. "I'm going to go up and see her, and I'll tell her you're all thinking of her and praying for her."

Claire's eyes were shut when they entered her room, but they flew open as if spring-loaded. "Sweet! Abbey!"

"Merry Christmas, Grandma," Mike said, dropping a kiss on her forehead. "How are you feeling?"

"Better. A little on the woozy side, so I'm afraid I'll have to pass on the ice-skating. Remember, Sweet, how we used to go ice-skating on Christmas Eve? The moonlight on the pond made it look like we were skating on a huge diamond."

Mike laughed. "I'd almost forgotten about that! We'd pretend that the diamond belonged to us, and we'd decide what we were going to buy with the money we'd get when we sold it."

Claire turned her bright blue eyes toward Abbey. "What would you buy?"

"Skating lessons, to start with. I'm afraid I'm probably the only Minnesotan who's a total klutz on the ice."

The elderly woman beamed happily at her. "When I met Arthur, I could have skated circles around any Olympic ice-skater, but I pretended I didn't know how, just so I could hold his hand. Silly fool, he fell for it. He couldn't skate for beans, but I sure did like to hold his hand."

A beeper sounded. Both women looked at Mike, who had the grace to be abashed about the interruption. "Sorry. I got this pager, but I never thought anybody would ever page me on it. Grandma, can I borrow your phone? It's the store."

After a quick conversation, he hung up the phone and turned to them. "I've got to run. The cash register won't start up. Abbey. . . ?"

"Oh, no." Claire looked as disappointed as a child who'd just lost out on candy. "I wanted to watch Abbey open her present from Luellen."

Abbey looked at Claire, at the forlorn expression on her face, and made a decision: "I'll stay. I can take a cab back."

Claire beamed happily. "Good."

Mike hugged his grandmother and promised to be back later. Then he left them alone together.

"Abbey, dear, I know you need to get to work, especially with this being Christmas Eve and all, so I won't keep you long. It's just that I'm so anxious to find out what Luellen gave you." Claire wiggled with barely-subdued enthusiasm.

At that moment, a health-care aide knocked on the door and entered, pushing a metal cart covered with a white linen napkin. "Claire, I have some breakfast for you. It's your favorite—French toast. I knew you had guests, so I brought some extra."

Claire's eyes lit up at the sight of the French toast, but she glanced at the Christmas present. She was clearly torn between finding out what was in the package from Aunt Luellen and having the French toast, so Abbey resolved the issue for her. "I'd be glad to join you for breakfast. We can open the package when we've eaten."

Abbey was amazed at how hungry she was, and she mentioned it to Claire, apologizing for gulping down her meal.

"Young people don't eat enough anyway," Claire said. "Everybody worries about being thin, although I don't know why. What's the point of dieting all the time? Especially when you can't have chocolate. I love chocolate."

Abbey smiled. Claire was really a dear.

"I know you have to get back to your store, Abbey, but I really do want to see what Luellen sent you. She always sends such interesting gifts." Claire motioned toward the tiny tree. "It's over there. Could you get it for me, please?"

The package was wrapped in gaudy green foil sprinkled with golden stars. "I wonder if this paper came from Brazil."

"Chile, dear. Luellen's in Chile. Open it so I can see what it is!"

Abbey pulled the paper off the box. Inside was an elegant leather-bound pocket calendar. "It's beautiful!" she exclaimed as she examined the burgundy, tooled leather. "Look, Claire, there's even a spot for one of those teeny electronic gizmo things that does everything but park your car!"

As she handed it to Claire, a piece of paper fell out. "Of course! It just wouldn't be a gift from Aunt Luellen without a note."

"What does it say?" Claire asked expectantly.

"Wow. This is short for Aunt Luellen. It just says, 'As you plan your days ahead,' and then 'This is the day which the Lord hath made; we will rejoice and be glad in it.'"

"Ah." Claire nodded her head as if that explained it all. "From the Psalms."

"That's the same one that was in—" Abbey said, stopping before she could spoil the surprise of Claire's slippers, which remained unopened under the Christmas tree. "But why—" And before she could finish the question, she answered it.

Because Claire, whose days were limited, looked forward, while she, who had her whole life ahead of her, planned only by an hourly schedule at work. The Lord, the one that Mike spoke of so easily, existed for her, too, and He gave her each day as fresh and new and bright as each day that He gave to Claire.

The same God made them all. The same God. This was why Mike and Claire were so happy—they were rejoicing in each day that the Lord had given them. It didn't matter if she had a thousand days. . .or one. They were all gifts.

The iron bars that had held her heart imprisoned fell away. She was free, totally free now to love. . .and to be loved. An aura of happiness and well-being surrounded her, too new and fragile to be analyzed or explained. She knew what she had to do. She had to tell Mike.

"Can I borrow your phone, Claire?"

Just exactly what she was going to say to him, she had no idea. She just knew she wanted him to be with her right now, to be at her side as she explored this wonderful sense of freedom.

But Mike wasn't at his store. The employee who answered the phone said that after Mike unjammed the cash register, he had run over to the church to drop off some toys he was donating for the Christmas Eve service. So Abbey kissed Claire good-bye with a promise to come back later and fairly flew down the hall to the lobby.

Too bad she didn't have her car with her. She could have zipped right over there, but instead she was forced to wait for a taxi.

And wait she did. She watched the clock over the door of the lobby as the minutes slowly ticked by. Selma assured her, when Abbey called every five minutes, that the store was doing fine. Both Selma and Brianna were on duty and wouldn't need Abbey there until noon.

Nadine, the desk clerk, emerged from the office with a young woman at her side. "Miss Jensen!" the teenager exclaimed.

Her face was familiar, but it took Abbey a minute to realize where she'd seen her before.

"I'm with the Jeremiah Group. Remember, you came out and talked to us?" She stuck out her hand awkwardly and said, "I'm Mona, by the way."

"Mona, it's good to see you again," Abbey said. "Do you work here?"

"I do now," the young woman declared. "Something you said got to me, and I had a talk with the career counselor with the Jeremiah Group, and bingo. Here I am. I want to be a nurse, I think."

"That's great! Nursing is a wonderful, noble career."

"I have you to thank for it, too," Mona added shyly, her eyes darting down to study her shoes.

Warmth surrounded Abbey's heart. "That's so sweet," she said. "Thank you for saying that. You know, I wasn't too sure that anything I said that evening had an impact at all."

"It wasn't anything you said. It was what you wore."

"Excuse me?" Abbey couldn't believe what she was hearing.

"Oh, not that it was gross or anything. It just made me realize that I didn't want a job where I had to dress up everyday like that. So when I thought about what I did want to wear, I always saw myself in a nurse's uniform. I figured, hey, nobody's going to come to my door and hand me one. So I decided to go out and get it myself. And this is where I'm starting. I've even signed up at the university to start on my degree."

Abbey was overwhelmed. She remembered Mike's words: "Who knows, you may very well have touched someone's heart here today in a way you can't know." And in turn, today, that someone had touched her heart.

"Mona, good luck on your new career. I know you'll be an outstanding nurse." She couldn't resist adding, "And you'll look smashing in a nurse's uniform."

Mona left with Nadine, and Abbey was left alone to wait for the cab. What a day this had been! Truly it was one to rejoice in!

While she waited, she prayed and rejoiced and turned her newfound knowledge over and over in her mind. At last the cab arrived, and Abbey decided to have the driver take her directly to the Word of Faith Community Church to save time.

The small church looked like Christmas itself, with glistening white snow drifted around the brick walls. The steeple sparkled in the morning sunlight, and the cross at the top of the spire pointed straight to heaven.

Mike was arranging gift-wrapped packages around a small tree in the narthex. He smiled when he saw Abbey. "How does it look?" he asked, stepping back to look at his handiwork.

"A pile of Christmas presents could never look bad," she said.

"You've definitely been with Grandma," he said. "Her Christmas spirit has been rubbing off on you! What happened to your humbug disposition, Scrooge?"

"It's gone. There's. . .something else there instead."

"Wow, that's a change. Cool!"

"That's not the only thing that's changed," she said, suddenly shy.

He stopped and stared at her, a gaily-wrapped package dangling from his fingers, forgotten for the moment. "What do you mean?"

"I mean I'm different. I mean that all the pieces fell into place. They've been there, bit by bit, but this morning it all came together. This is the day that the Lord has made, you know? Every day is the day. Every day is, all by itself, the most tremendous gift we have." She rubbed her forehead. "Am I making any sense?"

"Oh, yes," he said softly. "You're making a lot of sense."

"Good, because I want to talk about it, but I don't know exactly what to say. This Christianity thing needs some kind of manual."

"It has one. It's called the Bible."

"I don't know why I'm telling you this."

"I think I do," he said softly. "At least I hope I do."

He took her hand and looked into her eyes. "I have prayed for this moment for a long time, almost hoped against hope that this would be the one prayer that God would grant. And He has blessed me beyond belief. This is my Christmas gift from Him, knowing that you are His."

For a moment, neither of them spoke, until Mike broke the silence. "Would you like to go into the sanctuary with me?"

She nodded, and he guided her into the darkened sanctuary, with only the light from the stained glass windows to illuminate it. "I love that this room is called the sanctuary. I think of all it means—a haven, a safe place, a refuge—and I know that I'm in His presence."

They stood together, absorbing the atmosphere. "When I'm here," Mike continued, "the rest of the world falls into the background. I can focus on Him. It's a special place, beyond explanation. God is very real to me, Abbey, very real. I can't imagine trying to live without Him—or wanting to."

There, with the scent of the Christmas tree in the narthex, the wreaths by the coat racks, and the candles on the altar, Abbey thought of the little Baby who was born so long ago and yet had been born again two thousand years later in her own heart. She thought of His death and resurrection and knew, in that moment, that He lived in her heart. She gave her life to God, and her heart sang the wonders of the first birth long ago. . .and of the birth that had just happened in her.

❇

Mike watched her face as she was transformed. He had prayed for this. He knew that this was God's plan, and he was but a part of the plan.

I don't ask for much, God, he began, then almost laughed. That wasn't true. He'd asked for Claire's recovery only slightly more than an hour ago. *Okay, I usually don't ask for much,* he revised his prayer. *But if I could have one more thing. Just one more. . .*

He paused before proceeding. Was he asking too much? Would God reject his plea outright?

Abbey looked at him, her eyes glowing, and he knew he had to continue. *Please, God, let her love me.*

Chapter 17

Abbey stared at Mike. Could it be true? Was what she was seeing in his eyes real—or was it just a mirror of her own?

Without the prison walls around her heart, she could see so much more. Had she always loved him, or had it just happened? As she put out her hand, she realized it didn't matter. Either way, she loved him.

The words were extraordinarily simple. She loved him. And, possibly, just possibly, he loved her, too.

She felt absolutely liberated by the thought.

"Excuse me." A voice echoed in the empty sanctuary from behind them. "Mike, the store just called. The cash register is jammed up again."

The magic hovered around them a moment longer, until they both smiled.

"Tell them I'm on my way," Mike called back. Then his glance returned to Abbey, and so did the magic. "Can you come to the Christmas Eve service with me tonight?"

"I'd be delighted to." And she meant it.

Christmas was full of presents.

❄

The day flew by. Selma and Brianna barely had time to tease their boss about her new attitude. Abbey sang with the mall's Christmas carols. She bought a cinnamon flavored sucker at Lollipop Time, and by the time lunch rolled around, it was already gone. She got polka-dotted socks with individual toes in them for Selma. She stopped at Piñata Pete's and purchased a piñata shaped like a cow for Brianna.

It was Christmas!

But at last the mall closed. The recalcitrant metal grating slid down to close Trends.

"Whew!" Selma said. "I think we managed twice the sales that we did last year. At least that's what my aching dogs are telling me." She leaned over and massaged her swollen feet.

"We did do better. I haven't run the sales record yet, but—"

"What?" Selma said, in mock horror. "You, Miss Retail-Is-My-Life, you can't quote me our receipts? You're slipping, gal!"

Brianna pushed her coworker toward the door. "Leave her alone, Selma.

Can't you tell our boss is in love?"

"You two!" Abbey protested, but she couldn't dispute it. They were right.

"There's something else going on," Selma said thoughtfully. "Something else has made Abbey different. Softer."

"Love will do that," Brianna told her.

"Well, sure, but this is something else. What's up, boss lady?"

Abbey reached for her purse. "It's very simple. A Baby born in a stable touched me. A star over a small town on the other side of the world touched me. A flock of angels singing in the heavens touched me. Christmas touched me."

Selma and Brianna stopped. Then they looked at each other and smiled. "All right!" Brianna said, hugging her.

"Hallelujah!" Selma echoed. "That's wonderful news!"

"It is," Abbey agreed. "It is."

"We'd better get going," Selma pointed out, "or we'll still be here when people start rolling in with returns on the twenty-sixth. Eight a.m., right, boss?"

Abbey groaned. "Unfortunately."

The two women picked up their packages and purses and prepared to leave by the delivery door in the back of the store.

"See you two the day after tomorrow," Abbey said. "Have a very Merry Christmas!"

"And a Merry Christmas to you, too!" Selma called. Brianna waved a cheery farewell.

Abbey hurried down to Tuck's Toys. She walked through the gamut of the deserted kiosks, most of which would be gone after the returns and sales had ended in a week or two. She'd miss them when the mall went back to its normal schedule and appearance.

Unless, of course, the mall management decided to go with a King of Hearts theme or something equally as bizarre for Valentine's Day. She could see it now—Kiss Me Kandies next to Love in Bloom Florists.

But somehow it wasn't as dreadful as it had first seemed. Maybe falling in love had softened her.

She paused at the now-abandoned Candy Cane Calaboose and remembered the time she and Mike were locked in there together. Well, she mused, even the Candy Cane Calaboose wasn't bad if you could fall in love with your cellmate.

A horrible realization struck her. She didn't have a present for Mike.

On the wall, a poster for the Candy Cane Calaboose fluttered by a single staple. An idea struck her, but she'd have to hurry. She tore down the poster and ran back to Trends. One of the last shipments had been picture frames, and she held her breath as she looked through the display, searching for one in particular.

She breathed a sigh of relief. It was there.

The frame itself was a series of interlocking candy canes, and the poster fit perfectly inside it. She wound some tissue paper around it and stuck it into one of their gift bags. She dug through the remaining stock of complimentary small gift cards until she found one with a candy cane on it.

Abbey chewed on the end of her pen. She couldn't think of a thing to say on a card. "You're very sweet" was very dumb. "I CANEn't live without you"? "We were MINT for each other"?

It was always difficult to be clever. Sometimes it was downright impossible, and this was one of those moments.

She opted for no card at all. After all, she'd be handing him the gift in person.

Her eyes scanned the shop for a gift for Claire. Then she remembered something that had come in that morning's delivery. She had opened the box, but she had gotten so busy that she hadn't had the chance to unpack it and put the contents out. She dashed into the storage room and dug in the box until she found it.

It was a blue and white china jewelry box. The blue exactly matched Claire's eyes. Impulsively she tucked a gaily-striped candy cane pin inside it.

She tied it up in bright red paper, then wrote a sales receipt for the items so she could pay for them the day after Christmas.

"Ready to go?"

Abbey jumped as Mike's voice echoed throughout the cavernous mall. "You startled me!"

She shoved the hastily wrapped packages into a bag. "I'm going out the side. I don't trust this rusty old gate to work right tonight, and I sure don't want to be late."

He handed her a take-out bag as she met him in the mall corridor. "Not too fancy—just a burger and fries from Boomtown Burger. I've got two cans of soda in my coat pocket, too. We'll have to eat on the run, or I'm afraid we'll be late."

❋

The church service was wonderful, Abbey thought. The carols had a meaning far beyond what they had portrayed while they'd played on an endless loop at the mall, and she sang along with heartfelt gusto.

At the end of the service, ushers passed out small candles with circular cardboard drip-stoppers. The lamps dimmed, and the minister began: "I am the light of the world. . ." One by one the church members lit their candles from their neighbor's as the light was passed from the minister to the last guest, until the entire sanctuary was lit only by the glow of a hundred candles. And one by one they blew out their candles after the benediction while singing "Silent Night."

Abbey could not bear to speak until they had left the church and were standing outside, the cold air turning their breath into clouds. A light snow had fallen, making everything freshly white.

Her heart had opened honestly, and she needed to face life—all of it—honestly. She turned to Mike, her emotions overflowing, and started to speak, but he put his finger over her lips.

"Sssh," he said. "Listen."

From inside the emptying church, the faintest sounds of the last notes of "Silent Night" drifted out. "It's the Christmas prayer, the search for silence," he whispered.

She held his hand until the last notes faded away. "Thank you for giving me this Christmas Eve," she told him. "There's something else I wanted to tell you."

She had to open up, she simply had to, or she would burst with the joy of it. "Mike, I—"

He bent toward her, and time stood completely still. They were the only ones in the world. They were everyone. Then he kissed her.

It was true. She heard bells. Big loud bells that played "Joy to the World."

He laughed as their mouths separated. "Perfect timing," he said, motioning toward the spire where the bells rang out the Christmas carol.

If it were possible to save time, to press it between the pages of the calendar so that she could take it out and look at it again and again, this would be the moment she would save, Abbey thought. It was perfect, completely and totally perfect.

"Abbey, I think I'm falling in love with you." His words carried across the wintry night, and two of the people leaving the church heard and bent their own heads together.

There was so much she wanted to say, but the words stuck in her heart. Instead, she stood on her tiptoes and kissed him gently, reverently, in answer.

"I'd love to stay here and kiss you in the moonlight," he said at last, "but there's another woman in my life, and I've promised her I'd go out to Golden Meadows to play Christmas carols for a sing-along. Want to come?"

But Claire didn't join them in the Fireside Lounge. She was asleep, the aide told them. It was a calm, healing sleep, though, not the fretful tossing and turning that had signaled her illness initially.

The sing-along was attended by a majority of the residents, many with holiday sweaters and ties on. It was the perfect way to end the perfect Christmas Eve, like a bow on the present of life.

❄

The next morning, Mike picked Abbey up early. "Grandma's waiting, anxiously I'm sure, to open her presents. She likes to dig in before breakfast, but I've told her she'd have to wait a bit later today."

"She's like a kid about Christmas, isn't she?" Abbey asked. "It's wonderful to see that enthusiasm."

Claire was sitting up, looking much better than she had, when they arrived. "I've got the presents ready," she announced. "Let's go!"

At her insistence, Mike helped her out of the bed and into the overstuffed blue chair. Abbey suppressed a grin at the yellow frog slippers that she slid her feet into. Clearly Claire hadn't waited for her and Mike before starting to open gifts.

With a flurry of paper and ribbons flying, Claire unwrapped her presents. She oohed over the Wag-A-Muffin and the sweater that Mike gave her and aahed when she opened the jewelry box from Abbey.

"This has been a wonderful Christmas," Claire said. "And these are terrific presents. Thank you both."

"The best Christmas gift of all," Abbey said, giving Claire's hand a squeeze, "is seeing you healthy again." Then she looked at Mike. "Slight correction. It's one of the best presents."

"What? What?" Claire asked, her eyes glowing with excitement.

"This may be a bit premature, Grandma, since I haven't checked it out with Abbey, but I think there might be a wedding in the future." He dropped a kiss on Claire's forehead. "That is, of course, if we have your blessing."

Claire wriggled even straighter. "I have a problem with this, Michael James Tucker."

"You do?" Mike's face flushed. "Grandma—"

"I can't believe that you didn't ask her first!" Claire scolded. "Now get down on your knees and do it properly."

"Yes, ma'am!"

Mike gave her a jaunty salute and dropped to one knee. Taking Abbey's hand in his, he said, "Abbey, we've known each other since we were kids. We've been through many changes, some good, some bad, that have taken us apart from each other—and brought us back together again."

His voice caught in his throat, and he had to stop and take a deep breath to keep his words even. "I want to spend the rest of our lives together."

Abbey could only hold onto his hand as if it meant life itself. Her lips opened and closed, but no sound came out. Perhaps it didn't need to.

"Abbey?" His forehead wrinkled in concern. "Are you all right?"

"Yes," she said, her voice somewhere between tears and laughter. "Yes, yes, yes!"

"Kiss her," Claire commanded from her chair. "That's the next step. Sweet, do I have to think of everything?"

Mike playfully shushed his grandmother. "I know what I'm doing."

Claire gave a good-natured snort. "Ha. Well, it's a good thing I'm here in case you mess something up. Go ahead."

"Thanks," Mike said, grinning at her. Then he fished in his coat pocket and pulled out a box that was about the size of a small popcorn bag. "Okay, let me explain. See, when you've got two lovely women in your life, what are you going to do on Christmas? Clearly, get them the same thing. Abbey, here's your Wag-A-Muffin."

She opened the box and pulled out a pure white dove, embossed with a golden cross on the wing, a golden collar around its neck. "It's beautiful!" she said, running her hand down its back and watching the dove's tail move.

"I'm glad you like it. But now here's my dilemma. I got Grandma a sweater, and it just didn't seem right to get you one, too."

"It's improper," Claire interjected. "The first gift you give someone shouldn't be clothing."

"See what I put up with?" Mike said teasingly. "But then I realized that these old rules are for the birds, so I went ahead and got you something to wear."

Then he continued to stand there, his hands in his pockets, smiling at her.

"Where is it?" Claire asked impatiently. "I want to see!"

He didn't say anything for a moment, until at last he said, "Abbey has it already."

"I do?" she asked in surprise. "What?"

"Look closer at the dove. It's got a collar on. . ."

Abbey gasped as she realized what the collar was. It was a simple gold band set with a single clear diamond.

"If you don't like it, we can go pick out another one."

"I love it," Abbey managed to gasp, once her heart had returned to beating in a fairly normal pattern. "It's beautiful!"

He slipped it on her finger, and for a moment they stood together, their gazes locked in a timeless embrace. "Now do I kiss her?" he asked over his shoulder to his grandmother.

"Now would be a good time," Claire said, and before her eyes shut, Abbey caught a glimpse of Claire's satisfied smile.

"I have a present for you, too," Abbey said at last. She handed her gift to Mike. "I was going to wait, but now I think this is the right time."

Mike opened the framed picture and grinned. "I love it!" Then his eyes met hers. "Does this mean what I think it does?"

"I think I knew that you were my destiny when we were locked up together in that silly Candy Cane Calaboose. I thought I'd hate it, but deep inside me, I wanted it to go on and on." Abbey gave him a tremulous smile. "Isn't that funny? When I was locked up with you, I found my freedom."

Her heart was no longer imprisoned in its cage of defiance. She was free now, in so many ways. The walls were down; the door was unlocked and open, ready to welcome love.

"Grandma," Mike said at last, "you need to get healthy and stay that way. I think we have a wedding in our future!"

Claire wiggled her toes happily, and Abbey was sure she saw the frogs on the yellow fuzzy slippers smiling.

Epilogue

The Word of Faith Community Church was packed. A gentle snow had fallen, but it did nothing to diminish the happiness of those gathered within. It was December twenty-fifth, and this was a wedding. There was little that people liked more than a Christmas wedding.

It had been a year since Abbey had accepted Mike's proposal, and the days since then had flown by as if winged. The only change was that as the days passed, she loved him more.

The blessings in her life had grown and intensified since that amazing Christmas Eve. God continued to touch her life daily. She saw it in her work as well as her love. God did care for His own.

She'd gone back to college, preparing for the MBA she'd always wanted. Mike had come home one day with a brochure about distance education classes, and she'd signed up right away. They were perfect for her schedule.

After a period of relatively ineffective resistance, she'd answered the call to work with the Jeremiah Group. Her focus area was appearance, and she now advised the young women on the proper clothing to wear to work and how to find appropriate yet inexpensive apparel.

Mona had easily established herself as one of Abbey's favorites. Her natural affinity for the elderly served her well at Golden Meadows. Mona had even started college with a nursing degree as her goal, and Abbey was as proud as a mother peacock. As matter of fact, the young woman was presiding over the cake table at the wedding reception.

"Your veil's crooked." Selma's voice caught, and although Abbey saw the glimmer of tears in her friend's eyes, she knew they were tears of happiness.

"I can't go in with my veil crooked," Abbey teased her gently. "People will talk."

Selma sniffed back the threatening sobs. "They will anyway."

"Honey?" Her mother's hand caressed Abbey's cheek. "The usher says it's time to seat me, so I have to go. Abbey, I love you. Mike will be a good husband, I can tell."

"Any last words of motherly advice?" Abbey asked shakily.

"Just love him. That's it. Just love him."

Her mother started to go, then turned back. "I think I need to modify that a bit. Love him simply. Don't get carried away overanalyzing him. But also don't forget that you are a child of God, too. Be careful not to lose yourself." She paused. "I didn't know that when I first got married—or maybe I did, and I just ignored it—but it kept both Ed and me from having the best relationship we could, and that wasn't fair to any of us, including you."

Abbey saw tears pool in her mother's eyes. "Mom, I understand. And it's all right. Even when I was a teenager and fighting back against anything and everything, I still knew, in my heart, that there was love in our house."

"And one more thing, Abbey. Always, always trust God. Again, your dad and I didn't have that trust, and it made marriage just that much harder. But now we know, and life is better. I'm so happy to know you're starting your married life with God as the head of your household."

"Oh, Mom." It was all that Abbey could manage.

Her mother laughed shakily. "Look at me. The wedding hasn't even started, and already I'm a sodden mess. I need a handkerchief."

"So do I." Abbey confessed, feeling her emotions starting to crescendo. "We'd better get this show on the road," she told her mother. "If I start crying now, I'll have a drippy nose and swollen, red eyes by the time I get to the altar. Mike will turn and run."

Her mother smiled mistily, gave her a quick kiss, and left to be seated in the sanctuary.

"Ready?" Brianna spoke to them from the door of the room where Selma and Abbey had dressed. "We've got a church full of people anxious to see you. Some of them are worried about getting back to Golden Meadows in time for the Christmas party there, so I think you'd better get moving before they mutiny."

"All right. I'm ready. Nervous as a cat, but I'm ready." An entire flock of butterflies seemed to have made their home in her stomach.

Selma smoothed her red velvet bridesmaid's dress. "Next time, I get to be the bride, okay?"

"Okay. You've got to find your own fellow, though."

Selma made a face. "I knew there was going to be a catch somewhere."

Abbey enveloped Selma in one last hug. "I'm so happy," she confided. "I think I could burst."

"Well, don't," Selma said practically. "That's a new dress you've got on, you know, and white stains like nobody's business."

Abbey left the room with Selma and joined the rest of the bridal party in the small area behind the sanctuary, which was decorated in red and white. She adjusted her bouquet, which, like those of the others in the bridal party, included tiny candy canes sprinkled among the red and white carnations.

She leaned down and kissed her matron of honor, whose wheelchair was festooned with garlands of red and white tinsel.

The music started, and the four women proceeded down the aisle.

I should remember this, Abbey thought as she passed through the wedding guests. Their faces blurred, but she knew they were all smiling at her. *I need to remember this always.*

The minister was waiting for her at the altar. . .and so was Mike. He had never looked so tall, so capable, so trusting.

The minister began to speak the familiar words: "Dearly beloved, we are gathered. . ."

Her mind wandered back to the day the socks dropped through the grating, to the time of the blizzard, to the afternoon in the Candy Cane Calaboose.

"I do."

She looked at Mike, and the world got smaller, the congregation vanished, and there were only the two of them.

"I now pronounce you husband and wife. You may kiss the bride."

The world exploded with joy. The minister turned them to face the congregation. "I'd like to introduce to you Mr. and Mrs. Michael Tucker."

The organ burst into glorious song, a collection of Christmas carols, and hand in hand, Mike and Abbey rushed back down the aisle and into the narthex.

"We're married, honey," he said to her as he took her in his arms. "Now and forever."

He bent to kiss her, and as she lifted her lips to meet his, the guests began to file out.

Claire was the first to get to them. Abbey leaned down to hug her, and the older woman beamed at her. "Weddings are so romantic, aren't they?" she cooed. She blinked her eyelashes flirtatiously at her companion. "Albert, do we have something to tell them?"

The gentleman whom Abbey had met in the coffee shop during her first visit to Golden Meadows looked fondly at Claire. "Would that be advising them to keep Valentine's Day open?"

"What are you two planning?" Abbey asked. "A party?"

Albert and Claire's eyes sparkled with a shared secret. "Perhaps," Albert said.

"You could call it a party," Claire said, "except that we prefer to call it a wedding."

Abbey reached for both of them and enveloped them simultaneously in a bear hug. "I'm so glad for you!" She knew she was gushing, but she couldn't stop.

"And don't think you can just recycle the gifts from this shindig that you don't want," Claire said with an impish grin. "I'll be watching."

Abbey turned to Mike. "Did you know anything about this?"

He shook his head. "Nope. I'm as surprised—and as pleased—as you are. Grandma kept this locked tighter than the closet where she used to hide our Christmas presents."

"Well," Claire explained, "I had to get you two together first."

Mike grinned. "I don't know what to say, except thanks and congratulations!"

"By the way," Claire continued, "I do have another surprise. Want a hint?"

"Sure!" Abbey said.

"Okay, here it is: great hoppyness always." The elderly woman motioned toward the entry to the church.

Abbey turned startled eyes to the door. "Aunt Luellen! You came all the way from Brazil?"

"Chile, honey, and of course I did. I couldn't miss seeing my favorite niece get married!" The woman was tanned and fit and didn't look half of her eighty-something years. "And I can't wait for you to see what I got you!"

"If it turns out to be half as good as what you got me last Christmas," Abbey said, "I'm going to love it!"

Aunt Luellen looked confused. "I can't remember what I got you last year."

Abbey looked up at her handsome new husband. "Love," she said. "That's what you gave me."

JANET SPAETH

For as long as she can remember, Janet Spaeth has loved to read, and romances were always a favorite. Today she is delighted to be able to write romances based upon the greatest Love Story of all, that of our Lord for us. When she isn't writing, Janet spends her time reading a romance or a cozy mystery, baking chocolate chip cookies, or spending precious hours with her family.

A Letter to Our Readers

Dear Readers:

In order that we might better contribute to your reading enjoyment, we would appreciate your taking a few minutes to respond to the following questions. When completed, please return to the following: Fiction Editor, Barbour Publishing, Inc., P.O. Box 719, Uhrichsville, OH 44683.

1. Did you enjoy reading *Bittersweet Christmas*?
   ❏ Very much—I would like to see more books like this.
   ❏ Moderately—I would have enjoyed it more if _____

   _____

   _____

2. What influenced your decision to purchase this book?
   (Check those that apply.)
   ❏ Cover   ❏ Back cover copy   ❏ Title   ❏ Price
   ❏ Friends   ❏ Publicity   ❏ Other

3. Which story was your favorite?
   ❏ *One Last Christmas*   ❏ *The Candy Cane Calaboose*
   ❏ *Almost Twins*

4. Please check your age range:
   ❏ Under 18   ❏ 18–24   ❏ 25–34
   ❏ 35–45   ❏ 46–55   ❏ Over 55

5. How many hours per week do you read? _____

Name _____

Occupation _____

Address _____

City_____ State _____ Zip _____

E-mail_____

If you enjoyed

Bittersweet

Christmas

then read:

Montana

Mistletoe

Romance Has Perfect Timing
in Four Christmas Novellas

Christmas Confusion by Lena Nelson Dooley
Return to Mistletoe by Debby Mayne
Under the Mistletoe by Lisa Harris
All I Want for Christmas Is. . .You by Kim Vogel Sawyer

Available wherever books are sold.
Or order from:
Barbour Publishing, Inc.
P.O. Box 721
Uhrichsville, Ohio 44683
http://www.barbourbooks.com

You may order by mail for $6.97 and add $3.00 to your order for shipping.
Prices subject to change without notice.
If outside the U.S. please call 740-922-7280 for shipping charges.

inside *girl*

PERFECT MATCH

PERFECT MATCH

inside girl

a novel by **J. MINTER**

author of the insiders

BLOOMSBURY

New York • Berlin • London

BLOOMSBURY

Copyright © 2009 by J. Minter
and 17th Street Productions, an Alloy company

Published by Bloomsbury U.S.A. Children's Books
175 Fifth Avenue, New York, NY 10010

Library of Congress Cataloging-in-Publication Data
Minter, J.
Perfect match : an inside girl novel / J. Minter. — 1st U.S. ed.
p.   cm.
Summary: As Valentine's Day approaches and her friends have called a boycott on boys,
high-schooler Flan decides to dabble in matchmaking so all her friends can enjoy the
upcoming dance.
ISBN-13: 978-1-59990-335-4 • ISBN-10: 1-59990-335-0
[1. Dating (Social customs)—Fiction. 2. Friendship—Fiction. 3. Valentine's Day—Fiction.
4. New York (N.Y.)—Fiction.] I. Title.
PZ7.M67334Go 2009   [Fic]—dc22   2008039176

alloyentertainment

Produced by Alloy Entertainment
151 West 26th Street, New York, NY 10001

First U.S. Edition 2009
Printed in the U.S.A. by Quebecor World Fairfield
10 9 8 7 6 5 4 3 2 1

for Jordan, future heartbreaker

inside
girl

PERFECT MATCH

Chapter 1

Outside, behind the velvet rope on Houston Street, the winding crowd I'd just zipped past looked cold. But inside, at a private Screen Actors Guild party in the famously mod Angelika theater, things were getting hot, hot, hot.

"I want you to meet my girlfriend, Flan."

I know, I know, these words have been said about me before. I'll be the first to admit that I've had my fair share of boyfriends. But truthfully, the introduction had never sounded so sweet as it did when it was uttered by Alex Altfest, the Prince of New York, whose arm was lovingly curved around my waist.

We were standing in the glittering atrium of the theater, all dressed up to attend this very choice Hollywood-style event—made even more choice by the fact that it was hosted by one of Alex's friends to celebrate the premiere of his new film, *Cache Creek*.

1

The Angelika is most Manhattanites' destination for taking in classic artsy flicks—from foreign shorts to Woody Allen revivals. I loved seeing movies there, but until tonight I'd never thought about it as a hot spot for Hollywood types. With its high glass ceilings, multilevel cocktail bar, and black-tie waiter service, the Angelika really felt like a place to see and be seen. Which is why I was glad I'd decided to wear my new sapphire Tory Burch heels—and why I was even gladder to have the Prince of New York on my arm. I sighed contentedly and leaned into Alex.

"Flan?" Alex said, giving me a sideways grin.

Oh, right, introductions. I probably wasn't making a dazzling first impression by gazing off introspectively.

"This is my old crew from lacrosse camp—Brady, Saxton, and Phil. Brady's the one I told you about, the producer for *Cache Creek*." Alex moved his arm to my shoulders. "Guys, this is her."

The way he said it—*this is her*—like he'd spent enough time talking about me that his friends could now put my face to the girl in his stories—well, it sort of made me glow inside. I mean, I talked about Alex all the time to my friends, but until then, I hadn't considered that he might do the same thing.

Brady stuck out his hand. He was almost as tall as

Alex, with curly dark hair and dimples. "We've heard lots about you." He nodded at Alex. "In fact, it's kinda hard to get this guy to *stop* talking about you."

I could feel myself blushing. "I've heard good things about you, too," I said, taking a flute of acai spritzer from a passing waiter's tray. "Alex says the movie's getting lots of buzz."

"Nah," Saxton piped in, shrugging dramatically. He was blond and muscular with intense green eyes. "It was only *the* movie at Sundance last month, no big deal."

"And Brady only has Scorsese on his knees to direct his next film," Phil said, punching Brady's shoulder. "When are you going to break the news that you cast me as the lead?"

"Maybe when I find an actress worthy of your Yale drama school degree." Brady laughed. "Or at least one the studio can bank on, considering you're not exactly a household name." Brady shrugged apologetically as Phil feigned offense.

I was pretty impressed that Alex was friends with such a talented, artsy group of guys. Of course, I did have my token film-star best friend, Sara-Beth Benny. But SBB's movies weren't exactly the kind that got airtime at the Angelika. Although she had been moaning to me lately about her agent wanting her to do a project to up her dramatic cred—i.e., not another of her famous teenybopper blockbusters.

Hmm . . . If Brady was already working on another film, maybe I could find a way to introduce them? Not that SBB didn't already have an agent and a PR team and four personal assistants . . . but it'd be so cool to hook her up with a connection who could help her career. I'd mention it to Alex later.

Alex squeezed my shoulder. "Come on, I want to show you around."

As we mingled throughout the cocktail hour, I was struck by how great and attentive Alex was being. Even though he seemed to know everyone, he never left my side. As he spun me around the room for introductions, I got the feeling that a lot of people were sizing me—and my Tory Burch heels—up.

I'd been to enough parties and premieres to handle the scrutinizing gazes of the rich and fashion-conscious. Even so, there was something new about being introduced as one half of a couple. I wasn't used to it—my boy life and my socialite life had always been kind of separate entities in the past. But with Alex periodically planting his lips on my cheek and whispering funny details about all the people I was meeting—"that guy makes his driver take him to McDonald's in the Bronx so his nutritionist wife won't find out he eats meat"—I realized I was totally into being his other half.

"This is amazing." I turned to Alex, after I'd met more people than I could remember. "I'm so glad you invited me."

He smiled. "You're going to be even more glad when I tell you who else I invited."

I must have looked confused, because Alex spun me toward the entryway. My best friend, Camille, and her new boyfriend, Xander, were walking up the steps, hand in hand!

"Brady gave me two extra tickets to the screening at the last minute," Alex said. "Thought you might like to see a familiar face in the crowd."

"Hey, lovebirds," Camille called, flipping her trademark long gold hair. "Swank party, Alex. Ooh, swankier shoes, Flan. Bendel's?" she asked.

"Scoop," I corrected.

"Well, now that that important matter's settled," Xander joked, "should we watch this movie or what?"

The boys put their arms around us and our four-some joined the glittering, black-clad crowd at the doors to the theater. The only thing better than Xander finally asking Camille out was the fact that Xander and Alex went way back to their days at Little Red Schoolhouse, so they were almost as tight as Camille and me.

"We definitely have to start double-dating more often," I whispered to Camille as we entered the theater.

"I *know*," Camille said. "Friend time and boy time at the *same* time. What's better?"

The theater was already packed, and everyone was rushing to claim seats. As a friend of the producer, Alex had a group of reserved seats right in the middle. The four of us were able to sit down and relax with no problem, just in time to catch the scene unfolding in the row ahead of us.

A barrel-chested, bald man in Prada shoes and a tight pink T-shirt that read *Don't Mess with the Diva* had spread out his winter gear across four empty seats and was watching over them like a hawk.

"Um, excuse me," an equally muscular bald guy said to him in a huffy voice. "Where do you think you are, the high school lunchroom? You can't save seats in a New York City movie theater."

"I can if you knew who my friends are," Muscles Number One said defiantly, crossing his arms over his chest.

"That doesn't even make any *sense*," Muscles Two scoffed.

Camille and I looked at each other with raised eyebrows and I bit my lip to keep from laughing. It was a favorite secret pastime of ours—eavesdropping on Chelsea boys in catfights. Sometimes we staked out the back table at the Pinkberry on Eighth Avenue just to see what kind of drama we could witness.

But these two dudes were getting serious about the seats. One of them was rolling up his sleeves like he was about to throw a punch. That only happened at Pinkberry when they ran out of mochi. Just when I thought things were going to get ugly, Muscles Two said: "Wait a minute—you look familiar." He squinted at his opponent. "Did you do that Calvin Klein ad on the back of the M16 bus?"

Muscles One shrugged. "Maybe."

"Ohmigod, huge fan," Muscles Two said, making the I'm-not-worthy motion with his arms. Changing his tack, he sized up his opponent. "How about if I agree to find another seat, you agree to give me your number?"

Next to Camille, Xander leaned in to whisper, "You guys are so eating this up, aren't you?"

I giggled under my breath.

"Like it's Pinkberry," Camille replied.

"I guess love is in the air," Alex said, squeezing my hand.

He was right. Valentine's Day was a little over a week away. Even though I had a boyfriend, and so should probably have given the holiday some thought, I was mostly aware of how close it was because of my single friends at Thoney. They were already complaining about how depressing the whole month of February was unless you had a valentine.

I'd thought my friends were being dramatic, but maybe it was exactly this fear of spending February fourteenth alone that stopped the guys in front of us from clocking each other. Maybe Cupid made them take out their Palms to exchange numbers instead.

Just before the lights dimmed, Muscles Two snapped a photo of Muscles One on his phone. "Text me!" he grinned, before shuffling off to his seat.

"Classic New York," Camille said, whipping her hair into a giant bun and putting on her glasses to assume her I'm-watching-a-movie pose.

From the opening scene of the film, I was hooked—and even more impressed by Brady. It was the story of two star-crossed lovers, separated by distance, and family obligations, and some really incredible costume changes. *Hmm, I wonder where the lead actress got that belt. . . .*

But after a few minutes, I found myself distracted by a faint blue light in front of me. When I leaned forward, I realized that it was the glowing cell phone of Muscles One. How rude. Was he already texting

Muscles Two? Maybe if I leaned forward just a little bit more, I could make out what they were saying. It was bound to be hilariously racy. A little further . . . a little further . . . *oooph*! Before I realized what was happening, I'd fallen out of my seat. Everyone around us turned to look at me and held their fingers up to their lips.

"Shhhhhh," Muscles One said to me brusquely. Like he was paying *so* much attention to the movie!

Oh well, it served me right. I looked at Alex, who was shaking his head with a knowing smirk. I shrugged in apology, took his hand, and vowed to get back into watching the movie. No more spying!

But a few minutes later, I was distracted again by the distinct buzz of a vibrating cell phone. Now this guy was really being rude! But when the buzzing didn't stop, I realized that I was the culprit this time. Whoops.

In an attempt to be smooth, I reached down to turn it off. But before the screen went black, I noticed that I had four missed calls and three text messages from the girls in my Thoney clique. I couldn't help taking a quick glance.

From Harper: PARTY AT VANS. WE'RE ALL GOING.

From Amory: I'M GOING TO RICKY'S FOR PRIMPING PROPS. WHO WANTS GLITTER EYE SHADOW?

From Morgan: MEET ON THE CORNER OF PERRY AND WEST FOURTH. I HAVE THE CODE TO GET UPSTAIRS.

I looked over at Camille; I was sure the girls would have texted her as well. But she didn't seem to know or care about it. I kind of envied that she was able to focus on the movie. I was having a great time too, but now that I knew that all my friends were heading out to a party and assuming that I'd meet them there . . . well, my mind was sort of wandering. Should I let them know where I was? Would they be bummed that I couldn't make it? *Could* I make it, if we went right after the movie?

Wait, what was I thinking? It was just a party. I'd missed parties before and survived to tell about it. And here I was, at this amazingly fun event, with *Alex*, who I adored and who'd been cool enough to invite my best friend to join us.

Come on, Flan. Everyone in New York was looking for love and Cupid was actively smiling down on me. What more could I ask for?

*E*arly the next morning, I met Camille and SBB for brunch at a tiny East Village restaurant called Prune. They don't take reservations, so you have to get there right when the doors open at ten o'clock if you want to avoid standing in line for an hour. But they do have the best breakfast BLTs in the city, so it's definitely worth the early rising.

Luckily, all three of us arrived at the same time and SBB only had to sign three autographs and pose for two photographers on the way in, so we were able to snag our favorite sunny table under the hanging ivy plant by the window. The crowd was young and beautiful, mostly couples or small groups of girls. Each place setting contained the classic brunch trifecta: a frothy cappuccino, a pair of aviator sunglasses, and a PDA. The other groups of girls were all laughing as they dished out their tales of the

11

weekend's adventures, but I noticed that the vibe at most of the couples' tables was decidedly lower key.

"Is it me," I asked, smearing some of Prune's signature blood orange marmalade on a hunk of whole-grain toast, "or do the girls-only cliques seem to be having way more fun than the girls who are here with their boyfriends?"

"Probably because it's more fun to talk smack about your boyfriend to your friends than it is to actually hang out with him," SBB said thoughtfully, biting into her black bean flapjacks.

"Whoa, where did that come from?" Camille asked. "Is something going on between you and JR?"

SBB threw her head back in a laugh. "Not even. Jake Riverdale and I are more in love than ever. It's called *empathy*," she said, sounding out each syllable. Camille and I shared a secret smirk as SBB continued her explanation. "It's an acting term where you put yourself in someone else's shoes. I've been working on it recently at my agent's suggestion." She glanced around the room. "Take that couple over there." SBB nodded to her left at a couple so lifeless, they practically looked asleep. "Wouldn't you be Somber Sally if you were dating that dude? Wouldn't you rather be hanging with . . ." She scanned the room until her eyes landed on a group of girls practically falling out of their chairs with that laugh specific to inside jokes. "Them?"

I was used to SBB's "acting" terms and techniques, having been BFFs with the teen actress *Rolling Stone* had recently called "an intergalactic star" since we were both wearing training bras. But today, SBB's professional lingo made me wonder about life off-screen.

"Isn't it possible," I asked the girls, "to have as much fun with your boyfriend as with your friends?"

"Sometimes it seems like a lot more is at stake with boys," Camille said, looking down at her plate. "Like every word you say to each other *means* something, you know? It's easier to navigate when things happen with your girlfriends than with your boyfriend."

"Okay, your turn," I said to Camille. "I know you don't have SBB's excuse that your working on your act. Is everything okay with Xander? You guys seemed so good last night."

"We were. We are," she sighed, popping the last bite of her asparagus quiche in her mouth. "But after we left you guys at the movie, we both had messages from our friends to go to separate parties. And he wanted to go meet up with them and I didn't. I just got scared that I might be more into him than he is into me." She looked at me. "Do you know what I mean?"

The truth was, Alex and I had had the exact opposite conversation last night after the movie. But I knew that just because I thought it would be fun to meet up with friends after the movie, it didn't mean that I wasn't totally into Alex—and looking at Camille now, I was sure that the case was the same for Xander.

"Oh, you girls and your little worries!" SBB laughed, picking up the check. "I won't hear any more of it. You're beautiful and adored by your men, *capisce*?"

"Nice empathy, SBB," I joked.

"Empathize this: what we need is some retail therapy. Now, who knows what she's getting her man for Valentine's Day? *That*, ladies, is something worth stressing over."

As we stepped out of the warm, cozy restaurant into the harsh reality of February in New York, all three of us hustled into our hats and mittens. SBB whistled for a cab.

"Bloomingdale's on Broadway," she told the driver. Then she pulled out a thick packet of paper bound like a screenplay with three golden brads. But I doubted that anyone would title a script SHOPPING LIST. "What?" She shrugged at us. "I don't mess around with it comes to retail therapy."

When the cab pulled up to the great white building,

SBB got out first and started calling out a breakdown of the floor plan. "Boys first. We'll start at the third floor and move through the fifth. Then, once we've gotten the gift-buying work out of the way, we can reward ourselves with spa treatments on six and shoes on four."

Wow, it usually took me an hour just to make it out of the cosmetics section on the ground floor at Bloomingdale's. Since I had no good ideas about what to get Alex for Valentine's Day, I was pretty grateful that I had SBB-on-a-mission to keep me on track.

While we thumbed through piles of men's shirts and racks of ties and boxes of cuff links, I could feel my eyes glazing over. It's not that I wasn't interested in shopping for Alex—though I had to admit, high-heeled boots were way more fun to look at than cuff links. I mean, what *were* cuff links, anyway? But I just didn't think any of this stuff was quite right for Alex. And I wanted to get him something really special. What exactly that was going to be just hadn't come to me yet.

I looked at Camille to see if she was having any more luck. Her brow was furrowed in frustration.

"It's not just finding a Valentine's present that I'm worried about," she explained when she saw the concerned look on my face. She was holding up a hideously ugly brown sweater without even seeming to see it. "Xander's birthday is the week after next, *and* our one-month anniversary is right after that, but I don't want to go overboard with the gifts—especially if he doesn't think that one month is a big anniversary, 'cause you know, some guys don't really think about that, and—"

I had never seen Camille so unglued over a guy. I could always count on her to be the smart, balanced, carefree one. What was making her so nervous? I looped my arm through hers.

"Maybe you should follow SBB's lead," I suggested. "Put yourself in her shoes. Look at her. She's dating the most popular pop star on the planet and the only thing in her relationship that she's not completely confident about is whether JR would prefer the blue or the green Burberry scarf. You should get Xander what feels right. Try not to overthink it."

She nodded. "You're right." Her eyes finally locked on the mess of brown merino wool in her hands. "God, what am I doing with this awful sweater? Yuck. This is certainly *not* the answer." She tossed it back in the sale bin and sighed. "I'm going to go check out those money clips over there."

"Good idea." I smiled. Relieved that Camille seemed to have found her purpose, I looked around for a bench. It might have been the first time in my life that I opted out of shopping. I felt a little bit like my dad or brother when Mom, Feb, and I dragged them around department stores.

"Eeeek!" SBB came up from behind me and grabbed my shoulders. "Flan, thank you *so* much!"

"For what?" I asked, confused.

"For revitalizing my entire career!" She was bouncing on her Ferragamo heels. The last time I'd heard her so breathless, she'd just hurled herself over one of the blue *Village Voice* newspaper displays on West Broadway to avoid a Segway-riding paparazzo across the street. "Alex's friend, Brody? Or Brindy? Or, oh, Brady! Well, he just *inquired* about me. He got my agent's name from Alex . . . and he wants to audition me for a part! In his new indie film! Can you believe it? My agent said the script is totally smart and edgy. So it's basically the opposite of anything I've done before. It'll be groundbreaking! It'll be revolutionary! It'll be—"

"That's so great, SBB," I said. I was thrilled for her—and more than a little thrilled with Alex. I'd only mentioned SBB's career concerns in passing after the movie. It was totally sweet and perceptive of him to talk to Brady already, and without me even having to ask.

"So what's the movie about?" I asked. "What role are you auditioning for?"

"Oh, you know, it's a gritty drama, set in an all-American high school. And I would play the typical high school student. I'll just have to channel my inner—oh *no*! My career is finished!"

The color drained from her face and she sank onto the bench next to me.

"What is it?" I asked, holding her small body upright. I started to fan her with my mittens. "What's wrong?"

Very slowly, my little starlet eked out the words. "I never went to high school. I have no experience with 'typical.' I don't have a chance." SBB sighed wistfully.

I suppressed a grin. "SBB, high school is easy."

She looked at me doubtfully.

"Okay," I reconsidered. "It's not easy to *live* through, but I promise you, it will be a breeze for you to act. It's all your favorite stuff—boys, fashion, immeasurable drama." I patted her knee. "Trust me, with my help, you'll be the most convincing high school student the silver screen has ever seen."

SBB's eyes got all wide and dewy, the way they did when she felt really moved. "You'll help me, Flannie? I really want to prove that I can do this. I want to become a legitimate indie drama darling, the toast of the Independent Spirit Awards."

"Lucky for you," I said, "I'm something of an expert on high school drama. You can put your empathy skills to use on me."

As SBB gave me a tight side squeeze, Camille reappeared in front of us. "So," she said tantalizingly, holding her hands behind her back. "What do we think of this?" She held up a pocket watch dangling from a cool, sort of gaudy gold rope. "When you open it up," she explained while demonstrating, "there are three different compartments. The watch is one, and you can store two pictures on the sides. It's kind of a like a functional man locket. Weird or cool?"

"It's a mocket!" SBB squealed. "It's perfect! Where'd you find it? We'll take three, right, Flan?"

Camille led us over to the glass case where she'd found the golden mockets. I wasn't so sure this screamed *Alex*, but the other girls seemed so into it that I didn't want to argue. As the two of them brainstormed exactly which photos they'd put inside the lockets, I felt my phone buzz in my bag. It was a text from Morgan, whom I realized I hadn't seen all weekend.

YOU ALIVE? BEEN MISSING YOUR PRETTY FACE, she wrote. GRAB A COFFEE?

Morgan lived in SoHo, within walking distance from Bloomingdale's, so it'd be super easy for her to come meet up with us. But as I looked at my two friends gushing over their mockets, I tried to imagine Morgan hanging out in the men's section. All we were doing was talking about and shopping for our boyfriends. Of all my single friends, she seemed the most sensitive about her lack of significant other. I didn't want to blow her off, so I texted back:

HOW 'BOUT LATTES TOMORROW BEFORE SCHOOL? WE'LL NEED THE CAFFEINE TO GET THROUGH ANOTHER MONDAY

I knew I was doing Morgan a favor by opting to devote time to her solo, but something about my response felt a little forced. When had it started feeling like I had to dole out time with my friends based on whether or not they had boyfriends?

"Flan," SBB called me back to reality. "We're about to check out. You want in on the mocket, right?"

"Okay," I surrendered, feeling more enthusiastic about getting out of the men's department than about the gift itself. "Yes, I'll take the mocket." I was going to need some serious time in the shoe section to recover from this retail therapy session.

Chapter 3

A few hours later, I was holed up in my bedroom, avoiding my chemistry homework and holding up the mocket I'd just bought for Alex for the approval of my very discriminating Pomeranian, Noodles.

He was curled up in my arms, making his contented half-snore, half-purr sound (anyone who's met Noodles can attest to the fact that he must have been a cat in a former life). But when I showed him the mocket, his head perked up and he sniffed it suspiciously.

"It's all wrong, isn't it?" I asked, nuzzling his face.

Noodles barked twice in the affirmative. I lay back on my bed and sighed. It was a week and a half until Valentine's Day and after many hours of shopping for Alex I was back at square one. What's more, I was feeling incapable of taking my own advice to Camille. I felt like so much was riding on this gift. Since our

21

relationship was pretty new and I was still trying to feel things out, I just wanted to make sure to do everything right. The pressure was really starting to get to me.

A knock at my door interrupted my thoughts. "Flan?" My father stuck his head in. "We're ordering from Chin-Chin," he said. "You want the usual?"

Before he'd even finished his question, I had leapt from my bed to fling my arms around him. "Dad! When did you get back in town?"

More often than not, the rest of my family's professional globe-trotting duties left me sole proprietor of our way-too-big-for-one-girl town house in the West Village.

My dad shrugged. "Bolivia was way too hot for your mother. We flew back this afternoon."

It only took one look at my father to know that he spent very little time in the city during the winter. His neatly trimmed blond hair framed a face too tan for February in New York. His most recent hobby was buying mansions in foreign countries, declaring them fixer-uppers, and spending all his time renovating them. So whenever my parents made an appearance at our house, it was always cause for celebration.

"That beats the leftover pizza feast I had planned," I said, breathing in the familiar piney smell of my dad's aftershave. "I thought I was home alone."

"Far from it." My dad smiled, ruffling my hair. "We've got a full house, kiddo. Patch got in this afternoon from L.A. and he's meeting Feb at the airport as we speak. I think they're each bringing a *friend* home for dinner."

"They're not calling them *friends* anymore, Richard." I heard my mother's voice coming up the stairs. "You're so old-fashioned." She cupped my face in her cool, manicured hands and kissed both my cheeks. "Hello, darling," she said. "Isn't the new PC word for one's significant other *partner*? That's what Whoopi calls her boyfriend on *The View*."

"Wait," I said, trying to catch up to my in-on-all-the-family-gossip parents. "Patch and Feb suddenly have partners? And they're bringing them to dinner? Why didn't anyone tell me?"

My mother clucked her tongue. "Have you lost your flair for the impromptu dinner party? Didn't your father and I teach you anything? Have we been away too long?"

"No, yes, and yes," I said. "I'm so glad you guys are back, even if it's only for—"

My dad looked at his watch. "Fourteen hours. Why don't you give Alex a call? See if he wants in on this partners evening?"

When my parents went downstairs to get ready for

dinner, I slid the mocket into my underwear drawer and picked up my phone to text Alex.

DINNER PLANS? CAN I TEMPT YOU WITH GREASY CHINESE FOOD AND MY FAMILY?

I was trying to sound casual, since I knew it was a really last-minute invitation, but when Alex replied: WISH I COULD! COMMITTED TO GRANDMA'S TASTELESS CHICKEN TONIGHT, I couldn't help feeling a little bit bummed. My family was together so rarely that I hated missing the opportunity to have Alex at my side. Especially if Patch and Feb were both bringing home their, uh, *partners*.

Oh well—dinner with the fam, even as the seventh wheel, still beat microwaved pizza.

Soon a mess of voices filtered up from the first floor and I rushed down to meet my siblings, whom I hadn't seen in over a month. When I saw my older sister tripping over her suitcases in the foyer, a big smile spread across my face—then quickly turned into a laugh.

Feb was decked out in head-to-toe safari gear. A tall, blond guy standing with his arm around her sported a coordinating ensemble.

"So that's what you've been doing all month—hunting for ivory?" I joked, giving Feb a kiss.

"Not exactly," she said, shoving one of three massive

trunks against the wall. "Kelly and I just started a line of activewear with Karl Lagerfeld. It's inspired by the haute Australian bush hunter. You like?" Feb spun around to model, then put her hand on Kelly's chest. "Sweetie, meet my little sister-slash-protégé, Flan."

"Nice to meet you, Flan," the haute bush hunter boyfriend said. "And yes, before you ask, it's supposed to be ironic."

I smiled at Feb. "I like him already. Where's Patch? I thought I just heard his voice."

Feb rolled her eyes and flung open the door to the coat closet under the stairs. A huddle of bodies, one of which I recognized as that of my older brother, Patch, tumbled out in a lump.

"Remember when we used to wrap fruit roll-ups around our fingers and lick them off?" Feb muttered to me under her breath. I nodded, not sure where she was going with the question. "I think Patch's new girlfriend has him confused with a fruit roll-up."

I looked at Patch, who was bright red at having been busted making out in the coatroom. He did have a strange girl attached to his neck, but something else was different about him too. He was wearing a fitted yellow button-down and gray pin-striped slacks. I almost didn't recognize my vintage-T-shirt-only-wearing brother underneath the fancy clothes. Only a girl he really liked could get Patch to dress up for family dinner. At least his hair was still sticking out in all directions—that part I recognized.

Patch pulled away from the girl and gave me a friendly nod. "Hey sis. How ya been? This is Agnes." He sounded out of breath.

Agnes smiled at me warmly and said hi, but quickly turned her attention back to Patch. She focused on smoothing his hair out and giggling in his ear.

Feb made a gagging motion as my dad's voice called out from the kitchen.

"Mom's threatening to eat all the spring rolls if you kids don't get in here."

As the five of us headed into the dining room for dinner, Feb took me by the arm and pulled me back. She gestured at Patch and Agnes. "Never, I repeat *never* rent a houseboat off Capri for a week with those two."

"Why?" I said, wishing I wasn't always in school to miss the fun sibling bonding trips that Patch and Feb took every month. "That sounds so fun."

"Fun would require your brother to keep his hands off Hag-nes for more than three minutes at a time," Feb corrected.

"Ah, I can see that," I admitted, "but double-dating must be fun. Do you go on double dates with your other friends? Have they all met Kelly?"

Feb looked thoughtful for a minute. "To tell you the truth, Flan, since I started dating Kelly, I haven't really seen much of my friends."

Huh? But Feb had always been my friendship role model. She was legendary for her elaborate social circles. She had more friends on Facebook than anyone I knew!

"But what about Jade Moodswing?" I asked, remembering how tight they'd been at the French designer's fashion show just last month. "Or Opal Jagger?"

"I dunno." She shrugged. "We've sort of just . . . drifted apart. Nothing dramatic. You'll see when you get serious with someone. It's just one of those things."

I looked at my sister, who was back to giggling with Kelly. I had always looked up to her, but at that moment I found myself hoping I *didn't* end up like her. No matter how great things were with Alex, I never wanted to drift apart from my friends. It just felt so sad. There must be a way to strike a balance, right?

Trying to put her words out of my mind, I headed for my usual seat next to Patch. But Agnes—not surprisingly—had slid in before me.

"Hey Flan," Kelly said, pointing to a seat between himself and Feb. "Sit here."

"Everyone settled?" my dad asked. "Let's grub."

While he distributed chopsticks, the rest of us got to work opening up the stacks of steaming white boxes of food.

"No Alex tonight, Flan?" my mother asked. She'd changed into a black and white silk kimono and laced her chopsticks through her hair. "He's such a hunk, isn't he?"

"He's having dinner with his grandmother," I said, slurping a bowl of egg drop wonton soup.

"Awwww," everyone at the table seemed to say at once.

I looked up at them. "What?"

"That's too bad," my father said.

"Really sucks," Patch agreed.

"Would have loved to meet him," Kelly said.

"I'm sorry, Flan," my mother said, sounding like she'd taken empathy lessons from SBB.

"It's no big deal." I shrugged. "I saw him yesterday." I mean, it would have been great to have Alex there, but it wasn't like I couldn't function without him. Right?

"I'm just glad to be with you guys," I said, convincing myself.

"That's nice," my mother said. "Isn't that nice, dear?" she asked my father. When he smiled at her across the table, it was hard not to notice the silent closeness between them—between all the couples.

But then, midbite of her scallion pancake, my mother hopped up from the table. "I completely forgot to call Gloria about our donation to the Guggenheim's restructuring. BRB!"

As my siblings and I groaned at Mom's perpetual overuse of out-of-date slang, my dad sighed and picked up his BlackBerry. "Well, if your mother has permission to do business at the dinner table, I'm just going to send one quick e-mail."

I looked to Patch, who usually harassed my parents when they got bogged down by work during family time, but he was consumed—literally—by Agnes, who still seemed to have her lips attached to his neck.

Geez, if I was looking to my family for examples on how to be in a relationship, this dinner party was leaving me a little uninspired. I turned to Feb and Kelly, the last couple standing.

"So," I asked, trying to make normal conversation. "You guys have been traveling in the bush? Is it hot there or what?"

"Not really. It cools down at night," Kelly said.

"Are you kidding? It's been like living in a sauna," Feb said, oddly riled up. "And you never let us use the air conditioner! You wonder why I always have to wear my hair up!"

"We've been over this," Kelly said, shaking his head. "I think you know the carbon footprint of the average air-conditioning-using American."

Whoa, who knew I could hit such a sore spot by asking the most boring question in the world? If Kelly and Feb were fighting over the weather, how did they handle the hard stuff?

To diffuse the tension, I picked up the first tub of food in front of me. "More beef and broccoli, anyone?"

Feb looked at the food and then at Kelly with narrow eyes. "No thanks, Flan," she hissed. "We're *vegan* now."

"Oh, just lay on the guilt," Kelly moaned. "Everything is all my fault!"

A squeaky smooching sound—the parting of lips across the table—put a pause in their argument. Agnes was taking a breather from Patch and had turned to face us. "Could you guys keep it down over there?"

"Yeah," Patch agreed. "You're sort of harshing our mellow."

"That's it," my mother reappeared from the kitchen. "None of the brainiacs in the art world know how to read a simple e-mail. I have to dash uptown to straighten out this mess." She paused and looked around the table. "I'm so sorry to have ruined this lovely dinner. We'll reschedule, okay? And next time, Flan, you must make sure your partner can join us! You know what they say—nothing makes a mother hen happier than seeing all her chicks settled down. . . ."

Everyone around me seemed to take a cue from my mom and started stacking up the plates. Before I knew it, I was alone in the dining room. So much for a fun family dinner.

I was used to being alone at the dinner table, but I wasn't used to being alone when the rest of my family was *home*. I couldn't remember the last time I'd actually ended a family dinner feeling worse than before it. Was it because everyone was partnered off tonight except me? Or was it just because I hadn't had my fortune cookie?

Making jokes out of the cheesy Chin-Chin fortunes was usually our favorite part of the meal. I reached for the bag and pulled out one of the cookies.

I popped open the wrapping and performed my superstitious ritual of eating the whole cookie with my eyes closed before I unfolded the fortune. In a weird way, it felt like a lot was riding on this moment. Maybe if my family couldn't offer me relationship guidance, a generic platitude would do the trick. Slowly, I looked down at the slip of paper.

Have a wonderful night!

Lame! So much for guidance. I guessed that when it came to navigating relationships, I was on my own.

*A*n hour later, there was a knock on my door. Wondering if it would be the four-eyed, kissing Pagnes monster, or maybe Feb in tears after a blowout with Kelly, or possibly one of my parents checking in on my lonely evening, I opened up the door.

"Guess who?" Alex was standing in the hall outside my bedroom wearing his Hermès navy peacoat and a big grin.

"What are you doing here?" I asked.

"Kidnapping you," he said. "Come on."

I glanced back at the chemistry notebook on my bed, and took it as a sign that Noodles had crawled on top of it and fallen asleep. "I'll grab my coat," I said.

Outside my brownstone, Alex's driver was waiting in a town car. He opened the door for me and I slid in.

"Where are we going?" I asked—praying for

Scoops, my favorite ice cream store in the city. But then, we wouldn't need the driver to go to Scoops. It was just down the block on Bleecker Street. . . .

"You'll see," Alex said, raising an eyebrow.

The car hurtled south, through the West Village and into Chinatown, before taking a left on Canal Street. The streets were damp with slushy rain, and red and gold flags hung from storefronts, announcing the Chinese New Year. Even through the windows, the air was heavy with the scent of seafood shops lining Canal.

When the car pulled to a stop on a quiet street below Canal, Alex said, "I felt bad about missing Chinese food with your family, so I thought I'd make it up to you with Chinese dessert."

Ooh, he was good. He was very good.

"You mentioned once that you were on a quest for the best mocha chip ice cream in the city," Alex continued. "I know you think you've found it at Scoops, but you'd be cheating yourself if you didn't try this version."

We stepped off the damp street into the old-fashioned ice cream shop, loud with a surprisingly large crowd. All the flavors were written in Chinese on a huge whiteboard. I stood on tiptoe to kiss Alex on the lips. "This is so cool and authentic," I said. "I love it."

When I first met Alex, I thought he was your typical, partying bad boy. He wore designer motorcycle boots and played punk rock gigs at Hamptons parties. At first, I was impressed by the way he didn't care about the social rules that everyone else in our scene was so obsessed with—oh, and I was also super attracted to him. But mostly, I was intimidated.

But ever since our first date at Wollman Rink last month, I'd realized that for every thing about Alex that might paint him as a certain type of guy, he broke the rule by also being something completely opposite. Like, he wasn't just the captain of the Dalton lacrosse team—he was also an alternate on the math team. And his goal in life was to become a screenwriter, even though his dad assumed he'd go to law school and take over the family firm. And there was a really good chance he'd do all of those things. By now I knew that I should never assume I knew everything about Alex, because he always had a surprise up his sleeve. Kinda like how I shouldn't have assumed I knew all the good ice cream places in the city. . . .

Alex took care of ordering and handed me the bowl with tidy scoops of mocha chocolate chip. I grinned and took a bite.

"Omigod," I said with my mouth full of perfectly soft ice cream. "Scoops just got some serious competition."

"Save room," he said, snagging a spoonful. "This is not the last stop."

I took my to-go cup and followed Alex back to the car, excited to see what else he had planned.

"So how was dinner?" he said as we continued west along Canal Street. "What'd I miss?"

I thought about divulging how crazy my siblings were acting over their new S.O.'s but I didn't want to scare my still-new boyfriend, so I just said, "Oh, you know, the usual. Mom dressed in theme; Dad oversaw the passing of food; kids fought over the extra fortune cookie."

"I'm sorry I missed it," Alex said before telling the driver to take the Brooklyn Bridge. "I hope you got your hands on that last cookie."

As we drove over the bridge, taking in arguably the very best view of the glittery city, I thought back to my lonely moment at the dining room table. "Yeah," I said. "I guess I did."

"And?" Alex prompted. "What'd the fortune say?"

I laughed and started blushing for no reason. "It said, 'Have a wonderful night.' "

"Well," Alex said, as we stepped out of the car for the second time, on an equally dark street corner in Dumbo, "no one can say we didn't try."

The Brooklyn Ice Cream Company is legendary

for its no-frills flavors and amazing ingredients. It used to be a favorite of mine, but I realized I hadn't been back here since I was a kid—and I'd definitely never tried their mocha chocolate chip.

Alex and I strolled along the promenade and sampled the second contender's ice cream. "Hmm . . . It is chocolatier," I said thoughtfully. "And meltier . . . Hard to pick a favorite!"

"Don't pick a favorite yet," Alex said, steering me back toward the moonlit car. "If you think you can handle it, I've got one more place for us to hit."

"I think you underestimate my ice cream–eating capabilities," I joked.

We crossed the bridge back into the hustle of Manhattan and headed north again toward SoHo.

"This next place isn't technically ice cream—but the mocha chocolate chip is good enough that I think we should make an allowance."

"Ooh, I think I know where we're going," I squealed when the car stopped on Spring Street. We got out in front of the neon circular sign of Rice to Riches, a funny little café that serves dozens of crazy flavors of rice pudding.

By then, I was getting pretty full, so we decided to walk off all the mocha chocolate chip with a stroll around the neighborhood. Alex had his arm around me and I fed him spoonfuls of rice pudding—and only occasionally wondered whether this type of PDA would make Feb roll her eyes and vow not to rent a houseboat with Alex and me. I'd gotten as far as picturing the six of us, all hanging out on a boat for a week of island-hopping in the Mediterranean, when Alex came to a sudden halt.

"Look who it is," I heard a guy's voice say and looked up to see Alex's friends from Dalton—Remy Wise, Troy Fishman, and Xander. I thought Camille had said this morning that she and Xander had a study date tonight. . . .

"Oh, hey guys," Alex said.

"Hey Alex," Troy said, a twinge of annoyance on his face. "You know, your grandmother looks an awful lot like your girlfriend."

"Yeah," Remy said, crossing his arms. "You say you're having dinner with Grandma and then ditch us for Flan? Nice."

Alex looked flustered and shook his head. "Guys, I didn't ditch you. I *did* have dinner with my grandmother. I just picked Flan up a little while ago. What's the big deal?"

It didn't make any sense that the guys would think Alex ditched them. Had I done something to make them so cold?

"Whatever, man," Xander said, barely looking at me. "Seems like you're busy, or whatever."

Why was this black cloud hanging over the group? And why was it so easy for me to imagine this exact scene happening between me and *my* friends?

Alex looked stressed. He was running his hands through his hair. I put my hand on his arm. "Hey," I whispered, "I hope you didn't feel guilted into hanging out with me tonight. I didn't mean to—"

"No," he said quickly. "I wanted to hang out with you. I definitely didn't expect to piss anyone off by hanging out with you." He looked up at Xander. "Just because Camille . . ." He trailed off.

"Just because Camille what?" I asked. "Xander, where's Camille?"

Troy scoffed. "Like you don't know, Flan."

Xander was looking at his feet.

"Know what?" I asked. "What's going on?"

"I figured she would have told you," Xander admitted finally. "We broke up. A few hours ago."

I looked down at the remaining rice pudding in my bowl, which looked anything but appetizing. Alex's friends were all pissed at him for hanging out with me. Now Alex was squirming and clearly weirded out about missing post-breakup dude time. Worst of all, my best friend was probably sitting at home alone, heartbroken and miserable. And right before Valentine's Day! Poor Camille.

And did this mean I was now the only one in my circle of friends to have a boyfriend? That definitely wasn't going to make my balancing act any easier.

Chapter 5

The next morning, I set my alarm forty-five minutes early so I could be dressed and ready to hang with Morgan before school. We were meeting at Agata & Valentino's café on Seventy-ninth Street, and I didn't want to be late.

Ever since I'd enrolled at Thoney in January, Morgan had been a funny, comforting presence in my life. In fact, she'd been the very first person to be nice to me when I showed up shaking in my Moschino all-weather boots as a Thoney infant. I remember how nervous I was, not knowing how to get anywhere in the unfamiliar building. If it hadn't been for Morgan's peppy fashion compliment, I might still be frozen in the marble Thoney foyer.

My first month at school had kind of been a trial by fire—complete with an all-out election war over Thoney's coveted Virgil coordinator with Kennedy

41

Pearson and Willa Rubenstein (longtime frenemy and newfound enemy, respectively). But now that I was happily comfortable in my school life, I knew that I owed a big chunk of that happiness to my friendship with Morgan. Recently, though, I could tell she'd been kind of down. Last month, she'd gone on two dates with a random Exeter boy, only to hear that he'd been seen making out with a sophomore at a party three days later. None of our friends had even known she liked him that much, but there had definitely been a downward shift in the fun rating of the music she downloaded to her iPod.

For the past two weeks, she'd seemed to be actively trying to burst her eardrums with gloomy Cat Power music. I knew that her bubbly, indie rock–loving former self would be ashamed at some of her current musical choices, so recently, I'd been brainstorming ways to get the old Morgan back in business. I'd been meaning to plan something really fun for the two of us to do together over the weekend.

But now it was another Monday morning. How had a whole two days passed with us barely speaking? Morgan *had* been at her family house upstate on Friday night, and I *had* been with Alex on Saturday . . . and Sunday.

But this week I was determined to focus on our friendship.

I stepped into the newly revamped café of Agata & Valentino. It used to be just your run-of-the-mill gourmet grocery store. My mom and I would swing by for rotisserie chicken and grape gazpacho after she picked me up at my grade school, Miss Mallard's. But last year, the owners expanded the store to double its former size. Now there were a chic little coffee bar and pastry shop on the opposite corner from the grocery store. The place was always a little hectic with stroller pushing mothers and UES museum curators, but it was still the best spot in the neighborhood for a pick-me-up before school.

When I found Morgan in her gray Vera Wang toggle coat, she was waiting at the head of the line for her soy latte with hazelnut syrup.

"Morning, sunshine," I said, tapping her on the shoulder.

She turned and gave me her usual air-kiss, but she looked unusually tired.

"I'll believe the sunshine bit when I see it," she said, gesturing outside at the dismal gray February morning. "Can we make that a double shot in my latte?" she shouted over at the barista.

"I brought you something," I sang cheerily, holding up a new Vampire Weekend LP Patch had brought back from L.A.

"Oh," she said flatly, eyeing the CD. "Thanks, Flan."

"But you love Vampire Weekend," I said. "And this is an unreleased live album. Where's my frantic I-love-you-Flan jig?"

"God, that espresso maker's loud," Morgan said, clutching her temples. "Is it, like, insanely loud in here? Let's go outside. I can't hear anything."

I glanced at the terrace, where the iced-over patio furniture looked pretty forlorn.

"I guess we can just head toward school?" I said, kind of disappointed not to have a relaxing catch-up convo in the café. Instead, we grabbed our drinks and made for the door pronto.

"Sure." Morgan shrugged. "School. Where we'll be greeted by poster after poster after poster trying to sell us on how 'wild' and 'amazing' the Valentine's Day Dance is going to be."

Whoa. Someone had woken up as bitter as the unsweetened espresso I was drinking.

"Come on, Morg," I said. "Who cares what the lame student council posters claim? If we want the Valentine's Day Dance to be fun, all we have to do is show up and *make* it fun. Tell me you haven't lost faith in our powers of partying? Now, on to the important stuff," I said, tugging on her coat playfully. "What are you going to wear? You're the only one in our crew who looks good in red, so I nominate you to wear the bold and dramatic color of Cupid."

Morgan looked at me like I'd just asked her what she was going to wear to her beheading.

"You're joking, right, Flan? I thought we'd all agreed on this. None of us are going to that lame dance. Sadie Hawkins? For Valentine's Day? I mean, whose idea was that? Probably the dean's—the *male* dean."

"Morgan," I said, putting my arm around her as we turned onto East Eighty-eighth Street. "We're an all-girls school. If we don't ask the dates to our own dance, how are they supposed to know about it?"

"That's not the point," she huffed. "The point is—"

Uh-oh, Morgan's Random Exeter Boy baggage was rearing its ugly head again.

"The point is . . ." she repeated, unwinding her red Colette scarf from around her neck. Her face was flushed. ". . . that Camille has just been dumped by another typical jerky guy. We have to boycott the dance to show solidarity for our friend, and our gender as a whole."

Oh. Shoot! I could not believe I'd forgotten about Camille and Xander. I mean, I hadn't really forgotten—after Alex dropped me off last night, I'd only called and texted her about eleven times. Her mood online was still set to romantic—so obviously she wasn't ready to let the world know about her breakup just yet. I figured that maybe she just wanted a little time, that maybe she'd come to me when she was ready.

But Morgan seemed to know the gory details. Obviously, I was missing something. And had she kind of spat out those last words a little bit more viciously than necessary?

"Okay," I said, digging through my bag for my Chanel Tulip lip gloss so Morgan couldn't see the look of embarrassment on my face. "I guess I missed that conference call about the dance." I shrugged. "If you guys don't want to go for Camille's sake, of course I'll boycott with you."

But even as I said the words, I knew I wasn't hiding my disappointment very well. As we stepped into Thoney and walked through the entryway hall, Morgan swung by her locker. For the first time, I noticed all the posters that she'd had been talking about:

COME TO THE CUPID COTILLION!
TAKE ACTION—DON'T LET YOUR DATE GET SCOOPED UP BY ANOTHER WOMAN!

ROSES ARE RED, VIOLETS ARE BLUE, EVERYONE
WILL BE AT THE V-DAY DANCE—WILL YOU?

So they were a little dorky. The thing was, I *did* want to go to the Valentine's Dance. It had never occurred to me not to go.

Just then, Willa Rubenstein, class president and resident sociopath, brushed by in a swishy candy apple red Moschino skirt.

"Aww, cute," she said in her patented saccharine voice. "Cinderella wants to go to the ball. Too bad rumor has it none of your posse can get dates. Planning the cover-up girl-power night instead, I hope."

Before I could respond, Morgan squeezed my shoulder. Willa gave her coat a scrutinizing glare and swished away.

"I knew you wouldn't ditch us for some stupid dance just because you have a boyfriend," Morgan said, oblivious to Willa. "But it's gonna take more than a dance boycott to help Camille. You know how much of a wreck she is right now."

I did? Maybe I would know if Camille had returned any of my calls last night. Morgan had been so quick to point out the fact that I had a boyfriend. That couldn't have anything to do with Camille's silence, could it?

Morgan continued, looking more energized than she had all morning. "We'll have to do triage pretty much constantly until Camille is feeling better. Which is why we're scheduling an emergency cheer-up girl-fest today after school."

"We are?"

"Of course," Morgan said, looking at me like I was crazy not to recognize the need for immediate breakup triage.

"Of course," I echoed. We were standing in the hallway where we'd part ways when the first bell rang in a few minutes. Morgan would go to her Latin class and I'd go to AP French—but somehow, it seemed like we were already speaking different languages.

"So what's the plan?" I asked.

"After last period, we're meeting at the Bliss uptown. Harper scheduled group seaweed facials and body wraps. No boys allowed."

The thought of any guy actually wanting to witness five girls looking like monsters under a full body coating of green seaweed almost made me laugh, but when I looked at Morgan she was all boy-boycotting business.

"Got it." I nodded. "No boys."

As Morgan and I air-kissed good-bye, I thought I could sense a renewed purpose in her that I hadn't seen in weeks. It was great of her to take charge of Operation Heal Camille, but it felt a little like Morgan was *looking* for an excuse to drum up boy-hatred. Of course, I'd do whatever it took to be there for my friends, but I didn't think that needed to include swearing off all boys altogether.

Just before I stepped into my French class, I reached for my phone to put it on silent. While Morgan was telling me the details of our girls-only spa trip tonight, I'd missed a couple texts from Alex:

WE STILL ON FOR KOREAN BBQ IN MY HOOD TONIGHT?

Then:

HOPE YOU LIKE IT SPICY.

Double shoot. Would I ever stop constantly over-booking myself? Ugh. Alex had been talking up this Korean BBQ restaurant all week, and I really wanted to go. But . . . my best friend needed me. And it seemed like my other friends needed me to be there for her, too.

I wasn't exactly sure how spicy I liked my Korean BBQ, but I did know that if I wanted to keep the heat off myself in my social circle, I had only one choice.

How did you say "rain check" in Korean?

Sandwiched in the lunch line between my pals Harper Alden and Amory Wilx, I got a taste of just how widespread the anti-boy syndrome had become.

"I mean, Camille *trusted* Xander," Harper was saying as she readjusted her massive black Ralph Lauren sunglasses to hold back her straight golden locks. "And the way he just dropped her like that—it's completely disrespectful to her as a *woman*."

I loved Harper, but in some ways she was pretty traditional. Everything in her life had a mannered, high-society quality to it. I turned to Amory, who'd grown up with Harper and almost always called her out on her antiquated views of dating.

But Amory was nodding her head so enthusiastically, I thought her Candace Ang hoops might fall out of her ears.

"I know," she said, selecting a fruit salad from the

line. "It's like boys only want us on *their* schedules. They're are so capricious, just picking and choosing whatever girl, whenever they feel like it. Why should it be up to them all the time?"

I laughed and pointed at her fruit salad. "So says the girl who picks all the kiwi off one fruit salad and tosses it back with just cantaloupe left."

"Not the same thing!" Amory insisted, but she laughed. "Okay, maybe that was a little ruthless."

"This is why people shouldn't jump into relationships," Harper continued on her tirade. "My parents have a strict rule: no new guy can take me out until he has enough manners to show up at our house and introduce himself to my father."

"Geez," I joked, grabbing a bottle of iced jasmine tea. "If I had to wait around for my dad to be home to meet my new boyfriends, I'd never get a date!"

"That's not true, Flan," Amory said. "Alex has met your parents, hasn't he?"

"Briefly." I grinned, remember my mom talking about what a hunk he was at dinner last night. "He's pret-ty *amaz*—"

I froze midgush. Both Harper and Amory were staring at me as if I were praising my new pet tarantula. Whoops, better change the subject fast.

"Have we actually gotten Camille's side of this

story?" I asked as we paid for our grub. Both Harper and Amory looked at each other and shrugged. "I mean, so far, what we know about the breakup of the century is only conjecture, isn't it? Where *is* Camille, anyway?"

What if it wasn't that bad? What if, on her anti-boy rampage, Morgan had blown the story just slightly out of proportion? What if there was still a chance to hit pause on the man-hating DVD all my friends seemed to be tuning into? Maybe, just maybe, there was a way to turn things around in time for us to rock the Valentine's Dance like we had Virgil. . . .

Suddenly, Amory pointed dramatically.

"There," she gasped, breathless.

I followed Amory's finger toward the fourth table from the door, our daily lunch spot. Hunched over the table alone in her black Burberry trench was the shadow of my best friend. At that moment, Camille looked up to give us a full view of her tear-streaked face. We were on the other side of the cafeteria, but even if we'd been standing right in front of her, she still wouldn't have seen us. Her eyes were completely glazed over in misery.

"She needs us," Harper said, starting toward her. But before she'd even taken three steps, she turned back around to me. "And Flan, for Camille's sake, try to zip it on the Alex stories for like twenty minutes, okay?"

I blanched. That seemed a little uncalled for! But we were supposed to be uniting to focus on Camille, so I brushed off the harshness and just nodded.

As I followed the other girls toward the table, trying to imagine how things between Camille and Xander had fallen apart so quickly, I felt a sudden yank on my right elbow. I turned around to find the most un-Thoney-looking girl I'd ever seen within these walls.

She had bright red hair pulled into a high side ponytail and tied with a yellow ribbon. She was wearing a purple gingham shirt tied in a knot at her waist, and her face was dotted with a smattering of auburn freckles. Wait a minute—those freckles looked abnormally large and didn't exactly match her coloring. And underneath that thick mop of hair, I could have sworn I recognized . . .

A look of terror crossed the girl's face, and before I could say anything she clapped her hand over my mouth and dragged me—and my precariously balanced bowl of vegetarian pho—behind the vending machines.

"Don't make a sound," she hissed once we were alone. As soon as she uttered the words, I knew my suspicions had been right.

"SBB," I said, "*what* are you doing here? And *what* are you wearing?"

"I texted you an hour ago to see if it was okay if I came for . . ." She paused. ". . . a visit."

"I've been in chem lab all morning," I said, taking in her pleated jeans and old-school Keds. "And for the record, in the past, *a visit* means you stopping by with sushi and a cute bag you just picked up at Barneys. What's up with the gingham? I mean, I know urban cowgirl was in a couple seasons ago, but this seems like a stretch."

SBB sighed and collapsed pretzel-style on the parquet floor. "I know," she heaved. "I'm hideous. I just . . . I didn't want to be recognized on my first day of school! My audition for *Blinker High* is right around the corner. I know you said you'd help me unlock the mystery of high school, but I was just sitting around in my underwater pilates class this morning, feeling like every second that I didn't spend preparing for this part was a waste of time. I got so distracted, I almost drowned, Flannie! So I figured—I figured I'd enroll at Thoney with the very most wonderful high school student in the whole world." She looked up to gauge my reaction. "Just, you know, for a little while."

"Oh, SBB," I said, joining her on the floor and putting my arms around her. This audition clearly meant a lot to her. "Well . . . welcome to Thoney. I'm Flan and I'll be your tour guide through the treacherous world of high school." I tugged on her braid. "Lesson one: you don't have to dress like a complete geek—no offense—to avoid being recognized as your movie-star self."

"I don't?" she asked, wide-eyed.

"Uh-uh. Maybe start with a slightly less offensive wig and see how it goes?" I suggested. I slid the bowl of pho in between us and offered SBB first shot at the chopsticks.

"Wow, you have Vietnamese food in your cafeteria?" she asked, slurping up some of the spicy noodles. "This is *good*. I thought it was all Tater Tots and Jell-O."

"Lesson two." I held up two fingers. "Thoney is not your normal high school."

"Should I be taking notes?" SBB asked. "I've seen some girls walking around with *really* cute planners. I could get a planner like yours." She reached for my new Kate Spade notebook. It was flipped open to this afternoon, where I'd written: *Man-hating spa treatment with the girls.*

I sneaked a peek around the vending machines at my other friends. I knew I needed to be there for

Camille, but at least for now, the other girls seemed to have her tears under control. I didn't want to abandon SBB before she felt settled at Thoney.

"What's this?" SBB asked, pointing at today's box in my planner. "Does Thoney have an after-school spa club? Or are Bliss trips exclusive to Thoney too?"

"I dunno," I said. "I think boy trouble is pretty universal to high school girls. Although maybe not everyone does therapy via seaweed wraps . . ."

"Oh no," SBB said, snapping shut my planner. "Don't tell me something's wrong with you and Alex?"

"Far from it," I said, glad to be able to admit that. "It's Camille. She and Xander split up yesterday."

Before I knew it, I had spilled the whole story to SBB—from my early morning coffee and complaining session with Morgan, to my convo in line with Amory and Harper, to the sad sight of one very heartbroken Camille across the cafeteria, to the final realization that all of my friends wanted to boycott the first dance I'd every actually been excited about.

"But you *must* go to the Valentine's Dance, Flan," SBB said. "Think about how great you and Alex will look together all dressed up!"

"I know, but it won't be any fun if all my other friends bail," I said. I sneaked a glance around the vending machines to check in on Camille. She was dabbing her eyes with her handkerchief and Morgan was standing up, red-faced and waving her finger in the air—clear signs of an anti-boy tirade in progress. Making it to the Valentine's Day dance didn't look good.

"Flan," SBB said, looking at me like I was missing a really obvious solution to my problem, "how many times have you seen my movie *Heartbreak Hotel*?"

"Only about three hundred." I laughed, remembering SBB's role in last summer's smash hit about an eccentric millionaire living in the Beverly Hills Hotel. "You made me read Ronny Pepp's lines opposite you for a month before shooting started, remember?"

SBB nodded. "You do a really great Ronny Pepp," she recalled. "And you must also remember the brilliant idea that my character came up with when all her friends were heartbroken. . . ."

Simultaneously, SBB and I exclaimed: "She fixed them all up with dates!"

"Exactly," SBB said, looking proud of herself. "Look, you know a ton of guys. And all your friends are megacatches. I'm sure you could fix them up with Valentine's Day Dance–worthy dates in no time." SBB put her hand to her chest like she was about to make a grand confession. "I may not know high school—*yet!*—but I do know about matters of the heart. Trust me, all it would take to turn your crew around is a little bit of matchmaking."

I nodded. "You're so right," I said. "None of them would be anti-boy if I could find them the right boys! Flan the matchmaker. Why didn't I think of that?"

Feeling immediately more empowered about the fate of my Valentine's Day, I sneaked a final peek at my pals across the lunchroom. Everyone had stood up to recycle their trash—everyone except Camille, whose head was back in her hands in her Hunchback of Thoney pose. Hmmm. Finding a match for Camille should probably be my first priority.

"Flannie?" SBB asked innocently. "You're not going to tell anyone who I am, are you? I won't be able to really immerse myself if I know that my disguise isn't airtight. My Jakey-pie told me that I need to try to lose myself in my role while I'm here." She grasped my hands tightly. "You'll help me be a real live high school girl, won't you?"

Even as my mind was scrolling through all of the guys I knew, I had to laugh at SBB's earnestness.

"Don't worry, Not-SBB. Your crazy secret is safe with me."

Chapter 7

A few hours later, I was terry-cloth robe–clad and lounging in the ladies' waiting room at Bliss spa on Forty-ninth Street. Around me, Harper, Amory, Morgan, and Camille flipped through fashion magazines and munched on platters of olives, cucumbers, spicy hummus, and apple wedges. Usually, I loved this pre-spa treatment ritual at Bliss, but today I was consumed by the fact that I still hadn't gotten a chance to check in on Camille about how she was handling the breakup.

Across the room, I caught her eye. "Whoops," I said, looking down at my wrist. "Just realized I forgot to take off my watch." I cocked my head toward the locker room while holding Camille's eyes. "I'll just go throw it in my locker so it doesn't get all seaweed-wrapped."

"Me too," Camille said, stuffing her wrist in her

pocket to hide the fact that she'd already taken off her watch. "I'll go with you."

Once we were out of earshot of the other girls, I gave Camille a big, silent hug.

"Where've you been all day?" she asked, her voice breaking slightly. "I looked for you at lunch."

"I . . . uh . . ." I stalled, remembering SBB's plea for secrecy, even from Camille. "I realized I had to help Ms. Demsey with the layout for the newsletter. But I've wanted to talk to you all day. Everyone kept saying how bummed you've been, and after I saw Xander last night, I tried to call you, but—"

"Wait, you saw Xander last night?" Her forehead wrinkled and she bit her lip. "Why didn't you tell me?"

"I tried to call you all night," I said, putting my hand on her arm. "When I didn't hear from you, I figured you weren't up for talking. For what it's worth, Xander looked pretty upset about it."

"Good, I hope he looks upset." Camille crossed her arms, getting the giant sleeves of the terry-cloth robe tangled up in each other. "No, I don't. Yes, I do. I don't know, Flan. I've never been so confused."

"What happened with you guys?" I asked, helping to untangle Camille from her robe. "Everything seemed so good."

Camille nodded and sniffed. "He said it was *too*

good. He said he got scared. Does that sound like the biggest lie you've ever heard or what?"

I was about to say no, that in a way I understood what it felt like to be nervous about feeling so strongly about someone, but when I saw the fire in Camille's eyes, I knew that wasn't what she wanted to hear.

"I refuse to mope around forever," she huffed. "And I will *not* be one of those bitter girls who sits around on Valentine's Day, crying into a box of tissues, watching Lifetime movies and eating Lindt's."

The image of film-snob Camille watching Lifetime movies made both of us laugh.

"I need to snap out of this funk before you guys start thinking of me as your downer friend," she said, as if she were convincing herself.

"Camille," I said, tossing my watch in my bag and snapping my locker shut again, "I know you pride yourself on being the world's most positive person— and I love that about you. But this breakup just happened yesterday. You might need to give yourself a little time to feel it."

As soon as I said the words, I realized that completely went against the plan SBB had helped me hatch about getting my friends hooked up with new guys for the Valentine's Dance, but it felt like the right thing to say. Camille was going through something heavy. It might have to be up to her to decide when she was ready to move on. I realized then that if she needed me to skip the Valentine's Day Dance, I'd do it without question.

"Hey girls." Amory stuck her head into the locker room. With a grin, she attempted her Swedish masseuse impersonation, sticking out her chest, batting her eyes, and raising her voice intonations an octave. "They're ready for our treatment!"

We all cracked up. When I first met Amory, I was drawn to her funky style and effortless poise. Now what I loved the most about her was what a huge goofball she could be. She could always come up with something to lighten the mood.

"And," she continued, shimmying her shoulders, "guess who's working today?"

"Georgio?" Camille and I gasped at the same time. Georgio was an immaculate bronze god masseur from Greece. We hadn't seen him since the last time we'd all fought over which one of us would be the recipient of his magic touch.

Now Amory grinned and raised her eyebrows. "We all agreed to donate him to *you* today, Camille."

"Oh, you guys, I couldn't possibly accept such a gift," Camille said, swatting her hand. "Well, okay, if you insist."

But hey, if my friends wanted to nudge Camille

toward drooling over other guys, I was definitely all for that.

We filed down the tranquil hallway into the lavender candlelit group massage room. Five beds were set up like lotus petals, with all the heads facing one another so we could chat while the spa technicians worked their magic. We all lay down on our stomachs and grinned.

"It's been too long since we've done this," Harper said.

"Waaaay too long," Morgan agreed, closing her eyes. "The last time we were here, they were playing Carrie Underwood on satellite radio."

Leave it to Morgan to categorize time according to what music was in or on its way out.

"Maybe I should get dumped more often," Camille said. "You know, to give us a reason to indulge."

When everyone's face fell, she added, "I'm *kidding*, you guys. I don't want us all to feel like we have to tiptoe around it. Xander broke up with me. Life goes on, right?"

"Right," we all agreed, looking down at our beds.

In a rare moment of chattiness, Georgio leaned down to Camille and said, "Whoever hurt you is an idiot, Princess. A beautiful flower like you should have any man she chooses."

Even in the dimly lit room, I could tell Camille was bright red. But Georgio was right: Camille was a total catch. Maybe what she needed now was a guy who wasn't afraid to remind her of that. It was a shame Georgio wasn't a viable option.

Camille sighed. "Maybe I just need to, you know, put the whole thing out of my mind."

Exactly! I thought. Put Xander out of her mind with the help of an older, more mature, more Georgio-like guy.

"Exactly," Morgan said. "Which is why the rest of us have sworn off boys indefinitely to support you. Right, girls?"

"Right," Harper chimed in evenly, and Amory nodded in agreement.

"Right," I added. Sigh.

I looked up at the other girls to see if I could gauge what they thought of Morgan's guy-ditching doctrine. Harper looked stoic as usual. In fact, something about the way she was lying there, sheet-clad, reminded me of someone. . . .

It struck me out of nowhere. She looked exactly like the subject of a painting in our country house in Connecticut! Patch's artist friend Trevor had painted it last summer when he was studying at Julliard, and my mother thought he was so talented that she'd bought it to hang over our fireplace. I remembered my mother grilling Trevor about his blossoming talent, but when she'd asked him who his muse was, he'd blushed and stammered that he hadn't met her yet. He had just painted his ideal beauty.

I wondered if Trevor was still painting in New York. And I wondered how quickly I could arrange to introduce him to his future muse. . . .

"Flip," my decidedly un-Georgio-like masseuse commanded. I turned over onto my back so the hefty Swedish woman could slather the cool green seaweed mask on my other side.

I closed my eyes and continued to let SBB's matchmaking advice marinate in my thoughts. Where was I? I'd already come up with a type of guy for Camille—now I just had to think of the right older, handsome man for her. And Harper would be totally excited when I told her about my plot to make her an artist's muse. I craned my neck to the side to look at Amory to see if inspiration would strike a third time. She caught my gaze, winked, and stuck out her tongue at me.

Good, now what guy did I know who was as much of a ham as Amory? He would have to have the same stylish exterior and goofball interior—ooh! What about Alex's actor friend, Phil, from the movie premiere? He'd looked pretty amazing in his Kenneth Cole pin-striped suit. And he had been cracking jokes all night. I'd have to ask Alex if he was single. . . .

"Flan? Are you in?" Morgan's voice brought me back to reality.

I looked around the lotus of friends' heads around me. "Of course," I said, without having any idea what I was agreeing to. "Yeah, I'm in."

"Good," Morgan said. "I'll double-check with my parents that our cabin's free next weekend. We'll ski and drink hot chocolate and Jacuzzi and we won't even miss the Valentine's Day Dance at all!"

Wait—what? The Valentine's Day Dance was one thing, but had I just agreed to skip town with the girls the entire Valentine's Day weekend? How was I going to explain that to Alex?

As Morgan went on and on about how much fun we were going to have rejecting boys forever, I could feel my matchmaking plans slipping away from me. And I realized how fast I was going to have to act if I were to have any hope of salvaging the romance of Valentine's Day for my girls—and myself.

The next day after school, Morgan and I grabbed a cab and headed to SoHo, to the classy French bistro Balthazar. We were taking a photography class together and had to do a partners photo shoot where the focus was on food. Since Balthazar has some of the most gorgeous (and incredibly delicious) pastries in the universe, we figured there was no better excuse for a field trip.

"Oh my God, I love this song. Can we turn it up?" Morgan asked the cabdriver on the way downtown. She turned to me. "They never play the Kinks on the radio, can you believe this?" She grinned, singing along to the funky rock music.

I nodded in agreement, even though most of the time Morgan's music references were sort of over my head.

"My parent's have the best Kinks vinyl collection

at our cabin," she said. "I'll have to play some for you when we go up there next weekend."

"About next weekend," I started to say. I knew I had to come clean to Morgan that I wasn't as gung-ho as she was about abandoning Valentine's Day, but I wasn't sure how to bring it up.

"Oh, here we are!" Morgan told the cabdriver as we paused on Spring Street to pay the fare. "Let's just hope Balthazar has enough taste to spare us the Valentine overload."

"A romantic French café?" I joked. "That's likely."

Inside the restaurant, the red leather banquettes were packed with cappuccino-sipping power-lunchers, miniature poodles tucked into handbags, and a few saliva-swapping newlyweds. I thought the Valentine's decorations hanging from the ceiling were totally taste-ful, but Morgan looked at me and made a gagging motion with her finger.

We decided to eat before we worked, and slid into a booth as far away from the Cupid's arrows and groping couples as possible.

Morgan had just ordered a palmier and a latte, and I was looking forward to my linzertorte and Earl Grey tea, when I felt a strong hand grip my knee under the table.

"Flan, OMG." Morgan's face was white. "*Random Exeter Boy* is over there."

She pointed at a couple two tables down, though I could barely see the guy because his face was being swallowed by a waif girl with dyed red hair. I'd actually never had a chance to meet Random Exeter Boy back during his short-lived romance with Morgan, so I didn't know what to expect. I did know that Morgan was way cuter than the girl he was with today. I looked at Morgan to see how she was taking it, and to my surprise, the color seemed to be coming *back* into her cheeks.

"Hey." I grabbed her hand under the table. "How you doing? Do you want to leave?"

"You know what," she said. "I never liked the way he parted his hair. And look at how he kisses. It's all wrong. Yuck. He hated the Kinks too, if you can believe that! Plus, he does this really weird impersonation of his pet turtle that I just don't think I could ever be cool with."

"I'm gonna need a visual on that," I said.

Morgan scrunched up her lips and retracted her head back into her neck and started speaking in this really slow, hilarious, if-turtles-could-talk voice.

I started cracking up, and when Morgan saw my face, she started laughing too. By the time the waitress arrived with our snacks, we were practically rolling out of the booth.

"So yeah, enough said." I laughed, raising my mug of tea to cheers Morgan. "Looks like it's a good thing Random Exeter Boy didn't exactly come out of his shell. You should never be with someone who doesn't appreciate the Kinks."

When Morgan finally stopped laughing, she sighed. "You know, in a city this big, sometimes I think it really is fate when you run into someone you've been avoiding. Here I've been beating myself up for weeks imagining Random Exeter making out with someone else. Now that I've seen it up close, I'm so not worried about what I'm missing."

"Good," I said, offering her a bite of my linzertorte—and instead of disdaining the heart-shaped, red jelly–filled cookie, she took it.

"This is amazing," she said, wide-eyed. "I can't believe I've never tried one of these before."

"Wait—hold that pose," I said, pulling out the battered old camera I'd gotten for my birthday in sixth grade. "I think this could be just the look I've been trying to get." As Camille posed for delicate bites of the most Valentine's-y of cookies, I took almost a whole roll of film. With all the votives on the tables and the dusk outside, the lighting was perfect, and even more noticeably, something in Morgan's face looked lighter than it had just minutes before. I wondered if now was the right time to bring up the dance.

"Morgan," I said hesitantly, "I know we all agreed to go to your cabin next weekend, and it sounds really great, but—"

"But you want to go to the Valentine's Dance with Alex," she filled in. I nodded. "I know," she said. "I thought about that last night. Maybe I was a little too forceful with my whole solidarity thing. You shouldn't be punished for having a cool boyfriend."

"But I do want to be there for Camille," I said.

"Listen," Morgan said, taking a final shuddering glance at Random Exeter. "Next Tuesday is our pre–Valentine's Day Girls' Night Out. Camille was telling me all about how the two of you used to celebrate in middle school, and she wants to reinstate it this year."

I'd forgotten how much fun those nights used to be—no boy pressure, just exchanging valentines with your friends and doing the gushy stuff guys usually only pretend to like on Valentine's Day.

"We'll go all out for Camille that night and see how she's doing. We can adjust our plans for the weekend based on her needs."

That sounded fair. The bottom line was that we both did really care about Camille—we were just showing it in slightly different (and, well, personally gratifying) ways.

As we paid for our pastries and grabbed our coats, I said, "You know, it *might* cheer Camille up to go to the dance. What if I could find her a really amazing date? Doesn't any part of you want to go too? Especially now that you've got proof positive that you're over Turtle Man in there?" I stuck my thumb in the direction of the still-making-out prep school boy.

Morgan bit her lip. "Yeah, right, who would I even go with? I'm so sick of these private school boys who think they're so great. All they want to do is trade up. It's like, just pick a nice girl and stick with her—"

"Morgan," I called, "look out!"

Her tirade was cut abruptly off when she ran smack into a tall, dark-haired guy in a red ski cap who was turning the corner from Broadway.

"Whoops!" Morgan said. "I'm sorry."

"No," the guy said, "I'm sorry." He looked at me. "Flan?"

Huh? I looked more closely under the ski cap and noticed that the tall stranger was Rob Zumberg—Terrick Zumberg's cousin, whom I'd hung out with last fall in Nevis.

"Hey Rob!" I said. "Long time no see." I looked at

Morgan, who was eyeing her collision victim pretty closely. "This is my good friend Morgan. We go to Thoney together. Morgan, this is Rob. He was our resident brilliant musician in Nevis over Thanksgiving break."

"What do you play?" Morgan asked, looking super interested.

"Guitar mostly, but I can also play the saxophone and the accordion," Rob said. He was shifting back and forth on his feet and stammering a little bit. I'd forgotten how shy he was.

"Oh my God, I've always wanted to learn to play the accordion," Morgan said. At least she was giving him some positive reinforcement!

"It's really easy to learn," Rob said. "I could show you sometime."

Then both of them looked at me, either to seek my permission to hang out with each other . . . or maybe because I was getting in the way?

"You know what?" I said, catching the vibe. "I've got to head home and read up on how to develop these pictures tomorrow—"

"Oh no," Morgan said, looking stricken. "I completely forgot to take any pictures at Balthazar." She turned to Rob and laughed. "We were supposed to do a food photo shoot and Flan came all the way down to my neighborhood to go to Balthazar and then we started talking and—wow, that was dumb."

"You live around here?" Rob asked. "I'm two blocks up. Well, if you need another food subject for your shoot, I could show you my favorite French café. It's not as over-the-top as Balthazar, but—"

"Sounds perfect!" Morgan practically exclaimed.

"Okay, I'll just—" I started to say.

"Okay, 'bye, Flan." Morgan waved, grinning. "I had so much fun!"

I laughed and waved good-bye to both of them. I could tell Morgan was having even more fun since she literally ran into Rob.

Rob Zumberg! Why hadn't I thought of him before? I mean, he was a little on the quiet side, but he was sooo into music. He was such an obvious choice for Morgan. Everything about this afternoon seemed so serendipitous. Meeting Rob right on the heels of seeing Random Exeter boy? You couldn't write that kind of stuff! As I started walking up Broadway toward my house, I had to smile. My first real match had basically fallen into my lap.

Chapter 9

I was halfway home when my phone started ringing and the very adorable picture I'd snapped of Alex at Wollman Rink popped up on my screen.

"I've got a bone to pick with you," Alex said when I answered.

I froze in the middle of Washington Square Park South, nearly colliding with a pedicab full of tourists.

"What is it?" I asked, feeling my heart climb into my throat. "Is something wrong?" Had Alex found out about my friends wanting to ditch the dance?

"Yes," he said, sounding serious. "Something is very wrong. We've been dating for almost a month and I just realized that I have no idea whether or not you can bowl."

He was joking. My heart resumed its normal pattern as I mime-apologized to the red-faced pedicab driver.

"The thing is," Alex continued, "I'm kind of unstoppable on the lanes. So you have to be able to hold your own. I think you should probably come meet me at Bowlmor ASAP so we can resolve this."

"You only think you're unstoppable because you haven't seen my skills," I quipped back, regaining composure. "So wait, you're at Bowlmor right now?"

"Yeah." He laughed. "I'm with Saxton and Phil. And it'd be a whole lot more fun if you were here."

Hmmm, if Harper had been standing over my shoulder, she'd have told me that a boy is supposed to give you at least forty-eight hours advance notice if he'd like to take you out. But Alex had always chosen spontaneity over relationship rules. And I really did want to see him—not to mention destroy him at bowling in front of his friends.

"I'm on my way," I said, hooking a right on Eighth Street.

When I hung up the phone, I was grinning as I replayed the conversation in my head. It was cool that he was out with the guys and still wanted me to crash. And Phil was the exact friend I'd decided on fixing up with Amory! And Saxton, with his model frame and deep green eyes, might be just the thing to take Camille's mind off her Xander woes for a little while. But how to phrase this to make sure my friends wouldn't see this as a violation of their boy boycott?

NERVOUS TO MEET ALEX AND HIS FRIENDS AT BOWL-MOR TONITE. COME BOWL BADLY WITH ME FOR MORAL SUPPORT?

Luckily, within minutes I had an affirmative from Amory, who wrote: I'M DOWN, BUT CAN'T PROMISE I'LL BOWL BADLY—BOWLING TEAM CAPTAIN SEVENTH GRADE!

Two minutes later, Camille said: BEATS STUDYING FOR MY ART HISTORY EXAM ANY DAY. C U SOON. . . .

Perfect! And I'd thought the Morgan/Rob connection had fallen into my lap. Something in the cosmos must have wanted me to be a matchmaker. I should probably start my own business, get a Web site—

"Flan." Amory interrupted my thoughts at the swinging door to Bowlmor. "Think I can bowl in these?" She pointed at some truly amazing hot pink patent leather Betsey Johnson platforms. "I'm not so into the eyesore of the bowling shoe."

"If you can bowl in those, you might become my fashion idol," I said, giving her a thumbs-up. "Good timing," I said. "There's Camille."

Both of us leaned in to tag-team air-kiss Camille, whose hazel eyes looked bright under her lavender velvet hat. "So I haven't cried yet today," Camille said. "That's good, right?"

"Good! Great!" Amory and I cooed as we stepped inside the jerky red elevator that would spit us out at the lanes. Having a brokenhearted friend, I realized, was kind of like raising a small child. It took a village. And every minor moving-on achievement felt like a giant leap for womankind.

Once inside Bowlmor, we were bombarded by flashing disco lights, pumping eighties music, and the strangely pleasant scent of old leather shoes. As Camille and I ordered matching size-eight red-and-blue bowling kicks, Amory impressively avoided the shoe exchange altogether.

We grabbed a round of diet cherry Cokes from the bar and scoped out the scene for Alex and his friends.

"There they are," I said, pointing to the far lane, where Alex was programming the computer with names.

"Whoa," Amory said, fanning herself. "Who's the Adonis? He's almost as amazing looking as my shoes." She nudged Camille. "Do you *see* that guy?"

Camille nodded, though she wasn't even looking at Saxton. "Mmm," she mumbled without conviction. "He's cute."

"Hey guys," I called out to Alex and his friends. "I brought company."

"Oh," Alex said, taking in the even numbers. "Cool. Uh, Camille and Amory, these are my old lacrosse buddies, Phil and Saxton. Hey, Amory, aren't you into acting? You should talk to Phil. He's a pro."

Phil laughed. "I spent eight hours today 'working' as an extra on the Bohn Brothers' new apocalyptic movie in the Meatpacking District. I'm now the resident expert on how to collapse from radiation poisoning."

"At least you got to go out dramatically," Amory said, typing her name in under Phil's on the computer screen between the lanes. "My last part in the school play was as a corpse."

As Phil motioned for Amory to grab a seat next to him and started in with, "Let me tell you about my first role as a corpse," I looked at Alex. Had my boyfriend just jump-started the exact match I'd been about to initiate myself? Speaking of perfect matches! I pulled him in for a quick kiss.

"Hey you," he said into my ear. "You look pretty sweet in those bowling shoes. Too bad they won't help you beat me."

"I'll accept your apology for underestimating me after the game." I grinned, but my smile quickly faded when I looked at Camille, who was looking at her feet and twiddling her thumbs. I felt a physical pain at seeing my most fun friend having the least amount of fun imaginable.

"So, Saxton," I said, scrambling for conversation, "what position did you play in lacrosse? Camille and I just finished a pretty intense field hockey season."

"Cool," Saxton said, fixing his gorgeous eyes on Camille. "I was left forward; what'd you play?"

"Not very well," Camille responded.

Saxton nodded politely, but then said, "I think I'm gonna go grab a heavier ball."

The game got under way without any more painful moments with Camille. I was definitely enjoying watching Alex, who was, true to his boasts, by far the best bowler in our game.

"Okay, okay," I said, sidling up behind him after three straight rounds of knocking down only one or two pins. "I was all talk. I haven't bowled since back when it was still okay to use bumpers. Got any tips, Master of the Strikes?"

"I knew it was only a matter of time before you'd come crawling back to me," Alex joked. "Okay, the thing about bowling that most people forget is that halfway through the set, the scoreboard screen tells you exactly how to position your next ball toward pins you need to take out." We walked out to the line for my second roll. Alex stood behind me. "See, if you're looking at a six-eight-nine lineup, you want to look at the ball like this."

I wasn't entirely sure what he was talking about—though I did like his hands over mine on the ball—but I sure wished there was a magic screen somewhere telling me how to position my friends toward the right guys. Despite my confusion, with Alex as my good-luck charm, I managed to take out six whole pins that time.

"Oh my God," I exclaimed. "Bowling is so much more fun when you score!"

I looked over at Camille, who was fixated on watching the balls whirr out of the machine. Sigh. At least Amory and Phil seemed like they were hitting it off. I couldn't hear their conversation, but they were both making really exaggerated facial expressions and gesturing wildly with their hands. In just a few hours, I'd found a music freak for a music freak and a thespian for a thespian. I guessed Camille's case might just take a little bit more special attention. I wondered if I knew any guys who were desperately heartbroken and looking to be fixed up. . . .

During my next round of bowling, I'm sorry to say,

I did not achieve the same success I had immediately following my lesson from Alex.

"I'm starting to think you might just have to stand up there with me every time I bowl, like a tandem coach on a skydive," I said.

Alex nodded. "I have no problem with that."

Since it was now sort of a pattern with me to have a sweet moment with Alex and follow it up with a guilty glance at Camille, I looked over at my friend again. Oh good, she was talking one-on-one with Saxton!

I stepped closer to stealthily eavesdrop, but as soon as I tuned in to their conversation, I actually wished I hadn't.

"When he broke up with me," Camille was saying, her hand over her heart, "it was like a piece of me died. I've been walking around in a daze every since. Like I'm not even awake. Do you know what I mean?"

Saxton was nodding, but I could tell it was less of a sympathetic nod and more of a how-quick-can-I-bail-on-this-convo kind of nod. He looked at the screen and sprang to his feet.

"It's my turn," he said briskly. "I'll, uh, I'll be right back."

Camille didn't really seem to notice Saxton leaving or me plopping down in his seat. I put my arm around her.

"You know what the most fun thing about bowling is?" I said.

Usually Camille would have jumped to reply, "Obviously, watching everyone's butts." But today, she missed her cue.

So I had to use my fingers to rotate her head toward Saxton. He was bending over to bowl in some very fitted Diesel jeans.

"Now," I prompted, "isn't *that* more fun to look at than the ball-return machine? Don't you think he's hot?"

Just then, Alex appeared, holding a plate of jalapeño poppers with a stiff look on his face. He sort of half held out the plate to us, then turned and offered some to Amory and Phil first. That was weird.

Uh-oh—he hadn't heard me talking to Camille, had he? He couldn't really think I meant *I* was into Saxton.

It was time for my last frame and I nodded at Alex to join me. He didn't wrap his arms around me this time; he just told me which direction to aim for.

"Is everything okay?" I asked, while both of us faced the pins.

"Of course," he said. "Why wouldn't it be?" His voice sounded normal, but I wasn't convinced. I didn't want to make a big deal out of it; I could definitely just have been being paranoid.

After the game, when everyone grabbed their stuff and took the elevator back down to the street, he gave me a good long kiss.

"Saxton and I both live uptown," he said. I couldn't help wondering whether he was trying to gauge my reaction at the mention of his friend. "You'll be okay to get home if I share a cab with him?"

"Sure, yeah," I said. "Study date tomorrow?"

"Cool," he said. "See you then."

Camille, Amory, and Phil all shared a cab down the east side, but since I was going west, I decided to walk. I sort of wanted to clear my mind about how the night had gone. At least the Phil and Amory thing had felt like a success. And when Alex and I were bowling at the beginning together, I'd been having tons of fun. I just hoped I hadn't screwed anything up by trying to get Camille to focus on Saxton.

My cell phone buzzed and I pulled it out, hoping to see Alex's face on the screen, but it was a text from Morgan.

I'd forgotten all about her pseudo-date with Rob. I hurriedly read her message:

BE HONEST: WAS THAT WHOLE "RUN-IN" A PREMEDI-

TATED SETUP? HE'S NICE AND ALL, BUT I DON'T NEED YOUR PITY, FLAN. IT'S EMBARRASSING.

What? That was my least tactical fix-up ever! How had she gotten that idea? But knowing Morgan, this hiccup would seriously hinder any future attempts I might make at fixing her up by Valentine's Day. I guessed I was just going to have to find the *perfect* guy to make it up to her. But if not Rob, then who?

Chapter 10

On Wednesday, I showed up to my study date with Alex lugging two big tote bags full of books. I had tests in three of my classes over the next week, but lately the only work I'd been doing was Cupid's.

We'd agreed to meet at Westville café in my neighborhood, a tiny hole-in-the-wall that sold local art off its walls and had a never-ending stream of West Villagers rushing through its velvet-curtained entrance. The place was famous for the number of gourmet hot dog options on the menu, which was surpassed only by the number of body piercings sported by the waiters. I liked it because of the seasonal veggie plates, massive pots of tea, and out-of-this world carrot cake.

I grabbed a table by the window and was in the midst of talking myself into skipping the meal and moving straight to dessert, when the door chimes jangled, the velvet curtain parted, and my Prince of New York stepped into the bustling restaurant.

I once overheard my mom tell my aunt that every time my dad walked into the room, even after all these years, she still felt a little bit of a rush. I'd been about ten at the time, and remembered making a theatrical gagging motion while sprinkling crushed red pepper flakes on my microwave popcorn. But now, watching Alex scan the tiny restaurant for my face—then light up when he spotted me—I totally understood where my mom had been coming from. Something about the sensation made me feel really lucky to be exactly where I was.

"That's quite a load of books," Alex said, taking off his peacoat and black Agnès B. scarf and sliding into the seat across from me.

"Maybe it only seems like a lot because you didn't bring *any*." I laughed. "Don't you ever have homework?"

Alex shrugged. "You say 'study date,' I hear 'alone time.'" He leaned over the table to kiss me. "It is sort of hard to reserve you sans entourage sometimes."

"Hey," I teased, sliding down so Alex could hang his coat on the hook next to mine. "It takes an entourage-haver to know one."

"Touché." Alex laughed.

I was eagerly awaiting an appropriate moment to pump him for details on Phil. Amory had practically bombarded me after French this morning for information about Phil's status, relationship history, mother's maiden name, blood type, etc.

The waiter arrived, tongue ring flashing, and delivered Alex's medium-rare cheeseburger, no onions, and my large, gorgeous three-tiered slice of carrot cake. In fact, it looked so amazing that I took out my well-worn camera to snap a few pictures for the food assignment in my photography class.

Alex raised an eyebrow at me. "I know you like cake, but what are you now—the dessert paparazzi?"

"It's for a class," I told him. "And don't make fun of my crappy camera. It's practically vintage. Here, take a look." I pulled out the portfolio of Balthazar shots I'd developed in the darkroom at school earlier. Spread out on the empty table next to us, all the black-and-white photographs of shiny croissants, dramatic layered napoleons, and crusty brioches did look pretty striking.

Alex examined the pictures and then me. "You took all these yesterday? And developed them today? I'm impressed."

"Thanks," I said, glad that he thought they looked okay. "Morgan and I went to Balthazar after school yesterday. I didn't know the pics were going to turn out so well. I've never worked in a darkroom before."

I realized I was blushing. Even though I was really into the class, I felt sort of funny talking about it to Alex so seriously. So instead of getting all technical, I found myself blabbing about my *other* recent hobby.

"I left the restaurant with a roll of pictures," I said lightly. "Morgan left with a date. Well, it was sort of an impromptu date. And it didn't even turn out that well. She actually got sort of mad at me because—"

I looked up and could tell that I'd lost Alex somewhere along the way. He was giving me that smile that meant he was just this side of utterly confused.

"Hey," I said, changing the subject, uh, slightly. "Have you talked to Phil since last night?"

"Phil?" Alex squirted Tabasco sauce on his burger and looked even more confused. "I figured you'd be more interested in knowing about Saxton—"

"Nah," I accidentally interrupted him. "I figure that's a lost cause."

Alex didn't respond. He seemed to be taking a really long time to chew.

"Oh my God," I said, clapping my hand to my forehead. "I meant it seemed like a lost cause *for Camille*. And I was asking about Phil because Amory was into him. You didn't think I was—did you think I was . . ." I trailed off.

"Interested in them?" Alex said, putting the remains of his burger down to wipe his hands. "I don't know."

"Alex," I said, putting my hand over his. "Not even close. You have no reason to be jealous. This whole thing started because—"

"What whole thing?" he said.

I realized then that I hadn't really voiced my master plan to anyone since SBB concocted it on the fly behind the cafeteria vending machines. I took a deep breath.

"Well . . . I'm sort of on a mission to hook all of my friends up with dates before Valentine's Day." There, I'd said it. It didn't sound *that* crazy.

"That sounds crazy," Alex said, shaking his head. "I mean, your friends are great, but come on—some of them are pretty picky when it comes to guys."

"I thought being picky was a good thing," I said coyly. "That's how you ended up with me."

"Fair enough." Alex winked at me. "But why is it your job to find everyone a date?"

There was a time when I would have been too embarrassed to admit the girly truth to my boyfriend. There was a time when I might have come up with a really far-fetched story to explain it away. But tonight when I looked at Alex, I knew he'd appreciate total honesty the most.

"The thing is," I stammered, "after Xander and Camille broke up, my friends rallied behind her and . . . I know it sounds dumb . . . but they wanted us all to swear off guys for Valentine's Day."

"But you're not going to do that," he snorted, then paused. "Right?"

"Of course not," I said, forcing myself to look him in the eye, even though I was nervous. "I've been really looking forward to spending Valentine's Day with you. I just thought that if my other friends had guys that made them feel . . . you know . . . like you make me feel, they'd get over the whole boy boycott and then we could all just have an awesome time together at the dance."

"So that's why you brought the girls last night," he said, processing my insanity.

I nodded. "And that's the *only* reason I was asking about Phil and Saxton . . . and uh, checking out Saxton's butt."

Alex wiped his forehead with the back of his hand. "Well, *that* is a relief. I was wondering if I needed to be doing squats or something," he joked.

"So even if you don't manage to find dates for the

entire student body before next week, can we still spend Valentine's Day together?" Alex asked as I doggie-bagged the rest of my carrot cake to bring home to Noodles.

We shook on it. As he helped me into my coat, I realized that yet another study date had passed without either of us cracking a book. At least I'd come clean to Alex about the reason for my interest in his friends. And I *had* snapped that shot of the carrot cake for my photography class.

Outside, the night street was cold and quiet and we walked to the end of the block listening to our feet clack in unison on the pavement. The windows of the West Village storefronts were mostly dark, but you could still see signs of Valentine's Day in the displays.

Alex put his arm around me. "I guess the good-boyfriend thing to do would be to offer some help on the matchmaking front."

"Think of the perks!" I said happily. "If all our friends are hooked up, we'll have so much more time to hang out with each other."

"So you want me to talk to Phil about Amory?" he asked. "And I wouldn't necessarily consider Saxton and Camille a lost cause. I don't think her pout stopped him from thinking she was pretty cute."

As we turned the corner onto Perry Street, I faced Alex and put my arms around his neck. At that moment, we might have looked to anyone else like one of a million clichéd pairs caught up in pre-Valentine's bliss, but when Alex leaned in to kiss me, I felt like we were the only couple in the world.

Chapter 11

*I*n the halls the next morning, I could tell that Morgan was keeping her distance from me. Even though I'd apologized via a really funny e-card yesterday, we were giving each other some space. I was still getting used to Morgan's somewhat fiery temper, and knew that usually her little flare-ups lasted only about as long as a coat of mascara.

But two days after our tiff over Rob, her air-kiss didn't have its usual warmth, and she still hadn't shown me how her latest batch of photos turned out.

By lunchtime, I was anxious to set things right. When all my friends were seated at our table, I marched into the cafeteria with a peace offering of chocolate-covered strawberries, a bottle of her favorite Teavana iced tea, and a plan.

Just before I sat down, Kennedy walked by, glanced at the tray of chocolate-covered strawberries in my hand, and snickered. "At that rate, someone's not going to fit into her Valentine's Dress."

"Oh, I get it," I said evenly, relishing the fact that after so many years, I was finally able to snap back at Kennedy without breaking a sweat. "I guess the concept of sharing would be foreign to me too, if I had as few friends as you do."

"Slamming comeback," Amory whispered when I sat down at the table. She popped a strawberry into her mouth. "You're getting good at the Thoney social wars."

"I've definitely had enough practice," I responded, passing around the tray. "Who wants?"

"Thanks, Flan," Harper said, helping herself. "What's all this?"

"I have a confession to make," I said, meeting Morgan's eyes. She looked like she was s-l-o-w-l-y thawing out.

"What's up?" Camille asked, looking up from the notebook she'd been doodling in. Hey, that was classic Camille—I was glad to see even the smallest shift away from the droopy-eyed, catatonic woman of the past few days.

Here went nothing. For courage, I channeled last night's memory of getting Alex on board with my matchmaking effort—and the very amazing kiss that had come afterward. I took a deep breath.

"I promise I did not premeditate that run-in between you and Rob the other night, Morgan," I began. "But the truth is, when we bumped into him and I introduced you guys, I *did* think you two could hit it off. I know you don't agree, but I need you to believe that I didn't go behind your back."

Morgan sighed. "It didn't seem like something you would do," she said. "It's just that you rushed out of there so fast, I felt abandoned, like you just pawned me off on the first guy that came along."

For the record, this was not exactly true. From the way Morgan latched onto Rob, I'd thought she'd be thrilled to air-kiss me good-bye. But since I figured this was just her hurt pride talking, I said:

"Not even, Morg. Rob's so into music, I thought—"

"Most people on earth are into music," Morgan said. "Would you pawn me off on most people on earth?"

I looked at my other friends, whose faces indicated Morgan had a point. This was not going so well. Maybe I needed to find a new way in.

"The other day at the spa," I said, fiddling with the stem of a strawberry, "you guys were all so into the boy-boycott idea. I know I'm odd girl out because I want to spend Valentine's Day with Alex, but it's more than that. I want to go to the dance with all of you." I turned to Morgan. "The Rob thing happened by chance, but if I admitted that I have been thinking about fixing you guys up with dates for Valentine's Day—would you hate me?"

The table was quiet. No one looked ready to hurl a chocolate-covered strawberry in my face, but they also weren't jumping up and down with joy.

After what seemed like an eternity, I sensed a different kind of commotion out of the corner of my eye. When I looked over at the entrance to the cafeteria, I saw a girl with black pigtails and a green beret waving her arms at the French teacher, Madame Florent. The bereted girl was shouting in French—and I caught a few very choice slang words that they definitely didn't teach you in language classes at Thoney.

Omigod, was that SBB? She'd totally dropped off my radar the past couple of days. I sort of assumed she'd gotten tired of her undercover student project and rented *High School Musical* for research. Wrong. SBB's high school stamina was still going strong, and today it seemed refocused on playing as a foreign exchange student.

I looked at my friends, who still hadn't responded to my matchmaking proposal, and weighed my responsibilities.

"I totally forgot I have to check on something in

the darkroom," I said, slinging my bag over my shoulder. "Why don't you guys think over what I said—I'll be back in a few minutes and we can discuss."

Before they could answer, I hurried toward the spectacle of my starlet pal. I loved her, but the girl was like a wildfire. She needed to be managed before she spread.

By the time I reached her, Madame Florent had exited the scene and SBB was red-faced and huffy.

"Thank *God*," she cried when she spotted me. "Where have you *been*?"

"Shhh," I whispered, looking around at my classmates, who were taking a keen interest in the loud, kneesock-wearing girl who slipped a little too easily in and out of her French accent. "Maybe we should go somewhere more private." I tugged her back into the cafeteria and we ducked behind the vending machines.

"Good, yes, I can work in this space," SBB said, closing her eyes and breathing deeply. "It comforts me. And I have never needed comfort like I have these last few days. Why didn't anyone tell me how hard high school is?"

I laughed. "I rest my case of the past six months."

"At least you're a good student," SBB moaned. "I thought this research was going to be all about navigating the social jungle, but ever since I enrolled in this awful school, they've been springing these assignments on me. I failed my French test this morning. Do I look like the type of girl who can afford to fail a simple French test?" she wailed. "Look at me."

"It's hard not to," I said, taking in SBB's wild argyle knee socks, skinny tie, tortoiseshell glasses, and the large black mole she'd drawn in over her lip. "What are you going for with that look, early-nineties Cindy Crawford?"

"Hello—*French foreign exchange student*? Which is why it is not cool that I flunked that test today. Now Madame wants to call my mother! Imagine Gloria's reaction if a high school teacher called her to talk about my grades. Uh-uh, no way!"

As SBB rattled on about her academic struggles, I sneaked a peek at my friends around the corner of the vending machine. I was getting strangely used to the view from here. They looked engrossed in a conversation, and I really wanted to be over there to make sure it was going in the right direction. One pessimistic remark from Morgan could throw off the gravity of the whole table and send them back over to the dark side of the boy boycott.

"So I gave Madame your cell number." SBB was still talking. "So you'll remember to pretend to be my mother when she calls, right?"

"Huh?" I said, tuning back in. "You want me to what?"

"Is someone back here?" A throaty voice, followed by an unwelcome face appeared behind the vending machines. Willa Rubenstein looked positively devilish in her red Stella McCartney sweater. "Flan? Did you get a part-time job stocking the vending machines?"

SBB stepped forward and before I could stop her, she adjusted her beret and piled on the Frenchy. "I vas lost." She shrugged. "I am new and Flan iz helping me find my way to ze class."

Willa looked at SBB, then at me, then back at SBB. "Honey, if you want to get to know your way around Thoney, I'd suggest a better tour guide. *Au revoir.*"

After the she-devil disappeared, SBB winked at me. "I know you hate her, but don't you love how helpful she is to my research?"

I groaned and dragged her out from the vending machine hideaway just as the bell rang to announce the end of lunch—and the end of my chance to talk to my friends about Valentine's Day.

SBB was oblivious. She was tugging on my arm and looking at me with wide eyes. "So you'll help me, right? I need to focus on fitting in—not French class."

I was flustered by Willa and bummed at the sight of my friends heading up the stairs without me, so without thinking I jerked my arm away from SBB.

"Look, I don't really have time to be your mother right now, SBB. If your French is bad enough that you fail a French test, maybe you should have picked a smarter cover." I nodded at her outfit. "Anyway, you're drawing way too much attention to yourself to fit in here. I have to go."

I knew I'd left her stranded in the hallway looking stricken, but she wasn't exactly making it easy to help her. Plus, I had my own issues to take care of, not the least of which was the chemistry test I had to take right now.

I rushed to my locker to grab my periodic table, and when I opened it up, two notes fell out.

The first one was scrawled on loose-leaf paper in Amory's signature purple pen:

Okay, okay, we've agreed. matchmake us. May the best date win.
XO, Table Four

The second note was a postcard with a photograph of an old darkroom with black-and-white prints hanging to dry. On the back, it read:

It's coming into focus how great you are. Be my valentine?

Always,

Your secret admirer

My heart skipped a beat. Alex must have been thinking about the photos I'd showed him from the Balthazar shoot. I loved that he understood perfectly how important photography was to me.

If he could make me this swoony over a simple card, I couldn't wait to see what our first Valentine's Day would be like.

Oh, shoot. I'd been too busy to think about my (lack of a) gift for Alex until this little reminder. Valentine's Day was exactly a week away, and the only thing I had to show Alex how much he meant to me was the mocket I'd bought with SBB and Camille. It was more like a gag gift. The pressure was definitely on to find something deserving of a guy who left swoonworthy love notes in lockers.

With the stress of my chemistry test behind me, I took out my Kate Spade planner to pencil in a shopping trip for Alex's gift 2.0 after school. But first, I had a meeting for the Valentine's Day Dance committee. It was ironic to be planning an event that I might not even get to go to, but it was also the perfect way to make up for my dismissive behavior to SBB at lunch. She didn't know it yet, but being dragged to an extracurricular meeting was exactly the kind of drama that would bolster her understanding of the life of a high school girl.

Just before last period, taking a cue from the note-droppers in my life, I raised—or dropped—a white flag into SBB's locker.

When I found her after school, she was tapping on the padlock, murmuring what sounded like some kind of chant into the slats of her locker.

"What are you," I said, coming up behind her, "the locker whisperer?"

"What are *you*?" she replied. "The friend abandoner? How the heck do people open these things?"

"What's your combination?" I asked.

SBB looked confused; then a flash of recognition came across her face. "Oh, that's what those numbers are for?" She rummaged through her massive yellow JanSport backpack, and when she caught me giggling, she dropped the bag with a thud and said defensively, "What? The guidance counselor told me this backpack is really good for the spine. It distributes the weight evenly across your shoulders. I'm carrying a lot of heavy books here, Flan; it's not like I can be fashion-forward every second of my life—"

"Calm, calm." I coached, putting my hand on her shoulder. "Which is why I'm going to show you how to use your locker. You can keep some of your books in there."

She sighed. "I'm sorry. I'm just stressed." She turned and pointed a finger at me. "And you didn't make it any better. I've never been *dissed* in the hallway before! And even though, from an acting perspective, it was kind of good for me, from a friend perspective, *I did not like it*."

"I know." I nodded. By then, I had opened up her

locker. It was dusty and empty, save for my little white envelope. "Which is why I'm going to make it up to you now."

"What's this?" SBB reached for the envelope. "My first note! I wonder who it's from!"

As she tore into the envelope, I had to wonder whether she'd be disappointed when she found out that it was only from me, but when she read my message, her face lit up. "You want *me* to join you at a dance committee meeting? I'm so excited—see, this is the kind of thing I had in mind when I signed up for this torture. Okay, you're forgiven!"

As I pulled a happily chattering SBB down the hall to the student activities lounge, I wondered whether I should warn her about how to act in front of everyone on the planning committee. I was about to open my mouth to put out a few suggestions, when I felt a tap on my shoulder.

"What's all this?" Kennedy asked, waving her hand dismissively at SBB. "The dance committee is an elected position, Flan, and what goes on there is top secret. You can't just bring anyone you want to sit in."

Leave it to Kennedy to be a stickler for the rules as long as they worked against me.

"This is a new student, uh, Simone," I stammered. "She just moved here from—"

"Chicago," SBB responded, working the Midwestern accent. "The headmistress matched me up with Flan, since she was a former new student who adjusted really quickly—"

"That's debatable," Kennedy said, rolling her eyes.

"You debate with your headmistress?" SBB asked innocently. "Anyway, the headmistress told me explicitly that the best thing I could do for myself would be to follow in the footsteps of a model student like Flan."

Oh boy, SBB was taking this a little far. Now Willa had joined the conversation, and she was definitely going to remember SBB's French persona in the cafeteria. I decided to do some damage control.

"I'm sure if you have a problem with Simone sitting in on the committee," I told Kennedy, "you can take it up with the headmistress."

That might be enough to shut them both up. Ever since Willa had been implicated in a treasury scandal last month, both she and Kennedy were on academic probation. There was no one who made them more nervous than the headmistress.

"Whatever," Kennedy said, unlocking the student lounge and taking a seat at the head of the table. She gestured toward the back of the room, where a lone desk was set off from the conference table. "She can sit in the back if she signs a confidentiality agreement."

"Yay! I'll have my agent fax a standard nondisclosure—I mean, I used to plan dances all the time at my old school in Chicago, but—" SBB squealed until I nudged her to shut up.

Willa took a seat next to Kennedy and narrowed her eyes at SBB. "Weren't you the girl behind the vending machine at lunch? Weren't you *French?*"

Whoops.

"I just act French for an hour before and after every French class, to immerse myself." SBB tilted her head seriously. I wished she would just stop talking so she wouldn't dig herself in any deeper, but I was too far away to nudge her again.

"So the Valentine's Dance," I said, changing the subject. A few other girls from our class had filed into the meeting, and I didn't think everyone needed to be privy to SBB's methodology. "It's one week from tomorrow, and we still don't have a theme, right?"

"What about Romeo and Juliet?" my friend Dara asked, brushing her long black hair behind her ears. She was the secretary on the student council, so she referenced her notes from our last meeting.

"Lame," Kennedy dismissed her. "Shakespeare's not sexy."

I glanced at SBB, whose face had that "ooh, I know about Shakespeare from a movie I once made" look on it. Before I could stop her, she'd climbed on top of her chair.

"O Romeo, Romeo, wherefore art thou, Romeo," She spouted off the lines so theatrically that her beret fell down over her eyes. "A rose by any other name would smell as sweet—"

"*What* are you doing?" Willa asked. She and Kennedy were the only ones in the room nasty enough to ask, but I could tell from the other girls' faces that they were all thinking the same thing.

"We learned Shakespeare," SBB said, "at my old school . . . in *Chicago*. Yeah, I took a test over it and everything."

I covered my face with my hands. Maybe this hadn't been such a good idea.

"What's your point?" Kennedy said, then turned to glare at me. "Flan, your shadow is being disruptive."

"Uh," I stalled, "I think her point is that Shakespeare is romantic, right, Simone?" I raised my eyebrows at SBB to try to get her to sit down and just observe.

"No," Willa said flatly. "I'm class president and I veto that idea. Dara, what else do we have?"

As Dara flipped through her notes, SBB got back up on the chair. "That's dictatorial!" she said, throwing out a word she'd loved since playing Napoleon's mistress in a smutty period piece. "At my old school, in *Chicago*, we always voted to democratically settle such important matters."

"This isn't your old school, in *Chicago*," Kennedy hissed. "At this school, in *New York City*, we socially annihilate people who annoy us."

I had to stop SBB before she made any more of a spectacle of herself. I knew from experience that SBB had to feel needed in order to stay out of trouble. I racked my brain for a task to keep her occupied.

All I had in my not-so-good-for-the-spine Muxo schoolbag was the portfolio of prints from my photography class. Without much of a plan, I pulled them out and slid them across the table to SBB.

"Uh, Simone," I said quietly, "I was wondering if you could help me figure out which one of these to blow up and turn in for my final project."

SBB/Simone looked flattered and immediately set to work. For three blissful minutes, she was focused on flipping through my prints, and the conversation about the Valentine's Dance got shakily back on track.

"Kisses on My Pillow, Love Me Do, Red Hot Valentine . . ." Dara listed off the uninspiring ideas for themes.

"Who came up with these?" Kennedy demanded. "They're all completely forgettable."

I glanced at Dara's notes. Kennedy's name was listed next to each of the bad ideas we'd come up with at the last meeting, but I could tell Dara would rather take credit for them herself than point this out to Kennedy.

"The ideas themselves aren't terrible," I chimed in. "It's just they're sort of vague. We need something concrete. We need a concept. After that, coming up with the ideas for decorations, music, and activities should be easy."

"What about . . ." SBB/Simone said. The room waited impatiently for her to articulate. I just hoped she wasn't going to get back up on the chair.

"What about this one?" she finally said, laying one of my photographs on the table. Of all my prints, this one was particularly well shot and well developed. It was an image of the perfect Balthazar linzertorte.

"You're right." I smiled at SBB. "This is exactly the print I should use for my class."

"Not only that," SBB/Simone said, laying on the hard *a* in *that* like a true Midwesterner, "it's also the perfect theme for the dance: *Picture Yourself in Love*." She turned to the other girls on the committee, but stayed—mercifully—in her seat. "What do you guys think? We could blow up giant classy prints of romantic city shots and hang them on all the walls for decoration. We could have one of those photo button-making machines and give the buttons out for favors."

As I looked around the table, everyone seemed pretty intrigued by the idea. Even Willa and Kennedy hadn't thought of anything nasty to say—and that was huge.

"Ooh." SBB grinned. "And you know that song they keep playing on the radio, 'Picture You with Me'? Who's that by again—that really hot guy?"

"Jake Riverdale!" Dara chimed in. "Love him."

"Me too." SBB/Simone grinned. "That could be the theme song!"

I held back a laugh. The undercover pimping of her boyfriend's new hit single was definitely SBB's best acting of the day.

The whole table spoke up so enthusiastically that it was clear everyone was on board. I couldn't believe that by the time the meeting adjourned, the details for the Valentine's Dance had totally come together.

"Okay," Kennedy huffed, clearly pissed that allowing SBB/Simone into the meeting hadn't been a mistake. "We'll meet again on Wednesday to finalize the details. *Everyone* better be here."

As SBB/Simone and I walked out of the conference room arm in arm, I leaned in to whisper, "That was *amazing*. Are you sure you didn't go to high school?"

"Didn't you figure me out?" SBB asked. "I was just channeling you, Flannie. You're my high school role model. You know the way you get when you're planning something and your nose gets all scrunched up and serious." She laughed. "Do you think they bought it?"

Looking back at Kennedy and Willa huddled in the doorway, I was sure that they must have. SBB/Simone had been so convincing—even though it was a little embarrassing to learn that I did that scrunching thing with my nose.

But just before we turned the corner, I overheard Willa's voice and froze.

"I've got cousins all over Illinois," she hissed to Kennedy. "I'm going to put out some feelers about this *Simone from Chicago*."

I realized I'd better warn Simone that it might be time for a costume change.

Chapter 13

A few minutes later, SBB and I were waiting outside Thoney for her driver.

"Am I getting the hang of high school, or what?" she asked.

I was just about to tell SBB that tomorrow, she might even consider dressing like a normal New Yorker—instead of a professional student—when she pointed at the black town car slowing to a stop in front of us and clapped her hand to her forehead. "Shoot, is it a dead giveaway of my stardom that I'm being chauffeured home?"

I shook my head and laughed. "Are you kidding? At Thoney? Take a look around," I said, pointing to the line of town cars picking up the greater number of the girls who'd been at the dance committee meeting.

"Wow," she said. "High school and Hollywood

113

seem more and more similar every day. In that case—want a ride home?"

I looked down the street at the busy Park Avenue rush. It was nearly dusk, my favorite time of day in New York, and for a change, it wasn't bitterly cold outside. I shook my head and helped SBB into her car.

"Thanks, but I think I'm going to walk a bit. I've still got to find a Valentine's gift for Alex—" I caught myself. "I mean, to supplement the mocket."

SBB looked at me curiously. "Going above and beyond the mocket, huh? You must really like this one."

As she drove away, I started walking south on Park, trying to convince myself not to get too bogged down by the pressure of this Valentine's gift exchange. My family always said I had the magic touch when it came to gift giving. For as long as I could remember, every birthday and Christmas present I'd picked out had always received the most genuine oohs and ahhs out of anyone in my family. Part of that had to do with the fact that the rest of my relatives usually had their assistants do their shopping for them, but part of it also had to do with the fact that I put a lot of thought into my gifts. From the remote-control tracker device that I'd bought for my mom on eBay, to the chocolate fountain I'd given Feb for her twenty-first birthday, I always managed to come up with gifts that were personal and functional and unique.

Now, as the sun set in between the gray Midtown high rises, I moseyed in and out of the shops along Madison Avenue. I had made it all the way down to Midtown without finding anything, when I found myself in front of my favorite bookstore in the city, Rizzoli.

I stepped inside the impressive high-ceilinged shop, breathing in the crisp smell of new books and thinking that even if I didn't find something for Alex, I still wanted to check out their section on photography. I was sidling around a giant display of Valentine's Day books for children, when I hit a roadblock—a very tall roadblock.

"Excuse me," I said to the tall, dirty-blond-headed guy in a Weezer shirt. He was fully obstructing the only open path past the displays. I mean, who even wore Weezer shirts anymore? But I knew that Weezer shirt!

"Bennett?" I said as my ex-boyfriend spun around to face me.

"Flan?" he said. "What are you doing here?"

At first I felt guilty about admitting that I was here shopping for my current boyfriend—after all, Bennett and I had broken up because I was on the brink of a new romance with my *other* ex-boyfriend, Adam. Or did we break up before I met Adam? It was sort of hard to keep the timeline straight. The point was, I'd always felt a little bit of residual guilt/fear that I had broken Bennett's heart.

But looking at him now, he looked like his happy old Bennett self. Everything about him, from his chipped front tooth down to his worn T-shirt and frayed jeans, looked exactly the same as it had when I'd first fallen for him.

"Oh, you know, I'm just browsing." I shrugged. "What about you?"

From the way Bennett's face lit up, I thought he might tell me that he was shopping for his new girlfriend—not that that would bother me—but he just smiled and said, "I've been doing research on old film reels to try to learn more about the history of moviemaking. This place has a great section on old movie books. It's so cool, like a whole secret world."

"That's great," I said, wondering how genuine my excitement sounded.

Seeing Bennett all jazzed up about movies reminded me of all the ones he'd dragged me to watch last fall. He was the film editor of the *Stuyvesant Spectator*, and I'd always tried to support his passion for review writing, but let's just say after seven films about evil Russian clones, my enthusiasm had started to wane. For a second, the matchmaker in me came alive, and I thought that what Bennett needed was to be with someone who was just as into movies as he was—someone like Camille.

But then I remembered Morgan's harsh words in the lunchroom during the Rob Zumberg rift, and I pictured her standing over me saying, "A lot of people like movies, Flan. Are you going to pawn Camille off on just anyone who likes movies?"

No. I shook my head at the imaginary Morgan. I wasn't going to make that same mistake again.

So I looked at Bennett again and reconsidered my intentions. There was more to it than Bennett just being into movies. There was something specific about the *way* he approached his hobbies. He wasn't just interested in writing a good story or movie review; Bennett wanted to know the secret history behind everything he got involved in.

Which actually made him a way better candidate for someone like . . . Morgan! She was all about finding the secret anecdotes about her favorite bands. She spent more time poring over obscure music Web sites than she ever did on her homework. And she was forever telling us about which Beatle had written which song for which of his bandmates' wives. Totally something Bennett would do in his movie research. I also remembered the way Bennett had lightheartedly kidnapped and set free the frogs in my biology class last fall, when I'd been so stressed about animal cruelty. He was so laid-back that even when Morgan stressed about ridiculous stuff like extra-loud cappuccino makers at cafes, he'd be able to talk her down.

Bennett was grinning as he showed me one of the black-and-white books he'd found, and I caught a glimpse of his famous chipped tooth. Morgan *had* always had an unexplainable fondness for imperfect teeth. She claimed it was the Anglophile in her. It was undeniable: Bennett was the perfect match I'd been seeking for Morgan all this time.

He closed the book and looked up at me to see if I approved. "What do you think?" he asked.

"I think . . ." I said, grinning at him. "I think I'm wondering if you're seeing anyone."

Whoops, did that sound like a come-on?

"I mean, I've got this really great friend at Thoney, and I think you guys might be good together. That is, if you're single."

Bennett blushed and looked down at the ground. "Well, I mean, yeah, I am single. But . . . would that be weird?"

"I don't know," I said. "Would it?"

I couldn't tell from the tone of Bennett's voice whether he thought it would be weirder for me or for him. I didn't think it would be weird on my end, but I wasn't sure about Bennett. It wasn't really like me to think like this, but looking at his face, it crossed my mind that Bennett might not be over me.

Finally he shrugged. "It wouldn't be weird for me . . . if it wouldn't be weird for you."

"No," I said quickly. "It wouldn't be weird for me. It was my idea."

"Good," he said, thumbing through the books on the display case. "Okay, cool."

"Cool," I said, looking for something to keep my hands busy too. "So I'll text you Morgan's number and you can give her a call?"

"Sounds good." Bennett nodded. "Well, it was good to see you, Flan."

He gave me an incredibly awkward hug and hurried out of the store. I couldn't figure out which of us was responsible for that hug feeling so uncomfortable.

"I'm sorry, ma'am," a store clerk said from behind me. "We're closing. Did you want to take that *Mommy's Favorite Valentine* book?"

I looked down at the cartoon illustration on the

cover of the picture book I'd accidentally picked up while talking to Bennett. Not exactly the gift I had in mind.

"Uh, no thanks," I said, as she ushered me out the door to the dark street.

I guessed I'd have to put off my Alex shopping one more day. At least I'd gotten a little shopping done on Morgan's behalf. Now I all I had to do was convince her that this latest fix-up would be worth her while.

Chapter 14

*I*t was unseasonably warm the next day, so the girls and I decided to skip out from under the fluorescent cafeteria lights, grab some sushi from Haru, and park ourselves on the front steps of the Met during lunch.

Maybe it was the sunny weather, maybe it was just that it was Friday, or maybe it was the fact that I had very impressively arranged a slew of blind dates for my friends for tonight, but we were all having too much fun to think about going back to class.

Morgan had brought her inflatable speakers and was playing the Vampire Weekend CD I'd given her last week. Amory was making shadow puppets out of her sashimi. Harper was reading everyone's horoscopes off her BlackBerry, noting that all of our Romance Factor numbers for the day were abnormally off the charts. And Camille and I were participating in one of our favorite Met steps pastimes: selecting three guys off the street and playing Kiss, Diss, or Marry.

"Ooh, kiss," she said about a businessman crossing the street with an alligator Hermès briefcase.

"*What*? Diss—Camille, he's like forty."

"Forty and fiiine. Look at that luscious bottom lip." She pursed her own lips and made a smooching sound.

I pushed her playfully off the step and grinned. "I've missed this."

"What, me drooling over silver foxes?"

"You know what I mean," I said. "You being, well, you. I've been worried about you for a few days."

"It's still hard," she said. "Xander e-mailed the other day to see how I was doing, but I'm just not ready to talk yet. I'm trying to keep my mind off of it, you know?" I nodded. "Now remind me who this guy is that you're fixing me up with tonight?" she said.

"Camille," I said, incredulously, "it's Saxton. Alex's outrageously hot friend who you met at Bowlmor the other day? Don't you remember talking his ear off about your breakup?"

"Ugh." she shook her head. "Hazily. I guess I was still in a self-pity coma. Wait—I talked his ear off about Xander and he still agreed to go out with me?"

"He thought you were hot. Guys are able to over-look small flaws like emotional baggage to get a date with a gorgeous girl." I shrugged. "You're meeting at eight at Mary's Fish Camp. Wear that green leather skirt from Takashimaya, and just, uh . . . maybe try to focus on a new topic of conversation tonight?"

Camille nodded. "Got it. Okay, what about you, Harper? Who's our little yenta fixed you up with?"

Harper's cheeks flushed lightly. Even her embar-rassment was ladylike. "A painter," she drawled.

I'd managed to get Trevor's number from Patch, who confirmed that he was in New York and single. I wasn't sure Trevor would remember me, but when I called him last night, he actually sounded really excited. He said he'd had some bad experiences with blind dates before, so I'd agreed to show up with Harper for the first half hour to moderate their intro-ductions. It actually worked out perfectly, since Harper was a little wary of the whole blind fix-up thing as well. I knew once Trevor saw what a babe Harper was, and once she saw how cool and talented he was, they'd have no problem with me skipping out.

"I've never dated an artsy guy before," Harper was saying as she touched up her French manicure. "It feels so rebellious!"

"Just make sure you tell your parents that he also

graduated first in his class at Xavier so they'll let you out of the house," I coached. "You and I are going to meet at Grey Dog's at seven, and we'll have coffee with Trevor before I send you off on your own."

"What should I wear?" Harper asked.

I thought back to the image Trevor had captured in his painting. "Pearls," I said, glad that this request wouldn't be much of a challenge for Harper. "Pearls with something classy and black."

I turned to Amory, but before I could instruct her on the details for her date to see *The Adding Machine* with Phil, I spotted a familiar green beret dashing up the steps toward us.

Uh-oh. I'd been able to tone down SBB/Simone at the dance committee meeting yesterday, but I wasn't so sure I could maintain her cover in front of my friends. What was she doing here?

"Flan—here you are! I've been looking all over for you." SBB/Simone sank down on the steps. Today she looked like a schoolgirl from the fifties in an argyle cardigan, pleated gray skirt, and oxford shoes. Her hands were full of poster boards, Magic Markers, protractors, and a big Ziploc bag full of erasers. She looked like she'd just robbed a Staples store. And she clearly still hadn't figured out how to use her locker. In fact, she was so bogged down with school supplies, she didn't even notice the rest of my friends.

"After that committee meeting last night," she said hurriedly, "I decided that I need to join more clubs. That's the only way to round out this experience. So I signed up for the choir, the science fair, and the 4-H club. Did you even know Thoney had a 4-H club? Well, there's only one other member, but apparently that's all it takes to make a club so—"

Harper cleared her throat. SBB stopped talking and looked around, taking in my crew. For a second, I was sure her cover was blown. How were we going to explain this to my friends? I looked at Camille, who'd be the most likely of any of them to un-incognito SBB, but, amazingly, she seemed oblivious to the starlet in our midst.

Maybe it was because of how confident SBB was in her acting abilities. She just shifted her posture slightly, put on the Midwestern accent again, and stuck out her hand.

"I must have left my manners back in Chicah-go," she said. "I'm Simone, your new classmate at Thoney. You must be Flan's posse. She's told me absolutely everything about you."

I could tell my friends were a little thrown by a stranger knowing absolutely everything about them, especially when I'd never even mentioned having made a new friend. Still, they were polite enough to introduce themselves and act normal.

Which was more than I could say for SBB/Simone. After she pretended to learn everyone's names, she fixated back on me.

"So anyway, now I'm just stressing that I've signed up for *too* much. I feel put out, stretched thin, you know? I'm giving myself wrinkles and my face is insured. But then I remembered: overcommitments are my Flannie's specialty. So you can help me, right?"

"Um, actually," I said, looking around at my very confused friends, "I'm already a little overcommitted right now. I've fixed everyone up with dates tonight and I need to go over the details." I explained this last part slowly, to help jog SBB's memory that this whole matchmaking venture had been her idea—and that it was important to me, and my Valentine's Dance future, that everything go smoothly. Hint, hint. "Maybe we can meet up later?" I suggested.

"Oooh," she said, finally getting it. "I'll just wait here quietly until you're done."

Groan. Somehow I doubted that SBB was capable of waiting quietly for anything. I looked at my watch. We only had ten more minutes of lunch and I had a lot of dating ground to cover.

"Okay," I said. "Back to Amory. Your case is the easiest one, since you've already sparked with Phil."

"Oooh! Love those initial sparks," SBB cooed. I shot her a look to shut up.

"But what if Phil remembers me differently and doesn't like me this time around?" Amory used the last piece of her sushi shadow puppet to mime terror.

"Impossible," I said, shaking my head. "Just meet him outside the Provincetown Playhouse near NYU at seven-thirty, be your crazy self, and you'll be golden."

"Wear perfume," SBB chimed in again. "Actor boys love perfume."

"*Simone!*" I hissed.

"*Sah*-rry," she said sheepishly. "Shutting up now."

Luckily, after that, SBB stuck to her word, and I was able to get through the details of the final fix-up without interruptions.

"Morg, since you and Bennett are both crazy about Middle Eastern food, you're meeting him at eight-thirty at Moustache. You'll recognize him because he'll probably be wearing a Weezer T-shirt and, when he's waiting for someone, he always stands slightly slouched over, with his hands in his pockets."

"Oh, okay," Morgan said, sounding hesitant. "Remind me how you know so much about this guy?"

I'd conveniently decided to leave out the fact that Bennett was my ex. Morgan was already on the fence about being set up again, and I didn't want to do anything to tip the scales.

"Oh, you know, the usual," I said. "We had a couple classes together and a lot of the same friends at Stuy. He's great," I added. "You'll totally hit it off. But he likes really natural-looking girls, so don't wear too much makeup. And make sure to show up on time. He hates when people are late." I was trying to sound casual, but I could also sense the scrutinizing eye of SBB, who knew all about my history with Bennett.

Luckily, she came through for me and changed the subject. "So Flan, now that you've fixed up all your friends, do you get to spend some quality time with a special someone of your own tonight?"

"Actually, no," I said, almost wishing that I was the kind of person who could kick back with Alex tonight and not worry about how everyone's dates were going. But who were we kidding—this was me. And I'd put a lot of work into making sure everything went just right tonight.

I turned to my friends and shrugged. "I wanted to be around to check in on you guys. Did anyone notice how I conveniently arranged all your dates in the same neighborhood at half-hour intervals? Not that you'll need my help," I joked, then waited for my silent friends to reassure me.

"Of course not," Amory finally said, nodding as if to convince the other girls. "We'll be fine. Right, girls?"

"Right," Morgan said, looking nervous.

"We'll all bring our A-games," Camille said.

Under normal circumstances, I might have joked that hopefully Camille's dating A-game was better than her field hockey A-game, but she was biting her lip in this weird, nervous way, and avoiding my eyes by pretending to be very absorbed by the pedestrian traffic on the sidewalk below.

Why did my friends look so helpless and desperate? Gulp. I crossed my fingers that everything would go smoothly that night—and that I hadn't just made four big mistakes.

Chapter 15

At seven o'clock on the dot that night, Harper and I walked into Grey Dog's café on Carmine Street in the West Village.

"He's late," Harper whispered, looking around frantically.

"You don't even know what he looks like," I said, scanning the restaurant myself. "How can you tell he's not here?"

"I just have a feeling," she said. "If he were here, he'd have an eye out for us."

"So he's fashionably late," I finally admitted. "He's an artist—he doesn't live according to the clock in the same way other people do. It's better this way—we'll sit down first so there won't be that awkward shuffle at the door. Relax. I'll order you a soy latte."

As Harper worriedly picked out a seat, I headed

over to the coffee bar. I'd picked Grey Dog's because it was a total artist hangout, funky yet casual (which seemed to fit Trevor's personality) and because the giant chalkboard menu hanging behind the counter touted a huge selection of vegan-friendly sandwiches and salads (perfect for the nutritionally conscious Harper). True, she stuck out a little in her pearls and black Ralph Lauren sheath dress, but I knew that wouldn't matter once lucky couple number one hit it off . . . assuming he ever showed up.

"Flan," a guy's voice said behind me. Phew—it was Trevor. Oh, and he was hugging me. "Wow, *you're* all grown up. You look great!"

"Thanks," I said, paying for the lattes. "My friend Harper got us a table over there. Come on, I'll introduce you."

"Oh," he said, looking a little disappointed. "She's here already? Did I misunderstand? I thought the two of us would have a chance to catch up and your friend would show up later."

Yikes, thank goodness Harper was out of earshot. She would've been out the door quicker than you could say *gauche*. I glanced at her sitting over in the corner. She'd just spotted me talking to Trevor and gave a tiny wave.

"See?" I gestured at her to Trevor. She was a

knockout, even when she looked as nervous as she did now. "Now, don't you want to meet her?"

For half a latte, I hung around Camille and Trevor's cramped table to help make sure the matchmaking ball got rolling. Trevor seemed polite, if a little bit reserved. Harper was charming, but kind of stiff.

"So what are you painting these days, Trevor," I asked, when their conversation lulled for a moment.

"I've been doing some animal portraits," he said. "In fact, do you still have Noodles? I always had this vision of painting the two of you together."

I don't know why that comment took me by surprise, but I found myself stammering, "You know who loves Noodles? Harper! In fact, she loves all animals. So much that she volunteers at the SPCA on weekends. Isn't that right, Harper?"

Harper nodded, but chose not to elaborate.

"Cool," Trevor said. "So, this portrait of you and Noodles—"

I looked at my watch. Crap! It was already seven-thirty. I was going to have to book it if I wanted to check in on Amory before she and Phil went inside the theater.

"Actually, I've really got to run. Harper, tell Trevor about your Great Dane. I think that's a puppy portrait waiting to happen. Have fun!"

I ducked out of the café quickly, leaving them both with sort of stunned looks on their faces. But it would probably be a lot easier for them to talk if I wasn't there directing the conversation, right?

On my jog over to the Provincetown Playhouse on Macdougal, I pulled an SBB and went just a little bit undercover. I wanted to catch a glimpse of lucky couple number two without Phil recognizing that I was spying on him. Even though Alex was down with my project, I didn't want any crazy-Flan stories getting back to him. So I slapped on the biggest pair of black D&G sunglasses I'd been able to pillage from my mother's accessories trunk, and pulled a feathered fedora over my head. Not total incognito, but if I stayed far enough away, I figured no one would recognize me.

Luckily, when I spotted Amory and Phil, they were way more at ease with each other than Harper and Trevor had been. Amory looked like she was doing her impersonation of Hillary Clinton, and Phil was cracking up. Awesome—they were totally picking up where they'd left off at the bowling alley. My work here was done!

I decided I even had time to run to the bathroom before I dashed over to Charles Street to Mary's Fish Camp to observe Camille and Saxton. But just as I was coming out of the bathroom, I saw Phil heading to the men's room. Amory must still be waiting outside. I dropped my eyes, grateful for the fedora's cover.

"Flan?" he asked. "Is that you? Are you joining us? Great hat, by the way."

Whoops, maybe my cover wasn't as good as I'd thought it was.

"I forgot you two were coming here tonight," I lied, unconvincingly. "I just stopped in because I, uh, really love the fountain sodas they sell at the concession stand. But I'm on my way to meet a friend for dinner. Enjoy the show!"

"Wait," he grabbed my arm. "Before you go, I have a confession to make."

Huh?

"That note you got the other day from a secret admirer? I know you thought it was from Alex, but ever since I met you at the premiere, I haven't been able to stop thinking about you." He looked deep into my mortified eyes. "My cousin goes to Thoney and I had her slip it in your locker."

"But—" I stammered. "You're Alex's friend. And Amory's my friend."

"And she seems perfectly nice, but if you told me I had a chance with you—"

"No way! No!" I practically shouted. What was happening? This guy was definitely trouble.

Eventually, I'd have to break the news to Amory, but I could still see her waiting outside the theater for her dream date to come back from an innocent trip from the bathroom. The only thing I could do right now was get out of there. I looked at Phil. "Let's just forget this whole conversation ever happened, okay? I have to go."

"Flan—wait!" he called, but I was already dashing for the back door.

Out on the street, I did a few of the calming breathing exercises that SBB swore by before an audition. I was still a little shaken up by the time I got to Mary's Fish Camp, but in order to focus on lucky couple number three, I tried to put the whole Phil fiasco out of my mind.

Come on, Camille, I thought as I peered through the window of the tiny fish shack for her long mop of hair. *Please be your charming self so I can feel like at least one date is going right.*

Finally, I spotted her and Saxton sitting at the bar and sharing a plate of mussels Provençal. She'd taken my advice and looked like a total bombshell in her green leather pencil skirt. Whoa—and was that Saxton's hand I saw on her knee? Normally Camille played the prude card for at least three dates. But on-the-rebound-Camille looked down at his hand and even gave him an encouraging smile.

Well, I guess it was finally a score for Flan the Matchmaker. This was by far the date I'd been most wary about, but incredibly, it looked like Cupid had finally touched down. I decided not to jinx it by sticking around any longer and turned south on Seventh Avenue for my final check-in of the night.

During the five-block walk to Bedford Street, my racing around finally caught up with me. I was exhausted, and although I'd been watching other people eat a lot of food, I hadn't had a chance to eat a thing myself. Assuming my checkup on Morgan and Bennett went off without a hitch, maybe I could give Alex a ring and see if he wanted to meet me for a late dinner at Tartine, our favorite French place on West Fourth.

Rejuvenated by my plan, I sped up to tackle my last order of business. The restaurant Moustache was the preferred Middle Eastern joint among city foodies and right up both Morgan and Bennett's alleys. As I turned west on Morton, I expected to find the two of them waiting in line for a table outside and making hesitant introductory conversation.

Then again, I wouldn't have put it past Bennett to

suggest they make a quick stop at some of his favorite (i.e., dusty and disgusting) West Village comic book shops. I shuddered, remembering the way my allergies always acted up in those dingy basement shops he loved so much. Then again, Morgan might be much less allergic to superhero comics than I'd been back in the day.

But when I reached the meeting spot for lucky couple #4, what I saw stopped me in my tracks.

My ex-boyfriend Bennett and my ex-boy-hating friend Morgan were leaning up against a lamppost— totally making out!

I froze, then quickly ducked behind a parked car. I didn't want to look at them, but for some reason, I couldn't turn away. Bennett was doing that thing where he ran his fingers through her hair and—whoa, why did I feel really nauseated? Suddenly, meeting up with Alex for dinner was the very last thing on my mind. My heart was racing and my palms were slick with sweat. What was happening to me?

I couldn't possibly be *jealous* . . . could I?

Chapter 16

After a night of maddening, stressful dreams in which I was on one never-ending date with Alex, who kept turning into Phil, then Trevor, then Saxton, then finally Bennett, I wrestled myself out of bed. At least in my nightmare, I had looked like a goddess in a long, flowing dress and tiara. But when I looked in the mirror, I recoiled at the reality. My eyes were puffy, my skin looked washed out, and my hair was a tangled mess on top of my head. I didn't even know where to begin.

After my unexpected Bennett breakdown outside Moustache, I'd fled the scene and made for my bed as quickly as humanly possible. I'd put my phone on silent, even though I'd sworn to my friends earlier that I'd be available all night for postdate recaps. Now I had four unheard voice messages, most of which I didn't think I could bear to listen to. I wasn't ready to hear whether Amory had found out about what happened with Phil, and I definitely wasn't ready to listen to Morgan gush about what an excellent kisser Bennett had been.

When I noticed the phone vibrating on my nightstand now, I quickly prayed that it wouldn't be her. Luckily, when I looked at the screen, it was SBB. Phew. She seemed like the most likely candidate to take my mind off the weirdness of last night.

"Flan, I need a favor," she said immediately when I picked up the phone.

"What's up?" I asked, trying to avoid looking in the mirror.

"I need your opinion on something," she said. "But I'm at an undisclosed location. I've arranged a helicopter to bring you to me. You'll pick it up at the Chelsea Piers lighthouse in half an hour."

Normally, I might have asked SBB for a few more particulars, like why the trip required a helicopter—when she said undisclosed location, she could mean anything from Central Park to Cairo—but today I just dotted on some Prescriptives undereye cream and started rooting through my closet for a pair of clean jeans. This was one of those days where someone else's drama was going to be a welcome distraction.

By ten thirty-five, I was shivering on the dock

outside the lighthouse by the Chelsea Piers, wondering whether I'd gotten the wrong information from SBB.

Just then, a dark-haired man in tight white pilot pants approached me.

"Flan Flood?" he asked, showing a perfect chin dimple when he smiled.

"That's me," I said, smiling back.

"I'm Rich, and I'll be escorting you to your friend." He was very tan and very Hollywood, as all of SBB's "helpers" had a tendency to be. She'd probably met him on the set of that air force drama she'd been shooting last month.

He gestured to the helicopter that had been hidden from view until a large ship pulled out from in front of it. I felt a bolt of excitement. I'd ridden in helicopters a couple of times before, but never in the front seat, and never next to such an absurdly good-looking pilot.

Rich helped me into the passenger seat and soon we were lifting off into the crisp blue Manhattan air.

"I hope you're not afraid to fly," he said over the roar of the propeller.

"I hope it never ends," I shouted back, holding my hair out of my face and away from the wind. The view of the city was breathtaking, and I soon figured out that we were heading due east. I thought about asking Rich where we were going, but there was something about the mystique of it all that made the ride so thrilling.

Soon, we were crossing over the East River, so I ruled out all Manhattan destinations. I wondered just how far away we were going. . . .

But Rich began to lower the helicopter just behind the giant Coca-Cola sign that marked the allegedly up-and-coming neighborhood of Long Island City, Queens. I'd never really been over here before, but I had seen it showcased on a home makeover special with my mom last week, right before she jetted off to the mineral springs at Ojo Caliente.

SBB was waiting on the roof of a brand-new high-rise building, and when we touched down, she started jumping up and down.

"Hooray," she shouted, throwing her arms around me. "You're here! What do you think? Wait—don't answer that, you haven't even seen what I'm talking about. Close your eyes!"

We waved good-bye to Rich, and when SBB had positioned me where she wanted me, she took her hand away from my eyes. "Voilà!"

As I took in my surroundings, my jaw dropped. We

were standing in a massive empty loft with floor-to-ceiling windows that faced the East River and the vast Manhattan skyline behind it.

"Oh. My. God." I said, taking in the high ceilings, gorgeous hardwood floor, and immaculate kitchen against the wall facing north. "What is this place, SBB?"

"Mine," she gushed. "All mine after last night. Well, mine and JR's too. Isn't it heaven? It's ten thousand square feet of pure real estate bliss."

"You own this?" I asked incredulously. "What are you going to do with it? Are you moving out here?"

"Duh." She shook her head. "I could never leave my town house. How would you survive without me as a neighbor?" It was true. SBB had moved into the town house diagonally behind my family's a few months ago and I loved having her literally a cell phone's throw away.

"No," she continued. "My vision is to turn this place into a supertrendy socialite center. I want to have a restaurant, a lounge, a catwalk for friends to showcase their new lines; of course JR will need a poker table, maybe a spa . . ."

"Wow, SBB, that sounds incredible," I said. "It'll be like the YMCA, except for the young and famous!"

"I don't know what the YMPA is, Flannie, but if

you think this is a good idea, I'll feel way better about the investment. There's just one problem."

"What could possibly be a problem?" I asked.

"The landing pad on the roof only parks two helicopters at a time, so getting here could be a logistical disaster. You're realistic, Flan. Do you think people would really be likely to take a helicopter ride out just for dinner or a game of cards?"

"I think a lot of your friends take helicopters like the rest of the city takes the train—but if you're worried about it, you know, there's a subway stop right outside."

"There is?" SBB sounded honestly stunned. "I have a confession to make. I don't actually have any idea where we are. Are we still in America?" She lowered her voice to a whisper, like insurgents might hear us or something.

I started cracking up. "SBB, this is Long Island City." She still looked entirely confused. "Queens? Ever heard of it? It's part of New York City. You can take the subway. It's super easy. I'll show you on the way home."

"That won't be necessary," SBB said, waving her hand dismissively. "But I'm so glad to know about this subway development in case of emergency. Flan, how did you get so resourceful? And so good at geography? Queens, huh? Who knew?"

"I'm going to start calling you the Princess of Queens," I joked.

"Ooh, and you can invite the Prince of New York to visit my faraway palace next time. How is Alex, by the way? And how did all your friends' blind dates go last night? Step over to where the future lounge will be and tell me all about it!"

We plopped down on the hardwood floor. While we munched on pita chips that SBB pulled out of her massive Lancel tote bag, I told her the good, the bad, and the ugly details from last night's date-a-thon.

When I got to the part about Phil's crush confession and Trevor's overactive interest in painting a portrait of me with Noodles, SBB clapped her hands and laughed.

"It's just sooo fitting that all these silly little boys would fall in love with you, Flannie. Here you were trying to help out your friends and it all backfires. If I wrote screenplays, I would—"

"SBB, this is my life. And it's serious! How am I supposed to explain this to Amory?"

"Listen, honey, one thing they don't teach you in that dreadful high school of yours is that men are fickle, fickle, fickle. Not that you're not lovely and amazing, but it won't be hard to shift these pawns' attention toward the proper queen by Valentine's Day.

Don't even worry about it—I'll be at the dance too and would love to help you keep their hands and eyes where they belong. You would think with how much time boy drama demands of you that your school would devote a class to actually *educating* you girls. This is the first assignment I've been excited about since I started high school."

"Okay," I said, feeling better. SBB did have the magic touch when it came to getting guys to do what she wanted. "But what about Morgan and Bennett? Am I a terrible person for getting jealous of my friend and my ex-boyfriend?"

"Oh, Flannie," SBB said, braiding my hair while she talked. "I'd worry about you if you *weren't* a little bit jealous. These are two people who you care about. It's like, you want them to get along, but you also don't want to lose your place with either one of them."

"You're right," I agreed. SBB might technically have been my craziest friend, but she could also be shockingly wise. "I guess I also feel so weird about the whole thing because I'm so crazy about Alex that I got confused last night by my feelings when I saw Bennett."

SBB stood up and walked over to the window. She looked deep in thought for a minute.

"You know how many other actors I have to kiss for my career, right?" I nodded. "And you know that JR has to do the same thing with a variety of scantily clad idiot young actresses, right?" I nodded again. "Well, I thought I was used to it—until last month, when he got cast opposite Ashleigh-Ann Martin for an untitled romantic comedy set on the moon."

I gasped. Ashleigh-Ann Martin was SBB's known nemesis. "Tell me there's not a make-out scene!"

SBB shuddered and nodded. "But this is our life," she said finally. "I've realized that if I want to hold on to my man—which I do; he's *so* hot—then I have to learn to combat my jealousy. And what works for me is a lot of good old-fashioned quality time."

"You mean you just hang out with JR?"

"Why do you think we bought this giant palace in the land of Queens? I got jealous just last night—so we came out here and met with the real estate agent, and one thing led to another. . . . You don't have to buy a loft with Alex," she said, as if I were actually considering it. "Just give him a call, reconnect, put this weird Bennett thing out of your mind!"

Could the solution to my weirdness be as simple as QT with Alex? It definitely beat moping around the house.

"Thanks, SBB," I said. "I owe you one. Actually, I owe you more than one—"

"Promise to be the first patron at my palace when it opens, and I'll consider us even," she said.

We air-kissed to seal the deal.

Chapter 17

*A*fter journeying from Queens back into civilization again, I decided to follow SBB's advice. Me asking Alex out on a date was somewhat new territory in our relationship, but I bit the bullet and texted him Sunday morning:

HAVE A FUN IDEA FOR THIS AFTERNOON. MEET ME AT ELEVEN AT OUR SPOT IN THE PARK?

Alex wrote back almost instantly:

WEIRD—WAS JUST COMPOSING A NEARLY IDENTICAL TEXT TO YOU. I'LL BE THERE.

When we met up at the top of our favorite grassy hill near the east entrance on Sixty-eighth Street, there were only a few other souls braving the cold outdoors.

Alex greeted me with a kiss and an extralong hug to warm me up.

"So, what's your fun idea for the day?" I asked.

"Uh-uh," he said, "You first—your text beat mine to it."

Good, I'd been hoping I'd get to go first. I grabbed Alex by the hand and led him out toward Fifth Avenue. Just walking next to him made me instantly feel better about the whole Morgan/Bennett situation. Every time I glanced over at his stylish Bally's ski cap and killer smile, I knew that when it came to matches, Alex was the one for me.

When we got to Eighty-ninth Street, I stopped in front of the swirling modern exterior of the Guggenheim Museum.

"Aha," he said, holding open the door for me. "So she's beautiful *and* cultural."

"I was reading online about this really amazing photographer who's exhibiting her prints on the top floor of the museum. We've studied some of her techniques in my photography class. It's only on display this week."

The museum was crowded with buzzing New Yorkers, trying to keep warm with indoor activities. Since the date had been my idea, I stood in line to buy our tickets while Alex checked our coats. He held my hand as we wound our way up through the permanent collection toward the Guggenheim's top floor.

"I haven't been here in years," Alex said. "It was always my favorite museum as a kid because—"

"Because of the wacky winding ramp?" I said, and he nodded. "Me too! And my favorite painting in the whole city is right over—"

"Here?" Alex said. We paused in front of this tiny painting of a wave by an obscure Spanish artist from the eighteen hundreds. "I can't believe it. I've always loved this painting—how it captures the exact moment before the wave crashes."

I bobbed my head in agreement. "I think that's why I'm so fascinated by photography. I like the idea of searching for that one perfect instant to freeze in time."

Alex squeezed my hand. By then, we'd arrived at the top floor where the photographer, Anise Mapple-thorpe, had her sleek sepia prints on display. I couldn't help taking mental notes about some prints that might be the exact style we were looking to use for our decorations at the dance. There were lots of shots of food and even more dramatic cityscape images. I was enjoying the exhibit so much that I almost forgot to see what Alex thought, but when I looked over at him, his eyes were wide.

"I can see why you wanted to come here," he said when we came to the end of the exhibit. "Now, since

I'm going to drag you back out into the cold for my portion of the date, I figure I should sweeten the deal with hot chocolate."

Carrying our two giant Guggenheim café hot chocolates with extra whipped cream, Alex and I braved the cold again as he led me back into Central Park. We stopped in front of the duck pond at one of those telescope machines you pay a quarter to look into. I looked up at Alex, trying to guess what he had in mind.

"There's something I've wanted to show you ever since we started dating. Most people I know would laugh, but this is secretly my favorite place in the city." He slipped a quarter into the viewfinder, wheeled it to a stop, and gestured for me to look through it.

I pressed my nose against the frozen metal ledge and peered through. It was fixed on the top of a high-rise apartment building, and when I adjusted the focus, I could make out a mass of twigs near the edge of the roof.

"It's a nest," I said. "It's huge."

"It belongs to the only known red-tailed hawk in Manhattan," Alex said. "Usually they like warmer climates, but this one's been living there for years."

I looked up at him. A smile spread across my face. "You're an undercover bird-watcher."

"Guilty," he said. "It's pretty hard to be a bird

fanatic in the city, especially without binoculars." He shrugged and looked through the viewfinder. "But I'll take what I can get."

"It's amazing," I said. "I wish I had my camera to take a picture."

"It'll be here tomorrow," Alex said. "What *won't* be here tomorrow is the reservation that a friend of a friend got us for dinner at Nobu tonight."

"Seriously?" I asked. Nobu Fifty-Seven was this ridiculously amazing sushi place in Midtown. I'd been there once and the tuna belly sashimi literally melted in your mouth. I loved that place, but it usually took months to get a reservation.

"Seriously," he said. "I guess the look on your face means you like the idea."

As we started to walk toward the restaurant, I couldn't believe the sun was already setting. Throughout this entire epic date, I felt like Alex and I had gotten to know each other better and better. It was cool to discover new things we had in common even while showing off our separate interests.

At the edge of the park, we paused in front of a hot dog stand to take in the view of the horse-drawn carriages outside the old Plaza Hotel at dusk.

"This is my favorite hot dog stand in the city," Alex and I both said at exactly the same time.

"What??" we both laughed. "Jinx!"

"I can't believe you just said that," Alex said, shaking his head.

"I can't believe *you* just said that. I think it's the relish—there's just something about it."

"Exactly," Alex said, and we both started laughing. "Of all the hot dog stands in the city," he said. "This feels too remarkable to me to go uncelebrated."

"What do you mean?" I asked.

"I mean, who needs Nobu when we have this coincidental love for the same random hot dog stand. I vote we ditch that stuffy reservation and take two of these hot dogs, extra relish, on a carriage ride around the park."

I didn't know any Manhattanite who would skip out on a reservation at Nobu on a whim, but then again, I didn't know anyone else in the world like Alex.

"Sounds perfect," I said. And it was.

I was in such a haze of hot dogs and happiness that I didn't even think to check my phone until I got home at ten o'clock that night.

To my surprise, I had seven missed calls from SBB and fourteen text messages.

11:30 a.m.: NEED YOU.

11:43 a.m.: STILL NEED YOU.

12:12 p.m.: DID YOU FALL INTO A SAMPLE SALE RAB-
BIT HOLE OF SOME SORT AND NOT TELL ME ABOUT IT?

And so on.

Whoops—I felt bad that I had missed her, but I knew it was already too late to call her back. SBB required a lot of extra beauty sleep and was always in bed by the time *Desperate Housewives* ended on Sundays. Well, at least it had been her idea for me to put the Bennett weirdness out of my mind by spending the whole day with Alex. She'd understand if we just caught up tomorrow, right?

*F*ully rejuvenated by my fantastic date with Alex, I arrived at school Monday morning feeling more committed than ever to solidifying my crew's Valentine's Dance matches.

Standing outside of Thoney, I braced the winds to make a quick call to Feb, who'd emerged from couplesville to text me a few pictures of her dancing at some purple-lit nightclub in Shanghai.

"I can't hear anything," she shouted when she picked up. "Hold on, I'm going outside."

"I'm fine, thanks for asking," I said back, holding the phone out at arm's length to preserve my eardrums from the techno music drowning out my sister's voice.

Then there was a slight drop in decibel as Feb found a space outside to say, "Good timing. It's way too hot in there to dance to another eleven-minute techno song. Chinese ravers have insane energy. Insane. What's up?"

"Can you hear me well enough now to give some boy advice?" I shouted, becoming aware of what I might sound like to the other Thoney girls filing past me into school. But I needed a second opinion on the Phil fiasco, and I knew Feb had gotten her share of love notes from the wrong guy before. She'd know better than anyone how concerned I needed to be.

"This reeks of further drama," she said, when I'd finished. "For Amory's sake, I'd cut your losses and move on. She seems cool and there are way too many other, worthier fish in the sea. Look, Kelly's got some cute friends in the city. Why don't I text you some headshots and you can take your pick for a replacement, okay? But I gotta dash—I *love* this song!"

With that, the phone cut out. As Feb headed back into her nightclub, I sighed and headed back into the doldrums of high school. It was times like this when I felt far away from my sister's life, but I knew she'd always come through with some words of wisdom and/or headshots.

"Omigod, Flan," my friend Veronica said when I passed her in the foyer. "Hot trench."

"Thanks." I beamed, realizing with a grin that, even continents away, Feb was a lifesaver in more ways than one. Sometimes, when I missed her most, I did a little retail therapy in her raid-worthy closet full of unworn clothes. Like this morning's choice of the goat-suede Dior trench I'd dug up, rationalizing that since she and Kelly had sworn off animal products, *somebody* ought to wear it.

I opened my locker to hang up my coat and found a CD and, taped to it, a note scrawled in Morgan's hand.

A LOVEly mix to get us in the mood for Girl Valentine's Night tomorrow. Enjoy the tunes and don't forget—no dishing about Friday's dates until we're all together!

Sweet. Morgan always made the best mixes—and more importantly, I'd forgotten the girls and I had made that promise. This bought me a little more time to work on Phil 2.0—and to get used to the idea of hearing Morgan talk about Bennett. Things were looking up!

At my locker, I heard Dara's voice call out, "Supercute look, lady!"

I turned around to accept my second compliment of the morning, but before I could speak too soon, I realized Dara wasn't talking about my Dior trench at all. She was looking at another girl walking down the hall in a charcoal Balenciaga rubber dress that SBB and I had eyed on the runway at last month's fashion week.

Were my eyes playing tricks on me—or *was* that SBB underneath the black wig?

"Hey!" I whispered, when I was close enough to get SBB's attention. "I can't believe you got the dress. It looks *amazing* on you!"

SBB's eyes flicked over my trench coat, then looked past me down the hall. She said nothing, just kept walking toward her locker.

I followed her and put my hand on her shoulder. She shrugged it off.

"SBB," I said, feeling my nose wrinkle up in confusion.

"Don't call me that," she huffed.

"Sorry," I corrected myself. "Simone—"

"Actually, it's *Sally* now," she said coldly. "Things have changed."

"Huh? Look, I'm sorry about yesterday. I saw your messages, but it was too late to call you back. The good news is that Alex and I—"

"Zip it, Flan." She slammed her locker shut. "Do you have any idea what happened to me yesterday? I'll tell you. I ran into your favorite enemy, Willa, on the street—and she seized me. I was literally captive in her French-manicured claws. Thank God I had my wig tucked inside my Birkin for just such emergencies. Anyway, I could have sworn she was about to out me on that little Chicago fib. But instead, because she *hates* you so much, she spent all day giving me a makeover—so I could be 'cool' like her and not an 'FOF loser.' Sorry," SBB said, not sounding very apologetic. "Willa's words, not mine."

"An FOF loser?" I said. I was reeling from all this talk of Willa's seething hatred for me, but something about SBB's behavior was throwing me even more. "What does that even mean?"

"*Friend of Flan*," she said, looking around like she was making sure no one could see her talking to me in her new cool state. "After Willa put out tracers to all her bitchy cousins in Chicago, I had to scramble to come up with a story that I was just a normal girl from Hoboken. Like how I lied because you told me to, so I could seem more intriguing. I tried to call you all day, but you blew me off—and *not* for the first time since I've been at this school!"

"SBB, look, I'm sorry." I didn't like the idea of my friend spending all day with Willa, but I was trying to stay rational. Maybe instead of getting jealous again, what I needed was to schedule some QT with SBB, the way I'd done with Alex. "Let me make it up to you. Let's have lunch, just the two of us, okay?"

She shook her head. "It's just too little, too late. The thing is, after I started to go along with Willa's makeover yesterday, it was . . . fun. There, I said it. I had fun, with your enemy."

I sucked in my breath. That was harsh.

"I can't have lunch with you today." She paused dramatically. "Because I'm having lunch with Willa *and* Kennedy. They want to *include* me in their life— not keep me on the fringes of it. You never let me hang out with your friends."

"That's not true," I said, racking my brain. "You had lunch with us on the steps on Friday."

SBB rolled her eyes. "If you call wearing a virtual muzzle 'having lunch.' And that was only because I tracked you down. Because of you, I haven't had the high school experience I wanted at all. Do you know that six out of ten people at this school prefer a guy who shaves his chest? See, I'm learning things from Willa that will really help my career. When were you planning to teach me anything about being in high school?"

I didn't see what that statistic had to do with anything. And I definitely didn't see Willa as being all that in touch with the pulse of the student body here. But I could also see where SBB was coming from. Maybe I had been a bit preoccupied with my own pursuits during the past week.

"I'll fix this, SBB," I said. "Just promise me you won't let Willa suck you any further over to the underworld before I can make it up to you, okay?"

"Unlike some people," SBB said pointedly, "I don't feel comfortable making promises I can't keep."

"Sally, is that you?" I heard Willa's voice call out. "Awesome, I'm so glad you're wearing the dress. You're such a fast learner."

Shocker, Willa was being totally condescending, but for some reason, SBB seemed to be eating it up.

Then Willa glanced at me.

"I thought we agreed," she said slowly to SBB. "No more FOF-ing. It's not good for your rep."

"Sorry, Willa," SBB/Sally said. She'd lost all traces of her Chicago accent and was now another typical bitchy UES girl. "I was just saying good-bye." SBB turned to me. "So—good-bye."

Before I knew it, my best friend and my worst enemy were walking down the hall, arm in arm.

One day later, and one FOF down, the day that I'd been waiting for since I heard the words *boy boycott* had arrived. No, it wasn't Valentine's Day, but it was an important preliminary step: GVNO (aka Girls Valentine's Night Out, aka the night we'd agreed to gauge whether Camille was emotionally healthy enough to be dragged to the Valentine's Dance).

We were meeting at eight at Stanton Social, and I was the first to arrive. From the coveted back booth overlooking the entire scene, I reviewed the valentines I'd made for my friends. The sophisticated doily-laden Victorian valentine for Harper, the programmable singing card for Morgan, the sleek, modern postcard Valentine I'd picked out at Crane's for Amory, and the platonic Mad Libs love letter I'd written for Camille. When I'd bought the supplies over the weekend, I'd bought enough to make a paper doll Valentine for

SBB, but after yesterday, I'd reached the breaking point. I was so over fighting with Willa over something that should have been rightfully mine. And more than that, I was sick of trying to keep up with who SBB was supposed to be on what day of the week.

Now, as I looked around the room at the other glammed-up patrons in the restaurant—girls in flashy stilettos and Siwy jeans, and guys all freshly shaven and showing a very calculated amount of chest hair— I understood that SBB wasn't the only one in costume. To a certain extent we all were. But costume or not, I reminded myself, there was no excuse for the way she'd ditched me yesterday for Team Willa.

"Hey, there you are," Amory said as she slid into the booth next to me wearing a hot white Chloé slip dress with a plunging neckline. "Harper and Morgan are checking their coats. Where's Camille?"

"Right behind you," Camille chirped. "And I brought a guest Valentine."

She stepped aside to expose a very expertly done-up incognito SBB/Simone/Sally in a brilliant, shorter black wig and a Smart Fitzgerald patterned slip dress. She looked incredible again, but I had to muster some major willpower in order to suppress my groan. It was bad enough that she'd synced up with Willa; now she was moving in on Camille?

"Oh, hi—Simone, right?" Amory said, gesturing for SBB to sit down.

SBB shot me a nervous look. "Actually, it's Sally now. It's my middle name—Simone Sally . . . Struthers—and I think Sally's fresher, more New York, you know?"

As SBB babbled on about the very scientific explanation behind her name change, Camille pulled me aside. "I was leaving Thoney today and I spotted the poor, defenseless thing arm in arm with *Willa*. I figured since the headmistress assigned you to take Sally under your wing, I should help save her from the axis of evil. She's actually super nice—we should hang with her more often."

"Totally," I agreed halfheartedly. I searched Camille's face to see whether she was bluffing. It would be just like her to figure out who SBB was, then cover for me with a few covert winks. But Camille looked genuinely concerned about Sally's social acceptance into our clique. Exactly how preoccupied was she by all of this Xander stuff?

When we were all seated and had ordered enough Kobe miniburgers and halibut tacos to feed a modeling agency, we all passed out the valentines we'd made for one another. As I thumbed through the cards my friends had made for me, I realized that I wasn't the only one who'd personalized the cards based on distinguishing traits: all four of the valentines I received were matchmaking-related. Camille had even sketched out a scene from the *Fiddler on the Roof* as a joke.

"Okay, okay." I laughed. "I get it—you're sick of my obsession with fixing you all up with dates."

"Not even." Harper laughed. "We're just messing with you, Flan. I had a really good time with Trevor on Friday night. After you left, I even let him sketch my shoulder. He said I had remarkable clavicles."

"Oooooh," Amory teased. "You showed a boy your *shoulder* on the first date? Aren't you the girl who recently told me that boys don't buy the cow if they can get the milk for free?"

"He didn't get it for *free*," Harper said shyly. "He agreed to be my date to the Valentine's Dance." She quickly shot a look around the table. "I mean, *if* we decide to go."

"Maybe we should go," Amory said, sipping on her mango iced tea. "I'm sort of into Phil. He was so funny after the play; he was doing all these great impersonations of the characters."

Oh, crap—I *still* needed to figure out how to play off the whole Phil situation. Feb had sent a slew of pics of muscle-y Aussie men, any of whom would be a great substitution. My only problem now would be swapping Phil out without seeming suspicious. In my head, I started scrambling for a tactful way to talk to Amory, but I snapped back to reality when Morgan cleared her throat to speak.

"I know I was the loudest voice for the boy boycott last week." She looked at me and smiled. "But Flan did such a killer job setting us all up last week, I think I'm changing my tune."

"Morgan loves Bennett, Morgan loooves Bennett," Amory sang.

"We've been texting all week," she gushed.

While everyone else started oohing and ahhing over Morgan and her new love interest, I started to get that sinking feeling in my stomach again. Even in the guise of her new persona, SBB was watching me to see how I was coping.

She'd been remarkably quiet all through appetizers, but when she caught my eye, she spoke up. "So what's the problem here, girls? Sounds like you all want to go to this dance. Why the self-imposed boycott?" She flicked her eyes at me, and I felt like this was an attempt to get back on my good side.

The rest of the table had their eyes on Camille.

"What?" She finally shrugged. "It wasn't my idea to start hating all men in the first place. If you guys want to go to the dance, I'll go. I don't think Saxton's my next great love, but he'll do for picture taking."

I could tell that Camille, who thrived on being a good sport, was trying hard to take one for the team. But the fact that she didn't seem to care whether we all went to the dance or not reflected her general ambivalence toward everything these days. I wished there was a way to snap my fingers and take away the residual Xander pain.

"What about you, Sally?" Harper said to SBB, passing around a plate of fruit skewers. "Are you planning on going to the dance? Is there a special someone in your life?"

"You know, it's hard for me to date high school boys," Sally said, "because I have something of an obsession from afar with a certain movie star–pop singer. Confession: ever since I rented his film, *Demolition Dudes*, on DVD, I've been hopelessly in love with . . . Jake Riverdale."

The way she said it was so hilarious—especially because my friends all believed her pathetic crush-from-afar act—that even in my annoyed state, I had to join in with the rest of the table and crack up.

When the laughter died down, SBB/Sally turned to me and said, "You're quiet, Flan. Do you have a date to the Valentine's Dance?"

"Oh, Flan has the best date of anyone," Morgan said, shocking me with her enthusiasm. "She has this totally amazing boyfriend named Alex—"

"The Prince of New York," Harper chimed in.

"And he's crazy about her," Amory said.

It was hard to believe how much the tables had turned. Last week, my friends had been giving me death stares anytime I brought up Alex's name. Now they were cheering me on. It was funny how much easier it was to gush over your crush when your friends wanted to hear it.

"Things with Alex are great," I said, taking a final bite of my sinfully dark chocolate ice cream. "But we can hang out anytime. I'm just glad to hear you guys all get on board for the Valentine's Dance."

By the end of dinner, we'd sampled just about everything on the menu, dished on just about every boy in Manhattan, and come to the group decision that it was Valentine's Day Dance or bust. I buttoned up my Dior trench and we stepped back out into the cold.

"Which way are you headed, Sally?" Camille asked, hailing a cab.

SBB, who lived twenty feet away from me, would have offered to split a cab, but Sally squinted at me and skirted the question. She pointed at a black town car across the street. "Toward my driver. See you later!"

Everyone else grinned and called good night, but I couldn't help wondering about the icy distance between me and SBB. What if the new *Sally* didn't keep *SBB's* Valentine's Dance promise to help me keep everyone's dates fixed on the right girl? With my track record so far, I wasn't sure I could do it alone.

Chapter 20

On Wednesday, just before last period, I was thrilled to see my phone light up with the signature ring I'd set for my favorite French fashion designer friend, Jade Moodswing. Jade was an old friend of Feb's, and when she'd been in the states for Fashion Week last month, I'd lucked into a spot as a model in her show at the Armory. But ever since Feb had become Feb'n'Kelly, our household had been lacking its token ninety-seven-pound, chain-smoking, perpetually pouting designer.

"Coo-coo, *chérie*," her hoarse voice came across the phone. "Zere is small favor I need to ask. I must jet back to Paree *ce soir*, but my suitcase iz too full to fit in—how do you say—overhead compartment. Can you pleaze take a ball gown or two off my hands?"

"Let's see. . . . Um, where do I sign?" I responded, laughing.

I ducked out of school as soon as the bell rang and hailed a cab downtown to Jade's atelier in Chelsea. I was about to press the buzzer to her studio when I spotted a familiar profile peering through the windows of a store across Tenth Avenue.

What was *Xander* doing window-shopping at the 202 Boutique in Chelsea?

Before I knew was I was doing, I'd sprinted across the avenue to spy on him from a lesser distance. Why was he lingering in front of that one mannequin? And why did he have such a forlorn look on his face?

Then it hit me: 202 was Camille's favorite clothing store in the city.

"Xander?" I asked, tapping his shoulder.

He spun around. "What?" he said. His voice sounded strained and a little defensive. "I was just—I wasn't—"

"What are you doing down here?" I wasn't trying to give him the third degree, but I realized I sounded a little bit suspicious.

"I was . . . uh . . . looking for a present . . . for my mom for Valentine's Day. But this place doesn't have much." He turned back around and glanced at an amber and garnet necklace in the window that pretty much screamed Camille. "I'll probably just go to Louis Vuitton. She likes key chains and stuff." He was rambling, clearly nervous.

"Okay," I said, trying to put him at ease. "So, how've you been?"

"I've been good. I've been fine." He shot me a look. "Why? Did Camille ask about me? Never mind. Look, I should get going. Great to see you!"

Before I even had time to wave good-bye, Xander had taken off down the street faster than a Kenyan marathon runner. I knew I needed to tell Camille about the run-in, but since I couldn't exactly make sense of it myself, I wasn't sure how to position it to her.

Slightly shaken up, I crossed back over to Jade Moodswing's side of the street. When I got upstairs, she was perched on the windowsill smoking a cigarette and talking into a headset. A team of at least ten assistants ran around the room packing up dresses, tearing mock-up sketches off the walls, and stuffing fabric scraps into a giant platinum trunk.

When Jade saw me in the doorway, she waved me over to her, then gestured dismissively at the scene. "Iz always depressing to disappear from a place like zis. Two more hours in New York, then poof, we'll be gone."

"But you'll come back soon, right?" I asked. "Fall Fashion Week's only a few months away. . . ."

"We'll see," Jade said cryptically. "In the meantime, you must promise to wear the dresses well, *chérie*. I've arranged for a few of ze girls to model the line for you so you can select ze ones you want. Come, sit by me on ze ledge and take a look. Can someone bring Flan a Pellegrino?"

"Seriously?" I asked, plopping down on the sill next to Jade. This was almost more exciting than being one of Jade's models in the Armory show. It was definitely more relaxing.

"Do you want us to cue the music?" Jade's head assistant asked from the back of the room.

"Yes, yes, we spare no expense for Chérie," Jade said.

The lights dimmed, two flutes of Pellegrino arrived, and I tried not to laugh in disbelief. When I'd woken up this morning stressing over my Latin test and silly high school boys, a private fashion show of Jade Moodswing's latest formal-wear line had been the furthest thing from my mind. Oh, life . . .

Soon enough, the models filed out of a back room, pranced down an imaginary catwalk, and stopped right in front of Jade and me to pose.

"Oh my gosh," I said, breathing in the scent of all the haute couture. "Jade, you've outdone yourself."

"You like? They are all from ze newest line. I call eet *Jewel*."

I could see why. All the dresses were jewel-tone shades—deep sapphire, rose quartz, emerald, even an iridescent opal color, which I fell instantly in love with. Each gown also had a different signature touch—from a keyhole neckline, to a darted velvet bodice, to a layered petticoat that grazed the hardwood floor.

"These are amazing!" I said, a little breathless. "Each one is so unique, but they're still so totally you."

"I think zey are totally *you*, *chérie*. Maybe you will wear one on Valentine's Day for your *amour*."

"Actually," I said, eyeing the opal-colored gown, "we do have a Valentine's dance at school on Friday night." But then, I also couldn't stop staring at the emerald dress—or the sapphire dress. "Any of these would be perfect. I'm just not sure how to pick which one."

"Why do you have to pick?" Jade asked as the models continued to swirl around us. "To tell you ze truth, I don't really have room for any of zese. Take zem all, decide which one to wear later—give zem out to your friends as petite Jade mementos, *non*?"

My friends were all just as obsessed with Jade's couture as I was. The thought of showing up at the dance with an entourage clad in Moodswing couture made me bust out into a giant grin.

"That way," I said, rationalizing her gift, "even when you leave New York, you'll still be leaving a legacy of fantastic dress."

"*Parfait*," Jade said, snapping her fingers for an assistant to wrap up the dresses. "Everybody wins."

Blowing out a ring of smoke, Jade Moodswing might not have looked much like a fairy godmother, but I definitely felt like Cinderella. Only this time, real life trumped fairy tale, because I don't think Cinderella ever got to take four extra dresses for her friends to wear to the ball.

When the dresses were wrapped up and I had enough taffeta and silk to clothe a lesser borough, I leaned in to give Jade a thank-you kiss on each cheek. I skipped down the stairs to catch a cab. Maybe I could soften the blow of the cryptic Xander story by offering Camille first choice of the dresses for the dance.

Oh, shoot! The dance! With all the private fashion show excitement, I'd completely forgotten that I was supposed to go to a committee meeting today after school. And when I checked my cell phone in the taxi, I had the threatening text message from Willa to prove it.

IF YOU DON'T START PULLING YOUR WEIGHT, FLOOD, I DO HAVE THE AUTHORITY TO REMOVE YOU FROM THE COMMITTEE. PUBLICLY DETHRONED AT THE VALENTINE'S DANCE—WOULDN'T THAT BE EMBARRASSING?

Chapter 21

On Thursday morning, I woke up before my alarm clock to the sound of our repeatedly ringing doorbell.

"Could somebody get that?" I shouted in the general direction of the rest of my family. "Oh, right," I remembered aloud. "I'm the only one who's ever actually home. No offense, Noodles."

Yawning, I pulled on a sweatshirt and thumped down the stairs, thinking that whoever was cruel enough to ring someone's doorbell so many times before 8 a.m. had better have a pretty good excuse.

For a second, I thought that it might have been my dad. Even with his insane travel schedule, he tried really hard not to miss a Valentine's Day. But I knew that he had an important business meeting/golf tournament in Maui all week, for which he had already apologized profusely.

177

When I opened the door, I was greeted by a stranger in a Yankees cap.

"Can I help you?" I asked.

"I doubt it," he said flatly. "But they're paying me to help you." He reached behind him to pick something up off the stoop. Unceremoniously, he handed me the most enormous bouquet of red roses that I had ever seen.

"Omigod," I gasped.

"Omigod is right," the deliveryman said. "You must be pretty special. This guy got you the deluxe. Sign here." He held out a clipboard.

"I can see that," I said, signing my name and nearly buckling under the weight of the vase. "Happy Valentine's Day!" I said, overflowing with romantic wishes for everyone around me.

"Yeah, yeah," the guy said, starting down the steps. I guessed if I had his job, I might not have been so cheery, but as it was, I couldn't wait to read Alex's card—or to set the massive vase down before I dropped it.

The card was simple and white, but the message inside was anything but:

I know you think that I'm a guy who always breaks a rule.

But to deny you red roses on Valentine's day, I'd
have to be a fool.
Please don't expect a lot more verse from your
nonpoet boyfriend,
Just wanted to give you a romantic day from its
beginning to its end.

Can't wait to see you tonight.
—A

For the first time in my life, I was almost glad that my family wasn't around. If they'd seen me blush this hard over a love note from a boy, they never would have let me live it down.

By the time I met up with Alex after school, I'd stopped blushing and was just really excited to hang out with him. It had been such a long, fun, busy week of friends and fix-ups and dance coordinating, but now I was ready to dedicate my entire night to my valentine.

He'd left me a message to be dressed and ready to hit the town at seven o'clock, but at a quarter to seven, I was just getting around to wrapping the gift I'd rush-ordered online earlier this week. Five minutes later, I zipped up my brand-new soft pink flapper-style cocktail dress, and at six fifty-nine, I was smacking on my signature Chanel lip gloss. I had never been so punctual, but Alex always was, so I wasn't surprised when the doorbell rang just as I was blotting my lips with a tissue.

I dashed down the stairs and flung open the door. Alex had never looked better. He was wearing a dark gray Calvin Klein suit, a light pink button-down, and these really unique Euro-style black loafers.

"Whoa," we both said at the same time, taking in each other's outfits.

"I love your shoes," I said.

"You look beautiful," he said, stepping inside and looking around. "Do you still have the house to yourself?"

"Um, yeah," I said, wondering what he had in mind.

"Good." Alex turned around and picked up two hefty paper bags from Zabar's. "Point me toward your kitchen. I'm making us a Valentine's feast."

"Be gentle." I laughed, thinking about all the take-out food our house had seen in the past few months. "This room doesn't get a whole lot of use."

But as I led him back into our kitchen, I was secretly thrilled that he'd put more energy into planning our date than just making a reservation at some fancy restaurant. Things were already off to a really romantic start.

As it turned out, Alex was a real pro in the kitchen, which I added to the list of things that made him incredibly attractive. While he unloaded the groceries, I got to work picking out the music. Luckily, I had Morgan's latest mix on my computer, so I didn't have to play my typical embarrassing lineup of *American Idol* tunes.

"Do you like Al Green?" I called from the stereo in the living room.

"Are you kidding? Al Green invented the love song. He *is* soul."

"I'll take that as a yes." I laughed, pumping up the volume on the speakers. "Can I help you make dinner?" I asked, even though I hardly recognized most of the food Alex was unloading on my counter.

"Definitely," he said. "Do you know how to make aioli?"

"A-what-i?"

Alex kissed me and handed me a head of garlic and an apron. "Here," he said, laying down a cutting board. "I'll show you."

He wasn't kidding. For the next forty-five minutes, Alex showed me how to turn olive oil, an egg, and some garlic into the most amazing dip I had ever tasted. While I sliced the City Bakery baguette and some farmers' market veggies for the dip, Alex pan-fried an entire fish, filling the kitchen up with incredible smells of rosemary and sage.

By eight-fifteen, we were sitting down to a huge spread of amazing-looking food. It was the most romantic and intimate meal of my life—everything was so perfect that it almost made me nervous.

"Is something wrong?" Alex asked. "Did I over-cook the fish?"

"Not at all," I said, taking a bite of trout as proof. "Everything is perfect."

"Just wait," he said. "There's more."

"You always say that." I laughed.

"And don't I always come through?"

By the time we finished eating, I was ready to give Alex my gift. But right when I stood up to excuse myself and run upstairs, the doorbell rang.

"I'll get it," Alex said. Before I could protest, he was opening up the front door to let in a small man wearing black yoga pants and a black button-down shirt.

"Flan," Alex said, registering the very confused look on my face. "This is Paco. He's the best salsa teacher at Broadway Dance."

"No way," I gasped, guessing at what he was about to say.

Alex nodded. "I know you're always talking about how fun it'd be learn salsa, so I thought this might be a good time for a private lesson."

Paco stuck out his hand and looked at me seriously. "Nice to meet you, Ms. Flood. I hope you're ready to sweat."

Paco wasn't kidding. For the next hour and a half, he made us work up a pretty continual glow. Alex had some natural moves, but I was, embarrassingly, a little bit of a klutz. I kept tripping over my own feet and making Alex stumble with me. Alex thought it was pretty funny—Paco, not so much.

"Eyes up," he kept yelling at me. "What's with the elephant feet! Are you even listening to the music?"

Some girls might have gotten frustrated, but the tough love was good for me. By ten o'clock, I could make it through one whole dance routine without making either Alex or myself fall down.

At the end of our lesson, Paco turned to Alex. "She worried me at first—but she really stuck with it. I like it."

Alex laughed. "Well, thank you. I like it too."

After we showed Paco to the door, I turned to Alex.

"Thank you so much," I said. "I knew I was going to have fun no matter what we did, but this, I'll never forget."

"Hopefully we won't forget the moves either. I was thinking, if we want to show off our skills at the dance tomorrow night, we might need to practice one more time. Are you free in the afternoon?"

I reached for my planner on the mantel. I was learning—finally—to check my calendar before I made commitments. And it was a good thing that I did.

"Oh, I can't," I told Alex. "I'm stuck doing setup for the dance. I missed the committee meeting the other day, so it's Willa's form of punishment," I explained. "But it's actually going to be fun, because all the girls are going to come and help out."

"Ah, girl time, I get it," Alex said, looking disappointed. "They say you're not supposed to get jealous of your girlfriend's girlfriend time—"

"You," I said, putting my arms around him in the doorway, "have absolutely no reason to be jealous of my girlfriends. Practically all we do these days is gush about our boys. As soon as you show up at the dance," I promised, "I'll be all yours."

"I'm going to hold you to that," he said. We

kissed good night and I watched Alex walk down the steps.

It was only after I had shut the door that I realized I'd completely forgotten to give Alex his Valentine's Day present!

Luckily, I'd get the chance to give Alex his gift less than twenty-four hours later. I couldn't wait to see the look on his face when he opened it. By Friday afternoon, the little wrapped box was tucked in my oversize Chanel trunk—the only thing I owned big enough to cart around the *five* formal dresses I'd scored from Jade Moodswing.

When I'd texted the girls last night to meet me at the Rainbow Room to set up two hours before the dance—and to agree to let me dress them—not one of them had put up a fight. I felt reassured by their complete fashion trust. Hopefully it meant that they were feeling equally as confident about the dates I'd found for them.

To help us get in the setup mood, we'd blared cheesy romance songs—fighting over whether to listen to another Jake Riverdale song (Camille) or to

Donovan (Morgan)—and we ordered in sushi from Onigashima. Morgan and I hung all the black-and-white blown-up prints that our photography class had taken, while Amory and Harper blew up balloons. Everything looked so picture-perfect, I was almost glad Willa had threatened to smear my reputation if I didn't show up to handle the grunt work. Popping the final spicy tuna roll in my mouth and surveying our finished product, I realized that the grunt work had actually been really fun.

"Okay, Flan," Camille said, straightening a matted print of the Hudson River Park that Morgan had taken. "That's the last of the romantic photo decorations. Now can we *please* see our Jade Moodswing dresses?"

"*Please*," all the other girls echoed.

They started oohing and ahhing before I'd even unlocked the trunk. And when I pulled out the first dress—a deep sapphire floor-length gown, all four of them started screaming.

"I was thinking this one for Harper," I said, holding up the dress against her skin. "To accentuate her dramatic clavicles."

"Perfect," Morgan agreed. "She is so the muse of Trevor's dreams."

For Morgan, I pulled out a puffy, tea-length gown in a pretty shade of rose quartz. "Jade called this one the New Love dress," I said. I'd picked it for Morgan, my ex-bitter friend who'd spent all week forwarding me cute texts from Bennett. It was strange, because I'd never really seen that side of him, but I quickly shrugged that off, just happy that Morgan had found someone to get excited about.

As for Camille, all day she'd been a little blasé about her date with Saxton, but once I pulled out the dramatically sleek, backless emerald silk dress, there was no denying the excitement on her face.

"Okay, this just made everything worthwhile!" she said, hugging me, then rushing to slip into the dress.

Finally, for Amory, I doled out an amber-colored gown with a keyhole neckline. "Sheesh," she said, fanning herself when she saw it. "Is it hot in here, or is it my dress?"

Good—that was the reaction I'd been going for. Of all my girls, Amory was the only one I was slightly worried about. She'd totally dismissed the idea of any of Feb's Aussie model friends, claiming Phil to be her one and only valentine. I hadn't been able to bring myself to confess everything to her, so my new plan was to quit stressing, keep my distance from Phil, and find Amory a dress that Phil wouldn't be able to take his eyes off of. At least the dress part of the plan was taken care of. . . .

"That's it," I said happily. "Is everyone satisfied with her couture?"

"*Absolument!*" Camille said, crossing her legs à la Jade Moodswing. "But why are you holding out on us? We need to see your gown *immédiatement.*"

When at last I slipped into the brilliant opal ball gown, all my friends stopped fastening their own dresses to applaud. I loved that it fit me so well that I didn't even need a zipper.

"It's perfect," Harper said. "Alex is totally going to flip."

"That's the idea," I said, glancing down at my watch. "Speaking of which—he should be here any minute. In fact, all of our dates should. I'm going to go downstairs and wait for mine."

I tucked Alex's gift under my arm and took the looong elevator ride back down to earth. I couldn't wait to see him.

But apparently I was going to have to.

Ten minutes passed and he still wasn't there. Just before seven, several limos full of my formally clad classmates started showing up—including Sally, formerly known as Simone, formerly known as SBB. She was flying solo—I guess JR would have blown her cover—but she still arrived in the car with Willa and Kennedy.

As I tried not to fume, we exchanged icy stares as she passed. The vibe between us was as frigid as the weather, and neither one of us wanted to make the first thaw-out gesture.

Twenty minutes passed.

Standing alone on the curb in the freezing wind, I greeted Trevor and Saxton and even said a quick downward-gazing hello to Phil, who seemed to be avoiding my eyes too.

Still no Alex. Where was he? I'd left my phone in my bag, but it was all the way upstairs, and I didn't want to cross paths with him in the elevator if he showed up in the meantime.

I felt a familiar hand on my arm. *Finally*.

"There you are," I said, turning around.

Whoops—it wasn't Alex. It was Bennett.

I couldn't help it—my heart picked up. What was wrong with me?

"I was wondering," he said awkwardly. Uh-oh, was he going to ask me something about . . . us? Gulp.

"Have you seen Morgan?" he finally stammered.

"Oh," I said. "Sure, she's upstairs, I think—"

"Great, I'll go find her."

Just then a giant gust of wind knocked loose one of the primary bobby pins in my updo, and my formerly intricate braided bun came cascading down my shoulders. I was still holding Alex's present and didn't want to lose it in this wind, but I also didn't want to lose that bobby pin!

"Bennett," I called to him. "Can you help me? Just grab that bobby pin before it blows away?"

Bennett reached toward me as another gust of wind blew my hair all into my lip gloss. I hated that.

"Oh no," I said, trying to spit it out. "Help!"

"I'm trying," he said, brushing my hair out of my eyes. When he finally got it under control, I had spit all over him and he was holding my hair up in a mass above my head with both his hands. Our eyes met and we both started laughing.

An angry throat-clearing noise from behind us broke our moment.

Whoops. It was Morgan, and her face looked about as flushed as her gown.

"So it's true," she said. "I just overheard Sally talking about how the two of you used to date! Now I come downstairs to *this* scene? Nice matchmaking, Flan."

"Morgan, wait—" Bennett called, running after her.

It was then that I spotted Alex, who had picked the most inopportune instant of all instants to show up.

"Wow," he said, shaking his head. "I feel like such an idiot. Last night you were telling me how I shouldn't be jealous of the time you spent with your girlfriends. You didn't mention that I needed to watch out for your ex-boyfriends." He turned back to his town car and opened the door.

"Alex—it's not what you think!" I called, but he was already inside the car.

"I don't really feel like dancing anymore," he said, rolling up the window and driving away.

I was devastated. I looked down at the present I'd been holding out to give him—the very box that had caused this whole mix-up with Bennett and this stupid windstorm in the first place.

I couldn't believe that in thirty seconds, so much had fallen apart. I could either chase Alex's car down the street in my heels (not likely), or I could race upstairs to get my phone to call him—while simultaneously convincing Morgan that what she'd seen just now was *so* not what it had seemed.

After what felt like a year, I finally made it to the top floor and stepped back into the Rainbow Room. I couldn't even appreciate how elegant the place looked or how many of my fellow classmates were totally kicking it on the dance floor. I grabbed my bag from where I'd left it behind the bar and headed toward the ladies' bathroom. If I knew Morgan, she'd be there.

When I swung open the door, Morgan *was* there

(like I expected) crying (also like I expected) but she was flanked (*unexpectedly*) by Amory and Harper, who looked really pissed off.

Geez, the rumor mill must have been working faster than the elevator.

"Morgan—you have to believe me, nothing is going on with me and Bennett. It's so obvious that he's crazy about you."

"And it's so obvious that it drives *you* crazy. If you were over him, you would have told me that you guys had a history."

I looked to Amory for backup. She was always the voice of reason when my other friends got overdramatic. But she had daggers in her eyes for me as well.

"Don't look at me," she said. "You made such a big deal about picking the perfect dates for us all. If mine was so perfect, why did he ditch me for *your* friend Sally?"

"What?" I asked, my head spinning with the latest development.

"Trevor's been all over Sally too," Harper huffed. "It's hard for us to see how you didn't have a hand in all of this."

"You guys aren't being fair," I pleaded. "Where's Camille?"

"She bailed," Harper said. "She thinks Saxton is

totally boring and superficial. Is that the kind of guy you think is deserving of your friend?"

Looking at the three of them splayed out on the bathroom floor, part of me wanted to grovel at their feet, make up for this whole mess, and get their advice on how to dig myself out of trouble with Alex. The other part of me was furious.

"You've got to be kidding me," I said. "I have spent every waking minute of the last two weeks trying to make *you* guys happy—so we could all have a fun time tonight. I went through multiple Rolodexes for you guys. I hauled a giant trunk of couture across town so *you* could look fabulous tonight. I've been wearing myself to the bone for you all and this is how you repay me?"

The girls looked at one other and started to stand up and gather their things. "Don't bother storming out on my account," I said, ready to make an exit myself. "I'll save you the trouble."

Chapter 23

After a long, sleepless night, I lay in bed early Saturday morning, listening to the rain. I was feeling really low. I knew it couldn't have all been a bad dream, because I'd been tossing and turning all night. And when the doorbell rang this time, I was pretty sure it wasn't a flower delivery from Alex again.

After a few more insistent rings of the bell, I grudgingly climbed out of bed and headed down the stairs.

"Whoever this is had better have a really good excuse," I muttered under my breath.

"Hey kiddo," a familiar voice said when I opened the door. It was Patch, looking almost as sleep-deprived and tousled as me. "Sorry to wake you—I forgot my keys."

Before I could formulate a coherent sentence, I had burst into tears and flung myself into his arms.

195

"My life is over," I wailed. "All my friends and my boyfriend hate me."

"Oh boy," Patch said. "Sounds like we need air hockey and a large pizza from John's."

"Patch, it's seven-thirty in the morning," I said.

"Never too early for a pity party," he said, grabbing my coat from the closet and helping me into it. "A pajama pity party is even better," he said, taking in my attire as he sent a quick text.

I couldn't believe I was going out like this, but at this point, it wasn't like I had anything to lose. I followed my big brother across town to Ace Bar, his longtime favorite hangout in the East Village. The place was dingy and empty, and they didn't care if you had a pizza delivered while you played. And if you were Patch Flood, they didn't care if you texted two hours after they'd closed and said you were dropping by. Patch ordered a large pepper-and-mushroom pie and gave me a wad of singles to get quarters from the machine.

By the time we'd finished two games of air hockey (Patch and I were one and one), I'd spilled the whole story of the dance disaster. He hadn't said much yet, but he was being a really good listener. We paused in quiet contemplation and dug into the giant floppy slices. It was sort of amazing that pizza could still work its wonders so early in the morning.

"So how do I get my friends back? And what do I do about Alex? And BTW, how am I related to someone who eats the crusts first?" I said, handing Patch my crust so I could move on to another cheesy slice.

"The chick-fight thing isn't exactly my turf, little sis. Don't girls usually just make up with retail therapy?" He polished off the slice and slipped another couple of quarters into the pinball machine. "As for the romance trouble, I probably shouldn't be giving out advice there, either."

"Oh no," I said, feeling stunned. "You and Agnes broke up?"

"She didn't like that I needed a little bit of space every now and then. I guess I didn't do a good enough job convincing her that just because sometimes I had to eat and sleep and have conversations with other people, that didn't mean I wasn't crazy about her." He looked out the dirty window. "Does that sound crazy?"

I couldn't believe my big brother was asking me for relationship advice. Patch looked more pensive than I'd ever seen him. Part of me wanted to be compassionate, but another part of me just had to take advantage of his mood and score on him to win the game. This was definitely a morning of firsts for us.

"One thing is clear," I said, after Patch had recovered from his loss. "Both of us are going to have to do some serious groveling if we want to get them back."

"Doesn't quite seem like a Flood thing to do, does it?" Patch said, slurping up the last of his Coke.

"Maybe not, but we're bingeing on pizza and bad arcade games before nine a.m.," I said. "We're pretty pathetic without them."

"Speak for yourself," Patch teased. "This is totally normal behavior for me."

"You know what?" I said.

"I think we should get out of here and start the long groveling process," Patch finished for me.

I nodded.

"This might be the first time we've agreed on something." I laughed.

"Good luck," Patch said, messing up my hair again.

"You too. Keep me posted," I said.

I was eager to get to work fixing things with Alex. But first I was going to have to put on something other than these pajamas.

Back on the street, Patch gave me a fist bump before I hailed a cab back toward our house and he turned south toward Agnes's.

"Don't forget that Floods always get what they want," he called, zigzagging through traffic.

Fingers crossed that his brotherly advice was right.

When I got to my stoop, I spotted SBB sitting at the top of my steps. I had to do a double take before I realized that the girl sitting before me wasn't Sally, and it wasn't Simone. It was just my SBB.

She held up a doggie bag from EJ's, our favorite spot for brunch.

"Truce?" she asked.

I sighed. I was too tired to argue, too tired to explain that I'd already eaten, too tired to do anything but nod.

"Can we crawl into bed?" I asked.

"I thought you'd never ask," SBB said, racing me up the stairs.

Once we were tucked under the covers and tucking into our omelets, SBB looked at me with a devilish grin.

"What happened to you last night?" she asked. "You managed to miss all the drama."

I just about choked on a sautéed mushroom.

"Are you kidding? I thought I *was* the drama last night. What could I possibly have missed?"

"Oh, only that Willa's secret boyfriend secretly fell

for Willa's little protégé—that would be me—I mean, past-tense me. He basically accosted me in the coatroom. And when Willa came in to get her phone, she saw everything and *flipped*. Over a high school boy—can you imagine? No offense. Anyway, after that, Willa tried to engage me in a catfight, and it amounted to her yanking off my wig and exposing me in front of the whole class."

My head was spinning with all the details of her story. At least it sounded like my drama would *not* be the gossip everyone was talking about back at school.

Now I was just trying to figure out in what order all of these things had happened. If SBB had been unveiled early enough in the night—then maybe that would explain why Harper and Amory's dates had both been all over her.

"After that, it was only a matter of time before the paparazzi showed up. I ducked out before I could do any further damage," SBB said, wrapping up her story. She sighed. "So thus endeth my career as a high school student. But oh my God, what a thrill. Even though it ended sort of dramatically, overall it was such a good experience to add to the old repertoire. Have I mentioned that I love high school drama?"

"I'm glad *you* like it," I sighed. "My own drama was

a whole lot less fun last night. In fact, I'm pretty sure you're the only person in the whole school who's still speaking to me."

"And I don't even go to your school anymore," she chimed in.

"Yes, thank you for pointing that out," I said, offering Noodles the rest of my omelet. Either I was still full from the pizza, or I'd lost my appetite along with all my friends. "I'm just upset that my friends think I went behind their backs. They actually blamed me for their dates falling all over you. Like I can control what they do once they're at the dance."

"Whoops," SBB said. "Sorry about that. I was only trying to show them how we danced on the set of *Oh My Chocolate Pie* so they could try it out on their own dates. Sigh. I guess high school drama isn't all fun and games. Are you mad at me for drawing too much attention?"

"Of course not," I said. "You didn't do anything wrong. My Thoney friends said they trusted me, but it's plain to see now that they never did."

SBB got a funny look on her face and was quiet for a moment.

"Hello?" I waved in front of her face. "Anyone in there?"

"Oh," she said, sounding distracted, "I'm sure it'll

just work itself out. You guys can just all go shopping and make up over retail therapy."

What? Now she was sounding like Patch. That advice was so unrealistic—and unhelpful. Was she turning back into Sally again or something?

"Well, I should probably get going," SBB said, quickly packing up the brunch plates and grabbing her bag. "Now that I'm not in high school anymore, I have time to catch up on the rest of my life. Have a great day, Flan! Let's do lunch soon."

She disappeared more quickly than she could change costumes and before I knew it, I was back in my room alone.

I hated to break it to SBB but she was definitely going to have to work on that empathy thing some more. But before I could harp on how even more alone I felt after her visit, I finally fell into a fitful sleep.

*B*y Sunday afternoon, I knew I needed to pull myself together. I'd have to face my friends at school the next morning, and SBB/Simon/Sally wouldn't even be there for me to fall back on for moral support. Since I knew I'd feel much better equipped to make up with my girlfriends if I could get over the sinking feeling in my stomach related to the recent loss of my boyfriend, I decided to swallow my pride and try calling Alex—for the sixth time.

After the dance on Friday night, I'd texted him a few times but still hadn't heard back. I wasn't sure how many more apologetic voice mails I could leave, but I tried to remember what Patch had said. *Floods always get what they want.*

Okay, I told myself in the mirror, *I'm going to give it one more try.*

WILL YOU JUST GIVE ME A CHANCE TO EXPLAIN? I texted.

This time, the reply was instantaneous.

STEP OUTSIDE AND GIVE IT YOUR BEST SHOT.

What? After the hell of the last few days, this seemed too good to be true. Still, when I went out to the hallway and looked out at the street, the Prince's town car was stalled outside of my house.

I rushed downstairs.

"What are you doing here?" I asked, unable to decide whether my heart was racing because I was nervous or excited.

"*Not* giving you a chance to explain," he said.

"But—"

"Why waste time?" he shrugged. "I've already forgiven you. I think I might have overreacted on Friday night. What do you say we forget about it and go grab some hot dogs?"

"Umm, I say—" *Thank god!* "I say, let me just grab one more thing before we go."

I didn't know where the afternoon would take us, but I did know that I wasn't going to miss another opportunity to give Alex his gift. I grabbed my bag and slipped the little box inside.

"You might want to bring your heavy scarf," Alex said, pointing at the sky. "It feels like snow outside."

When the town car dropped us off at the world's best hot dog stand, I could tell Alex was right. There was that electricity in the air that usually meant a rare Manhattan snowfall. I gripped his hand with excitement. It felt so good to have him back—almost too good to be true.

"I know it's freezing," he said, rubbing my hands as we waited for our two hot dogs with extra relish. "Should we get these to go and eat them in the car?"

I shook my head. "We can't go inside now. There's nothing better than being in Central Park to catch the first few flakes of snow."

Alex gave me that you're-kinda-insane-but-I-like-it smile and we grabbed a seat on the bench to dig into our hot dogs. It was pretty amazing how much better food tasted now that the giant lump in my throat had dissolved and I could actually swallow it.

"So can I ask what made you forgive me?" I said. "I was sort of looking forward to this whole groveling act I'd worked up."

"You should file that act away in case you need it next time," he said, then nudged me. "I'm kidding." Alex looked down at his shoes and started swinging his feet. "Well, partially it was that I kept replaying that scene with you and that guy Bennett in my mind. I knew something about it wasn't right, but I couldn't put my finger on what it was. Then, last night, I was playing pool with Phil and Saxton, and Phil sort of came clean about the note he sent to you last week."

Oh, crap.

"I was pissed at first," Alex continued. "But when Phil told me how you reacted, how it was never even a question in your mind, I knew that my instinct about Friday night was right. I had to come make it up to you."

I breathed an enormous sigh of relief. "Well, you just about covered all of my groveling points anyway." I laughed.

"I'm sorry, Flan," he said, leaning in to give me a kiss.

"I'm sorry too," I said.

At that very moment, the first snow began to fall.

"Wow, it's like this is out of a movie," I said.

Alex held up a finger. "Just wait—" he said.

"Don't tell me," I guessed. "There's more?"

This time, I was ready to insist on being the one to top the perfect moment with my belated Valentine's gift.

But once again, before I could take it out of my bag, Alex was standing up and holding his hands out to me. "I need to whisk you away to a secret destination and I need you to not ask any questions."

"But what—"

"Uh-uh." He shook his finger at me. "That sounds suspiciously like a question." He held open the door to the town car. "Hop in."

"More ice cream?" I guessed.

"No questions," he said, shaking his head.

The car started rolling east, and as I looked excitedly out the window for clues about our destination, Alex thwarted me again by pulling out a blindfold.

He shrugged. "How can it be a secret destination if you know where we're going?"

I considered protesting, but I could tell from the look on his face that he was enjoying this whole game, and the truth was, I was kind of into the mystique of it too. I leaned my head forward and accepted my blindfolded fate.

When the car finally came to a stop, Alex hopped out and took my hand so I could stumble out too. Even blindfolded, I could tell that we were on the water, because the wind was really biting into our faces. I could also tell that we weren't alone—there was a buzz in the air that wasn't just the snow's electricity.

"When am I allowed to ask questions?" I said to Alex.

"Patience," Alex said, reaching around the back of my head to untie the blindfold. "Not yet, not yet."

Standing in front of me on a dock facing the East River were Camille, Morgan, Harper, Amory, and SBB dressed as herself.

Before I could ask questions, a small fleet of helicopters swooped down to land next to us on the dock. Their propellers were loud, but my friends were louder, and they all held out their hands and yelled, "SURPRISE!"

Chapter 25

"Okay," Alex said. "Now you can ask questions."

I was perched in the cramped backseat of a helicopter, flying over the East River next to SBB, Camille, and Alex. From the devilish look of excitement on SBB's face, I had a guess that we were headed toward her palace. But for the life of me, I couldn't figure out why—or how all of my friends had agreed to come after the debacle on Friday night.

"Will someone just start from the beginning?" I said.

"Well, remember how I said I was playing pool with the guys—" Alex started to explain, but was quickly interrupted.

"Morgan and I were midfume at H&H the next morning and—" Camille said at the same time.

"Excuse me." SBB's loud stage chirp silenced the other two. "As the mastermind behind this operation,

I believe I've earned the right to speak first and freely. Agreed?"

The rest of the helicopter's occupants giggled and nodded.

"So . . ." SBB turned to me. "Remember my awkward shuffle out of your house yesterday?"

"I don't think I could forget it." I nodded. "That was definitely some Oscar-worthy awkwardness."

"I know," she sighed. "It was weird, and I'm sorry for that, but when I get an idea as good as this one, I need to act on it without hesitation. You know that. Carpe diem!" She straightened her sequined headband and took a deep breath. "I bailed on you yesterday because I realized that I could fix *everything*!"

She looked at Camille. "What you girls didn't know was that I'd promised to help Flan keep everyone's date's eyes on the right girl on Friday. But after what happened with Willa, and then my unmasking—er, unwigging, which really hurt by the way. *Never* glue on a wig. Anyway, things got a little out of control—"

"You're a movie star, guys have no choice but to fall all over you, say no more," Camille finished. "I'm just baffled that I didn't pick up on your true identity earlier." She shook her head. "Either I've been *way* self-involved this week—or you, my dear, are an excellent actress."

"Thank you," SBB said seriously. She turned back to me. "Anyway, I dropped the ball at the V-Day ball, I know, so when I heard the whole rundown from you the next morning, I knew I had to let your friends know that your intentions were always good."

"So she hijacked us yesterday and took us to Fig & Olive to explain," Camille filled in.

SBB shrugged. "I just told them over pink peppercorn soup how hard you'd been working to find everyone's perfect match. And that you were putting in all that effort while simultaneously trying not to blow my cover—no small feat. *And* you did it even after my short-lived foray to the axis of evil—whoops!" she rambled on. "Obviously, after it was all out in the open, everyone instantly forgave you."

"You went to my favorite restaurant without me?" I asked, thinking about how I loved to sit at the antipasto bar at the sleek Meatpacking restaurant. It was weird to imagine SBB and my Thoney friends making dinner plans sort of behind my back. "How did that play out? What did the other girls say?"

"It helped," Camille continued, "that Bennett called Morgan twenty times to grovel and reassure her that he only had eyes for her."

Hearing Camille say that, I thought I might have had a different reaction. But all I felt was relief. Finally, things were as they should be—and now I could just put all that weirdness with Bennett behind me.

When Alex put his hand on my knee, I knew he was the one I really wanted.

He leaned in and said, "While we're on the subject of groveling, you should probably also know that I convinced a very pathetically depressed friend of mine to go grovel in front of Camille," Alex said.

"Huh? Do you mean Saxton?" I asked, not so sure whether Camille would really be into that.

"Actually . . ." Alex looked at Camille and winked. "I mean Xander."

Camille turned beet red and started fiddling nervously with her hair.

"You and Xander got back together??" I squealed, looking at my friend, who was suddenly all nods and shyness.

That the best news I'd heard all day.

"So everything came together," SBB said, clapping her hands. "Just exactly as I planned. I'm in high school for what, a week? And I've already perfected the social graces."

We all laughed, and as the helicopter started to descend, I turned to SBB.

"I'm still a little jealous that you guys went to Fig & Olive without me," I said. "But I guess I'm glad it resulted in this. Wait," I said, finally taking in the fact that we were landing on SBB's rooftop pad outside her palace in Long Island City. "What exactly *is* this?"

"Duh," SBB said as we touched down. "Don't you know about the only family tradition I have with Gloria?" she asked.

I shook my head.

"After every major blowout fight, we make up and have a lovefest," SBB said, as if it were common knowledge. "Remember our brawl after she got the same tattoo as me—and then my subsequent Sweet Fifteen birthday party in Cairo?" She shrugged. "Make-up lovefest."

Camille put her arm around my shoulder. "Consider this your we're-sorry-Flan lovefest," she explained. "SBB suggested we throw a party at her palace, and we all jumped to start planning."

"And don't worry," said Alex, who'd been awfully quiet. He gestured at my jeans and black turtleneck sweater. "We thought ahead. The Jade Moodswing dresses are waiting for you inside."

"Love that your boyfriend was the one to come up with that idea." Camille laughed.

"Me too!" I said, thinking about how important it was to have a good time in my opal dress so I wouldn't forever associate it with Friday night's drama.

Alex hopped out of the helicopter and helped each of us down to the windy patch of concrete. My hair was blowing all over the place, and I was still a bit overwhelmed by the forgiveness backstory I'd just been fed, but it didn't stop me from feeling like Cinderella being helped out of her carriage by the prince. It was definitely a moment deserving of a kiss.

"Someone pinch me," I said to Alex. "I'm worried that this is all a dream—or that the helicopter is going to turn into a pumpkin any minute or—"

"I'll give you a reality check." SBB gestured behind her. "Since you last visited the palace, I had a whole row of landing pads installed. Now up to ten helicopters full of revelers can land at a time. And Cinderella won't have to take the subway home—you can just stay a princess for good!"

Chapter 26

*H*arper, Morgan, and Amory arrived on our heels in a second helicopter and twenty minutes later, my friends and I emerged from the ladies' lounge. We were reoutfitted in our Jade Moodswing jewel-tone dresses and ready to party. SBB had brought over her team of stylists to get us glammed up in a jiffy, and we were all sporting her newest fragrance, Starlet.

The palace looked amazing, with white leather couches and deep purple and gold lighting. JR's latest CD was blasting, and there were candles shaped like skyscrapers dotting the banquet tables and lining the catwalk.

Wow, I'd thought the Rainbow Room looked pretty swanky on Friday night, but this put our crepe paper, balloons, and matted photos to shame. The palace walls were even sporting some particularly notable décor from the Valentine's Dance: five of the NYC prints I was most proud of from my photography class.

Camille put her arm through mine. "We all put so much work into making the dance decorations really amazing. It seemed like a waste to abandon them even after most of us abandoned the dance." She shrugged. "So we asked SBB if we could use them here. It just seemed like the perfect match!" We stepped back to admire the black-and-white cityscapes hanging from the wall next to the real cityscape visible through the floor-to-ceiling windows.

"Okay you two," SBB said, grabbing our elbows and leading us over to the bar where Harper, Amory, and Morgan were waiting with flutes of champagne. "You can admire your own photographs later, Flan—"

"Hey!" I said.

"I'm kidding," SBB said, hands on her hips all mock indignant. "I've been admiring them all day! But right now, it's time for a toast."

I looked around for Alex. Where was he?

Reading my mind, Camille said, "Don't worry, he didn't go far. The rest of the party's about to arrive. Alex just went upstairs to let everyone in."

"And before all the boys show up, I want to propose a toast," SBB sang out.

We raised our glasses.

"To Flan," she said, "whose intentions are always good, even when her matchmaking choices are spotty."

There was a time when I would have taken this remark too seriously, but tonight, looking at all of my grinning, glamorous friends, I realized that I wasn't the only one who'd been through a lot this week. Even after all the drama, we'd come out smiling and with more than a few funny stories to tell.

"And to you guys," I said holding my glass out to clink. "For putting up with my obsessive matchmaking."

"You know what they say," Amory said. "Practice makes perfect. Even though Phil turned out to be a total frog, I can't say I minded kissing him to find that out."

Modest little Harper's jaw dropped, and Camille slugged her playfully on the shoulder.

"Don't act all prude, Miss Blueblood. You were totally pimping out your clavicles to Trevor just because he claimed to be an *artiste*!"

I busted out laughing and said, "Okay, okay, so Trevor and Phil and Saxton were lame. But look at Morgan and Bennett. My track record's not *all* bad. In fact, if anyone wants to go out with a really cute Australian guy, I could set it up—"

"NO!" All my friends cried at once, but all of us were laughing.

"Point taken." I shrugged. "Cheers."

"I can see we're right on time," Alex's voice called from the doorway. Bennett and Xander and JR were all next to him, along with a few guys I sort of recognized as Daltonites but didn't really know.

"Is there enough champagne to go around?" Xander asked.

"At our palace," SBB said proudly, snuggling up to JR, "there is always enough champagne."

The guys filed in and everyone took a glass. The room was heating up with chatter and expensive formal wear.

"Omigod," Amory whispered. "That's Jason James. He's JR's costar from *Demolition Dudes*. Huge obsession. How's my hair?"

"Flawless," Harper assured her. "And isn't that Rick Fare, the tennis player? I think he goes to my country club."

Camille looked at me. "Our friends might not need your matchmaking anymore, but I must admit, the whole experience worked wonders to lift the boy boycott."

Xander was at her elbow. "I nabbed you a lamb chop lollipop," he said, looking proud of himself. "There were only a few left on the tray, and I know they're your favorite."

Camille grinned and snapped up the hors d'oeuvre. "Actually, there is something I like even more than lamb chops," she said flirtily. "Wanna dance?"

Speaking of dancing . . . I spotted Alex sitting at a booth next to SBB and JR and sank down next to them.

"There you are." He put his arm around me.

"You guys," I said, "this party is amazing. And this place looks incredible. SBB, how did you do it so quickly?"

SBB shrugged. "Jade Moodswing's personal assistants were desperate for work after she went back to Paris. I just made a call. She definitely trained them well: at the first mention of the party being in your honor, they got down to work like busy little worker bees. I'll have to send Jade a thank-you gift," she said, pulling out her BlackBerry to make a note.

Speaking of gifts, I was not going to wait any longer to give Alex his!

But just then, a waiter approached, bearing a giant red box tied with a white bow. "For Miss Flood," he said. "Special delivery."

I looked at Alex, but he just shrugged. In fact, he looked a little uncomfortable. Oh no, I *really* hoped this wasn't another valentine from an unwanted admirer. But everyone's eyes were on me—I had to open it.

Nervously, I broke the seal on the envelope, but

when I opened the card and saw the familiar hand-writing, I breathed a giant sigh of relief.

I hate to miss a Valentine's Day with my favorite youngest daughter. Here's a token to help you capture it until I can get the full report!
Love,
Dad

Inside the box was the new Nikon camera I'd been admiring for months. It probably wouldn't have occurred to me that I needed a replacement for the battered old camera I'd been using, but now I was super psyched to trade up, thanks to Dad. And when I showed Alex the card, he looked even more relieved than I was.

"Well, I guess I can share you with your family," he joked. "Now, I hope you won't be too embarrassed, but I asked the DJ to play the salsa song we practiced to the other night. Do you still remember the moves?"

"You lead," I said. "I'll, uh, try to follow."

After JR's hip-hop song came to a smashing close, the familiar music came on and I could hear Paco's shouts in my head. My heart started racing. I really didn't want to be accused of having elephant feet again, especially not on an empty dance floor in front of all my friends!

But when Alex put his arm around my waist, all the moves came right back to me. Soon we were spinning around the parquet floor. I was grinning and a little dizzy, but then I reminded myself that Alex made me feel like that most of the time, even off the dance floor. Before I knew it, the music had ended and I looked around at all my applauding friends.

"Encore!" Camille shouted.

It was a little embarrassing, a lot exhausting, but mostly it was just a blast.

Alex and I slid into some open seats by the bar and ordered two large ice waters to catch our breaths.

"Breaking news," JR said, coming up behind us with SBB. "The weather just got too wild to fly anyone home. Looks like we're going to have to keep this party rocking till broad daylight."

I looked out the windows and couldn't believe my eyes. I'd been having so much fun I hadn't even realized how hard the snow was coming down. I also couldn't believe it was already midnight.

"Oh, these pilots *claim* they don't want to fly until it calms down for so-called safety reasons." SBB gestured over at her fleet of sexy dark-haired pilots. "Personally, I think they just don't want the party to end," she said. "You should see how much caviar they've eaten!"

"Either way," Alex said, leading me over to the windows to watch the snow, "I can't think of anyplace I'd rather wait out a storm."

Chapter 27

*I*t was a good thing that most of the partygoers agreed with Alex, because the snow didn't let up until almost sunrise.

We rocked the dance floor pretty hard until about three in the morning, but eventually exhaustion caught up with everyone. Well, almost everyone.

Bennett and Morgan were huddled near the bar, gazing into each other's eyes and having a heart-to-heart. But Camille and Xander had passed out on the lounge next to window, and Amory, Harper, and their newfound crushes looked like sardines, sleeping in a row on the catwalk. SBB and JR were wearing matching sleep masks and had changed into matching gray Ralph Lauren pajamas. Even I, who had a hard enough time sleeping in the world's most comfortable bed, found myself dozing on Alex's shoulder.

By five-thirty, he was shaking me awake.

The helicopter pilot was standing over us.

"The storm's letting up. You guys want to take the first flight back to the city? Best view in the world."

Alex and I looked at each other and shrugged. How could we argue with that?

I went over to the sleeping SBB and planted a kiss on her forehead. "Thank you for everything," I said. "Thank you for being SBB."

"It's Sally," she murmured in her sleep. She was going to have to break the habit soon enough.

I laughed and took Alex's hand as we walked out to the roof.

The city had never looked so beautiful. As the last few flakes fell around us, the gray glint of sky behind us started to glow a pinky yellow. Thick, powdery snow coated the treetops and cars below us. Even the East River looked shockingly pristine.

"It's so quiet," I whispered.

"It's so perfect," Alex said, taking my hand as we took off. "Look out there, near the Fifty-ninth Street tram. I think I see a raven's nest—that's a-mazing."

"Wait," I remembered. I was glad that I finally got to be the one to say, "There's more."

When I reached into my tote to reveal a gold-wrapped gift with a bow the size of the small box, Alex's eyes lit up.

"I didn't get to give this to you on Valentine's Day," I explained. "Or at the dance, or at the hot dog stand. I'm not going to let another minute go by."

"You didn't have to get me anything, Flan."

"Yeah, right!" I said. "You have no idea how much I stressed over what to get for you—or what I bought initially and had to return when I came to my senses." I shuddered, remembering the mocket, which seemed like years ago. "But when this idea came to me, I knew you were going to love it."

Slowly, Alex unwrapped the box. As soon as he pulled out the compact pair of binoculars I'd special ordered from GRDN, a hipster nature store in Park Slope, a huge grin spread across his face.

"Do you have any idea how long I've been wanting these?" he said, holding up the binoculars to his eyes.

"Only about as long as that red-tailed hawk's been in Manhattan," I guessed. "Look," I said, gesturing to the box. "There's even more!"

Alex pulled out the Audubon *Birds of America* guidebook I'd bought him to go with the binoculars.

"I hope you won't regret giving me this," he joked. "I'm going to be dragging you back to the park all the time to go bird-watching now."

"As long as there are hot dogs involved, I won't mind at all."

We were flying directly over the park then, and Alex held the binoculars to my eyes so I could look down. The view of the barely waking-up city was unbelievable—and the binoculars were pretty sweet too.

Soon the helicopter started dipping back down near the Hudson River piers. I couldn't believe our spectacular sunrise flight was coming to an end.

"Before we land, there's one more thing," Alex said, reaching under his feet. "I didn't get a chance to give you my gift yet either."

He pulled out a long, thin shiny silver-wrapped box, which I promptly tore into.

"Oh my gosh," I gasped, catching a glimpse of the corner. Even before I'd fully unwrapped it, I knew exactly what it was.

It was a framed print of the Spanish watercolor of the tidal wave that we'd been admiring at the Guggenheim last week. I'd always wanted to buy some of the artist's work to hang in my room. This was even more special because now I could think of Alex every time I looked at it.

"Do you know what I think?" I asked Alex.

"What?" he said, taking my hand.

"I think these gifts are the perfect match."

"Kind of like another duo I know," he said. My perfect match leaned in to give me the perfect kiss. The helicopter had just touched back down on solid ground, but I was pretty sure I was still flying.

Find out how it all began in the Insiders series, also by J. Minter